The F...... y . ....ingo

As he stepped forward, she barred his way, making
him halt again. Shafts of moonlight now highlighted the shimmer of tears on her cheeks.

'Don't make me invisible, Kit. Not you, too. I
couldn't bear it.'

The yearning in her voice echoed the same desperate loneliness he had often experienced. It
touched him so deeply; so deeply he offered
instinctive comfort. Her innocence had been
deceptive, however. She was more woman than
child, he realized, as the light kiss he offered was
returned with growing response. Only when the
screech of a hunting owl overhead brought him to
his senses, did he break away with a feeling of
shock. This girl he was swiftly subduing was only
sixteen. What was more, her name was Kirkland.
Both facts put her out of bounds to him, dangerously out of bounds.

THE FLIGHT OF FLAMINGO

Elizabeth Darrell

ROWAN

A ROWAN BOOK

Published by Arrow Books Limited
20 Vauxhall Bridge Road, London SW1V 2SA

An imprint of Random Century Group

London Melbourne Sydney Auckland Johannesburg
and agencies throughout the world

First published in Great Britain by Century 1989
Rowan edition 1990

© E. D. Books 1989

The right of Elizabeth Darrell to be identified as the
author of this work has been asserted by her in accordance with the Copyright, Designs and Patents Act, 1988

Printed and bound in Great Britain by
Courier International Ltd, Tiptree, Essex

ISBN 0 09 959930 9

PART ONE

1

The Kirkland launch glided through the stillness of a dreamy English summer afternoon towards Sheenmouth Abbey, her gleaming white bows breaking reflections of willow-lined banks and pale heat-hazed sky into shimmering images which spread in ever widening circles. Donald Kirkland and his friends were now as dreamy as the atmosphere. They had been up-river to an island owned by their host's father, where they had picnicked, splashed in the shallows, and danced to music from an ancient gramophone whilst sipping cocktails. They were now returning to prepare for the further delights of the evening. It was 1929 and life was there to be lived to the hilt.

Leone Kirkland was not finding it easy to emulate them, as she lay back against the royal-blue cushions gazing at Guy Kingsford who was, in turn, gazing at Mitzi Fennemore. The ache of loneliness had spread from her breast to tighten her throat. Today had been a failure. Although several of Donald's friends had made faint attempts to acknowledge the presence of a thirteen-year-old girl, the blond, brooding embryo poet had totally ignored her. Being ignored during school holidays in the place she could never think of as 'home' was no new sensation to Leone, it was simply more painful, in this instance. Guy was neither a business giant nor an aviation genius such as her father invited to the ancient abbey he had converted into the Kirkland residence; and

7

he was different from the male friends Donald frequently brought here during the university vacations. Leone had had great hopes of finding a soulmate in this silent, seemingly unhappy young man, until she had discovered him writhing in desperate passion amidst the undergrowth on the island they had just left. Leone had only identified the girl beneath him by the pale-blue shoe on the left foot which had beat rhythmically against the ground in either protest or ecstasy, she could not decide which. Guy seemed no happier from the encounter, despite Mitzi's frequent vamping smiles in his direction, so Leone still could not guess the girl's feelings. She knew her own too well.

Twisting away to hang over the side of the boat, Leone realized her attempt to drown her misery with rapid and generous indulgence in the potent cocktails had failed as signally as her efforts to find a companion of her *own*. Her schoolfriends had ceased to accept invitations to the draughty sixteenth-century monastery, which might as well still be inhabited by monks for all the lack of fun and entertainment it offered them. It was not even within easy reach of a city providing such things. Sighing heavily, Leone thought yet again how much easier life would be if Donald had been a nineteen-year-old sister, instead. Being the only girl in a stronghold of self-absorbed males was unbearably lonely: being ignored by every one of them was painful enough to make her long for a return to Switzerland for the new term. She would instantly accept Zöe Charterhill's invitation to spend Christmas with her cousins in St Moritz. Anyone's cousins would be a more attractive prospect than a grey, gloomy yuletide at Sheenmouth Abbey with no company other than cigar-smoking financiers and Donald's undergrad friends who appeared more lecherous than poetic.

Her introspection was interrupted when the launch slid alongside the private jetty. Old Walter, who had been their boatman for years, came forward to pull them in and hold the vessel steady while they all scrambled ashore. Leone was the last to leave because she now realized the full effects of the cocktails tossed defiantly down her throat. In a state Donald would term 'half-cut', she somehow managed to walk the jetty without falling into the water, then began to plod behind the laughing group towards the great yellow monastery high on the bank of the River Sheen near the eastern border of Devon. The buttercups dotting the lower meadow began to swing around crazily as the heat combined with her intoxicated state to induce dizziness. Misery was complete as she realized no one was aware that she had dropped far behind them all, nor would they care that she was now feeling very drunk. Longing to reach her room, stand beneath a cool deluge of water, then flop on to her bed to sleep off the unpleasantness of threatening nausea, Leone toiled up the path crossing the meadow, then tackled the long flight of stone steps which led to the flagged terrace running along the south side of the building.

Entering the great hall patterned with colour from stained-glass windows, where a branched staircase gave access to the upper galleries, she found the entire group halted on the stone flags just inside the entrance. Leone stopped also, swaying slightly. Then she heard her father's voice break the sudden silence.

'I'm sorry to spoil the light-hearted mood of your day, Donald, but I'm afraid there's been a tragic accident. I must ask you to leave your friends to amuse themselves for a while. Please excuse us, ladies and gentlemen. The freedom of house and grounds is yours, but I must ask you to stay clear of the chapel. Restoration is not yet complete, so there's a real danger of falling masonry. My staff will be happy to bring anything you may require, and my son will join you shortly before dinner. Drinks will be served in the baptistry at seven-thirty.'

Leone pushed her way unceremoniously through the cluster of guests just in time to see her father and Donald heading towards the library at the far end of the vast hall. With a sudden rush of resentment she stared at their backs. What kind of tragic accident had occurred? How did it affect Donald? Although her brother was destined to inherit Kirkland Marine Aviation after working his way through Cambridge and the company's design office, he was not yet allowed a hand in controlling the family organization which built seaplanes. However, if the tragic accident did not concern the business, why should it affect Donald and not herself? She was as much a Kirkland by birth as he. Resentment burst into open protest at this further instance of ranks closing to shut her out, and inebriation made her pugnacious. She set off determinedly towards the library, her soft-soled shoes making no sound to betray her.

Sir Hector pushed open the heavy studded door of the ancient book-lined room to allow Leone a glimpse of someone waiting there. Vision was cut off by the closing door but, as it was not closed completely, she had no hesitation in widening the gap enough to peer through. The visitor came as a great surprise, for he was a youth standing awkwardly on the mustard and black carpet which had been especially woven in Axminster. This boy was vastly different from Donald's university friends. His face was ashen, his dark eyes wide with some kind of shock as he gazed at the Kirklands. The clothes he wore were cheap and ill fitting. Bony wrists stuck from the sleeves of his tweed jacket, and the collar of his shirt, wrinkled and grubby, looked tight enough to choke him. The brown shoes had scuffmarks on the leather; the heels were worn down unevenly.

Leone gazed at the stranger, fascinated. Then Sir Hector turned to explain his presence to Donald. 'Geoffrey Anson met with an accident in the workshops this morning. It seems he had been drinking more heavily than usual, lost his footing, and fell into one of the machines. He had no chance, of course. Nothing could be done until the machine had been switched off. The shock from such terrible mutilation would have mercifully killed him instantly, but the men are all very shaken by the affair, as you can imagine. I've closed the workshop for today, and sent them all home.' Shaking his head, he said heavily, 'What a senseless tragedy! He had been warned several times about drunkenness during working hours – once by me personally – so he knew quite well the risks he was running by pursuing that course. As everyone knows, the poor man went downhill fast after his wife left him. I was loath to fire one of the most gifted designers in the country, however, even though his work was suffering from the systematic decline.'

'Good God, sir,' exclaimed Donald, apparently only just taking in the implications of what he had been told. 'Surely we are safeguarded against industrial accidents.'

'For those who are sober, yes,' came the sharp reply. 'Anson was not in command of himself, so there'll be no obligation for company compensation, I assure you. Teale has already compiled the report exonerating Kirkland's from all blame. Even so, the man had been with us a long time. I regarded him almost as a friend, which leaves me with some sense of obligation, despite the circumstances.' His outflung hand indicated the white-faced boy. 'This is Kit Anson, Donald. His father's sudden death has saddled him with debts he can never hope to repay. It has also left him alone in the world. A few minutes ago, I offered him a home here, and the opportunity to continue his engineering studies at the company's expense.'

Shaken by his father's words, Donald stammered, 'I . . . beg your . . . your pardon, sir, but are you saying you've . . . *adopted* him?'

'Not officially, but I trust he'll find it possible to feel like one of the family before long. He may not look the part right now, but we'll soon get him some decent things to wear and polish him up enough to meet Kirkland standards.'

At that point, Leone slid back through the door to

lean against the thick stone wall, heart thudding. Her father and brother had discussed something totally bizarre. Her father had just declared that he would have that gauche boy looking and feeling just like one of the family. Donald had been thunderstruck, as well he might. To have some kind of unofficial brother thrust upon him at a moment's notice must raise all manner of fears in his mind. A drunkard's orphan in their midst could make little difference to her own future, but could he possibly shake Donald's?

The three came from the library at that point, and headed for the stairs. Her father had a reassuring hand on Donald's shoulder. Kit Anson walked like an automaton several paces behind them.

'I've instructed Maitland to install him in the bell-tower suite,' Sir Hector was saying. 'The light's particularly good there, and that small look-out halfway up the intermediate steps will serve as a study, where he can set up his drawing board. He brought a few things with him, but Maitland has the rest in hand. You'll have to find him a dinner jacket and stiff shirts until he's properly kitted out. No need for riding breeches or tennis flannels yet awhile. The boy can't decently indulge in such things until after the funeral. I've arranged for that to be held on Thursday.' Reaching the foot of the stairs, they all halted. 'There'll have to be an inquest, of course. Teale assures me it'll be no more than a formality and, for young Anson's sake, he'll ensure that the affair is kept as private as possible. No point in raking up Anson's past history. I never believe in looking back. What's done can't be altered. One must always look to the future. Far more rewarding than wallowing in regret.' He began turning away. 'Well, take him up and settle him in, my boy. I'll be studying Willard's latest report, so won't be dining with you. It'll be your duty to introduce young Anson to your friends.'

Addressing his father's back, Donald asked stonily, 'What do I introduce him as?'

Sir Hector turned. 'Eh?'

'What do I tell my friends?'

'Tell them. . . .' He let out a rich laugh. 'Tell them to take a good look at him as he is now because they won't recognize him in three years' time. He might well be our leading designer one day, if he's inherited his father's brilliance . . . and if he takes full advantage of his new status.'

Leone waited until they had all vanished from sight then, lost in speculation, made her way to her rooms. She sprawled on the green cushions of the window seat to gaze at the bell tower rising at the far end of the front façade, the threatening nausea dispelled by the drama she had just witnessed. Sir Hector Kirkland was universally known as a ruthless unforgiving man, who would tolerate neither weaklings nor tricksters. Why, then, had he taken in the penniless son of an employee who had often been warned about his drinking and whose work had suffered because of it? It made no sense. Her father reputedly never made a move unless it brought some advantage his own way. What could an orphaned engineering student deeply in debt offer a man who could snap his fingers and make practically anything happen? All manner of wild theories flew through her fuddled brain. Could Kit Anson be her own illegitimate half-brother? The fact would explain the mystery and fit well with the information that Daisy Anson had left her husband, forcing him on the path to drink and ruin. Leone was thrilled with the notion, until reason told her that Kit's mother would surely have taken her love-child with her and that Geoffrey Anson was unlikely to have continued to work for his wife's seducer. The death blow to this attractive theory was the knowledge of her own father's complete rejection of women after the death of his wife when Leone was no more than an infant.

Rolling away from the window, dissatisfied with her lack of a solution and unable to forget that glimpse of someone destined to become one of her family, she decided on more positive action. Still in her crumpled shorts and sun-top, she ran on bare feet along the upper gallery to the bell tower. It did not occur to her to knock on the curved door. Pushing it open, she climbed the six spiral steps to the set of rooms normally used only for bachelor guests of youth or no great importance. Leone liked the suite on three levels, with a marble bath in the smallest of the circular chambers just beneath the arch containing the original monastery bell. The ingenuity of the modernization appealed to her love of the quaint. It seemed to have overwhelmed the sturdy figure standing by a sconced window set in the thick curving yellow stone wall. He was staring from it like a resigned prisoner.

Unbidden rapport arose in Leone at the sight. 'Don't you like it here?' she asked in quiet sympathy.

He spun round nervously, startled by her unsuspected presence, and she saw that his square face was still ashen around a mouth tugged down by shock. Even so, the dark stony eyes missed no detail of her crumpled, expensive leisurewear.

'This is the original tower, you know,' she continued, when he remained silent. 'The huge cast-iron bell is up there directly above where we're standing. Don't worry. There's no chance of it falling. Father ensured that it's securely held in place. The monks used it to summon everyone to vespers, or whatever it was they had. It was also rung as a warning of fire or flood or any kind of disaster.'

After several moments during which Leone wondered if shock had robbed him of speech, he said, 'You must be Miss Kirkland. My father said there was a daughter as well as a son.'

His voice, surprisingly deep, contained a strong Devonshire accent which reminded her of the inexplicable circumstances of his installation here. He looked extremely rough around the edges and totally out of place in these surroundings.

14

'I'm sorry about your father,' she offered. 'It must be terrible for you.'

When he merely nodded, she flopped on to one of the chairs covered in ruby velvet and drew up her knees to study him over the top of them. 'My mother also died in a tragic accident, you know. I was a baby when it happened and I wasn't orphaned, of course, which is a bit different, but it means we have something in common, doesn't it?' Thinking of his father's drinking, she added, 'She was drowned when her lover's yacht sank in a storm off the coast of Naples. It caused a frightful scandal.' She thought that information might ease his embarrassment over having a father who was a drunkard and a mother who had abandoned him. 'I'm not supposed to know about the lover – Father never speaks of her or the tragedy – but the facts are common knowledge so I soon heard them.' Hugging her knees tighter, she asked, 'Are you really all alone in the world?'

'My mother's around somewhere, I suppose,' he admitted.

'Doesn't she ever get in touch?' she asked accusingly.

He shook his head.

'Heavens, how odd.'

'There's nothing odd about it. She married again. Started a new life.'

It was defence of the woman who abandoned him, made in aggressive tones. Leone resented his attitude and thought it time to remind him where he was. Fixing him with a stern look, she said, '*You're* starting a new life now. Sheenmouth Abbey dates back to 1584 and much of it is unaltered, you know. The monks weren't always as pious as they should have been, according to legend. Smugglers used to bring contraband goods up the Sheen at night and store them in the grounds. There's a network of tunnels still in existence beneath the building, although Father sealed the entrance when he moved in, and our boatman, Walter, has papers showing that his ancestors were once chased and shot at

15

by excisemen. The monks are known to have brewed medicines here, so how easy it would have been for them to bottle rum or cognac snatched from wrecks along the coast, then sell them under the guise of herbal cordials.'

He appeared unimpressed. 'I've lived in Sheenmouth all my life, so I've heard the yarns. Most of them are nonsense invented by the local fishermen to impress summer visitors.'

'No they're not,' she cried, furious at his dismissal of the legends which gave her family home the only touch of romance she could find in it. 'The bell in this very tower used to toll the go-ahead for the smugglers waiting further down-river with their contraband cargoes, telling them all was ready to receive what they had brought. One of the monks who was more pious than the rest was so filled with remorse after ringing the bell one night, he hanged himself with the rope. Since then, the bell has been known to ring at midnight. A slow dong-donging, as if a heavy weight is swinging on the end of the rope. It's his ghost.' Undulating her arms several times very slowly, she uttered an eerie wail. 'Wooooo!'

Something about the way he looked back at her caused her to fall silent, and she realized the effect of too many cocktails was making her behave very foolishly. It was also bringing a return of nausea. Putting her feet to the floor she sat up straighter, hoping to ease the unpleasantness. The movement merely induced giddiness. Trying to correct the impression of immaturity, she changed the subject abruptly.

'Are you studying engineering at Cambridge, or at Oxford?'

'Neither.'

'Where do you study, then?'

'At home . . . by correspondence course.'

She gazed at him incredulously. 'You mean you actually send questions and answers back and forth by *post*?'

He stiffened. 'How you give the answers to their ques-

16

tions is immaterial. So long as you get them right, you eventually qualify.'

Giving him a frank look, she told him, 'You'll have to do something more impressive than that if you're going to be one of us. Father will insist. You do realize that everything about you will have to change from now on, I hope.'

Shaking his head, he murmured, 'I haven't had time to take it all in yet.'

'Poor you,' she offered, feeling sorry about his total unsuitability. 'Father must have made you aware that you'll never do as you are, if he really does intend to make you into a Kirkland.'

When he ventured no reply, she studied him closely, head on one side. Tall and chunky, in greasy unpressed grey flannels and a faded blue shirt with ragged cuffs, he was as different from Donald as a stray mongrel from a pedigree hound.

'Just why have you been taken in by the grand Sir Hector Kirkland?' she asked curiously.

'For my father's sake, I suppose.'

'Rot,' she declared, getting to her feet so suddenly the room began to spin. 'He has never done anything for someone else's sake in his life. There's a deep mystery behind all this, and I'm going to get to the bottom of it. *I am*,' she emphasized, as she realized that her stomach was finally about to reject the cocktails, and headed for the door. 'I fully intend to befriend you, Kit Anson, because no one else in this house will. After all,' she reasoned, over her shoulder, 'we're going to be like brother and sister, aren't we?'

'I shouldn't think so,' came his low comment, as she hurried down the spiral steps and fled for her own room.

By dinnertime Leone was feeling fine again. After being sick, taking a shower, then lying on her bed for an hour making elaborate plans, she dressed in a deep-cream layered chiffon dress with a frilled bodice, and sallied

17

downstairs eager for action. As the only guests were Donald's, she was perfectly at liberty to dine with them in the refectory now thickly carpeted in tobacco and beige, and hung with silk-embroidered tapestries. The long oaken table with its set of five dozen chairs had been carved by a local craftsman and his two sons. Above the table hung five circular flambeaux, with wall sconces to match, and the lofty chamber was heated in winter by giant tiled stoves imported from Poland.

The house-guests had gathered in the adjacent octagonal room, to stand around drinking sherry or to sit together on scattered church pews lavishly padded and covered in dull green-and-gold brocade. They were all speaking in loud brittle voices as they drank and smoked, but none made any secret of the universal curiosity in the dark young man standing self-consciously beside Donald, the sleeves of his borrowed dinner jacket well down over his square workmanlike hands. Although he also held a glass of sherry, Kit Anson appeared not to have tasted it.

Leone paused on the threshold, comparing her new brother with the existing one. Donald was the taller by some inches, and as fair as the other was swarthy. His physical grace and air of assurance emphasized the gaucheness of a companion who now totally resembled a drunkard's orphan who had been offered charity. Leone bit her lip thoughtfully. Donald had either recovered from the shock of several hours ago, or he was putting on a brave face in front of his friends. It was impossible to tell his true feelings. She did not know her brother well. A six-year age gap had effectively separated them from birth, before the sex barrier had risen to shut her off from the other residents of Sheenmouth Abbey. Donald was easygoing, fond of *girls, gin and gee-gees*, like most of his contemporaries, and confident of his future planned by their father. Beyond that, Leone knew little of his thoughts and feelings. He was always perfectly nice to her, if somewhat condescending, but presumably had no more interest in the deeper side of her personality than she had in his.

As she now walked into the room, her arrival made no impression on anyone save the unhappy Kit Anson. He frowned as he gazed at her across the heads of three girls sitting on a pew facing him. He seemed unsure of whether she was the intoxicated person who had burst into his room that afternoon, so she walked straight to him determined to confirm her vow to befriend him. He certainly looked in need of a friend right now.

'Hallo, Kit,' she greeted warmly. 'Have you been introduced all round?'

'Yes, but I can't remember anyone's name,' he murmured, still frowning.

'Heavens, who can? They call each other *old thing* or *sweetie* or *honeybun*. Don't they, Donald?' she asked her brother.

'Mmm,' he agreed absently, his gaze following the advance of Maitland Jarvis, their father's personal assistant. 'Wonder what old Maiters wants now.'

The sandy-haired man came up to address Kit in his clipped impersonal tones. 'Sir Hector would like to see you in his study. Dr Gibbs has the death certificate, and would like to discuss it with you both. It won't take more than a few minutes, Mr Anson.'

Fully confident that his polite request would be seen as a command, the man turned away. Kit hesitated as he looked for somewhere to put his full glass. Leone took it from him, with a sympathetic smile. Mention of a death certificate had reminded her of the morning's tragic accident, and remorse hit her. She had been too drunk to take in the emotional significance of the astonishing decision to 'adopt' this orphaned boy, and realized she had probably seemed rather unfeeling during their initial meeting.

'We'll wait until you get back before starting dinner,' she promised. Then, when Kit had gone, turned to Donald. 'Isn't it a bit much to expect him to socialize

19

tonight? His father was mangled up in machinery only twelve hours ago.'

Her brother's pale-blue eyes regarded her shrewdly. 'Fat lot he'd care. I thought everyone knew there was no love lost between them.'

'Everyone save me. I've never even *heard* of the Ansons.'

'Why should you have? They didn't concern you in any way.'

'They do now. He's suddenly become my brother.'

A strained smile crossed Donald's attractive features. 'Oh, grow up, Leone!'

'Then what is he? I've ruled out the possibility of his being our half-brother, so what other reason could there be for taking in an employee's orphan and making much of him? He's not exactly the usual kind of *child* orphan, is he? At his age he could get a job, and live in digs somewhere. Lots of people of his class do it, so why not him? Father doesn't make generous gestures like this; he just doesn't! What's behind it, Donald? If I have to treat him as one of the family, I think I'm entitled to hear the facts.'

'You don't have to treat him as one of the family, you idiot,' said Donald acidly, seizing her arm and dragging her out of earshot of the three girls blatantly listening to their every word. Halting in an alcove, he took out his silver case and lit a cigarette from it before saying, with barely contained irritation, 'This doesn't really concern you. You're no more than a child. But, to prevent your inventing romantic notions that Father has a paternal obligation to take the blighter in, I'll tell you what I know. It won't fit your fanciful ideas, because it's a pretty sordid history.'

'Tell, just the same,' she urged, imagining all manner of scandals surrounding the Anson family.

Exhaling smoke, her brother said, 'I knew old man Anson, of course, but I'd never met the son. Seemed something of a spineless sort, from all I'd heard.'

20

'Why?'

'I don't know. Just an impression I had. Geoffrey Anson was loaned to the company just before the end of the war, when we won the contract to build our first seaplanes for the RAF. He stayed with us when peace came, and became our senior designer within a very short time. I was too young to know him in his heyday, naturally, but it appears that success went to his head and he began gambling. He started with small bets on horses. Then, growing addicted to the thrill of games of chance, he took to travelling to Torquay at weekends, to visit the casino. Placing bets with the local bookmaker was one thing, but nights at the gaming tables brought the additional temptation to drink when luck wasn't running his way. Soon, that had also become an addiction, and I gather no one was really surprised when Daisy Anson went off with an itinerant artist who was working in Sheenmouth one summer.'

'Didn't she care about her son?' Leone asked immediately.

Her brother shrugged. 'Who knows? Maybe he was a sullen blighter even in those days. Anyway, she eventually divorced Anson on the grounds of his relationship with a waitress at the casino, and the old boy went downhill fast after that.'

A loud whoop of laughter from a nearby group of his friends took Donald's attention, and he showed every sign of moving off to join them. Leone grabbed his arm quickly.

'Come on, finish the story before you walk away. You can't leave it there.'

Glancing back at her irritably, he said, 'You know the rest.'

'No, I don't. You suggested just now that Kit wouldn't care about his father's death, because they hated each other. Why?'

Donald's long graceful fingers crushed out the cigarette in an ashtray, and he sighed in a long-suffering

21

manner. 'When Daisy Anson left, they were living in a very comfortable place up on the cliffs at East Sheenmouth, but Geoffrey soon owed so much he was forced to sell it. He didn't settle his debts, however. Like all compulsive gamblers, he believed he would one day break the bank and win a fortune. Good money went after bad, until the pair were even forced to leave the cheap rooms they then occupied after old Anson engaged in a drunken brawl with the landlady's husband. When he was also refused further admittance to the casino, he tried to do himself in.'

'Heavens!' cried Leone aghast. 'How?'

'Walked into the sea one dark night. Unluckily for him, some local fishermen spotted him and hauled him out.'

'Poor Kit!'

'Poor Kit, be damned! When the old salts turned up at the shack the Ansons then called home, there was the deuce of a row between the half-drowned father and his son. The story goes that the young blighter had already packed his bag and was on the point of leaving. When they turned up with old Anson still alive and kicking, he was furious, apparently.'

'I suppose he had some reason to be,' offered Leone, not liking what she was being told about someone she had decided to befriend.

'All I know is that his attitude didn't go down very well with those who had plucked his father out of the sea. Despite his faults, Geoffrey Anson was a pleasant chap, well liked by those who met him, and immensely popular down in Sheenmouth.'

'Buying drinks all round in the Smugglers' Inn with the money he should have spent on his son?'

'Well, possibly,' conceded Donald grudgingly. 'It's true that Kit had to abandon his hopes of signing on at the College of Engineering in Exeter, and take a job instead. That hardly improved relations between them.'

Certain her brother was on the point of returning to

the social gaiety of his friends, Leone asked urgently, 'So where does Father come into the affair?'

Donald's roving gaze returned to fasten on her face. 'In view of the long-standing association Kirkland's had had with old Anson, Father decided to step in, in an attempt to stop the rot. He offered the pair, rent free, that disused old boathouse down on our north boundary. It has living quarters above it. In my opinion, it was a jolly decent gesture in addition to giving Kit a job in the workshops, at a time when the recession was making hopes of employment very slight. In return, old Anson walked the straight and narrow for a while, turning in some first-rate work on a new design. As a result of generous advice from Father on some prudent invest-ments, the Ansons were gradually able to pay off what they owed and even start to accumulate. Kit wasn't in the least grateful, however. He made it very clear to the men in our workshops that he deeply resented doing dirty manual jobs, while his father was up in the design office rubbing shoulders with the executives. There are stories galore of heated arguments at the old boathouse between the pair, with Kit even knocking his father down during a row.'

'Where is the boathouse?' asked Leone curiously. 'I've never come across it.'

'You wouldn't. It's beyond that belt of thick copse. No one ever goes there.'

With the sharpness of the adolescent, she asked, 'If no one ever goes there, who could have overheard heated arguments between them?'

'Don't split hairs,' Donald said impatiently. 'They hated each other all right. Chaps in the design office reckon it was their enmity which drove the old chap back to the bottle. He turned up for work half cut one morning and when they hauled young Kit up there to deal with him, Geoffrey kicked up a hell of a stink and flatly refused to let his son near him.' He gave a cold laugh. 'Can't actually pin anything on Kit regarding the affair this morning, because the blighter was conveniently late for work and therefore not in the machine shop at the time. If he possesses any finer qualities at all, which I doubt, he ought to be feeling pretty sick about it, however. No one doubts that he's basically to blame for Anson's death.'

'That's a terrible thing to say,' cried Leone, in a brave attempt to stick by her vow to befriend the intriguing Kit, despite her uncomfortable suspicion that he must be as black as her brother was painting him. 'If it's true, why has Father brought him here to live, and why is Maitland ordering clothes and things which will turn him into someone resembling a Kirkland? It doesn't make sense, does it?'

Donald looked even more strained, as he shrugged once more. 'There was a strong bond between Father and Geoffrey Anson. I suppose he feels it's the least he can do for a man who had a rough deal from life.'

'Phoo,' she declared. 'No one *forced* Kit's father to start drinking and gambling. He had only himself to blame for driving his wife away and turning his son against him. Life didn't hand him a rough deal: he dealt the cards himself.' She felt rather pleased with that quote from a film she had seen recently on much the same theme. Carried away, she went on, 'If you ask me, *he's* the one who's spineless, not Kit. You're basing your opinion of him on things other people have said, which might not be true at all. Anyway, if Kit has been working at Kirkland's, how is it you've never come across him before?'

'He's only a greaser in the workshop. I have no reason to deal with people like that.'

She frowned. 'You'll have to now, won't you? There's more behind this than Father deciding to be kind to an orphan. If I were in your place, I'd be very keen to find out what it is. Kit may not be offered the Kirkland name but, for some strange reason, it looks certain he's going to be offered everything that goes with it. Where will that leave you, Donald?'

Kit did not return. Although Leone tried to persuade her brother to delay the meal, he brushed aside her plea and spoke hardly another word to her that evening. It followed the usual pattern. No one really appreciated the four courses cooked to perfection, and the diners gathered eagerly after the meal to indulge their particular brand of high jinks. A raven-haired girl called Julia spilled coffee down her ivory satin backless evening dress and thought it hilarious. Then, one of Donald's undergrad friends, whose father was a colonial ambassador, accidentally set fire to Mitzi Fennemore's georgette stole with his cigarette, causing shrieks of excited laughter. During the resultant uproar, Guy Kingsford wandered outside moodily, wearing his persistently tragic expression. Leone wondered why he had seemed so fascinating this afternoon. Kit Anson intrigued her far more. She wondered yet again where he could be.

When the others crowded on to the terrace to dance to the gramophone, Leone slipped away unnoticed and made straight for the bell tower. Her quarry was not in his sitting room, so she climbed the spiral steps to the bedroom. He was not there, either. In the open wardrobe hung the borrowed dinner suit. The shirt, stiff front, and bow tie had been flung on to the bed with the onyx cufflinks and shirt studs. Kit's own clothes were nowhere to be seen. Leone might have believed he had run away if it had not been for two cheap suitcases beside the chest of drawers, and for the worn leather case containing draughtsman's instruments which lay alongside a number of rolled sheets of paper. There was a wooden toolchest bearing the initials C.P.A. What was his middle name, she wondered. Peter . . . or Philip? Surely not *Percival*! Far too stuffy for her intriguing new brother.

Up in the circular bathroom she found a cheap shaving brush and razor standing defiantly beside the boxed set from Harrod's provided for the use of guests. The tangy lotions had not been used, for no lingering scent hung in the air. He appeared to have taken advantage of the other facilities, because the maroon bathmat and towels were wet, and the large tablet of quality soap lay in the bath near the plughole. Hanging alongside the maroon bathrobe was a navy-blue plaid dressing gown with a frayed cord trailing from one of its loops. Leone stared at it. He must have had it for years! It was at least two sizes smaller than Kit. Maitland would soon instruct Coombes, the visitors' valet, to dispose of *that*.

Returning to the bedroom, Leone sat on the floor to investigate the contents of the two suitcases. The first was filled with textbooks, piles of notes and technical drawings, and letters from his tutors commenting on his work. He was an excellent student, judging by their comments. There was an old photograph album which she pored over with intense curiosity, identifying Kit as the small boy with floppy dark hair. She guessed the woman in several pictures with him was his mother. She looked quite respectable; plump and blonde, with a shy smile. Not the type to have abandoned her young son, surely. But she had, so the pictures must give a false impression, Leone decided. There were several studies of elderly people who were probably his grandparents. Where were they now? Had they died or, like her own, simply lost interest in the child their daughter had left to fend for itself? A large number of blank spaces in the album suggested that photographs of Geoffrey Anson had been removed. Had father and son truly hated each other, as Donald said?

The second suitcase contained clothes. These were all fairly dreadful, and smelled damp. Holding up a pair of quite astonishing underpants, Leone sighed. Did he really wear such antiquated horrors beneath his trousers? Coombes would faint away with shock at the sight of them. The bathing trunks with a striped belt were almost as ancient, and when she spotted a clumsy darn in the most vital area, Leone had to fight the desire to giggle. Her new brother really would not do, if this was his idea of a wardrobe. To be on a par with the Kirklands, he would have to change beyond recognition. She frowned momentarily, remembering her father saying no one would recognize Kit in three years' time. Why, *why*, was this boy being given such bounty?

Beneath the folded clothes she came upon a framed photograph of a seaplane, and she recognized the background of hangars and slipways owned by Kirkland's. It was a graceful little machine with high wings, and floats almost as long as the aircraft. Even she had heard of *Diadem*, for the company's most famous design had been internationally blazoned in magazines and newspapers when a competitor in the Schneider Trophy Race had blamed his failure to win on the fact that his team had not been flying the sleek little seaplane produced by Kirkland Marine Aviation. To prove his point, the pilot had flown *Diadem* over the designated course on the following day, exceeding the speeds claimed by the trophy winner. The stunt had caused worldwide publicity for Kirkland's, but it was not thoughts of that which occupied Leone as she stared at the framed picture. Inserted into the corner of the frame was a slip of paper. Written on it in a youthful hand was: *Dad's finest design*. So Geoffrey Anson had created *Diadem*! That slip of paper proudly stating the fact did not fit in with the description of a boy who hated his father enough to be glad he was dead. What was the truth about Kit Anson?

After exploring all manner of theories concerning Kit's adoption by her father, Leone had fallen asleep with no firm conclusion. It led her to rush downstairs for breakfast next morning, in the hope that he would be there for her to question. She was delighted to see his solitary figure, at the octagonal table in the room used by those who disliked eating in bed. He got to his feet as she entered, and all she could think of was his terrible under-

27

pants. His top clothes were little better: a crumpled grey shirt, grey flannels and a striped pullover with ribbing that had been stretched into flutes. He was still very pale.

Noticing the empty plate beside his cup filled with strong tea, she asked kindly, 'Don't you want any breakfast? I'm *starving*.'

'They brought me some tea, but haven't asked if I want anything else,' he said. 'I wouldn't mind something to eat.'

'Well, have something, silly,' she cried, crossing to the sideboard. Lifting the lids of the silver dishes one by one, she recited, 'Scrambled eggs, mushrooms, tomatoes with bacon, kedgeree, poached haddock . . . oh, and there's porridge to start with, if you want it.'

He flushed. 'I didn't realize.'

'Don't expect to be waited on for breakfast,' she informed him. 'We all come down when and if we feel like it. The meal can sometimes go on for hours, and the staff have other things to do. Come on! Take what you want. I'm not intending to hold these lids up for ever.'

He crossed to the sideboard, and selected eggs, bacon and tomatoes. Then, when she asked if he wanted porridge first, he nodded and spooned some into a bowl to carry back to his place at the table.

Watching him attack it hungrily, Leone sighed. For someone who was extremely clever at engineering, he was awfully slow in other areas. Had he really intended to go without breakfast, when it was there in front of him? The dishes were big enough for anyone to see.

'Where did you go last night?' she asked, as the butler entered with her customary coffee, setting the silver pot and milk jug by her right hand. 'I was afraid you'd thought better of Father's offer, and gone home again.'

'I did go home,' he confessed, glancing up from the fast-dwindling porridge. 'Dr Gibbs needed certain documents . . . for the inquest.'

'Heavens, I'd forgotten that. How awful for you!'

'Sir Hector says I won't have to attend. It'll be no more than a formality, apparently, and his legal people will handle it.'

'They always do,' she informed him matter-of-factly, as she added cream to her coffee. 'What are your plans for today?'

'I don't know. I intended to go to work, as usual, but your father told me I'm not to do that any longer. Mr Jarvis is going to arrange for me to attend the engineering college when the new term begins.'

Leone thought it time to tell him a few useful facts about life in the Kirkland household. She might save him awkwardness. 'You must stop calling him *Mr Jarvis*. Only the servants do that. There's a choice between "Maitland" or "Old Maiters", as Donald calls him. If you're going to be one of us, you'll have to forget you were ever a greaser,' she added, recalling her brother saying that he never mixed with such people. 'I'm glad about the engineering college,' she said generously. 'It'll be much better than taking exams by courtesy of the royal mail.'

When he made no comment, she tried another tack. 'Would you like to come riding with me when we've finished eating? There's sure to be something in the stables to suit you.'

Dark eyes regarded her warily. 'I haven't had much experience.'

'What does that mean?'

'I've only ridden the Sheenmouth donkeys.'

Her burst of laughter coincided with a forkful of scrambled eggs, as she spluttered, 'You really are funny.'

'It wasn't meant to be a joke,' he said stiffly. 'I've fed and exercised them every evening for three winters. Mr Moxy paid me enough to buy my textbooks.'

'You buy your own textbooks?' she exclaimed, sobering slightly. 'Heavens, how quaint!'

'Every student buys his own books.'

'I don't. Heiterman's provides everything.'

'Only because the ridiculous fees your father pays cover all you need. There's a great difference between your fancy high-class Swiss school and a correspondence course, you know.'

Resenting his preaching tone, she fired up swiftly. 'Congratulations on realizing *that*, at least. It's a pity you're not so sharp about everything else, Kit Anson. If I hadn't come down to breakfast, you'd still be sitting there like a bumpkin waiting to be served.'

His mouth tightened in anger, and he slammed his knife and fork on to the tablecloth. 'Now, look here, you little. . . .'

His outburst was halted by the entry of Maitland Jarvis, looking fresh, alert and supremely assured, as usual. He nodded a brisk greeting to Leone, then addressed Kit.

'The fitter from Sir Hector's tailor has arrived with samples of cloth. He wishes to measure you, Mr Anson. A manicurist is also waiting to attend to your hands.'

'My hands,' he echoed hoarsely. 'What's wrong with them?'

Maitland gave his irrefutable reply to all such awkward questions. 'Sir Hector has requested it.'

He turned away and Kit got to his feet immediately, leaving his breakfast on the table. As he walked off, Leone studied his hands. They were ingrained with grime from the greasy machinery he had been handling day after day in the Kirkland's machine shop. Next minute, she was alone in the room. Dropping her fork forcefully into the plate of cooling eggs, she left the table to go to the window seat and flop on to the cushions. Leaning back against the stonework, arms folded in vexation, she sighed heavily. He had trotted off obediently, like a dog at Maitland's heels. They would have him performing tricks all day now.

'Oh, *blast*,' she cried softly. 'He's going to be like everyone else. *Sir Hector has requested it.* So they go off with Maitland and don't reappear for the rest of the day. I thought he was going to be interesting . . . and *company*.'

The silence in that room seemed to mock her, so she left it swiftly. It was no better in the massive hall. Donald and his friends were all sleeping off the intoxication of the night before, and probably would not descend until lunchtime. Her father would already be at his desk, where he must never be disturbed, and her chosen candidate to help her fill in the long hours was now being manicured and measured. Even the thought of the fitter's pained expression at the sight of Mr Anson's underpants failed to raise her spirits. Kit might be a bit of a simpleton and, as Donald claimed, a sullen blighter, but he had been someone to talk to and investigate as a mystery. That was better than no one at all.

Walking moodily to the stables, she told Porter to saddle Jemima, then rode off towards the copse. Even her attempt to take a look at the old boathouse where Kit had lived until yesterday was thwarted, however, for the area was so overgrown there was no passage through to the far side. Changing direction, she went to the Kirkland jetty where she tied her mare to a rail and called to old Walter to bring out the speedboat used by her brother for streaking back and forth on the river.

The boatman shook his head as he looked up from polishing the brass on the larger of the two launches. 'No, Miss, that I can't do. If you was Mr Donald, now that would be a different thing, but I dursn't hand over that streak o' lightning to you. 'Twould be the end of me, I knows. Strict orders I was given about that pesky boat. Mr Donald or his friends, and nacherly your father himself would be perfectly fine, d'ye see, but not you, Miss. Sir Hector pertickly requested it.'

Foiled, she then demanded that Walter row her up as far as the old boathouse. He shook his head again.

'I've not the time. There's a party of very important gennelmen coming to visit the works today, and they're

31

a-coming up to the Abbey for lunch. This launch got to be spick and span, and there's barely a ha'porth of time to do it in. Come back later on and p'raps old Walter'll take you up there, tho' why you'd want to see that tumbledown place I don't know. Up a narrow inlet, it is, and that dark and gloomy it fair gives me the goosies. Folks say 'tis haunted, d'ye see.'

'You'd think every building in Sheenmouth was haunted, from what people say,' she retorted crossly. 'It's a pack of lies to attract visitors, that's all. No one's ever seen a ghost. Not a *real* ghost. Why can't we have something really exciting in Sheenmouth?'

Walter paused in his polishing, his faded blue eyes growing dreamy. 'There's talk they be holding one of they flying races here. That'd be an attraction, all right.'

'Gazing for hours at a series of circling dots in the sky! I don't call that exciting,' was Leone's disgruntled verdict of the Schneider Trophy Race. 'Why can't we have a gruesome murder, or smugglers in the tunnels beneath the Abbey again? Tell me about your great-great-great-*great*-uncle, who found the body of the monk swinging on the bell-rope, Walter.'

His head in the shabby peaked cap bent to the work in hand once more. 'Not today, Miss. I got to get this craft ready for young Philips to take down-river for Sir Hector's guests. You go off now and enjoy yourself.'

Jumping from her perch on the wooden pile, Leone untied Jemima and rode moodily back to the stables. She next took a solitary swim in the pool designed to resemble a Roman bath, then ate a bar of chocolate whilst sprawling disconsolately on a gilt lounger. If a party of important men was arriving for lunch, she would be expected to eat hers in her room and keep out of sight during their visit. Donald would have to desert his friends in order to join the lunch guests, so they would be scattered in various rooms engaged in the usual flirtatious tomfoolery. How would she occupy the rest of the day? Renewing her vow to befriend the boy her father had thrust upon them all, she jumped up with the intention of dressing then visiting the bell tower once more.

The circular suite was empty, and Kit's cheap suitcases were no longer there. The textbooks, photograph album and framed picture of *Diadem* were on the dresser, but his clothes must have been thrown out already. The drawers were now neatly filled with new shirts, ties and handkerchiefs alongside smart underwear. Up in the bathroom the plaid dressing gown had been replaced by one of dark-green spotted silk.

Wandering slowly back down the spiral staircase, Leone went across to pick up the framed picture of a seaplane. *Dad's finest design*. Swallowing a lump in her throat, she acknowledged that the mysterious Kit Anson was speedily being changed into yet another unreachable male in the Kirkland dynasty. Sir Hector Kirkland, self-made millionaire who had turned a disused fish factory into a prosperous marine aviation company and been knighted for his work during the war, had taken in a stray mongrel to add yet another masculine member to a household where only Mrs Roberts, the housekeeper, broke the monastic atmosphere. A drunkard's orphan with grimy fingernails and an uneducated voice was in the process of being given all the daughter of the house possessed, plus something she had striven in vain for. Kit Anson was having *attention* lavished upon him. The new brother had been snatched away greedily and set on the path to his glittering future before she had had a chance to get to know him. She was as alone in that ancient monastery as she had ever been.

The lump in her throat grew larger. At first, she had been intrigued and prepared to offer sympathy, seeing the ashen-faced Kit as another lonely misfit in the unemotional regime which turned Sheenmouth Abbey into a business headquarters rather than a home. Now, she resented him deeply. Within a few hours he had been absorbed into the brotherhood manipulated by Sir

33

Hector. His daughter remained as invisible to his eyes as before.

2

Nothing appeared to have changed much during the three years since Leone had last been in Devon. The seven-mile drive from Axminster took her past familiar landmarks: villages with lyrical names, comprising thatched colour-washed cottages whose gardens were filled with rambler roses, lavender, delphiniums and night-scented stocks; ancient oak-beamed inns with adjacent grassy areas dotted with benches, where children could play as their elders drank; homely sub-post offices providing anything from knitting wool to a packet of biscuits, along with the postage stamps; bow-fronted teashops for gossip over tea and fancies; a saddler's rambling premises with a smithy run by all the men of one local family; small tranquil churches where villagers were baptized, married and finally laid to rest. Between these tiny unchanging communities the road undulated through open downland white with grazing sheep, to climb eventually to the long stretch of high ground which ended in red cliffs above Sheenmouth sands bordering the waters of Lyme Bay.

As Meader turned the car from the road leading down to Sheenmouth, at the junction where a finger-post indicated the narrow lane to Magnum Pomeroy, Leone reflected that if nothing in Devon had changed, she certainly had. At sixteen, she was now one of the senior girls at Heiterman's, enjoying the privileges maturity brought even to schoolgirls. Freedom at weekends, a room of one's own rather than sharing with three others, and permission to arrange meetings with boys – or *young gentlemen*, as the staff preferred to call them – providing some responsible person would also be present at the rendezvous. All in all, life had grown very enjoyable amongst her multi-national friends, so Leone had eagerly accepted invitations to spend school holidays in Athens, Corsica, Florence, Heidelburg, Paris, Monte Carlo, and even one very exciting Christmas in Tunis, where a friend's uncle was the British Consul. Maitland had always cabled her father's permission to stay with this succession of wealthy influential families, and she had never failed to express her thanks in her next obligatory monthly letter home. Whether or not Sir Hector Kirkland bothered to read his daughter's letters, she had no idea. Replies were rare, and then couched in unmistakably 'Jarvisonian' terms. Cards and presents arrived on the appropriate occasions, almost always from an exclusive Swiss store, and Easter never passed without a lavish gift of chocolate in a be-ribboned basket. Her father, at least, fulfilled his paternal rôle albeit through a third party. Between herself and Donald there had been no communication whatever since that summer of 1929, when the curious 'adoption' of Kit Anson had taken place.

Whatever the initial reason behind her father's surprising move, he was now apparently reaping rich rewards. After Kit had been snatched up by the system operating in her home that summer, she had returned to school vowing not to court such loneliness by spending another vacation there. The vow had held good until some of her schoolfellows had begun sighing over photographs in society magazines of a dashing young British aviator, who was fast making a name for himself in speed flying. Slowly, it had dawned on her that the subject of their hero-worship had the same name as the drunkard's orphan who had ridden only the donkeys on Sheenmouth sands. Doubting that the 'Keet Ansong' the girls adored could possibly be the one she knew, Leone had studied the pictures closely, trying to identify the laughing young man in a leather flying helmet with the white-faced boy she could now hardly recall. Yet the text had claimed him to be the test pilot for Kirkland Marine Aviation, whose latest unofficial speed trial suggested that he would soon make his all-out attempt at the world's speed record. He would fly the exciting new seaplane *Aphrodite* designed by Donald Kirkland, son of a man who owned the company pushing to rival the top manufacturers. Only then had Leone realized how long she had stayed away from that monastery in Devon. Life there had been marching along in her absence.

Curiosity had driven her home. If Donald had actually designed this new aircraft, he must have abandoned his sybaritic life and got down to some serious work. Without a host of undergrad friends surrounding him, and her own maturity putting her in the adult league now, she might have a chance of drawing closer to her brother. Certainly, her father could no longer deny the presence of a grown daughter among his influential guests. Both he and Donald would find her a person to reckon with, she told herself, and undertook the long journey with all the aplomb of a much-travelled, sophisticated and extremely determined girl on the brink of womanhood. In a tussore-silk Paris costume which emphasized her developing figure, and with the confidence of personal popularity with her European friends, Leone vowed to tackle the brotherhood at Sheenmouth Abbey and gain entry, at last.

The late May sunshine was striking the south side of the building with its bell tower in the eastern corner when Meader drove up between the cedars to the massive studded door. The yellow stonework appeared to glow with light as Leone studied her home with faint surprise. Had it always looked this impressive and beautiful? Maybe it truly had changed during her absence. When the chauffeur came round to open her door, she swung her legs to the ground and stood for a few moments gazing down the sloping meadows to where the river shimmered between the young green of the trees bordering its banks, and beyond that to the little town of East Sheenmouth. There was a sense of tranquillity, broken only by the far-distant calls of a flotilla of moorhens as they sailed past the Kirkland jetty, which reminded her that no other place she knew had quite the same mesmeric quality on early summer sunshiny days. As the soft breeze ruffled the tendrils of hair above her ears and shifted the calf-length fluted skirt against her legs, she caught herself sighing with unexpected pleasure.

Her mood was broken as Clunes and Meredith came from the house to greet her with impersonal respect, then take from Meader the vast number of leather trunks and bandboxes stacked atop and behind the car. Gazing around the vaulted hall with its chequering of colour from the stained-glass windows, Leone marvelled that it could appear so different now. Had she seen it with the vision of a child before? On being informed that Sir Hector, Mr Kirkland and Mr Anson were all at the works, which disappointed but did not surprise her, Leone told Clunes that she would have a tray of tea in her sitting room, and set off up the stairs, unpinning her burnt-straw hat as she went.

When she entered the suite of connecting rooms which had been hers all her life, her three-year absence was even more abundantly apparent. She found herself surrounded by the trappings of girlhood. The wardrobes were filled with dresses covered in frills and bows, tailored skirts in navy, white or grey with racks of blouses which hung straight, without bodice shaping. The evening gowns had high waists and puff sleeves, bringing a smile from her at the thought of those presently in the trunks being brought upstairs one by one. Even the former treasures lying about the room – a harlequin doll with a china face and floppy limbs, a trinket box of inlaid mother-of-pearl, an ivory buddha whose stomach she would rub for a wish to be granted, a tennis racquet reputed to have been owned by Suzanne Lenglen, a photograph of John Gilbert – all these spoke of a girl Leone had practically forgotten. Had the entire household forgotten her, too? She would soon awaken it to her presence!

After taking a shower and dressing in a blue linen frock, she drank her tea. The four tiny sandwiches and the dainty fingers of honey cake remained on the plate as she finally admitted to herself her true reason for coming home. Unable to resist the impulse, she made her way to the bell tower. Presumably, he still occupied the tiered circular rooms. As she climbed the six spiral steps to the sitting room, a curious wave of apprehension swept through her. Kit Anson had been no more than a gauche white-faced youth of nineteen. Who was this man he had apparently become within three short years; a man who was more a member of her family than she?

He was certainly not a tidy person. Although his valet would have removed any shoes or clothing left lying about, he would not be permitted to touch letters, papers or items of a professional nature, and the chaotic state of both desk and adjacent study proved that point. Open textbooks, charts, diagrams, newspaper clippings, files spilling letters written on headed notepaper, vast numbers of gilt-edged invitations, a great many photographs of aircraft, most with neatly printed data clipped to them, and several grease-smeared logbooks all jumbled together to give the impression that the occupant was either totally unorganized or so busy he had no time for order. An aroma of shaving lotion mixed with petrol hung in the room, as she gazed around at this evidence of unquestionable ownership by Kit Anson.

Then she spotted the framed photograph and moved to pick it up. Recollection of him flooded back at the sight of *Diadem* and the slip of paper in the corner of the frame. *Dad's finest design*. Yet he had reputedly hated his father, had once actually knocked him down, and been furious when fishermen had prevented the older man's suicide. That pale face, badly cut dark hair and loud tweed jacket from which grimed hands had jutted, came back in her memory so clearly she marvelled that they had not been constantly with her.

'Well, you've got more nerve than the rest, I'll say that for you,' pronounced a voice containing a faint Devonshire accent from behind her, making her swing round so swiftly she almost lost her balance, 'I don't know how the hell you slipped in past the servants without being seen, but I promise you they'll certainly see you on your way out, young lady,' he continued forcefully, advancing to pluck the photograph of *Diadem* from her hand. 'Come on, out you go!'

Next minute, this thickset dark fury of a man seized her by the collar of her dress and the seat of her panties to frogmarch her across the room then down the steps to the door. Robbed of clear thought by his preposterous behaviour, Leone found herself halfway along the upper gallery before it occurred to her to struggle. It did no good. He had too firm a hold of her in strategic places. Whether or not he would actually toss her bodily from the premises she had no chance to discover, for Meredith appeared with one of her pale leather bandboxes which had been overlooked.

'Black marks all round,' her captor told him sternly, in passing. 'You know the tricks they get up to, so how is it none of you spotted this little miss sneaking in?'

'But . . . that's Miss Kirkland, sir,' announced Meredith faintly.

'Never mind who she is, she should have been prevented from breaking into my rooms,' came the firm directive, as he halted momentarily. 'Someone must have seen her . . . unless she climbed up the bell-rope. I wouldn't put it past her.' Then, in the act of moving off again, he asked curiously, 'Who did you say she is?'

'Sir Hector's daughter, Mr Anson. I understood you to be acquainted with the news of her expected arrival

40

today,' Meredith added, with awe at such conduct towards the only female member of the family he served.

Loosening his hold on the back of her skirt, Kit tugged at Leone's collar until she was facing him, saying to the servant as he scrutinized her closely, 'Are you playing straight with me, Meredith? She hasn't bribed you to say she's Leone Kirkland?'

Meredith was affronted. '*Certainly not, sir*. I'm holding an item of baggage in my hand now.'

A grin broke over Kit's face as he murmured, 'So am I.'

'If you value your toes enough to prevent their being stamped on, you'll quickly let it go,' said Leone, coming to terms with the situation at last. As Kit's hand dropped to his side, she stepped away from him, saying, 'That'll be all, Meredith.'

As the servant moved off with the bandbox, Kit began to chuckle, scrutinizing her from head to foot. She told him coolly, 'Your toes are still in grave danger, Mr Anson.'

Holding up a defensive hand as he edged away, his humour nevertheless increased. 'Be fair. You've changed rather a lot.'

'So have you.'

'You were a pert child.'

'You were a stray mongrel.'

Tipping back his head as laughter got the better of him, he gave Leone the uncanny feeling that although he had no pedigree he had somehow become a champion of his breed. As she continued to watch this irrepressible stranger, who bore little resemblance to the boy of three years ago, she realized that laughter of such a spontaneous genuine nature had had no place in the sober atmosphere of her home in the past. He could only have challenged it and been the victor. Now he had done the same with her, because laughter was starting to bubble in her own voice, as she said, 'I think I'm entitled to know why I was about to be thrown out of my own house.'

He nodded, dark eyes still lively with mirth. 'You are, indeed, although I doubt the explanation will endear me to you.'

'I doubt *anything* will do that after the way you've just treated me, but tell me just the same.'

Putting his hand beneath her elbow, he began to lead her back along the gallery. 'Aviation is a hazardous profession, Miss Kirkland. Although I'm not afraid of a challenge, a chap can be hugged almost to death by squealing girls and kissed practically unconscious by those who are really determined to have their pictures in the newspapers. You wouldn't believe the tricks these sensation-seekers employ. One even tried to post herself to me in a giant parcel.'

Leone looked up at him suspiciously. 'You're lying.'

'Cross my heart and hope to die,' he assured her. 'So when I walked into my rooms just now and found a neat little blonde baggage making herself at home, what was I to think? Girls have tried it before, believe me, which is why I've told the staff to be on the look-out for soft cuddly intruders.' Reaching the bell tower, he ushered her through the door and up the steps, studying her expression. 'Have I succeeded in making you understand my reaction?'

She waited until they had re-entered the cluttered room before answering, 'You've succeeded in making me think you're disgustingly conceited.'

He grinned. 'So girls are constantly telling me.'

Inviting her to sit down, he shrugged off his expensive Harris tweed jacket, then dropped on to a velvet-covered chair as he tugged the green silk cravat loose and tossed it on to a nearby pile of books. Watching him, Leone was filled with sudden strange fascination. The pure physical impact of this man was like none she had encountered in those of her own set. His tanned face was vivid with undisguised eagerness for life; expressions

42

chased across his features to betray his true feelings with no hint of affectation. Taller and even more muscular than before, Kit Anson had somehow retained the intriguing hint of origins which lay deep in the yeomanry of Devon, despite the assurance of someone who was now a Kirkland in all but name. Her sense of faint shock deepened as she recalled how he had seized and ejected her from this room a moment ago. Smiles might come readily to this reckless aviator, but there was an aggressiveness about him which suggested that anger could rise as swiftly as laughter and prove just as devastating. A powerful personality to confront!

'I can't believe that you and the boy I recall are the same person,' she murmured, almost to herself.

'We're not,' he responded firmly.

'Tell me what happened.'

Leaning back with one leg resting across the other knee, he said, 'When those summer holidays ended, that boy was sent to an engineering college for the final year of studies. By the time he had gained his qualifications, he had discovered the true love of his life. His benefactor had provided him with the funds to afford flying lessons, and the aforementioned disgusting conceit allows me to tell you that everyone soon realized that he was a born pilot with exceptional aptitude. When he joined Kirkland's there was just one job he wanted, so he demanded it with great temerity. A short period of corrective punishment followed but, I regret to admit, it didn't cure his determination to have his way. Taking matters into his own hands, he defied orders and took up the company seaplane to demonstrate what he could do with it. Despite the fact that he damned near broke his neck in several very risky manoeuvres, the stunt so impressed the great Sir Hector that a truce was declared. Kit Anson became the test pilot for one of the most advanced marine aviation companies in the country on the following day.' Leaning forward to grasp his knee, he spoke with sudden depth of feeling. 'I count myself one of the most fortunate men in the world, although I have finally given up pinching myself to prove I'm not dreaming it all.'

She asked him the question which had never been answered. 'Why did Father take you in three years ago?'

Glancing down at his linked hands, he said, 'God knows . . . but I've made sure he's never regretted it.'

How could he have regretted it, Leone thought, as she studied the explosive quality of this person who had changed so totally since their last meeting. There was an assurance, a sizzling vitality, an air of iron determination about him which surely only Kirkland influence could have generated. She had come home ready to resent a stranger who had captured all she had consistently been denied; ready to fight him for the place he now occupied in her family. Instead, she was swamped by feelings she had least expected.

'The European magazines suggest you might soon challenge the air speed record,' she said. 'Is there any truth in that?'

His square face was alive with an astonishing pride. 'It's not usual for company pilots to compete in that area but, after a few more trials, I'm going to have a crack at it, yes.'

'In *Aphrodite*?' she asked, to show that she was au fait with family affairs despite her three-year absence.

'Of course! She's a siren of a machine; a temptress who offers paradise to the man who dares give her her head and manages to hold on to his own,' he declared fervently. 'Just as I believe I've mastered her, she demands more of me. The perfect union is only a matter of days away. As soon as we reach that balance of wills, I'll tell Sir Hector to fix the date.'

'You speak as if she were a woman,' Leone said, strangely envious of his sensuous description of a relationship she did not comprehend.

He shook his head. 'Women are easy to handle. *Aphrodite* is a goddess.'

'You mean, you can't grab an aircraft by the seat of its pants and give it a piece of your mind?'

A grin dawned on the face that surely could never once have been ashen with shock and awe. 'I'll not be forgiven for that, I can see, unless I use excessive charm.'

'My brother designed the seaplane,' she said, reverting to a safer subject. 'Does he share your love affair with this combination of wood and metal?'

'Ah, designers are a different breed altogether,' he informed her, lying back in the chair and crossing his legs in the perfectly tailored flannels. 'They are bewitched by line and elevation, by thrust and power ratio; they worship at the shrine of positive and negative Gs, wing curvature and structural equilibrium.' Then he added, with apparent seriousness, 'Designers create a stunningly beautiful virgin, then stand back to admire her from afar. It's the pilot who woos her, urges her to give her all, and finally conquers her, losing his own heart in the process.'

With her earlier curious sense of envy deepening into something remarkably like jealousy, she said, 'If you've given your heart to a flying machine, small wonder you treat women so badly.' When he laughed, she left the subject again swiftly. 'I still can't imagine Donald worshipping nuts and bolts.'

'All right, perhaps he's more prosaic than my father was, but *Aphrodite* is the result of designing brilliance, take my word. When I break the speed record, it will be as much a triumph for him as it will be for me . . . and Rolls-Royce, naturally, for without their supercharged engine especially designed for us there'd be no point in trying.'

'What *is* the point in trying, Kit?' she asked. 'There must be a reason other than doing it for the fun of it.'

'Certainly. Attention will be focused on Kirkland Marine Aviation as a contender for inclusion among the real giants such as Hawker's and Supermarine. Sir Hector has been highly successful with his foreign investments during this recession, but the company has been suffering like all other British Industrial firms. Kirkland's is his favourite baby, and he wanted a means of pulling it out of the red. This could be it. By making the affair as sensational as possible and sinking money into a flight taking no more than an hour to complete, he could bring off exactly what he hopes for. Orders for the standard *Aphrodite* model should come in from all over the world, Sir Hector will save his company, Donald will be recognized as one of our most talented designers, and I will hold a world record many men presently covet. Not bad reasons, are they?'

'No . . . but they're all dependent on you. Suppose you fail at this "sensational affair".'

'I won't. *Aphrodite* is the fastest thing in the air ever produced. I'll take the record, and your father will feel more than satisfied with the stray mongrel.'

'I'm sorry, I shouldn't have called you that,' she said swiftly.

'It's an apt description.'

'Not now.'

'Wait until you've more knowledge of me before you change your opinion,' he warned. 'I can tell you with confidence that Kirkland's has an exciting future ahead. With Donald designing, and me testing, then suggesting refinements, there's no limit to the kind of machine we'll be producing a few years hence. By that time, my dear girl, you'll be one of the most courted women in Europe.'

'I'm already doing quite well in that direction,' she told him smartly. 'I don't need the help of that dynamic duo Kirkland and Anson, nor do I need a pilot to woo me, urge me to give my all, then finally conquer me, thank you.'

He laughed. 'I'm glad to hear it. It means we can enjoy being just friends.'

Knowing already that she could never be that, she shook her head. 'Your whole life is devoted to a goddess.'

'I still need friends to cheer my lonely moments.'

'You're practically one of the family now. How can you possibly be lonely?'

'You *are* one of the family, and still manage it,' he pointed out.

'That was when I was a child,' she declared. 'I've changed.'

'Outwardly you have, I can't deny, but I suspect you're still the same pert, slightly arrogant, eager outsider seeking a way to enter the charmed circle.'

Judging it time to leave, she got to her feet. 'You might have reached perfect understanding with a seaplane, Mr Anson, but *I* suspect your understanding of women is limited to brute-force tactics which usher them from your hallowed presence as soon as possible.'

She descended the steps with as much dignity as the memory of his hand clutching her panties would allow, but he had the last word.

'Don't destroy yourself in the attempt, Leone. Admission to the reigning dynasty is strictly limited, I've discovered.'

Brother and sister met again after three years, in the octagonal room adjoining the refectory. They eyed each other in surprise as the evidence of the time lapse since their last meeting became clear to them. Leone realized how alike they were now she had matured: tall, slender, blond and graceful of limb, blue-eyed with golden skins. There was no doubt of their kinship.

'My word, you look very grown up, Leone,' said Donald, after studying her mauve chiffon dress with broad bands of silver and amethyst beading around the hem and half-sleeves.

'So I should. I was sixteen in February.' She smiled. 'I like the new moustache. It suits you, despite making you look older than twenty-three and rather studious – like a professor.'

Closer scrutiny of her brother's face showed her a curious lacklustre quality in eyes which used to be bright with zest, and fine lines spreading around them to rob him of that air of youthful exuberance she had seen in Kit. Still too involved with girls, gin and gee-gees? Surely the rigours of being 'hugged to death and kissed almost unconscious' would have wreaked as much havoc on the vital man she had encountered this afternoon. No, Donald's condition must be the result of long working hours and concentration on the success of his brain-child.

'How's school?' he asked then, irritating her with his reference to something which almost contradicted his earlier compliment.

'Oh, blackboards and desks and inky fingers,' she replied coolly. 'You can't have forgotten, Donald. You were a student for far longer than I've been.'

'Grown rather tart with your riper years,' he commented, further ruining her intention of warming to the brother who had stood aloof during her childhood. 'What's brought you home after all this time?'

'Pour me a sherry and I'll tell you,' she replied, settling on one of the pews and wondering why he seemed so aggressive and jumpy. 'I prefer it rather dry.'

He poured two drinks and handed her one, before taking a cigarette from an embossed case and lighting it. Then, settling in the other corner of the pew, he said through the smoke, 'You stayed away so long I drew the obvious conclusion.'

'Which was?'

'That you couldn't accept the new addition to the household.'

Enlightenment dawned. Donald clearly never had, and understandable resentment of a brother who was not a brother burned within him still. All the same, Kit was a pilot and employee of the company. Donald was heir to it and all that went with it; he was a designer with no longing to fly faster than any man in the world. Kit hardly threatened Sir Hector's legitimate son too seriously.

48

'Didn't it ever occur to you that it was the entire household I couldn't accept?' she asked quietly, wanting to confess her loneliness to someone who would now surely understand it. 'I was unhappy here.'

'Unhappy – a child who was given everything she wanted!'

'Was she?'

'Come off it, Leone, you only had to express a wish and Maitland was instructed to make it reality.'

'Exactly,' she said with emphasis. Then, unwilling to pursue the subject, she turned to something which would bring better results. 'Actually, I was driven home by curiosity. They're probably rather late, but I wanted to give my hearty congratulations.'

He looked startled. 'Good lord, who told you?'

'Not you, which was a bit mean, I thought. No, it was in all the magazines, so I guess it's pretty common knowledge everywhere.'

'I don't understand,' he said in plain confusion.

'*Aphrodite*, you chump!' she said laughingly. 'The glossy magazines were full of glamorous pictures of Kit, accompanied by superabundant praise for everyone concerned with the project. The whole world must be aware that you've designed this terrific seaplane.'

Confusion was replaced by a surprising suggestion of unease on his fair handsome face, and he tossed back the remainder of his sherry in one gulp. Twisting to put the glass on a small table, he said, 'I thought you were referring to Steph.'

Taken aback by his response to her genuine enthusiasm for his achievement, and by his total lack of interest in taking up the chance to recite an ode of praise for the machine – as Kit had done – she asked curiously, 'Who's Steph – someone in the design office?'

Thinking better of his empty glass and taking it across to the decanter to refill it, he made a surprising announcement. 'I shall celebrate my engagement to Stephanie Main at the reception to be held here to celebrate the breaking of the speed record earlier that same day. Maitland has all the arrangements in hand; invitations written, caterers booked, band engaged, bubbly on ice. All we need is the go-ahead from our pilot, who's as temperamental as a bally prima donna when it comes to pinning him down to a date.'

Thrown off balance by news of another milestone in Donald's life which neither he, nor any other member of this household, had bothered to write and tell her about, and noting the significance of his references to Kit as 'the new addition to the household' and 'our pilot' rather than by name, Leone began to realize that things had not changed much in her home. She was still very much an outsider, it seemed.

'I'm somewhat out of touch, Donald,' she told him, trying to curb her anger. 'Who is my future sister-in-law? Someone Father approves, or you wouldn't be planning to make that kind of announcement on that kind of business occasion.'

'Old man Main is the head of Allied Nordic Banking Corporation. Steph's his granddaughter. Her people run an estate in Northumbria: father's a stockbroker, mother's one of the Stanwell-Turners.'

Leone's eyes widened. 'No wonder Father approves.'

'It cuts both ways,' he said tightly.

'Mmm. Brilliant young designer due to inherit a growing aircraft company, and a converted monastery along with huge foreign investments,' she mused, recalling all Kit had told her this afternoon. 'Yes, I suppose she's doing rather well for herself, too.'

'My God, you've turned into a cynical little tyke,' Donald cried in such savage tones that Leone was unable to control herself any longer.

'Are you trying to tell me that this union is based solely on starry-eyed romance with a capital R? From the information you've just given me, I'd say Father regards it more as a business investment.'

'Ha, that's a typical comment from someone who

spends her time with the precocious daughters of the filthy rich! You have no notion of the reality of life. Father should have chosen a decent English school instead of that highly expensive place in Lucerne.'

'An English school would have been too near Sheenmouth,' she retaliated swiftly. 'I might have turned up unexpectedly on the doorstep at the worst possible moment.'

'Isn't that what you've done now?'

She stared at him, deeply hurt. In three years he appeared to have changed so radically there was no means of reaching him. What had happened to make him so bitter and defensive? Pushing down her desire to lash back in the same manner, she tried once more to break through the barrier she had always come against in this place.

'Donald, please don't let's quarrel,' she began. 'I came home determined to. . . .'

Further words were prevented by the entry of Maitland Jarvis in dinner jacket, bow perfectly tied with ends equidistant from both silk lapels. It was typical of a man who rarely erred, a man Leone had always distrusted without knowing why.

'Good evening, Miss Kirkland,' he greeted with the usual urbane smile. 'Welcome home.'

'Thank you . . . but I appear to have chosen the wrong time for a family reunion,' she replied, still churned up over Donald's aggression.

'I'm afraid we're all very tied up with the speed trials, at the moment. It has become inexpressibly vital to set a firm date.' Turning to Donald, he went on, 'Sir Hector has just received secret confirmation that the Italians plan to put their man Benzini up in a bid for the record sooner than we expected. *Aphrodite* must be ready in time to beat them to it. If we exceed the record by a large enough margin, they'll be so disheartened they'll call it off. It will almost certainly persuade them to put in further work on their machine. Your father's in a fighting mood. He'll want a good reason why we can't go for it before the middle of the month, so I hope to God there is one if Anson says no.'

'He wants another slight modification to the rudder,' Donald told him, with a scowl.

'In that case, do it, boy. Do it!' said an autocratic voice Leone recognized well. 'Why are you standing here drinking sherry when you should be working on it?'

Sir Hector Kirkland had a neat but powerful frame which looked impressive in suits cut by a master tailor. His thinning fair hair had turned grey since Leone last saw him, but his strong features presently wore a vigorous expression which belied his years. It was a look which told those who knew him that he was spoiling for action.

Donald defended his presence there. 'He's merely dreaming up reasons for delaying the moment of truth. We've modified that rudder three times already. I think he's funking it.'

'Why should he?'

'Afraid of failure.'

'He won't fail,' snapped Sir Hector. 'I say he won't; he says he won't. What's up with you, boy? Don't you have any faith in your own creation?'

Donald flushed slightly, and said, 'He's making an issue out of a trifling point.'

'Never mind. Give him what he wants,' came the crisp command. 'Maitland, ring the bell. We'll have dinner right away, then you can get Johnson back to the works, Donald, and drive him all night, if necessary.'

'There'll be no need for that, sir,' Kit assured him, arriving at that moment. 'It's only a small mod. An hour or so should be adequate enough to do it in.'

Casting him an assessing glance, as if checking that he was properly dressed with everything respectably buttoned up, Sir Hector told him, 'That's all to the good, because I've set the date as June tenth. One of my

52

secretaries is driving to Axminster post office at this moment with the invitations for the reception.'

Kit frowned. 'That allows us only twelve days.'

'Precisely. You've been shilly-shallying long enough over this. I'm not going to permit Benzini to steal our thunder when we're so close to success.'

'He will, if I fail due to lack of preparation.'

'Don't use that tone with me. I've made the decision, and you'll do as you're told.'

'I'm the man who'll be making this attempt,' Kit reminded him.

'I'm the man who's paying you to make it. Never forget that, boy.'

'I never forget who calls the tune, sir, but you'll be throwing your money away if I'm not ready by the tenth. To go up in a machine unable to fulfil its true potential may result in my taking the record, but it'll be by such a narrow margin Benzini will take it from us before your bubbly's gone flat.'

Sir Hector smiled at him. 'If you're *not* ready by the tenth, it'll be not only my money that's thrown away, but your job. Grab this thing by the throat and go for it. Stop being so pernickety.'

'Being pernickety, if that's how you like to regard it, is behind the success of any pilot,' Kit countered, growing heated. 'It's not only your prestige and the boost to Kirkland's sluggish trade which will be at stake when I take *Aphrodite* up. My life might seem a trifling consideration against all that, but I'd prefer to hang on to it for a few years more.'

For several moments the two men confronted each other, then the older one smiled again. 'Now then, boy, simmer down. We're all getting stage fright, which is why I propose to ring up the curtain. I have utter confidence in you. The whole team has. Let's have dinner, then you can take yourself off to bed while Donald puts this modification in hand. Test it tomorrow when you're less jumpy.'

Turning away from Kit with the intention of moving into the refectory, her father then caught sight of Leone, still sitting on the adjacent pew. A suggestion of minor shock passed fleetingly over his face, then he said in unusually quiet tones, 'By George, how much you've grown to resemble your mother!'

She rose, acknowledging to herself that she had half expected him to imagine that she was one of Donald's friends. 'How are you, Father?'

'Very tied up with an event of acute importance, as you've probably deduced from all this technical argument. Dining with us, are you? Come along then. Time is a luxury none of us can afford, at the moment, so the sooner we sit at the table, the sooner we can leave it and get back to work. Except you, boy,' he added, in Kit's direction. 'A nightcap and bed is your after-dinner schedule every night until the tenth. Your women'll wait for you, never fear. They'll probably welcome a rest, too.'

To her astonishment, Leone found her elbow being taken by her father, who walked her into the adjacent stone dining hall in which five places had been set at the long table. As they progressed, he asked how she was, how she liked school, and what the channel crossing had been like. She answered in dutiful tones, reflecting that they could have been strangers recently introduced, who were making polite conversation.

Then he smiled with a semblance of affection. 'Now you're here, have you everything you need?'

'Not really, Father,' she told him impetuously. 'I've outgrown Mrs Roberts, who never did much for me, anyway. I've always been provided with a personal maid at the homes of my friends.'

'Then you shall have one here. See to it, Maitland,' he commanded, as they all sat at the table. 'No moon-faced local girl, of course. Contact a London agency for one. French, if possible.'

'Certainly, Sir Hector,' said his assistant, shaking out

his napkin with such a precise flick of his wrist, the starched linen cracked like a whip.

'The jewellers will be sending a man down with the ring on Thursday, Donald,' said the man of the house, apparently considering his daughter's needs now taken care of, and concentrating on his son. 'We were wise to select a solitaire. Always a better investment, in my opinion. Nothing flashy, just a top-quality stone in a good setting. You'll place it on the girl's finger as I make the announcement, so the newsmen can take a few pictures.'

As his monologue continued, Leone glanced at the two men facing her and asked, 'What's Stephanie Main like?'

'Very charming and well connected,' Maitland told her smoothly.

Kit offered a more comprehensive version, as they sipped chilled vichyssoise. 'Rich brown hair – masses of it. Eyes the colour of vintage sherry. Slender, intelligent. A voluptuous dancer when the wine has been flowing. Lovely arms, skin like cream satin. . . .'

'That'll be enough to be going on with,' Leone told him tartly. 'I thought you only waxed lyrical over flying machines.'

'Ah, if you want real lyricism, I'll describe *Aphrodite*,' he offered with his wicked grin.

'I'll form my own impression of her, thanks,' she replied, feeling decidedly aware of his impact in a well-cut dinner jacket. 'You seem to get too carried away by your appreciation of beauty.'

Sir Hector broke into their conversation, taking up her last line. 'He can forget all that for the next twelve days, as I just now told him. Now, Maitland, I want you to ring Miss Main and ask her the colour of the gown she'll be wearing on the tenth, then order a basket of appropriate flowers to be brought in when the announcement is made.'

'Certainly, sir,' came the response, the request apparently being stored in the filing cabinet of his brain.

After a meal of soup, an asparagus soufflé, local fish with summer vegetables grown on the estate, and various cheeses during which talk was concentrated on the coming speed attempt, the gathering immediately broke up. Donald was posted off to the workshops down-river; Maitland disappeared with his employer in the direction of the office suite on the third floor of the monastery with only a brief goodnight. Left alone with Kit, Leone found him looking apologetically at her.

'Not much of a first-night reunion, is it? I did warn you.'

'Father's insistence on setting the date has produced worries, I understand that,' she said, trying to sound sincere.

'I'm afraid I'm going to have to leave you, as well.'

'That's right,' she agreed hollowly. 'A nightcap and straight to bed . . . *alone*.'

He overlooked that jibe in surprising manner. 'I must go down there with Donald to keep an eye on what they're doing to *Aphrodite*. I have to fly her in twelve days' time. She has to be perfect by then.'

Anxious to keep him there a little longer, she asked, 'Is flying really as dangerous as you suggested? Your life at stake, and so on.'

'No, dear girl, flying isn't in the least dangerous. Crashing is. That's what I hope to avoid when I push her to limits no other aircraft has reached.' Touching the top of her head lightly with his hand, he added, '*Goodnight, sleep tight. Hope the bugs don't bite.*'

'What?' she asked softly.

'A little rhyme I used to chant as a boy. I'd forgotten it until now.'

He walked away, leaving her with the thought that while Donald's future bride and an aerial goddess could inspire poetic odes to their charms, all she could coax from him was the memory of a rather vulgar rhyme from his dubious past. With a sigh, she made her way up the branched staircase, feeling as excluded as if the monastic brethren still inhabited her home.

When Kit went for his morning swim he was lost in thoughts of the coming twelve days. The modification had been done the night before, and he intended to take *Aphrodite* up as soon as today's tidal flow provided the right conditions, but he was unhappy over Sir Hector's high-handed attitude towards this speed attempt. Kit knew his own caution was being viewed in some quarters as self-doubt or even fear of failure, but a pilot must be allowed his own judgement over something which would be followed by the eyes of the world and which also constituted a considerable risk to his life. He knew he was capable of exceeding the present record of just over 407 m.p.h., but his love affair with *Aphrodite* instilled in him the strong desire to display her full glory when he launched his mistress on her glittering path to fame. So jealous of their relationship was he, any attempt by another man to intrude on it aroused the martial instinct in him. How dare old Kirkland try to stamp his avaricious, insensitive will upon a union which was so delicately balanced? When Kit climbed into the cockpit later that day, he would have to speak love words to his temperamental lady; coax her, woo her with honeyed promises of paradise if she would consent to their ultimate consummation within a matter of twelve days. When it did occur, with a sea of upturned faces studying every movement they made, he wanted the whole world to hold its breath with wonder. Sir Hector had no understanding of this. Kit's demonstration of his commitment to *Aphrodite* would be vastly different from that of Donald's to Stephanie Main on the same day. It required more than a shrewdly chosen solitaire and a basket of flowers to match his lady's dress. Kit's soulmate needed constant pampering, warmth and protection from the elements, sleeking down with soft cloths and clear golden oil, gentle words of adoration and encouragement as she purred quietly over the sparkling river before her orgasm of excitement, which would lift them both into a heaven precluding any other person as they dipped and soared as one. Small wonder he was preoccupied that morning, as he swam back and forth in the Roman-style pool.

The morning ritual was not due to a passion for swimming; it was part of his necessity to keep fit. To fly an aircraft might suggest no more than the ability to sit in a small leather seat and move one's arms, but a pilot needed to be mentally alert, strong enough to hold his machine steady in an emergency, and physically sound. Kit underwent a regular check at the Sheenmouth Cottage Hospital, ate well, and exercised daily. His eight hours of sleep might often be taken alongside a soft female form, but he counted that as additional exercise and a very definite contribution to his sense of general wellbeing.

Between now and the tenth of June, however, there would be no sexual exercising, he was just reminding himself, when a girl's voice called out a good morning to him. Turning his head towards the far end of the marble pool, he was in time to see Leone Kirkland, in a very stylish scarlet bathing suit, make a perfect swallow dive into the ripples caused by his own progress through the chilly water. Unlike most girls, who shrieked and splashed in flirtatious manner, this one was a very good performer both from the diving board and the depths of the pool. Then he remembered that she had been born to this, whereas young Kit Anson had been obliged to tramp from East Sheenmouth to a stretch of riverbank facing the aircraft works where his father was employed, with an old pair of darned bathing trunks wrapped in a coloured towel under his arm. He had had friends in those days. After his mother had run off, and his father had started drinking, other boys to swim with had been hard to find. When he had found them, they had taunted him until there had been no alternative but to fight.

58

'Hallo,' said Leone, arriving beside him as he floated on his back. 'I'm glad you like swimming. It's nice to have company.'

They moved slowly side by side until they reached the rail along the shorter side of the pool. Gripping it with a hand that had pink-tinted fingernails, she turned to him eagerly, her youthful oval face at variance with her sophisticated manner, he felt. Right now, in a scarlet rubber bathing helmet with a tiny peak, and with lashes and lips wet, she looked no more than a disturbingly pretty adolescent girl. He caught himself wishing that lack of affection had not made her so brittle. That would come soon enough to someone destined to be one of society's darlings.

'Did they do the modification?' she asked, her legs scissoring in the clear water.

He nodded. 'I shall be testing her later this morning, if the weather holds.'

'You mean, you're going up?'

'That's the only way to do it, silly girl.'

'I'll come and watch you.'

'I haven't yet heard you ask for my permission.'

She smiled disarmingly at him, all glow and water-drops. '*Please* may I come and watch you?'

He began to tingle with awareness. 'Does your father allow you to visit the workshops?'

'I've never wanted to before. Surely you haven't forgotten that I'm a Kirkland, Mr Anson.'

'I suppose I have,' he admitted, heaving his dripping body up to sit on the side. 'You're a little different from the others.'

'In what way?' she demanded, shifting so that her hands were then on each side of his legs, and her face was tilting directly up at him.

'You have curves where the others haven't.'

It did not bring the giggle he had expected. Her eyes seemed to be searching for something behind the teasing,

59

and her voice had lost its earlier vitality when she said, 'The practised philanderer. I *had* forgotten that.'

'Never forget it,' he advised quickly, touched by the first suspicion that her loneliness might lead her to imagine his friendship was deeper than it could be. Sixteen was a vulnerable age, and this girl was looking for any kind of warmth she could find. 'Flattery rolls off my tongue like drops of water from your bathing helmet. Ask any girl within fifty miles of Sheenmouth.' Getting to his feet, he looked down at her pale shape in its scarlet costume, distorted by the ripples created by the withdrawal of his legs from the water between her outstretched arms. 'Come and see *Aphrodite*, if you want to, but don't expect a VIP welcome. When I'm with her, I don't see anyone else.'

Pulling on a robe, he slung a towel around his neck and headed for his rooms, where breakfast was served to him at seven every morning. While he ate, he read the morning papers. Each of them contained a short paragraph speculating on an Italian attempt at the speed record presently held by an RAF pilot named Stainforth. No wonder Sir Hector was growing anxious over the national interest in another country's advances in aviation. The Italian Benzini could easily steal Kirkland thunder, and ruin everything. Because of a general recession at the turn of the decade, British government expenditure on aircraft development had been drastically cut back. They had even pulled out of an obligation to finance last year's Schneider Trophy Race which the British team had looked certain to win, and the event would have been cancelled if Lady Houston had not generously given £100,000 so that it could be staged.

British pilots were among some of the finest in the world – consider their sensational exploits during the war – and they deserved national support as well as every opportunity for aviation pioneering. Everyone knew the aeroplane would play a vital part in any future war. Other nations were investing money and manpower in the industry with that in mind. As was often the case, Britain had her head in the sand. Kit, like all his countrymen with an interest in the future of flying, was very bitter over the situation and wanted his own coming attempt to go some way towards focusing attention on the potential of the nation's pilots. The tenth of June had to be a day of total glory, so a massive lead on Stainforth's record was essential. Sir Hector had possibly been right to force the issue, but the outcome rested in Kit's hands alone.

With that on his mind, he dressed in casual clothes before making his accustomed sprint down the winding path to the boathouse. As he approached it, he spotted a girl in cream flared trousers and a blue-and-beige striped top sitting on one of the jetty piles.

She smiled as he arrived on the weathered planking. 'Very athletic! Are you planning to *swim* down to the workshops?'

'You know the answer to that, or you wouldn't be here fully dressed,' he replied, not too happy about her presence. 'You're brighter first thing in the morning than most girls I know.'

'You'll discover I'm brighter in many ways than the kind of girl who'd try to post herself to you. I can think of much easier methods of reaching the fascinating Kit Anson than trusting the royal mail to deliver me into his hands.'

She fenced too cleverly with emotive words for a schoolgirl, he decided. The Kirkland arrogance was there beneath that beckoning exterior. He looked for the boat, which Walter normally had tied alongside in readiness for him. Leone enlightened him.

'I told Walter we'd take *Columbus*, this morning.'

'I'm not permitted to use the family boat,' he told her swiftly. 'He knows that very well.'

'I'm going to take you, silly,' she announced, jumping from her perch to stand beside him. 'Walter's afraid I can't handle it but, heavens, in Monte Carlo last summer

61

Raoul let me take control of his latest acquisition without a qualm. It was a giant of a thing!'

'Raoul is to be congratulated on his iron nerve,' Kit replied dryly, realizing that here was a very worldly, experienced schoolgirl. 'His bank balance also earns my admiration, if it can risk writing off his latest acquisition without noticeable loss of naughts.'

The throaty roar of a powerful speedboat engine heralded the emergence of *Columbus*, probably the fastest craft on that stretch of the Sheen. As Walter taxied it alongside the jetty, he registered Leone's excitement and looked up at Kit unhappily.

'I don't rightly know my duty, Mr Anson, I tell you straight. Miss Kirkland always be too young a lady afore, which was why Sir Hector give pertickler instructions, d'ye see. But . . . well, she *do* be one of the family, and says she'll be as safe as muffers in this speed machine. Here she is wanting to take you along, and I don't see there's any way of stopping her, sir.'

'There isn't, Walter,' Kit told him caustically. 'She's a very determined young woman, with astonishing confidence in her own ability. Let her have her way. If she should be overestimating her prowess, I'll be on hand to take the wheel. I'm sure she'll absolve you from blame if her father should kick up a dust when he finds out. Isn't that right, Leone?' he asked pointedly.

Jumping into the smart scarlet-and-white craft, the girl cried, 'What a fuss you men always make! We could have been down there by now. Come on, Kit. Get in, or I'll go without you.'

'Is that a genuine offer?' Kit asked with feigned optimism. 'I'm no Raoul, I must warn you.'

Revving up with a roar, she put out her tongue at him. Awareness stirred in Kit once more as he stepped in beside her, and took the rope Walter uncoiled expertly from the mooring post. Whoever the courageous Raoul might be, perhaps he had taught the girl the basics of propulsion, he thought . . . amongst other things! It suggested only the other things, when they shot away with such force, Kit was thrown backward into the scarlet leather seat.

'Whoops! Sorry,' Leone called over her shoulder. 'It takes a while to grow used to the feel of any boat.'

'Let me know when you do, just in case I don't notice the difference,' he said, back on his feet and moving up beside her as she swung round into mid-river.

'Are you always so beastly superior towards women?' she demanded.

'Yes, always,' he told her.

It silenced her for a moment, then she tilted her face up to him with a delighted smile. 'You're quite nice, apart from that.'

'So are you,' he responded involuntarily. 'So stop acting like the high-powered Kirkland girl!'

They headed down-river as the sun appeared over the high ground to their left, where East Sheenmouth sprawled in an expanding mixture of old-fashioned rows of boarding houses, and brash modern hotels offering cocktails and jazz each evening. At that hour the numerous small craft of holiday sailors had not invaded the peaceful reaches of one of the south coast's most scenic rivers. The glossy red-and-white boat cut through the water effortlessly as it ran between the steep wooded slopes dropping down from East Sheenmouth, and the more gentle banks to their right where the wealthy or retired had built themselves riverside retreats, from which they pottered about in boats of every size and description.

Kit knew them all, which meant he was well versed in who could navigate competently and who could not. Brigadier Bunce, late of the Lancers, imagined he could sail a boat the way he rode a horse, and could stop it just as quickly. Kit always gave the old cavalryman a wide berth on water, and also socially. He was an inveterate bore with a reputation for pinching plump female bottoms. The Reverend Glade always behaved on water as if in a car, shooting out his left or right arm to indicate that he was about to veer. As he needed both hands to do this, there followed a long period suggesting that he was doing his daily exercises, as he tried to indicate and tack simultaneously. There were those who rowed, those who sculled, and others who punted. There were madcaps, fainthearts, and downright fools who took to the water for fun. Those who used the river regularly could identify them a mile off, and muttered good salty oaths as they passed.

This morning the river was empty, save for the many waterbirds who enjoyed the shallows and inlets in that stretch of the Sheen. The sky was clear, promising a sweet golden day such as the end of May could often bring. The elegant riverside homes all had private jetties and large sloping gardens, which were presently filled with rioting orange, pink, red and white azaleas and rhododendrons. Floral bridal veils covered the almond trees, and there were beds of early roses, forget-me-nots and pinks. Dogs were already out in some, their early morning inquisitiveness driving them to sniff the scents of those who had trespassed on their personal patches during the night. Dressing-gowned residents, drawn on to their sun-washed terraces by the deep-throated roar of the Kirkland boat, waved in friendly fashion as they passed. Leone waved back with high spirits.

Kit enjoyed it all, confident now that Raoul had known what he was doing when entrusting his vessel to this girl. Watching her thoughtfully as the breeze ruffled the waves of her short blonde hair, it was difficult to form an opinion of the daughter of his benefactor and stick to it. Was she a precocious little baggage, or merely a child of wealthy society? Would she one day find the soulmate she craved, or go the way of most of her kind in the heartless desperate search for excitement to hide the loneliness? He suddenly recalled their first encounter, when she had burst into his dazed misery and prattled about a monk who had hanged himself from the

64

bell above his rooms. What had happened to her in the three years since then? Who had cared? Was she really as sophisticated as she liked to pretend, or was it possible for her to be deeply hurt? Glancing comprehensively over her trim curves, he told himself Raoul must have been either a fool or a man of unusually strong principle if all he had taught her was how to steer a boat.

Her head turned, surprising him in his study of her lithe body. Flushing faintly, she asked, 'Do you approve?'

'Of your seamanship, yes. I award full marks, Miss Kirkland,' he responded, deliberately steering away from that kind of intimacy.

Accepting his rules, she then asked, 'Are you likely to be ready by the tenth?'

'Sir Hector has requested it, so it's a foregone conclusion. Unless some disaster occurs, I shall have to ensure that I am.'

'May I watch you fly this morning?'

He smiled. 'If you can bear to hang around for hours while I check that all the conditions are right. Look, there she is,' he added, nodding towards the distant bright yellow aircraft lying on the water alongside the collection of grey buildings comprising the hangars, workshops and offices of Kirkland Marine Aviation. 'Isn't she the most exquisite creature you've ever been privileged to see? Study the beautiful line of her hull, the elegance of her high wings, the magnificent manner in which she rides the tide on those long stylish legs, the wonderful. . .'

'Oh, don't start eulogizing again,' said Leone, almost snappily. 'It grows a bit sickening, after a while.'

He fell silent, studying the present love of his life as the brilliance of her design hit him yet again. How his father would have rhapsodized over this perfection, he thought, as a fresh view of the little seaplane was possible when Leone swung the speedboat in a starboard turn to head for the Kirkland's jetty. Then, as they curved towards the slipways running down from the hangars, sending ridges of foam up on their port side, a small powered vessel shot out from behind an ancient barquentine reputed to have taken contraband liquor up to the Abbey in the old days, which was permanently moored mid-river. At the wheel of the shabby craft was a typical two-weeks-every-summer sailor. He saw the red and white rocket hurtling towards him, and forgot all the rules of navigation. Zig-zagging frantically on the same course, he gave Leone only one chance of avoiding him. Swinging the wheel hard over with commendable calm, she straightened from the turn to roar past the terrified novice, trying to throttle back as they closed in on the workshops at full speed. Kit knew they would never stop in time, and so did she. Heaving the wheel round in the opposite direction, she re-entered the starboard turn she had broken but, by now, she was too near the bank. *Columbus* scraped one of the concrete slipways, leapt into the air, then smacked back into the water to career headlong at the yellow seaplane moored just ahead.

'*Turn! Turn!*' yelled Kit, his heart plummeting at the inevitability of what was about to happen. '*For God's sake, turn!*' Then he seized the wheel where Leone, white-faced and desperate, was trying to pit her strength against a high-powered engine and the weight of wildly undulating water. Their combined efforts succeeded in making the powerful craft almost stand on its side with the violence of the turn, but still it clipped one of *Aphrodite*'s floats as it sped past.

There was a bang, followed by the sound of rending metal. Kit twisted frantically to look behind him, fear beginning to gather in his throat. His beautiful mistress, his hope of triumph was starting to tilt in alarming fashion. He watched her go over, feeling sick and trying to pretend it was not happening. So lost in painful disbelief was he, he hardly noticed the gradual slowing of the speedboat, the roar of the engine quietening to little more than a purr, or the overreaction of the man who had begun shouting abuse at them from his hired holiday boat. People came running from the workshops and hangars to stare aghast at the disaster, and Kit found himself actually blinking back tears as the full import of what had occurred ran through his stunned brain. Months and months of work destroyed in a moment. The pride, enthusiasm and skill of several dozen men dealt such a blow, it would fill them all with bitter disappointment. The Italians would have a free field, and his own dreams would remain no more than just that.

The sound of sobbing broke through his despair, and he turned to see Leone, pale and tear-stained, crouched on the seat.

'I'm sorry,' she offered, in deep distress. 'I'm *so* sorry. There was nothing I could do to avoid it. Oh, God, I could kill myself.'

Swallowing the lump in his throat, he turned back to *Aphrodite*, saying tonelessly, 'The sensation created by your suicide might just compensate your father for the loss of the world air speed record . . . but I wouldn't bank on it.'

3

The team which had conceived, created, then perfected
Aphrodite tenderly amputated her crushed foot and made
her whole again. It took time. The weight factor had to
be taken into account, along with the vital consideration
of balance both on water and in the air. Only the pilot
could confirm when this had been achieved. It was a
period of tension all round as the tenth of June drew
nearer. Press exposure, which had sensationalized details
of the collision and Leone Kirkland's 'madcap spree in
the family speedboat', built up extra tension by setting
the British public agog to know whether or not the
attempt on the record would still be made on schedule.
Anyone who knew Sir Hector, already had the answer
to that.

The engineers and mechanics worked unremittingly
to have the seaplane ready. Kit, fighting the desire to
stay with his mistress day and night to protect her from
further harm, tried instead to relax between test flights
and put his trust in those of his colleagues who had no
need to maintain top physical form for the momentous
day. They could afford to work themselves to a standstill
during the run-up to the tenth, but his own maximum
effort would have to come then.

At Sheenmouth Abbey an army of professionals was
slowly transforming the designated rooms into a tasteful
but sumptuous setting for an evening reception worthy
of the triumphant occasion Sir Hector had determined

it would be. A raised platform for the dance-band was erected in the great vaulted hall, whose stone floor was to be covered with polished wood panels. Denouncing floral decoration as too pretty-pretty for the theme of the day, the owner of the monastery had chosen instead plaster figures from Greek mythology set in a series of tableaux, each with the goddess *Aphrodite* as the central subject. The creators of these managed to introduce a touch of living growth by twining greenery around the sturdy pillars of the hall, and by placing white waterlilies in the several mock-marble pools where small fountains played. The refectory, where a lavish buffet would be offered, received the same thematic treatment. Artificial grass would cover the stone slabs of the floor after the carpet had been taken up. The long oaken table, which would bear the superabundance of food, was augmented by a number of ornate mock-marble benches set beneath arbors of greenery where lifeless gods and goddesses posed in near-naked splendour. The main terrace, and the floodlit swimming pool, were encompassed by tall Grecian columns supporting a theatrical backcloth which effectively closed off from view those trappings of modern life, the tennis courts and glasshouses. As a final dramatic touch Sir Hector had decreed that his guests should arrive up-river from Sheenmouth on decorated barges, and be transported from his private jetty to the foot of the steps leading into the monastery in small Grecian chariots.

These arrangements, together with the preparation of a covered stand on the promenade beside Sheenmouth sands, where Sir Hector, and senior staff of Kirkland's would watch the event in company with high-ranking officers of the RAF, representatives of the Air Ministry and the leading aircraft manufacturers, engine designers, investors, socialites and junior ministers in the government, all went ahead without a hitch. A light luncheon would be served in the stand an hour before take-off, and field-glasses would be on hand to allow guests the most advantageous view of *Aphrodite* in mid-air. Even the ultra-efficient Maitland Jarvis was a little worried over this aspect of the day. The organization at Sheenmouth Abbey was totally under his control, but the stand on the promenade was producing some niggling little problems. As the seafront esplanade was not owned by Sir Hector, it had been necessary to ask the permission of the Mayor of Sheenmouth to put up several rows of seats shielded by an awning beneath which food and alcohol were to be served. He had readily agreed, expressing great gratification on behalf of his wife, three children, mother-in-law and several town councillors over the front seats he felt sure they would be offered for the most spectacular event the little resort had ever known. Protocol demanded that he be invited into the VIP area, naturally, but a bumptious seaside optician who happened to wear a chain of office around his bullish neck threatened to regard himself and his uninvited family as the guests of honour amidst men of great wealth and international repute, several of whom were barons. The urbane personal assistant said nothing to his employer, knowing he would simply be told to 'put the little bugger in his place', but it was knowing what his place should be on an occasion such as this which was the crux of the problem. Sir Hector tended to brush such things aside, but it was not always possible to solve them in that manner.

In the case of his daughter, it was. Never a man to wring his hands over irretrievable situations, his reactions to the grave news of damage to *Aphrodite* was to marshal every effort towards repairing her, wasting no time on an inquest into how it had happened. Leone had sent the family's fastest craft slap bang into the company's greatest asset. Never mind the circumstances, she had done it and risked his every hope for the future. Those who dealt such blows to Sir Hector Kirkland were never castigated, neither were they ever forgiven. He merely shut them completely from his life. As Leone had never really been part of it, little changed between them.

Within the girl herself, however, was a sense of distress which threatened to destroy that determination to take her rightful place at Sheenmouth Abbey. It had been an unavoidable accident, as even Kit had later acknowledged, yet she could not forget the sight of that little yellow seaplane tilting beneath the water. There seemed no means of assuaging her sense of guilt in a household where she was the only person unoccupied during those frantic days leading to the tenth of June. How could she have made such a disastrous start to the visit designed to establish family unity? Donald had been aggressive even before the accident; now he was ignoring her whenever they happened to meet. Her father's brief warmth during her homecoming dinner was never likely to be repeated. Kit was either down at the workshops, or shut in the bell tower for the rest essential in preparation for the feat he would attempt. She had several times tried his door, but it was locked whenever he was in there. Even her usual pastimes were prevented by an army of caterers, electricians and gardeners who swarmed over house and grounds.

As the days dragged past, she both dreaded yet longed for the moment to come. Sir Hector Kirkland had set his heart on gaining this distinction for his company, and Kit was the sole means of providing it. All her thoughts, day and broken nights, were for the young man who had made such an onslaught on her senses from the day of her arrival. Suppose she had made success impossible with her headstrong behaviour? What would happen to the stray mongrel if he failed? Retribution was usually swift, where her father was concerned, and he had made it plain that Kit's job depended on obeying his employer's orders. Kit must be aware of the stakes involved, yet success was equally precious to him. He would surely risk everything to snatch it. What if he took too great a risk? That prospect was too painful to

71

consider, which was why she ticked off the days with such confused feelings.

June tenth dawned cloaked in mist from the sea. Even Sir Hector Kirkland could do nothing about the weather and, whilst all the preparations had gone ahead on well-oiled wheels, no one had dared to mention the one factor which could delay everything. The British were accustomed to braving the elements for outdoor events. Many family picnics were determinedly eaten in a howling gale, or the Inter-Varsity Boat Race watched, shivering, from beneath a raincoat draped over the head, so the grey damp shroud was no deterrent to those who flocked by train, car, bicycle and small boat to Sheenmouth, bent on having a wonderful day. Half of them had only a vague idea of what a seaplane actually was, and were uncaring of whether or not it broke this speed record – or even if it actually flew that day. The major aspect was that there would be excited crowds, plenty of razzamatazz, every kind of seaside delight on offer, and the chance of spotting someone famous among the VIPs. Of course, if this aeroplane with the funny name did manage to fly, there was the additional chance of excitement if it crashed; the thrill of being able to say you had witnessed a drama certain to be on the front page of the dailies next morning!

Many of those who made the journey to the coast that day, however, cared only about the hope of Kit Anson breaking the air speed record by so much the Italians would be forced back to their drawing boards in despair. Encountering the mist as they approached the coast on their journey, these people's hearts sank with disappointment.

Teashops in Sheenmouth's cobbled streets did a good trade in providing warming drinks, hot toast or teacakes, and even eggs and bacon for those who had hiked or cycled there after a very early start. Along the promenades on both sides of the mouth of the river, seafront cafés almost obscured by the mist were also full, to the disgruntlement of the ice-cream sellers huddled into their thick woolly jackets. The bunting strung all along the beach areas hung damply between lamp posts, a sorry sight on a festive day. The small pier ran out into obscurity. It could have been three miles long, or only five hundred yards for all anyone could tell. It made no difference. By ten o'clock, spectators were gathering and jostling for advantage, enjoying every suspenseful moment. Cigarettes were exchanged, so were items of gossip. Young men winked at the girls. They either gazed back haughtily, or gave the green light with their mascara-lined eyes. Mothers carrying babies fell into discussions on ancient remedies for thrush, whooping-cough and thumb-sucking. Their husbands were soon arguing companionably about the government, the worrying situation in Germany, the cricket scores, how to grow marrows, and the price of beer. Children gravitated towards each other and invented games with toffee-apple sticks, or seashells, to keep themselves amused while the adults talked, talked, *talked*! Soon, everyone crowding whatever open space could be found along that stretch of coast, had settled happily to their national pastime of waiting for the weather to clear so that something could happen.

The atmosphere was vastly different in the VIP stand when dignitaries and their wives began arriving just before noon. The mist had lightened from grey to white, and the Met men promised a clear afternoon once it had dispersed, but a cold buffet and chilled wine did little to warm them now they were no longer within the plush interiors of their cars. The more elderly men in pin-stripes and morning coats worried about their joints; their ladies in flowery silk costumes and elegant straw cloche hats smiled stoically, whilst wishing men would stop trying to prove they could do something better or faster than anyone else – or would at least do it indoors. Sir Hector assumed a confident relaxed manner to cover his tension, as he ably hosted what he intended to be a flattering, impressive show of hospitality. Maitland Jarvis ping-ponged between the true guests of honour and the mayoral upstart, who was growing more and more obnoxious as he availed himself of the chilled wine. The cold appeared not to discourage him, or his plebeian retinue, unfortunately.

Leone, in a dress of pale-blue silk-embroidered Swiss lace, was so nervous she shivered as she wandered among the guests with the same canapé in her hand for more than half an hour, and drank so much fruit punch she then suffered the agony of a full bladder, whilst unable to escape the pontification on overseas investment from a junior government minister her father had told her to entertain. Sir Hector was certainly aware of her existence today, even if he only saw her as someone to take care of his lesser guests. It was some comfort to know that he, like herself, Maitland, and the staff of Kirkland Marine Aviation was also inwardly tense as they all waited for a message from Donald, who was at the work-shops with Kit and his team. He would telephone to a mechanic waiting in the pier ticket-office when the go-ahead was given by the man who, alone, would make the decision.

Before going to bed last night Leone had given Coombes a sealed good-luck note to put on Kit's break-fast tray this morning. All week, however, flowers and parcels tied with ribbon had been arriving from female well-wishers until the gallery had been filled to over-flowing. She hoped Kit had bothered to read her mess-age, and that it had cheered him more than the extrava-gant tributes from adoring females, many of whom had managed to sneak into the grounds and mob him as he set off for the workshops at the crack of dawn. She had watched the mass worship from her window, and now fully understood his reaction on finding her in his room on the day of her arrival. She was less understanding of the pain such worship had induced in her. The pain was still there as she studied the shrouded promenade. If

74

only it were over; if he had broken the wretched record and landed safely. She could then happily be sick with relief and look forward to the evening celebration of his success.

The sun eventually broke through at two-thirty. A ragged cheer rose from the main promenade, as well as from the less fashionable one on the East Sheenmouth side of the estuary. It was now possible to see those who had decided the best view would be had from the cliffs. An exchange of friendly waves was made as a charge of expectancy ran through the patient spectators, and everything began happening. Small boats put to sea to take up positions near the marker buoys. In them were the officials who would time the seaplane's three runs in each direction, a doctor to administer emergency resuscitation, if needed, Kirkland's mechanics to deal with technical faults, and men from the broadcasting service. The Sheenmouth lifeboat was also run out by its enthusiastic crew, and a clangour of bells announced the arrival of the ambulance from East Sheenmouth Cottage Hospital, closely followed by the local fire engine.

After that flurry of activity, the waiting resumed. There was an air of suppressed excitement about it now, however, as heads were constantly turned towards the river mouth for a first sight of the seaplane and its dashing young pilot. In the covered stand they all waited for a runner from the pier ticket-office with news of the go-ahead. When the man finally arrived, breathless with tension and physical exertion, he was seized by the inebriated mayor who demanded to hear the news first. Leone's knees turned weak as the word was passed around. *They're setting off now!*

In the mysterious way such things happen, the information immediately ran through the crowds like lightning over a wire fence, and the vast band of people compressed into a thin line as those at the rear pushed forward to crane their necks for a better view. The whole of Lyme Bay then seemed to ring with cheers, as the little waterborne procession emerged from the estuary and turned into the open sea lapping Sheenmouth sands. Heading the flotilla was a boat containing Donald Kirkland, designer of *Aphrodite*, and an expert from Rolls-Royce, who had made the engine for the seaplane. Behind them came a boat towing the pontoon on which the delicate, streamlined and immensely powerful machine was secured, watched over by overawed mechanics. Following closely was the Kirkland launch, which seemed to be filled to overflowing with so many people it was not clear whether Kit Anson himself was among them, or with the mechanics on the pontoon. Bringing up the rear was a veritable armada of hired craft containing newsmen and photographers anxious for sensation of any kind. These craft were ordered to keep well clear by a policeman with a loud-hailer, who was standing in the stern of the Kirkland launch.

Unable to see very well from her relegated position in the stand, Leone climbed on to a chair. Her heart was pounding; her throat was dry. Could that flippant young man she hardly knew really fly that machine and do what he claimed? It was no trifling feat, it was a world-shattering one. Suppose he failed? *Suppose he crashed?* While she watched the water-borne procession drift to a halt, followed by the tedious business of final preparation, something extraordinary occurred. Remembering that ashen-faced boy in a cheap jacket and grubby shirt, who had stood in the library whilst her father had discussed him with Donald in brisk, dispassionate terms, tears began to blur her vision. It was now clear what this day was really all about. There was a world record to break; a company to promote. What Kit was about to prove, however, was that he was as good as any Kirkland. In three short years he had done what she still found impossible. The stray mongrel was now running with the pedigree hounds before the eyes of the whole world.

A cry went up all along the promenade as *Aphrodite*'s

engine roared into life. Next minute, a thickset figure wearing dark trousers, a flying jacket and leather helmet clambered on to the pontoon, where a short ladder enabled him to reach the cockpit hardly large enough for a man of his size. Once he had settled inside, little could be seen of him, and the growing roar of the engine was almost drowned by the crescendo of cheers. Everything now lay in the hands of the daring young aviator.

Suddenly, the pontoon tilted, the ropes were snatched away, and *Aphrodite* slid into the sea. She began surging forward in a great fountain of spray that practically hid her from view, and everyone realized the vital moment had finally come. After a bad tilt to port which drew gasps from the spectators, the machine righted itself and sped over the sea until she lifted and became no more than a yellow moth against the pale blue of the sky. It was a shimmery kind of moth, so far as Leone was concerned. Tears multiplied as she watched that flying capsule climb and turn into the sun. It dawned on her, with a brand of shocked wonder, that the man crammed inside *Aphrodite* was the first person for whom she had cared so deeply in all her sixteen years.

On the cliffs above Sheenmouth sands, Warren Grant was being practically strangled by his girlfriend, Mona. She clasped him tightly around his neck as she hid her face in his best pullover.

'I can't bear to watch,' she gasped into the rust-coloured wool.

More intent on following *Aphrodite*'s progress, as she circled in preparation for the straight stretch between the buoys marking the actual speed course, Warren pushed down the brim of his sweetheart's hat, which was obstructing his view through the binoculars.

'You've been waiting more than three hours to see it,' he murmured abstractedly. 'Don't be silly.'

'What if he crashes?'

'Whether you're watching or not won't change the

fact. Phew, just look at that fuel ejecting from the ex-
hausts as he turns! That special mixture in the tanks
might produce exceptionally high speeds, but he'll have
to watch his temperature at full throttle. Just look at that
beauty!' he marvelled, studying every line of the sleek
machine with floats so long they looked like two
additional hulls.

For months Warren had spent every spare moment
sitting on the banks of the Sheen near the Kirkland
Marine Aviation hangars, studying *Aphrodite* in all stages
of development. This morning he had been there to
watch the activity prior to the actual event. Once he had
known it was under way, he had raced to this vantage
point on his motorbike, pushed his way to the front of
the crowd, and waited. Mona had suffered it all for the
sake of spending the day with him, but she had no real
interest in something she regarded as her rival in his
affections. Warren supposed she was right. It was more
the aircraft itself, than the man flying it, which was
creating the flame of excitement in his chest. He naturally admired Kit Anson's skill and courage, along with
everyone else, but fascination with the quest for speed,
greater manoeuvrability, steeper climb and dive
capacity, and the ultimate in aircraft design had been
instilled in him as a boy by his stepfather. Lieutenant
Beamish Doyle, a Canadian in the RFC, had occupied
no more than three years of Warren's life before being
killed in Mesopotamia, but in that short time had given
the dreamy lad visions of future machines which would
weave magic in the skies. *Aphrodite* looked set to do just
that, and the debonair giant in smart pilot's uniform
would have revelled in the occasion as Warren did.

The seaplane had made one run in each direction, and
was still losing what looked suspiciously like ejections of
fuel on the turns, when Warren's experienced eye
detected a forward spurt which told him Anson was now
fully under way.

'*Here he goes,*' he breathed, grabbing Mona's hat from

78

her head and dropping it on the grass, to prevent any risk of his missing what was plainly to be the first of the really fast runs in the bid for the record.

From the promenade below rose a roar, growing progressively louder as the streaking seaplane passed over the first of the buoys. Flags and hats were waving like a sea of colour above the cheering spectators growing almost hysterical with excitement, but Warren calmly set his stop-watch as he followed *Aphrodite*'s progress through his powerful lenses, his passion for design teaching him the wider implications of what he was witnessing. If Anson did break the record, it would be broken yet again before long. Men were sending machines faster and faster through the air. This yellow beauty would have her day, then a new goddess would take her place. What he would give to have a hand in creating her!

'Is he all right?' asked Mona, from the region of his chest.

'Stop being silly and see for yourself,' he told her, twisting to the right to study Anson's turn in preparation for his next run. 'He'll do it! By George, he's definitely going to do it!' he murmured, as his aviator's eye calculated the speed his stop-watch would verify. 'He must be going well over four hundred.'

Scribbling the time of the run on the small notebook he had given Mona to hold for him, he resumed his scrutiny through the binoculars as his girlfriend drew away to risk being a spectator to anything which might now happen.

'Oh, he's not going all that fast,' she complained. 'I thought it would look like a yellow flash passing by.'

'Not from this distance,' he told her with accustomed patience. 'Take my word for it, he's really moving. I don't like the look of that starboard float. That's the one they had to replace when the Kirkland girl drove into it last week.' Pushing the knob of his watch, he glanced down quickly to read out the figures. 'Write that down underneath the first lot, will you? That ought to show you how fast he's going.'

'Well, it doesn't,' came the bored reply. 'When's it going to be over?'

'Shh!' he admonished. 'Here he goes again.'

Mona remained silent, whilst all around them people developed a frenzy of excitement as *Aphrodite* flew back and forth over the designated distance once more. Then she circled and began to lose height, indicating that Kit Anson had made his bid and was coming in to land. Torn between desire to watch the pilot touch down, or make an amateur calculation of his average speed over the three runs, Warren finally decided to keep his binoculars trained on the yellow seaplane until it rested tranquilly on the water. By doing so, the judges beat him to it with their signals of success. The spectators had no idea by how much the record had been broken, but to know that it was was enough to set them kissing each other, dancing a jig, or surging forward into the water in the hope of hearing the precise details.

Amidst the euphoria all around them, Warren sat down on the grass feeling a glow of quiet triumph. A boat that could fly; an aircraft that could float! It was a brilliant combination of design and engineering. What if the technique could be further developed until there were passenger liners which could take to the air? Imagine that: long graceful hulls with massive wings, and four, maybe even six, engines to propel them half-way across the world! Travellers could reach India within a matter of hours; be in England one day and Africa the next. Just imagine it!

'Warren, what's up with you?' cried Mona impatiently, looking down at him. 'He's getting out into a rowing boat now, and everyone's rushed on to the beach to cheer him in. Aren't you going to watch?'

'No,' he murmured, visions of the future refusing to be banished by her words. 'Is there any tea left in the Thermos?'

'Oh, you really are the limit! This is the best bit of the day, and all you can think about is tea.'

He blinked up at her in a mild manner. 'Is there any?'

'See for yourself,' she told him, returning her attention to the sands where a few of the more extreme spectators, mostly young women, were trying to swim out to meet their conquering hero as he was brought ashore. Despite the attempts of two local constables and several men from Kirkland's to protect him, Kit Anson was immediately mobbed and lifted on to the shoulders of stalwart admirers, who bore him ecstatically over the sands towards the VIP enclosure where a bottle of champagne awaited him. By the time he was deposited there beside Sir Hector Kirkland, who shook him enthusiastically by the hand, a chant was beginning to make itself heard above the cheers. FOUR ONE SEVEN . . . FOUR ONE SEVEN.

While all those responsible for the day's endeavour congratulated each other, and baptized their laughing champion with champagne until he was drunk with it and his own happiness, and while a succession of young girls somehow managed to reach their hero to plaster his face with their scarlet lipstick, Warren sat on the cliffs drinking lukewarm tea and thinking about that figure of four one seven. Anson had just added 10 m.p.h. to the world record, to make *Aphrodite* the fastest flying machine ever built. Surely the man who must presently be feeling stunned by his own achievement was Donald Kirkland. At a mere twenty-three years of age, what a glittering future lay before him. With family wealth and influence to back his immense flair, he was the man who would one day design those majestic liners with wings to encompass the world. Lucky devil!

Mona dropped on to the grass beside him, taking from him the empty cup to screw back on the flask. 'They'll be moving off soon. Can we go down and watch the VIP cavalcade on its way to Sheenmouth Abbey?'

Made aware of time passing, Warren reached for his

leather coat. 'Gosh, no. The road'll be blocked all the way from Magnum Pomeroy to Sheenmouth with people wanting to do that. Come on. Unless we leave right now, we'll never get through.'

'We're not going straight home?' cried Mona, disappointment all over her round flushed face.

'Sorry,' he said, shrugging into the motorcycling jacket and picking up his goggles. 'I've got a lesson at half-past seven.'

'Oh, Warren, surely not! Whoever would want to fly on a day like today?'

'Budding Kit Ansons – although this particular chap hasn't a hope of ever getting his flying ticket. The best instructor in the world couldn't turn him into a pilot, take my word.' On the point of crossing to his motorcycle, his dreams of the future had faded enough to allow him to realize how long-suffering dear Mona was, and how very upset she looked. 'I daren't skip the lesson. Mr Mason would fire me. You wouldn't want that to happen.'

Her drooping carrot-red head shook, as she let out a heavy sigh. 'I wish you could get a proper job instead.'

'This is a proper job,' he reasoned, taking one of her hands. 'I'm paid for every lesson I give . . . and there's the pieces I do for the *Rowmead Quarterly*. They bring in a bit more.'

Looking him sulkily in the eye, she reminded him that the *Rowmead Quarterly* was published only four times a year, and the editor did not always remember to pay him. 'You had to go to their offices and demand it last time,' she complained. 'By the time you'd bought petrol for the ride, what they gave you wasn't worth going for.'

'But they always head my piece *From our Air Correspondent*,' he pointed out in defence of the tiny publication.

'Huh!'

As he was desperately anxious to get away before the

narrow lane down to Sheenmouth became congested with traffic, Warren decided on more positive action. It had the desired effect, although Mona put on a pretence of modesty which belied the glow in her eyes.

'Warren, you shouldn't do that in public.'

'Everyone's kissing each other, so why shouldn't we? Anyway, I couldn't help it,' he added, shamelessly setting about getting round her. 'You've been so patient today, and I thought it was time to show you how grateful I am.'

Her cheeks grew pink with pleasure. 'I didn't mind you watching it at all, silly. I just thought we'd be going into Sheenmouth to see all the crowds and the fun afterwards.'

That reminder of congested streets led him to take her elbow and lead her across to the motorbike, trying not to betray his urgency.

'I'm sorry, Mona, but I daren't risk losing my job. I'm lucky that Mr Mason still employs me considering the small number of new pupils registering for lessons. If I turn up late today, and the man gets ratty over waiting, I'll be out on my neck.'

Luckily, most of the crowd which had been watching from the cliffs had decided to stay for a picnic tea before winding their way back to Sheenmouth, so Warren was able to make good progress through the downhill lanes. Mona was silent until he recklessly decided to gain time by leaving the road two miles outside the little resort, and making a bumpy descent of Rigger's Hill, at breakneck speed. Her arms tightened around his waist, and she shrieked with excitement all the way down. He caught himself laughing at her. She loved speed. It was another thing they had in common. He was very fond of Mona. In fact, he thought he might even be in love with her. Certainly, he had never felt the same way about any other girl.

He eventually pulled up in the small paved area beside the office where rowing boats could be hired for an hour or so of fun on the river. Warren always left the bike there, and walked the short distance to the tiny office of the *Sheenmouth Clarion*. Mona's father was the owner/ editor of the weekly paper, and therefore a man of some substance. He was also a person of strong opinions, especially where his pretty young daughter was concerned. One of these was that she should not be exposed to the dangers of a motorcycle. Although many local people spotted her on the pillion seat behind Warren, none of them passed the information to Jack Cummings who was universally disliked for his rudeness, harsh judgements and total lack of tolerance.

Whereas the little town had been prepared to make allowances for the man when he returned from the war, crippled by severe leg wounds, only to discover his wife pregnant by another man, compassion had slowly petered out when bitterness became his god. With her mother driven from the house, the red-haired toddler had had a stern upbringing. Small wonder the residents felt sorry for the girl, and did nothing to spoil her romance. They thought it time she had some fun from life and the young flying instructor seemed a likeable fellow.

As Warren helped her from the pillion seat he found his resolution weakened by the sight of her lovely rosy cheeks and bright eyes. On impulse, he suggested that they had an ice cream down by the river before he took her home. It was some compensation for all she had put up with from him that day, he thought. She was thrilled, and gripped his hand tightly as he led her down the steps to where the Italian ice-cream man always stationed his wheeled barrow. They were greeted by an empty space. Moriano had guessed the river would be deserted on an occasion like today's, and was probably on the promenade or sands.

Warren sighed as he studied Mona's disappointment. 'It's no good suggesting a cup of tea, instead. We'd never get served in time.'

84

'Bother the ice cream and cups of tea,' she told him heatedly. 'I don't care about that; I just want you to stop a little longer. Everyone else is having a good time today. The real fun's only just going to start . . . and *you* have to give a silly old lesson.'

Feeling guilty, he said, 'I could come back later on for an hour, if you like.'

'You won't get through the crowds,' she pointed out, wandering moodily along the towpath. He followed her in time to catch her next words. 'Sometimes, I wonder if you really are fond of me, or if you say it to get your own way.'

He overtook her, bringing her to a halt. 'Of course I'm fond of you. Look, I know today hasn't been much fun for you – hanging around by Kirkland's waiting for the mist to lift – but it wouldn't have been the same for me without you. I like having you with me. I like sharing things with you, talking to you about them.'

'Well, then?' she prompted softly, moving dangerously close to him and making it perfectly plain that she expected to be kissed.

Unable to afford the time, yet unhappy over her disappointment, he drew her into his arms and touched her full mouth lightly with his own. 'I'll get what you call "a proper job" soon, I'm sure. I'll only give lessons at weekends then. I'll be able to afford something better than that attic at Mrs Bardolph's; some place where we could be together whenever we wanted.'

'When?' she demanded, pressing her body against his in a disturbing manner.

'I've tried,' he protested. 'You know I have. It's hard for men to find work these days. Your father prints enough news about the recession, so you must realize it's not because I'm lazy.'

'I've never said that, Warren,' she told him softly. 'It's just that I do like you so very much, and we've been going out together for six whole months. That's a long time, isn't it?'

Her mouth was almost touching his, so it was impossible not to kiss her again. She responded with such startling fervour, pressing herself against him, that his arms tightened around her to the extent of his fingers finding contact with her breasts. The elation of the day acted as a spur to desire, and he began to lose his head. On that deserted towpath, where willows hung over them to provide a green bower, the embrace turned into a passionate overture to forbidden actions. As his mouth sought the soft, warm hollow at the base of her throat, his hands were feverishly pulling her blouse from the waistband of her skirt until they encountered the smooth satiny skin of her back. Her soft cry of pleasure was like a green light to his heightened senses, and he felt his head begin to swim with notions he had always denied.

Into that wildness came a sonorous repetitive sound which told him a message he could not ignore. The church clock was announcing the three-quarter hour from almost above their heads. He had to get to the Aero Club for that lesson. Putting Mona gently away from him, he was dismayed at what he had been doing. She appeared even more dismayed because he had stopped.

'Gosh, Mona,' he exclaimed, 'you make it hard for a chap to be good, you know.'

'Do I?' she asked, in thrilled tones.

'I'll say. It's just as well I've got to get going, or who knows what might have happened.'

'Going?' She was looking at him hungrily, which made things worse.

'To the Aero Club . . . for the lesson.'

Reality overtook her, and her eyes filled with surprising tears. 'You beast!' she cried emotionally. 'You beast, Warren Grant! That's all you ever think about: *flying*.'

'It's already a quarter to six,' he said. 'Didn't you hear the clock just now?'

For some reason he did not understand, his words caused her to cry in earnest as she turned away, furiously

86

tucking her blouse back into her skirt. When he went to her, she shrugged him off with a tearful 'Leave me alone!' Conscious of time passing, yet riddled with guilt over the way he had treated her, he stood irresolutely on the towpath. But he had to do something about the situation, and swiftly.

'I'm sorry I've upset you, Mona,' he began tentatively. 'You . . . well, you were so loving, I got carried away.'

All she did was cast him an accusing agonized glance, then faced the river again.

'Mona,' he coaxed, 'please don't be like this. I'm only human, and we have been going out together for a long time.'

'Long enough for you to know I'm not that sort of girl,' she told him in muffled, angry words. 'Perhaps you should try Rosie Higgs down at the Monks Arms, if that's all you want to do.'

She had touched his Achilles heel, and he felt his colour rise. 'I don't want Rosie Higgs, I want you. Not for that,' he hastened to assure her. 'I want your company . . . your friendship.'

It seemed to be impossible to placate her, for she burst into fresh tears at that. When he tried to take her hand, she pulled it away, saying, 'You've got to get to your silly old Aero Club, remember.'

He had not forgotten. Sighing heavily, he asked, 'Will you let me walk you home?'

'I suppose so. Dad'll ask questions if you don't.'

Jack Cummings believed that girls should be called for and escorted home by their young men, so Warren was obliged to take valuable time in accompanying a silent, mutinous girl to her front door. Girls really were the devil when in this mood, he told himself, still feeling guilty for having caused it.

They were nearly at the *Clarion* office, when he tentatively asked, 'Shall I come back later, or not?'

'Please yourself,' she replied coolly.

Tempted to suggest that Rosie Higgs might be more

enthusiastic over his offer, he thought better of it. There was no point in starting the whole thing off again. He had no time. If he lost the job at the Aero Club he really would be in a jam. His rent for this week was overdue, because he had bought the paint to finish the model seaplane he had designed and put together. What he would be paid for today's lesson would at least enable him to offer Mrs Bardolph an instalment on the rent, to keep her sweet.

The door of the little newspaper office stood open. Jack Cummings appeared to be waiting for someone within the dingy room which served as his editorial office, separated by a low screen from the counter where members of the public handed in advertisements, or entries for the Births, Marriages and Deaths column. As Warren offered Mona an ultra-polite farewell, he was accosted by her father.

'Just a minute, young man. I'd like a few words with you before you skip off.'

'Could you make it some other time, Mr Cummings?' he asked swiftly. 'I've a lesson booked for seven-thirty, and I must allow for the roads being jammed today.'

'No, I can't make it some other time,' came the stern reply from someone unable to accept or forget what life had done to him. 'Unlike you, I'm a working man whose time isn't his own. Come in and shut that door! All that racket from people who swarm in here to gawp at some fancy show laid on by the Kirkland family, then go back to their big-town houses leaving Sheenmouth littered with their rubbish. I suppose you took my girl to see it.'

'Yes. Anson broke the record by ten miles an hour.'

'I know that,' he roared, in sudden fury. 'Do you think the editor of the local newspaper wouldn't hear that kind of news before anyone else? Nothing but bally-hoo, in my opinion. Aviators were more nuisance than they were worth in France. Always coming down to ask the way because they were lost, or wanting transport back to base because their machines were full of holes and wouldn't fly. Don't ask me what good they ever did, all dressed up in their fancy uniforms and thinking they were very fine fellows with the ladies.'

Warren fired up immediately, which caused him to slam the door as he closed it behind him. 'My stepfather was killed after wiping out a Turkish gun emplacement which could only be approached from the air.'

The other man's mouth twisted. 'Six of my pals were killed doing the same with a German one. That was *after* the RFC had telephoned to say the weather wasn't nice enough to enable them to do it.'

There was no effective reply to that, so Warren got down to more urgent matters. 'What did you want to say to me, sir?'

'What are your intentions towards my daughter?'

It was dark in the cramped front office, so Warren hoped old Cummings could not see his expression too clearly. 'I don't quite understand,' he hedged, wondering wildly if someone had seen him with Mona just now and rushed to tell her father.

'Then you're a dolt!'

'I'm very fond of Mona.'

'I should hope you are. She's been giving you a great deal of her company over the past six months.'

'*Dad*,' put in Mona, with obvious embarrassment.

'Keep quiet, girl, and you might find out what this young man with his head in the air plans to do about your devotion.'

In putting his hand on a nearby bench, Warren accidentally knocked over a pot of ink. It began spreading over some sheets of newsprint beside it. From his wheelchair, Jack Cummings probably could not see what had happened – Warren hoped!

'Yes, I'm very fond of Mona,' he repeated with a show of confidence. 'I'd like to continue taking her out, sir.'

'Then I suggest you buy her a ring, so that she and the residents of Sheenmouth know how she stands.'

'*Dad!*' cried Mona again, plainly distressed over such a demand.

'Well?'

There was no way out of it this time. 'I'm only twenty-four, Mr Cummings.'

'Old enough to get a girl into trouble, aren't you?'

Warren swallowed. 'I wouldn't do that to Mona.'

'Is there something wrong with you, then? Different from other men, are you?'

He felt his colour rise. 'No.'

'Is there something wrong with my daughter? Does she lack what all other girls have?'

Deeply sorry for Mona who was being discussed so frankly in her own presence, he hardly knew how to answer. 'No . . . I mean, I don't know . . . no, of course not.'

'Then you either buy Mona a ring and set the wedding date, or you'll say goodbye to her right now.'

'Dad, *please*,' begged the girl tearfully. 'He'll ask me . . . when he's able to.'

Her father turned on her, his face harsh. 'He'll ask you now, or go. Where's your pride, girl?'

The clock on the wall above Jack Cummings' head showed Warren it was now six o'clock. He grew desperate. If Mason sacked him for missing a lesson, his situation would be hopeless. All the same, he felt as if he were dealing Mona actual blows as he said stiffly, 'If those are your conditions, Mr Cummings, I must accept them. At present, I'm in no position to consider marriage. My earnings barely cover my personal expenses. I couldn't possibly support a wife, much less provide a comfortable home for her. If I sold my motorbike, I daresay I could get a diamond ring for Mona, but it wouldn't be fair to her. It might be years before we could marry, and other chances could pass her by while she was tied to me.' Conscious of Mona's distress, he tried one last shot. 'I'd like to assure you that I've always treated your daughter with the greatest respect, sir, and

I'd continue to do so if you'd allow me to go on taking her out. I really am extremely fond of her.'

Cold eyes looked back at him across the dusty room, while revellers began pouring into the cobbled street outside from the direction of the sands.

'Goodbye, Mr Grant.'

Mona seized his arm. 'Warren, don't go,' she pleaded. 'Let's talk about it some more.'

He slowly shook his head. 'Your father's right. You deserve some kind of promise after six months. I'm so sorry I can't give it to you.'

Warren reached the small house on the outskirts of Sheenmouth after fuming and cursing his way through celebrating crowds, who had no understanding of his urgency. From the *Clarion* office to his digs, it was necessary to drive right into the centre of the resort and then take the main road to Axminster leading out of it again. The traffic was worse than any he had encountered during the seven months he had lived there, so it was gone half-past six when he parked his motorbike in the little alley leading to the rear entrances of the terrace of Edwardian houses. Even so, he paused a moment before going round to the front steps of number twenty-two, where he rented an attic room. Mona had become part of his life. Without her, it was going to be very lonely. There were plenty of other fish to fry and, in the summer months, fun-seeking girls with liberal attitudes could be picked up along the promenade very easily. However, if that was all he wanted, he would never have started taking Mona out. She was a really nice girl – loyal, loving, and very genuine – the sort of girl who made everything he did seem doubly enjoyable or interesting. He could talk to Mona, explain complicated things to her so that she understood and enjoyed them as he did. The knowledge that she would always be there when he called in at the newspaper office created a warmth inside him, a sensation of emotional confidence.

Kicking moodily at the back wheel of the bike, he

castigated himself. How could he have fooled himself that such a situation could last indefinitely? Old Cummings was absolutely right. Look at what had happened down by the river! He had been finding it more and more difficult lately, especially when Mona made no effort to stop his wandering hands. He sighed. Although it was true that he was financially unable to consider marriage, it was also true that he had no wish for such a commitment yet. Even to Mona. There were ambitions to pursue; dreams to turn into reality. Even so, being forced to end his friendship with Mona so abruptly and totally was quite painful. A yawning chasm of loneliness had opened before him now.

Treading heavily up the front steps of Mrs Bardolph's house, he let himself into the tiled hall as the chiming clock told him it was now a quarter to seven. His depression deepened. He should never have stopped by the river. Valuable time had been wasted, and it had served no good purpose. Mona now believed he had only wanted one thing from her. Perhaps he *would* be better off with Rosie Higgs from the Monks Arms.

'There you are, Mr Grant,' exclaimed his landlady, coming from the parlour as he began to climb the stairs. 'I expected you earlier than this.'

'I was held up by all the visitors,' he told her gloomily. 'Sheenmouth's packed with people all coming from the beach.'

'Never seen so many,' she agreed. 'Came past here all through the morning in sharrybangs, they did. Still, it's good for trade. With things being so bad lately, it's just what the town needs. I've kept your tea hot for you. A nice little lamb cutlet with some bubble and squeak, then plum tart and custard to follow.'

He halted halfway up the stairs. 'I won't have time, I'm afraid. There's a lesson booked for seven-thirty. Could you manage a cup of tea and a sandwich instead?'

'That's not enough for a growing man,' she ruled sternly. 'You can't go flying an aeroplane with no more

than a sandwich inside you. Mr Bardolph says that Mr
Anson has orders from Sir Hector Kirkland to eat three
proper meals a day and drink plenty of milk to make
him strong. I'm not saying that you can be compared
with a champion like him, but a couple of slices of bread
and some cheese won't be enough to . . .'

'Please, Mrs Bardolph, there won't even be time for
me to eat that soon,' Warren interrupted impatiently. 'If
I miss that lesson, I could be fired by Jim Mason.'

'Who else would he get?' she called after Warren reassuringly, as he set off up the stairs again. 'I'll get you
some tea . . . and a nice thick sandwich. Mind you eat
it before you go.' Then she remembered something. 'Oh,
Mr Grant!'

He paused to look down the stairwell at her neat figure
in its brown skirt and figured pin-tucked blouse. 'Yes?'

'I had a little accident in your room just after dinner.
You left that toy aeroplane of yours right on the edge of
the cupboard, so it was no wonder my sleeve caught it.
I'm ever so sorry, but it was under my feet before I
knew. Still, you can soon make another, can't you? It's
not as if it was valuable. Well, I'll go and pop the kettle
on right away.'

Feeling sick with apprehension, Warren raced up the
remaining two flights to his large room in the roof. He
was almost afraid to open the door. Breathing hard,
he stared at the dresser where the three-foot model of
Seaspray, the seaplane he had designed and painstakingly
built to scale over the past six months, lay as a pile of
balsawood on the polished surface. The pride of his life,
the great hope for his future, the minuscule outlet for
his frustrated creative drive had been smashed to pieces.
Hardly aware of closing the door behind him, he moved
to gaze miserably at the pieces shaped with such care
and concentration, then painted in silver and sea-green
only last night. Finishing his own goddess of the two
elements had been symbolically timed to coincide with
the flight of *Aphrodite*. How could she be so ingloriously

destroyed when the other had this afternoon flown to universal acclaim?

Sinking on to a chair, he hunched over his knees in a state of misery. He was doomed to mediocrity, it seemed. After Beamish Doyle had been killed in Mesopotamia, Warren's mother had enjoyed the attentions of a number of men on leave in London, who were looking for a brief affair with no promises attached. They had tried to win over her son with sweets, and tales of their supposed daring, but Warren had grieved for his RFC hero as the only father he had really known, and held aloof from their approaches. With puberty, he had realized what his mother had virtually become. His disgust had been more due to what he saw as her insult to the memory of the brave Canadian flier rather than to a feeling of moral outrage. It was not as if she went soliciting on the streets. Packing a suitcase when she was out one day, Warren had left home with the intention of lying about his age in order to sign on with the crew of any ship going to Canada. His stepfather had once mentioned a sister, so he hoped to trace her with the help of the Air Ministry who might have a record of her address. The Air Ministry had instead returned him to his mother, via the Fulham Constabulary.

He had left home again a year later, but all his inquiries at the docks had met with the same reply. *Join the end of the waiting queue of men after jobs*. With no money, and nowhere to go, he had returned home of his own accord determined to make the best of things and save hard. His mother's various lovers had been generous men, so their apartment had been very comfortable and they had lived well. In a period of deepening recession, it was only through the continuance of her amours that Vera Grant was able to accumulate a considerable sum, and support her son in comparative luxury while he studied aerial engineering. During those student days, Warren had worked as a copy-boy on the nightshift of a large newspaper – a post gained for him by his mother's most persistent admirer, who preferred not to share the apartment with his mistress's son during the hours of darkness. Study during the day and working nearly every night was tiring, but the money earned in the newspaper offices was enough to allow Warren to save with the intention of taking flying lessons.

Vera Grant had died of consumption early in 1930, and Warren had found himself comparatively well off. Despite a deep-rooted sense of abhorrence over the means by which his mother had obtained the money, he had immediately contacted an aero club and learned to fly. Six months later he had gained not only his pilot's licence but his engineering degree, and all had seemed set for launching himself into a career in aviation when fate had taken a hand in his affairs. An influenza epidemic had made him one of its victims, and his neglect in summoning medical aid had resulted in pneumonia. Things had gone from bad to worse after that. Weeks in hospital had cost him his job with the newspaper; lack of income had forced him to move to a cheaper apartment. A second severe winter had laid him low again and the doctor, diagnosing a permanent weakness in his chest, had advised him to move south away from London fogs, where the climate was more gentle and the sea air would be beneficial.

After much thought, Warren had bought a motorbike, packed up those few things he valued and set out for Sheenmouth with high hopes. That had been seven months ago. High hopes had yielded low returns. Applying straight away for a job at Kirkland Marine Aviation – his reason for choosing to live in Sheenmouth – he had been told that the company was already reluctantly having to shed some of its existing employees so, however good his qualifications, would not waste their mutual time in giving him an interview. Deeply disappointed, he had inserted a small piece in the *Clarion* outlining his capabilities and stating a willingness to do any kind of work, even if it was purely seasonal. Mona

95

had been there behind the counter and, reading his piece back to him for confirmation, had suggested that he try Mr Moxy, the donkeyman, who was always looking for people to clean out and groom the animals during the winter. However, Mr Moxy already had someone for the donkeys. Going back to tell Mona the fact had merely been an excuse to talk to her again, and their friendship had blossomed immediately. She had helped him through the first part of this year, when the deserted promenade had been lashed by rain and the chairs in the beach cafés had remained upturned on bare tables. His savings had dwindled drastically by the time Mona had arrived at Mrs Bardolph's one afternoon, full of excitement over a notice she had just been given to insert in that week's edition of her father's newspaper.

'Go up there right away,' she cried, 'before someone else reads it in the *Clarion* on Saturday. You can fly; you're just the person he needs. Oh, Warren, you've just got to get this job.'

He had, and she had been thrilled . . . *then*. Today, the job at the Aero Club had been dismissed as quite inadequate for a prospective husband. It was, of course; yet it was a godsend for a budding aircraft designer waiting for his great chance. That was to have been in several days' time, when Warren had intended to take his model of *Seaspray* to Donald Kirkland, who would surely have been impressed enough to recognize his potential. It would take weeks to re-construct the model. Next Monday would see the commencement of joy-rides from the club airfield, which would occupy him in the dreary business of taking up a succession of people for ten-minute circular flights over Sheenmouth sands. He was dreading it, despite the extra money he would earn. Young boys would dangle dangerously over the side, girls would giggle or be sick, pompous asses would give him orders. All the time, he would be longing to get back to work on *Seaspray*.

A discreet tap on the door heralded Mrs Bardolph

with a pot of tea and a doorstop sandwich. He felt too sick to eat it now. Dragging himself to his feet, he mumbled incoherent replies to his landlady's light-hearted references to his 'toy aeroplane', then realized it was five past seven.

'Oh, *hell*,' he swore, as the woman departed. 'Double hell and triple damnation! I'll never get there in time.'

Only by struggling over several stiles with his motor-bike, and bumping across fields in a series of shortcuts, did Warren manage to arrive at the Aero Club no more than fifteen minutes late. His pupil, a fat, monocled landowner from Magnum Pomeroy whose route to the club had not been congested by returning spectators, made his annoyance obvious. He also allowed it to affect his deplorable skill to the point of endangering both the aircraft and their lives. Several times Warren was forced to snatch control from his pupil at the last minute, and the half-hour lesson was made even worse by the fact that this pitiful attempt to fly a solid dependable machine was being made in the same airspace in which Kit Anson had taken his glittering yellow goddess faster than anyone in the world.

After collecting his money and suffering a severe telling-off from Jim Mason, who threatened to sack him the minute he found another pilot, Warren mounted his motorbike, adjusted his goggles, and set out in a very black mood to face the crowded road back to his lodgings. Then misery swamped him. He had lost Mona, and could not face the wreck of *Seaspray* tonight. The only thing to do was to drive into Magnum Pomeroy and spend the money he had just earned in the Buck and Hounds. To hell with paying his rent. Ma Bardolph did not deserve it after what she had done today.

Turning left instead of right on leaving the airfield, he gave the machine full throttle and fairly raced along the narrow lane which led to the village, and thence to Forton, Biddlecombe-by-Sheen and Packhampton, past the old monastery where high jinks would celebrate

Donald Kirkland's achievement tonight. Thoughts of that occupied his mind to such an extent, only reflexes saved him from hitting a girl standing beside a large Bentley as he rounded a curve flanked by high summer hedgerows. Swerving as he squeezed his brake, he screeched to a halt, engine racing, with his front wheel stuck in the blackthorn. It was all so sudden, he had not even begun to extricate himself when the girl appeared beside him.

'Thank heavens you came along,' she cried delightedly. 'Do you know how to repair this car?'

Thinking of all the names he would like to call her, he pushed up his goggles angrily. The sight of her robbed him of speech for a moment. Short golden hair, huge blue eyes, a superior kind of expression, and a blue lace dress which must have cost a fortune. He found his tongue. 'I could have killed myself trying to avoid hitting you.'

The gorgeous eyes filled with impatience. 'Please listen. The car has broken down. We've been stuck on the road from Sheenmouth for absolute *hours*. When we finally turned off it, a kind of banging started under the bonnet.' Gripping his arm as he straddled the bike, she gave him a dazzling smile. 'Be a dear and have a look at it.'

Deciding that he was quite entitled to be angry with her, he plucked her hand from his arm and gave it back to her. 'I'll be as dear as you please, but all that'll happen if I look at it will be that it'll look back at me,' he lied, having no inclination to mend anyone's car in his present mood.

'Don't you know *anything* about cars?' she demanded desperately.

'No . . . only motorcycles. Now, if you'll excuse me, I have an important appointment at the Buck and Hounds,' he told her, backing from the depths of the hedge into the road again.

'I'll come with you,' she declared and, before he could

stop her, she had climbed on to the pillion seat and settled behind him, clutching him around the waist and displaying a delectable amount of silk-covered legs.

'Just a minute,' he protested.

'Oh, please,' breathed her sweet voice in his ear. 'I just *have* to get to the Abbey, which isn't far past the Buck and Hounds. I'm absolutely desperate. We've been delayed so long, it's now practically a matter of life or death. Please, *please* say you'll take me.'

The mood he was in now inspired the reverse reaction. This girl was undoubtedly one of the Kirkland set. The way she spoke, the expectation that others would jump to her bidding, and the dress which had that unmistakable touch of class he had seen in big London stores, all spoke of wealth without the proof of that Bentley a few yards away with its bonnet up. Playing knight-errant to this girl might be fun. He would get a peek at the Kirkland home and, if it really was a matter of life or death, her father or someone interested in the affair might give him half a crown for his trouble.

'All right,' he agreed impulsively. 'Hold on!'

Partly because she had told him the case was urgent, but mostly to show her a thing or two, he opened the throttle and attacked the road in unusually reckless manner. Like Mona, this girl plainly loved speed. Her exhilarated laughter in his ears partially negated his depression, so that he soon began to catch the feeling of vital urgency. Racing through Magnum Pomeroy, he brought indignant looks from drinkers outside the Buck and Hounds, and set the landlord's two red setters chasing after them, barking hysterically.

'You're absolutely *splendid*,' cried the girl, in his ear. 'How fast are we going now?'

'Much too fast,' he yelled over his shoulder. 'If old Harry Jupp sees us, he'll report me to Sergeant Phipps at Sheenmouth police station. I'll be in jail by Saturday.'

'I'll come and bail you out,' she promised. 'Turn off here, down that lane. *Heavens!* You cut that very fine.'

99

'Yes, didn't I?' he agreed proudly, completely caught up now in the absurdity of what he was doing.

His hope of roaring up to the front door of the old monastery was thwarted by the presence of people in evening clothes, who were strolling in the grounds and along the driveway. He made a reasonably spectacular arrival, however, by scattering several elegant groups with blasts on his horn, then came to a halt outside the massive yellow stone building from whence came the sound of a dance-band playing superbly. The girl scrambled off to stand beside him. She looked wildly attractive with her hair windblown and her cheeks flushed by speed and excitement. Warren had never met anyone like her, and felt quite giddy from the experience.

'Come on,' she said, in the authoritative way she had. 'You deserve a drink after that.'

'Thanks, but I couldn't go in there dressed this way,' he told her regretfully.

'Nonsense! No one will look at you, they'll all be swarming over Kit Anson tonight. *Come on*,' she urged, practically dragging him from the saddle.

Disentangling his legs from his machine, he asked, 'Do you know him?'

'Who . . . Kit? Heavens, he's practically one of the family. Do you want to meet him?'

Stumbling along beside her as he pulled off his goggles and gauntlets, he expressed his doubts again about entering. 'I don't think it'll work, you know. They'll think I'm a gatecrasher.'

She shook her head. 'They'll think you're another pilot when they see the goggles and leather coat.' Gripping his arm as he hesitated, she dragged him forward across a wide flagged terrace. '*Come on*. I'll introduce you to my brother Donald, and he'll give you a drink while I dash upstairs to change.'

'Your brother Donald?' he asked, his heart quickening.

'Donald Kirkland. He designed the seaplane Kit

broke the world record in this afternoon. You *must* have been watching. It was thrilling!'

As they walked in on a scene such as he had never ever imagined, Warren told himself that before Mrs Bardolph had dusted his room today this would have been the chance of a lifetime. He had nothing to offer Donald Kirkland now, and he certainly did not want half a crown from *him* for bringing his beautiful crazy sister home. He wanted a job. *Seaspray* might have got it for him.

4

Warren's first impression of the great hall decorated with half-naked plaster figures posing rather suggestively in discreet alcoves, while large numbers of excited young people threw themselves about to the music of a lively dance-band, caused him to wonder what the ghosts of the former monks thought of such irreverence. Dazed by the noise, the colour, the absolute excess of everything, he forgot his initial reservations and drank in every detail as he stood just inside the door, a curious spectacle himself in breeches, blue-check open-necked shirt, pullover hand-knitted by Mona, and leather boots and jacket.

Nobody appeared to notice his entrance. The band, on a raised platform, was almost certainly not a collection of amateur musicians like they had at the local dance-hall. Their impressive yellow dinner jackets blended with the predominantly primrose-coloured decor – the shade of world success this afternoon. The royal-blue velvet cloths attached to their music stands and stamped with the glittering gold initials P D, suggested to Warren that he was seeing and hearing the renowned Phil Davenport, who normally played only in the kind of clubs and hotels he had never been able to afford. A thrill ran through him. This was far more exciting than slipping back for an hour with Mona this evening.

'Come on,' said the girl beside him, using what

appeared to be her favourite term of command. 'I'll hand you over to Donald, then dash off to change.'

Following her around the edge of a joyously bobbing crowd of dancers, he asked in loud tones, 'What about this matter of life or death?'

Her gorgeous smile hit him again as she angled her face his way. 'Kit broke the air speed record, even though I crashed into *Aphrodite*, and I haven't congratulated him yet. When they carried him up in triumph to the stand for champagne, I had passed out with relief.'

Reaching a tall, fair-haired man, the girl Warren now knew to be Leone Kirkland tapped his arm to draw his attention from the young couple speaking to him. When Donald Kirkland turned, Warren was struck by the resemblance to his crazy sister, and it then truly dawned on him that he was face to face with a man he admired and deeply envied.

'The traffic was impossible,' the girl told her brother, shouting to be heard above the band. 'Then we broke down in the most isolated spot on the Pomeroy road, and I was just growing really desperate when. . . ' She broke off to turn to Warren. 'What's your name, by the way?'

Bemused by the unbelievability of what was happening, he gave it in full. 'Warren James Bartholomew Grant.'

She turned back to her brother. 'When . . . *he* came along on a motorcycle to effect a gallant rescue. He's been absolutely *splendid*. I've promised him a drink and an introduction to Kit. Look after him for me while I dash up to change.' Twisting to smile at Warren with devastating effect once more, she told him, 'There you are! Now I really must get into something a little more suitable.'

Feeling the remark was slightly ironic coming from a girl who had just told him he would not look out of place dressed as he was, Warren could not believe Kit Anson would hold attention tonight when this girl was in the vicinity, whatever she was wearing. With her departure, cordiality also appeared to vanish, however. Donald Kirkland betrayed a disapproval verging on disgust as he looked Warren over from head to toe. Telling himself that it was more important to impress this good-looking graceful young man with his ability than with his appearance, Warren smiled.

'How do you do, Mr Kirkland. It's a very great privilege to meet the designer of *Aphrodite*.' As the other man reluctantly shook his hand, he added, 'As a designer myself I fully appreciate the brilliance of your work. I've watched her development every step of the way, and she flew like the supreme champion she is this afternoon. Congratulations.'

'Thank you, Mr . . .?' he replied, in cultured but defensive tones. 'I'm afraid my sister failed to make a formal introduction.'

Warren gave his name again, leaving out the James Bartholomew this time. Donald Kirkland seemed less than impressed.

'Forgive me, Mr Grant, but I thought I knew all the leading designers in this country. Are you, perhaps, with a foreign company?'

If only he had had *Seaspray* to offer! 'Actually, I'm an independent designer,' he said, finding inspiration just in time. 'I hate being tied down.' Seeing the other's expression he kept talking fast, wishing it were not necessary to shout in order to be heard. 'As it happens, I've just finished developing a new seaplane I call *Seaspray*. I was intending to contact you shortly to offer you the first opportunity to study it.' Knowing that what he said during the next few minutes would convince his doubting listener of his knowledge and competence, Warren then launched into an involved technical description of wing elevation, propeller displacement and the perennial problem of cooling at high speeds, which he believed he had solved in *Seaspray* by fairly simple means.

Carried away by his unusual but sound theory, it was some time before Warren realized that his companion was showing signs of acute boredom. Lapsing into silence, he told himself that even if he looked like an out-of-work country bumpkin in the midst of this elegant party, any man wholly concerned with aviation development could not fail to take an interest in his ideas, even if it was to disagree and point out the drawbacks. Donald Kirkland was not even listening, as he gazed around the room with a trapped expression on his fair-moustached face. His roving glance finally settled on what it was seeking, it seemed, because he beckoned a sandy-haired man in a spotless dinner jacket. He came across immediately, past groups of dancers who appeared to part like the waters of the Red Sea to allow him through.

'Yes, Mr Kirkland?'

'My sister was apparently rescued by Mr Grant, who brought her home on his motorcycle. She would like him to be given a drink and an introduction to Mr Anson before he leaves. Would you see to it?'

The man turned to Warren with the impersonal politeness of a well-trained subordinate. 'Would you come with me, sir? I'll take you to Mr Anson, then send a waiter to you with cocktails.'

Warren had no choice but to walk away from the man who should have changed his life for him this evening. It always happened that way in films and books. A cocktail and an introduction to the famous Kit Anson was a great deal more than the half-crown he had flippantly imagined a rescued damsel's father might offer, yet this suggestion of a gratuity for services rendered had now somehow taken on a slightly insulting flavour. If he had not felt an obligation, as well as a very strong desire, to wait for the Kirkland girl to reappear, Warren would have walked out there and then, mounted his bike, and paid a belated visit to the Buck and Hounds. People were certainly beginning to notice him now, but showed no more than mild curiosity over what appeared to be a dispatch-rider being conducted to whoever was to receive the message he was delivering. They soon turned back to the real business of the evening.

Kit Anson was eventually found in an octagonal room which appeared to be furnished with church pews – rather a weird idea, Warren thought. The hero of the day was under siege. Pretty girls gathered in open worship around him, while the male contingent mostly smoked as they silently studied this man whose courageous quest for speed had sent him faster than any man through the air, in a machine so delicate it was hard to believe that he had performed the feat and returned to the water with *Aphrodite* and himself still intact. Telling Warren to wait on the periphery, his companion moved expertly through the group to approach Anson and speak in his ear. The pilot glanced across at Warren, then nodded his agreement before excusing himself to those surrounding him, and stepping out through a nearby heavily studded door standing open to the evening. Warren was then beckoned by the sandy-haired man he strongly suspected of patronage and therefore disliked, to be told that Mr Anson would see him out on the terrace.

With a twitch of his lips, the man then added, 'After you have drunk your cocktail and spoken to Mr Anson, there's no necessity for you to come back into the house, sir. I'll pass your thanks to Mr Kirkland, along with your farewells.'

Giving no opportunity for a suitable reply, the man then threaded his precise way back to the noise and hectic activity of the dancing. Feeling very definitely insulted by now, Warren walked from the curious room with the intention of offering congratulations to the pilot who had plainly been told to give him five minutes of his time, then leaving Sheenmouth Abbey by pretending that he had an important appointment elsewhere. 'Elsewhere' would be the Buck and Hounds.

The plan was instantly discarded when Kit Anson

smiled warmly at his approach, and said, 'My grateful thanks for allowing me to escape for a while. My head was starting to spin with the sound of so many voices speaking at once.'

He had seen Kit Anson many times through his binoculars while he had watched the activity at Kirkland's slipway during trials on *Aphrodite*, but now the great man was beside him Warren was very conscious of his considerable strength, both physical and personal. Small wonder women made fools of themselves over this man who, he reminded himself, was no more than twenty-two – two years younger than he was. How marvellous to have reached such a pinnacle so swiftly.

'I watched your performance this afternoon,' he said admiringly. 'As I'd studied *Aphrodite* throughout her trials, I knew you'd do it. An extra ten is no mean achievement, though. Congratulations.'

The pilot nodded an acknowledgement, but said nothing as he studied Warren through dark eyes betraying his tiredness.

'I thought I spotted fuel coming from the engines on the turns,' Warren continued, keen to find the cause of it. 'That mixture you used was probably a little too volatile at full throttle, although you'd probably never have reached four one seven on anything less. Did you get the breeze up, at all?'

There was another nod from the man in well-fitting evening dress. 'I was petrified throughout the entire flight. The cockpit grew so hot, it was like sitting inside a furnace which could blow up at any time. When I landed, the spray actually spat and sizzled as it hit the sides.'

Warren whistled through his teeth. 'Frightening!'

The other man looked back at him almost dreamily. 'Exhilarating! I believe I lived half my life up there this afternoon.'

'I've designed a machine which would enable you to live the other half,' he said, on impulse. 'The drawings

107

are at my lodgings. I tried to interest Mr Kirkland just now, but he plainly thought I was just an upstart who happened to have given his sister a ride home. That stuffed shirt was told to palm me off on to you, give me a drink, then send me on my way.'

Kit Anson's brow furrowed as his weary brain tried to fathom the sense of those words, then he moved away along the terrace. 'Let's take the weight off our feet, shall we? That "stuffed shirt" is Maitland Jarvis, Sir Hector's right-hand man,' he added, as he reached a wall shunned by other guests, and sat. 'He gives the impression of being little more than a robot, but he can be dangerous. His head is a filing cabinet. You have been duly registered, then inserted under the letter U.'

'Why U?' asked Warren, sitting beside this man he found such surprisingly easy company.

'U for upstart.' He gave a faint smile. 'That's what you said, if I remember correctly.'

Warren smiled back. 'Very definitely . . . but the way I'm dressed gives credence to that theory, I suppose.'

'Well, it certainly wouldn't help you to capture Donald Kirkland's interest in any project you might have. You've chosen just about the worst time, anyway. He's preparing to announce his engagement this evening.'

'Just my luck,' said Warren resignedly, 'although I didn't actually choose the time to offer him *Seaspray*. Miss Kirkland dragged me inside and introduced us, so I thought I shouldn't let the opportunity pass.'

'Miss Kirkland dragged you in? You're one of Leone's friends?'

'I wish I was,' he replied with feeling, reminding himself that he wanted to see her again before he left. 'Her car had broken down on the Pomeroy road, and I damn nearly ran her over when I took a corner. Before I knew it, she'd jumped on to the pillion and said she had to get here on a matter of life or death.'

'Really? What was it?'

'She didn't reveal it, at the time, but I found out just now that she hadn't yet offered you her congrats, and was very anxious to do so.'

The other man began to laugh softly. 'That girl really does invite a tanning sometimes, but just as you're about to administer it, she goes all haughty on you so that you remember who she is. Why has she deserted you?'

'To go upstairs and change into something more suitable, she said. Although, several minutes earlier, she had assured me that no one would notice anyone but Kit Anson this evening. I guess she was right.'

'Yet it was Donald Kirkland who held more interest for you.' Giving Warren a speculative look, he said, 'Care to tell me about this machine of yours? *Seaspray*, I think you called her.'

Thrilled that his companion had noted the name, and knowing that his was the type of interest he had been expecting from the designer of *Aphrodite*, Warren needed no second bidding. Going into great depth of technical detail which he knew any pilot would understand, he outlined the development of his own seaplane from conception to birth, answering the informed questions put to him as he went along. They argued a little over some points he made, developed others to conclusions which surprised and excited them both, and discussed the subject of waterborne aircraft with such deep mutual interest, the sun went down and lights sprang up all along the terrace without their noticing the change. Finally, after shifting his position for the tenth time, Warren's companion stood up with a smile.

'That wall is growing very hard on the backside. I suggest we find more comfortable seats where drinks are on hand.'

Warren got to his feet, also. 'The stuffed shirt was supposed to send over a cocktail for me.'

Taking him by the arm, Kit Anson said, 'I can find you something more substantial than that.' Then, as they walked together over the flagstones, he added, 'You're a flier as well as a designer, that's obvious.'

'Yes. I give lessons at the Aero Club near Magnum Pomeroy.'

'You have my sympathies. You know, I'm really keen to see those drawings of *Seaspray*!'

'I had a model of her until around two this afternoon. My landlady dusted my room without due care, and trod on what she calls my "toy aeroplane". It'd take me a while to put her back together, I'm afraid.'

'What filthy luck!'

'It's been that kind of day, actually,' Warren went on, finding it easy to confide in this man who was not at all the unapproachable hero he had every excuse to be. 'I lost my girlfriend, because her father told me it was a diamond ring or else. Then, congested roads made me late for a lesson with a silly ass who can't grasp even the basics of flying, and Jim Mason threatened to replace me as soon as he found another pilot. On top of that, I used my rent money to buy paint for the model of *Seaspray*, so I'm a week overdue. Being dragged here by Miss Kirkland saved me from drinking myself silly in the Buck and Hounds.'

'I know the feeling,' came the sympathetic comment, as the man of the moment made to lead him inside the Abbey.

Warren stopped him. 'Look, I really don't think I should go in there again. It's been marvellous talking to you, and I'd be thrilled to show you my drawings, but this outfit is a bit too much for an elegant affair even if attention is mostly focused on you tonight.'

'Wouldn't you like to stay? I'm sure Leone will be expecting you to.'

He shook his head. 'Even an inflated ego like mine can't blind me to the fact that it would be out of the question, dressed as I am.'

'That's no problem.'

'Eh?'

'My dear fellow, the Kirklands keep a wardrobe for guests who remain overnight unexpectedly. If you'd like to stay – and I hope you will, because I'd like to continue our discussion – I can hand you over to Coombes, who'll fix you up with what you need. What do you say?'

Overwhelmed by the notion of anyone keeping a wardrobe filled with clothes for visitors, sensing that the rapport he had established with this speed champion could lead to an interesting, productive relationship, and wanting very much to see Leone Kirkland in her 'something suitable', Warren could only stammer his thanks.

Kit Anson smiled. 'Good. I'll find Coombes and get him to do the necessary. By the way,' he added over his shoulder, 'you've given me the name of your machine, but not your own.'

Warren told him, adding, 'Didn't the stuffed shirt say who I was?'

'Do you really want to know what he said to me?' came the challenge.

'Might as well.'

'He murmured in my ear that Miss Kirkland had brought in someone who was making himself a nuisance, so could I give him my autograph then chuck him out?'

Warren caught himself laughing. 'Why didn't you?'

'Because you represented salvation with a capital S. You know, I'd much prefer to spend tonight in lone communion with *Aphrodite*. I'm dog tired and highly emotional. If I were a woman, I'd break down and weep. Talking to you has been the next best thing, because you appear to be just about the only one here who'd understand how I feel.'

Warren was touched. 'That's a great compliment from someone of your calibre, Mr Anson.'

'Not at all, it's that sense of rapport one flier has with another . . . and you'd better start calling me Kit, if we're going to work on that seaplane of yours together.'

Leone took a long time over making herself beautiful

for Kit. At first, she had despaired over the series of events which had culminated in being stranded by the roadside while he was being 'hugged to death and kissed unconscious' by as many girls as could lay their hands on him. The misery of the days following her crash into *Aphrodite* had left her unable to eat, or to sleep much during the short summer nights, while she worried about whether or not all would be ready for the date fixed by her father. When it was known they would be, fears for Kit's safety had continued the pattern of denial. Whilst waiting for the mist to clear today, she had drunk too much and not eaten enough. Small wonder that excitement and relief when it was over had taken their toll. A doctor amongst her father's guests had recommended that she should lie down for at least an hour, so she had been taken to a room in a seafront hotel where she had been given a white powder and told to sleep. Meader had been instructed to wait until she had recovered enough to be driven home. Everyone else, including Kit, had returned to Sheenmouth Abbey by boat.

The powder must have been a sedative. When she had awoken, it was seven o'clock. By then, all roads out of the resort had been jammed with cars, motorcycles, charabancs, bicycles, and even those forced to walk back to Axminster because they had missed the train. She had practically wept with frustration. When the Bentley had broken down soon after they had finally branched off on to clear roads, it had seemed the last straw. The young man on his motorbike had represented a knight in the shiniest armour imaginable, when he had crashed into that hedge beside her.

Now she was home, it occurred to her that the delay might be to her advantage, after all. Everyone else would have mobbed Kit ages ago, so her own congratulations would receive more attention from him. Instructing the maid Maitland had hired for her to put away the dress she had intended to wear, Leone impulsively took from her wardrobe a wildly sophisticated ballgown she had

112

bought in Zürich. The black chiffon dress, cut in a severe figure-hugging line which swept into a small train covered with black satin roses, made her look at least eighteen. It was sleeveless and practically backless, with a stark décolletage softened by a diagonal line of matching satin roses. The mannequin who had modelled it had worn emeralds. Leone had none, so decided that the fairness of her skin and hair contrasted so well with the black she needed no jewels to complete the stunning effect she wanted to create. At the last minute, however, she fixed an ornament of diamanté, pearls and tiny black feathers just above her right ear, before snatching up a shimmering bag on a silver chain handle.

With her heart beating fast, she hurried along the gallery and down the wide flight of branched stairs, searching the sea of faces for the one person she longed to impress. Kit was nowhere to be seen among the couples dancing a foxtrot.

'Looking for me, beautiful?' murmured a voice in her ear. 'Seek no further, you've found me.'

She was swept into the arms of a young man with olive skin, patent-leather hair, and sickly good looks, whose shirt studs were diamonds and whose breath smelled strongly of gin. They foxtrotted for several minutes as if glued together, while his damp hand explored her bare back. Then, when the slow sentimental tune came to an end, he flicked the lobe of her left ear with his tongue and offered to show her a cosy little spot he had discovered.

'It's the cell of one of the monks who used to inhabit this place aeons ago. Believe me, darling, theirs was no life of denial. I could tell you tales of this place which would literally leave you gasping.'

Leone struggled free, saying, 'No, they wouldn't. I live here.'

Any further exchange between them was prevented by a roll on the drums, which defied even the most persistently garrulous guest to ignore the call on his attention.

113

All heads turned to the band where space was being made for several people mounting the steps to the platform. As Leone watched from the midst of the revellers, a curious pain burned in the region of her breastbone. Her father, Donald and Kit were now taking centre stage amidst roars of approval and thunderous applause. The pain spread to her throat. Never had her exclusion seemed more total than it was now, in the presence of so many people. Why had they said nothing to her; why had no one attempted to find her? Donald knew she had arrived, at last. She had crashed into *Aphrodite* and been punished for the problems and anxiety she had caused. During the past days she had accepted solitude without complaint, knowing everyone was laden with the burden of preparing for this day. But *Aphrodite* had been successfully repaired, and Kit had flown her to prove himself wildly victorious. All should be forgiven her now, surely. Tonight was made for Kirkland celebration, and she was one of the family, to be recognized as such. Her sense of excitement, and of pride in Kit, was so strong she could only relieve it by being part of the limelight illuminating him.

Attempting to push her way through the clustering guests, she was defeated by sheer numbers. Then, swallowing the lump in her throat, she told herself that this occasion truly belonged to only the men. Kit was heroic, Donald was brilliant, and her father was now lord of all he surveyed. All that could be said of her was that she had damaged the aircraft at the eleventh hour and almost ruined what had been achieved today.

Standing motionless in the spellbound crowd, she then realized that her father was the only one of the three who was smiling. Donald looked pale and nervous; Kit was not the laughing jubilant man he had every right to be tonight. Strained and tight-jawed, he appeared dangerously exhausted. Leone's heart went out to him.

Sir Hector held up a hand for silence, then embraced the guests with his satisfied smile. 'Ladies and gentlemen, this has been a day the whole world will remember. As the cheering and shouting fade, I offer a more humble personal tribute to these two young men. Donald Kirkland is a name on everyone's lips tonight, as they extol the skill and brilliance of someone who must hold the future of marine aviation in his youthful hands. I share that universal claim for his ability. But he is also my own son, so my pride in his triumph is primarily that of a father.' That comment was augmented by a paternal grip of Donald's elegant shoulder. 'How many men are lucky enough to know that their life's work will be continued and even extended beyond our present vision, by a son with the qualities I see in my own? I count myself greatly blessed.'

During the slight pause while applause rippled through the hall, it seemed as if emotion got the better of him. Then he loosed his grip on Donald and turned to Kit.

'The name of this young man is also on everyone's lips tonight. The fastest man in the air the world has ever known.' A cheer rang through the vaulted hall, and he allowed time for it to die down before giving a smiling nod. 'Yes, I share your acclaim for his personal courage and daring, but Kit Anson is also the test pilot for Kirkland Marine Aviation, so my pride in his achievement is also on behalf of the company I started in a disused fish-canning factory and built up into what it will now be – one of the nation's leaders in marine aircraft development.' Putting his hand on Kit's shoulder, he went on, 'Ladies and gentlemen, three years ago I took into my home the orphaned son of a highly valued employee and gave him every advantage a young man could desire. It was a risk, of course, like any investment, but I think you'll agree that it has yielded rich dividends.'

Fresh applause greeted this, but Leone stood quite still, gazing at Kit's face. So this was why he had been brought into her home on that unforgettable day. Not as her bastard half-brother, not as an official second son, not even as the fortunate recipient of a generous gesture towards a lamented friend. Kit Anson was simply one of Sir Hector Kirkland's investments. If he had not guessed it before, he had just been made publicly aware of the fact. Poor Kit! Yet, perhaps not so deserving of sympathy, since he had yielded rich dividends. The daughter borne by Marina Kirkland had little hope of emulating his success . . . unless she somehow made her mark as stunningly as he had.

The murmur died as movement caught everyone's attention. Leone studied the girl her brother was bringing up the steps to join him. Stephanie Main lived up to Kit's lyrical description in every way. The halo of tawny hair around her oval face suggested nostalgic Edwardian beauty. Tall, almost majestic, her figure also suited that bygone age. Her handspan waist, swelling bosom and hips, and graceful neck were enhanced by a dress of rich pink beaded satin which highlighted her creamy skin to perfection. Leone was too distant to check Kit's claim of sherry-coloured eyes, but they were certainly wide and lovely.

The pain of exclusion returned in full force as she heard her father express his pleasure in welcoming the future bride into the Kirkland family. This moment had nothing to do with aircraft or flying. A stranger was being fêted and acknowledged as Sir Hector's new daughter-in-law, while his true daughter was being ignored. Leone became a pillar of ice in that overheated hall, as the flashing solitaire was placed on Stephanie's finger and she exchanged kisses with Donald, Sir Hector and, finally, a hesitant Kit. The newsmen were all highly delighted with their pictures. The basket of flowers Maitland had chosen was then presented, after which the radiant recipient was asked to pose with her fiancé, and with her future father-in-law. Only when the photographers insisted on pairing Stephanie with the aerial hero of the day did Leone begin to suspect something agonizingly

116

unacceptable. Was this engagement the reason for Kit's tight-jawed expression, for his lack of vitality? He had extolled her beauty and charm in lavish manner, yet was Stephanie Main the one girl who did not want him?

Horrified by a rush of tears to blur the vision of her family on a rostrum she could not reach through the press of guests, Leone found her pride rising, replacing the need for emotional release through tears with release through anger. She had come home fully determined to take her place here, and take it she would. They would *not* continue to exclude her, especially when another female was on the brink of breaking through the male ranks of this monastic regime. Tonight was the perfect occasion for something dramatic to happen, and she would be the instigator.

The ceremony was over, and the band was striking up a twostep, by the time she had pushed her way through the milling people to reach the raised platform. Kit had vanished, and her father was deep in conversation with several serious-faced businessmen several yards from the spot. Donald was about to take his future bride on to the dance-floor for the twostep, so Leone crossed swiftly to them and summoned a bright smile to suggest that all was well with her. It was vitally important to hide from this Edwardian girl, who was soon to become her sister-in-law, the fact that she was regarded as unimportant by the men of her family.

'Congratulations,' she said, in a carefully controlled voice. 'Sorry I couldn't join you for the presentation of the ring and family groups all embracing, etcetera, but I was cornered by a persistent journalist who wanted the story from my angle. You know: *Daughter of the house tells of the private anguish behind aerial triumph.* Don't worry, Donald, I was terribly discreet.'

Stephanie, whose eyes really were the colour of sherry, studied her with an amused smile, but Donald glared at her with the same animosity he had worn since her crash into *Aphrodite.*

117

'For God's sake, Leone, this is a celebration not a wake. Wherever did you find that funeral dress?'

His words cut even deeper into her wounded senses, coming as they did in front of this girl who apparently succeeded where she had always so dismally failed.

'It took some finding,' she retaliated swiftly. 'I scoured Zürich for it and realized that it was just right for the sad loss of my dear brother. Now I've seen Steph, it seems I haven't lost a brother but gained a sister.' Maintaining the same breezy manner, she said to the other girl, 'You've no idea how glad I am to get some female support, at last. Being the only woman in this dismal place has been frightfully dreary at times.'

The girl in pink satin gave a smile so dazzling, Leone told herself that if this was what Kit admired in a woman, she stood no chance whatever of gaining his interest.

'I can well believe it, having been the only woman here myself on several occasions. The only solution is to forbid all talk of aircraft and turn their minds to more entertaining subjects, I've discovered. They soon thaw.'

They would, Leone thought furiously, wondering what entertaining subjects this seductive creature dreamed up to bring about the miracle. Her next words suggested that she planned to set to work on Leone next.

'I shan't force my friendship on you, my dear, but I'll be very glad to advise you on the painful business of growing up.' The celebrated eyes took in every detail of the sophisticated black dress. 'One can make so many embarrassing mistakes at the age of sixteen.'

All hope of friendship with this girl died instantly, and Leone sharpened her blade ready for battle. 'You plainly speak from experience, Steph. When's the wedding, by the way . . . or hasn't Father told you the date yet?'

Stephanie took that on the chin as she slipped her arm through the crook of Donald's possessively. 'We thought an October ceremony would be rather lovely. The resto-

118

ration of the chapel will be complete by then, and I adore the Abbey surrounded by dew-laden meadows and autumn leaves. It has an ethereal beauty perfect for bridal veils and the sound of organ music floating on the still, crisp air.'

'Heavens!' exclaimed Leone before she could stop herself. 'You're as poetic as Kit. You two should get on very well.'

'We do, my dear Leone. Believe me, we do.'

The manner in which it was said suggested that the words were a gross understatement of the depth of her relationship with the main hero of the moment. It was the salt to increase the agony of her wounds this evening, and she was driven to say, 'As you're another of Father's risky investments, I suppose it's not really surprising.'

Donald turned on her furiously. 'You insulting little beast! I can only believe you've had too much to drink again. This morning you embarrassed Father by obliging one of his principal guests to dose you and put you to bed, then you had the nerve to bounce in dragging some country numbskull by his oil-stained hand and rudely interrupt my private conversation in order to palm him off on me, while you went up to change into something which makes you resemble a West End tart. If you can't behave decently, clear off to bed.'

'Sweetie!' protested Stephanie, in faintly amused tones. 'Don't be harsh on the child. It's been a very exciting day for everyone.'

'Then let's celebrate it,' he growled, sweeping her into his arms and joining the dancers swiftly.

Leone remained where she was, as stunned by the encounter as if he had struck her on the cheek. Since her arrival he had been surprisingly moody and belligerent, and his fury over her damage in his aircraft was probably excusable. Tonight, however, he should be on top of the world. Wide professional acclaim and a brilliant marital match, plus the renowned Sir Hector proclaiming him a son in a million; what more could any man want? There was no possible reason for a brother to crush his sister so completely, unless she had given him good cause for the attack. She knew she had not; knew that she posed no threat to the pinnacle on which he now stood.

Still stunned and near to tears, she tried to make sense of his behaviour. Then it occurred to her that she might have taken the lash earned by someone else. Surely not Kit. He had just been publicly proclaimed an investment, not another son. His daring flight had brought him a victor's laurels, but it had also enhanced the designer's reputation a hundredfold. Was Kit truly a rival for the silky smooth Stephanie? No, the solitaire had clinched ownership, and Kit was unlikely to crave forbidden fruit when ripe, luscious plums were apparently dropping in his lap daily.

Who else could threaten Donald? Not the father who would hand him the moon on a plate; not the invisible sister. Not the stray mongel taken in as an investment. The future Mrs Donald Kirkland was the only remaining candidate. Beneath that old-fashioned exterior probably lay a woman as emancipated and calculating as any in this modern age. Was Donald having to give more than a good-quality diamond in order to have and hold her? At that point, it dawned on her that after that dewy mist-laden October wedding in the restored chapel, the pair would be living here in Sheenmouth Abbey. The faint hope of female friendship to aid her own bid to break the masculine monopoly had been crushed by the recent confrontation, so what were the prospects? If Donald's future promised to be glittering, her own looked a duller shade than ever. Why, then, had he hit out at her in such a humiliating manner?

Someone appeared before her. 'Hello. I was hoping to find you again.'

'Were you?' she murmured abstractedly.

'I wasn't sure it was you, at first. Gosh, no one's going to look at anyone else tonight, now you're around.'

The warm admiration in his voice was so unexpected it captured her attention. She gazed in curiosity at a young man with slicked-down brown hair, whose face was vaguely familiar. His eyes were a dreamy blue-grey, fringed by dark lashes which made them his main feature. Right now they were filled with exactly the kind of wonder she had hoped to see in Kit's when she congratulated him.

'Would you care to dance?' he asked hopefully, just as her brother and Stephanie swung past laughing together.

'All right,' she agreed defiantly.

They had moved no more than several yards when the twostep ended. His disappointment was marked. 'I suppose you're not free for the next dance, are you?'

'I have to find Kit,' she told him, gazing around the vast hall.

'I was introduced to him, thanks to you.'

Her attention was drawn back to her companion. Where had she seen him before? 'Thanks to me?'

'Yes, indirectly. I liked him tremendously, and found it hard to believe that he was the man who had flown *Aphrodite* this afternoon. I imagined he might be rather unapproachable.'

'He is, when in the vicinity of that seaplane. That's all he thinks about.'

'That's understandable.' He gave a shy smile. 'He offered to look at my drawings. I'm a designer, you know.'

Leone began to lose interest in him. Flying and the machines that did it appeared to be the only topics of interest in Sheenmouth. Would she be acknowledged a Kirkland if she sat in a seaplane: would Kit be interested in her if she offered him some drawings?

'I suppose you're brilliant, too,' she muttered.

He shook his head. 'Fame's still a long way off, I'm afraid. I was on my way to the Buck and Hounds to drown my sorrows when you stopped me.'

'Heavens, you're him . . . he! The shining armour on

121

a motorcycle; the person with a long name,' she exclaimed in surprise.

His smile was still shy. 'I don't know why I said it all. Warren will do. I know I look more respectable now Coombes has kitted me out, but I didn't realize you had no idea who I was.'

'You said you were a designer, so I thought you worked for Kirkland's.'

'No such luck! I'm an unemployed designer, when I'm not giving flying lessons at the Aero Club.'

'Flying, flying,' she cried. 'Is that all men ever think of?'

'Not when they're standing next to a girl who looks as stunning as you do in that dress.'

The wonder in his dreamy attractive eyes was like balm to ease the multiple blows of that endless day. He offered the only hope of enduring the remainder of it, so she seized it eagerly. With a warm smile, she said, 'How lucky I was to run into you tonight.'

'I was the one who ran into you,' he reminded her. 'I could have killed you.'

'You very gallantly hit a hedge rather than me, and I think you're an awfully nice person.'

Flushing slightly, he said, 'So are you, Miss Kirkland.'

'Shining armour people are allowed to call me Leone,' she offered, desperately glad of his presence beside her. Then, seeing Stephanie watching her from across the shoulders of several men clustering around the engaged couple, she said impulsively, 'They're starting a foxtrot. Are you any good at it?'

'Rather! May I demonstrate?'

'If you like.'

He had not lied about his prowess, and he was equally expert at the waltz which followed. Leone complimented him generously.

'My mother had lots of friends to stay in our London apartment, so I used to spend the evenings when I wasn't

122

studying at dance-halls. You get to learn every step in the book in those places.'

Intrigued, she asked against his shoulder, 'Do you mean those public affairs where people pay to enter? Whatever are they like?'

'Some of the bands are really good, and it's a marvellous way to meet people if you go there on your own. Mind you, the more high-class ones wouldn't let girls enter without a partner.'

'That seems awfully unfair,' she protested. 'What if they were on their own and wanted to meet people?'

He flushed again. 'They wanted to avoid . . . well, they didn't want girls who weren't exactly respectable.'

'But they didn't mind admitting men who weren't respectable?' she asked indignantly, before it dawned on her what he was trying to say. 'Oh, I *see*.' Then, because she was reminded of Donald's reference to a West End tart, she fell silent for the rest of the waltz. When they stood side by side again, she beckoned one of the hired waiters bearing cocktails. They both took a glass from his tray, and Leone pursued another of his comments. 'You said your mother had an apartment in London. Have you both moved to Sheenmouth now?'

He shook his head. 'Mother died last year. I've found digs here, but I'm a bit fed up with my landlady today. She knocked *Seaspray* on to the floor, then trod on her. It'll take me weeks to rebuild her.'

Sipping her cocktail, Leone asked, 'Knocked *what* on the floor?'

'The model of the seaplane I've designed.'

'Oh, not back to flying,' she grumbled.

He lowered his glass. 'I'm sorry, but it was a terrible blow after the hours of work I'd put in on her. I was intending to show her to your brother, but he didn't seem interested, anyway.'

Unwilling to pursue that subject, Leone said quickly, 'Tell me more about your youth in the public dance-halls.'

'I didn't spend my entire youth in them,' he protested.

'You must have taken your own partners sometimes. Were they pretty?'

There was no guile about him, for she read his expression quite clearly. 'I suppose I thought they were. Now I've met you, I know I was wrong.'

Strangely emotional in a matter of seconds, she asked impulsively, 'Shall we be friends, Warren. Really good friends?'

'Yes please,' he answered. 'I'd like that very much.'

They drank in silence for a few moments, until the mood was broken by the band embarking on its next number. It was a tune Leone did not know – she was familiar with very few of the popular songs unless they were European in origin. Warren apparently knew it, and his face came alive.

' "Lady of Spain" is one of my favourites,' he told her, raising his voice in order to be heard. 'Some of the bands used to let me play with them, you know, and I always enjoyed this number.'

'Heavens,' she returned, trying to take in what he had said, 'you actually played a musical instrument at these dance-halls?'

He nodded. 'The trumpet.'

Finding him more intriguing by the minute, she urged him to elaborate. Watching his expression, she guessed his days in London had not been totally happy. Had his mother neglected him in favour of her many friends? Never having really known her own mother, and feeling as she did about Kit's, she had decided long ago that they were a curious breed.

'My stepfather used to play in a band before the war. When he was killed in Mesopotamia, one of his friends brought his trumpet home and gave it to me with a note Dad had written. I couldn't just put the thing away, could I?' he asked in appeal. 'He had shown me the basics, so I taught myself the rest. It's the most volatile instrument, and Sonny Montana – he's one of the bandleaders I got to know very well – Sonny taught me a superb arrangement for "Lady of Spain".'

All at once, Leone saw her chance to make her mark this evening. Donald could dazzle to his heart's content; her father could bask in reflected glory. She would capture attention by introducing a friend who could play the trumpet, in addition to designing seaplanes.

'Will you play it now?' she asked eagerly. 'Will you go up there with the band and play it for me?'

'Good Lord, no,' he said swiftly. 'That's Phil Davenport. He's the best. In any case, he'd never let me.'

'He'll have to if I say so,' she said with great authority. 'My father's paying him to do what he's asked tonight.'

'Your father's not paying me,' Warren pointed out. 'I couldn't, Leone.'

'Yes, you could,' she argued, catching him by the hand and dragging him forward. 'Come on, it's not much to ask you.'

Only her determination forced the unwilling young man to mount the steps to where they were almost deafened by the volume of the band in full swing. Over the sound, she shouted her request in Phil Davenport's ear. The bandleader's raddled face was schooled into the polite expression he was being paid to wear in this abbey, but he shook his head whilst continuing to conduct his musicians.

'Sir Hector would never approve,' he told her.

She stood her ground. 'I'm his daughter, and my friend has played with Sonny Montana.' She hoped the name she emphasized really was an impressive one. 'He would now like to play with you.'

Visibly unhappy, the man conducted several more bars before signalling his band to stop. Lowering his voice accordingly, he began his professional diplomacy.

'It's not that I have personal objections, Miss, it's just that . . .' he glanced over her head to Warren in appeal. 'I'm sure you understand my situation, sir.'

'Yes, of course,' he agreed. 'It's perfectly all right.'

'It's not perfectly all right,' cried Leone, holding Warren's arm as he made to leave. She was so thrilled by her plan now, no one was going to be allowed to spoil it. All she hoped was that her new friend could really play the trumpet well; well enough to cause a minor sensation in this old monastery. 'Think how proud your stepfather would be,' she said persuasively, before turning back to Phil Davenport. 'Give my friend a trumpet and let him play. You'll soon realize how brilliant he is.'

Warren stood uncertainly, his gaze on the bandleader's face. The dancers, waiting curiously in the centre of the floor because the music had ceased in mid-chorus, were also all gazing at Phil Davenport.

The dark-haired man sighed. 'Have you really played with Sonny, sir?'

'Oh yes,' Warren assured him. 'He even wrote a special arrangement of "Someone to Watch over Me" for me to play with his band.' Enthusiasm overcame his modesty. 'It was the hit of the evening each time we did it.'

'What did I tell you?' demanded Leone triumphantly.

The battle was won. A trumpet was handed to the young man who had given Leone a promise of friendship, and she moved aside as Warren had a short technical discussion with the musicians. Then, wearing a long-suffering expression, the bandleader lifted his baton to start the introduction. Warren put the trumpet to his lips. Soon, the sweet mellow notes of the instrument echoed in the vaults of the great ceiling, and bounced back off the ancient stone walls.

The resulting magic caused everyone in that hall to fall silent, more spellbound by the music than the sound of their own voices, for once. There was a haunting, poignant quality about the arrangement that caught at Leone's throat and set her heart yearning in a way she had never before experienced. All at once, she longed for something she found difficult to identify; ached for an alien fulfilment just out of reach. That pain in her breast returned so strongly, she realized tears might be the only means of easing it. They were almost there on her lashes by the time the final note died, and a total silence hung in the smoke-filled atmosphere of an ancient stone chamber where monks had once walked so softly.

Next minute, there was uproar as the guests went wild with enthusiasm. Flying, seaplanes, Kirkland Marine Aviation were all forgotten in the thrill of this impromptu performance. Warren Grant was a sensation to these elegant, sophisticated people pressing forward to cluster around the platform and gaze eagerly up at the young man who was laughing with delight. Phil Davenport recognized what was happening and, after a brief word with Warren, struck up 'Alexander's Ragtime Band'. The result was electrifying. The youthful flying instructor in borrowed clothes became another person as he fingered the gleaming instrument. Someone began to clap to the rhythm. Soon, the beat was taken up by guests who had forgotten the symbolism of the surrounding Grecian grottoes. They were now in another world, where the goddesses were on celluloid.

With a final resounding top note, Warren lowered the trumpet to face an ecstatic reception and cries for more. His bow tie was tugged free, his top stud undone as he prepared for another encore. His eyes now contained reveries of times Leone had not shared; his brown hair had sprung back into its normal wiriness. He looked young, triumphant, king of his own castle, as he embarked on a sentimental lovesong. Voices began to take up the refrain very softly, as those gazing up at him started to sway together. In that enchanted moment, no one noticed a young girl in a sophisticated black dress descend the steps at the rear of the platform and slip out to the moonlit grounds of her home.

Leone could watch and listen no longer. Tonight, she had found a friend; someone who wanted her company alone. Then her ridiculous desire to make her mark as a Kirkland had led her to give him away to the entire assembled company. All she had succeeded in doing was to set yet another male on a triumphant pedestal in Sheenmouth Abbey, where women apparently had no place whatever.

Kit found even the distant sounds of the party disturbing, so he walked on in the starlit darkness until he was blessedly alone in a silence broken only by nocturnal rustling and the whirr of night wings. He envied those birds their freedom to fly; yearned to be up there among the stars with *Aphrodite*. Exhaustion had finally driven him to seek solitude before he risked passing out in public. The stress of the past weeks, the nerve-stretching delay this morning, the concentration, tension and physical effort of what he had achieved were all now taking their toll of him.

In those first minutes after learning that he had added an entire ten miles an hour to the existing record, jubilation had possessed him. The cheering crowds, the glowing faces of those who had worked with him on the project, and the congratulations of Sir Hector had been as intoxicating as the champagne they had used to baptize him. The adoration of young women who had kissed and clung to him had added to his sense of conquest, both as a pilot and as a man. He had flown faster than anyone else in the world. *Anyone else in the world*. It was a fact still too momentous to take in, despite the constant references to it since he had come down from that aerial union with his goddess. It had been no easy conquest. *Aphrodite* had demanded more from him than any mortal woman. She had lived up to her reputation of orgasmic challenge in every way, and driven him hard. Every muscle of his body, every facet of his senses, every cell of his brain had been called into action against her precocious flirtation with everlasting sleep. Now he was totally spent, and filled with such longing to be alone with her on this night of triumph the ache was almost unbearable. His head was spinning with the echo of so many hundreds of voices; his right arm felt like lead after being pumped up and down so vigorously for hours. The uninhibited adulation of the women who had kissed, touched and almost stripped him on the beach, had been continued by the evening guests, whose hands and eyes had ravished him without pause. Escape had been the only solution.

Highly emotional over the laurels he had won this day, three parts drunk on champagne, and sexually aroused to a high degree, only communion with *Aphrodite* would ease his condition. Only she would understand that he needed to relive those moments of dangerous glory in his memory; only in her presence could he allow victorious tears to spill over. Even so, as he tilted back his head to gaze at the stars, they suddenly multiplied as moisture blurred his vision. It had been a long humiliating struggle to reach this moment. If his father was up there somewhere, looking down, perhaps he would be proud of him, at last.

Control was finally lost. This day, with all its conflicting implications, now extracted its price. As he turned into the ruin of the abbey chapel, where bars of moonlight through the pane-less arched windows offered striped seclusion, his shoulders began to heave as sadness and elation merged to remove time, even reality, beyond his present reach. Up there with his erotic goddess there was no doubt in his mind that he was a god. With his feet on the ground, he was someone quite different, someone he could not yet define. After today, who would he be, where would he belong? What road could he possibly follow from here? Had he gained the final summit, or was there another pinnacle beyond this which reached into the unknown? These questions were all unnecessary when he was in the skies above the sea, confronting destiny unhesitatingly. Only when he returned to earth did identity elude him. The relief of tears somehow eased the ache in his limbs, but not the one within, which needed the answers to those questions, on this momentous night.

The sound of stones rattling on the far side of the chapel caused him to turn smartly, appalled at being caught out in his moment of weakness. A girl stood uncertainly, framed in the arched stone like a cameo, matching the atmosphere in that hallowed ruin. Her pale hair was like the moonlight; her black dress the shadows. Her intrusion, therefore, did not seem entirely unwelcome. For a moment or two, they both stood silent, caught up in the rare, questioning encounter, on a night when nothing appeared to be quite real.

'I've never seen a man cry,' she ventured, with hushed awe in her voice. 'Is it because you're sad, or because you're too happy?'

He brushed his wet cheeks with the back of his hand. 'I suppose it's a little of both.'

'It must be a great deal of both, to affect you so much.' As she drew nearer, her face, paled by the silver light, searched the shadows in the hope of a clearer view of him. 'How long have you been out here all alone?'

'Too long, that's quite obvious,' he told her with feeling. 'I've just made a fool of myself in front of you. I thought the days of doing that had long passed,' he added, remembering their initial introduction three years ago.

'I don't think you're foolish; just rather wonderfully human.'

Silence fell between them again. She looked absurdly desirable: a child-woman in a dress whose ultra-sophistication only served to emphasize the untouched quality of her youth. Those large shining eyes, that soft wilful mouth suggested innocence waiting to be broken. A dangerous combination, when a man was as vulnerable as he was now.

'I wanted to be the first to congratulate you, yet end up being the last.'

'I doubt that,' he said, as lightly as he could. 'Until

130

someone snatches the record from me, people will go on doing it.'

'And girls will want to kiss you?'

'Most probably.'

'*I want to kiss you*,' she whispered.

The mesmeric quality of that moon-dappled cloister open to the stars was enough, without this girl's naïve sensuality to add to his sense of confusion tonight.

'This is dangerous,' he told her swiftly. 'Your father has warned us often enough not to come here until restoration is complete. We must go.'

As he stepped forward, she barred his way, making him halt again. Shafts of moonlight now highlighted the shimmer of tears on her cheeks, also, as she put her hands on his arms.

'Don't make me invisible, Kit. Not you, too. I couldn't bear it.'

The yearning in her voice echoed the same desperate loneliness he had often experienced. It touched him deeply; so deeply he offered instinctive comfort. Her innocence had been deceptive, however. She was more woman than child, he realized, as the light kiss he offered was returned with growing response. Highly aroused by confusing emotions himself, what had begun as a fond embrace now turned into an extremely provocative sharing of passion. Only when the screech of a hunting owl overhead brought him to his senses, did he break away with a feeling of shock. This girl he was swiftly subduing was only sixteen. What was more, her name was Kirkland. Both facts put her out of bounds to him, dangerously out of bounds.

5

Kit awoke to find himself shrouded in mist. The chill dampness had penetrated his bones, and his lashes were edged with moisture. It was not tears. The moment of weakness had brought an unexpected hazard into his life last night, and there was no chance of his risking such a thing again. Heavy-headed, and with cramp tying knots in his left calf, he opened the door of his sports car and scrambled painfully to his feet to rub the affected muscles. Then, reaching for the only available liquid, he relieved the dryness of his throat from the hip-flask kept in the leather pocket of the door. The hair of the dog, he thought wryly. His watch showed that it was nine a.m. Another hot sunny day when this mist cleared. A day in which he must face the implications of his success.

Stamping around on the grassy hillside to rid himself of lingering cramp, he shivered. This time yesterday he had been totally dedicated to achieving just one single aim. It had brought professional triumph for himself, and the much-needed boost for the company. Sir Hector would reap all manner of benefits from the worldwide publicity and Donald, as heir presumptive, would now be firmly established as the golden boy of aircraft design. Kit did not delude himself, however. Records existed to be broken. A pilot was only as good as the aircraft he flew and his 417 mph would soon be exceeded by another man in a seaplane with even sleeker lines and a more powerful engine, fuelled by an inspired mixture which would allow undreamed-of speed through the air. Then, yet another man would make even that seem slow. The feat was thrilling, prestigious, and immensely romantic but, like scaling untrodden peaks, had little lasting value.

Aphrodite had been streamlined and super-powered to achieve racing speeds. The standard seaplane she had been at birth was a useful little machine which could be adapted as an air-ambulance for use in terrain where rivers or lakes were the only means of access to isolated communities, or for carrying a limit of two passengers or the equivalent weight in cargo by an island-hopping air service. Rescue groups found them invaluable along stretches of rocky or sheer coast, and the RAF still used seaplanes in areas which precluded the use of wheeled aircraft. Even so, Kit was not so in love with his goddess that he could not see that her day was almost over. The advantages of aircraft which could land on water were very clear, but size, not speed, would determine their future. The *Aphrodite*s of the aviation world were built for glory, glamour and national pride. If Kirkland's was to survive into the future, attention must be turned to flying boats. Large, graceful, dependable ships with wings. Runways were unnecessary. They could land on any handy stretch of water, and there were oceans, rivers and lakes galore all over the world.

He shivered again, so began trotting around his mist-enveloped car in an attempt to warm up. It was an easy exercise. He was extremely fit. He was also only twenty-two, with an uncertain future. The task he had set himself yesterday had been done to the best of his ability. His name would be placed in the record books, his photograph would continue to appear in newspapers and magazines, invitations would now pour in naming him as guest of honour or asking him to speak at distinguished gatherings. Women with little better to do would chase him shamelessly. Some would probably catch him. Yet, what did a professional flier do after he had done his

utmost? Slowing to a halt, he sighed. What did a moun-
taineer do after he had climbed the highest crest; look
for a higher one, or seek a different challenge altogether?

Turning back to his car he climbed in again, knowing
he must wait for the mist to clear before attempting to
drive off. In these conditions he could easily plunge into
the sea. Blowing on his chilled hands he gazed into the
greyness. Fortune, albeit with conditions attached, had
smiled on him three years ago. Sir Hector never did
anything unless it would bring some kind of reward for
himself. If Kit wanted fortune to continue smiling, it
was imperative for him to offer some further, attractive
return on the three-year investment his benefactor had
so publicly revealed last night. The gauntlet had been
thrown at his feet on that platform. He must take it up,
or ignore it at his peril.

After some minutes of casting around in his weary
brain for inspiration, the memory of a young man in
motorcyling clothes came back through the confusion of
last night. They had not met again after Coombes had
taken the uninvited guest off to be suitably clad, but
that had been Kit's fault. After Sir Hector's speech he
had had more than enough of that party, and not
returned.

The stirrings of a rare kind of guilt assailed him once
more. Whether Leone had followed him to the ruin, or
merely come upon him by chance, he could not decide.
Either way it had led to disaster. She was a minor; a
schoolgirl! In the cold light of day he could not conceive
how his comforting embrace had so swiftly flared into
full adult passion, yet it had. He thought it unlikely that
she would relate to anyone, especially her father, what
had occurred. There would be hell to pay if she did. It
did mean, however, then he would either have to be
very cruel or hold her at arm's length until she returned
to Switzerland. The latter would be difficult, because of
her determination, and was sure to hurt her to a degree.
Yet he could not bring himself to plunge a knife right

into her heart. He had taken the coward's way out last night. After forcibly escorting her back indoors, he had hurriedly changed, taken his car from the garages, and driven to this isolated spot to spend what had remained of the night. His only hope was that her astonishingly mature response to his embrace had been induced by drink, but he somehow felt it was a vain hope.

Pushing such thoughts aside, he followed those which were more productive. The motorcylist, Warren – he could not recall his other name – had designed a seaplane he had hoped to show to Donald. From their conversation, it had been plain he had known what he was talking about and some of his theories were worth pursuing. Apart from the fact that he had digs in Sheenmouth, owned by a landlady who apparently had no idea of his talent, all Kit knew about him was that he gave flying lessons at the Aero Club. Taking another drink from his hip-flask, Kit settled back in the car to wait for the mist to lift. While he did so, he elaborated on a vague plan based on the brief meeting last night.

The terrace of houses looked neat and clean enough, but they induced unpleasant memories in Kit as he trod up the steps of number twenty-two. He saw again a tight-mouthed boy dragging his inebriated father away from the vengeance of a man with a cut lip and a bloody nose, watched by the residents of the terrace who had been drawn to their doors by the sounds of aggression. The victim's wife had tossed their suitcases down the steps after them, shouting abuse. Pushing such thoughts aside, he rang the bell on the red-painted door.

The woman who answered it was cast in the same mould as that long-ago landlady: respectable, law-abiding and demanding from her tenants the same consideration she extended to them. Her suspicion of an unkempt, unshaven young man was immediate.

'What can I do for you, may I ask?'

135

'I'd like to see Mr Grant,' he told her quietly. 'Jim Mason at the Aero Club gave me this address.'

Her untinted lips pursed. 'Done nothing wrong, has he?'

Kit smiled. 'On the contrary. Is he in?'

Nodding her crimped head, she said, 'Fast asleep, I shouldn't wonder. Came back in the dead of night, waking the whole neighbourhood with that motorcycle of his. Then he fell over his feet climbing the stairs.' Disapproval was in every word as she added, 'I always thought he was a Temperance man, but he certainly deceived me in that direction.' Making no sign of allowing him entry, she asked who he was.

'Kit Anson.' He tried the softening effect of another smile.

This was one woman who was impervious to his charm. 'Oh, are you? I wasn't born yesterday, young man. That was him who flew the aeroplane across here and broke a record.'

'That's right. Were you watching me, Mrs. . . ?'

'Bardolph.' She peered closely at his face. 'You're not really him, are you?'

'Of course. I must see Mr Grant on a matter of some importance that we discussed at Sheenmouth Abbey last night. Sir Hector Kirkland also wishes to thank him for rescuing his daughter and escorting her safely home.'

Name-dropping succeeded where masculine charm had failed, and she stood aside to let him in. 'Right up the stairs. Top floor,' she called after him. 'If he wants a cup of tea, he'll have to come down and fetch it. Breakfast was over long ago, tell him.'

Warren was in bed, as his landlady had predicted. He sat up in confusion as he recognized his visitor, colour flooding his face and neck.

'Gosh, how did you trace me?' he mumbled with embarrassment.

'Through Jim Mason,' Kit explained, smiling to put

136

the other man at his ease. 'Finding you was easy; gaining admittance was a definite challenge.'

Warren's colour deepened further. 'I made a terrible noise last night, apparently, so I'm not very popular with the terrace.'

'Were you very tight?' Kit asked, with interest. 'You took a bit of a risk on the motorbike, didn't you? If you're like a lot of pilots I know, you probably drive as if you're flying, anyway. I've been told I do.' Seeing the other's continuing awkwardness, he offered to return later. 'You look exactly the way I've often felt, so perhaps this isn't the best time for a get-together.'

'No, it's all right,' said Warren hastily, climbing from the bed with a hand clutching the waist of pyjama trousers that were on back-to-front and in danger of falling down. 'Sorry about this mess. I'm not usually as untidy as this. It must look like a slum to you.'

'I've seen worse,' he said abruptly. 'I haven't always lived at Sheenmouth Abbey, you know.'

Sweeping his goggles and leather jacket from a chair Warren invited Kit to sit down while he slipped along the landing to tidy up. 'It'll only take a minute or two, then I'll be pleased to talk about anything you like.' Halfway across the room, he paused, still clutching his trousers. 'I could ask Mrs Bardolph to bring us some tea.'

Kit adopted a high voice. 'If he wants tea, he must come down and get it. Breakfast was over long ago.'

It induced a rueful grin. 'You sounded just like her. Won't be a tick.'

Kit glanced around the room while its occupant was in the bathroom. Warren Grant possessed some good things. Expensive binoculars in a leather case, a pair of silver-backed hairbrushes, a set of encyclopaedias with spines tooled in gold. There was a pile of aviation manuals that cried out for a shelf, a well-worn musical instrument case with the initials B.D. and an antique silver frame containing a photograph of a smiling man in RFC uniform. If Warren was hard up now, he had not always been, Kit deduced. Who was he? What was his background? Why was he giving lessons at the Aero Club when his real interest was in design?

There was a vast improvement in Warren's appearance when he returned. The striped trousers had been reversed and were now securely tied by the cord, his crisp hair had been damped into a semblance of order, and he smelled of carbolic and toothpaste. Kit felt filthy, in comparison, and said so.

'I don't usually make morning calls on people, in this state,' he confessed. 'I slept in my car up on Bickham Hill.'

'Ended up tight, too, did you? You had more reason to be than anyone else,' Warren declared, more at his ease now. 'Tell you what, I'll nip downstairs for two cups of tea while you clean up a bit.' Taking a fresh towel from a drawer, he tossed it over. 'Second door on your right as you go out. Take as long as you like.'

Feeling a new man, Kit returned to the attic room to find his host, in flannels and a blue shirt, sitting with a tray containing tea and a plate of rock cakes.

'Good lord, I must be losing my touch,' he told Warren. 'Your landlady would have none of me, even when I assured her that I was "him who flew the aeroplane yesterday", yet a fallen Temperance man like you is plied with tea and buns.'

Warren laughed. 'Have faith. Delayed hero-worship overcame her. These buns – her speciality – are specifically for you.'

'Liar!' said Kit comfortably, sitting in the other chair. 'I'm sorry we didn't meet up again last night. It was my fault. Things got on top of me, so I made my getaway.'

'A party of that size must have been a bit much to take after the stress of the flight,' Warren agreed, biting into a rock cake. 'Surely the Kirklands realized that.'

'I haven't had a chance to find out yet. They'll soon let me know their feelings on the subject, believe me.'

Kit stirred his tea with the spoon from the sugar bowl. 'What happened to you? Coombes did fix you up, didn't he?'

'Mmm, rather,' Warren told him, with his mouth full. 'I looked so dapper, Leone spoke to me for five or ten minutes without recognizing me.' He drank some tea, then said, 'As a matter of fact, I intended to send a note of apology to you, and to her. You see, once I got up there with Phil Davenport, I was sunk. They kept demanding more and more. When I eventually climbed down I was hauled off and monopolized by a group of total strangers, who pressed drinks on me while they told me their life stories. Later on, I looked for you both, but neither you nor Leone was anywhere to be found. I had to give up the search and come away when the party began to break up.'

Steering away from the subject of where he and Leone had been, and puzzled by what he had been told, Kit coaxed from his host the surprising story of his impromptu concert on the trumpet. This led to the disclosure of his youth spent in London, and the explanation of a trumpet case bearing someone else's initials. Soon, he had learned a great deal about Warren, which strengthened his belief in the plan he had hatched on that misty hillside.

'I came this morning in the hope of seeing your drawings,' he said eventually. 'If they're as good as I suspect they are, you should be doing something other than teaching people to fly for fun. Have you them handy?'

Warren crossed to a table covered with a brown chenille cloth, lifted it, and opened a cutlery drawer. Bringing a roll of papers back to Kit, he looked at him apologetically.

'My draughtsmanship isn't one hundred per cent when done on a flat table in poor light, I'm afraid.'

'To hell with draughtsmanship, so long as the detail and specifications are there. Workmen find fault with

139

drawings, even when they're perfect. It's one of their professional foibles. Right, let's spread them out and take a look.'

Half an hour later, Kit knew he was on to a winner. He set about putting the next part of his plan into operation. With barely concealed excitement, Warren listened as he outlined the scheme from start to finish.

'Of course,' Kit concluded, 'you realize that I haven't yet approached the Kirklands, so nothing is definite. You'd like the job if they offer it, wouldn't you?'

'You know damn well I would,' came the fervent reply. 'I'd give my eye teeth for it.'

'You'll be expected to give a lot more than that if you work for Kirkland Marine Aviation,' he warned. 'Sir Hector will expect you to devote your whole life to his company.'

Warren grinned. 'Suits me.'

Kit then sat back and spoke of something else he had been considering. 'It seems to me that these digs will be a bit inconvenient. To get to the workshops from here you'd have to go down into Sheenmouth, then out again on the Toddington road until you get to Riggers Hill, then up across Giddesworth Downs on that narrow track before linking up with Riverside Road. It's a hell of a journey each day. In winter it'd be damn near impossible, if Giddesworth Downs were covered in snow.'

'I suppose I'll have to try to find somewhere nearer,' Warren agreed thoughtfully. 'This side of the river's a bit tricky. I suppose East Sheenmouth would be a better bet. I could come down Duckworth Hill on the motorbike, then take the ferry over.'

Kit looked at him frankly. 'There's a better solution, if you'd be interested. I haven't always enjoyed luxury, you know. Before I moved into Sheenmouth Abbey, I lived in a boathouse about half a mile up-river on the Kirkland boundary. When my father was killed in a works accident, Sir Hector said I could keep the place so long as I undertook the maintenance and repairs. It was of no use to him, and would have fallen into decay unless looked after by someone. I've only been over to it now and then – too many memories – but it might be the very place for you, Warren. There are two large rooms above a spacious store, which my father and I used to tinker about in. The lavatory is a bit primitive, and the bathroom is no more than an outside wash-house, but we occupied it for more than two years without suffering too much discomfort. You're welcome to use it. We paid no rent to Sir Hector so, now it belongs to me, the same terms apply. I believe a drawing board and several other useful things are still there. You can utilize them, if you wish. The greatest advantage of the place will be that you can come down to Kirkland's on the boat with me each morning. Well, what do you think?'

Warren seemed uncertain of his reply. Then he said, with some diffidence, 'Leone told me about your father and the accident. I'm sorry. It must have been terrible for you but, if you don't mind someone else living in your place of sad memories, it would be the perfect answer. If I get the job, that is.'

'The offer isn't dependent on your getting a job with Kirkland's,' Kit told him, wondering what on earth Leone knew about his father to tell this chance acquaintance of hers. 'You could save on rent, and have much more room to work on designs. There'd be no clumsy landlady to step on your models, either.'

'Gosh, it's really jolly nice of you,' said Warren, flushing with pleasure. 'I can't think of adequate words to tell you how grateful I am.'

'That's just as well. I've taken a leaf from Sir Hector's book, and decided never to do anything unless there's some advantage in it for me. You, Warren my lad, are going to help me to achieve my next ambition,' Kit told him, getting to his feet. 'I'll go back now and take the first step towards it. I'll be in touch as soon as there's any news.' Turning at the door, he smiled. 'It looks as though we have the makings of a fine team. Thanks for the tea and buns.'

Warren came across to him swiftly, his colour deepening once more. 'Would you give my . . . my best wishes to Leone, and tell her I'll write to explain what happened last night.'

Feeling sorry for him, Kit asked, 'You really like her, don't you?'

'Rather! Don't you?'

Avoiding an answer to that, he said quietly, 'Perhaps you aren't aware that she's only sixteen, and still a pupil at a very expensive Swiss school. She'll be going back there in September for the new term.' Seeing the dismay on Warren's face, he felt his own duplicity as he added, 'If you're going to forge close ties with the Kirklands, you'd better cool off where she's concerned. I'd hate you to land yourself in a fix over her.'

The dismantling and cleaning-up processes were taking place almost everywhere on the ground floor when Kit returned to Sheenmouth Abbey. Knowing that a few guests had stayed overnight with their host, and would almost certainly have a light luncheon before they set out for home, he went to his bell tower quarters to shave, take a bath and eat a substantial meal to compensate for missing both breakfast and lunch. After sleeping for over an hour, he dressed in fawn slacks and a cream-and-brown checked shirt to go in search of Sir Hector. He was where Kit had expected him to be, no matter that he had not retired until just before dawn, and had been entertaining guests until only an hour ago. With him in his office suite were Donald and Maitland, and there was a definite morning-after-the-night-before aura about all three when Kit walked breezily in.

Sir Hector looked up to scowl at him. 'Where the hell have you been?'

'Recovering from last night.'

'You weren't here last night, damn you! Who gave

142

you leave to slip off halfway through the evening? People were asking for you, wanted a few words. Wives expected to dance with you. It was your duty to do so. Made me look a bloody fool.'

'I'm sorry, sir,' said Kit. 'I was doing my duty until well past two.'

'I was doing mine until five this morning . . . like everyone else save you.'

'You and everyone else didn't fly *Aphrodite* yesterday,' he pointed out calmly. 'And if *I* hadn't done so, there'd have been no reason for the party. While you and your guests were eating and drinking beneath a marquee on the prom, I was flying around in circles within a red-hot cockpit to make Kirkland's world famous. I was still going around in circles while you and your guests were indulging in more eating and drinking last night. I left, rather than embarrass you by passing out in the centre of a Grecian grotto. We would both have looked bloody fools then.'

Sir Hector grunted. 'Very smooth, very smooth. You're beginning to sound like a Kirkland. You're not, and don't you forget it.'

'No, sir, you already have one application for membership under way.' He turned to Donald. 'Where is Stephanie? Sleeping off the excitement of becoming engaged to you?'

Donald's scowl was a replica of his father's. 'She apparently has more stamina than you. We've already played two sets of tennis this morning.'

'In the mist? How did you decide which of you won?'

'The mist lifted just after eleven,' came the sharp reply. 'If you had left your bed a little earlier, you'd have noticed.'

'You didn't overdo the exercise, did you, Donald?' he countered. 'You're looking very pale.'

'So would you, if you had managed to stick it out to the end last night.'

'The end *this morning*,' Kit reminded him, then

143

relented to say, 'I suppose it's a bit much to handle when you become recognized as one of the world's hopes for the future, and also win the hand of a very beautiful girl on the same evening. In all the excitement of yesterday's quick-fire events, I don't think I actually offered my congratulations to either of you. Please accept them now.'

'Thanks,' was the brief reply, before Donald got to his feet ready to leave. 'I think I'll find Steph and go for a swim.'

'I was hoping to discuss something with you,' put in Kit swiftly. 'Can you spare half an hour or so?'

'Can't it wait?'

He countered that with the reason which brooked no argument in this household. 'It's business.'

'Sit down, Donald,' his father told him. 'Yesterday's success can't be left to stagnate. That's where a number of men go wrong. They puff up and tell themselves what fine fellows they are, then wake up one day wondering why they're in a backwater. Yesterday we made the world sit up and take notice of us. We have to keep it sitting up!' Waving imperiously at the chair his son had just vacated, he added, 'That girl of yours will have to learn to wait, so she can start now.' Turning to Kit, he showed some signs of testiness. 'I hope this means you've been doing something useful all morning, when you should have been here.'

Taking his time to sit in a vacant chair, Kit nodded. 'I've been following up a contact I made last night.' Unable to resist the temptation, he glanced across at the immaculate personal assistant. 'You'll probably remember the fellow, Maitland. He rescued Leone when the Bentley broke down, and she invited him in to meet Donald. You brought him across to me with the message that he was making himself a nuisance, so would I give him my autograph then chuck him out. Good thing I didn't, because he told me about a new seaplane he'd designed. Seemed very disappointed that he'd been unable to interest you in it, Donald.'

Into the heavy silence which followed, Sir Hector said, 'What is that sly piece of screw-twisting leading to, boy?'

Reminded that his benefactor was no fool, Kit then got straight to the point. 'I roused him out early this morning, and he showed me the drawings of his seaplane. We discussed it in full detail and, in my opinion, I've come across the very man we want. He has flair and originality, based on a good sound knowledge when it comes to design, with the added advantage of being a qualified pilot. Taken together, they add up to the opportunity of a lifetime for Kirkland's.'

Sir Hector poured water from a flagon on his desk, and drank slowly as he shook his head. 'Wrong! Kirkland's has no use for another seaplane, and we already have a top designer in Donald.'

'A top designer of seaplanes, yes,' Kit agreed, with emphasis, 'but Donald admits to being confronted with insoluble problems over the flying boat project we now badly need to get under way. As you just now said, sir, we have to follow yesterday's success with something truly exciting. I agree wholeheartedly that another seaplane would be a waste of time. Benzini is certain to take the record from us within a year from now, if not sooner, and the Americans are using their vast resources for aircraft development which will quickly outstrip our limited efforts in this country. Look, sir,' he continued, growing enthusiastic, 'you've wanted to expand to the development of flying boats for some time. The future for such machines is very rosy. Warren and I discussed this very thoroughly, and he's full of ideas, having realized himself that the possibilities for passenger transportation are endless. I happen to have touched on the great dream he's had for several years. Put him in our design office with Donald, and we'd have the opportunity to lead the world with our "passenger liners with wings". His expression!'

Sir Hector drank more water whilst staring straight ahead, as if seeing the actuality of what Kit had described. It was an excellent indication of his deep interest. Donald, now looking paler than ever, Kit thought, watched his father with an expression bordering on apprehension.

'Passenger liners with wings,' mused the older man. 'A nice turn of phrase, that. *Passenger liners with wings!*' Focusing on Kit, he said, 'Get him up here, boy. I'll talk to him.'

'It wouldn't work, Father,' cried Donald immediately. 'We can't have two designers at Kirkland's.'

Sir Hector's sharp eyes swivelled to study him. 'Why not?'

'I don't want anyone else.'

'Nonsense! Two minds are better than one.'

'Two minds think in different ways,' came the stubborn reply. 'I couldn't possibly work with him. The entire scheme is out of the question, especially as this man is a pilot, as well.' Casting a sour look Kit's way, he added, 'I had enough trouble with the pilot of *Aphrodite*. They're never damn well satisfied with any machine.'

'This man wouldn't be flying it; he'd be designing it.'

'No, Father, I have to do it on my own.'

'Then do it! Don't keep coming to me with the excuse that there are too many problems each time I ask about progress. If you want to do it alone, solve the bloody problems.'

When Sir Hector began to pin down people in this ruthless manner, those who knew him recognized defeat and quickly surrendered. Donald was surprisingly deaf and blind today, Kit thought, watching the contest avidly.

'They're insuperable,' Donald insisted mulishly. 'Engineering and construction limitations are the same for any designer, no matter who he is or how many assistants he has.'

'Limitations are there to be overcome! Good God,

146

boy, the wheel would never have been made if man had accepted *limitations*.' He leaned heavily on the desk to make his next point to his son. 'I want a passenger liner with wings. It's the best idea I've ever been offered. You'll make me one, everyone realizes that, but you'll make it a hell of a sight quicker with this man on your staff . . . *if he's as good as I've been told*.'

Looking desperate, Donald jumped to his feet again. 'No, sir. I can't work with anyone else. You're asking too much.'

As if oblivious of Kit and Maitland, the pair confronted each other in a battle of wills. The hardened businessman and holder of the purse-strings was certain to win, but Kit had never known Donald to show such lengthy and violent opposition to the man who could make or break him.

'Asking too much, am I? Is it too much to ask you to put into the company no more than a fraction of what you'll get out of it?' demanded Sir Hector, face and neck purplish in colour as he moved in for the kill. 'Kirkland's constitutes your future, and a glittering one it is. Yesterday covered you with glory, and never forget who it was who ensured that it did. That girl you're going to marry will provide you with the perfect social back-up for your career. This abbey will pass to you when I go, and a great deal more beside. I had to build this up from a disused fish-factory,' he reminded his son, in a voice rising with anger. 'You will get it handed to you on a plate, boy. We are on the brink of world greatness, and all I'm asking you to do is to recognize that I know what I'm doing when I rule that this man will work with you. *This man will work with you*. Do I make myself clear?' he ended on a roar.

Donald's collapse was nothing if not spectacular. 'Yes,' he snapped, and immediately left the room.

With his gaze on the door through which his son had just vanished, the victor said, 'Maitland, send a message to this man telling him to see me as soon as he can get himself here. Where does he live, boy?'

Kit gave the address, then found himself being fixed with the cold eye as the personal assistant left on the heels of the son of the house.

'You'd better be right about this.'

'I am. Absolutely right.'

'Cocky bastard,' came the gruff comment. 'You haven't yet explained what part you expect to play in this scheme.'

Kit sat back in his chair, prepared to enjoy himself. 'My part will be to undertake a world promotion tour for Kirkland's, by accepting all the invitations I'm going to be sent to fly *Aphrodite* in displays and competitions. While I'm doing that, I shall canvas orders for the flying boat from international passenger lines. By the time I return, the plans for a prototype should be ready. I shall help to build her, then demonstrate her qualities on a proving flight from here to Africa.'

'You're raving mad,' cried Sir Hector, excitement flaring in his eyes at a thrilling prospect beyond present possibility. 'It could never be done.'

'They said that about travelling through the air at 417 m.p.h. but I did it only yesterday. When that prototype is built, I'll fly it from here to Africa.'

'Damn you, I do believe you have the guts to try!'

'I'll try, and I'll succeed,' Kit told him, with matching excitement. 'How would that seem as a dividend on your initial investment?'

'By God, you're more of a Kirkland than . . .' The other man broke off and turned away abruptly. 'Don't grow too damned big for your breeches, boy. Never forget who you are.'

Excitement vanished beneath the swift violent anger which swept through him at those words designed to keep him at arm's length, where he had always been.

'I never wish to forget,' he cried. 'I made the name of Anson respectable again yesterday. It'll be more, much more, than respectable by the time I've finished with it, believe me.'

Leone dressed for dinner with great care. The sophisticated dress of last evening could not be worn again, of course. Not that it would be suitable for a quiet family meal served in the ornate Roman pavilion beside the swimming pool, as a private celebration of her brother's engagement. Stephanie would be at Sheenmouth Abbey for the next six weeks while the complicated arrangements for the wedding were argued and decided upon, but it was highly unlikely that everyone would be present around a dining table simultaneously again during that visit. Leone guessed tonight was only possible because an inevitable hiatus had been caused by the tremendous events of yesterday.

For herself, a circle of the deepest red would be for ever around the date 10 June 1932. It had been the most momentous day of her life. The memory of those moments in the chapel chilled and thrilled her. She had walked away from a young man creating unexpected musical magic, to wander heavy-hearted beneath the stars, as lonely as ever in this place she never really thought of as home. Movement over by the ruin still in the process of restoration, had sent her across to warn the trespasser of his danger. What she had seen, however, had rendered her silent.

A tall, strong, courageous man slipping away from public adulation to weep beneath the moon! Surely no other woman had been privileged to witness his deep innermost feelings, to glimpse the person beneath the jaunty, debonair hero. In that poignant moment, Leone had seen again a white-faced stunned youth standing in the bell tower with no more than two shabby suitcases and an old photograph of his father's seaplane to mark his past. Maturity had suddenly made her see how thoughtless, perhaps even selfish, she had been three years ago when curiosity had outweighed any sense of real compassion for someone she believed would become an unofficial brother. Last night she had gone to him with that belated sympathy, her tears matching his. What had happened between them had been explosive. That kiss had dissolved all pain and anger.

She had slept late this morning, and awoken full of wonder. The fumbling experimental embraces she had exchanged with Raoul in Monte Carlo, and with Lorrieta Montero's handsome hot-headed cousin in Barcelona, had stemmed more from eager curiosity than from strong emotion, but the passion she had experienced in Kit's arms last night established a deep bond between them which could never be broken. He had needed her; needed comfort from the one person who knew the boy he had once been. The bevy of adoring women who clustered around him wanted only the dashing flier with dark good looks, money in the bank, and a faintly ruthless attitude towards them. Leone had caught him with his defences down last night. They could never be rebuilt between them now.

She had not seen him since he had marched her back to the safety of crowds, plainly disturbed by the way he had betrayed himself to her. When she had slipped along to his room this afternoon, his door had been locked. She guessed that he might now feel disgusted and embarrassed, because he had let his pose of sophistication slip to expose his naked desire for love and understanding. Who better than she knew the pain of that desire? It was essential that she should convince him that the secret they now shared would remain theirs alone. It was of utmost importance to give him the sense of assurance that he could turn to her, offer confidences, seek consolation of any kind from her without fear of betrayal. When he had taken off yesterday morning and headed into the sky alone, she had known she loved him. Last night in the ruined chapel, that love had become passionate enough to fulfil her longing for identity.

Choosing a romantic dress of sea-green georgette,

which had sheer half-sleeves and a trailing scarf, Leone then made her way downstairs wondering how Kit would treat her tonight in the presence of others. Only Donald and Stephanie were there when she reached the floodlit swimming pool. The engaged couple were chatting quietly together as they lounged in the gilded Roman chairs, enjoying a pre-dinner drink. Tonight, she saw Stephanie through different eyes. Kit might have rhapsodized about her beauty, but would never allow this girl to reach beneath his guard. She was, therefore, no threat to Leone.

'Hallo,' she greeted, in deliberately friendly manner. 'Making plans for October?'

Donald's expression suggested that he was unhappy about whatever subject was under discussion. A lovers' tiff already?

'I hope you're feeling in a better mood tonight,' he said sourly.

'I hope you are, too,' she retaliated.

Stephanie smiled. 'I'd very much like you to be one of the bridesmaids, but will you be able to come over from school to attend?'

Telling Dayley that she would have a pink gin, Leone then sat beside her future sister-in-law.

'I naturally took it for granted that I'd be asked, so I've planned everything. Heiterman's is frightfully prestigious and all that, but there are colleges in England which are every bit as good.' Taking the glass from Dayley, she said, 'I'll transfer to one near here. There you are, problem solved! May I choose my own dress?'

'We'll choose it together with my cousin, who's about the same age as you. I don't want to force either of you to wear something you hate. The four younger girls will be in champagne-coloured organdie, but I wouldn't inflict such "dolly dresses" on you and Jane. She's blonde, like you, and I must say that's a very pretty colour you have on. It suits you beautifully.'

'Thanks.'

151

Stephanie could afford to be generous with compliments, thought Leone dryly. She looked sensational in clinging amber slipper satin and heavy gold jewellery. With her long tawny hair, vivid make-up, and elaborate gold kid sandals studded with mock topaz, only Cleopatra herself could have looked more exotic against this poolside setting.

Sipping her drink, Leone asked her brother if the chapel would be fully restored in time for the wedding. 'It still hasn't a roof,' she pointed out.

Donald gazed gloomily at her. 'You should know better than to ask a question like that. Father has made up his mind that we shall be married in it, so it *will* be ready.'

'It seems a pity,' she reflected dreamily. 'A ruin is far more romantic.'

'Not if a lump of masonry falls on the bride,' he retorted. 'Have you spoken to him about not returning to Heiterman's?'

'How could I? He's been obsessed with *Aphrodite* and the speed record, like everyone else here. Still, it was frightfully thrilling. What a pity you arrived too late to see it, Stephanie.'

'I did see it, my dear girl,' Stephanie told her, in surprise at her ignorance of the fact. 'Kit invited me to the hangar to watch preparations, and I was in the boat with him and Donald when *Aphrodite* was towed out for take-off. I kissed him for luck the moment before he climbed into the cockpit. You're right, it *was* frightfully exciting.'

Leone drank the rest of her pink gin rather quickly and asked Dayley for another, trying to smother her jealousy by thinking of the kiss Kit had received from *her* last night.

'Ought you to be drinking at that rate?' asked her brother. 'The evening has hardly begun, and you'll end up half-cut, as you were yesterday.'

Ignoring him, she concentrated on Stephanie. 'Do you plan to be married in white, or otherwise?'

The bride-to-be put up a graceful hand tipped with long scarlet nails to push back her hair as she replied. 'I've spoken to Paulo Zardini, and he's very enthusiastic. You see, as the setting for the marriage is so steeped in legend and antiquity, I felt my gown should complement it. Together, Paulo and I have decided on gold antique lace with a matching veil worn over a wimple.'

'Heavens!' Leone exclaimed. 'A nun being married in a monastery! It sounds marvellous, but isn't it very slightly shocking?'

'What's very slightly shocking?' demanded Kit's voice from behind them, amusement uppermost in his tone. 'Is it suitable for my ears?'

'Your ears, darling, are hardened enough to cope with anything Leone might say,' Stephanie told him.

The Edwardian face became more alive than before as she looked up at him, and Leone had to acknowledge that she was all Kit had claimed. In short, quite stunning. As Kit joined the group, she had to extend that description to him. In well-cut white dinner jacket, which enhanced his dark looks, he would disturb the peace of any woman, she decided. He most certainly disturbed her own as he smiled her way.

'I understand your gallant rescuer yesterday turned out to be a genius with the horn. The lad asked me to apologize and explain to you that he was literally borne off by over-enthusiastic guests, who plied him with drinks until he was most decidedly confused.' Sitting beside her, he took from Dayley his usual glass of pale sherry before adding, 'Warren's landlady has decided, rather to her disgust, that he's not a Temperance man, after all.'

Leone was so surprised by his words, she forgot her resentment of the other girl's endearment to him. 'How do you know all this? Have you seen Warren today?'

He nodded. 'We had a long fruitful meeting this morn-

153

ing over tea and rock buns. He's a very talented young man. With any luck, he'll soon be working for Kirkland's.'

'There's no luck attached to it,' said Sir Hector, arriving at that moment. 'I took him on this afternoon. He starts tomorrow.'

'Tomorrow!' exclaimed Donald sharply.

'There's no point in delay. He's a good sound man with ideas and ambition. I liked him. Knows what he's talking about.' Turning to Kit, he nodded. 'You were right. Good thing you met up with him.'

'I met up with him first, Father,' Leone said, primed by two pink gins in quick succession, and by the tingling proximity of the man who had kissed her so possessively last night. 'He came along on a motorbike, so I stopped him and made him bring me home. He'd been so sweet. I brought him in and asked Donald to look after him while I changed. Why did you send him over to Kit with instructions to throw him out?' she demanded of her brother, in retaliation for his comments about the two gins.

'He was dressed in boots, breeches and a leather jacket,' Donald claimed in self-defence. 'Everyone was staring at him.'

'Kit arranged for him to change. Why didn't you?'

'Why didn't you? You were the one who invited him in.'

Sir Hector studied Leone keenly. 'Are you in the habit of stopping young men on motorbikes, and hopping on the pillion?'

'I've only had the chance to do it once, so far,' she told him, 'but I expect I could easily form the habit. Stopping them is the difficult part. Once they're safely stuck in a hedge, climbing up behind them is very easy. They can't refuse to take you where you want to go, when your arms are around their waist. Warren surrendered in a very short time.'

'Artful young miss,' commented her father thoughtfully. 'Don't do it again. Motorcycles are for men, not girls.'

'Father, that attitude surely went out long ago. Women do anything now. I don't see why a girl shouldn't one day fly a seaplane and break Kit's speed record.' She turned to the man beside her. 'Would you be upset?'

'Thinking of trying?' he teased.

'I might,' she declared, teasing him back.

'If you flew a seaplane with the same deplorable lack of skill you used in the speedboat, your neck would be the only thing you'd break,' said Donald.

'Sweetie,' protested Stephanie gently, 'that's a little unkind. From what Kit told me of the affair, it was an unavoidable accident.'

'Whatever it was, it's over and gone,' Sir Hector decreed. 'It's my policy to put the past behind me and get on with something more productive. Donald, young Grant will be at the office by nine tomorrow. Be prepared to outline the main problems, so that he can start giving them some thought. I want you there, boy,' he added, waving his glass in Kit's direction, 'so don't take off like you did last night. The women will have to wait. Daresay you'll survive without them for a few days more.'

'Will the women survive without Kit?' queried Stephanie softly.

'By the way, sir,' said the subject of this speculation on his sexual affairs, 'I've offered Warren the tenancy of the old boathouse. His present digs are extremely inconvenient for the journey to the workshops, and he'll need the extra facilities for a drawing board, and so on. I know you told me the place was mine, but I thought you'd like to be made aware of his presence there. I can take him down in the boat with me each morning, and he'll be on hand should he be needed after working hours.'

'Excellent,' said Sir Hector, almost glowing with satisfaction. 'By God, we'll get this flying boat under way at last. I want an all-out effort from everyone.'

'Father, we have given an all-out effort on *Aphrodite* for the past eighteen months,' Donald said, with some force. 'Surely we deserve a short break. The record was broken only yesterday.'

'And I was delighted. That was yesterday, however, and now I'm looking to tomorrow.'

'But, sir, Steph and I have to work on the arrangements for the wedding. She's on an extended visit so that we can.'

Sir Hector smiled. 'Stephanie is an extremely capable and intelligent woman, who understands the need for priorities. That's why I'm confident that she'll make the perfect wife for a man like you. My dear Donald, you may safely leave the nuptial arrangements in the hands of your beautiful fiancée, while you attend to something which will affect your future together most significantly. Weddings are affairs best handled by women, anyway. Dresses and posies and iced cakes – hardly masculine concerns, are they? Ah, here's Maitland!' Turning to Dayley, he nodded. 'We'll have dinner now.'

As the neat and spotless personal assistant arrived beside him, Leone's father asked, 'Did you get through to them?'

'Yes, Sir Hector. As you predicted, there'll be everything possible laid on. They'll confirm dates just as soon as they've planned a programme.'

'Good, good,' was his gratified response as he moved towards the three steps leading up to the pavilion, where the marble table was set for six with the Venetian dinner service in red and gold, and matching ruby goblets enhanced by gold filigree embossing.

In her youth Leone had always felt it was perfect for a Roman orgy, and had longed to be allowed to join her father and his guests for an evening there. Now, she found the Roman pavilion, the tasteful table settings, the charm of massed candles, and the summer sunset reflection in the pool before them so romantic, she longed to be alone there with Kit in a continuation of their unity last night. She was particularly irked by the presence of Maitland Jarvis at what was, after all, supposed to be a private family celebration. Although Kit was not a Kirkland, his status at Sheenmouth Abbey was higher than that of a mere employee. He had every right to join them. Maitland gave the evening a business flavour which somehow jarred in such an evocative atmosphere. What jarred even more was the suspicion that Maitland fully expected to be included in the private celebration, even though he never overstepped the mark by behaving as anything other than an employee. Her father spoke quite freely in his presence then, next minute, barked orders at him. Maitland never showed resentment or gratification over the way he was treated. He held a unique place in this masculine household, mused Leone with slight irritation.

Throughout the four courses which ended, as a concession to Stephanie's presence, with a wonderful mousse of fresh apricots and grand marnier, Leone tried to forget Maitland. For once, conversation ranged over many subjects which had no connection with flying, and she was able to contribute a great deal because of her wide circle of European friends and the many social connections she had made whilst holidaying with them. After a while, she realized her words were being heeded, and serious replies were being given. That knowledge, plus the presence of Kit at the candlelit table, suddenly ignited a spark of unusual joy within her. She sensed acceptance, at last. A rare warmth spread between them all as laughter, rarely heard even at the dinner table in that old monastery, rang out in the still June air as night finally extinguished the sunset.

After coffee and liqueurs beside the pool, Sir Hector had relaxed so much he declared his intention of indulging in a rare early night. Getting to his feet, he gripped

Donald's shoulder to keep him in the chair beside Stephanie.

'No need to get up. Stay there with that lovely young woman of yours, and take it easy. Enjoy the rest of the evening. You've earned it, my boy, and tomorrow you'll embark on a project which will consolidate the reputation you established for yourself yesterday. Trust my judgement, Donald. It hasn't let you down yet, has it?'

A cloud passed over Donald's attractive features as he murmured, 'No, sir.'

'Goodnight, my dear,' Sir Hector said to Stephanie, in a tone bordering on satisfaction. 'I couldn't be better pleased with my son's choice of bride, and I can promise you a very exciting and distinguished future as a Kirkland. These are pioneering times, and this family will play a starring rôle in them.'

The girl gave him one of her dazzling smiles. 'After yesterday, who could doubt that?'

'Mmm, pity your people are in Kenya and missed it all.'

'They'll be back long before the wedding. Mother will be desperate about clothes. She'll want to contact all the female guests and somehow worm out of them details of what they intend to wear, rather than suffer the nightmare worry of being outshone as mother of the bride.'

Sir Hector smiled at Donald. 'I told you weddings were affairs more suited to women. Leave well alone and concentrate on your first priority.' Turning to Kit, he said, 'The same applies to you, boy, and it is *not* wenching. That's for leisure time, as I've had to remind you on many occasions.'

It said something for the happy mood of the evening, that Kit stood up with a grin on his face. 'It's part of a flier's job to keep the ladies happy.'

'Cheeky young devil!' was the surprisingly good-natured response. 'When you embark on this proposed world tour Maitland is successfully organizing, I suppose you'll spend half your time in dalliance. Well, I'm not financing that, I assure you. If your pockets are in their usual state, it should put severe limits on entertaining the fair sex.' Jabbing a finger in his direction, he concluded, 'Be there at nine tomorrow – sharp!'

'I wouldn't miss it, sir, after playing the vital rôle in getting Grant for the company.'

'Wrong, boy,' he declared. 'My daughter had the sense to nab him whilst he was stuck in a hedge, then bring him here. Isn't that correct?' he asked Leone, with a light-hearted warmth she found so very pleasant.

'Yes, Father,' she replied, smiling up at him. 'Kidnapping useful young men is another thing women do, besides arranging weddings. We're rather good at it.'

'Possibly . . . but I sincerely trust this will be the only time you do it, Miss. Too young for such things. Still at school, aren't you?'

'I have to talk to you about that,' she said.

'Not been thrown out, I hope.'

Smiling as she rose from the gilded lounger, she knew she must take this opportunity of a hearing while he was in such a mellow receptive mood. After nine a.m. tomorrow he would be unapproachable again.

'No, of course not. Stephanie has asked me to be a bridesmaid, but I shall be back in Switzerland before October.'

'I'll arrange a ten-day leave of absence for you. No problem whatever.'

'Father,' she said urgently, as he began to turn away, 'I don't want to go back to Heiterman's.'

He frowned. 'Someone upset you? Rules too strict? It's all experience of life. We all need little setbacks to strengthen our characters. They give a person determination, the will to succeed against all odds. Running away is never the answer.'

'It's nothing as complicated as that,' she protested, following him as he moved away. 'I've had enough of Europe. I've seen all I should, and met almost everyone in the social set over there, but I realize I've seen very little of my own country and hardly anyone here last night knew my identity. I had to practically swear on oath to Phil Davenport that I was a Kirkland.'

Sir Hector drew to a halt at the end of the pool. 'Never heard the name. Don't know him myself.'

She laughed lightly. 'He's not one of your aviation people. Phil Davenport is the leader of one of the most exciting dance-bands of the day. I have that on the authority of Kirkland's new designer. Warren's an expert on musicians.'

Her father's frown deepened. 'I've arranged for him to work for me, not to give my daughter silly ideas about wanting to leave one of the best schools in Switzerland. How old are you?'

'Sixteen.'

He sighed heavily. 'By George, you look like your mother did when we first met. She was nineteen.' Reaching for one of her hands, he patted it in an unprecedented gesture. 'Don't try to grow up too soon. The world and its temptations will wait for you, never fear. There are better fish in the sea for you than young Grant, so go back to school and forget him. You're far too young for ideas along those lines, as I shall swiftly tell him if he forgets his place.'

'You're wrong,' she told him with a touch of impatience, unable to reveal that it was Kit not Warren she wanted to be near. 'There are other schools as good as Heiterman's.'

Letting go her hand, it was plain he was losing interest in her. 'If you claimed there were some better than the one I selected for you, your case might have more strength. I see no sense in changing a perfect arrangement at this stage. Maitland will request your leave of absence for this frilly-frock affair.' Turning to his assistant who had been standing nearby throughout this conversation, her father said thoughtfully, 'Perhaps we should run through that report of Teale's before I turn in. There won't be a lot of time in the morning and it can't wait.'

The two men walked away deep in conversation, leaving Leone wondering if she had dreamed the last two hours of rapport with her father, who must surely have driven his wife to the life of pleasure and rumoured infidelities which had led to her death. If Marina Kirkland had continually been relegated to the background in the name of BUSINESS, small wonder she had sought affection elsewhere. Turning back disconsolately to the others, she found her brother and Stephanie dancing to the soft strains of music from the hidden loudspeakers around the pool. It struck her that they were a golden pair – the girl in shimmery amber and topaz, Donald with blond hair gleaming against his lightly tanned skin. Her father was right in this instance. They were well matched in every way. As she watched their bodies move gracefully as one, her own began to ache from the desire to be held close by Kit once more. She moved across to where he sat watching the dancers appreciatively, and cut off the vision by standing before him.

'Do you think Father would consider that dancing with me came under the heading "wenching"?' she asked pertly. 'As you've been forbidden to indulge in it, I very much hope not.'

He gave her a long level look, then rose and held out his arms. 'I think I'm safe enough. No one would classify Leone Kirkland as a wench.'

'Not even you?' she murmured, closing with him eagerly.

'Especially me!' Before moving off he asked, 'Are you a good dancer, Miss Kirkland?'

'Absolutely divine. How about you?'

'Oh, a.d. too, naturally.'

Loving every moment of his nearness, she tilted her face up to ask, 'What did Father mean about your world tour?'

'That was rather an expansive description,' he said

lightly. 'I shan't cover the whole world. I've already received a number of invitations from Europe, Scandinavia, America, and even Australia to take *Aphrodite* for exhibition flights at all manner of fancy occasions. More are certain to come in after yesterday. I suggested to him this morning that acceptance of them all would not only promote the company, but would allow me to stir up interest in the flying boat we all so badly want to manufacture. I'd be a kind of Sales Ambassador. Unlike Amy Johnson, who uses these kind of opportunities to bang the drum for aviation in general, my motives would be far more mercenary, and therefore less admirable. However, your father was very keen on the idea. As you doubtless heard, Maitland has been put on to it immediately.'

Her heart sank. 'How long will you be away?'

'Six months, at least. More, if I can manage it.'

'So long?' she cried in dismay. 'When will you set off?'

'Not for a few weeks. Even the redoubtable Mr Jarvis needs a short time of preparation for such a complex project.'

It was some consolation, but she was still unhappy. 'What about the wedding?'

He shook his head. 'Business and matrimony don't mix. I'll have to forego the boon of watching the incomparable Miss Main become Mrs Donald Kirkland. Even more, I shall be sacrificing the once in a lifetime thrill of discovering whether or not the mother of the bride succeeds in finding a dress not remotely similar to that of any of the guests.'

Leone stopped dancing, forcing him to a halt as she studied his face in annoyance. 'Kit, why are you adopting this elaborate social pose with me?'

'This is rather an elaborate social occasion, isn't it?'

'Not as elaborate as the one last night . . . and you were vastly different then.'

His expression hardly changed, but there could have

162

been a fleeting shadow in the brown of his eyes as he said, 'Don't judge me on last night, Leone. I was three quarters drunk, maudlin with anticlimax . . . and I *did* mistake you for one of my wenches.'

'No, you didn't,' she contradicted softly. 'What happened between us was very, very special. Don't worry, I would never tell anyone. I understand why you did it. I'll always understand, darling, so please don't pretend with me any longer. I'm the girl who knows the *real* you.'

Putting his hand beneath her elbow, he led her to the far end of the pool where shadows made the night even more enchanting for her. For a wild moment, she believed he was going to kiss her again. Instead, he turned her to face him and stood holding her arms while he spoke to her very seriously.

'Your father was right when he told you not to try to grow up too soon. It can be dangerous. What happened last night is the perfect example of that risk. You *don't* know the real me. I'm only twenty-two, yet my name is in every newspaper across the world today. For me, that's only the beginning, however. When your father took me in three years ago, my dreams and ambitions suddenly took on the gloss of reality. He and Donald have made it possible for me to pursue the love of my life; exploration of the sky. That is my *only* love, Leone. I now have money, social connections, and every advantage enjoyed by those lucky enough to bear the name of Kirkland. Life is exceptionally good for me right now, and that's the way I want it to continue. "Wenching", as your father called it, is part of it, and a most enjoyable part. I want that to continue, also.'

'Go on,' she prompted, thrilled by every moment of his heart to heart confession which strengthened her knowledge of the person she knew him to be.

With fresh determination, he said, 'There'll be women galore on this tour. I'll be expected to charm them in the name of the company. I'm extremely good at it, as you discovered, because I can turn it on at will. There'll also be a great many opportunities to further my own career and reputation. I'll grab them all hungrily, believe me, and when this flying boat is built, my name will be headlined across the world again as they rank me with the great pioneers of aviation.'

'Why?' she asked, breathless over the prospect, for his sake.

'Because I intend to make flying history. The name of Anson will be there with Mollison and Lindbergh and Wright – to say nothing of the incomparable Amy.' Fervour highlighted his dark attraction even more, as he added, 'Even the ambitious Sir Hector Kirkland was rendered inarticulate for a moment when I outlined my plan.'

'Tell me!'

He shook his head. 'It's too far in the future, but I'll do it, I swear.'

'I know you will,' she assured him dreamily.

'That's the real me, Leone,' he insisted, reverting to the original topic. 'Kit Anson is searching for fame, fortune and the pathway to the stars. He's ruthless, opinionated and extremely fickle.'

She smiled her love at him. 'He's also a very accomplished liar.'

Releasing his hold on her, he studied her with exasperation. 'Haven't you listened to a word I've said?'

'Yes, and I was delighted by it all. Even the piece about women galore. You've forgotten that I've had a taste of the way you deal with girls who pursue you too closely – my collar still bears the evidence of your rough handling, and so do my panties – so I'm not too worried about you in that direction. Darling Kit, it's because of such women that you're fickle . . . and why shouldn't you be opinionated? You have every right to be after yesterday. As for being ruthless, I think you adopt that manner as a means of defence.' She took one of his hands in her own. 'Please stop trying to bluster your way through excuses for last night. It wasn't in the least dangerous. You're not the first man in my life, you know. Father might think of me as a schoolgirl, but Jose Montero certainly didn't . . . and neither did Raoul!'

'Dear God,' he exclaimed forcefully, 'the careless, irresponsible Raoul needs a hearty kick on his backside, in my opinion.'

They were marvellous words to her ears. 'I hope you won't be as jealous of Warren's interest in me. Father wouldn't like his new discovery to be treated to a kick in the pants.'

'I've already spoken to Warren about you,' he told her sternly. 'He's not used to rich, precocious girls who order him about. I gather he got rather carried away last night. Leave him alone. Your father won't want his blue-eyed boy to have the wrong ideas where you're concerned.'

'His eyes *are* blue, aren't they?'

'I'm serious, Leone.'

'Good,' she retaliated delightedly. 'You've stopped pretending, at last.'

Movement towards them heralded Stephanie, saying, 'Hey, you two, what about a swim? It's always heavenly by moonlight.'

'A marvellous idea,' agreed Kit, with relief touching his voice and expression. 'It might cool everyone down a little.'

Although she resented the other girl's intrusion into her exchange with Kit, Leone had to own it was an inspired suggestion. They split up to don bathing suits hanging in cupboards within the separate changing rooms. Leone chose her usual scarlet. The other girl maintained her shade of the evening in a smart costume of beige, with chocolate-coloured swathes across the hips.

'You didn't dance for long,' Stephanie commented from the adjacent cubicle. 'What was the deep, serious discussion about?'

'Our plans,' she called back airily. 'It's the first real chance we've had.'

'Oh?'

Leone smiled at the curiosity in that one word. 'Kit's been so busy with *Aphrodite*, and now there's the new project starting tomorrow. Men never have any time, do they? However did you and Donald ever meet, by the way?'

'At the Chelsea Arts Ball. A mutual friend introduced us because I was dressed as Queen Nefertiti, and Donald had come as an Egyptian slave.'

'Mmm, and the relationship has stayed that way ever since,' she commented mischievously.

'How astute of you to recognize the fact!'

Leone picked up her bathing cap and went out to wait by the mirrored area, where lotions and perfumes stood on a marble table for use by guests after swimming. Within several moments another image appeared beside her own, and a little of Leone's sense of satisfaction evaporated as she was forced to recognize that she looked very much the young girl against the rounded maturity of someone soon to become a Kirkland. Stephanie would one day be mistress of Sheenmouth Abbey, where a young sister-in-law would play an even less important rôle than she did now. With a surge of apprehension, she wondered what rôle Kit would then play. At present, he treated this place as his home.

'Someone walk over your grave?'

She turned to Stephanie. 'What?'

'You wore a very odd expression just then; as if you'd seen something unpleasant. Anything to do with your plans?'

'No, those are all extremely pleasant.'

'For you, or for Kit?'

'You'll see,' she said enigmatically. 'Come on, I can hear them splashing around out there.'

The two men were swimming energetically, breaking the reflections of floodlights into tiny gleaming fragments as they disturbed the clear water. Leone climbed to the highest board and dived, swimming effortlessly underwater to surface beside Kit as he turned at the far end of the pool.

'How about a race?' she invited eagerly.

'All right, mermaid, but I'll win.'

That he did so was only due to his superior physique. His compliment on her prowess pleased her, so she challenged him to a diving contest. On hearing of it, the other pair decided to join in, but none were a match for the girl who had spent lonely hours with little else to do but amuse herself in this pool. Tonight, it was especially thrilling to show off in Kit's presence. She used the opportunity to the full, ending her display with a spectacular triple somersault she dared them all to emulate. Only Kit was game to try, and listened intently while she explained the complications of the dive.

'Go ahead and break your neck,' invited Donald, heaving himself out and getting to his feet beside Kit on the marble surround, 'but be there at nine a.m. sharp . . . with your head tucked under your arm, if necessary.'

Kit laughed, and walked away from him to climb the steps of the diving board. Leone watched intently, suddenly chilled by her brother's words. Such things happened. After flirting with death in the sky yesterday and returning safely, he could now attempt this dive, with tragic results.

'Kit, don't,' she called after him fearfully. 'Come back and let's have some fun instead.'

He smiled down at her from the high board. 'Afraid of losing your crown as queen of the springboard?' he teased.

'No.' It was only a whisper as she watched him stretch both arms and poise, ready for the swift series of rotations. How would she carry on living, if anything happened to him? Fear and elation merged to quicken her heartbeat as he leapt into the night air. When he cut the water cleanly, it was after only two somersaults.

167

Discretion had apparently overridden valour. He came to the surface shaking water from his dark hair, laughing at his own faint-heartedness.

'I now have to suffer the humiliation caused by misdirected bravado,' he called to her. 'Only a fool willingly exposes himself to it . . . especially before the eyes of the fair sex.'

'Don't be silly,' she managed to call back, still shaking. 'You attempted it, which is more than Donald did.'

Her brother, towelling himself down, said calmly, 'I never feel the need to display my prowess to ladies.'

'My God, he really is a magnificent specimen,' murmured Stephanie at the rail beside her. 'Stripped down to the bare essentials like that, it's dramatically obvious.'

Donald had always been graceful rather than powerful in build, but Leone had to admit he looked attractively well-proportioned as he stood holding his towel, gilded by the floodlighting. Yet, when she turned to Stephanie, she saw that the girl's eyes, sparkling with a strange excitement, were gazing at Kit as he climbed from the pool with water gleaming his muscular body and plastering the dark hair to his sturdy limbs. Sharp jealousy mixed with her own swift violent reaction to his basic sexuality. It gave birth to a deep suspicion. Kit had sung a hymn of praise to Stephanie's beauty; he had invited her to watch his flight yesterday from the boat he had travelled in. She had kissed him for luck; she had earlier this evening called him darling. Now, she had just sung a hymn of praise to *his* beauty. What exactly was the relationship between this man she now loved, and her brother's future wife? Moving through the water to grip the rail on the far side of the girl about to mount the steps, Leone confronted her.

'I get the impression that you know Kit well. How is that?'

Stephanie smiled and pushed out into the water to pass her and gain the steps. Leone followed her up, determined on an answer. She received it once they were both standing on the marble slabs surrounding the pool.

'We've known each other for more than eighteen months. Kit was the mutual friend at the Chelsea Arts, who introduced me to your brother.'

The information came as something of a shock. In the lingering echo of her physical desire for him, she caught herself saying, 'You knew Kit first, yet chose Donald?'

Pulling the rubber cap from her head so that the tawny hair tumbled loose over her shoulders, the other girl gave her a shrewd glance. 'My dear Leone, women don't *marry* men like Kit, they simply enjoy them. You'll find out.'

She was filled with disgust at such a comment in connection with Kit. It suggested that he was some kind of shallow plaything; almost a gigolo. Leaping to his defence, she began, 'That last comment was . . .'

'Modern?' suggested Stephanie swiftly. 'As you said to your father, women can do anything, these days. At last, we are able to emulate what men have been doing for centuries – marry suitably, but continue to find pleasure elsewhere with those who are specifically designed to give it. Kit is immensely exciting, but his future is so precarious.'

Furious, Leone cried, 'That hasn't stopped a great many women from marrying pilots.'

'Dear girl, you misunderstand,' the other girl said calmly. 'I wasn't referring to the dangers of flying. Kit is a charity boy; everyone knows that. Charm is his passport to survival. He works hard at it, believe me, and never more than on your father because, if he ever puts a foot wrong where Sir Hector is concerned, everything will tumble down around him leaving him the way he was three years ago. I shouldn't care to be anywhere near him if that happened.'

6

When Warren took up residence in the old boathouse on the Kirkland boundary, he still found it hard to believe his life had changed so much. It was as if Midas had touched every aspect of it, although it was Leone Kirkland he credited with the golden fingers. If she had not jumped on to his pillion that evening and imperiously ordered him to take her to Sheenmouth Abbey, life would now have been very bleak. Because of that chance encounter he had a job such as he had dreamed of for years, enough money to live very well, and a quaint, roomy home he had been told he could do anything with in order to make it comfortable. He also had the famous Kit Anson for a friend. Small wonder he lived in a daze for a while, travelling up to Kirkland's by boat each morning to discuss, plan and offer his opinions to Donald and Sir Hector, with Kit backing him up. Then, he would return exhausted but radiantly happy to his new home by the river, to marvel yet again at his astounding good fortune.

Kit had warned him that he would be expected to give almost his entire life to any job offered him by Sir Hector, and he had found that to be true. He gave it willingly, not simply out of gratitude, but because this flying boat project was one he could not bear to leave alone. The dream machine possessed practically every waking thought because, unlike *Seaspray*, he was designing an aircraft which would be built, and would be flown.

Sir Hector had guaranteed that. There were not enough hours in each day for Warren. After two weeks on the job, he was driven to clear the ground-floor storeroom the Ansons had used as a workshop-cum-office so that he could work at night, so full of theories and ideas was he.

His living quarters above the boathouse were reasonably cosy, although what they would be like in winter he could not guess, but the storeroom virtually on the riverbank smelled dank, and the surrounding copse must have overgrown considerably in the three years since the Ansons had occupied the place. Leaving the heavy workbench and tools where they were, for the moment, he moved the drawing board up to his sitting room where the light was much better. That done, he decided the flat-topped desk with its four drawers should join it. It was a heavy piece of furniture, so he removed each drawer to take up separately. Then he secured the desk shell with ropes and hauled it to the next floor by means of one of the pulleys installed for slinging boats up while repairs were done. He felt very satisfied with his evening's work once he had arranged everything in the room for his greater convenience, and made himself a mug of cocoa while he took a rest.

Sprawled in one of the old armchairs, he sipped his cocoa whilst his mind grappled with the main problem facing them on this project. Kit had vowed to fly it from Sheenmouth to Africa. The distance was nothing – the whole world had been encompassed by air through the daring exploits of aviation's pioneers in tiny machines – but what Kit was promising Sir Hector was to take a 'passenger liner with wings' over to that dark continent. Warren's own description of an airborne concept had fired everyone's imagination and, whilst it was naturally inconceivable to carry the hundreds accommodated in ships, the new Kirkland's flying boat would have to provide passage for many more than the half-dozen daring souls who could presently be taken across the

Channel in floatplanes. Any man with engineering skill and flair could design a hull with the capacity to seat, perhaps, up to twenty passengers plus the requisite crew, but it required a near genius to then provide large enough fuel tanks to feed a probable four greedy engines, to design wings strong enough to support such engines yet light enough to maintain the essential balance of the machine, and to produce floats capable of keeping the huge aircraft steady when taxiing across the water. When all that had been accomplished, it then required a miracle-worker to work out how such an enormous, heavy machine would ever rise into the air after ploughing through the sea at increasing throttle.

Lost in speculation for some time, Warren realized how it must be done. They would first have to design a ship, then an aircraft, merging the two by selecting the essential demands of each. Whereas a seaplane was really a straightforward aircraft with floats rather than wheels, what they now had in mind was a ship which had wings rather than sails. The approach to this must be vastly different from that towards *Seaspray* or *Aphrodite*.

At thought of the famous yellow seaplane, he frowned. The only slight damper on his new sense of joy was Donald Kirkland's lack of cooperation. Warren was aware, through Kit, of the man's fierce opposition to his father's decision to bring in another designer, and he sympathized with such reluctance, to a certain extent. However, during the two weeks they had been exploring the possibilities and drawbacks of the project, Warren had found himself puzzled on several occasions by the younger Kirkland's lack of contribution to the discussion. Kit was a qualified engineer, well versed in the 'nuts and bolts' aspect of construction and, as a champion pilot, offered the benefits of his knowledge from the practical angle. Donald remained obstinate about not wishing to form one of a team. Warren preferred to believe it was that rather than a somewhat immature possessiveness over a brain-child because, in his opinion, the brain-child was not worth such guarding.

So far, Donald had consigned the basics of flying boat design to paper, but the machine he appeared to be advocating seemed to be little more than the standard *Supermarine* model already in service, blown up to several times its existing size and with two wing-mounted propellers to augment the one fixed behind the cabin. His ideas, such as they were, were sound enough in theory yet showed no touch of the brilliance he had shown with *Aphrodite*. Warren had been so eager to work in harness with this gifted designer, he took the man's refusal to give rein to his flair and imagination as a heavy snub to his own ability. His attempts to coax the secret theories from Donald Kirkland by offering several of his own had met with failure. Kit was wildly enthusiastic and outgoing, like himself, yet Donald was like a bottle of rare wine with the cork so firmly in place it prevented even a single drop of the precious contents from spilling on to the tongues of those thirsting for the privilege of sharing it.

A unique family, the Kirklands, Warren had decided. Its menfolk were unbelievably determined and exclusive, convinced of their own superiority. Yet the only girl tempered these same qualities with a generous warmth and vivacity which endeared her to one immediately. He had certainly fallen beneath her spell, unaware of her extreme youth until Kit had warned him. The spell was still strong on him, even knowing that she was no more than a schoolgirl, so he had avoided all risk of their meeting. Kit had several times asked him up to his quarters in the Abbey to chew things over privately, but Warren had suggested that his friend come, instead, to the boathouse. As each was reluctant over the suggested rendezvous, they had driven in Kit's fast car to the Buck and Hounds where the convivial atmosphere offered no more serious threat than inebriation. On those return journeys Warren had had ample evidence of Kit's admission that he drove a car as if flying a seaplane. However, since his own style on a motorbike was flamboyant enough and he intended to change the machine for a sports car as soon as he could afford it, Warren found no fault with his friend's attack on the narrow country lanes. In fact, he found no fault with any angle of his new life save Donald's refusal to share his skill. His foolish attitude was delaying solutions to design problems, which could be better thrashed out with several minds throwing in ideas and theories. As the senior designer, Donald had the power to approve or veto proposals, but he would not even accept that Warren had sufficient skill to make any. The only answer was to develop them here in his new isolated home. Then, with Kit behind him, he would present his finding to Donald when Sir Hector was present. It would probably serve to worsen relations between himself and the heir to the company, but it might start a flying boat on the way to being built. Finishing his cocoa, he went straight to work at the desk without bothering to replace the drawers. They remained in a pile on an old sofa.

The work went so well, he refused an invitation from Kit to drive with him into Torquay on the following Saturday, where his friend wanted to buy a few things for the overseas tour he was to embark on shortly. Even the offer to introduce him to several pretty, fun-loving girls did nothing to persuade Warren to give up the chance of a full day's work on his private theories. He rose early on a morning of grey skies and sheeting rain, made himself thick lumpy porridge the way he liked it, fried eggs and bacon to put on a plate beside a full pot of tea, then carried it all to the desk where he promptly let it grow cold while he grappled with a very tricky weight ratio. Solving it was such a triumph, he happily cooked a second breakfast to eat hot, only to realize that it was then practically time for lunch instead. Adding several apples to his meal solved that problem very

174

speedily, and he was about to return to his desk when he heard movements on the ground floor.

Thinking Kit had changed his mind about driving to Torquay in such heavy rain, he called out, 'Come on up! I've got some good news for you.'

The footsteps on the wooden stairs sounded light for a man of Kit's size, and Warren was dumbfounded when a pale round face plastered by very wet red hair appeared through the aperture in the floor to stare apprehensively at him.

'Don't be angry, Warren,' she begged. 'Mrs Bardolph told me you were here . . . and all about the job at Kirkland's. I wanted to congratulate you.'

He went forward with his hand outstretched, to help her up the last few steps. How could he have forgotten this girl he so nearly loved? Yet, since meeting Leone Kirkland on the Magnum Pomeroy road, so much had happened so fast, he had not given Mona a single thought. Guilt swept through him as he saw her sodden state: shoes and stockings splashed and muddy, the thin raincoat clinging to her sturdy shape, and the water dripping from her hair on to her cheeks.

'However did you get right out here?' he asked roughly.

'You're not annoyed, are you?'

'Why should I be? Mona, you're wet through! Take off that mackintosh while I fetch a towel for your hair.'

Still shaken by the realization of his total exclusion of her from every aspect of his life since that evening her father had presented his ultimatum, he walked through into his bedroom to collect his remaining clean towel, smitten by the unhappiness in her eyes. While the most marvellous gifts had been falling into his lap, Mona had plainly been distressed and lonely. He had not even written to her after declining to buy her an engagement ring. That might have softened the break a little. Returning with the towel, he saw the torrential rain had penetrated through to her green-and-white spotted dress. She was now shivering, possibly because of her daring in coming here, but also from the chill.

'How did you manage to get so wet, silly girl?' he asked, with a more gentle approach than before.

'Haven't you looked outside? It's absolutely pelting!'

'I've been so busy, I haven't noticed the weather. Here you are. Dry yourself a bit with this.' He held out the towel. 'This place is practically inaccessible. However did you make your way here on foot?'

Taking the towel, she began to rub at her hair with brisk movements. 'Mrs Bardolph knew you were in an old boathouse on the Kirkland boundary, and Jake Meakins at the ferry knew near enough where it was. He told me to get off at Forton, then follow the river up to the inlet. He forgot to say that the path is so overgrown it's practically impassable, in places.' Her face peered up at him from the depths of the towel. 'Once I'd come so far, I was more frightened of turning back than I was of facing you.'

Feeling even more guilty, he went across to take the towel and begin rubbing at her bright hair himself. 'Fancy being frightened of me, you goose! You should have written. We could have met somewhere easier to reach than this place.'

She put up her hands to still his, gazing in troubled fashion into his eyes through the tangle of red strands. 'Would you have met me, after what Dad said to you?'

He made no immediate answer to that. Now she was here there was little he could do about it, but would he have met her if she had written to ask?

'What made you call on Ma Bardolph?' he asked, to change the subject.

'There was a job vacant up at the tractor works. It wasn't flying, but it was to do with engines. I wanted to let you know about it before I put it in this week's edition. Of course, I didn't know you'd gone up in the world, mixing with the Kirklands.'

'I'm not,' he protested. 'At least, only at work.'

'Oh.'

She was still shivering, and he felt even more remorseful at his neglect of her now he knew she had tried to help despite three weeks of silence from him.

'You'll catch a nasty cold unless you get out of those wet things,' he told her fondly. 'Go into my bedroom and take off that wet frock. There's a dressing gown you can wear while we dry it. I'll make some tea.' Placing his hands on her rounded bottom, he urged her forward. 'Go on, do as I say!'

While he made tea on the small stove rescued from a boat, according to Kit, Warren recalled the many happy times he had spent with Mona and how she had made his first months in Sheenmouth bearable. Through her, he had heard of the job at the Aero Club. She had done so much for him, how could he have left her lonely and miserable after that scene with her father? She led a cheerless life at home but, being a girl, could do little to change it. His momentary thought that Leone Kirkland would soon change her lot if it were as cheerless, was pushed aside by acknowledgement that Mona was one of the world's givers and Leone most probably one of its takers. Jack Cummings would doubtless wring every drop of duty and compassion from his daughter, until her own life had practically passed her by. Poor Mona!

'Do you like living in this queer place?' asked the girl, as she returned to hang her dress over the back of a chair. 'Who does the cleaning and cooking for you?'

'I do.' He grinned. 'Actually, I haven't got round to much cleaning yet, as you can see.'

Her nose wrinkled. 'It smells a bit damp.'

'That's because it's raining. It's nice on dry days.'

'There's extra space,' she conceded, 'but it was more comfortable at Mrs Bardolph's.'

'I had to pay rent there. Kit lets me live here for nothing.'

'Kit?'

'Kit Anson.'

'Oh.'

He reached for her hand. 'Come on, don't go all pi-faced. I'm still the same person I always was, and he's not in the least lofty or la-di-da, you know. You'd like him, Mona.'

Her smile finally broke through. 'No one's called me pi-faced for ages.'

Drawing her nearer, he said, 'Maybe I'm the only one who makes you that way.'

'You make me happy, Warren,' she confessed, her smile starting to fade. 'I've missed you ever so much.'

He turned from that hazard to pick up the tray containing tea and biscuits, then carry it across to a large lumpy settee, where a low table stood beside it covered with books.

'Push those on to the floor,' he instructed her. 'I haven't sorted them out yet, so it won't matter.'

'How did you manage to make friends with someone like Kit Anson?' she asked, as she carefully unloaded the table and placed his books in neat piles beside it.

He poured tea, relating to her the story of how Leone had stopped him and demanded to be taken home; a circumstance which had led to his present good fortune.

'We're working on this exciting new machine,' he added, 'because Kit apparently made Sir Hector crazy to have what I had called "a passenger liner with wings". I'm determined that he'll have it, despite Donald's refusal to cooperate.'

'He sounds a very stupid person,' Mona commented, busily rolling back the sleeves of Warren's dressing gown so that her hands were free to hold the cup and saucer. 'Sir Hector sounds greedy and hard as nails. That girl sounds very selfish and a bit crazy.' Her gaze challenged him. 'How can you like people like that?'

'I don't have to like them, just work with them.'

'Even that girl?'

'She's not "that girl", Mona, she has a name,' he told her firmly. 'Of course I don't work with her. In fact, I

178

haven't set eyes on her since that first evening . . . and I don't want to,' he finished enigmatically.

That information pleased Mona, and she drank her tea whilst remarking on the state of the room.

'It's disgracefully untidy. How do you manage to find anything?'

'I haven't had to look for anything yet. I've been so busy since I moved in, all I do is eat, work and sleep. The Ansons left some stuff here, and I keep meaning to ask Kit if he wants to sort it out and keep any of it. Apart from my books and clothes, all I brought with me was a box of provisions which Ma Bardolph got in for me.'

'You shouldn't call her that, Warren. She's been ever so good to you.'

'It isn't meant to be insulting. The other tenants called her that . . . and I know she was good to me,' he said, in his defence. 'There's a canteen at Kirkland's so I have a hot meal there at midday, and one of the estate gardeners brings me eggs and vegetables when there are any to spare. I'm fine here.'

'It's a bit lonely, stuck out here in the middle of nowhere.'

'I've been so busy, I haven't had time to feel lonely.'

She put down her cup and saucer, then turned to him. 'That's the third or fourth time you've said you've been so busy you haven't noticed anything else. Does that mean you've been too busy to think about me?'

It was a tricky question. If he answered yes, she would be hurt and upset; if he answered no, it would be a lie and lead to more tricky questions. He hesitated.

'I've thought about you . . . every day and every night,' she confessed, in low tones.

'Oh, Mona,' he exclaimed remorsefully, 'you know why I've stayed away. Your father was right about the situation. I *was* beginning to make unfair demands on you.' In an attempt to lighten the atmosphere, he added,

179

'I've even been too busy to follow your advice to take out Rosie Higgs from the Monks Arms.'

She turned a faint pink. 'I'd forgotten I said that to you.'

'How is your father?'

'The same.'

'He hasn't any idea you've come here?'

She shook her head. 'I told him I was meeting someone I'd known at school, who was down here on holiday. I don't think he's heard that you're working at Kirkland's. He'd have told me.'

She leaned forward to take a biscuit, and the dressing gown parted a little to reveal the lace edging of her bodice which lay around the curve of her breasts. Warren could not take his eyes from the sight. Work had occupied his thoughts to the extent of forgetting pleasures of that nature. All at once, he was acutely aware of how much he had missed them.

Mona surveyed the room again as she nibbled a ginger-snap with her strong teeth. 'If it was done up a bit, I expect it could be quite nice. Pretty curtains at the window instead of those plum-coloured repp, and cushions to match. You'd have to get new furniture, of course. These old chairs smell of mildew. You might not be aware of it, but it's very noticeable when anyone first comes in. You'd also need a nice carpet instead of these dingy old rugs.' Her gaze rose to the plain wood walls, then on to the beamed roof where Warren heard rats scampering at night. 'You could put planks across to make a proper ceiling, then it could all be painted a nice bright colour.' As she turned to him, her face was filled with the glow it had worn on remembered occasions. 'It's plain no woman has ever lived here. It needs a feminine touch to make it into a real home.' She put her hand over his. 'I could come at weekends and clean it up for you; make it cosy and comfortable.'

It sounded marvellous. Faced with an even more revealing glimpse of her bodice as the dressing gown parted further, thoughts of just how cosy and comfortable she could make him at weekends warmed his mind.

'I couldn't ask you to do that,' he murmured.

'You don't have to. I'm offering,' she told him just as softly. 'The bedroom is in an awful mess. Fancy leaving coils of old rope in the corner! And there aren't any curtains at all at that window. I'm making a new pair for my room at home, but I'll bring them here instead. They'll be long enough. When the floor has been scrubbed, some nice rugs put down, and a white counterpane thrown over the bed, it'll start looking quite attractive.'

Apparently oblivious of the way he was now fondling her hand and wrist, Mona studied the jumbled corner which served as a kitchen.

'That's an utter disgrace! It needs a new stove, and some cupboards to pack away the china. Not that any of those things are worth keeping. I've heard stories about old Mr Anson smashing plates and things when he'd been drinking, so I suppose these were the only pieces left. Now you've got a proper job, Warren, you can afford to buy a nice tea and dinner set.'

All at once, Warren saw which way her mind was working. She was planning a home for *two*. It came as a shock to realize that there was now no real obstacle to buying her a diamond ring and setting a date for the wedding. As she continued speaking of her ideas for making the boathouse into a charming, unusual riverside home, he tried to rationalize his thoughts. He would very much like to live in the place she claimed she could create from these utility rooms. It would be nice to have someone to cook, clean and care for him. Even if Kit decided to ask for rent later on, he could afford to pay it. With what he presently earned at Kirkland's, plus the bonus he had been promised by Sir Hector when the prototype flying boat went into production, his financial future was rosy. He was extremely fond of Mona; he found her sexually beckoning. Since leaving London he had not been to bed with any girl. Even in the capital, he had only done it on two occasions, and then with a strange sense of guilt at treating the girls as other men treated his mother. His feelings for Mona had been alto-gether different, based on fondness and the attraction of generous innocence. He wanted what she offered now. There was a certain incitement in the sight of his own clothes draped over her curves in a manner which emphasized her femininity. A diamond ring could gain him all these advantages, and a few more which were probably less obvious.

'Don't you agree that it would be better than the dump it is at the moment?' she asked him, turning eyes shining with wonderful visions towards him. 'Oh, Warren, it would be the cosiest little house you've ever known. In time, we could make a garden by clearing some of the trees along the bank . . . and we'd have our own boat to take us down to Sheenmouth, like the Kirklands do,' she elaborated, carried away on the tide of her dreams. 'It would be the perfect spot for a couple of dogs, and for . . . well, later on, who knows?' she finished shyly.

He knew, well enough. Since his present enthusiasm was for the activity which came before what came later on, he delayed an immediate response, whilst taking in the glowing attraction of her face surrounded by the fluffy red hair drying like a halo.

'Darling Warren, I do so love you,' she murmured, closing against him with her arms sliding around his neck. 'The last three weeks have been the worst of my life, and I'd have gone to Mrs Bardolph's even if there hadn't been a job vacant. I couldn't bear it without you any longer.'

Her urgent kisses brought an immediate response in him. Returning them with growing hunger, he sensed her surrender even at that point. It was easy to slide the dressing gown from her plump freckled shoulders, as his mouth opened hers and his tongue tasted the sweetness of the pink lipstick she wore. Her bodice was buttoned at the front, and she gasped with relief as his hands bared her breasts which were taut with desire for his touch. Knowing that he would meet with no opposition, Warren struggled with his own clothing as he reduced her to a state of sexual frenzy by an assault with his mouth and teeth on her half-naked body.

Then, tugging the dressing gown cord free, he pushed it from her legs to leave her dressed in no more than a pair of cotton pants. Mona clung to him, wriggling with the longing to be completely free and increasing his urgency to spill the tide rising fast within him. Unbuttoning his own underclothes, he pulled them off before getting to his feet to carry her through to the bed, tearing off her frilly panties and dropping them on the floor as he went.

The climax came almost immediately and, to his astonishment, they achieved the elusive simultaneous orgasm. Mona cried out with wonder, and the pleasure-pain of it, while he lay across her damp body, marvelling at the difference between this union and the others he had experienced. Once was not enough to satisfy either of them, and Warren was able to take his time during the repeat pleasure. If their points of climax did not exactly match, this time, they were close enough to bring total contentment which lulled them both to sleep before they were aware of it.

Warren awoke to find the sun streaming through the uncurtained window. Turning his head on the pillow, he saw a girl beside him. Recollection came swiftly, and with it a strong sense of guilt. He had just used Mona as men had used his mother; traded on her weakness to satisfy a basic need. Oh God, what if he had just made her pregnant? He would have no alternative but to marry her. He sat up quickly, filled with something bordering on panic. Jack Cummings would march him to the altar before he knew what had hit him.

With passion well and truly spent, he began to count the cost. Even if there were no repercussions from what he had done this afternoon, Mona would expect him to produce the diamond ring, together with the date of the imminent wedding. Nice girls only surrendered to men they trusted to honour the union. Putting his head into his hands, he told himself she had planned this all along. The minute she had heard he had what she called a 'proper job', she had arrived to set her trap. He had walked straight into it like a gullible fool. The Kirkland family had dangled the golden future before him, and the Cummings family meant to snatch it from him. He would lose the hope of fame and fortune in exchange for a few curtains with matching cushions. Anger swamped him. Why should he have to give up all he wanted? After all, he had given Mona as much pleasure as she had given him just now. Why should he have to offer the rest of his life by way of thanks?

His swift movement to leave the bed roused Mona. She smiled dreamily as she studied his nakedness.

'I never knew men could look beautiful,' she murmured, 'but you do right now.'

He glanced around for his underpants or trousers, but they were back in the sitting room where he had dropped them. It seemed a little ridiculous to pull a sheet over his vulnerable parts, so he brazened it out as he said, 'We slept too long. It's almost five. Shouldn't you be getting back?'

Mona apparently sensed the change in him immediately. Pushing back the sheet, she moved across the bed on her knees until she reached him. With her swollen breasts touching his chest, and her damp thighs temptingly close to further invasion by him, she put her hands on his shoulders as she gazed up in troubled fashion.

'What's wrong, darling? You've grown all distant.'

'Nothing's wrong. I'm just worried about getting you home before your father grows suspicious and asks too many questions.'

Her smile was like that of a mother for a foolish child.

'He can ask whatever questions he likes now, silly, and it won't matter.'

'Of course it'll matter,' he said sharply. 'You can't tell him what we've just done. He'd half kill us both.'

She was still smiling. 'I wouldn't tell him *that*. I wouldn't tell anyone. It's our marvellous secret. It'll always be our own marvellous secret.'

The trap seemed to be closing fast. 'Mona, we both got very carried away,' he told her with a tone nearing desperation, because her naked nearness was beginning to arouse him again. He was acutely startled by his own virility this afternoon, and swiftly backed away from her before adding, 'You'd better not come here again. It's far too risky.'

Stepping from the bed, she pursued him and made matters worse by sliding her arms around him, feathering his chest with her moist lips as she murmured, 'If you find it too risky for me to come here like this, we'd better get married as soon as possible. Then we can do this all the time without worrying.'

'It's not as simple as that,' he told her, disentangling himself. 'I've only just started working for Kirkland's, and Sir Hector demands that I devote all my time to the job. I need to concentrate for hours on end when I get back here each day, and I'm more or less at his beck and call at any time of day or night. As Kit says, that family expects total dedication from people who're fortunate enough to be taken up by them.'

Mona grew so still she could have been a nude alabaster statue, as his words began to make shattering sense. The glow of lingering sexual pleasure faded from her eyes, and she shivered involuntarily as if he had thrown cold water over her. Then, as she crossed her hands over her breasts as if to protect them from further assault, the silence was broken by a light voice calling Warren's name. Almost immediately, Leone Kirkland appeared in the doorway, dressed in riding clothes, with a small basket of peaches in her hand. Her blue eyes widened with shock as she gazed first at his naked body, then at Mona's, and finally at the tumbled bed.

'Heavens!' she whispered in hollow tones, 'I had no idea you were . . . oh, how . . . how . . .'

Turning on her heel, she fled from the doorway with the basket of fruit still in her hand, leaving Warren feeling exposed and humiliated to face the pain of the girl now crouching on the bed beneath the protection of a sheet, as she broke apart.

Warren sat up for most of that night. His new golden future had just been tarnished by two girls: his self-esteem had been wrested from him by one act of spontaneous pleasure. He tried in vain to put from his mind that scene with Mona which now left him feeling guilty, angry and bewildered. Turning on him like a wildcat when he had swiftly dressed and tried to comfort her, she had betrayed the other side of her personality for the first time. Warren could still hardly believe such words could have come from the girl he thought he knew. Her vindictive accusations had first wounded him, then made him angry enough to suggest that she had fully intended to be seduced so that she could then force him to marry her. They had said many hurtful things, yet Mona had always managed to turn every point so that Warren emerged the only villain. Finally, she had stormed from the place, claiming it was a filthy, disgusting centre for his filthy, disgusting behaviour with any girl in sight, including that wealthy tart, Leone Kirkland.

Any hope of working had been destroyed for that day, so he had sat trying to come to terms with the situation. Mona had been a sweet and marvellous girlfriend for six months, at a time when he had been too impecunious to offer her marriage. Why then, now that he could afford to keep a wife, and when she had proved to be a highly enjoyable sexual partner, had he instinctively backed away from commitment to her? She would make the boathouse into a most attractive home in no time, she would cook and iron for him, ensure that he always had a clean shirt, and make him very happy in bed. The list sounded irresistible, yet he could not help adding that she would also deplore his untidiness, scold him if he arrived home late for the dinner she had lovingly prepared, and would find it impossible to let him work at home without interrupting him every few minutes with some domestic triviality. She had already indicated that she wished to fill the place with noisy children and dogs. Time would make her plump, rosy and demanding. Many men might still consider that a well-balanced bargain, but Warren now admitted to himself that his sights were on the stars. Any girl who might one day share his life would have to want those glittering prizes, also . . . a girl like Leone Kirkland, for instance.

He sighed heavily. After three weeks without making contact, Leone had to choose that precise moment to pay him a visit. Mona had believed her to be the next candidate for his bed. What did Leone now think of him? A girl of sixteen, no matter how sophisticated, must have been shocked to walk in on a man and a girl stark naked beside a rumpled bed in mid-afternoon. Mona had felt unbearably humiliated; he had been acutely embarrassed and dismayed. What if Leone returned to the Abbey to relate her experience to Sir Hector or Donald? Would they imagine he was bedding a series of girls on their property; using the old boathouse as a den of vice? What if she told Kit of it? Would his friend feel he had abused his generosity in letting him live rent-free here? Suppose Leone remained silent on the subject, but saw the affair as his betrayal of her offer of friendship on taking him into her home. There were many subtle ways a girl in her position could punish him, or even hold him to social blackmail, if she chose.

What a fool he had been to jeopardize his hopes for the future! Suppose Mona went home and told her father? For simple sexual relief, he should have gone to a girl who demanded his money, not his whole life in return. The men who had enjoyed his mother's company had known what they were doing. A brooch, a chiffon nightdress, a few roses, and they were able to walk away from her to do as they pleased. None of them would have been swamped with guilt afterward. None of them would have stayed up half the night, wondering about the possible actions of a vengeful father. He had not even been a vengeful son, Warren realized then. He had allowed himself to be dispatched from his home at night to work in a newspaper office. Yet, what else could he have done at the age of fifteen? His mother had not wished to be avenged. She had enjoyed her mode of life, and any attempt at noble interference by him would have been countered with the advice to grow up and gain some experience of the wicked world.

At three a.m. he decided to make himself some cocoa and stretch out on the sofa. The bed seemed a most undesirable resting place, for the moment. The cocoa-tin was empty, and there was not even enough milk left for a cup of tea. This small deprivation ignited his smouldering temper, as he recalled the rude remarks Mona had made about his living conditions. He had no need of her to make it bright and comfortable. He had no need of any girl. Driven by anger, he began to bring order from chaos. With fierce determination he stacked books neatly on any flat surface handy, shifted furniture, swept floors, dusted, folded away or hung up clothing, took the offending coils of rope from the corner of the bedroom to drop into the workshop below, changed the sheets on the bed, hung an old tablecloth left by the Ansons over the window bare of curtains, washed and stacked the chipped china Mona had criticized, then finally started putting the four drawers back into the shell of the desk.

They contained bottles of ink in various colours, old nibs, wall-charts with yellowed edges dating back to the Twenties, packets of drawing pins, blotting paper and any number of indiarubbers. The latter brought a faint twitch of amusement to Warren's tight mouth. Old Anson must have altered his designs a great deal to require such a supply of erasers. The last drawer did, in fact, contain several rolled drawings marked by dampness and age. Curious to see the work of the man who had designed *Diadem*, then tragically died before his brilliance was further consolidated, Warren unrolled the stiff sheets covered with precise lines, curves and figures. The series of plans was for a seaplane, but it was not the early, successful *Diadem*. Geoffrey Anson had scribbled the name *Solitaire* beneath the full sketch-plan of the graceful little aircraft, but as he studied the details, Warren experienced a growing sense of unease and disbelief. Was he holding in his hands the explanation of Donald Kirkland's reticence on the flying boat project? Was this the cause of so many curious aspects of the man's behaviour? Had he possibly stumbled upon the inconceivable truth about the heir to Kirkland Marine Aviation?

7

On the fourth day of the following week, Warren and Kit worked late in the design office. A heated argument with Donald in the middle of the afternoon had sent the man storming out to streak away up-river in *Columbus*. In Kit's view, the younger Kirkland was lovelorn due to his father's refusal to allow him enough time with his fiancée. Such deprivation led to bad tempers and lack of concentration on his work. The remedy, he opined, was to lock the pair in a bedroom for several days, from which Donald would emerge inspired, glad of the opportunity for occupation for the brain rather than the body. Warren had a vastly different theory, of which he was now so certain, it had changed his approach towards his employer's son to the extent of forcing the point which had sent Donald off in a furious mood.

After the events of Saturday, Warren had spent Sunday resolving several issues, the main one being what he should do with Geoffrey Anson's drawings of *Solitaire*. After much thought, he had decided to hand them over in very casual manner, saying nothing of his suspicions. They were more his friend's concern than his own. If his theory was proven, Kit was the right person to either speak out or let sleeping dogs lie. For his own part, pretending ignorance was the safest course. All the same, his secret knowledge made a deal of difference in his approach to his work on the flying boat design. Nothing had been said since Monday, when he had given

Kit the rolled drawings, so he guessed they must have been put aside without inspection.

Nothing had been said on the subject of Leone's visit to the boathouse, either, so Warren breathed a sigh of relief, thanking both his lucky stars *and* the Kirkland girl's silence. The affair had comprised the second issue he had thrashed out on Sunday. Knowing he would have no option but marriage if Mona should tell her father what he had done, he had waited all that day for Jack Cummings to come after his blood. When Monday also passed with no sign of the wrathful father, it seemed certain Mona had also kept her own counsel over Saturday's lovemaking. Strangely, Warren felt a sense of anti-climax almost amounting to disappointment.

After working on a knotty engineering problem until they had solved it, Warren and Kit returned on the boat, chilled and hungry. His friend dropped Warren off and headed back to the Kirkland jetty, saying he intended to eat a hearty dinner in his quarters whilst checking through the itinerary for his forthcoming tour, then write some overdue answers to letters. Warren watched Kit take the boat back down the inlet, envying him the occupation of letter-writing. It was something he, him-self, never did because he knew no one. Turning into the boathouse on this July evening of overcast skies which were bringing darkness too early, he felt loneliness more strongly than he had ever done.

Since Mona's visit the place seemed to accuse him; fill him with doubts and a peculiar sensation of incomplete-ness. She had painted a bright picture for him, and he had turned it to face the wall. The longing to turn it back, to enjoy its warmth and colour, was growing daily stronger. Their union had been so perfectly attuned, so stimulating, he was now sexually restless. Sleep had become elusive; his body longed for further excitement. He could have all she had offered – someone to love and care for him, a clean, comfortable home, companionship and her eager limbs to satisfy the hunger she had aroused in him. All he had to do was ride into Sheenmouth to buy a diamond ring, then set a date for the wedding. Why not do it, he urged himself. He missed her, he wanted her. They could build a very happy life here together, and she would have the children and dogs to keep her occupied and fulfilled whilst he built his career. With a surge of eagerness he decided he did have a letter to write, after all. He would ask her to meet him in Sheenmouth on Saturday to choose a ring, and then to plan a most important date.

There was an envelope lying on the workbench, and he instantly imagined it to contain a letter from Mona. Instead, it was a summons to meet Sir Hector on a highly urgent matter. The emphasis on immediacy was so strong it left no margin for misunderstanding. Yet it was less a sense of obedience than a desire to have the interview over so that he could write to Mona, which led Warren to wash his face, comb his unruly hair, and set out right away, pushing his motorbike through the copse and on to the muddy track leading to the Magnum Pomeroy road.

It was the first time he had been inside Sheenmouth Abbey since causing a stir with his trumpet concert. It looked vastly different tonight. The gaiety, the noise, the Grecian grottoes were gone. The false floors and pseudo-grass had been loaded into lorries and taken back to the warehouses. The vast hall tonight seemed gloomy, almost oppressive. His footsteps echoed on stone slabs, as he crossed to the branched staircase rising to corridors lit by sconces to brighten the dimness. Sir Hector's business suite lay on the third floor, he had been told by the servant – a sour-faced individual whose expression made no secret of his opinion of anyone who dared to visit the owner of the Abbey dressed in a thick woolly jacket, and grey flannels as spattered with mud as his scuffed brown brogues.

Warren was slightly apprehensive as he made his way through the silent building, following the directions he had been given. He hoped most fervently that he would not come face to face with Leone. Such an encounter would be awkward, in the extreme. He also hoped he was not about to be told off for daring to cross swords with the senior designer after working for Kirkland's only a month. Perhaps Sir Hector was about to challenge him to explain why he had not yet produced specimen sketches for the passenger liner with wings he had boasted of designing. In either case, a reply would be difficult. His employer ruled both home and business with inflexibility. Warren had no illusions. His good fortune could end as abruptly as it had begun. Kit had advised him to walk the tightrope with extreme care, performing tricks only when they had been first approved by the ringmaster. He had heeded this warning, and was prepared to be even meeker than before in order to hold on to what he had, if it was in jeopardy. All the same, what he had learned four nights ago had prompted him to challenge Donald today with that knowledge to support his boldness. Unfortunately, he dared not offer it to Sir Hector as an excuse, because the man believed his son unrivalled in the field of aircraft design. If and when the storm broke, Warren determined to feign ignorance. His future had been too precarious in the past for him to risk losing its present security. He would have to tackle this mysterious interview by using his wits and offering up a few prayers.

If the remainder of Sheenmouth Abbey had been restored and decorated in the style of its original religious purpose, Sir Hector's business suite contained every modern item found in thriving company offices. The man Warren had dubbed 'the stuffed shirt' admitted him on his knock. Without a smile or word, Maitland Jarvis then quietly entered an inner sanctum to emerge again and beckon the visitor forward. Passing through a large carpeted room containing three desks with typewriters, telephones and card-files, two of which were still occupied by male secretaries working like robots, Warren entered Sir Hector's office. On the day he had been interviewed and engaged, the meeting had taken place in the grounds, beside the ruined chapel. It had seemed, to Warren, to be a very casual conversation, conducted in between Sir Hector's comments to the workmen restoring the old building. Tonight's interview was very evidently to be vastly different.

The owner of Kirkland Marine Aviation sat behind a desk laden with files, a dictaphone, four telephones in varying colours, cigar box, gold and tourmaline lighter, and a copy of *Who's Who*. He looked a formidable figure in a plum-coloured smoking jacket and heavy horn rimmed spectacles but, contrary to Warren's expectation of being kept standing while he deliberately studied some report – a favourite practice designed to turn the culprit's legs to rubber before the actual reprimand – Sir Hector watched his entry and attacked immediately. The shot came from an entirely unexpected quarter.

'Read this!' Warren was commanded, being handed a sheet of paper.

He took it with a slight frown, and read the message stamped on it in printer's ink.

DO YOU KNOW WHAT YOUR DAUGHTER GETS UP TO IN THE OLD BOATHOUSE? SHE IS A TART. ASK YOUR NEW DESIGNER WHAT GOES ON BEHIND YOUR BACK BETWEEN THEM AT WEEKENDS.

It came as a total shock, and it was some moments before he could even accept that it had happened. He read the words again and again in disbelief that Mona could have done this to him. It could not be the work of her father; Jack Cummings would have wreaked a different form of vengeance than this. Swallowing hard, he realized then just how much Mona had loved him, and how very deeply he had hurt her. He also realized that she was irrevocably lost to him.

'If the sender is a man, I want his name from you because he is plainly a crank who covets my daughter.

194

If some silly venomous bitch is behind it, I want you off my property tonight. That boathouse is no more use to me than to anyone else. The bloody thing will be pulled down, and you can go to hell!'

Warren tried to think, but the shock of such betrayal from a girl as sweet and loving as Mona still robbed him of his senses.

'I have not insulted my daughter by telling her of this, but you had better have an explanation for this outrage, or you'll pay dearly, I swear. There'll be no scandal attached to any member of my family.' Sir Hector rose in the full flush of his anger. 'You'd better say something very soon or I'm liable to choke the words out of you.'

'It's a lie, naturally,' Warren blurted out. 'Miss Kirkland has never visited me in the boathouse. We met on the night of the world record attempt, when I brought her home on my motorcycle. We have not even spoken to each other since then.' (That was true enough, since he had not answered her shocked comments last Saturday.) 'I'm as appalled and furious over this as you are, sir,' he continued, gradually regaining his composure at the thought of a scandal which could very possibly be attached to this family. If that ever came out, his position at Kirkland's would be highly unenviable.

'I admit that I did receive a surprise visit last Saturday from the girl who works in the office of the *Sheenmouth Clarion*. We know each other quite well because of my frequent visits to insert ads, or to answer vacancies for jobs during the months that I was looking for work.' Talking fast to avoid interruptions from the violently angry man, he went on, 'Miss Cummings had accepted notice of a vacancy at the tractor factory, and went to my former lodgings to tell me of it before the *Clarion* was issued this week. The landlady gave her my new whereabouts so, as she had to visit someone in Forton, she decided to come on to the boathouse.' He forced a half-smile. 'I thought it frightfully good of her, especially as her good intention came too late. She was unaware,

195

of course, that I was now employed by you. I felt a bit ashamed that I hadn't bothered to drop in and tell her, after her past kindness, but I've been so busy settling in and putting in evening work on the project, it had gone from my mind.'

His grim-faced employer said, 'That might explain a girl at the boathouse, but what has it to do with this obscene message?'

Warren took a deep breath and offered the first of the prayers. 'A great many men in this area are out of work and desperate, as you know, so isn't it possible that the note could be from someone who passed along the river on Saturday, saw me talking to Miss Cummings, and believed he had the means to vent his resentment and envy of my luck in being employed by Kirkland's? I know it's despicable, but a hungry family and loss of pride make men do insane things. If I knew who he was, I'd deal with him myself, sir.'

Struggling on despite the sense of shock and guilt multiplying with every minute, he ended on a note of remorse. 'I'm extremely sorry that you have been subjected to receipt of such a letter, Sir Hector, and I can only give you my word that Miss Kirkland always has and always will be treated with my deepest respect.'

There was no more than a moment of silence before his employer made a typically swift decision. 'I believe you, lad. The shock you had on reading that filth was obviously genuine. The matter is now closed, but I'll say one thing to you before we get on to business matters. My daughter is a minor. She will be returning to school in Switzerland in September. I'm well aware that she is growing very lovely, and has a provocative personality, but her name is Kirkland. That puts her out of your league – now and at any time in the future. Do I make myself clear?'

'Perfectly, sir,' Warren murmured, hardly believing he had come out of the situation so easily. Either his prayer had been very promptly answered, or Sir Hector wanted his flying boat more desperately than he had imagined.

'One more thing. It is not through *luck* that you are working for Kirkland's. I want a passenger liner with wings, and you have sworn to give me one.' He sat down again. 'Now, what was all the fuss about this afternoon?'

With the confidence of sound engineering knowledge, plus recognition of his chance to put forward his findings without Donald's damping influence, Warren launched into an enthusiastic account of his work with Kit after Donald had left the office, and also of the sketches and calculations he had been doing in the evenings at the boathouse. When he left Sheenmouth Abbey several hours later, it was with Sir Hector's praise ringing in his ears, and a very tasty supper inside him. Still, as he drove his motorbike along the dark lanes, his sense of wellbeing was not quite strong enough to cover the growing distress over Mona's act of vengeance. She had succeeded no better in her attempt to destroy him, than in winning him.

Kit put aside the neatly typed itinerary of his imminent tour with a sense of excitement. Whatever else Maitland was, there was no doubt of his thoroughness and efficiency. Nothing had been left to chance. The times of his flights coincided with tides and were augmented with alternative dates in case of bad weather or mechanical problems. Hotel bookings allowed two days at either end of the proposed stay, for the same reasons. In each case, a suite had been reserved so that he could entertain privately those with business interests in *Aphrodite*, or in the new flying boat under development. Where he had been invited to stay as a personal guest, Maitland had entered the fact in red, with a lengthy note concerning the background of the prospective hosts, a brief description of the house, and an account of the style of living to be found there. Comments like *Fairly formal* or *Rigid etiquette*, and even *Dead, but they won't lie down*, which betrayed a sense of humour one would not suspect of a man who rarely smiled.

It was to be a long, hectic tour covering Belgium, Holland, Italy, Germany, Egypt, Africa, Ceylon, Singapore and Australia. Kit knew it would demand a great many flying hours, yet he saw them as the best part of the six-month trip. In the air, he was totally fulfilled. On the ground, he was obliged to act a charade. Even in bed, he never forgot that he must not offend the wrong people. Getting away on this tour would be a godsend in that very respect, because Leone was pursuing her misguided path where he was concerned, despite his efforts to disillusion her. He bitterly regretted that kiss in the chapel, but could not make her accept that it had been a result of the mood of the moment. He liked her well enough; she had certainly blossomed since that evening. However, she was endangering them both by her adolescent infatuation. Donald must surely be aware of it; Stephanie most certainly was, and delighted in taunting him over it. He would be glad to put distance between himself and her, too. They had been lovers on numerous occasions, even after Donald's courtship had begun, but she seemed to think the affair could continue now, with Donald's expensive solitaire on her finger and a wedding being planned. He was finding it difficult to hold her at arm's length, because she knew far too well how best to arouse him. She had even been hinting that a word in Sir Hector's ear about his daughter's imminent deflowerment by an ungrateful protégé would cause an interesting diversion. He did not really believe she would carry out her subtle threat, but he did wonder how long it would be before Maitland felt obliged to ensure that Sir Hector was made aware of Leone's youthful adoration. Woe betide them both, if and when he did. Of what use would it be for Kit to deny it, when Leone would almost certainly reveal that he had treated her to very adult passion on the night of his world success?

All in all, Kit was counting the days to his departure,

even though he was disappointed in the lack of progress on the flying boat project. The tour had been planned as an advance promotion for the new machine, in addition to a sales bid for the standard *Aphrodite* seaplane. He had hoped to have some idea of the scale of the proposed machine before setting off. As it was, details would have to be relayed to him en route. Like Warren, he was annoyed by Donald's stubborn attitude against working as one of a team, although he had already experienced the man's stonewalling tactics over modifications to *Aphrodite* and had learned to overcome them by bringing up the subject in Sir Hector's presence. Kit had advised Warren to do the same, or no progress at all would be made whilst he was away.

Finishing the last of his letters, Kit reflected on the friendship between himself and the young designer, which had sprung up so swiftly. Perhaps it had been due to the fact that he had sensed a similarity in their lives; that there, but for the grace of Hector Kirkland, would he have been in that attic room in Sheenmouth, lonely and struggling for recognition. Thank God for that meeting! Warren showed every sign of vindicating his own belief in his ability. Once Donald came round, they would surely form the most amazing and successful team.

Sealing the final envelope, Kit put his letters on the tray for collection by Coombes when he came to wake him in the morning. He was thinking of turning in, when he spotted the two rolls of drawings Warren said he had discovered in a drawer of the old desk at the boathouse. Everything about that place held black memories for Kit. He had not even gone down there with Warren to inspect the state it was in; simply given the other man the key and told him he was welcome to the place if he thought it habitable. Picking up the rolls of paper, he was tempted to stuff them in the hearth and put a match to them. Any reminder of his father was deeply disturbing . . . and yet he could not somehow

199

bring himself to destroy his work, which was the only gold among the dross. Against every inclination, he pulled free the tapes confining the broad sheets, and spread them out on his desk.

The series of plans and detail sketches were for a seaplane named *Solitaire*. Kit frowned. He had heard nothing of the model, so it must be one abandoned on the drawing board. With professional interest, he studied the lines and dimensions to see if he could figure out why the project had been dropped. One by one, he absorbed every detail of the drawings and calculations made in his father's shaky hand. Then, almost like an automaton, he reached for the second roll and searched every line on the sheets contained in it. The room turned cold; his body slowly grew icy. His mind tried to shy from the hideous truth, but it shot round to confront him on all sides. Here in his hands, he finally had the reason for Sir Hector Kirkland's great generosity in taking him in on that shattering day three years ago!

He stood like a pillar of ice as those memories he had buried so deep raced to the surface. Geoffrey Anson, a wonderful, laughing man with whom a small boy could share so much fun and all his youthful secrets, had suddenly become famous. His picture had been in all the papers alongside the magic machine called *Diadem*, which he had designed and which had flown at speeds faster than those during the spectacular Schneider Trophy Race. The son of such a man had almost burst with pride and reflected glory: he had been the envy of boys at his school, and the headmaster had even made an announcement during morning assembly concerning Mr Anson's wonderful contribution to the nation's advance in the field of aviation. Fame had brought its drawbacks. A new grand house in the best part of East Sheenmouth; a better school for Master Anson. Other boys at the new school had important fathers, so some of the glory faded. During the holidays, his old friends no longer wanted him. *Toffee-nose*, the girls had called him. The boys had shouted things like *clever-arse* or *piddle-pants* as he had passed in his long trousers and smart blazer. Worst of all, the paternal companion, the sharer of masculine delights and adventures, was seldom at home.

Puberty had brought awareness of deeper emotions between people, and also a curious shyness of the mother who still tried to pet or kiss him. Although the only two in the house for most of the time, they gradually drew further apart. Whenever Father did put in an appearance, the house rang with quarrelling voices. *But you've got everything you ever wanted now . . . I haven't got you . . . You never wanted me before . . . I do now . . . Everything's changed . . . I'll say it has! . . . I'm damned if I know what you do want. First you moan that we can never afford anything, now we can you're still not happy . . . You're never here . . . If you weren't always nagging, perhaps I would be . . . You've got some other woman . . . No, Daisy, I'm too fond of you . . . Tell it to the Marines!*

The implication of the Royal Marines had been a total mystery to him until a schoolfellow had explained the meaning of the phrase indicating absolute disbelief. He had not shared it: his father could never be seeing another woman. That was a sin, surely. Later on, the quarrelling had altered course after several ornaments and items of furniture had vanished.

I had to pawn them. The bank wouldn't let me have any money and the boy has to eat . . . You don't give a damn about the boy. That money's gone on your back, to impress some man . . . It's certainly not to impress you, you wastrel . . . I'm trying to win back all I lost . . . You won't, and you'll never give it up, will you? Doesn't it bother you that you'll put me and your boy out on the street? . . . He's your boy, too . . . He's never been my boy. To him, you're God Almighty, and I'm just some incestuous bitch anxious to handle his privates . . . My God, you've grown common since you started going around with that pimply painter. Oh yes, I know all about that! . . . From your drunken pals at

201

the Smugglers Inn, I suppose. They'll say anything all the time you're paying for the drinks.

So it had continued. He had lain in bed discovering the real people he had always known simply as Mum and Dad. He had come home one day to find there was only Dad. Mum had gone away with the pimply painter, and the house had been sold. They had moved into a broken-down cottage in the poorer part of East Sheenmouth, and he had been told he was to go back to his old school after Christmas. The two terms leading to the long summer holidays had been purgatory. No one had dared to actually fight him, because he had been boxing champion at the other school, but children can be more cruel with their tongues than their fists. He had shed shameful tears in his room on many occasions. All the girls had liked him a lot, but he had spurned the company of all but one, for fear of being called a sissy for being with girls all the time. May had been irresistible, however. He had grown really keen on her, and when several boys taunted her for going around with him, he had defended her with his fists. After that, he was condemned for being the worst two things a schoolboy could be – a swot and a bully.

Fortunately, a perceptive teacher had recognized his ability and arranged for him to enter for a late scholarship. He had won a place at a grammar school in Axminster but, on hearing the news, his father had told him he could not attend because the train fare was too expensive. Cleaning out the stables and grooming the seaside donkeys throughout the winter had earned him enough to buy a second-hand bicycle, which had given him the means to cover the six miles to Axminster and back each day. During those two years at the grammar school, they moved house three times, until they rented just two rooms in a boarding house near the sands, and far too close to the Smugglers Inn. He had watched his father's gradual degeneration helplessly. The love and admiration had turned first to pity, then to disgust that a man with such capacity for brilliance could throw the gift away. Any lingering remnant of gentler feeling was destroyed when his hard-earned savings from the donkey job, which would have enabled him to attend an engineering college in Exeter, had been taken by his father and lost on a desperate wager. He could stand no more, and had packed his bag during his father's absence one evening. On the point of leaving, some fishermen had arrived with the man they had dragged from the sea, half-drowned and as drunk as a lord. Kit had not dared to threaten to leave again.

They had been ejected from the boarding house after another drunken scene and, to his everlasting shame, had been forced to sleep in the donkey stables for a week. Then, miraculously, Sir Hector Kirkland had offered them the use of the old boathouse and life had begun to look up again. The place was well isolated, and had a workshop where his father could occupy himself usefully. By accepting a job as a greaser at Kirkland's, where some of his workfellows taunted him on his past history and made his days very miserable, Kit had been able to afford to pay for a correspondence course in engineering. He and his father tolerated each other, no more, but both welcomed the calmer period. Geoffrey Anson had begun working on something at weekends and evenings, hinting that it would show everyone he was not done for yet. He had also hinted that his friend, Sir Hector, had given him a good tip which would make his fortune before long.

They certainly had more money, and their living standard improved dramatically. He had met up with May again, and they began going out together in a serious way. Then, he had returned from one exhilarating Saturday date with her to find his father had been drinking very heavily, and was extremely abusive. The resulting quarrel had been violent, with many home truths hurled in both directions. When his father had run amok and started smashing the china, he had not hesitated to land a well-placed punch on the older man's jaw to knock him out cold. The story had leaked out somehow, and the men in the machine shop had ostracized him. By then, he had been past caring what anyone thought so when, a few weeks later, he had been met at the door of the workshop by Sir Hector as he arrived late after oversleeping, the expectation of being given the sack was almost a welcome one.

Told of his father's death in a gruesome accident whilst blind drunk, he had been stunned by the violent end of a wasted life. There had been little sense of personal grief for a man who had lost his ability to care for others, and had consequently crushed the love he had been offered beneath the weight of his selfishness and greed. Even so, the drastic event had robbed Kit temporarily of the power to come to terms with his uncertain future, and it had been in a dazed state that he had allowed himself to be controlled by the man who had taken charge of the situation so smoothly. The astonishing sequence of events that had led to him being installed at Sheenmouth Abbey had left him still in that dazed state. Later, they had inspired a dog-like sense of gratitude for every scrap thrown his way by his master.

The stray mongrel, Leone had called him, and it was an apt description for the nineteen-year-old who had been taken in to run with the pedigree hounds. He had kept pace with them, even though he had never been allowed to forget his mongrel roots, and finally overtaken them on June tenth this year. He had never really under-stood why the chance had been offered him, and the answer had been in the old boathouse for the past three years. It might have remained there for ever, if Leone had not seized a young man on a motorcycle and obliged him to bring her home.

So many things now made sense – sickening, humiliat-ing sense. A great cry of protest began to build inside him; a surge of deep belated grief for a man he had once been so inordinately proud of. A strange rattling noise began, and he realized the papers he held were shaking violently. His body was rigid although his hands moved convulsively, and he had to release tension with a long sigh of distress. Only then did anger begin; a brand of anger which made any other he had felt mild by comparison. It was not the hot, impetuous anger created by rising temper, but the ice-cold deadly variety born of uncontainable rage. It drove him from his room to seek and destroy.

It was almost as if it had all been planned to happen on that particular evening. After searching every likely place, Kit found both his victims in the library where he had stood three years before whilst one had explained to the other that he was to be taken in, given some decent clothes, and polished up to meet Kirkland standards. Father and son turned in astonishment from what was plainly an unhappy discussion.

'I didn't hear your knock,' snapped Sir Hector.

For a moment or two, Kit truly believed he would physically assault the man. However, he had words with which to batter them both near to annihilation. They tumbled out in icy, precise sentences.

'For three years, I've lived here ostensibly as one of this family. You've been at great pains to impress everyone with your great generosity to the son of a dead friend and colleague. No one knows how I was made to earn my place here, which was certainly never as one of the family. I took all your careless insults without retaliating. I obeyed your cool commands, I silently accepted your offhand criticisms of what I wore or how I behaved, I bore the insufferable public references to my private affairs with women. For three years, I allowed myself to be treated by you both as a charity case who must be grateful for every day you chose to allow me to remain in your hallowed midst. I put aside my pride and self-esteem, because I had the opportunity to redeem the name of Anson, which had earned such disgust and derision over the years. Probably, not one person watching me break the speed record that day knew that I was as concerned with that as with gaining personal glory.'

Sir Hector, in plum-coloured velvet jacket, gave him a steely look. 'Now you've made two people aware of it, so get out. We're discussing a family matter.'

Kit took a step towards the two figures standing before shelves lined with valuable antique books, which were never read. 'You bastards! You despicable cheating bastards!' His hands holding the rolled plans were shaking again. 'For three years you've made me lick your boots for fear of being sent away as suddenly as I arrived, and all the time you've been hiding your abominable secret from the world. My God, no wonder you kept me here on a chain. I did the refinements on *Aphrodite*. I suggested the modifications, sought out her weaknesses. It was my advice handed to Rolls-Royce when they asked for a revised stress factor.' Turning his attention to Donald, he cried, 'You loathsome lying tyke! All you are is a very standard engineer who happens to know a nut from a bolt. You couldn't design a toy soldier, much less a seaplane conceived by one of the most talented men this country has ever known.' He took another step forward, seizing Donald by the lapels of his smart jacket. 'I'll force you to confess, even if I have to choke the truth from you.'

Struggling from Kit's hold, the pale-faced Donald moved back fast.

In disgust, Kit threw the rolled plans at their feet, saying in a voice grown husky, 'There are the drawings for a machine my father named *Solitaire*. You stole the design, changed the name to *Aphrodite*, and claimed worldwide credit for it.' Concentrating on Sir Hector, he continued. 'Your son hasn't the guts to do such a thing of his own accord, so it's obvious the damnable crime was hatched by you. Geoffrey Anson was a brilliant man. He was also a drunkard and a gambler, but you robbed him of his right to redress in the eyes of the

206

world. I'll never forgive you, and I'll make you pay for your contemptuous pretence of deep friendship when he was killed, in that same workshop which built his last and most triumphant machine. When I've finished with you both, the whole world will know what you've done.'

Sir Hector smiled – actually smiled. 'Spoken like a true nobody! You burst in here with the manners of a mongrel, throw some rolls of paper at my son's feet, and create a histrionic scene crying vengeance. I'll accept that you've inherited your father's weakness for alcohol, and overlook it just this once. Now get out!'

'Father, he knows,' cried Donald, who looked ashen. 'Don't you realize, *he knows?*'

'Knows what?' barked his father.

'He's not a fool!'

'He's more than a fool, he's a bloody imbecile.' Swinging back to face Kit, Sir Hector brought into action the personality which had gained him all he had coveted. 'Without me, you'd now be following in your father's footsteps, living in some cheap room, up to the hilt in debt due to your weakness for women, and despised by the entire neighbourhood. You're in bondage to me, and don't you ever forget it! You'll pick up that paper you've thrown on the floor and tear each sheet into pieces in front of us, before carrying it over to the fireplace and putting a match to it. Then, you'll apologize separately to me and to my son for your insufferable behaviour, before expressing your humble gratitude for all you've been given during the past three years.'

Kit looked back at him with murder in his heart. 'Go to hell!'

Sir Hector smiled again. 'Pack your bag and leave within the hour. Hell is where *you'll* be heading, boy.'

'I'll take you both with me.' He bent to pick up the plans. 'When the news of this outrage breaks, you'll be finished.'

'News? What news? Stick your head under the tap and sober up, for God's sake. Living here for three years has given you delusions of grandeur. You're the whelp of a drunken sot, and everyone knows it. You were brought here as a surly, orphaned ruffian with dirty fingernails and cheap underpants. Of course you licked boots: it brought you what you wanted, didn't it? Christ Almighty, in three years you've advanced from being a greaser in my workshops who slept with the Sheenmouth donkeys, to becoming the holder of the world air speed record, living in a suite of rooms in this house and preparing for a tour of half the world as the conquering hero. What more do you bloody well want, you ungrateful brute? I'll give you a choice. You can tear up those drawings and set them alight, then apologize for being a worthless, insolent bastard, and I'll allow you to retain your quarters here in addition to making this tour, as planned. Alternatively, you can leave these premises within the next sixty minutes or risk being physically ejected by my son and Maitland at the end of that period. You'll have no money. I shall ensure that no one will be willing to employ you. The newspapers will be told of your deplorable alcoholism, worsened by the fame and adulation after breaking the speed record, which now makes you a danger in any aircraft. The claim will be backed by a full unexpurgated account of your parentage and unsavoury background, which will explain your eventual reversion to type. *You'll* be finished, not us.'

Kit had been too outraged and grieved to think deeply of the full consequences of his action. He was still too emotional to care. 'You're not God, although you tend to think you are,' he retaliated, gripping the rolled plans so hard they had grown flat. 'I believe you could do all that to most people, but I have built a reputation in the world of aviation which would survive your most damning accusations against me. Jim Mollison really is a drunkard, and a greater womanizer than I am, but he is still lauded for his aerial feats. I'll leave here well within the hour, I assure you, and the newspapers will have a story from me, also. It'll make taller headlines than the one you have in mind.'

A sneer touched the other man's mouth. 'Very, very few people are in a position to hurt me, and a snivelling little runt like you would be kicking his own arse to attempt it.'

'Perhaps . . . but I can hurt Donald so much it will be the end of him. I've put his lack of cooperation down to resentment and the same insufferable conceit evident in anyone named Kirkland. Now I know the truth. How long do you think it'll be before Warren Grant sees through his pathetic attempts to hide the fact that he hardly knows more than the basics of design?'

'You'd back your word against mine? Laughable!'

'Your word – even your wealth and influence – can't put into your son what you find unable to accept that he lacks,' Kit told him, with cutting clarity. 'Donald is a dud, a failure. Your son is the biggest setback of your life. He's weak, has little ambition, and is no more than a mediocre engineer. When you die, all you've achieved with greedy, ruthless determination will collapse, because your heir won't give a damn about holding on to it. Accrediting him with my father's brilliance is evidence of your Achilles heel, and if it's now your plan to hold Warren "in bondage" by giving him a place in your charmed circle, with the intention of allowing him to design a flying boat you will claim as your son's brainchild, I shall go all out to destroy any hope of it. *That* is well within the power of a surly orphaned ruffian with dirty fingernails, because Warren is a friend of mine and Donald is already terrified. Just look at him! Is *he* the reason for criminal theft of another man's genius? You'd do better to make Leone your heir. She's honest, daring, perceptive, and full of Kirkland pride. What's more, she's a real girl, not a man full of feminine weakness.'

Before he knew it, Sir Hector had stepped forward and struck him hard across the face two or three times. Kit's fists bunched instinctively, but he was holding the plans his father had drawn; the evidence of a crime no one would believe. Words were his best weapons.

'Your Achilles heel, as I said just now,' he rasped. 'I'll accept that I'm no match for Hector Kirkland, but your son will destroy himself without help from me. It's too late for my father to receive recognition for his superb design, but you allowed me to fly it in a bid to break the world record without knowing the truth. A son making aviation history in a machine created by his father must constitute another world record, apart from being a superlative achievement for the Anson family. That's the crime I'll never forgive – *never!*' His voice threatened to break under the stress of his grief. 'You'll probably do your damndest to make things impossible for me in this country, but even Hector Kirkland can't bribe the whole world. My reputation is such that any number of foreign companies will be delighted to persuade me to work for them. While I'm deciding which offer to accept, I'll need finances. I'll sell you the Anson *Solitaire* for ten thousand pounds,' he said, holding out the two rolls of drawings. 'It will let Donald off the hook on that one, at least, until he puts the rope around his own neck over this flying boat Warren will be expected to design for him.'

'Give it to him,' Donald told his father, in shaky tones. 'Pay him off – give him anything he wants to keep quiet. Then toss him out on his ear.'

Sir Hector ignored his son while he looked Kit over with his habitual scrutiny, as if checking that he was clean, presentable and with his trousers properly buttoned up.

'I wondered how long it would be before you got to the root of the matter. All that filial nobility and outrage didn't deceive me for an instant, you spineless mongrel. So it's now blackmail, is it?' His expression hardened further. 'All I need do is ring this bell, and I can have Maitland here to help us hold you, douse you in spirits, then throw you out into the Sheen to be picked up by a passing boat, like your father once was. If you're not on your way to pack by the time I've counted ten, that's exactly what will happen. *GET OUT!*'

Kit left the library on the count of five. In the grip of that brand of fury which will not heed common sense, he raced up the stairs to his rooms, threw into a bag his books, shabby case of drawing instruments, the family photograph album, and the silver-framed picture of *Diadem*, then snatched up the keys to his car. It was then that he made the greatest mistake of his life. Going up to the shadowed floor where the offices were situated, he let himself into the deserted suite, switched off the theft device, and opened the safe hidden beneath a stone slab. Taking several thick wads of five-pound notes to stuff into the bag with his few possessions, he closed the safe again and re-set the alarm before leaving the office and locking the door behind him. Still with the madness on him, he descended the fire escape and hurried down the path around the north wing of the Abbey, to the garages. There he encountered a tawny-haired girl in a ruby velvet evening coat over a long dress of shimmering silver beads, who was climbing from a dark-green coupé rather unsteadily.

'Well, well, well,' she mumbled, her eyes very bright in the light cast by sconces inside the extensive garage. 'Where are you going to at this time of night, lover boy?'

Throwing the bag into his car, Kit climbed over the small door to flop into the driving seat, and started the engine with a roar. Stephanie came alongside to drape herself over the windscreen, covering his hands with her own as they gripped the wheel. The low-cut dress revealed that her breasts were naked beneath it, and there was the giveaway aroma of gin on her breath as it fanned his face at her soft laugh.

'This damned monastery is too cloistered for my taste,' she confessed. 'I've been to Torquay for some fun, but they're all in bathchairs there. C'mon Kit, let's have some *real* fun and excitement. I'm so sexually frustrated,

211

I swear I'll explode if someone doesn't take me to bed soon.' She leaned closer so that her breasts hung, full, rounded and luscious, tipped with rigid nipples, within reach of his mouth. Lowering her voice to a husky whisper, she pleaded with him. 'C'mon Kit, show me what a real man can do with a woman as hungry as I am. Donald has to get permission first, and Daddy obviously hasn't told him what your daddy told you, darling. C'mon Kit, let's set each other alight, like we used to.'

He leaned across to throw open the other door. 'Get in,' he invited. 'I'll set you so well alight, they'll see the glow for miles around.'

The car raced away from Sheenmouth Abbey and on to the Magnum Pomeroy road, but he turned in the other direction which led to the river and the collection of villages alongside the Sheen, which were served by ferries calling four times daily. Soon, they were running beside the dark shimmer of the river as he stepped on the pedal and threw the car around the bends in the unlit road, to the delight of his passenger.

'You're the only person in that place who isn't a monk,' she gurgled. 'God, it's wonderful to be with a man who doesn't give a damn; a flesh and blood *male*.' Her hand came up to fondle his hair, then slid down to his ear and neck. Next minute, she was nuzzling his throat as her fingers busily unbuttoned the front of his shirt in her eagerness for him.

The night breeze buffeted him as the madness possessing his mind found partial relief in action. He was out to break the speed record in a machine his father had designed. The Ansons would show the stuff they were really made of now. He would travel through the air faster than any man in the world. The girl beside him began to laugh exultantly as she caressed his bared chest.

'This is crazy, darling. That's what I find so exciting about men like you. While you'll do anything to be in the limelight and stay there, beneath that aura you're so divinely *earthy*.'

He hardly heard her. He was reaching full throttle now. The cockpit was growing overheated; the machine was starting to shake with the stress of the forward thrust. This was his greatest moment. His hands could hardly hold her steady as he saw the dark water flying past below him, yet he knew he had done it. Once more, he felt that incomparable sense of total fulfilment, and tears formed on his lashes as the immense emotion of the achievement overwhelmed him. Diving, he took *Aphrodite* in to land on the shimmery surface of the water. Then there was a terrible sound of screaming in his ears. It was followed by complete silence, and darkness blacker than any he had before known.

Leone awoke that morning with a sense of foreboding. Since her visit to the old boathouse last Saturday, she had not been sleeping well. The night-time longings she had experienced since puberty, had grown so strong, dreams and fantasies had haunted her hours of darkness. The memory of that naked pair facing each other in the aftermath of what had plainly been a complete sexual union on that tumbled bed, excited and disturbed her to the point of wanting to relive it. She deeply envied the girl her knowledge of life; she yearned to see again the vital masculinity usually hidden. Thoughts, fantasies and rioting imagination jumbled together until she was sighing with the pain of unfulfilment, born of her brief passion with Kit in the ruined chapel. The love she had discovered on that momentous day had comprised deep admiration for his courage and daring, strong physical attraction, and the wish to protect and console him. All that had now suddenly been swept aside by overwhelming sexual desire for him. Shades of loving, the gentler brand of tenderness and understanding, were swamped by her violent yearning for something her woman's body demanded but her schoolgirl's mind did not yet totally understand.

Tossing restlessly in her bed, tormented by recollections of that scene, Kit replaced Warren and she became that unknown red-haired girl. She was obsessed by the longing to witness Kit's nakedness, to experience the full depths of exploration by him in that same boathouse. In her wilder fantasies, it happened before the eyes of that other pair, so that they would know she also possessed the secret of full sexual union. In others, her lover was Warren, who passionately possessed her on that tumbled bed while Kit stood by naked, looking on. During those five days and nights, she had grown feverish to the point of desperation, because Kit had either stayed late at the office down-river, or remained in his locked room occupied with plans for his tour. Those few occasions on which she had been in his company had only served to increase her fever for him. Knowing that he would be setting off within a few weeks, and would be away for six months or more, Leone decided that she must satisfy her yearning soon or go mad.

Last night, she had been able to hold back no longer. Slipping from her bed at two a.m. she had peeled off her nightgown and wrapped a thin robe about her trembling body before making her way to the bell tower, smothered in French perfume and wearing a great deal of bright lipstick. The door had been unlocked, so that Coombes could enter to wake the occupant in the morning, so she had sidled in to grope her way across the dark lower room to the staircase leading to Kit's bedroom. By then, she had been so excited, her legs were weak and desire had become an unbearable pain in the pit of her stomach.

Her intention of waking him, then dropping the robe to reveal herself fully to him for the first time, had been thwarted. His bed had been empty, still neatly turned back with pyjamas laid out ready for him. It had been a physical blow; an unacceptable setback. Her plans had allowed for anything but his absence. With a soft moan, she had sunk on to the bed to clutch his pyjamas in an attempt to ease the drive for sublimation. So great was

214

the agony of his involuntary rejection, tears had run down her cheeks to soak into the sheets which had covered the body other women had known yet she was denied. Only when all the tears had been shed and her limbs had felt chilled and leaden, had she returned to her room exhausted and suffering from violent jealousy of the woman he must have been with at that moment. Emotion of any intensity had never bothered her in her sixteen years, until then. The anguish of caring so deeply almost frightened her.

This morning, overtones of the previous night's events put heaviness in her heart. Perhaps loneliness had been more bearable than love. Even so, she made her way down to the pool, where she had so often been certain of encountering Kit taking his morning swim. Of late, Stephanie had also been there, no doubt to admire the man she considered a 'magnificent specimen when stripped to the bare essentials'. The blue water lay disturbed by no more than the slight breeze. The gilded loungers and the changing cubicles were deserted. A strangely ominous silence seemed to hang in the air.

With her heart heavier than ever, Leone wandered back indoors knowing her quarry always breakfasted in his room. The door was sure to be locked, and he would be feeling highly pleased with himself this morning, she thought bitterly. As she crossed the hall her bleak thoughts were interrupted by an imperative call from her father, who stood in the doorway of the octagonal room with Donald. She crossed to them listlessly, wishing she had used the side door instead. They looked very straight-faced. Crossing swords on the wedding plans again, she supposed. Marriage, the union of a happy couple, was the last thing she wished to discuss, at the moment.

'You'll have to know this,' her father began, without preamble, 'so there's no time like the present. I'm afraid we've been very badly let down and deceived by the orphan I took in and treated like a son.'

Leone gazed back at him, whilst trying to make sense of what he was saying. He could only be talking about Kit. That sense of foreboding increased.

'His father was a drunkard and a gambler; he is a drunkard and womanizer. Gaming tables and women are equally expensive so I wasn't surprised when he was soon as deeply in debt as his father always was. There is the faint chance of recouping losses on a lucky wager. Mistresses with extravagant tastes *never* give anything back. I knew the state of his bank balance and several times tried to warn him of his folly. He never heeded my warnings any more than his father had. After claiming the speed record, fame went to his head. Money-lenders refused him further loans, however, and even began demanding payment. His banker then declared that he would no longer honour his cheques because of an impossibly high overdraft.'

It all sounded a complete fabrication. He could not possibly be referring to Kit. Yet the fact that her father never actually called him by his name, told her that *was* who he was describing. He was mistaken, of course, quite mistaken.

'Last night, he burst in on us during a private conversation. It was very evident that he had been drinking heavily. He was aggressive and arrogant enough to demand from me the sum of ten thousand pounds, claiming it as his due for gaining the speed record for Kirkland's. When I reminded him that I was already financing a world tour which would enhance his reputation further and boost his personal wealth considerably, he turned extremely nasty and indicated that unless I handed over ten thousand pounds there and then he would refuse to undertake the tour. I had then to tell him that he was not the Almighty, and that the company had another pilot in young Grant, who could soon replace him. He then grew highly abusive; threatened to blacken the name of Kirkland and seek employment with a rival company unless I handed over the money

216

he so badly needed. Knowing full well that he had no intention of settling his debts, and would only go straight out to spend it on more wine and women, for his own sake, I still refused.' He sighed and licked his lips in a gesture of regret. 'I'm very sorry to report that he then assaulted Donald in his uncontrollable rage – he was an aggressive boxer in his youth. I was compelled to eject him, with the advice either to sober up and apologize, or seek employment elsewhere. He has gone, my dear, and I trust we see and hear no more from someone with such total lack of loyalty or gratitude.'

Leone was torn by conflicting feelings as she gazed first at her stony-faced parent, then at Donald's ashen features. It could not be true, it could not. Yet, why would her father fabricate such a wildly improbable story? It was not in the least like Kit, not the man she loved so fiercely, not the man who had cried with joy beneath the moonlight on the evening of his great success. He was not disloyal. She recalled his once telling her that he counted himself one of the most fortunate men in the world, even though he had finally given up pinching himself in case he was dreaming. So why was her father saying these terrible things? Why had Kit gone? She gripped the skirt of her dress with agitated hands as she grappled with confusion and shock. When had he ever been so drunk that it was apparent to everyone? He had taken to locking his door lately, however. Why? He had willingly confessed to being an inveterate chaser of women, who fully intended to do so during his tour. He had repeatedly told her she did not know his real self; had warned her not to trust him. Yet he was so vital, gentle, full of laughter and golden dreams. Or were they really relentless ambitions he would stop at nothing to achieve? No, not the wonderful courageous man she had grown to love.

A small voice told her that she had believed Warren Grant to be a gentle, enthusiastic person longing to be her friend, until she had discovered him naked with a red-haired girl last Saturday afternoon. Suddenly, that vision which had seemed so dangerously exciting lost its allure. It now seemed sordid, almost disgusting. Lust on a rainy afternoon! Dear God, she had fully intended to emulate them with Kit last night. If he had been in his room, she would now be just one more of his many conquests. How could she have rolled about his bed clutching his pyjamas against her nakedness, weeping for elusive violation? Her cheeks grew hot at the thought, and yet that vulnerable first love struggled to survive. It had been so very, very precious.

'He's not really like that,' she heard herself say, in a hollow voice. 'He'll come back. There must be an explanation. He *must* be intending to come back and give us the truth.'

Sir Hector's expression darkened further. 'The truth is that we've had our charity flung back in our faces. Like father, like son. He's a liar and scoundrel, who has more sense than to come back here . . . *ever!*'

A flurry of movement in the hall heralded Merrydew accompanied by a brace of uniformed policemen, who began to cross towards them all. Their footsteps beat an irregular tattoo on the stone flags. Leone's heartbeat slowed as the sensation of foreboding deepened into real fear. Her father stepped forward to confront the approaching group.

'What is it, Merrydew?' he snapped.

The ageing servant looked extremely doleful. 'These men insisted that the matter was urgent, Sir Hector, and as you were in clear view they gave me no chance to ask you if you were in.'

'Now they know I am, I'll see them in the library.'

'It does concern the whole family, sir,' the police sergeant said, in his slow Devonshire accent. 'I'm afraid there has been a motor accident. No need for alarm, though. Both are certain to recover from their injuries. Unfortunately, the car wasn't discovered until the first ferry set off up the Sheen this morning, so they'd been trapped in the vehicle for some hours and were suffering from loss of blood as well as exposure to river mist when the ambulance reached the spot. They're both safe in East Sheenmouth Cottage Hospital, and in no danger, according to the doctor who examined them. Mr Anson came off worse due to being pinned beneath the vehicle. There's an arm and leg broken, as well as serious concussion and a great many lacerations. He was lucky, nevertheless, to escape with no worse. Miss Main has minor injuries to hands and face, but is suffering from shock.'

'*Miss Main?*' thundered Sir Hector.

'My God, he took Steph with him.' Donald seemed beside himself with passion. 'He did it to get at me. It won't stop there, you know it won't. We should have given him what he wanted, done as he said.'

Leone's cry of protest was silent and infinitely anguished. Kit lay broken and bleeding beside another woman. Whilst she had been rolling over his bed in orgasmic yearning, he had been racing recklessly away from her with the girl he had so openly admired – the girl who was engaged to marry Donald. How could she understand this? How could she find an explanation which would allow her love to survive these facts?

Oblivious to the effect his words were having on them all, the sergeant took the leather bag held by his subordinate. 'We had to go through this for identification, sir, and I thought it best not to leave it at the hospital. Apart from a few personal belongings, there's a large sum of money in it. It's not safe to leave so much lying around unguarded.'

'Money . . . what money?' asked Donald in strangled tones.

The man's placid face gave no hint of his thoughts as he said, 'I had to count it, Mr Kirkland. It's regular procedure, so that someone can sign a docket to put with our records. There's nine thousand, nine hundred and twenty-five pounds altogether,' he told Sir Hector. 'All in fivers.'

'Oh God,' exclaimed Donald, turning even paler. 'He meant what he said. He won't stop now until he's . . .'

'Be quiet,' snapped his father, holding out his hand for the bag. 'Where's the receipt you want signed?'

'Just here in my pocket-book, sir . . . oh, and there was something else I thought best not to leave at the hospital.' The constable held up two rolls of papers tied with tapes. 'These seem to be plans and suchlike, Sir Hector. I thought you'd prefer to have them here in case they're important.'

'They're damned important,' cried her father in tones of curious triumph. 'These are the plans for Kirkland's new seaplane, still in the stage of development. My God, if these had reached the hands of my rivals . . . Sergeant, I want Anson and that woman placed under arrest. Immediately. Not only did he steal these drawings, he most certainly took from my safe the money in this bag which amounts to the sum he last night demanded from me with threats. Miss Main is his accomplice in crime.'

'No!' cried Donald. 'Steph would never do that.'

Looking totally shaken, the policeman questioned the charge. 'You do understand, sir, that I'm speaking of Mr Kit Anson. The famous pilot who recently broke the speed record in your seaplane. The Mr Anson who lives here in the Abbey.'

'I know only one Anson,' came the cold response.

'You want him *arrested*, sir, and charged with the theft of money and secret drawings?'

'I do.'

'You're quite certain about this, Sir Hector?'

'For God's sake, man, don't you understand simple English?' her father cried explosively. 'The man is a thief. He is also a liar and a drunkard. Last night, he assaulted my son whilst under the influence of alcohol. You may add that to the charges against him. I want him under lock and key immediately.'

'Not while he's in a hospital bed, sir,' the confused sergeant ruled, with a shake of his head. 'He needs medical attention.'

'Then put a man beside his bed until he *is* fit to be locked up! I intend to telephone the editors of several national newspapers. When this story is printed, the cottage hospital will be swarming with reporters intent on digging out every detail of this disgraceful affair. By the time they've finished with him, he'll be begging for the sanctuary of a cell, believe me.'

Leone heard all this through a daze of misery. Pounding through her brain was Stephanie's claim that she would not wish to be near Kit, if he ever put a foot wrong with Sir Hector and set everything tumbling around him. She had also claimed that charm was Kit's passport to survival, and he worked hard at it. Last night, he had ceased to use it. The price he would now pay was very high.

The uniformed men departed leaving the rolls of drawings, but retaining the money to be used as evidence. Donald grew almost incoherent as words tumbled from him the minute they were alone. In a state bordering on frenzy, he condemned his father's action and pleaded with him to reconsider before it was too late.

'Pull yourself together, boy! Don't you realize that he's cut his own throat by smashing up that car? By the time he's sufficiently recovered to know what's happening, he'll wish he'd killed himself in that accident.'

'But you can't punish poor Steph.'

'She did you a very good turn by going off with him. You have every excuse to end a relationship which was making a fool of you.'

'Father, I love her.'

'*Love?*' he roared in anger. 'There's only one thing worth loving in this world, and that's success. Where's your bloody pride, man? This sister of yours isn't full of protests. She's accepted the evidence of their treachery which is staring her in the face. She has Kirkland pride.

221

If *she* were my heir, I might have some hope for the future.'

Leone walked away from their angry exchange. Her own hope for the future had been destroyed in the most brutal manner. The upper corridor seemed to mock her with its silence as she dragged her feet along it towards the bell tower. Opening the door, she walked inside to drive the truth home even more painfully. The circular rooms still held the scent of his presence, and she knew they would contain another ghost beside that of the hanged monk. Echoes of his voice and laughter hung in the air. Visions of an ashen-faced boy in dreadful clothes mingled with those of an arresting young man who had seized her by the seat of her panties, intending to throw her out. How hard he had worked to charm her! How easily she had succumbed! Kirkland pride was stronger in her than in Donald, it seemed, for her love had flown on the wings of humiliation.

There was a drawing pinned to the board, his hand-writing elucidating the aspects of a wing skeleton marked by arrows. The old box of draughtsman's instruments was no longer beside it. Up in the bathroom, a cake of soap still lay near the plug-hole of the bath, and the smart silk dressing gown hung on the door. The memory of an old plaid woollen one, several sizes too small, returned strongly enough to hurt her. Going back to his bedroom, she pushed open the wardrobe. It was filled with expensive clothes and racks of hand-made shoes. Nothing appeared to have been taken. The bed was as she had left it last night; rumpled and creased. His silk pyjamas lay where she had thrown them in a fury of frustration. On the dresser were silver-backed hair-brushes, and a leather box containing fancy studs and cufflinks. Only one other item appeared to have been taken by the man who had deceived them all. A picture in a frame. *Dad's finest design*.

Kit Anson had vanished with no more than the meagre possessions he had brought with him. He had left here

222

all those things which had made him the person she had believed him to be. She slowly sank down on to the bed where her surrender to him was to have taken place last night. If only she had remained invisible! By revealing herself, she had become a target for the cruellest darts life could produce. She would not return to this place until the wounds had completely healed.

PART TWO

8

Sir Hector Kirkland died on Christmas Eve 1937. Doctors had warned him to slow down or risk the consequences. Having taken risks all his life and rarely having heeded unwelcome advice, he had continued accelerating the pace his quest for power had demanded. The heart attack had killed him immediately, during a dinner party at the home of a man he had hoped to persuade to invest in Kirkland Marine Aviation. The funeral on December thirtieth was attended by more than three hundred people, none of whom felt any great degree of sorrow over the passing of one of aviation's aspiring giants. The heir to the throne was a more likeable person, but avaricious competitors stood ready to move. Donald Kirkland was never likely to be a giant.

At her father's funeral the Kirkland girl made an unexpected appearance. She had left England shortly before Kit Anson's sensational trial, and had not returned since. The owner of a villa overlooking Lake Lugano, she was often to be seen in glossy magazines which specialized in upper-class tittle-tattle. Rumour had it that she was gaining a reputation for breaking engagements to wealthy eligible men. Now almost twenty-two, it seemed she might be following in the footsteps of her mother so tragically drowned on the yacht of her lover, and was either very promiscuous or particularly hard to please. Although the bereaved daughter looked pale and distrait during the service and

227

subsequent gathering in the London mews cottage, masculine interest was nevertheless captured by her striking blonde beauty against the severity of her black, sable-trimmed suit. If she happened to be unattached now, there were those standing ready to chance their luck in a bid for admission to the Kirkland dynasty before she returned to Europe.

The day had been endless. Leone had felt chilled to the marrow in the huge draughty church. Cold weather in England seemed damp and cheerless. In Europe it invariably brought sunlight sparkling on snow, trees glistening white against skies as blue as the Mediterranean, huge log fires to fill the house with the scent of pine forests, and the exhilaration of skiing, ice-skating, racing through the still nights with sleighbells ringing merrily, or careering downhill by moonlight on toboggans guided by reckless young men. London at the tail end of December was grey, depressing and alien. The mourners in heavy dark clothing were the same.

The funeral service for the man she had never been permitted to love had been long and solemn. In her father's mews cottage, the traditional gathering of principal mourners for warming drinks and cocktail fare had hardly been less long and equally solemn. Leone had recognized only three people present: her brother, Maitland Jarvis, and Warren Grant. After five years, they had seemed like strangers. Donald had his own reasons for holding aloof, Maitland seemed even more supercilious and unlikeable than before. Warren was now a successful designer of almost thirty, with eyes as dreamy as before and shyness which was even more pronounced. He had returned to Sheenmouth with Maitland on the late train. She and Donald now sat together before a dying fire, in the masculine atmosphere of their father's sitting room. Sir Hector's strong personality haunted that low-ceilinged room as they sat in silence, each stunned by the terms of a will intended to ensure that Kirkland Marine Aviation would continue as he wished.

Sir Willard Jameson, the family solicitor, had explained the significance of the legal document, then outlined the options open to them. They had been advised to discuss them most fully before making a very far-reaching decision. Donald had been deeply upset, to the point of declaring that he would challenge the state of his father's mind when dictating the will, as he had been under extreme pressure recently. Sir Willard had then pointed out that the document had been ratified five years ago. Donald was still visibly upset, and Leone had a certain detached sympathy for him. Although she doubted there had ever been warm affection between father and son, her brother had worked in harness with him for seven years and must have achieved some depth of understanding with a man who had believed love to be a form of weakness.

However, as she curled up in the leather armchair with a crystal goblet containing brandy, Leone was more concerned with her own reaction to all their solicitor had told them. Wearing a ruby velvet loose gown, into which she had tucked her feet, she was warmer than she had been all day as she gazed reflectively into the fire. The only sounds were the ticking of the clock and the occasional rustle as the embers shifted in the hearth. The will had been made five years ago, after events she had deliberately shut from her mind until now. An echo of the pain she had felt then had been revived by the extraordinary revelation late this afternoon.

Throughout the sensational proceedings which had led to the eventual destruction of Kit's character and professional career, Donald had acted as their father's puppet, saying and doing all he was told in public but collapsing into astonishing apprehension when alone. Leone had returned to school before the actual trial, delayed until the accused man had sufficiently recovered from the car crash. She had not been expected to give evidence, but she had coldly endorsed to anyone who had asked, the newspaper reports of his drinking problem, his unbridled passion for women, his quick temper that often found expression with his fists, and the many ways he had exploited the man who had treated him like his own son.

On the overwhelming evidence given by Sir Hector, Donald and Maitland Jarvis of the events of that night in July, plus the presence in the wrecked car of the exact sum missing from the Kirkland safe along with secret plans of a new seaplane also missing from Sir Hector's office, Kit Anson had been found guilty of assault, theft and attempted industrial espionage. There had been an additional charge of forcible abduction brought against him by Stephanie Main, who had convinced a jury that her former lover had been insanely jealous since her engagement to Donald Kirkland and had forced her into his car using threats and brute strength. For that, he had received an additional prison sentence and been ordered to pay compensation for the injuries she had sustained through his reckless driving.

Those few who had spoken in his defence could give no account of the events which had taken place at Sheenmouth Abbey on the night in question. Neither could they actually deny that the record-breaking pilot had been known to drink heavily, that he enjoyed sexual conquest, and that he had been boxing champion of his school and therefore fearless when confronting other men. The judge had been very harsh in his opinion of someone who had been given everything a young man could want and repaid his benefactor with greed and violence. He determined to make an example of a person who had received public adulation, then disgraced his obligation to live up to it. Heroes should not have feet of clay, he had ruled, or they were unworthy of the pedestal of fame. Kit had been ignominiously removed from his and placed behind bars.

Thinking now of that first vulnerable adolescent love which had been so cruelly crushed, Leone recalled the morning when the truth had been revealed. Her father had applauded her silence and condemned Donald's cries of distress, saying that he wished she were his heir instead. He had done the next best thing. Tonight, she and her brother were joint owners of Sheenmouth Abbey, this mews cottage, an apartment in the City, an ocean-going yacht, a fleet of smaller boats, and six cars. They were also joint owners of Kirkland Marine Aviation. It was that which had stunned them both. Donald found it impossible to accept, but accept it he must, for the will was binding. They both had to find the best means of resolving the problem; now, he could make no business move without her approval.

Thinking deeply whilst sipping her brandy, the revival of those five-year-old memories showed Leone why her father had done it. Her silence that morning had suggested the Kirkland traits her father admired: pride, determination and ruthless lack of forgiveness towards those who betrayed her trust. Donald, on the other hand, had almost wept for the loss of a promiscuous fiancée whilst begging their father to hush it all up. This dual rôle had been forced upon them in an attempt to combine their characters and produce something near to his own personality when handling business. Donald possessed the technical knowledge; she had been seen to have the clear-headed unsentimental attitude her brother lacked. Could they merge to produce another Sir Hector, she wondered as she gazed at the pictures in the fire? The hearth contained an alpine scene with mountains tinted by the setting sun; a scene she knew well and would almost certainly witness again on many occasions. Each time with a different man beside me, she added on an inward sigh.

The giant ruby missing from her finger signified another hope shattered. Lars had gone the way of all male flesh, where she was concerned. Their engagement had lasted longer than usual, so her consequent disillusionment had been all the more bitter. The news of her father's death had awaited her at the villa in Lugano, where she would have spent Christmas alone, licking her wounds. But for the desire to get right away for a while, she might not have come home for the funeral. No one would have missed her; they never had before. Thank heaven her misery had driven her to cross the Channel after shunning it for so long.

'I think there's only one satisfactory way out of this absurd situation,' said Donald, breaking into her reverie. 'With New Year upon us, nothing can be done for a day or two, but as soon as Sir Willard returns from Scotland, I'll get him to draw up the necessary papers. You aren't intending to dash back to Baron Whatsit's castle in Sweden right away, I hope.'

'He's not a baron, and it was an ancestral pile in Denmark,' she said quietly. 'I'm not going back there. It wasn't a home, but an expensive suite of offices.'

Donald's mouth twitched. 'I see. You weren't the love of his life. Just an injection of much-needed cash for his ailing business?'

'Something like that.'

'Poor Leone! Still struggling to be all-in-all to some man, and no one will take up the offer?'

'I'll survive.' She shifted position to ease her back. 'What papers do you suggest Sir Willard should draw up?'

'The only ones possible, under the circumstances.' He frowned as he studied her by the room's low light. 'It's out of the question for me to buy your shares in Kirkland's. I haven't that kind of cash available, for one thing, and the company is going to demand all I can lay my hands on in order to get *Flamingo* successfully launched. After taking almost four and a half years to develop and produce her, it's imperative to win massive orders. Father put everything behind this flying boat, so we have to earn back our investment at least twofold.'

'Or go under?' she asked in surprise.

'Not exactly. Well . . . possibly,' he amended with reluctance.

'My shares wouldn't be worth a penny then, so why not leave things as they stand in case you can get them for nothing later on?'

He was in no mood for frivolity. 'For God's sake, Leone, we're not talking about some piddling little village smithy. Kirkland's is fast becoming one of this country's leading aircraft companies. We're considering millions while sitting here this evening.'

'So was Father when he made that will,' she pointed out.

'That was five years ago. We've expanded considerably since then.'

'By what means? If you've been occupying four and a half of them in the development of a flying boat, how have these millions accrued?'

'You wouldn't understand.'

'I won't if you refuse to explain.'

He shook his head. 'Women shouldn't involve themselves in business.'

'I've just inherited half of one.'

'Which underlines how ludicrous this situation is. Father must have been mad,' he said explosively, for the fourth time since hearing the news.

'There's often a method in madness.' She held out her glass. 'I'd like another brandy.'

'Leone, there's only one way open to us,' he said, ignoring her outstretched arm, 'and that's Sir Willard's other option that you retain your shares, thus reaping the dividends and so on, but give me written power of attorney on all company decisions.'

Uncurling herself, she swung her feet to the ground and crossed to the decanter. Pouring a modest amount of brandy, she then turned to say, 'You still haven't answered my question. How has Kirkland's been expanding?'

Avoiding her direct gaze, Donald addressed the fireplace as he fingered the fine cut glass which sparkled with diamond flashes as it caught the light.

233

'Although the *Aphrodite* affair created worldwide interest, we were unable to take full advantage of it. Warren offered to fulfil some of the engagements Maitland had organized in Europe, but he was inexperienced in seaplanes so couldn't show off the machine's full potential.'

'He also had the wrong name, hadn't he?' she suggested in quiet tones.

'We had to do something quickly,' Donald continued, still staring at the embers. 'Warren produced drawings for a light racing seaplane he'd designed and called *Seaspray*. Father put it into production, and we sold models all over the world to wealthy men who fancied the new sport of air racing. We then streamlined it even further, and they all wanted the new version. So fierce is the competition between them, we're continually being asked to produce individual models for those prepared to pay a fortune for even the slightest modification which will produce additional speed or manoeuvrability.'

Leone resumed her seat in the hard leather chair facing Donald. 'Raoul de Montfort killed himself in an attempt to fly beneath a low bridge near his château. One of the floats touched a rock. What drives a man to risk his life at the age of twenty-four by a compulsion to perform senseless tricks in the air?'

'Search me,' he replied, finally meeting her eyes. 'I'm not a pilot.'

She was suddenly curious. 'Your whole life is spent designing machines which fly, yet you make no attempt to take them into the air. Why not?'

'I prefer to stay alive.'

Sipping her brandy, she took the subject further. 'Do you ever take a risk of any kind, Donald?'

'Where's all this leading?' he asked irritably.

'Father took risks.'

'And died before he was fifty-five. I aim to become an octogenarian, at least. No, I don't take risks, Leone, which is why you can leave your half of Kirkland's safely

234

in my hands. Once *Flamingo* is successfully launched, you can rest assured that Father's death will not reduce the flow of cash you need to comb Europe seeking that elusive soulmate.'

Put into words, her future sounded even bleaker than her past. She faced him frankly. 'What about your soulmate? She appears to be somewhat elusive, too.'

He scowled. 'I don't need one. As soon as *Flamingo* hits the market headlines, I shall announce my engagement to Anita Bergenstein.'

'The American heiress!' she exclaimed, in astonishment. 'You dark horse.'

'There's nothing dark about me. You simply haven't been here to know that our relationship is no secret.'

With that comment emphasizing her own growing awareness of inner isolation, she could not resist using his approach of a moment ago. 'Is Anita the love of your life, or a much-needed injection of cash for an ailing company?'

'Kirkland's is not ailing,' he said, firing up immediately. 'Father risked all available capital on his dream of a passenger liner with wings. We gave him one. Now, we're left with the task of making the dream work.'

'We?' she queried, suddenly seeing the dual ownership in a startling new light.

'Warren Grant played a strong rôle in designing *Flamingo*, so I suppose he's almost as responsible as I am for her success.'

'So it's an all-male concern.'

'What else could it be?' he demanded irritably. 'That's why it's essential to get the deed of attorney drawn up and signed as swiftly as possible. Then I can get on with establishing the new hierarchy.'

'When you marry that sweetly feminine wad of dollar notes, what rôle will your wife play in the hierarchy?' asked Leone, growing more thoughtful by the minute.

'For heaven's sake, will you be serious?' he demanded. 'My marriage won't affect you in any way.'

235

'Of course it will!' she contradicted, studying his elegant form in tailored dinner jacket and expensive braided trousers, as he relaxed with one ankle resting on the other knee. 'If Anita Bergenstein is as shrewd as I've heard, she'll take on more than the Kirkland name in return for her investment. Shall I be obliged to give her power of attorney, too? What if you don't realize your ambition to become an octogenarian, and pop off before your time? The widowed Anita could then be making my decisions for me in good old rip-roaring Yankee manner.'

Her brother straightened in his chair, and put the goblet on the small table beside it. 'This week has been unbearably hectic, and Father's will has proved the last straw. Will you stop being so bloody facetious so that we can get down to the real business between us?'

'You remarked just now that women shouldn't be involved in it.'

Donald got to his feet in one furious movement. 'Is it impossible for you to take anything seriously? While you've been doing your damnedest to outdo Mother with your escapades with Europe's idle rich, Father and I have been working like slaves for the company which provides the wherewithal for your self-indulgence. I'm asking you to make it easy for me to carry on doing what I've done, so that you can continue doing what you've done. It's little enough to demand of your featherweight brain, surely.'

She rose to face him, clutching the goblet so tightly her fingers ached. 'As I haven't been here to know about your wooing of a girl designed more as a business investment than a bride, so you haven't been in Europe to know about my life, Donald. How dare you speak to me as you have just done? Whilst you have been "working like a slave" for Kirkland's, I have been earning the wherewithal for what you term my self-indulgence. For two years I travelled everywhere with George Markham, translating papers and documents into English for his

236

trilogy on the history of European culture. When he returned to Boston I became a translator for an archaeologist involved in work on the site of a possible Roman pavement. For the last fifteen months, I've assisted Contessa de Palveri with her attempt to trace her family history. During the course of my work I met and became engaged to three wealthy men dubbed by society magazines as playboys. I made three serious mistakes, but I am now known as a playgirl because of them. I am not. Neither am I self-indulgent. My villa in Lugano was bought with my own money. My car and speedboat I also paid for from my earnings. The allowance Father gave me has paid for my clothes, that's all. If I've spent a great deal of time in châteaux and villas owned by people society pleases to regard as the "idle rich" it's because they have invited me and made me feel more welcome in their lavish homes than I ever felt in Sheenmouth Abbey.' She took a deep breath. 'Perhaps you'd care to apologize now.'

'All right,' he said reluctantly, still tight-lipped, 'but it doesn't change this impossible situation. As the will stands, it means I can't make a move without you. It's absolute madness.'

Out of the blue, Leone made a decision. 'I mean to observe Father's wishes, Donald.'

'You *what?*'

'I've decided not to give you power of attorney.'

'You're mad,' he whispered, stunned for the second time today.

'Like Father was?' she returned, assessing the implications of her impulsive decision.

'How can you . . . it's ludicrous,' claimed her brother in growing protest. 'Leone, you can't do this to me, you can't tie my hands so tightly. Often, company decisions have to be swift or the chance is lost. If I were forced to telegraph every château and ski-lodge in Europe for your go-ahead on something you knew nothing about, it would mean certain death to the company. Is that what you want?'

'No, Donald, I want to help you to run it.'

He turned away, gripping his hair in anguish. 'Dear God, you know nothing about aviation.'

'I'll learn.'

A cold laugh escaped him as he swung to face her again. 'The only interest you've ever shown in the subject was to make a fool of yourself over the company's test pilot five years ago. There's a hell of a lot more to it than that.'

Amazingly calm in the face of his contempt, she said quietly, 'That was another of my serious mistakes. It won't happen again, believe me. You won't have to telegraph every château. I've decided not to return to Europe. It's time I did something more fulfilling than putting my trust in men who never live up to my expectations. I intend to go home to Sheenmouth Abbey, which is also half mine now, and start learning the art of making aircraft.'

'Learn the art of . . . you're *mad*!' he cried again, despairingly.

'No, Donald, I think I've just discovered my sanity. For years, I've been the invisible Kirkland but, oh boy, is the world about to see me now!'

Warren had slept badly again. Since Hector Kirkland had died, he had been deeply worried. The life force of Kirkland Marine Aviation could not have chosen a worse time to bow out. More and more of the world was becoming accessible by long-range aircraft as commercial airlines vied with each other to establish new routes across the Atlantic and to all points east. Short Brothers and Vickers Supermarine were developing new flying boats, as well as modifying their earlier models to meet the demand for bigger, more spacious, long-distance machines. If Kirkland's did not break into this lucrative market now, the chance would almost certainly be lost.

The company was presently like a flying boat with only half its quota of propellers, well able to move across the water but lacking the impetus to take to the air. Donald was a sound, competent man in all aspects of the business, but he did not possess the flamboyant drive needed right now. *Flamingo* was a combination of advanced design, great power, and absolute reliability which had taken almost five years and Warren's total dedication to perfect. She sat in the company's number-one hangar, waiting for someone to sing an aria to her countless virtues. The operatic baritone who would have done so had just taken his last curtain call, and an ineffective reedy tenor was left to take his place. Donald's voice would fall on deaf commercial ears; it would be drowned by the chorus extolling other ships of the air.

As Warren climbed from the motorboat on that first day of 1938 he was preoccupied, hunched against the cold wind whistling up the estuary. *Flamingo* had been created during fifty-four months of mental and physical anguish, when all else had been sacrificed to the drive for design perfection. Every single moment had been worth the cost to his health and happiness. He had truly created a passenger liner with wings, as he had dreamed of doing. The Canadian stepfather he had known so short a while would be amazed at the way in which flying machines had developed, especially in the mind of a small boy who had hero-worshipped him. A hangar had had to be built to cope with an aircraft of mammoth proportions compared with the fairylike seaplanes the company usually turned out. Extra hands had been employed once production had begun. The precise cost of this beautiful water-bird was probably known only to Sir Hector's worried accountant and banker, but Warren was unhappily aware that the company could stand or fall on this one aircraft. She was a fine machine, with several aspects which made her vastly superior to some already in use on international routes, but men spending millions tended to prefer the tried and tested product

239

unless they were convinced that the returns for backing something new would be increased and guaranteed. Who, or what, would convince customers that *Flamingo* constituted the finest investment with wings they would find in the world today? Donald had neither the personality nor the drive of a tycoon to sell her with silver-tongued words. Warren had reluctantly test flown his own prototype, but he was unhappy in marine aircraft and *Flamingo* was incredibly heavy to handle for a man more used to dual-controlled light monoplanes. He was well aware that he could never dazzle prospective customers with a flying display. That needed a Kit Anson.

Walking across the company slipway, Warren entered the vast hangar frowning. Guilt always arose swiftly whenever he thought of Kit. Although he had not been present on that fatal night five years ago, he was reasonably sure that the cause of the quarrel between the Kirklands and their test pilot had been Kit's discovery of their theft of his father's design. Whether or not he had actually stolen money from Sir Hector's safe and brutally forced Stephanie Main into his car, Warren could not guess, but the so-called 'secret plans' found in the crashed vehicle must almost certainly have been those handed over by himself to Kit after stumbling on the awful truth. No one had suggested that he should give evidence at the trial. He had known the accused man for too short a time. So, he had stayed silent, reasoning that if Kirkland might and influence could succeed in discrediting a man of Kit's standing, going in to court with the story of design theft would result in no more than losing his own chance of a lifetime. Kit had not attempted to exonerate himself, possibly also knowing that the facts would never be believed in the face of such incriminating evidence. Warren had maintained his silence while his friend's reputation and character had been torn to shreds before the awarding of a two-year prison sentence. Guilt had prevented his visiting Kit in jail, although he had written to him, at length, declaring

240

his belief that a dreadful mistake had been made some-where along the line.

Kit's fate had alerted Warren to the dangers of close involvement with Sir Hector, making him tread extremely carefully despite the knowledge that his employer wanted the flying boat design so much he might overlook a great many things in order to get it. However, now knowing that Donald was uncooperative through lack of skill and not because he resented work-ing in harness with an unknown designer, the knowledge had led Warren to forge ahead with his own ideas on no more than token agreement from the younger Kirkland. If Sir Hector and his son suspected that he knew Donald had little design talent, they gave no sign of it. Neither did he. On the theory that mutual silence on the subject was the most profitable policy, *Flamingo* had been designed by Warren, drawn up in plan by Donald, but attributed to Kirkland Marine Aviation. As *Seaspray* had been so unexpectedly taken up by Sir Hector, and credit given to his sole genius, Warren was happy to let sleeping dogs lie. Fame mattered little to him. Successful creation was all he cared about, and an ugly possibility had now reared its head. If *Flamingo* remained as a one-off proto-type, Kirkland's might not survive. With proven design-ers already well entrenched in any company with enough cash to develop new models, Warren might well be back to giving lessons at the Aero Club. It was not a happy prospect with which to start the new year.

In company with the three men who had worked most closely with him, Warren spent several hours fussing over the giant aircraft in the manner of a besotted lover who cannot bear to leave his mistress alone even when passion has been spent. They eulogized, examined, pol-ished and oiled until they could delay departure no longer. None of the four was happier when he headed for home. The problem caused by Sir Hector's death remained. Warren felt even more depressed on the return journey up-river in the dismal afternoon. His chest, always susceptible to damp chilliness, began to wheeze on each breath by the time he reached home.

Distrust of the Kirklands, plus the fate of Kit Anson, had governed his determination never to move into Sheenmouth Abbey beneath Sir Hector's sharp gaze. An intense antipathy towards Maitland Jarvis, and the desire to avoid any social intercourse with Leone, had been additional reasons for remaining in isolation. Ownership of the old boathouse had been transferred from Kit to himself by Sir Hector after the trial, but Warren had taken the precaution of insisting on payment of a nominal sum in return for a deed of ownership before spending more on making the place a home. The success of *Seaspray* had made him a reasonably wealthy man, by his past standards, and the boathouse was now exceedingly bright and comfortable. The old workshop on the ground floor was also fitted with superb tools, workbenches and arc-lamps.

He ran the little boat into the shed, tied it up and crossed to close the outer doors before entering the workshop. There, he mounted the steps leading to the overhead apartment. It was nice and warm to greet him. Mrs Chubb, his housekeeper, had put more coal in the stove he had designed and installed, before leaving for the day. There was an appetizing smell filling the tiny kitchen, but his appetite was tempered by a heavy-heartedness today as he peered inside the oven at a cheese and leek pie keeping hot. Tugging the long woollen scarf from his neck and slipping free of his overcoat, he poured himself a tankard of ale before flopping down into a chair to stare at the fire. Damn Sir Hector! Why had his ruthless heart given up before *Flamingo* was safely launched? The man was well known for never doing anything to oblige anyone else, and success was no use to him now. He would not give a damn for the predicament of those left behind. Holding a belief that what was done could not be altered therefore a man must look forward, he would expect the project to go ahead. He had been no fool, however, so how would he deem that it could go forward with Donald's ineffective weight behind it?

The smell of burning reminded him of the pie. He hastily rescued it from the oven and tucked into the part still edible, following it with a helping of fruit fool from the refrigerator he had designed and manufactured himself several months ago. Several cups of tea whilst reading back numbers of aeronautical journals finished off his meal, then he stacked china and glass in the kitchen to await Mrs Chubb in the morning. By nine o'clock he had washed himself in 'Grant's Patent Showerbath' before donning pyjamas and dressing gown to sit before the dying embers in further gloomy contemplation of his future. So deep were his thoughts, it was a moment or two before he registered that the knocking noise was being made by a human hand on the underside of the trap-door entrance several feet away. He rose and crossed to the rope pulley in faint alarm. The only reason anyone would come for him at five to ten on New Year's Day was because an emergency had arisen over *Flamingo*. He tugged the rope which raised the door, then stared in astonishment at the face tilted to look up at him through the square opening in the floor.

'May I come in?' asked Leone, not waiting for his reply and climbing up to stand beside him.

Warren felt instantly embarrassed, and tugged his dressing gown securely over the area most required to be covered.

'I'm so glad you're now accessible by car,' she continued, with a smile. 'Maitland told me you'd tarred a driveway down from the Magnum Pomeroy road. Even so, I almost missed it in the darkness. Places look so different after a five-year absence.' Casting a glance around the room, her voice took on an enthusiastic tone. 'My goodness, you've made this extremely cosy. It used to be so tumbledown, if I recall.'

So far as he knew, she had only been there once before – on an occasion when the area required to be covered

243

had been very fully exposed. His embarrassment doubled.

'I thought you were still in London, Miss Kirkland.'

Her large blue eyes appealed to him. 'You used to call me Leone. We agreed to be friends, didn't we?'

'Is Donald here?' he asked, his senses totally scrambled by her unexpected presence.

. 'In the boathouse?' she teased. 'No, he's at the Abbey having a *frightfully* deep conference with Maitland. May I sit down?'

'Er, yes . . . yes, of course,' he mumbled, letting the door down with a bang as he released the rope to move across the room. 'I'm sorry. I should have asked you to come in right away. You must find me very dull after the people you usually mix with.'

'I find you refreshingly natural,' she told him. 'Poor you! It's extremely bad-mannered of me to arrive uninvited at this hour. I had no chance to say much to you at the funeral, and it's a long time since we last met, isn't it? I suppose we're both different people now.' Flopping down into the chair he had just vacated, she stretched her elegantly booted feet towards the fire. 'Mmm, you've been keeping this chair nice and warm for me.' She angled her face towards him again. 'Do you still play the trumpet so brilliantly?'

'Only for my own amusement. Never in public. Look,' he said awkwardly, 'I think I'd better slip next door and get into something more suitable.'

'Suitable for what? Do sit down. I want to arrange something with you, and I can't if you persist in hopping about like that.' She smiled encouragingly. 'I've seen men in their dressing gowns before, you know, and you look extremely neat and respectable in yours.'

Flushing a little, he sat carefully in the other chair. Girls played little part in his life, so he felt ill at ease in her company under these particular circumstances. Leone Kirkland had fascinated him from the moment she had caused him to drive into a hedge to avoid her.

After five years, she fascinated him more than ever. In a black ankle-length divided skirt, matching fitted jacket and a small hat with veiling which covered her face, she looked fatally attractive. It seemed incredible that she should be sitting with him now as if they were close friends.

'Are you planning to stay at the Abbey for a few days before going back?' he asked, trying to subdue his excitement. 'Donald didn't think you'd bother to travel down to Sheenmouth, especially at this time of year. He said you'd never liked it.'

'I'm planning to do things to the Abbey so that I shall,' she replied enigmatically. 'Warren, you'll know this eventually, so I'm jumping the gun to tell you that Father left everything he owned equally between Donald and me. I've decided not to return to Lugano. Instead, I'm going to run Kirkland's in harness with my brother.'

Warren was dumbfounded. He could do no more than gape at her. She appeared to be expecting this reaction, for she continued with hardly a pause.

'I know what you're thinking. Donald feels the same way about it. It'll take a long time for me to learn something of the technical side of the business, but I can be very helpful on the clerical and social aspect. From the little I've heard from Donald so far, I gather there's an urgent need to stir up interest in *Flamingo*.' Her lovely smile broke through again. 'My decision will create something of a stir in press and business circles so, while Kirkland's is hitting the headlines on that score, we'll do something sensational with the flying boat. Between us, we should come up with an original idea.'

All this was said in tones of such complete assurance, Warren was swept along on her wave of confidence. It sounded believable. He desperately wanted it to be believable.

'Yes,' he began thickly, then cleared his throat. 'Yes, between us we should.'

Rising as if to leave, she paused to say, 'You're still as nice as you were when you rode into a hedge to avoid hitting me. I think you must have lied when you said you couldn't mend the Bentley, however. An aircraft designer must surely know enough about cars, too. I'll forgive you for that, if you'll agree to do something for me now.'

'Of course . . . anything,' he murmured.

'Will you give me flying lessons?' she asked, making him nonplussed for the second time in very few minutes. 'Donald has never thought it necessary to learn, but I feel the owner of an aviation company should show confidence in what it manufactures by taking to the air herself, don't you?' As she moved across to the trap-door on a waft of French perfume, she added, 'Besides, it's always been apparent to me that in order to prove one's existence in this world, knowledge of flying is number-one priority.'

After Leone had gone, Warren put more coal on the fire. He was too worked up to consider going to bed yet. He would ring Jim Mason at the Aero Club in the morning to hire one of his trainers. January weather would interfere with a course of lessons, unfortunately, but it would be good to have something to take his mind off *Flamingo* for a while. Women often became very skilled pilots; especially those with determination and daring personalities. Leone Kirkland seemed very strong on both points.

He sat for a long time, marvelling at this astonishing turn of events. The depression following Hector Kirkland's death began to lift. A spark of optimism, a curious excitement, began to glow inside him. This girl could be the means of changing the course of his life . . . in more ways than one. Her father had once warned him that Leone was a Kirkland, and therefore out of his league. But Sir Hector was dead, and Leone was putting herself very firmly into it now.

9

It was a clear crisp late January day providing perfect visibility for flying. Warren had delayed her lesson two hours due to the very low temperature which had created the conditions. Going up before the sun had warmed the air a little could be risky, he ruled. Not only would Leone become dangerously chilled, there was the slight chance of ice forming on the wings if she climbed too high. When she had pointed out over the telephone that men had flown over snowcapped mountain ranges quite successfully, his uncompromising reply had been that she was neither a man nor experienced enough to fly over Bickham Hill in freezing conditions, much less a mountain range. It had brought a smile from her. Her relationship with Warren had strengthened greatly in the past four weeks. Having lost his sense of awkwardness in her company, he had become the nearest to a male friend she had ever known, turning into a veritable angry bear when dealing with anything concerned with flying or aircraft. During her eight lessons, they had crossed swords frequently over his tendency to growl at her whenever she made a mistake. Normally gentle and sweet-tempered, he forgot all that when sitting in the rear cockpit. Once, he had snatched the controls from her with an oath she had never expected to hear from a man of his type. Back on the ground he was prone to read her a stern lecture on all she had done wrong,

247

accepting no excuses for her errors. It made him an excellent instructor, she supposed wryly.

When she eventually climbed into the front cockpit with a noonday sun warming her face, she appreciated the wisdom of delay. Her heart suddenly lifted. Flying was fun; it was exhilarating. Why had she waited so long to take to the air? The answer lay deep within her and refused to be recognized. Warren stood on the wing to check her straps, reciting the usual list of dangers to avoid. She nodded when he asked if she was sure of the course and flight plan he had devised for today, and obediently repeated it to prove that she was. Impatience always ruled her at this point, but he had impressed upon her that three quarters of any pilot's success was due to pre-flight thoroughness.

Finally, he appeared satisfied and lowered himself into the tutor's cockpit behind her. She switched on and began taxiing out to the runway marker, where she would turn into the wind. Her take-off was near to copybook perfection. She smiled, well pleased with herself. He could not possibly grumble at her today. Up they rose over the village of Magnum Pomeroy which stood out as clearly as if every building and field had been recently washed and polished, then she made her first turn over Sheenmouth Abbey where the river lay beside it like a silver ribbon. The beauty beneath, and the cold glory of the cloudless azure sky all around her, put unexpected yearning in her heart.

As she flew on with the intoxication of the rarer atmosphere luring her into thoughts more fanciful than concentration on altitude, bearing and forward thrust, she saw the past few years for what they had been. Fluent in most European languages, she had used her abilities to gain employment which had kept her occupied and provided her with the money she had needed to live a life independent of the family which had never wanted her. She had been a proficient and efficient translator, but had found limited personal interest in George Markham's pursuit of European culture, the documents concerning Roman mosaics or those tracing the ancestors of an eccentric and rather objectionable contessa. Three times she had imagined herself in love with men who had promised escape; three times she had been disillusioned. One had sought only a cultured attractive hostess for a succession of parties at his château, where guests indulged in deep play at the gaming tables or in the numerous bedrooms. The second had expected a sexual slave to his virility – one of many slaves, she had soon discovered. Lars had seen marriage as a business investment which would inject cash into his ailing motor company. There had been no escape possible with any one of them.

Escape from what, she was asking herself, when a series of loud thumps on the fuselage behind her brought her back to the present with a start. Growing hot with guilt, she realized that she had been flying with total lack of concentration. The altimeter showed she had descended when she should have climbed, and the view below revealed the sea lapping Sheenmouth sands two miles west of where she should presently be.

'Oh *hell*,' she whispered explosively. 'I should have turned over Giddesworth Downs. He'll be livid!'

The thumps were Warren's usual method of telling her to look round at him for a directive signal. Knowing too well what she had done wrong, Leone ignored the command and quickly entered a right-hand turn, climbing as she did so and concentrating on the tricky manoeuvre which should put her back on course. Making a face at the prospect of what he would say when she landed, she headed for the next landmark, reminding herself of the dangers of what she had just done. If she had been flying solo, escape might have been all too easy to find – permanent escape in a crash!

For the following forty minutes the small aircraft responded to her determined touch, and Leone began her descent over the church and Dobbs Farm feeling she had quite redeemed her earlier carelessness. All that was needed was a faultless landing, and Warren would surely overlook her one error. Slowly and carefully she dropped towards the Aero Club, watching the speed and altitude with hawklike gaze. With fifty feet to go she began to wobble slightly, and a voice from the rear called out calmly, 'Watch that throttle!' He sounded very reasonable, so she relaxed with confidence enough to set down on the hard grass in almost exemplary style. Smiling with satisfaction, she reduced speed until the tiny machine rolled to a halt near the club hangar. After cutting the engine, she pushed herself up from the cramped seat and clambered in her neat blue flying suit on to the wing, before jumping to the ground well pleased with herself.

Warren came up to her pulling off his thick gauntlets. He was scowling. 'Just what the devil do you think you were doing up there?' he demanded.

'My mind wandered for a moment or two, that's all,' she told him.

'That's all! If we'd been in mountainous country we could've flown into one while your mind was wandering. If we'd been over a city we could've wrapped ourselves around a cathedral spire.' He flung out an arm with a pointing finger. 'If we'd been three miles west of here we could've hit the lighthouse on Craggy Point,' he raged. 'In the cockpit of an aircraft a pilot must *never* let his mind wander, even for a moment or two. I thought you had enough intelligence to absorb that fact.'

It was all true. Knowing it was caused her to hit back. 'All right, all right, you've made your point. There's no need for a long speech on the subject.'

'Yes, there is,' he retorted, his chill-flushed face wearing an uncompromising expression. 'My life is valuable to me. If you're intent on throwing yours away, don't do it when I'm in the back seat. Understand?'

Furious, she snapped, 'Don't treat me like a child, Warren.'

He pulled off his leather helmet from which his unruly hair sprang up to gleam brown in the sunlight. 'A child, Miss Kirkland, would be absorbed in what she was doing – totally absorbed. You weren't, and endangered both our lives.'

'Don't be ridiculous!' Then, as he began to turn away, she cried, 'If you feel that way about it, I'll find another instructor.'

'I wish you would,' he flung over his shoulder. 'I could be confident of a future then.'

Nonplussed momentarily, she then ran after him with a weak defence. He pulled up as she barred his way determinedly. 'Neither of our lives was in danger, now was it? I'm sorry. I felt so exhilarated by the sunshine and the thrill of being up there in a clear blue sky for the first time. It looks so beautiful; I hadn't realized. There have always been clouds when we've gone up.' He still looked very much the way he had when she had forced him to ride into a hedge on his motorcycle – mutinous and unimpressed by her approach. 'Oh, for heaven's sake, I missed a landmark, lost a little height and was late making a turn. You're acting as if we escaped death by inches. We didn't, and I thought my unscheduled turn on the climb was rather good. Besides,' she added persuasively, 'my landing was the best I've ever made, wasn't it?'

He seemed immune to her cajoling. 'Why didn't you look round when I banged on the fuselage?'

'I realized what I'd done wrong. It was more important to correct that than to get signals from you telling me what I already knew.'

'Oh, really?' he commented, his breath frosting in the chill atmosphere. 'What if I'd been trying to draw your attention to the fact that I was overcome by cold, that I needed oxygen or I'd pass out? What if I'd been trying to tell you I'd been gripped by cramp, or had a serious nosebleed due to the rarefied air? What if I'd suffered a minor heart attack and was trying to warn you that I'd be of no help to you up there? You ignored me and climbed even higher before completing the course and landing smugly satisfied with yourself.'

She sighed with exasperation. The day was so lovely – a shining blue jewel among so many grey winter hours – it was unreasonable of him to adopt this pugnacious attitude to spoil everything.

'Why is it that anything connected with flying and the machines which do it turns ordinary men into opinionated brutes?' she demanded of him.

His unwavering gaze challenged her. 'You've avoided the issue. One of the most vital rules in the air is that signals of any kind must be observed. Why did you ignore mine?'

'I didn't,' she countered immediately. 'I acted on it and got straight back on course.'

'And if I really had had a heart attack?'

She swung her helmet and goggles airily in her left hand, and said just as airily, 'I'd have got you down all in one piece, don't fret.'

He looked at her keenly. 'Prove it.'

'Eh?'

Taking her elbow, he began walking back to the aircraft. 'Prove to me that you could do what you've just claimed. Take her up over that same course without me behind you.'

'You're mad!' she cried, trying to stop in her tracks but being pushed on by him. 'I couldn't go solo.'

'You'd be on your own if I was ill in the rear cockpit.'

'This is ridiculous,' she cried. 'Whatever's come over you today?'

Reaching the aircraft, he nodded at the front cockpit. 'You asked me to teach you to fly, and you've just boasted that you could do it without my help. Get in there and prove it . . . unless, of course, you're prepared to admit that you'd be hopeless if I weren't there ready to take over when you made a mistake like you did this morning.'

Leone stood irresolute. Warren would never make a challenge of this sort if he felt there was any danger involved. It was herself she had to convince. The idea was terrifying. All alone way up in the sky. What if the engine suddenly cut out, or one of the wings dropped off? Every aspiring pilot had to go solo sooner or later. Leone would prefer to make it later.

'Come with me and pretend you've had a heart attack,' she suggested. 'It would be the same thing, really.'

He shook his head. 'Oh no, it wouldn't. Where's that Kirkland confidence which was so pronounced a moment ago? Was it just bluff to pull the wool over my eyes?'

'Right,' she said decisively. 'I'll show you, Mr Grant.'

Jamming the helmet back on her head, she climbed into the aircraft once more and waited while Warren checked that her straps were properly fastened. Her heart was hammering as he gave her the word to go, and her hand was slightly unsteady as she switched the ignition to bring the engine back to life. Feeling she must have taken leave of her senses, she taxied forward to the marker at the far end of the field. With her teeth gritted determinedly she opened the throttle and moved forward with increasing speed, concentrating on avoiding all the dangers possible during take-off. She was up and smoothly away, turning over her home before real panic overcame her. The emptiness of that rear seat practically seared her back like a flame. Although Warren was normally not visible back there unless she looked over her shoulder, knowing he was still on the ground gave her a sensation of frightening isolation in that endless blue heaven she had found so thrilling earlier.

That fearfulness lasted until she had climbed to eight hundred feet and levelled out, when it came to her that isolation was no new experience for Leone Kirkland; she had been alone all her life and managed to survive. Her confidence returned. She would show Warren the folly of throwing the gauntlet at *her* feet.

Climbing further and turning correctly at Giddesworth Downs, she headed for Forton Fort which stood a clear sight on a rise beside the river. Exhilaration filled her anew. The engine sang sweetly; the wings seemed securely fastened still. Another turn over the fort put her on a course to fly above the river towards Axminster. She wondered what Warren was thinking as he waited for her to reappear, then reminded herself that she must not let her thoughts wander. *Concentrate*, she breathed sternly. Climbing over Axminster, then diving quite steeply back towards East Sheenmouth as part of today's practice, she circled above the cliffs right on course for Magnum Pomeroy. Only then did she think about the landing and that empty rear seat. Apprehension returned.

Warren was a dot on the small airfield as she descended over Dobbs Farm, but she was too tense to think about him. *Watch your height . . . ease that throttle . . . pull very gently on the stick*. His voice seemed to be reciting these instructions as the ground raced up to meet her. At the last minute, she worried about her speed. The wheels touched the grass, left it again, then thumped down to jar her every bone as the aircraft hurtled towards the hangar. Fighting the onward surge with gritted teeth, Leone brought the machine to a standstill ten yards from where the figure in overalls and leather jacket stood shading his eyes against the lowering sun.

Shaking with a sense of anticlimax and upset because she had made such a deplorable landing, she switched off the ignition and slowly climbed to the ground. It was infuriating. Warren would have seen nothing of her perfect turns, the copybook climbs and dives, the careful manner in which she had banked over Forton and sideslipped after passing East Sheenmouth. He would judge her performance on the landing he had just witnessed. She could see it written in his expression as he approached, so she attacked first.

'All right, you don't have to say it. I know that landing was deplorable.'

He gave his usual rather bashful smile. 'Not half as terrible as mine when I first went solo. I had to make two approaches, and even then I did a kangaroo hop twice as high as yours.' As she gazed at him in bewildered disbelief, he said, 'Apart from daydreaming, your first flight was so good I knew you were now ready. I thought you might turn into a jelly if I suggested going solo, so I had to play on your Kirkland pride a little. Congratulations. You're a very competent pilot, Leone.'

'Thank you,' she said thickly, turning from him to walk towards the clubhouse so that he would not see her tears. Suddenly awed by what she had dared to do, she realized that recognition had come at last. Yet learning to fly had simply made her one of the boys. What must she do to gain recognition in her own right?

As she walked through the upper galleries, Leone reflected that she might have bitten off more than she could chew by insisting on helping to run the company. Her decision had brought the predicted headlines, but they had not enhanced Kirkland's prospects. Grave doubts were expressed over the future of a company half-owned by a girl who knew nothing about aviation. Her record of broken engagements suggested that she was quickly bored and sought fresh excitement, so her whim in joining the family firm might last no longer than her romances. Caution was recommended until boardroom battles had subsided, and Donald Kirkland was left to pick up the pieces in the wake of his sister's return to Europe. Leone was not so much angry as dismayed by this. What might have begun as a whim had strengthened into determination to succeed. Public opinion must be overcome somehow. It did not help that her relations with Donald were still very strained. They quarrelled over his persistent refusal to take her seriously enough to discuss any business matter with her, and the situation was greatly worsened by her resentment of Maitland. Donald hardly made a move without consulting the man, and Leone felt that her rightful position in family affairs was usurped by someone who had always occupied a curious place in the household. Indeed, he was a curious person. He was always immaculately dressed in clothes bearing the hallmark of high-quality tailoring, yet their conservative style was nevertheless in keeping with his subordinate position. Maitland took his meals with his employers, had his own suite of rooms, a valet and a sedate but expensive car, yet he addressed Donald as Mr Kirkland or sir. He was equally courteous to Warren, who invariably sported bright woollen pullovers with tweed trousers, an old scarf several yards long which he coiled around his neck, and a leather coat. To hear Maitland address this dreamy man, ten years his junior and with an unpolished accent, as 'sir' suggested the deference of a valet or footman. Yet in business discussions or dining table conversation, Maitland always spoke with an authority and assurance which contrasted strangely with his position. Leone had challenged Donald to define the man's status. His reply had been that Maitland was completely indispensable. She had then challenged the salary he received, giving her opinion that it was over-generous in view of the fact that they also provided him with luxury living quarters, a servant, and a modern car.

Any criticism of Maitland Jarvis fell on deaf ears where her brother was concerned. Her suggestion that they could dispense with his services and employ a younger local man instead to save the company a considerable amount, was met with Donald's stubborn refusal to even consider it. Maitland knew the business inside out; his mind was a complete filing cabinet for everything connected with it. Nothing Leone said could move her brother on the subject of a person she resented more and more each day; on any matter unconnected with business, he was usually prepared to give ground. Leone had retired Mrs Roberts, with whom she had never seen eye to eye, and employed as housekeeper a brisk competent woman from Axminster, who had run her own hotel until it had been destroyed by fire. Mrs Marshall was a divorcée, whose disillusionment with the male sex made her an excellent ally in Leone's determination to rid her home of its monastic tendencies. Menus now included variations to suit the lighter palate, flowers placed in all the main rooms were arranged in romantic style to add a feminine touch to the austere building. Swiss embroidered table linen replaced the severe starched white, which had suited a hostelry rather than a home. Leone had also taken on a rosy-cheeked girl from East Sheenmouth, enjoying her ingenuous manner after so many aloof, temperamental European boudoir maids. Nancy had proved to be an apt and eager pupil.

The same could not be said of herself, Leone mused ruefully, as she continued along the gallery towards the stairs leading to the third-floor office suite. After six weeks at the helm of Kirkland Marine Aviation, she still had no idea how to steer it. The new partner could speak French, German, Italian and Spanish, she could converse knowledgeably on art, music and literature, she could paint attractive watercolours, play a bruising game of tennis, ride with as much skill as a potential champion, and choose clothes with individuality and flair. None of these talents were in the least use when learning to understand aircraft manufacture. She had been conducted over *Flamingo* by Warren several times, but still found it impossible to understand his eulogy on statistics and design developments. The flying boat's elephantine grace, spacious interior and latent power all excited and intrigued her, so she readily accepted the word of the two designers that the aircraft was a potential champion of the air. How to prove the fact was the problem presently facing them all. Today's meeting was for the purpose of reaching a solution, at last. Already well into February, the promotion would need to enter the planning stage now if *Flamingo* was to be launched in the spring. Leone had racked her brains for a brilliant solution, but all she had offered so far was that a lavish party should be held at sea on board the flying boat, to which they should invite men of wealth and influence. Donald had immediately pointed out that a lavish party needed space, and even *Flamingo* could not cope with an elaborate buffet and bar, and a supply of stewards to serve the large number of guests required to make the evening worthwhile. As the wives of such men usually expected to be invited to such affairs, he had added, the guest list would necessarily be very short. Warren had then remarked that a rough sea on the vital night would probably prostrate most of the guests, anyway, and the idea was discarded.

At present, the best suggestion had been made by Maitland: that a demonstration flight over Sheenmouth, followed by a lavish party at the Abbey along the lines of June tenth 1932 when *Aphrodite* had taken the speed record, would be easy to organize yet attract a great deal of interest. Warren had flatly refused to fly his creation, saying that he was no Kit Anson. A short silence had followed, as it always did at any mention of that name, until Leone had ruled firmly that another pilot of equal skill must be hired to give the display. The matter had been left in abeyance, as it seemed to be no more than an unimaginative repeat of what had been a triumphant world-shaking event. No one went so far as to say that it would almost certainly revive interest in the scandal with its echo of that other time. Yet a better idea still eluded them.

Entering the outer office, where Willard and his two male secretaries immediately rose to their feet, Leone answered their greetings quietly, reminding herself that she must replace one of them with a girl. The masculine flavour was still too strong in the business area of her home. Warren was alone in the austere room furnished with a large walnut table and matching high-backed chairs. He stood up, giving her his warm, enthusiastic smile.

'Hallo, Leone.'

She smiled back. 'Did you come through the copse to get here?'

'The copse?' he echoed, mystified.

'You have snippets of twig in your hair, and on your sleeve.'

'Oh.' He put up a hand to brush the top of his head. 'I came in too close to the bank and collided with the undergrowth. Too engrossed in this insoluble problem to look where I was going, I suppose.'

Crossing to him, she began picking the twigs from his springy brown hair. 'How you've avoided a sticky end, I can't imagine,' she scolded. 'You need someone to look after you, Warren.' Meeting his glance, she asked, 'Why aren't you married?'

He pulled a face. 'Who'd want a chap who thinks of nothing but wing stress and cruising altitudes?'

'How about that redhead?' she suggested teasingly. 'She seemed very taken with you, if I recall.'

His colour rose swiftly, taking her by surprise. She had not seen a man blush for years, and she realized once more that Warren was vastly different from the suave sophisticates of her acquaintance.

'Sorry. Your private life is your own affair,' she told him hastily, 'and I agree it would have to be an exceptional woman who would live with aviation as a constant rival. I experienced it as a girl, and discovered that there was no means of ousting it.'

'Is that what you're attempting to do here?'

She shook her head. 'My only hope is to catch the epidemic, too. I'm finding even that more difficult than I imagined.'

'Only because you refuse to put in enough study of the manuals,' he said severely. 'You're a very competent pilot. Going solo after eight hours is most commendable,

259

but you'll not be granted a licence until you know the mechanics of what you're doing.'

'So you keep telling me,' she said ruefully, perching on the edge of the table. 'I drive my Austin very successfully without knowing what's happening under the bonnet.'

He groaned with exasperation. 'If your car breaks down, you simply send for a mechanic to get you going again. If the same thing occurs mid-air, the pilot has to be able to deduce the probable cause and get himself safely down. There are no helpful mechanics in the sky, you know.'

'I do try hard to take it in,' she assured him, 'but I suppose my brain isn't the kind to understand aeronautics.'

'And so say all of us,' commented Donald from the doorway, where he had just entered with Maitland.

'Give your sister time. She's had a great many problems to deal with since Sir Hector's death, and none of us learned the subject in six short weeks,' put in Warren, swiftly defending her. 'She can, at least, fly the machines the company produces.'

'No, she can't,' argued Donald, dragging out a chair and sitting at the conference table. 'A trainer at the Aero Club is nothing like flying *Flamingo*.'

As Maitland stood clutching several folders, waiting for her to be seated, Leone cried, 'That's it!'

'That's what?' demanded her brother, in offhand manner. 'Leone, if you'll sit down we can get started. We're already ten minutes late.'

Too full of her idea to point out that he was the cause for the delay, Leone sat on the chair Warren pulled out for her and made her triumphant announcement.

'I'll do the flying display in *Flamingo*.'

The three men gazed at her incredulously, apparently all lost for words. She took advantage of the silence.

'I know the basics of flying. Warren says I'm good. He could teach me how to handle the controls of *Flamingo* by the time we're ready to launch her, and *I* could do the demonstration flight.' At the sight of their expressions, she added, 'For heaven's sake, I'm not suggesting that I'm skilled enough to dazzle onlookers with aerobatics. Warren could do that if he weren't so obstinately modest. A hired genius could do even better than he, but we've already decided that the affair would be too much like a repetition of another occasion. Don't you see, though, that the event would become sensational and draw all the attention we could wish if Leone Kirkland was scheduled to fly *Flamingo*?'

'You'd crash,' commented Donald dryly.

She raised her eyebrows. 'Even greater publicity.'

'For a machine we would no longer have because it was at the bottom of the sea with you?'

'You'd never gain your licence in time,' put in Warren, in kindly tones. 'In any case, you're not robust enough to handle *Flamingo*. It needs strong wrists and a fairly tough physique. No girl could possibly fly a boat of her size.'

'Has a girl ever tried?' she demanded.

'Cut it out, Leone,' her brother demanded. 'You're wasting valuable time with this Pankhurstian attitude. We all gave that scheme a pretty good thumbs down two weeks ago. Even you attempting aerial suicide wouldn't give it the required boost.' Starting a cigarette with the heavy silver desk lighter, he leaned back to squint at her and Warren through the cloud of smoke. 'What we really need is an inspired suggestion.'

'She made a very courageous offer, nevertheless,' Warren said.

Leone lit her own cigarette, reflecting that they were drawn up like opposing armies; Donald and Maitland facing herself and Warren. Was it possible for any suggestion, however inspired it might be, to find favour with them all?

'Do you have one, Donald?' she asked, holding her filter-tip elegantly to one side.

'A courageous offer?'

261

'An inspired suggestion.'

'Ah, one of those. As a matter of fact, I have.'

How very attractive he was when he smiled, she thought. Possessing the grace and charm their father never had, Donald could become a successful man if only he were more adventurous. Maybe the marriage to his American bundle of dollars would do the trick . . . unless she ran off with another man before the wedding, like Stephanie Main had!

'Are we going to be privileged to hear it?' she prompted.

'I suggest a challenge, my dear Leone. In the Great War, flying aces would drop a metaphorical gauntlet on the enemies' airfield, naming date, time and map reference. It was a morale-booster, of course, but made in the very best spirit of rivalry. I propose that we issue a challenge for any pilot to bring a flying boat to Sheenmouth on a given date, and attempt to prove his machine superior in every way to ours.'

'Good God, no!' cried Warren in alarm. 'Do you want to put us out of business?'

Donald's smooth brow furrowed beneath its sweep of blond hair. 'I did emphasize "superior in every way".'

'I won't do it, and that's flat.'

'We'll hire a flying ace to do it.'

'No!'

Leone turned to Warren in confusion. 'You constantly sing *Flamingo*'s praises. I don't understand why you're so upset.'

He got to his feet in great agitation, walking back and forth as he spoke in heated manner. 'The approach is totally wrong. Those wartime challenges have been exaggerated, I assure you. That phrase "morale-booster" is extremely telling, because that's what they were: desperate attempts to prove to themselves that they were superior to the enemy. This would be seen in the same light, Donald.' He clutched his hair as he continued pacing. 'Christ, we'd have each of our competitors using the occasion to demonstrate the merits of his own machine – at our expense, financial and commercial. *Flamingo* is above that kind of razzamatazz favoured by the Americans.'

Leone looked at her brother. 'Inspiration from Anita, by any chance?'

Donald ignored that. He was angered by Warren's reaction. 'May I remind you, you're not a partner in this company.'

'You're not the designer of the machine.'

After whipping out that emotional riposte, Warren halted to gaze at Donald in something approaching shock, and he wore much the same expression as he gazed back. Leone was deeply puzzled by the exchange. *Flamingo* was the result of their dual genius, surely. She was still trying to make sense of it when Warren sat beside her again, and began fiddling with pad and pencil.

'I'm sorry, Donald, but I feel very strongly that it would be unwise to give competitors a free opportunity to display their own wares,' he mumbled. 'Whatever we do should focus attention solely on *Flamingo*.'

Tight-jawed now, Donald asked, 'Are you implying that she couldn't stand up to competition?'

Warren's head came up swiftly. 'No! She's the best boat on the market today. Taken all round, she's the best.'

'Perhaps Mr Grant feels he would prefer to make further tests before deciding on a definite plan,' put in Maitland quietly.

'What Mr Grant feels appears to be totally misunderstood,' Warren growled, attacking pencil and pad once more.

Donald drew nervously on his cigarette, tapping ash from it with his long elegant fingers. 'Stop acting like a prima donna and clarify your objections. Time is running short, and time is money, remember.'

'Heavens, how much like Father you sound,' declared Leone, getting to her feet in exasperation. 'To use

263

another Americanism, "OK baby, so time's running short." So apparently, are our ideas. I've offered to fly the damned thing myself, and been laughed out of court. Maitland thinks Warren needs more time, but Warren is hurt about being misunderstood. You, Donald, propose some kind of Red Baron challenge, which could push sales of every other boat and leave us facing bankruptcy. Warren feels hurt and misunderstood over that, too. To think I had always imagined businessmen to be so capable and clever!' Relenting slightly, she put her hand on the young designer's shoulder. 'I know you love that machine as if she were a woman, but all you've done today is object to all our suggestions without offering one of your own.'

He glanced up at her with such fervour in his eyes, she was instantly and unpleasantly reminded of another man who had loved an aircraft with obsessive passion.

'*Flamingo* is superb. Whether or not you've been laughed out of court here, Leone, the authorities would never permit you to fly her without a licence, and they wouldn't grant you one on the little experience you could gain in the time available to us. No further tests are needed, Maitland,' he added, glancing across the table at the dark-suited assistant. 'My objections to an aerial challenge are based on known facts. Boats already on the market can fly faster over short distances, climb at greater rate, perform tighter turns, and can even maintain greater stability on rough seas. None can claim all these virtues, just one, but spectators at a gathering such as Donald suggested would simply see *Flamingo* outshone in almost every respect. That type of event would provide no opportunity to prove *Flamingo*'s capacity for long-distance flights, for her astonishing stability in the most turbulent aerial conditions, for her cargo capacity and the luxurious comfort of the spacious passenger cabins, plus the tremendous advantage of power which can lift her from the water after a very short take-off run. Her rate of actual climb might be slower than some other boats, but she reaches lift-off remarkably quickly, which allows her to land and depart from smaller lakes and waterways than can any other boat of similar size.' He got to his feet beside Leone, making a great point of pushing his chair back very neatly beneath the table before looking directly at Donald across it. 'Kit Anson vowed he'd fly our passenger liner with wings from here to Africa when she was built. I think we should arrange a proving flight along those lines, fill *Flamingo* with likely customers, and bally well show them what a bloody fine aircraft they're being offered.'

There was a short silence between them all. Leone's mind immediately filled with all manner of exciting ideas, but her brother sounded perfectly calm when he asked, 'Will you fly this route?'

Warren shook his head. 'I'm not happy in boats, you know that. Besides, I'd have to be on hand to answer queries from the passengers as we progressed. Some are certain to have investigated the virtues of other boats before the flight, and will ask very probing questions. I couldn't fly and sell *Flamingo* at the same time.' Having picked up a pencil from the table while speaking, he fiddled with it until it snapped. Looking abstractedly at the broken pieces in his hands, he said, 'As we'd need an entire flight crew with stewards to wait on passengers, serve drinks, and so on, I suggest we approach one of the smaller airlines to see if we could hire one of their experienced crews for the occasion. Searching for individual people would be time-consuming and chancy. In any case, even if we were fortunate enough to get the top man in each field, they might not work together well as a team. Far better to employ people who know and respect each other.'

There was another short silence before Donald asked the man beside him, 'What would it cost, Maitland?'

The sandy-haired assistant replied calmly, 'I'll have the answer for you in two days, Mr Kirkland. I take it you're speaking of *total* cost – fuel, catering, docking charges at the stops en route, transport to and from Sheenmouth for the guests, in addition to the hire of a crew.'

Donald looked surprised. 'Good lord, can you do all that within two days?'

'Oh yes, sir,' came the smooth answer. 'I should need details of the proposed route, however.'

'That's no problem. Here, Warren, come and take a look,' he invited, getting to his feet and crossing to the wall at the far end of the room. Reaching it, he tugged a cord until the rotation of maps produced one of the area under consideration. Leone walked over to join them, feeling that she had now been excluded by the three men. An idea was fast taking shape, and it was essential that she should first know the route they planned before she placed it before them.

'Naples, Athens, Cairo, Khartoum, Mombasa,' Warren quoted, moving his hand over the map.

'Out of the question,' Donald said immediately. 'It'd be far too expensive.'

'Maitland hasn't done his sums yet,' came the protest. 'Whatever we do is going to cost a lot.'

'Just look at the distance!'

'*Flamingo* is a long-distance boat. That's what we'll be out to prove.'

'So what if they're all greatly impressed by that, but place no orders at the end of it all?'

'They will,' Warren assured him heatedly. 'I defy any man to take a trip like that and fail to fall beneath the spell of one of the finest marine aircraft ever built.'

'What of the women who'll be making the trip?' put in Leone at that point. When they turned to look at her in surprise, she went on, 'You surely weren't proposing to fill *Flamingo* with a group of cigar-smoking top businessmen, who'd eat and drink their way to Africa and back whilst making private deals amongst themselves, then thank you for a most enjoyable trip and walk off highly satisfied with the contacts they'd made at our expense?' Seeing that she now had their full attention, she stubbed out her cigarette and elaborated. 'You've just mentioned a route comprising some of the most romantic places on earth. In order to make your passengers appreciate the fact, it's essential to include some women to liven up the male ranks. Some wives, wealthy widows with money to invest, an actress or two to provide glamour, and some eccentric socialites will give this flight the sense of excitement and novelty we want to create. What you propose is no better than an aerial gentlemen's club. Warren has eulogized over the luxurious aspect of the passenger cabins, so let's show this aircraft for what she is. The main objection to Donald's idea of a challenge with other boats giving of their best was that we must keep all attention focused on *Flamingo*. We won't do that by providing an airborne clubroom for portly businessmen to eat, drink and snooze their way across to Africa. They have to be continually aware of the comfort, luxury and delightful entertainment of travelling the world in one of our wonderful flying boats. To do that, we have to simulate a normal passenger service flight, not a boring, endless all-male club meeting!' she said emphatically.

Walking to the large window overlooking the Roman-type pool, she said as she gazed down at it, 'Father was never a man sensitive to atmosphere, but he had *style*.' Swinging round to face them again, she said eagerly, 'That's what we need now. A flamingo is a graceful water-bird with feathers the colour of beautiful pinks. It is found in large numbers in Africa. See how appropriate it is that our *Flamingo* is flying to Africa! We must decorate the interior in contrasting pinks, and the cuisine must reflect the same theme. New drinks with names to suit the stops en route will be served. Special dishes must be presented – *Steak Athenia* . . . *Filet of sole Napoli* – you know the kind of thing. Heavens, if they can name peaches and ice cream *Pêches Melba* after Dame Nelly,

I'm sure we can engage a chef with great imagination and a deal of impudence to do something similar for us.'

The blank unresponsive expressions on their faces drove her to demand, 'Do you want to sell this machine, or not? The trip is the ideal solution, but it has to have a quality of opulence which will flatter those who travel in *our* boats. Warren said just now that others can outshine ours in various respects. What they *can't* do is offer glamour, romance and the kind of swankiness which makes passengers the envy of their friends. Only the presence of women on this flight will highlight those aspects. For God's sake, the men you want to persuade to invest in our machine have got to have the trip of their lives – something they can't wait to repeat – if we hope to succeed. They have to leave *Flamingo* on their return to Sheenmouth, having been totally seduced by the days they've spent aboard – to say nothing of the nights,' she added emphatically.

'Leone,' cried Donald in disgust, 'we're trying to discuss an important question here, and you rant on about creating a pink aerial upper-crust *bordello*.'

'That's quite ridiculous, and you know it.'

'All right, but can you deny what you're suggesting is nothing more than a flying restaurant?'

'Why not, Donald?' she cried. 'Why not a flying restaurant, a flying bar, a flying club . . . a flying Orient Express? Why not imply that to fly by *Flamingo* makes passengers into pampered darlings throughout the journey? That *is* what she's supposed to be, isn't it – a passenger aircraft?'

As Donald walked away, thrusting his hands into his pockets angrily, Warren said in thoughtful tones, 'I think Leone's on to something good. Your father told me all along that he wanted a "passenger liner with wings", and that's what we've produced. So she has to have all the glamour and luxury found on ocean-going ships. I think the scheme is an excellent one.' He turned to her, and his eyes had never held such a wealth of dreams. 'Any additional ideas?'

'Naturally,' she responded with a smile. 'I haven't spent the past five years as an exile in Europe without making my mark. Africa is still the Dark Continent of my experience, but Naples, Athens and the Mediterranean are more familiar to me than Sheenmouth. I'm known at all the grandest hotels, so a word from me would have the management of each eating from my hand. Our passengers will stay in their best suites, dine at tables decorated suitably whilst being served with any dish I care to order.' Casting a serene glance over the three men, she concluded, 'Maitland can do the sums, Donald can concentrate on business contacts and invitations, Warren can fuss and worry over the competence of the hired crew, but the glamour aspect is very definitely my province. Well, what do you say?'

'Fine . . . fine,' conceded Donald slowly, and very grudgingly. 'It sounds like a winner. There's just one snag. Where do you imagine the company will find the money to finance these frills and furbelows in flamingo-pink?'

'I'll provide it,' she told him, the thrill of anticipation bubbling inside her. 'The sale of some jewellery and furs should fetch more than enough, I imagine. I no longer have any use for them. They're part of a life I've put behind me. I have no intention of ever returning to it.'

Kit began his descent, flying parallel with the long stretch of sand-fringed coastline lapped by the translucent turquoise seas around Portugal. Lisbon was no more than fifteen minutes away. He arched his back to ease the stiffness in his shoulders after the long flight. It had not been the easiest he had ever made. The machine was old and tired; needed a complete and expensive overhaul before a disaster occurred. His mouth twisted. Tom Digby would not be losing much if it did. An obsolete floatplane flown by a pilot no one else would

269

employ hardly constituted a great asset, he reminded himself as *Gina* glided down towards the mouth of the Tagus, where Western Mediterranean Air Services slipways and hangars nestled the shore. Bathed in brilliant sunshine, the buildings stood out clearly against the dark green trees forming a windbreak behind them.

Alongside the main jetty lay a great yellow flying boat, which formed one of a fleet owned by his friend Tom. It reminded Kit of *Aphrodite* because of the colour and diminished size from above. He was always reminded of that seaplane designed by his own father whenever he looked down upon these yellow craft riding the water. As Tom's chief pilot, he had test flown each of the machines and also trained young men of mixed races to fly marine aircraft. He had trained them too well, which left himself the only man experienced in handling *Gina*, the ex-RAF floatplane used for transporting special consignments of cargo. Today, he had aboard a full load of special wine from Madeira ordered by a Portuguese aristocrat for the forthcoming wedding of his only daughter. The precious bottles stood in straw-lined crates bolted to the floor of the cargo bay, and probably constituted the only items of value aboard – apart from the life of Morris Snaith, his navigator and radio operator, who had never been in prison and whom anyone would be glad to employ.

Kit frowned as he dropped lower and lower, until the boat began to feather the surface before settling to send spray flying out on both sides of the hull. As he taxied *Gina* past the yellow machine which dwarfed her, he told himself he was lucky to be at the controls of any aircraft. The estuary was busy with small boats set rocking by the wash from the old machine he was piloting. On shore, Tom's warehousemen were coming from the large sheds on tractors towing trolleys. The wine would be loaded on to these, along with a great number of baskets and trays of orchids on ice. These blooms had been grown in the nurseries of one of the large estates

270

on Madeira. There had been no invitation to stay over-night in the grand villa, where three unmarried daugh-ters were carefully protected from airmen who came and went so spasmodically. Instead, he and Morris had occupied airless rooms in the heart of Funchal, where sleep had been interrupted by noise from the adjacent cantina.

Morris was Kit's regular navigator; an Englishman who had married a beautiful Portuguese girl who had unfortunately brought her entire family to live in the home he had struggled to provide. Gradually, poor Morris had been relegated in his own home until he now shared a room with a crippled brother-in-law. His bride slept in the master bedroom with her mother and two unmarried sisters. One of the sisters was occasionally tucked up with Kit, but Morris' plea to make it a perma-nent arrangement cut no ice with him. The two men liked each other, and worked well together on these individual flights. It was important for men to feel confi-dence and rapport when their lives rested on such a relationship.

The tricky business of docking was completed satisfac-torily, to both men's relief. It had been a hot uneventful flight, and they were tired. Leaving the aircraft, they headed across the hangar aprons to the company offices built in a tower. As they climbed the steps to the Oper-ations Room on the floor below Tom's office, Morris betrayed his reluctance at being back.

'I swear I'll stay in Madeira next time,' he grumbled, plodding two steps behind Kit. 'Each time I return, I expect to find my bed is now out in the courtyard. That's only one step to the street outside my own house.'

Pushing open the door, Kit entered the large room spread with windows. 'Assert yourself, man! Kick out ma-in-law, Rosa and Alia, then move determinedly back to the nuptial chamber.' He nodded a greeting to the men on duty, then crossed to an ancient lift which served the upper floors. Jabbing a finger on the button, he turned to confront Morris. 'I can't understand how a man who is decisive and highly intelligent in an aircraft, can go to pieces when faced with a parcel of women.'

Morris' long face lengthened further in a grimace. 'You know where you are in a flying machine. It's impossible to have the same depth of understanding with a female.'

The lift arrived, and they entered to rise up with much shuddering and knocking. Kit made no further comment: he knew exactly what his colleague meant. Although *Gina* was little more than a flying coffin, in his opinion, he felt the usual sense of anticlimax now he was back on the ground. It was always the same. Being earthbound gave a man too much time to think.

Tom greeted them genially, listened to their report on the flight and Kit's complaints about the old floatplane, then astonished them by offering them a drink.

'Very amusing,' Kit responded dryly. 'Is it the new company policy to make your employees so inebriated they don't realize what death traps they're flying?'

Tom laughed, and set up three glasses on his desk. As he poured whisky for them all, Kit reflected that his friend was a most enigmatic person. No more than thirty-five, Tom Digby was an aerial buccaneer of the most admirable kind. The discredited son of a merchant banker, he had flown all manner of aircraft for princes, potentates, emirs and any man of wealth or eccentricity willing to pay a large sum for his services. A distant scandal over a woman he had loved very deeply had left him emotionally scarred, determined never to return to his homeland. A big, rangy freckle-faced man with bright red hair, he had flown in combat during the Spanish Civil War. It had cost him the sight of one eye during a crash over mountainous terrain. Having accumulated a vast fortune from his former mercenary career, Tom had crossed into Portugal and started an airline of his own. With flair, and with the help of many influential friends he had made along his chequered path, he was building a formidable company. Right now, he appeared to have something to celebrate. Leaning back in his chair with a generous measure of whisky in his hand, and a self-satisfied expression, Tom explained his unusual generosity.

'I have just won a prestigious contract from beneath the noses of rather glossy rivals. Not only will it boost the income, it'll give the company exactly the kind of publicity it needs. You two lads will earn a tidy little bonus for making the flight of a lifetime.' Raising his glass, he smiled. 'Here's mud in your eye.'

'What's the snag?' asked Kit warily, not touching his drink.

'What's the cargo?' asked Morris, even more warily.

Tom let out a shout of laughter. 'Where's your spirit of adventure, you cautious sods? You resemble a brace of maiden aunts, instead of the two daredevils I took you for.'

'Our spirit of adventure has just been exhausted on a trip to Madeira in your aerial sarcophagus,' Kit responded. 'Like maiden aunts, we'd be more interested in the prospect of a brand-new boat, and a leisurely trip along the Med with luxury accommodation at each stop.'

'That, my lad, is exactly what you're going to get,' cried Tom triumphantly. 'I was asked to tender a quote for the price of a first-class crew to take a prototype passenger boat on her proving flight. The proverbial little bird told me what other companies were asking, so I undercut them by quite enough to ensure the contract. It's still a damned tidy sum for Western Med. The crew will earn bonus payments at the end of a successful flight, naturally.'

Stifling a surge of excitement, Kit pointed out something their employer appeared to have forgotten. 'You've just split up your crews and rearranged the flight schedules. After telling me I've trained your boys so well they can manage without me beside them now, you put me at the controls of a broken-down old machine to haul wine and flowers for weddings. I assumed that I'd been put out to grass.'

'Spare me the hearts and flowers rubbish,' Tom said, growing serious. 'You've done worse than that in your day, and you damn well know it. This contract is the chance of a lifetime to show company worth and reap all the publicity the trip will draw. Much as I hate to feed your inflated egos, you two are my best pilot and navigator. Why else would I send you on flights such as you've just completed? I wouldn't trust any of the others to handle that old bucket. Yes, I admit *Gina* needs expert handling. You're getting your reward now. This proving flight is something really special, so I'm prepared to send my prime men. I'll give you back young Joss Hamilton as your co-pilot, Kit. Morris'll be your navigator, and the rest of Joss' crew will back you up. While you're away, I'll organize the overdue service on *Gina*, and give Pele Rosario the chance to fly the Thursday service to Alexandria. He knows the ropes well enough.'

Kit still had not touched his whisky, but his excitement was gathering fast. Morris had gulped his drink, and looked ready for more to cope with his incredulity.

'I'll arrange to get you two and Joss over there in April for flight trials. The rest can join you a week before the actual trip scheduled for early May.'

'Over where?' asked Kit, with interest.

'The motherland.'

His excitement began to fade. 'For the company's chance of a lifetime you're risking it by sending me, aren't you?'

Tom gave him a level look. 'Whatever else was questioned, it was never your skill as a world-class pilot. That's what I'll be sending over.'

Morris, who knew Kit's history almost as well as Tom, asked in bemused fashion, 'It's a long way to send us just to make a proving flight.'

'Not this proving flight,' his employer told him with great relish. 'This is going to be something very special.

274

Naples, Athens, Cairo, Khartoum and all points back to Sheen . . . back home,' he amended, his gaze on Kit's face. 'A hell of an opportunity for a man to prove himself, along with the aircraft he'll be flying.'

Something inside Kit began to freeze up as he recalled himself saying, '*I'll fly your passenger liner with wings from here to Africa.*' Tom's slip of the tongue, coupled with a proving flight to Africa, was too much of a coincidence. Surely his friend would not be so lunatic as to attempt such a deception!

Growing colder by the minute, Kit asked tonelessly, 'Is the manufacturing company of this new boat situated on the Devon coast, by any chance?'

Tom nodded.

'Kirkland Marine Aviation?'

'You know damn well it is,' Tom told him quietly.

He rose to his feet. '*That's* the snag. I knew there'd be one.'

'Kit!'

'I won't do it, Tom.'

His friend rose to face him. 'Do you really want to be stuck here with my company all your life?'

'I won't do it,' he repeated.

'We'll lose the contract.'

'Joss is perfectly able to command a crew. Send him with a co-pilot.'

'If you don't go, the whole deal's off,' Tom told him heatedly. 'Good God, man, I'm not operating a good-works society here, you know. Kirkland's have developed a top-class boat called *Flamingo*, which you should already know if you're as sharp as you should be, and this proving flight is planned to be something quite stunning. The passenger list will be as diamond-studded as that of any court occasion, and the whole damned interior is to be decked out in all shades of pink. The overnight accommodation will be booked in the most splendid hotels available, all along the route.' He sighed heavily. 'It sounds a hell of a good idea, and only a superb crew will ensure total success. I happen to employ a bunch of men who could do the whole thing with their eyes closed better than any other crew, and the boost this company would get from world news coverage comprises the best piece of luck to come my way for years.'

'I won't do it, and that's flat,' Kit told him, slamming the full glass on to the desk.

'Think of Morris . . . and Joss,' pleaded his friend.

'You think of them,' Kit countered, his anger mounting further. 'When you accepted this bloody contract you knew you were putting your head into a noose. Even if I were fool enough to go ahead with this piece of stupidity, what do you imagine would happen when *I* cruised up the Sheen and presented myself as their hired pilot? No, Tom, you go jump off a cliff.'

The other man adopted a voice loaded with tragedy. 'My life savings are sunk into this company; my reputation has been laid on the line with the signing of this contract. I'd captain the crew myself, except . . .' He put his hand over his blind eye theatrically, a trick he used in the hope of gaining sympathy when outnumbered.

It angered Kit further today. 'Don't play that game with me, Tom. You knew damned well what you were risking when you agreed to the terms of that contract. One look at me in connection with any of that family's dealings, and they'd have your guts for garters, you fool. Send Joss over to captain the crew of their glittering, glamorous pink machine, because nothing in the world would make me do it.' Pushing the full glass towards Tom, he added, 'I've nothing to celebrate . . . and I'll drink my own, thanks.'

He left the office, slamming the door on his friend, the Kirkland family, and Warren Grant's *Flamingo*.

10

For once, Kit drove along the rutted coastal road with great care. Those in hamlets he passed through, who were used to his friendly wave as the car roared past, shook their heads in mystification. Only a man in love could be so lost to his surroundings, they all agreed. Alia Terrazi had surely not captured his heart after failing for so long, so the lady must be someone very special who had, perhaps, arrived in one of the great yellow flying machines today. They were pleased. Senhor Anson needed a woman to look after him, and little Alia was not suitable for a man of his calibre. A young, strong, handsome fellow who could make a big metal bird rise into the sky and descend to alight on the water, deserved a woman of beauty and culture.

Kit drove with care only because he was so deep in thought he did it automatically. He was not really angry with Tom; they were too close in friendship to fall out for long. The scene he had walked away from had revived memories and inspired introspection. Both were affecting him deeply, as he took the shabby Bugatti over the track which ran alongside clear turquoise water shimmering in the cool sunshine. The breeze ruffled his hair, and he could have been flying *Aphrodite* over Sheenmouth on a June day after mist had cleared to leave blue sparkling clarity wherever he looked.

His vision suddenly blurred. He lifted a hand automatically to polish the lenses of his goggles, found he

277

was wearing none, and wisely swung the car to a halt facing the sea on a small overhang. For a moment or two, he sat bringing himself under control. Tom had been right. No aviator fascinated by marine aircraft was unaware of new designs being developed. So she was finished! Warren's promised passenger liner with wings. The proving flight to Africa had been his own idea, although he had not imagined glamour and pink fizz. Leone's suggestion, of course. The trip was certain to cause a sensation – another connected with the Kirkland name.

Resting his head back on the seat, he gazed at the sky. He could already see her up there – a great, graceful white water-bird gliding majestically across several oceans and continents with all four engines humming sweetly. Did she retain any of those features he had initially conceived with Warren? How long had it taken before his former friend had realized that Donald was not the brilliant designer the world believed him to be? Kirkland's must have been expanded to cope with the production of this prototype. Memories of the company slipways and hangars came rushing back to overwhelm him. The hours he had spent there fussing over *Aphrodite* prior to that record-breaking flight! Then the morning of the attempt; mist hanging over the Sheen and himself shivering with nervousness as he waited for it to clear. The greatest day of his life! Whatever they had done to him afterwards, that day would always be his and his alone. Although the Italians had taken the record from him two years later with an astonishing 440 m.p.h., the Anson name would grace official records for ever. Even the Kirklands could not take the achievement from him.

Frustration escaped in a deep sigh. Whatever had possessed Tom to tender an offer to Kirkland's knowing what he knew of the affair? Although Kit owed his present employment to the red-haired man who had befriended him, the debt was not so great that he would expose himself to Kirkland ruthlessness once more.

Donald would never risk any association with a man named Anson, either. That contract had been doomed from the outset. Young Joss Hamilton was a good steady pilot, but lacked the wider experience this job demanded. What a flight! What an opportunity for any pilot to gain an international reputation! What a wonderful prospect for any man who was not called Christopher Paul Anson!

Straightening up and turning the ignition key, he backed the car on to the track and drove to the isolated two-roomed villa he rented from a local landowner. Mrs Valenques, the woman who cleaned and cooked for him, would have seen him pass her stone house and would come before long to get him a meal. The place smelled airless, so he left the door ajar and opened the windows despite the chill of the day. Filled with a sense of pointlessness, he gazed around the room as if seeing it for the first time. Mrs Valenques had tidied it in his absence, but she knew better than to touch the roll-top desk which would not close because of the piled books and wads of papers stuffed into it. He went across, fingering the dusty covers of manuals on aeronautical engineering, aerial navigation and the theory of flight. Maps, charts, tide-tables, a list of international radio signals, notes on nautical hazards, and information on tidal flows, prevailing winds and time differentials for most of the world all crowded together in organized chaos. He knew where to lay his hand on any of them immediately. The collective essentials of a profession he could not abandon! His gaze then shifted to the desk top and the framed picture standing there. *Dad's finest design*. The photograph was now one of *Aphrodite*, with himself waving triumphantly from the cockpit. He might never be able to reveal the truth to the world, but he wanted it there before his own eyes every day of his life.

Turning to face the room, this opportunity he could not take suddenly became unbearably beckoning. Five years ago he had vowed to take a flying boat in triumph

279

to Africa and back. Now, but for a name, he could fulfil that vow and make aviation history again. Walking into the bedroom, he took from the wardrobe a full bottle of whisky. Settling himself fully clothed on the bed, he put the neck of the bottle to his lips and began to drink in an attempt to blot from his mind all thought of a draughty, ice-cold enormous cockpit housing the controls of the latest, most exciting flying boat anywhere in the world – a cockpit he burned to occupy.

The two years he had spent in prison could have been worse hell than they had seemed. Sir Hector Kirkland had had no influence over convicted criminals, and Kit had been regarded as a hero still by his fellow prisoners. His jailors had also maintained a reasonable attitude towards him, giving opportunities for additional study or exercise when they could. He had even been asked twice to lecture the more privileged inmates on aeronautics. Only during his last three months had a new prison officer made his life total purgatory, due to an inborn resentment of anyone he regarded as a 'toff'. The entire twenty-four months could have been like that, Kit knew, but the real hell had been incarceration. For a man who only came fully alive when rising up into the vast open heavens, imprisonment had bred a kind of madness constantly beneath the surface of his outer calm. It had attacked his subconscious, making him awake screaming on many occasions. It still happened now and then, which was why he kept the whisky in his bedroom.

He had returned to the world on a bitter November day in 1934 to find unemployment rife, and Europe in turmoil. Rumours of another war in the near future affected the stock market and industry, as Adolph Hitler and his Nazi party took control of Germany backed by the growing might of its armed forces. Britain had no money for military expansion, so the problem was shelved. Her aviators were still being treated lightly by the government, Kit had discovered, despite remarkable development of aircraft by the leading companies. He had read the details eagerly, but the full extent of Kirkland power and influence had been realized when he presented himself at the offices of these firms. Even at small private airfields, the name Kit Anson registered negatives. Pride would not allow him to change it. Finally, after a period of deepening degradation, resulting in eating at soup-kitchens and sleeping where he could, which had reminded him of bedding down with the Sheenmouth donkeys, he had been offered a job as a greaser in a canning factory in Wapping. The girl who worked in the office became friendly with him after he had rescued her from the unwelcome attentions of the head storeman, and only her intervention with the manager had saved Kit from being sacked on the spot. Meg had offered him a bed in a house owned by her aunt. Soon, they were sharing it regularly. Then her aunt had discovered them together, and agreed to let him remain on condition that she shared the bed in place of her niece. He had left the house and spent that night in the garden shed.

Almost two years of desperate half-life had followed, until Kit had read of the young Englishmen flocking to join the International Brigades to fight the Fascists in Spain. Those organizing such irregular bands welcomed any man willing to risk his life in the cause they championed. Although Kit's name was known to them, too, they saw him in a vastly different light. He was sent out to join a squadron of buccaneering, eccentric pilots who gladly flew any machine available to them in bombing and machine-gunning raids. To be in the air again, albeit in slow, outmoded wartime models, was the first sensation of freedom Kit had felt since leaving prison. The company of other aviators had completed his cure. One of these had been Tom Digby and, on a night when they had both been highly elated with battle success, Kit had confided to his new friend a truth he had spoken of to no one save his solicitor, at the time of the trial. Then,

281

he had been advised not to attempt to save himself with such a story since it was certain to add to his discredit.

Kit had been flying alongside Tom when his friend had been shot down, so had been able to pinpoint the crash for the Spanish rebels who had gone into the mountains with mules and brought the wounded man in. Realizing that his flying days were over, Tom had decided to start his own airline in neighbouring Portugal. He had asked Kit to join him as his chief pilot, and they had been in operation for six months. Franco was pushing ahead with his bid for control of Spain, despite the collection of assorted foreigners who were still attempting to help the Republican forces. Adolph Hitler was pushing ahead with his bid for control of all he could get, in addition to lending troops to Franco, and the possibility of another war in Europe seemed stronger with his every move. There was little doubt in Kit's mind that his combat experience in Spain would one day stand him in good stead, yet his love for marine aircraft kept him yearning for something beyond his reach. Today, Tom had offered it to him on a plate, and he was forced to refuse it. He tipped the bottle again.

Two years in prison had forcibly changed his drinking habits. Two further years of such poverty he could not afford to buy it had left him well able to do without alcohol for most of the time. In consequence, however, on those few occasions when he needed the oblivion it brought so easily, he became very inebriated in a short time. Today, he deliberately set out to empty the bottle as he stared steadfastly at the photograph of *Aphrodite*. Dad's finest design flown by his own son! Sir Hector was dead, so only himself, Donald and Tom Digby knew the truth now. God, but it would be wonderful to vindicate the Ansons and make the surviving Kirkland pay for what they had done.

Gulping more whisky, he began to grin. Imagine terrifying the wits out of young Donald by taking command of his brand-new prototype on its proving flight! Imagine being the pilot hired to take assorted Very Important Persons halfway across the world, in a pink-lined flying boat upon which all Kirkland hopes were centred! The grin turned into a chuckle. Imagine being a thorn in the Kirklands' side throughout the entire trip! Donald would never be sure of his captain, never know what he might do or say, never know if he was flying in the right direction and whether he would land where he should. Just think of the public sensation at the news that Kirkland and Anson were joining forces again. If publicity for the flight was what they were after, they would get it in full!

Kit's chuckle then turned into full-blooded laughter that echoed louder and louder in his head. Then he felt himself falling.

He hit the ground with a tremendous thud which knocked the breath from him, but he still appeared to be alive because he could hear voices speaking his name. Hands seized his arms and legs, then he felt himself floating through the air as those bearing him along spoke a lot of nonsense to each other. He was lowered into a remarkably uncomfortable seat which appeared to be fashioned from stone. Next minute, he gave a gasp of shock as a cold deluge hit him and continued in some force, until he was shaking and spluttering uncontrollably. Next, he was hauled upright and stripped naked, before rough hands lifted him again. Something soft and warm folded around his body as scalding liquid was forced down his throat. He now felt too weary to care what was happening, yet each time he began to drift away into flamingo-pink fluffy clouds, he was shaken until his head rocked back and forth.

'Come on, man, sober up!' commanded a voice in his ear. 'We're not letting you alone until this has been thrashed out.'

With sleep consistently denied him and cup after cup of black coffee disappearing down his throat, he reluctantly faced the fact that he was in his villa at Lisbon feeling very sorry for himself. The flight of *Flamingo* had been no more than fantasy, and he was still the man the Kirklands had tried to destroy, and damn near did.

He studied his friends morosely as he clutched the thick towel around his shoulders. 'I suppose you expect me to say thanks.'

Morris shook his head. 'We know you too well for that.'

'And I know you too well to believe you all came here purely out of concern for my welfare,' he responded. 'You're wasting your time. I won't do it.'

'You're a fool,' Tom declared. 'I didn't expect you to jump at it – knew I'd probably have to twist your arm a little – but this reaction is damned ridiculous. It's also extremely unfair on your crew, Digger, Morris and Joss, who're faced with the chance of their careers right now.'

'I'm not stopping them,' Kit murmured, rubbing ineffectively at his wet hair with the towel. 'They're welcome to take a trip in a fine pink Kirkland creation. I wish 'em the best of luck!'

'I wouldn't offer to take command of a boat like that,' Joss said frankly. 'My experience is too limited.'

'Yes, it is, but if you're dead set on this trip, you'll have to overcome your shortcomings,' Kit said forcefully. 'Excuse me, but my bladder is now bursting. If you're all gone by the time I get back, I'll quite understand.'

In the tiled bathroom he also towelled his hair dry, brushed his teeth, and donned the thick robe hanging on the back of the door. Returning to his sitting room, he found them all drinking coffee and munching the meat patties Mrs Valenques had brought in for him.

'Make yourselves at home,' he told them sarcastically. 'As you appear to like it here so much, I can always leave instead.'

'Sit down, you stubborn bastard,' said Tom, 'and listen to some sound advice.'

Morris leaned forward with his arms along his thighs

to speak seriously to Kit. 'I don't know the full ins and outs of your quarrel with the Kirkland family, but you don't seem the kind of chap to rat on people who befriend you, as they apparently suggested. Your refusal to meet up with them again makes me feel those two years in the clink didn't solve anything. All the same, this contract means a lot to all of us – especially Tom, who also befriended you – and you're the only thing stopping us from taking it up.'

Joss coloured slightly at Morris' ruthless criticism of a man he deeply admired. He was still young and rather sensitive.

'The company has no other pilot of your standing and skill, Kit, and truly I'd be terrified of taking command of *Flamingo*, even with Pele or Juan as my second,' he said.

'If you haven't the necessary guts to take on the job, Kirkland's will have to offer the job elsewhere,' Kit said then. 'Spare me all this "hearts and flowers" stuff. It's having no effect on me whatever.'

Tom got to his feet. 'OK, so your friends mean nothing to you. We'll have to learn to live with that. Let me just outline something for you before we all leave. You once held the world air speed record. That makes you one of the finest fliers of marine aircraft alive today. In Spain, I saw you remain cool and controlled in emergencies which made other men panic. Whoever flies *Flamingo* on this exacting trip will gain an experience second to none. Now, my friend, you have a score to settle with that family – you confided in me one night, if you recall – and it's a bloody big score, in my opinion. I'm offering you the chance to do it in the most satisfying fashion, with the added bonus of enhancing your reputation even further with this single flight. Unlike Morris, Joss and the rest of the world, I know you didn't rat on those who befriended you – quite the reverse – so go over there and fly their prototype while you watch them squirm. I'll read the newspaper accounts of your triumph with the utmost relish.'

Although Tom was actually outlining what he, himself, had imagined whilst getting drunk, Kit still objected. 'One sight of the name Anson on the flight list would cause a storm of protest.'

'I don't have to supply your names,' said Tom calmly. 'Just so long as I list your official ranks – Captain, First Officer, Navigator and so on – then supply age, qualifications and experience. I don't think anyone at Kirkland's will care what you're called. The chap I've been dealing with – a pompous ass named Maitland Jarvis – behaves as though aircrew are faceless creatures who operate in the nose of the aircraft and won't be seen by the VIP passengers.'

'They might not care about names, but they'll bloody well care about my face, when they see it, Tom.'

His friend grinned. 'By then, time will be running too short for them to do anything about it. They'll be stuck with you, old son. Aren't you avid to see whether or not they panic when brought face to face with Kit Anson after all these years?'

Looking around at Morris' lean, hopeful face, Joss' youthful eagerness, Digger's challenge and Tom's confident, amused expression, he heard himself say, 'It's no good, I won't do it. *And that's final.*' Somehow, even to his own ears, it did not sound in the least final now.

There had been heavy rain for two days, and the Sheen was swollen. The high spring tides often coincided with a spell of typical April weather, but floods rarely occurred along this stretch of the river because both banks rose quite sharply. Only when quite exceptional conditions prevailed did the low-lying area around Forton sometimes vanish under the water. At the moment, the level on the company's slipways was much higher than usual, but it simply meant that the aircraft launched quicker. There was little fear of the hangars being invaded by the river at high tide. With only four weeks to go, worries were plentiful enough without that additional one.

The morning was like polished glass; everything stood out clean and sparkling in the welcome sunshine. Leone rode home fast across the downland bordering the Magnum Pomeroy road just beyond the Abbey boundary. It was pure joy to get out into the fresh air after the past two dismal days, and Jemima appeared to share the feeling. The mare could not share Leone's desire for escape from the other occupants of the monastery, however. As the departure date drew nearer, tempers were growing shorter, including her own. Warren, having adamantly refused to fly *Flamingo* himself, was fussing and fretting over the proficiency of the hired crew despite his own admission that their listed qualifications and experience could hardly be bettered. Donald was predicting disaster from every direction, checking facts he knew to be sound, and lying awake at night worrying about failure and possible closure of Kirkland's. Only Maitland remained calm, supremely assured, and ready to metaphorically soothe brows. Strangely, it was his attitude which most ruffled Leone's nerves. Why did the man never betray human feelings like everyone else? After two days being cooped up with his unctuous perfection, she had escaped to the more natural variety to be found out of doors.

Cantering over the moist turf in jodhpurs and scarlet jumper, with the breeze ruffling her hair, she found herself able to think clearly about the subject causing so much anguish and anticipation. She had gained her way over the glamour aspect of the flight. Warren had been a surprising ally in that, whether through enthusiasm for the idea or for herself she was unsure. That he was growing fond of her was very apparent. She told herself that she should do everything to discourage him. The knowledge that his admiration was genuine, and given with no idea of reward, made it too precious to discard lightly. He was a sweet shy person, who laid himself open to the kind of deep hurt she had so often suffered through misplaced affection. Today's world had no use for sincerity and devotion, she had discovered. Only when dealing with his beloved creation did Warren grow assertive, stubborn and almost ruthless. He, at least, should be happier after today. The crew hired by Maitland was to present itself at Sheenmouth Abbey this morning.

Donald had invited an impressive selection of guests, all of whom had leapt at the opportunity to make this maiden flight. Although he had not acceded to Leone's suggestion that an actress or two be included, he had secured the acceptances of an émigré Russian countess, and a celebrated society hostess known to her friends as 'the even merrier widow'. Leone had met her at St Moritz, Monte Carlo, and Heidelberg but, like most of that set, knew Monique Carlyon-Bree more by what was said of her than by personal knowledge of the woman. Countess Renskaya had not graced the younger strata in which Leone had moved, but Donald had met her socially and commercially, for she dabbled in all manner of investments.

The sale of her furs and jewels had brought Leone a large sum, and further funds had been gained by disposing of the London apartment which both she and Donald felt was superfluous when they had the mews cottage. Leone's approach to the hotels they would use en route had been highly successful. Anything she desired could be provided by those managements used to catering for the whims and eccentricities of those with wealth or title. The notion of a party of influential guests arriving by pink flying boat, which would anchor offshore to attract public excitement, appealed to their love of the grand style. They rose to the challenge magnificently. The decor and upholstering of the aircraft's interior had now been completed, although the finishing touches had still to be added. Leone was highly delighted with the outcome of her inventive plans.

Slowing her progress as she neared a small band of copse marking the Abbey boundary, she sighed with pleasure at the visual glory of the morning. The trees were yellow-green with their first new foliage, and lamb's tails hung fat and fluffy from many branches. Larks had risen at her progress across the downland, and still sung joyously now they were no more than tiny specks high above her. A vee-shaped squadron of ducks came in to land on the river, with feet outstretched, as she broke through the copse into the grounds of her home. Greetings were quacked between those already on the Sheen and the new arrivals. The ferry on its way up to Forton scattered them as it came in closer to the Kirkland jetty than usual due to the high water. The Abbey was always a landmark of interest to those travelling the river, and it had been even more so recently. Leone had no doubt that the departure of *Flamingo*, with her distinguished passengers, would bring visitors to Sheenmouth in their hundreds to witness the event.

Turning Jemima towards the stables, Leone reflected that the tradesmen of the little seaside resort would welcome the invasion of sightseers at the start of the summer season, despite the weekly condemnation of the whole project by the *Sheenmouth Clarion*. The editor wrote almost vitriolically of the Kirkland family, the company, the arrangements for the flight, and the money being spent on 'ridiculous pampering of those who expect to bathe in pink champagne while ninety per cent of British people could not afford a bar of plain soap'. Leone had been infuriated, but Donald had advised her to ignore such nonsense, adding that Jack Cummings, the editor, had been a rank socialist since returning from the war so had always conducted a campaign against the most prominent family in the district. Where he learned much of what was correctly quoted, they could only guess.

Handing Jemima over to Porter at the stables, Leone

walked slowly alongside the north wing of the Abbey past the swimming pool and tennis courts, where she had spent so many hours of her lonely school holidays. Although emotionally bereft still, there was a new sense of purpose in her life. All she did had some practical use now. Given time, she felt confident of learning more about the business of manufacturing marine aircraft. She enjoyed flying, although what Warren called 'the schoolroom learning' was very unpopular with her. Try as she might, understanding the contents of the manuals he had given her was still very difficult. Handling an aircraft was one thing; understanding why and how it did what she wanted was a different matter altogether. She had used the flight of *Flamingo* as an excuse to leave her studies, yet she would never gain her licence until she had mastered the technical aspect of navigation. When she returned from Africa, a determined effort must be made to reach the standard required for a pilot's licence. All in all, however, life was good. She was happier than she had ever been in her life. There was no thought in her head as she entered by the studded door in the north wing, that it had been merely the calm before the storm.

Making her way through the ground-floor corridors to the central vaulted hall, she admired Mrs Marshall's choice of floral decorations in the niches which, doubtless, had once contained religious objects. The woman was a gem after the prune-faced Mrs Roberts. Crossing the stone floor tinted with colour from the sun on stained glass, Leone saw her brother come from the library as if in a trance. He looked rather pale, and stared at her with blue eyes as expressionless as pieces of china.

'You look very odd,' she commented. 'What's happened?'

'Eh?' Her voice appeared to bring him back to awareness of his surroundings.

'Is something wrong? Nothing has happened to *Fla-*

mingo, has it?' she asked anxiously, it being the greatest disaster she could think of, at present.

Donald shook his head slowly. 'The pilot we hired to fly her has arrived.'

'The man from Portugal?'

'He's . . . it's Kit Anson.'

She gazed at him, turning cold. 'If that's your idea of a joke, I can think of funnier ones.'

'He's in the library with Warren now. No one's laughing, I assure you,' Donald told her in vague tones, obviously deeply shaken and upset.

'He's in the library? *Kit Anson is in our library at this moment?*'

'Yes.'

'Then he can leave immediately,' she said, through a tightening throat. 'Why haven't you already thrown him out?'

'I can't. We've engaged him to fly *Flamingo*.'

'We've engaged a pilot from a Portuguese airline.'

'He is a pilot from a Portuguese airline.'

'We'll have to get a different one.'

'Maitland signed a contract.'

'Tear it up!' She ran a distracted hand through her shoulder-length waved hair. 'My God, this is ridiculous! It's totally ridiculous. How can that man be here?' Looking at Donald wildly, she cried, 'Maitland arranged all this, didn't he? Ha! At last, the perfect, infallible, sickening Maitland has made a mistake. He'd better rectify it pretty damn quick.' Highly worked up, she walked back and forth with the sound of her angry steps echoing from the vaulted ceiling. Eventually, she turned to plead with him. 'Donald, how can he be a pilot from Portugal? He was imprisoned, disgraced. Who would employ a man with his record and put him in charge of an aircraft? There must be some mistake. Maitland must have gone completely mad!'

'Don't blame Maitland. He had no idea this could happen. The airline based in Lisbon is a reliable and

291

growing company which offered us the best terms for a crew whose combined experience and qualifications were most impressive. There were no names given on the contract, just ranks.'

Swinging round in the middle of her pacing, she cried, 'Then we're under no legal obligation to accept him. Don't you see that? Tear up that contract and we'll go elsewhere.'

'There isn't *time* to go elsewhere,' he told her wearily.

'Make the people in Lisbon send another pilot.'

'He's the captain of an entire crew. They'd all have to be replaced.'

'Then replace the whole bally lot,' she said through her teeth. 'Haven't you any pride at all, Donald?'

Goaded from his stunned acceptance, he said furiously, 'I have a prototype flying boat on which the future of Kirkland Marine Aviation and this family depends. So much ballyhoo already surrounds this flight to Africa, we can't possibly postpone it while we find another pilot and crew of equivalent skill and experience who will accept the sum this airline agreed with us. The harm's been done, you must see that. It'll cause as much publicity if we fire him as if we go ahead and let him take the flight.'

Unable to believe what she was hearing, Leone went for her brother's throat with her next words. 'I hold a fifty per cent share in *Flamingo*, don't forget. My vote rejects this crew. I refuse to have any member of it on this flight.'

'This flight is vital to the survival of all of which you own fifty per cent,' her brother told her wearily. 'We *can't* reject this crew. We need the best . . . and Warren says we've had the good fortune to be offered it. Anson simply has to pilot the machine. He'll be up in the flight cabin all the time, with no chance to leave it and mix with the passengers.'

Still fighting a sense of panic, Leone said urgently,

'Donald, he stole Father's money, some drawings, and the girl you loved. Haven't you any pride at all?'

'Not when I'm faced with the unavoidable. That's half your trouble, Leone. No wonder you can't find anyone to share your life. No man on earth could ever live up to your requirements.' Taking her arm, he turned her to face him. 'We all knew about your adolescent worship, which received a severe slap in the face when the hero turned out to be the villain, instead. Was it because he took Father's money, or because he took Stephanie that makes you unable to face him now?'

With reaction fast confusing her clarity of thought, she mumbled, 'You can't do this against my will. My vote cancels yours.'

'Oh, for Christ's sake,' Donald swore, losing the last of his patience. 'OK, go ahead and fire him!' Waving a hand at the library door, he repeated, 'Go ahead and fire him. All you have to do then is find another pilot and crew for the same price by Friday. They'll need a minimum of two weeks to familiarize themselves with and test fly *Flamingo*, study the route, tides and prevailing winds along the flight paths. If we have more weather like we've had the last two days, they won't be able to take her up at all, so you'll have to allow another week on top of that. Use your damned fifty per cent . . . but if any action of yours ruins this venture, it'll be fifty per cent of nothing at all.' Turning on his heel, he finished harshly, 'Go ahead and fire him. Tell yourself you're Father's daughter, if that's what you want to believe, but he'd take this on the chin and turn it to his own advantage. What's done is done, was his philosophy. Men never let emotion make fools of them when it comes to business.'

The sound of his footsteps receded as he reached the branched staircase. Soon, the distant sound of a slamming door cut him off completely, and Leone was left in that great draughty hall with his last words ringing in her ears. Here, in this same hall, she had been told of

Kit's treachery. Surely her father would want her Kirkland pride to overrule Donald's weakness now.

Gripping her riding crop tightly, she moved towards the library door and pushed it open. Ridiculously, she somehow expected to see an ashen-faced boy dressed in cheap tweed from which bony wrists projected too far. Instead, standing beside Warren was a tall sturdy man in a well-tailored dark-green uniform embellished with gold insignia of rank on sleeves and lapels. As she halted just inside the door, he studied her silently for a moment or so before moving forward.

'Five years have wrought changes in you, Leone. I would hardly have known you,' Kit said, in the voice which still contained the soft Devonshire accent. He offered his hand. 'How are you?'

Nothing had prepared her for what she felt on confronting him again. With heartbeat racing, she studied his face for signs of the treacherous charmer he was. All she saw were lines of experience where there used to be laughter lines, a mouth which was straight and tense instead of curved into a disarming smile, and familiar dark eyes which gazed back unflinchingly at her. The shock of his betrayal might have been that moment inflicted, it hurt her so unbearably, as she stood there still loving him and realizing why her life had been so empty and unhappy for the past five years.

Kirkland pride finally came to her rescue, making it possible for her to say, 'You're fired.'

His hand dropped to his side. 'We've already thrashed that out with Donald.'

'I'm the other half of the partnership. The half which refuses to allow you to fly *Flamingo*.'

Warren moved up to them. 'Leone, there's no time . . .'

'Keep out of this,' she told him, her gaze still on Kit. 'This is a matter between management and a prospective employee. Your application is rejected, Mr Anson.'

'*Captain* Anson,' he informed her quietly. 'You'll never find another crew by your departure date.'

All at once, she saw the truth. 'You knew that all along! You deliberately omitted the names on that contract so that we'd be forced to let you take this vital flight.'

Warren was shocked. 'You don't know what you're saying. Kit wouldn't . . .'

Rounding on him, she said tautly, 'I'll deal with this my own way. It doesn't concern you.'

'Oh yes, it does,' he returned heatedly. 'I designed *Flamingo*, and I insist that she be given every opportunity to display her top-class qualities. Kit's the right man to do that. He was in on her conception – it was through him that I was given the job by your father – and he even made some of the initial developments with me. He's one of the finest pilots in the world when handling marine aircraft.' Putting his hand on her arm, he continued forcefully, 'Our only concern now should be the total success Kit can make of this proving flight . . . not some silly affair which happened five years ago.'

'*Some silly affair!*' she cried, shaking his hand from her. 'He stole ten thousand pounds, the plans for a new seaplane, and my brother's future wife. He threw Kirkland generosity back in our faces. What makes you imagine I'd agree to have him anywhere near me again?'

Sensing slight movement beside her, she turned back to find Kit's expression had hardened. 'My God, they really hated me, didn't they? You were little more than a child, who should have been kept right out of it.'

'The shocking details were in all the newspapers for any child to read. Womanizing, drunkenness, *lies*,' she flung at him. 'I suppose I should be glad you took Stephanie as part of your Kirkland haul, because she would otherwise be married to Donald by now.' Trying to retain control of herself and the situation, she added with a tone of breathless finality, 'I won't have you on this flight, neither will I have you in this house a moment longer.'

Kit gazed at her for a long while, an incomprehensible emotion darkening his square face. Then he said, 'You've plainly been indoctrinated with the Kirkland ten commandments. One day, I'll tell you what they really are. I'll leave your house right now, but only to go down to the workshops to look over *Flamingo*. Whether you like it or not, you'll have to accept that I shall be flying her to Africa and back. If you find that impossible, you had best stay here in your ivory tower, while the rest of us make further aviation history.'

11

Although the weather was extremely chill for May, it discouraged none of those bent on seeing *Flamingo* set out on a flight wrapped in glamour, intrigue and bravado. Newspapers had been full of details. Hardly a day had passed without an item covering some aspect of a journey which had captured the nation's interest. The notion of a flying boat with pink seats and walls, filled with financiers and diamond-decked ladies destined to be served *haute cuisine* meals in mid-air, was a dazzling enough prospect for anyone. When news of the most bizarre aspect of the flight had been announced in headlines an inch high, even those who had been dismissive of the affair began to find the flight of *Flamingo* highly intriguing. With the revelation of Kit Anson's contract to fly the prototype came speculation on the astonishing liaison between this particular man and the Kirklands, after the scandal of the past.

For days, the stretch of water between Sheenmouth Abbey and Kirkland Marine Aviation had been patrolled by photographers with eager journalists. The monastery itself had been under virtual siege, with newsmen chasing every car seen leaving it, day or night. It was the same at the company workshops, and Kit had been forced to ask for police patrols to keep the sightseeing boats clear of the water channels during the many trials, after two near accidents with small boats.

On the morning of departure Sheenmouth residents

recalled the events of almost six years before when the little resort had been filled with visitors eager to see Kit Anson either break a record or his neck, according to how bloodthirsty they were. Once more, the roads leading down to the coast had been jammed since just after breakfast, and cafés were doing a roaring trade in tea and toast. By ten thirty, just an hour before the scheduled departure, spectators had crowded the banks of the Sheen near Kirkland's to await the arrival of the passengers. From the company slipways, right up to the Abbey itself, any stretch of the riverbank accessible to determined people provided a viewpoint. Riverside residents were outraged when total strangers asked to be allowed to watch the waterborne procession from their neat, sloping lawns. When these same strangers began assembling in private gardens uninvited, the owners accepted the inevitable and even provided tea and biscuits at a shilling per head.

With attention focused on the Sheen and the Abbey, the crew of *Flamingo* hoped to be able to reach the workshops via the narrow road across Giddesworth Downs without trouble. However, coming from their hotel on the promenade, they were immediately mobbed by girls who had discovered where they were lodged and lain in wait for them. The appearance of these tanned young men in green and gold uniforms, led by the rakish, notorious Kit Anson, put the girls in a frenzy of excitement. Young Joss Hamilton went over in the rush, Morris was dazed into submission, and Digger Rathbone, the Australian engineer, kissed as many as he could whilst wishing they had arrived the evening before so that he could have taken greater advantage of their enthusiasm.

Kit experienced an unpleasant sensation of *déjà vu*, as he fought his way through the press of eager young women leaving lipstick smears on his face, neck and shirt collar. The past four weeks had proved to be more difficult than he had feared, and today was certain to revive that other occasion far too painfully. He longed to reach the cockpit, start those four powerful engines and rise up into the sky in the direction of the Mediterranean. Returning to Sheenmouth had been a most unhappy experience. The Abbey had held too many memories of a young man doing anything save lick Sir Hector's boots, to show his gratitude for being taken in by the great man of aviation. Maitland had been as supercilious as ever. Donald had swiftly collapsed beneath the inevitable, but had since spoken only through an 'interpreter' in the guise of Warren or Maitland, which was even more insulting than treating him as a servant.

Leone had been an initial shock. At twenty-two, she was strikingly changed from the young girl he had tried to prevent from hero-worshipping someone she hardly knew. Today's Leone had even greater determination, and an excess of pride which already hinted at another ruthless Kirkland in the making. Her adolescent adoration of him had vanished beneath an astonishing reverse emotion. He regretted her presence on this flight. Donald and Maitland he could handle well enough, because their behaviour was predictable. The girl had always been precocious; now she had power to back her whims and fancies. That made her potentially dangerous on an occasion as important as this. Already, she had ruled that his duty was simply to fly *Flamingo* to Africa and back. At no time would he or members of his flight crew mingle with the passengers. His colleagues had immediately demanded that he tell her it was usual for the captain and first officer to do so, if only to reassure those whose lives were in their hands. He had refused. Members of the Kirkland family made laws, not requests, he had advised them.

As he presently escaped the clutches of a girl bent on removing his tie for a memento, and scrambled into the front seat of the first of the waiting taxis, he told himself he had no wish to leave the cockpit to socialize with those who would regard him as nothing more than an interesting specimen. At the controls of *Flamingo* he would be as happy as a man could be. That was where he planned to remain during this flight. He was a simple flying boat pilot now, not a record-breaking hero of the skies. All the same, if massive orders were not placed at the end of the unique flight, it would be through no fault of his own. *Flamingo* was as superb as Warren had claimed. The rapport between himself and the young designer had instantly revived and, apart from the satisfying thrill of flying a world-class boat, their friendship was the only aspect which had made his return home bearable.

Joss, Morris and Digger piled into the back seat, and the taxi nosed its way forward slowly until several girls pulled a suicidal friend from her seat on the bonnet. She left sticky red imprints from uninhibited kisses on the windscreen in front of Kit, much to the disgust of Gerry Maggs who owned the cab.

'No shame, some of 'em,' he grumbled to Kit, whom he had known since his boyhood. 'You should see the sights on the beach come summer, these days. In a darn sight less than they should be, they are, gigglin' and throwin' theirselves at young men, with no thought of the consequences. It's the poor lads'll be blamed when they find theirselves in the family way, you mark my words. I don't agree with it, Mr Anson. Remember those days when you used to exercise the donkeys? Didn't never see young women prancing about around you like they did just now, did you? Stands to reason the world was better off when they did as they was told.'

'They still do when you handle them the right way,' Digger called from the back seat.

'My right pocket's practically torn right off,' marvelled Morris. 'I wish Marie had seen those adoring girls. Might have made her think.'

Glancing over his shoulder, Kit said, 'There are other ways of making her think, and I keep suggesting them to you. It's like talking to a brick wall.' Seeing his co-pilot's bemused expression, he grinned. 'Squeezed in rather a sensitive place, were you?'

The youngster coloured. 'I've been flying the Lisbon to Alex route for several months, but I've never had a reception like that at either end.'

Digger asked dryly, 'You don't think they were there to see *you*, do you?'

'I don't care who they came to see, it was very enjoyable to get the leftovers,' Joss said. 'Can we pretend we've forgotten something, and go back?'

'And risk Miss Kirkland's wrath? Just pray she doesn't see us in this state,' advised Morris.

'She has to be strict,' Joss replied, in her defence. 'For a young girl, she has a tremendous amount of responsibility.'

'Not half as much as you have at the controls of a flight to Alex, and you're much the same age,' pointed out Kit quietly.

'Ya, you're talking to a lovesick lad,' Digger said carelessly. 'He won't hear a word said against Luscious Leone.'

'Shut up!' commanded the blushing Joss.

'I intend to concentrate on the walking tiaras,' Digger continued, unabashed by the youngster's fury. 'With my craggy good looks and Outback charm, I should catch the eye of some lonely widow looking for the spice of life before she pegs out.'

'You won't get the chance,' Kit told him, as the taxi climbed up to Giddesworth Downs where he used to court young May after school hours, and where he had once fought a boy for calling his father a drunken sot. 'We've had our orders to stay away from the passengers. I suggest we comply with them.'

He lapsed into silence as they crossed a stretch of high ground he knew so well. Twenty-two years of his life had been spent at Sheenmouth, the only happy ones being the first seven and the last three. Especially the last three. They had been glittering years. Like a bauble on a Christmas tree, he had been covered in the shining, shimmering dust of glory, suspended in time and space for all to see and admire. Then, those who had once ridiculed him had been dazzled by his achievements; others had been brightened and enriched by them. That festive period had been so triumphant even he had forgotten how fragile a blown-glass bauble could be, how precarious on the end of a branch easily snapped from the sturdy powerful trunk. The Kirkland family had dashed him to the ground. Prison boots had trampled the shattered pieces until they were no more than dust. There was no way of putting those motes together so that they shone and sparkled as before. Returning to Sheenmouth had simply highlighted that fact. He should never have come home.

The taxi reached the far side of Giddesworth Downs and began its descent of Riverside Road, which led to the main gates of Kirkland Marine Aviation. Nearing the works, they found the road blocked by half a dozen people who appeared to be waiting for them. These were not hero-worshipping girls, but men with angry faces. Gerry was forced to halt. His blast on the horn failed to make them fall back, and they crowded forward to peer in at the passengers. Kit recognized most of them at the same time as they recognized him. Residents of Sheenmouth, young and old, determined on venting old grudges against Geoffrey Anson's son. They shouted insults at him, thumping the window with bunched fists.

'Go back where you belong, in prison' . . . 'Sheenmouth doesn't want jailbirds here' . . . 'All the Ansons are rogues' . . . 'Thief and drunkard' . . . 'Gave the town a bad name' . . . 'Go to Africa and stay there'.

An ear-splitting blast on a horn behind them announced the arrival of the second taxi, driven by Gerry's nephew. The realization that they were now outnumbered, plus the fact that Phil Maggs was a bruiser of more than six feet, weighing fifteen stone, persuaded the men to withdraw up the sloping banks bordering the road. The two cars then drove forward to the gates, which were opened then swiftly closed behind them. Gerry swung his vehicle around to pull up with a jerk at the entrance to the main hangar.

'I'm very sorry about that, Mr Anson,' he said in a tight angry voice. 'The Kirkland's people should have cleared them off before we arrived.'

'Some of them were Kirkland's staff,' Kit pointed out harshly.

'They didn't mean anything they said, sir. They were just worked up.'

'Oh, they meant it, Gerry. They've been waiting a long time for an opportunity like this.'

The old man was very shaken. 'Please don't let it upset you; not when you're just about to take that great machine up into the air.'

Kit climbed from the car, saying over his shoulder, 'Nothing upsets me these days, Gerry. Forget it.'

At that moment, something struck him on the left temple. He ducked far too late as the stone landed several feet away. When he looked swiftly across at the gates, the sole man left on the bank had no weapon save his right hand, which he used to signal expressively in case the stone had not made his message clear enough. Ignoring his colleagues who were gathering around him, Kit walked purposefully through the hangar to the slipway beyond. *Flamingo* had been launched, and was anchored mid-stream awaiting the crew and passengers. Making for the small boat which would ferry them over the short distance, Kit asked himself savagely what he had imagined he would prove by returning to Sheenmouth. His decision had merely caused the press to reprint the lies they had reported five years ago, and given the people of his home town another chance to air their opinions of the Ansons. It had done nothing towards repairing his professional reputation. That was plainly damaged beyond recall.

303

Warren had been inside *Flamingo* since early that morning. He had supervised her launch half an hour ago, and now sat watching the boat approach with the crew in their distinctive green uniforms of Western Mediterranean Air Services. On this greatest day of his life he was feeling suicidal with nervousness. Kit's presence aboard would make all the difference. He was so full of self-confidence and so enthusiastic about *Flamingo*. Nothing could possibly go wrong with a man of his calibre at the controls, backed by a crew as good as the one he had brought with him.

Warren could still hardly believe the stroke of luck which had brought them together again on this vital trip. The only aspect marring the pleasure of their renewed friendship was his own sense of guilt where Kit was concerned. If only he had destroyed those plans for a seaplane called *Solitaire*, which had been stolen to become *Aphrodite*, instead of casually handing them over to Kit and leaving fate to make the running! Unaware that Warren knew the truth, his friend had remained his friend, although vastly changed. Youthful exuberance and easy charm had been driven from Kit by the intervening years, yet when it came to aircraft and things aeronautical enthusiasm and the natural brilliance of the man overcame all else. Warren sensed that it was these qualities which had kept him going in the face of Kirkland insults, and despite the memories his return here must have exhumed. Yet it seemed only right that, as Kit had persuaded Sir Hector to employ an unknown designer to create a passenger liner with wings, and had also worked on the embryo aircraft with him, so should he be the man to make this historic proving flight.

The crew clambered aboard in silence. When they made their way through the lower cabin and climbed the steps to the upper deck, led by Kit, Warren discovered the reason for their subdued behaviour.

'Whatever happened?' he asked, getting to his feet in

alarm at the sight of his pilot with blood running down his face, and with spatters of it all over his clothes.

'Slight accident, that's all,' Kit replied tersely. 'It's not as bad as it looks. Most of it is lipstick.' Placing his bag on one of the pink seats, he unzipped it vigorously. 'You don't look too hot yourself. Rather like a playwright waiting for his masterpiece to be performed for the first time.'

'It's the same kind of thing,' Warren responded, unsettled by this curious start to something of such importance to them both.

Stripping off his green tunic, Kit tugged at his tie before unbuttoning his red-smeared shirt. 'You've no need for first-night nerves. *Flamingo* is a sure-fire winner, and you know it.' Bare to the waist, he walked into the crew's toilet to run water into the small basin. 'Seems a shame to ruin one of Miss Kirkland's pretty pink towels before we even take off, but the first rule of a captain and his crew is to look clean and smart. For some reason, passengers have more confidence in the ability of tidy men than scruffy ones.'

While Kit washed, Digger murmured to Warren, 'We ran into some blokes who didn't share our admiration of him.'

'Good lord!' he exclaimed softly. 'Did they set about him?'

'Only once. They'd have had the rest of us to tackle if they hadn't run for it.' Then, in normal tones, Digger said, 'I thought you planned to come up in the launch with the nobs.'

'I funked it, at the last minute,' Warren confessed, even more unsettled by this hint of animosity towards Kit. 'You've no notion of what's going on back at the Abbey. It's like a breakfast cocktail party.'

'Any fast-goers among the women?' asked Digger hopefully.

'I'm sure you'll find the answer to that before long,'

Morris said, taking Kit's place at the washbasin to scrub away the lipstick smears.

'Get a move on,' Kit advised in clipped tones, as he tucked the tail of a clean shirt into his dark-green trousers and expertly flicked another tie into a knot. 'I'm leaving here dead on eleven, and you'd all better be ready when I do.'

'I've never been on a flight like this one,' mused Joss, shaking his head in wonderment. 'Posh passengers in pink seats! It's like something dreamed up by Disney.'

'It was dreamed up by your current pash, lad,' Digger reminded him, 'and your hopes will be totally doomed if she comes up here and sees you looking like a refugee from a babe's brothel. Go in there and clean up, you disgusting lecher!'

Warren left their comradely banter behind as he followed Kit on to the flight deck forward of the upper cabin. When his friend took the pilot's seat, Warren sat in the right-hand one beside him. Now something was happening, he was starting to feel better. Waiting was nerve-racking, and he had waited almost six years for this. Kit betrayed no sign of nervousness as he embarked on the lengthy preparation for flight. Warren was content to watch him in silence. When Joss scrambled up to take his rightful place, Warren then vacated the seat and stood behind them as both pilots passed vital figures and information to each other in the countdown to starting the engines. The youthful first officer had become a different person. His wide, innocent-looking eyes missed nothing, and his brow beneath the fine, pale hair was furrowed as he compared instrument readings with the list in his hand.

Their assured voices helped the muscles in Warren's stomach to relax. He had flown *Flamingo* himself on test flights, so knew the routine well. Now he was handing her over to others, like a man relinquishing a beloved mistress to lovers who would fulfil her better than he ever could. He looked ahead through the windows, along the great blunt nose, to the mouth of the river. The sun was shining spasmodically, and the chill breeze was ruffling the surface of the water. Just the conditions *Flamingo* liked best. Spectators were thronging both banks, and the sands were sure to be filled with those waiting for the great white bird to taxi slowly out into Lyme Bay, ready to rise into the sky. On the cliffs above the sands, he could see dots moving around. Momentarily, he recalled himself up there with Mona, watching *Aphrodite* and dreaming of a passenger liner with wings. He little thought that almost six years later, others would be there watching for the substance of that dream to appear. Taking him unawares, tears filled his eyes so that the Sheen now had a myriad ripples to blind him.

'Come on, you stupid blighter,' said Kit, getting to his feet. 'It's time you left us and carried out your part of this affair. The launch is practically here. Get down those steps and welcome everyone aboard.'

Warren swallowed his unwelcome emotion, and turned to walk past the tables where Morris and Digger were settling in. At the door which shut off the flight deck from the upper cabin, Kit halted him with a hand on his arm.

'I know just how you feel,' he said quietly. 'Tears'll come thicker and faster when we get back, and people clamour to place orders for a magnificent piece of design engineering.' He paused momentarily before asking, 'How long was it before you realized that Donald was no more than a good draughtsman?'

As Warren stood nonplussed, Kit frowned. 'I'm pretty certain why you've allowed everyone to believe this boat is a dual creation, but I know you must earn total credit. *Flamingo* will be a sensation, I promise you. I hope you'll then feel strong enough to defy Kirkland greed and stand on your own brilliance. I'll do everything I can to help you.' Holding out his hand, he smiled. 'Good luck and happy landings.'

As he shook the hand his friend offered, Warren's old

sense of guilt rose swiftly. On the brink of confessing what he had known for almost six years, he was prevented from doing so by Kit's gentle push into the cabin. The metal door was closed, shutting him off from any control over his splendid creation.

Leone's legs felt weak as she stepped from the launch in to the spacious lower cabin, any pleasure and excitement she had felt over this flight buried beneath the distress of Kit's re-entry into her life. The past four weeks had been hell. With all the meticulous planning done, and with invitations enthusiastically accepted, they had had no choice but to agree to the unacceptable. Donald had appeared to come to terms with it better than she, but her brother had not discovered that she was impossibly in love with the man who had tricked them into this intolerable situation.

Time and again she asked herself how she could feel such overwhelming yearning for someone she had despised for six years. Daily she questioned her lack of pride and self-respect. The answer to this stern cross-examination was the same each time. Kit Anson filled her mind, her every waking thought. He ruled her dreams. It was unthinkable, yet her heart raced at the sound of his voice, her blood surged faster through her veins at the sight of his powerful figure, and her senses sang wild songs each time his dark gaze challenged hers before moving on with his thoughts still hidden. All she knew was that somehow a long-ago love had survived the bitter winter to bloom even more gloriously. Small wonder no other passion had lived up to what she felt now. With the prospect of two weeks in tantalizingly close proximity to Kit, Leone longed for the flight to be over, and for him to return to Lisbon leaving her to lick her wounds in the solitude of a former religious retreat. Meanwhile, she must somehow endure the coming days with a smile and a poise which would hide the truth, in particular from the man who had already betrayed her trust once.

Wearing a pale-green braided silk costume trimmed with silver fox she dutifully donned both smile and poise to welcome the ladies aboard. Their arrival prompted the appearance of two handsome Portuguese stewards who proceeded to assist the removal of coats and fur stoles with a smiling deference which went down very well with women used to the good things in life. When the men climbed aboard accompanied by Donald and Maitland, they seemed equally impressed by the stewards' services. Declining the proffered seats, the guests stood in small groups gazing around and discussing the merits of all they saw. Some chose to wander through the large hull, opening doors to inspect every aspect of the craft under their sharp scrutiny. Before long, the interior of the aircraft resembled a continuous cocktail party, with people kaleidoscoping to talk to each other in very loud voices.

The chatter was brought to a sudden halt by a burst of thunderous sound, which set the hull shuddering around them. Then, the thunder doubled to deafen them. The shuddering increased as the whole machine appeared to come alive. The passengers' voices returned. They told each other, full of excitement, that the engines had started. That was why they could see fine spray flying past the windows. Everyone rushed to see the fine spray. Those on the upper deck called down that there was a better view of the engines from where they were. There was a rush for the steps. An elderly gentleman at the bar was demanding a whisky and soda to help his 'queasiness'.

'Never been a good sailor,' he confided to the barman, to help his case along.

The steward shook his head and explained once more that it was too dangerous to serve drinks during take-off, but that he would bring a drink to the gentleman the moment Captain Anson gave his permission.

Seeing Warren nearby, Leone went across to him. 'This is little short of a nightmare. I never expected them to roam all over the aircraft like curious children. Just look at them!' Gazing around, she went on, 'Donald's been cornered by those two men from Anglo-Asiastic for ages, and seems unable to control this situation. Maitland looks green around the gills, and I sincerely hope he is starting to suffer from seasickness.'

'Maybe it's envy,' suggested Warren vaguely, seemingly bemused by what was happening.

'What can we do? If this is an example of what the next two weeks will be like, I think I should have flown a suicidal display in *Flamingo*, after all. It would have been less stressful.'

At that moment, a member of the crew appeared at her side. She recognized him as the co-pilot, Joss Hamilton. He was very businesslike today, she discovered.

'The captain is ready for take-off, Miss Kirkland,' he announced above the babble of the milling passengers.

'We're not, I'm afraid,' she confessed ruefully. 'When we've managed to get everyone settled in seats they feel happy with, we'll let you know. Then we can start.'

The boy looked most unhappy. 'I'm afraid you can't do that. It's the pilot's prerogative to tell you when he intends to leave. He's in total command once everyone's aboard.'

Tired after entertaining twenty-four assorted guests for breakfast, and deeply unsettled over the many hazards of this trip, she promptly sank on to the nearest pink seat and looked up at him in weary defiance.

'Tell him to take command, in that case. I wish him luck in his efforts.'

Young Hamilton looked relieved. 'Thank you, Miss Kirkland.'

As he pushed his way back through to the steps leading to the flight deck, Leone reached up to touch Warren's arm. 'Sit here and hold my hand. You look just about as apprehensive as I feel.' As he sat down, she produced a strained smile. 'As soon as we're safely up, I'm going to have a giant pink gin. The only way to get through the next fourteen days might be to get blotto, then stay that way until we touch down on the Sheen again, don't you think?'

He shook his head as he took her hand in a firm clasp. 'There's too much at stake – for us all. I have to prove to myself that I really have designed a championship-class aircraft. Donald has to sell it in large enough numbers to save the company. You have to vindicate your claim that you can earn your half-share in Kirkland's by making a valuable contribution towards running it. In addition, Kit has to demonstrate that he's still one of the finest pilots of marine aircraft in the world, despite what it chooses to say of him.'

Right on cue, Kit's softly accented voice filled the hull over the relay system. 'Ladies and gentlemen, this is Captain Anson. Please take your seats immediately. I am about to taxi to our take-off position, and it is *essential* that everyone aboard should be sitting during that vital procedure. There will be ample time for you all to inspect this splendid aircraft during the coming days and ask any questions you wish of myself or any member of my crew. Please occupy the nearest available seat now, as we shall be underway in two minutes. The tide is falling rapidly. If we miss it, we may have to delay for eight hours. Thank you.'

Incredibly, order emerged from chaos at mention of an eight-hour delay. The passengers sat obediently, as docile as rebuked schoolchildren, well within the two-minute deadline. *Flamingo* began to move slowly down the Sheen towards the open sea like a graceful galleon. Leone gazed from the window where water was beginning to surge up higher and higher over the broad white hull as their speed increased. People lining the banks began waving madly. Their open mouths suggested that they were also cheering. They were on their way, and there was no turning back. *The pilot is in total command once everyone is aboard*. That was why she needed a giant pink gin; why she would need to produce an inscrutable

311

smile while she longed for the flight to be over. More wounds were certain to be inflicted by this man preparing to take them all up into the element he loved more deeply than any woman.

Lunch was served as they crossed the coast of France. Chilled celery soup, local lobster, and Crêpes de Sheen. (The chef was as impudent as Leone could wish.) This was complemented by appropriate wines, and rounded off with cheeses, petits fours and liqueurs. The meal was presented in impeccable style on Wedgwood china, by the Portuguese stewards who knew exactly how to make men feel highly sophisticated, and how to treat even the plainest woman as a raving beauty. A flash of their dark eyes, an understanding smile, deference without servility, and efficiency which had them appearing at exactly the right moment then melting away unobtrusively, all contributed to the relaxed atmosphere now prevailing. Captain Anson's crew members were proving themselves as skilled as he at managing large numbers of passengers. At the end of the meal, the gentlemen moved to the smoking saloon, where cigarettes or Havana cigars were available. The ladies changed seats to form small gossiping clusters, or stretched their legs in pairs along the promenade running practically the entire length of the aircraft.

Leone had abandoned the pink gins after downing three in swift succession. From the moment of departure, the passengers had been charmed by everything. The take-off had been highly exciting, even for those who had flown before. *Flamingo* had risen from the water in a remarkably short time for such a large craft, after an initial powerful surge which had set up a great flying cloud of spray and had had those aboard gasping from the thrill of it all. Once in the air, she had climbed at a more majestic rate, so Kit had turned and flown back along the entire length of Sheenmouth sands at cliff-top level. Watchers on land had waved caps, scarves and cardigans as the huge white bird had glided past close enough for them to see the faces framed by the windows. In their sense of elation, the passengers had waved back. The cheering crowds along the route, their own genteel salutes in return, suggested royalty acknowledging their subjects' enthusiasm. It gave them the first hint of the éliteness of travelling by luxury flying boat.

Three hours into their journey, and with a splendid meal inside them, the time had come to mix, socialize, investigate and ask questions. Most of the male passengers had flown before, although not necessarily in marine aircraft. Two were ex RFC pilots, who had entered the civil industry after 1918. They, and the representatives from aircraft companies around the world, kept Warren virtually under siege with questions of performance and statistics. The bankers and financiers, who knew little of aviation technology and were more interested in the arithmetic of investment in *Flamingo*, mainly centred around Donald. Maitland, Leone noted with grim glee, was very definitely unhappy in the air. After working for an aircraft manufacturer for more than fifteen years, this was the first time he had ever left the ground. Though he was manfully doing his best to maintain his ultra-perfection, Leone nevertheless felt it would not be long before he would be driven to seek a quiet corner in which to ride out his misery. Maybe it would do him good to realize that he was actually a man, not a walking miracle, she told herself.

Her own rôle was to chaperon the ladies. All but two of the twelve had never before taken to the air, and were finding the experience eye-opening. What spaciousness; what comfort! What attentive service from the two *divine* stewards, my dear! Countess Renskaya was deeply impressed by a mode of travel she had always associated with 'gentlemen clad in leather garments, squeezed into tiny seats hollowed out from machines shaped like a cigar'. She confessed to Leone that she had packed into her luggage many thick woollen socks, and a copper foot-warmer heated by candles.

'Now I see that I shall not need such things,' she chuckled, fingering a huge black diamond on the pearl choker around her wrinkled throat. 'This is the only way to travel across the world. The only way. I am completely enamoured of it already. The whole continent is there at my feet, instead of a copper pan warmed by candles!' Leaning confidentially towards Leone, she said, 'Your brother is a very beautiful young man. He is like my Grigor – as graceful as a blond antelope. So strong, he was. So . . . how do you say . . . full of exercise?'

'Athletic?' suggested Leone, very taken with the description of Grigor.

'Exactly!' The lined face grew soft with recollection. 'What a lover! He first seduced me on a gondola during a Venetian carnival. He was killed by the Bolsheviks as we all crossed the frozen river, and my heart died with him.' Wiping moisture from her eyes, she added, 'It is for his sake that I decide to give your beautiful brother the money I brought with me from Russia. He will not seduce me – I am too old – but he will give me his gratitude, which is all I can expect from any man now. With my money, he will make more of these machines that have no shape of the cigar. I shall instruct that he names one "The Countess Renskaya", and I shall travel twice a year in it. That will please me very much.'

Knowing the news would please Donald immensely, Leone felt a thrill of excitement. *Flamingo* was already successful, after no more than a few hours of this proving flight. Surely it was an excellent sign that Kirkland Marine Aviation would win the orders so badly needed.

'My brother will give you more than his gratitude,' she said with a smile. 'Your investment will reap good dividends, I assure you, Countess.'

'You have this same look as he, my dear,' the ageing Russian continued. 'Have you ever been seduced in a gondola?'

Leone shook her head. 'What a pity we're not scheduled to call in at Venice. I might have been fortunate enough to have the experience.'

The Countess chuckled. 'Lovely . . . quite lovely. I must have you to some of my parties. But you must promise to bring your brother.'

'I promise,' she replied, delighted by the old eccentric who then struggled to her feet clutching an enormous black spangled handbag.

'I shall now find the smoking saloon, and enjoy a cheroot,' she announced. 'What a pleasure this *Flamingo* is. I shall travel on her twice a year. Yes, definitely twice a year.'

After pointing her in the right direction, Leone looked around for Donald so that she could break the news to him. He was discussing the contents of the sales brochure with two men from an American company. Leone had her doubts about them. If aircraft development in the United States was as far advanced as she was frequently being told, why was such interest being shown in *Flamingo* by men from that country? Were they industrial spies? Would they return armed with information on Warren's wonderful design, then produce their own aircraft along the same lines? It *was* done. Kit Anson had attempted it by stealing the original drawings of a new design. But for that car crash, he might well have succeeded.

She sat in one of four empty seats facing each other in pairs, and gazed from the window. That part of the world presently at her feet had been her playground for five desperately lonely years. France, Switzerland, Austria, Italy. Her first seduction had not taken place in a gondola, but in Raoul de Montfort's Lagonda. They had been swimming, diving from the rocks into a sea which had shimmered with the lights from his uncle's château way above. The water had been dark, deep and dangerous on that rocky promontory, but they were both very strong swimmers and both drunk enough to

315

surrender to the call of wild excitement. Closing her eyes, Leone pictured him climbing from the car and stripping off his clothes as he urged her to join him. His strong naked body outlined by the moonlight had reminded her of Warren and the red-haired girl; reminded her of how she had yearned to repeat that scene with Kit. Knowing she must find the answer to that elusive total experience, she had dragged the evening gown from her shoulders and followed Raoul out to where the silver and black sea beckoned as irresistibly as that union she had never savoured.

The chill and physical exertion of the swim had sobered them, so that they had both been highly aware of each other when they emerged and returned to the car. Raoul had been as wild in love as in everything he did, but Leone had soon discovered that he regarded it as simply another craving to be indulged whenever the mood took him. When he had been killed in a seaplane several years later, she had attended his funeral along with all the girls who had been willing partners to his charming immorality.

'Ah, there you are, Leone,' said Monique Carlyon-Bree, arriving to sit facing her. 'Monte looks so different from the sky, doesn't it?'

Coming from her memories, Leone gave a faint smile. 'This is how those who lose a fortune and put a pistol to their heads see it, I suppose.'

Monique laughed. 'Quaint girl!'

'Are you enjoying the flight?'

'Immensely, my dear . . . save for that ghastly woman in yellow.'

Pointing from the window, she said, 'Isn't that the de Pechards' villa down there – that white monstrosity right on the headland?'

'I suppose it must be,' agreed Leone, looking down at the sweep of coast bordering the sparkling Mediterranean. 'Which ghastly woman did you mean?' she probed, returning to the subject of a moment before.

316

Monique adopted a frothy social guise when she wished, but she was a shrewd woman commanding a double fortune inherited from two elderly husbands, who also had friends in all the right places. It was important to keep her happy on this trip.

'Little plump pigeon of a creature with platinumed hair. Could be a wig, come to that. Certainly isn't natural in a woman of her age.' She gave a throaty laugh. 'Crikey, I could be describing myself, couldn't I?'

At that moment a steward came to fasten a table between their seats and announce that he would be serving tea very shortly.

'How delightful,' exclaimed Monique, responding to the man's flashing smile with feminine enjoyment before looking back at Leone. 'The woman in yellow? My dear, apparently she once travelled to Marseilles on a flying boat, and is driving us all potty with non-stop tales of her *experience*.' That last word was uttered in throbbing melodramatic tones as her hand clutched her bosom.

Leone sympathized openly. Monique had been an air passenger so many times she deserved her own pair of wings. She must be protected from irritation by this 'travel bore' or the entire flight would be ruined for her. The steward arrived with tea, finger sandwiches and miniature cream-filled meringues. As he departed another figure took his place beside their seats. The woman was wearing a yellow dress with matching loose coat, which did nothing to flatter her short plump shape. Monique's foot jabbed Leone's significantly.

'Miss Kirkland, I've been looking for you,' accused the new arrival. Recognizing her as the wife of a director of Anglo-Asiatic, Leone's heart sank. Monique was important because she travelled a great deal and mixed with wealthy influential people, but if Mrs Harmesworth should be upset, she could influence her husband's decision on whether or not to invest in *Flamingo* for his airline's Asiatic routes. An order from Nicholas Harmesworth, and his colleague Sir Mallard Frencham, would keep *Kirkland's* in business for several years.

Leone obediently smiled at the woman. 'I'm sorry if I seemed elusive, Mrs Harmesworth. Monique and I were just chatting about you, as a matter of fact.'

'Really?' exclaimed the other eagerly, sitting next to Leone. 'I'll join you both for tea and elaborate on anything you wish to know.'

Trying to ignore the stormy look from her companion on the opposite seat, Leone signalled the steward to bring additional china.

'It's such fun to see the Med from above, don't you think?' she commented smoothly. 'Why were you looking for me? Can I help you in some way?'

In contrast to Monique's preserved beauty, Mrs Harmesworth had gone to seed. Self-indulgence was written all over her, and Leone realized she could cause trouble in all manner of ways if things did not go her way on this flight.

'Well, my dear, I felt you would be grateful for a little tip from an experienced traveller,' she began, helping herself to two of the sandwiches as the steward poured tea for her.

'I'm sure I should,' Leone said tactfully, as Monique's foot pushed hers once more.

'We have been in the air four hours already, yet the captain hasn't introduced himself to us and ensured that we're all comfortable.'

Growing wary, Leone said, 'He's the pilot, Mrs Harmesworth, and can't leave the controls.'

Round nondescript eyes gazed at her in apparent shock. 'Surely there's a first officer; another pilot aboard.'

'Naturally.'

'Then Captain Anson should have made his rounds by now,' was the firm declaration. 'My husband observed that the operational crew appeared to be making themselves very scarce on this flight, for some reason.'

'The reason is because I requested them to do so,' Leone said, furious with the woman and trying hard not to show it.

'Good gracious, did you? It's usual for the pilot to speak to his passengers, Miss Kirkland. After all, if we have to place our lives in their hands, they should have the courtesy to let us see in whom we've put our trust.' Helping herself to a meringue, she continued with hardly a pause. 'In this particular instance, it's more than ever essential that we should meet this man. No one denies his skill as a pilot, of course, but he has been in *prison*, hasn't he? I must suppose that you and your brother have good – if somewhat baffling – reasons for employing him after what he did to your father, but that's not really my affair.'

'It's not anyone's affair what members of the crew have done in the past,' put in Monique sweetly. 'On the numerous flights I've made, I've never known passengers to expect to probe into the background of the man at the controls. You must have travelled on a very curious airline to Marseilles, Mrs Harmesworth.'

The other woman turned on her angrily. 'It was my husband's line, Anglo-Asiatic. Perhaps you've never experienced the privilege of travelling as a VIP, Mrs Carlyon-Bree.'

'*Lady* Carlyon-Bree,' corrected Monique, even more sweetly than before.

Sensing the kind of trouble it was her duty to avert, Leone felt between the devil and the deep blue sea – the devil being Kit Anson and the sea certainly not the sparkling Mediterranean so vivid below them. Summoning all her self-control, she offered the Harmesworth woman another meringue.

'When you meet Captain Anson, I'm sure you'll feel every confidence in his ability to fly us safely to Africa and back.'

'*That* has never been in any doubt, Miss Kirkland. It's his other qualities I tend to question.'

Swallowing her antipathy towards the woman, Leone beckoned the steward across. 'Tell Captain Anson his presence is required in the cabin . . . *at once*,' she snapped, to relieve aggression she could express no other way.

Monique beamed at her across the small table. 'Must we hide our handbags, and strip off all our diamonds?'

It was a piece of frivolous teasing she could not accept. 'Excuse me,' she murmured, getting to her feet. 'Mr Grant is signalling for my assistance. Enjoy the rest of your tea.'

Warren was with three men all greatly enjoying a hilarious discussion on the lucky escapes each had experienced whilst learning to fly. Donald was enduring a monologue, accompanied by much finger-jabbing on the tea table, from a vigorous senior official of the Air Ministry. He gave Leone an expressive movement of his eyebrows as she passed, but could not escape to join her. The remaining passengers were happily enjoying the informal tea taken twenty thousand feet above the Mediterranean, so she moved out to the promenade where she attempted to calm down after Monique's remarks about hiding her handbag and diamonds from a man known to have been in prison for theft. For some inexplicable reason, she could not accept such comments, even when they were made in a light-hearted manner. Why, when he had been caught red-handed with the spoils and subsequently ruled to be guilty?

When Kit then appeared from the flight deck, his height seemed to fill that narrow walkway as he came towards her. There was no smile of greeting as he paused beside her.

'Rather a rapid change of management policy, isn't it?' he asked, with a hint of derision.

She straightened up. 'Some passengers have hinted that they'd feel safer if you put in an appearance, that's all.'

'It's usual,' he conceded, 'although it sometimes has

the reverse effect. They worry about who's flying the machine while the pilot's socializing.'

Still upset by the references to his prison record, Leone said sharply, 'There's no question of your *socializing*. A polite word here and there is all that's required of you.'

He leant his shoulder against the bulkhead and looked down at her shrewdly. 'What are you afraid of, Miss Kirkland?'

'I've no idea what you mean,' she snapped. 'And the passengers are waiting.'

Making no move to go, he raked her with a gaze which seemed to look beyond what he saw. 'Donald is trying to accept the inevitable with fortitude, but you are still fighting my presence on this flight. Why? I'm no threat to you as I am to your brother.'

'You're no threat to either of us,' she countered, coldly avoiding his challenge. 'You're being paid to fly this aircraft and do as you're instructed. Put a foot wrong, and your employment can be terminated, you know. While you're working for us, you'll have to recognize your place and keep to it.'

He shook his head. 'Sacking me would cause the kind of publicity you'd do anything to avoid. My place, as you so slightingly suggest, is to captain this entire flight to the best of my ability. That requires me to assume total command on board this flying boat, which means that I can overrule any instructions given by Donald or by you. Stop playing the part of company executive, my dear girl, and face the fact that you haven't the first idea what it entails.'

Feeling as if a rug had been pulled from under her feet, she struggled to follow his firm rebuke with something approaching control. Before she could speak, however, he straightened up to slide past in the narrow space available, saying as he practically brushed her body with his, 'While I reassure the passengers, you should take the opportunity to powder your shiny nose. On this vitally important flight, even Leone Kirkland can't afford to put a foot wrong and look less than immaculate. You're on this trip to provide the glamour, aren't you? Go to it, then.'

He left her standing to suffer the first of the wounds she had expected during the coming two weeks. Lost in recollections of six years ago some words came back to her suddenly. *Women don't marry men like Kit, they simply enjoy them.* Stephanie had certainly been enjoying him, while a yearning, passionate young girl had been tiptoeing to the bell tower in trembling anticipation of what would have been her first and lasting surrender. Thank God he did not know that. Her sense of humiliation now would be doubled.

Tea was cleared away, and still Kit remained in the cabin. She could see him presently sitting with Donald and the men from the Air Ministry, deep in conversation with them. He had run the gamut of eager ladies who had each coaxed him to sit beside her for a chat. They had been visibly charmed and gratified by his attentions. He was doing his job supremely well; she should be pleased. Why, then, was she furious with their reaction to his easy attraction?

Turning away, she headed for the washroom reserved for Kirkland use. After running cold water over her wrists, and touching up her face, she emerged to see Kit climbing the steps to the flight deck again. Donald came hot on his heels, looking flushed and angry.

'He said he was carrying out your orders. *Did* you tell him to wander around speaking to anyone he fancied?'

'No, I did not! That obnoxious Harmesworth woman made a song and dance because he hadn't made his rounds. I had no option but to send for him. What a hypocrite she is! Far from hiding her valuables, she looked set to give him anything he wanted. All the women did.' Putting on a bright smile, she added, 'He always had phenomenal success at what Father termed "wenching", didn't he?'

322

Donald scowled. 'He had the damn nerve to take over my conversation with Sir Henry and old Marshall, giving them the facts I'd already discussed at great length. He's been with *Flamingo* no longer than a few weeks, yet speaks as if he's an expert on her.'

'According to Warren, he is.'

'I could wring Warren's neck,' Donald told her explosively. 'He's spent the past two hours guffawing over hairy flying yarns with Blenkinsop, Maters and Stanhope instead of helping me to sell *Flamingo!*'

'We're only six hours into this flight. They won't sign cheques yet. Stop being impatient. Exchanging flying yarns is as important as stunning their brains with statistics. Anyway, I've a piece of good news for you. Countess Renskaya is so impressed by the spacious comfort here, and by your similarity to her former lover, she's prepared to invest in the company providing you name one of the boats after her. Isn't it grand?'

Donald seemed unimpressed by this exciting prospect. 'Huh, I just hope she's still of the same mind when we reach home.' Running an agitated hand through his hair and glancing over her shoulder, he added, 'Where the *hell* is Maitland?'

'I sincerely hope he's suffering from violent airsickness. If my prayers are answered, for once, it will afflict him continuously until we get back to Sheenmouth.'

He scowled again. 'You treat everything as a huge joke.'

'And you go to pieces. What a pair we are, and how Father must have despaired over us.'

He looked away from her through the window, silenced by that for a while. Then he said, 'We're coming in to Naples now. I hope to God he knows what he's doing at those controls.'

'Of course he knows,' she murmured, moving forward to stand beside him. The incredible hue of the fabled bay with an ancient terraced city rising from it, stood out brightly against the purple background of Vesuvius.

'A member of the crew told Warren that Kit's been flying boats with their company for more than a year. Before that, he fought with the International Brigade in Spain, taking to the air in all kinds of obsolete machines. Did you know that?'

'He's not fighting Spaniards now, he's about to land our valuable prototype on a vast expanse of very deep water,' came the edgy response.

'Whatever else he might be, he's a brilliant pilot, Donald. Even we have never denied that,' she said, in surprising defence of Kit.

They began to drop lower and lower towards the tiers of colour-washed buildings curving around the bay, where marker buoys indicated their landing area. Her brother bent over for a better view through the porthole.

'It looks as though half the town has turned out to watch this. There'll be hell to pay if he muffs it in front of all those eyes.'

'I know how to bring an aircraft down safely,' she responded coolly, 'and Kit appears to be doing all the right things. He won't muff it, Donald, and you damn well know it, otherwise you'd have fought the contract we were tricked into signing. If I recall, you left me to do all the protesting on that score.'

As *Flamingo* swept in a descending turn which would put them on course for landing, Leone was surprised at the enthusiasm of those crowding the tiny jetty which had been placed at their disposal by the port authorities. Interest in the arrival of an aircraft on a trip which had been publicized in worldwide press coverage was understandable enough, but this ecstatic reception seemed a little overdone. However, she reminded herself that Italians were excitable demonstrative people, and their enthusiastic reception could only add to the prestige of this trip.

They dropped lower and lower towards the cobalt sea, and the voices in the cabin behind them registered the thrill now being experienced by the passengers over their first landing in this wonderful new aircraft. Leone appreciated the steadiness of the machine during this vital manoeuvre, knowing it to be due to the pilot's skill and confidence. She had none of Donald's doubts that Kit would not make the perfect landing on every occasion. In this one direction, she trusted the man implicitly.

Soon, they were no more than a few feet above the water gilded by the lowering sun. Then, with a gentle thump, *Flamingo* began to skim the waves, sending high-flying white foam over the windows to obscure their sight of the shore at their first port of call. With a loud roar, they de-accelerated with astonishing force, to demonstrate one of the aircraft's great virtues, until she slowed to no more than a cruising glide beneath the shadow of the pastel-tinted terraces of Naples. The foam subsided to no more than two white streaks beneath the floats, and Leone then saw that the spectators were holding aloft several banners with bold lettering on them. She read the Italian phrases of welcome and adoration for Kit Anson, the hero of the skies and leading aviator, and her throat tightened.

'Donald, look!' she directed in faint tones.

Her brother appeared to freeze as he stared from the window to read this visual acclaim for an ex-hero. It was now possible to hear the passengers all exclaiming over this unexpected reception which was apparently for their pilot alone.

'What does it mean?' she asked. 'Why are these people making such a fuss, and how did they know about him?'

'They've read the papers, like everyone else,' Donald said, still staring at the banners. 'I imagine the fuss is because Naples was Benzini's home town. What other reason could there be for this ridiculous demonstration?'

Leone frowned. 'Benzini? Wasn't he a rival for the air speed record?'

'He killed himself in an attempt to take it from us in 1933.' When Donald turned to her she was astonished to see something remarkably like apprehension on his face. 'Whose bloody trip is this, ours or Kit Anson's?'

12

Warren stood on the balcony of his hotel room in the beguiling warmth of that May night, gazing down on the lights of a festive city. It was a moment he knew would live with him for ever. He had flown in a machine of his own design which had roared gracefully into the sky from a chilly blue-grey estuary, cruised across France, then glided down to touch the blue Mediterranean with the sureness of a homing sea-bird. His ache of success was now accentuated by the balmy, blossom-scented dusk, the throb of cicadas, and by the unbelievable opulence of a hotel hanging high above the sea. Kit had predicted tears of pride on their return to Sheenmouth, but they already hung on his lashes at the sight of *Flamingo* illuminated by buoys as she rode the waters of the bay. This one day had been enough to confirm his claim to have produced a superlative aircraft. Almost six years of total dedication to a belief, a cause, a tribute to that young Canadian who had briefly given affection to a boy surviving on dreams, had culminated in this heady, magical night.

With his gaze still on *Flamingo*, he recalled rounding a bend on his old motorcycle and hitting a hedge to avoid a girl in an expensive blue dress. That chance encounter had led to his standing here on a balcony in Italy, en route to Africa; the first time he had ever left his native land. On that other evening, he had been dragged into Sheenmouth Abbey wearing oil-stained clothes, to be dazzled by a glittering crowd dancing to the music of Phil Davenport. Then, he had been hastily handed over to the hero of the evening, who had been told to give him a word then throw him out. Kit had ignored the advice and, tonight, Warren was the hero. Tonight, he would be correctly attired for an occasion when the glittering crowd would be offering *him* their congratulations. He, Warren Grant, was perched on the pinnacle of achievement, and he had the momentary wish that Sir Hector could have been there to witness the fact.

Next minute, a slight cloud obscured his sunny horizon as he recalled Kit's words just before take-off this morning, which had raised the question of Donald's minimal contribution to the design of *Flamingo*. With an unwelcome honesty, Warren realized he had been playing safe, as he had done on discovering those drawings of Geoffrey Anson's in the old boathouse. He would not be the hero tonight, because he had allowed Donald to claim a half share of his creation. Kit had correctly guessed his reasons for doing so, and suggested that he should now be strong enough to break free. However, Kit himself was a prime example of what Kirkland power could do to a man who thought himself able to defy it.

Until this moment, Warren had felt it did not matter who laid claim to the design so long as the craft was built and allowed to fly. Suddenly, on this haunting unforgettable night, he wanted *Flamingo* to be his alone; wanted it with such strong, possessive passion the tears returned to his lashes. Even so, he knew in his heart that it was too late to claim her, as Kit had discovered it too late to claim *Aphrodite* for his father. His friend had paid a terrible penalty for trying. Warren would not risk a similar fate. Unlike Kit, he had an additional reason for dreading a break with the Kirkland family. He was in love with the female half of it.

Staring out at the velvet dusk, he owned that his desire to lay bare the truth tonight was partially due to the wish to impress Leone in the only way open to him. They were good friends, and it was clear her feelings covered no more than a fond impulse to mother him. Each time she straightened his tie, smoothed his unruly hair, or tucked his scarf more securely around his throat, the intimacy of her touch tormented him. Yet he dared not reveal his feelings. To be offered her sympathy would be as bad as her ridicule. On this very special evening, when romance in all its anguished glory hung in the still air, he might have shown her a more heroic image without Donald to steal half his claim to it.

As if that were not bad enough, there was a third hero tonight, albeit a tarnished one. Kit Anson had been greeted with banners, cheering crowds, and showers of blossoms that had lain like bridal confetti on his cap and shoulders. He was presently being fêted by the men of Benzini's team, his widow and family, and the people of a Neapolitan suburb. Like her brother, Leone had appeared highly annoyed by the lionizing of a man they had once disgraced. Yet Warren could not forget her expression when she had walked into the library to face Kit again after almost six years. How could she possibly be in love with a man she professed to hate? If she ever discovered the truth about that past affair, Kirkland passions would truly be roused . . . and his own hopes of winning her would die.

Turning back into his elegant cream and blue room, he sensed that such hopes would plague him on this night containing all the elements of elation. Until now, he had banished physical demands by concentration on an alternative love affair with a flying boat. Only the inhibitions born of spending his youth in an apartment used by his mother's numerous lovers would prevent his seeking a girl in the streets of Naples later this evening. Kit would probably not be hindered by instinctive reluctance to take what a woman offered, then walk away. He would doubtless be a hero in more ways than one tonight.

In evening dress and with his hair slicked down, Warren later trod down the wide blue-carpeted marble staircase towards the grand salon lit by massive porcelain and crystal chandeliers. The pastel murals formed the perfect background for those already gathered there in small exclusive groups. He spotted Leone at the same time she saw him. Breaking from the circle, she came across swiftly, and he was reminded again of their first meeting. She was now dressed in sophisticated black which made her so stunningly lovely he knew she was the only girl who could satisfy him, tonight or any night. Her dress shimmered with jet beading until it flared into a swirl of ostrich feathers from the knee, and the deep vee of her bodice accentuated the gracefulness of her throat fully revealed by hair drawn back into a chignon. Her smile warmed him like a heady red wine.

'I'd forgotten how handsome you can look when you're all togged up,' she said, tucking her hand through his arm to draw him further into the room. 'It's a great boost to your winsome charm, and you must use it to the full tonight. From what I've heard, you impressed all the men very greatly during the flight. Now you have to win over the ladies.'

His heart sank. 'You know I'm hopeless at social chit-chat, and these people are so worldly and sophisticated. I can talk the hind leg off a donkey in a discussion on anything to do with flying, but know I haven't the first idea what to say when faced with gushing females used to places and occasions like this.'

'Leave the talking to them, sweetie,' she advised, untouched by his plight. 'Smile devastatingly whenever you can, and encourage them to rattle on as long as possible. You'll come into your own after dinner. I've already told everyone how marvellous you are on the dance-floor. When you sweep them off in your arms, remember to look as if you think each one is absolutely divine.'

'Leone, I. . .'

'I've also had a word in the ear of the orchestra leader,' she ran on enthusiastically. 'He's quite happy to let you play a solo or two with them.'

'Oh no,' he said, halting determinedly. 'That's right out of the question.'

There was concern in her study of his face, as waiters scurried past with trays of drinks for guests whose conversation level was rising with every glassful. 'This isn't the time for one of your displays of stubbornness, Warren. You've made an excellent impression, so far, and you *must* follow it up tonight.' As he made to speak, she continued in urgent tones. 'I never expected them all to be eating out of our hands so soon, but they are. It's vital to keep them in that state. We'll all be working hard and doing things we don't particularly want to do. You said only this morning that so much is at stake during this flight, remember? Donald is manfully exposing himself to a barrage of searching questions from experts, whilst being as charming as he can be when he tries towards the more boring women. I'm flirting hectically with the men when their wives aren't around, and soothing ruffled hen feathers when I'd far rather leave them to scratch each other to pieces. All I'm asking you to do is woo them like mad when you clasp them against you on the dance-floor. *Please*, Warren.'

Helpless in her hands, and longing to tell her he wanted to woo her like mad instead, he weakly surrendered. 'All right. I'm not very experienced at flattery, but I suppose my dancing is up to scratch. I'll partner them all, Leone, but I won't play with the orchestra. I'm here as an aircraft designer, not as an entertainer.'

Her lips brushed his cheek gratefully, accelerating his downfall. 'You're a darling,' she breathed, 'and you must see how important it is to show them you're *human* beneath all that aeronautical brilliance. When you get up there and play your golden horn, they'll be stunned and thrilled.'

'I can't. . .'

'Yes, you can,' she insisted, urging him forward again. 'It's already arranged, and I'm counting on you to provide the final touch to their delight in this first day.' Tilting her lovely face to his, she added softly, 'I'll never forget that night the air speed record was broken. I found a friend, then immediately lost him to the crowd when he cast a spell with music.'

'You didn't lose me,' he managed, as they neared a group of their passengers.

His remark was lost beneath the gaiety of her intervention in the conversation of the two men from the Air Ministry, the wife of one of the former RFC pilots, and the Harmesworths. Warren smiled obediently as he responded briefly to their greetings, but he could not help reflecting on how adroitly Leone had avoided any mention of Kit when speaking of the air speed record. Yet the two were inseparable, surely. With half his mind on unhappy speculation, and telling himself he should have been more assertive with her a moment ago, he stood with an aperitif in his hand feeling more than ever that he was wandering in the realms of unreality. With memories of that other occasion so sharply revived, he recalled Kit confessing to him that he longed to be alone with *Aphrodite* in that moment of triumph. How well he understood that need now. If only he could escape this side of the proving flight of his brain-child.

They were ushered in to dinner by the maitre d'hotel, who treated Leone, Monique and several others in their party as old friends. There was a ripple of delighted appreciation from them all, as they took in the sight awaiting in the alcove prepared in accordance with Leone's wishes. The artistry of a local florist had swiftly created *Flamingo* in white blossoms to suspend above a horseshoe of tables. These were set with pink linen garlanded by white flowers, heavy silver cutlery, and rose Venetian glasses inlaid with silver tracery. Equally spaced around the inner curve were four table-fountains in rose-coloured glass, the three tiers of each sending down miniature cascades of pink water into the lowest levels illuminated from beneath by lights nestling amid white gardenias.

Warren was seated between Countess Renskaya, in silver pleated silk with rubies, and a shy woman in olive-green with no jewellery who was married to Sir Mallard Frencham of Anglo-Asiatic and reputedly a millionairess in her own right. Overawed by this woman's wealth and by the Countess's frank, rather eccentric conversation, Warren found the meal an ordeal despite the novelty of the many dishes.

When the long dinner ended, they all gathered merrily in the Florentine ballroom, where dancing was already in progress. Dutifully obeying Leone's wishes, Warren offered to partner any lady who wished to dance. Although his grace and skill were plainly admired by those who had been told of it in advance, his difficulty with small talk was aggravated by the sight of Leone gliding past in a succession of male embraces which entailed the placing of their hands on her bare shoulder-blades. She had an irresistibly beautiful back, he decided, only half-heeding Mrs Harmesworth's complaint about the inappropriateness of Captain Anson's absence.

'It's only a rather dubious *peasant* celebration of a feat he achieved so long ago everyone else has forgotten it,' she declared. 'After all, Mr Grant, he is the captain and should be on hand in case any of his passengers need advice or assistance. One doesn't find the captain of a ship neglecting his duties in such fashion, when in port, does one?'

'I've never been on a ship, I'm afraid, so one doesn't know what the captain's duties are,' he murmured absently, hating the young Italian with sapphire shirt studs, who was trying to nibble Leone's ear as they foxtrotted by.

To forestall any further complaint from this dumpy woman in blue lace, he tightened his hold around her

333

rigidly corseted waist and embarked on a series of involved turns and crossovers, which had her striving to follow him without twisting her right leg around her left and resembling a flamingo herself. Mutinous after enduring that second dance with her, he returned her to her influential husband, then crossed to where Leone was still being held against the fiery Italian while he released what could only be a torrent of passion in her ear. Glaring at the man as he approached, Warren wished he had been a boxing champion at school, as Kit had been. He would enjoy knocking this fancy fellow down with a well-placed hook. Leone seemed pleased at his intervention, however, and almost floored him with her smile.

'You poor thing! Gino and I sympathized when we saw you with that terrible Harmesworth creature for the second time. Duty is a harsh taskmaster.' Turning to the Italian, she said, 'Ask her for a dance, sweetie, and I might just believe you'd do anything in the world for me.'

Gino's views on the subject were easy enough for Warren to understand when he embarked on a flood of expressive Italian. When he then moved off towards the door in sulky fashion, Leone chuckled softly.

'That woman has her uses, after all. What an easy way to be rid of him.'

Despite those words, Warren was still jealous enough to ask, 'Who is that Neapolitan Valentino?'

'The son of the proprietor. He asks me to marry him every time I stay here. Do you approve of it?'

'The hotel, or that gigolo repeatedly asking you to marry him?'

Still chuckling, she placed her fingers lightly on his lips. 'Shhh! Don't let Franchini hear you speak of his adored son in those terms. At least, not until we're ready to depart in the morning. I want him on my side the whole time we're here. He's produced marvels so far. Wasn't that soufflé a masterpiece of culinary art?'

334

He was weary, confused, and filled with longing he could not banish, so he spoke instinctively. 'I wish you wouldn't keep up that social pose with me. It's so artificial.'

The amusement faded slowly from her face, and he felt guilty enough to add swiftly, 'I much prefer the real you.'

'Who is she, Warren? I wish you'd tell me,' she responded in almost dreamlike manner.

Being no skilled spinner of words, that challenge was beyond him. After several awkward moments during which they both hesitated on the brink of speaking, she reached out for his hand.

'You mentioned Valentino just now, and they're embarking on a tango. Let's show everyone how it should be done, shall we?'

The sensuous movements of the dance heightened the pleasure of holding her in his arms. Dipping and twisting to the sultry beat of the music in perfect harmony, Warren forgot everything but the desire for her which had come to the fore this evening. Tendrils of her hair teased his skin as they advanced cheek to cheek, before swiftly spinning to return in similar fashion across the polished boards. Her thighs brushed against his each time they dipped low, and when she arched gracefully backward across his right arm, the curve of her breasts and the slender pliancy of her body heightened that desire until he wondered how he would get through the night without her. Maybe it would be necessary to seek a girl in the streets, after all, and pretend she was Leone.

When the dance ended, she began walking towards the tall open doors leading to the terrace. 'Let's find a little peace and solitude, shall we?'

He followed her on to the broad stone area where trailing jasmine and oleanders scented the darkness, and where there appeared to be stars above and below them. She walked to a far corner bedecked with geraniums. The scent of lemons wafted on the slight zephyr as he recognized the distant sound of a Neapolitan brass band, and voices raised in laughter and song. A hero was being revived down there tonight. Almost a thousand feet below them, the sea whispered rhythmically as it met the shore. All around the terrace, couples in shadowy embraces murmured in the language understood by every man and woman in love. There were no words between himself and Leone as she stood lost in some vision which lay beyond that darkened bay, and he stood no more than a few feet behind her fighting the pain of it all.

Eventually, she asked softly, 'Are you still there?'

'Of course.' He moved nearer, wondering if he dared draw her back against him.

Still gazing ahead, she said, 'My mother drowned out there in those beautiful blue depths.'

The words came as a shock and broke the mood he had imagined between them. Disappointment kept him silent.

'I never really knew her. I'm not sure I would have wanted to.' She paused before adding, 'Mothers are universally portrayed as loving, caring people who protect their children fiercely. That can't be true. Mine went off with all manner of so-called friends, with no thought for me. Or for Donald.' She paused again, then continued in strange faraway tones. 'Daisy Anson ran off with an artist. That always struck me as extremely unmotherlike behaviour. Donald and I were very young, of course, and we had a nursemaid in full charge of us. Maybe there's an excuse for Marina Kirkland. But *he* was eleven or twelve when his mother left, and she'd brought him up herself. Don't you think that seems particularly heartless? Perhaps that's why he . . .' She broke off and turned to face him suddenly. 'You're the only person I know who lived continuously with his mother until she died. Did she love you very deeply?'

The question touched an exposed nerve. His reply was very abrupt. 'I couldn't say.'

'But did she do what mothers are supposed to do: cuddle you when you cried, kiss you better when you fell over, read you stories, show you off to all her friends?'

'What's this all about?' he demanded, having a very good idea of the answer and finding it unwelcome.

Her eyes were a deep luminous blue as she gazed up at him with disconcerting sadness in her expression. With the low lights sheening the hair drawn back to reveal her face stripped of its social mask, she looked lonely, lost and unbearably lovely. To his dismay, Warren realized there would be no one but her for the rest of his life despite her passion for the man who had been practically destroyed by her family.

Stepping so near they were almost touching, she suddenly asked desperately, 'Would you like to kiss me?'

Uncontrollable anger raced through him, taking them both by surprise. 'No thanks, I don't kiss by invitation. I'm not Gino . . . or any one of those groping nibbling fancy boys who like to surround you.' He took a deep breath. 'And I'm not a substitute for Kit Anson, either.'

The outburst appeared to shock her deeply. For a moment she held her breath, then spun swiftly to face the dark void above an even darker sea. Warren stood with his heart thudding, knowing he should now walk away. Instead, he reached out to seize her bare shoulders, tugged her round to him, and kissed her with the fierceness of long denial. She froze in his arms then, as his passion mounted, her body slowly melted against his, as if in relief. Breaking apart eventually, they regarded each other with mutual wariness as the carnival in praise of a past hero rioted noisily distant through the streets way below.

'That was quite a kiss from someone who doesn't do it by invitation,' she breathed. 'Was it inspired by anger?'

'No, something quite different,' he told her roughly. 'Why do you profess to hate him so much?'

'Who?' she asked, still seeming breathless.

337

'You know who! You put on a very good act most of the time, but I saw your expression when you walked in to the library and found him there.' When she remained silent, still looking lost and desperate, he went on angrily, 'Don't worry, *he* has no idea of the way you really feel about him. All he has on his mind is redeeming his reputation with this flight – a reputation your father broke six years ago. I can see the truth only because I'm in the same condition over you.'

The words were out and there was no way of retrieving them. He could have bitten his tongue out when he saw the pity in her eyes.

'Poor Warren. It's hell, isn't it?'

'So you try to ease it by hitting out at him whenever he comes near? That's no solution.'

'It's only for two weeks; just fourteen days.'

'It's for a whole lifetime if you shut it away. Bring it into the open and see what happens,' he advised, telling himself he was crazy to suggest the move he had just made so impulsively. It was the last thing he wanted.

Her face was shadowed with pain as she said, 'He'd only hurt me unbearably all over again.'

'Then you'd really hate him . . . and we'd both be happier.'

She could have been talking to herself with her next words. 'I don't understand it. It's madness; it's totally inexplicable. He betrayed us . . . the whole family.'

Warren stood in the enchanting persuasiveness of the scented darkness knowing that the moment to tell her the truth about Kit Anson hung there between them. He remained silent, helplessly silent, and it served to condemn the man over again in her eyes.

'All I can do is protect myself with cold words and hostility. Somehow, I have to get through this flight which is so vitally important to us all. Help me, Warren,' she pleaded. 'If you truly do love me, help me to survive this incomprehensible passion for someone who has no idea of loyalty. You're the only person I can trust.'

With his sense of guilt clutching at his throat, he was spared the need to answer by the arrival of Maitland with a message from Donald. The Frenchams were asking for Leone; would she go immediately. The girl summoned a smile and donned her social guise as swiftly as she had shed it.

'Tell my brother I'm on my way,' she said brightly. As the suave assistant turned away, she hesitated momentarily, her eyes large and appealing as she studied Warren. 'Neapolitan nights are dangerous. They tend to induce all manner of romantic confessions which you see for what they really are in the cold light of dawn. Take my word for it, Warren. I've been here before, and I know.'

He was left on the terrace to watch her tantalizing silhouette disappear in to the bright lights and even brighter laughter. There was a saying; see Naples and die. Perhaps he just had.

Kit awoke with a monumental hangover and only faint recollections of the night before. Beside his bed was a pretty doe-eyed girl of around seventeen, who smiled shyly as she told him it was 'seven of the clock, so he was woke of his request and must have the brekfuss'. The sheet appeared to be tightly wound around his naked body, so he prudently remained on his stomach until the girl had left the room.

The people of Benzini's native suburb had made him extremely drunk last night, and he was now suffering. Still on his stomach, he squinted at what he could see of the whitewashed room in the villa near the harbour, where accommodation had been reserved for the crew. One of them must have put him to bed, but the clothes he had been wearing were nowhere in sight. The shuttered doors had been flung wide when the girl had placed a tray on the small table out on the balcony, and brilliant sunshine was flooding in. Kit wished it were a grey, overcast morning, instead. Closing his eyes against the brightness, he lay counting the rhythmic thuds in his head until the girl's words began to register.

'Hell!' he swore, rolling on to his back and fighting free of the sheet. His travel clock showed him the girl was wrong. It was now seven fifteen of the clock!

Despite the sunny aspect of the morning, there was a thunderstorm in his head as he got to his feet and padded across to bring the coffee pot inside. It was his intention to close the doors, then drink the entire contents in blessed semi-darkness. Halfway across the room, he spotted an ample woman beating rugs on the opposite balcony, so swiftly wrapped a towel around his waist. It was insecurely fastened, however, and began to slip as he took up the tray. When it dropped to his feet, he held the tray at groin level as he returned her friendly 'Bongiorno!' At that point, the door of his room opened, and he swung round automatically to see who had walked in without knocking. Delighted laughter came from the facing balcony, making him step forward quickly to kick the door to behind him.

'Do you make a habit of exhibiting yourself to the neighbours first thing in the morning?' asked Morris calmly.

Kit scowled. 'What I most dislike about you, apart from your deplorable navigation, is your twisted sense of humour.'

'God, it's stuffy in here,' his friend said, going across to fling back the door again. Then he sat on one of the chairs in the bedroom, looking at Kit. 'Know what I most dislike about you? Two small drinks and you're helpless – I mean, quite paralytic! A man should be able to hold his liquor. Even young Joss stayed on his feet all evening.'

Kit poured more coffee. 'He's going to have to fly us to Athens today, because I'm damned if I'll attempt it in this condition.'

'The lad'll be petrified.'

'Do him good,' was his unsympathetic response, as he

downed more black coffee. 'Did I make a fool of myself last night?'

'Not half! They all loved it, although we had to rescue you from Benzini's youngest brother. He took a great fancy to you, and we suspected he had more than Continental salutations in mind when he kept kissing you.'

Kit was alarmed. 'I didn't kiss him back, did I?'

'You were too drunk to be more than the passive recipient of all manner of adoration. Boy, did the women make a feast of you!'

'Where were my pals; the loyal crew whose duty it is to support their captain?'

Morris grinned. 'Enjoying some of the crumbs left over from the feast.' He began buttering a roll from Kit's breakfast tray. 'The Italians are lovely people, aren't they?'

'Except for Mussolini and his followers. The Neapolitans are fun-loving and affectionate, but in some other parts of Italy we might not have been made so welcome,' he pointed out, walking to the tiny bathroom to put his head under a cold deluge. Towelling it gingerly, Kit stood in the doorway watching Morris enjoy the breakfast he could not himself face. 'Be under no illusions, if Adolph Hitler gets the war he's determined on the Italians will back him against the rest of Europe. My own participation in the civil war in Spain is enough to arouse hostility from ardent Fascists in this country. If I really was no more than a passive recipient last night, I was fortunate to risk nothing more dangerous than ravishment by Benzini's young brother.'

Returning to the bathroom, he began shaving with extreme caution. The Kirklands were furious enough over the reception awaiting their arrival yesterday; it would not do to present himself this morning with sticking plaster on his face to suggest a drunken punch-up last night. He paused, razor in hand, relishing the memory of Donald's face as he had conducted his VIP passengers into the launch to the sound of spectators

341

chanting the name which must turn a knife in his stomach each time he heard it. Sir Hector might have had no conscience where the Ansons were concerned, but guilt and shame were lurking in Donald's eyes each time they met his own. With a sigh, he continued his careful removal of the dark stubble which gave him a villainous aspect when combined with bloodshot eyes.

Calling through to Morris, he asked, 'Are the boys all up and about, and clear-headed?'

His friend came to lean against the door jamb, still munching. 'Of course. They can hold their liquor like real men.'

Kit splashed his face with water, then said into the towel, 'They've never been deprived of it for four or five years. It takes a while to get used to it again.' Walking past Morris, he took clean underpants and a white shirt from his bag. 'If you've finished gorging my victuals, go and round up these "real men" who comprise my crew. I've a launch organized to take us out to *Flamingo* at eight.'

He was tying the smart green and gold tie before Morris spoke again. 'I know they found you guilty on the strength of incriminating evidence, but I've never believed you capable of stealing their damned cash.'

'You're a fool, then,' he declared into the mirror. 'I did steal it, and would have spent the lot if I hadn't driven my car into the Sheen. Don't turn me into a hero.'

'I don't have to. The affectionate people of Napoli did that last night,' was his friend's quiet reply. 'The lads have now realized what an exceptional man they have in command of this flight.'

Kit had no idea what to say to that, so he continued dressing in his uniform trousers and black shoes until he heard the door close behind Morris. Straightening from tying his laces, he stared out at the pretty colour-washed houses straggling down the slopes while his head continued to thud. Last night had put him back on his pedestal for a while. The cheering of those ashore as the launch had carried him towards them, the claps on the back from young men, the adoring girls, the triumph of being carried shoulder-high whilst showers of petals had rained on him, had been thrilling. A dead hero had been reincarnated. Also revived was the awareness of how much the Kirkland family had taken from him.

This morning, his mind was full of memories of their greed for power and recognition which had robbed him of his professional integrity and standing. Those years in prison, and the degrading ones which had followed, had robbed him of his youth. Last night, he had laughed joyously for the first time in far too long. In the old days, he would have drunk his crew under the table, and awoken with a girl beside him in the bed. Now, he became senseless after a very small amount of alcohol, and regarded women as no more than an occasional necessity. Even Morris' sister-in-law, Alia, made all the running. What had happened to that warm, delightful quality known as 'pleasure'? The Kirklands had banished it from his life, and the nearest he got to it now was when he was at the controls of *Flamingo*. Even that would be denied him today.

A glance at his clock showed him it was now fifteen minutes to eight. After brushing his hair with slow careful strokes, he packed his things, slipped on his jacket and cap, then walked downstairs to the tiny courtyard where an old man was watering the geraniums. There, he found the entire crew awaiting him in spruce, immaculate style, drumming their fingers or tapping their feet impatiently. At his appearance, they studied their watches in unison.

'Cheeky sods,' he said gruffly.

The girl who had brought his breakfast appeared with his clothes of the night before, cleaned and pressed. He thanked her, and reached in his pocket for money.

'No,' she cried swiftly. 'Mama say no give nothing.'

343

Blushing faintly, she moved nearer. 'Last night many girl kiss you. I like kiss you. You say please?'

Looking into her eager adolescent face where dark shining eyes mirrored her hero-worship, he was briefly reminded of an equally young girl in a sophisticated black dress begging to be allowed to kiss him in a moonlit ruin. He shook his head gently.

'Save your kisses for a man who really deserves them.'

The launch was waiting by the sun-washed jetty, and they were soon out to where *Flamingo* rode the slight swell. Conditions for take-off were perfect. Once they were aboard, they tackled their respective tasks with the industry of bees in a hive. A succession of small craft came out with fresh vegetables, rolls and the table linen which had been laundered overnight, during which time *Flamingo* was taking on fuel. Digger went on his inspection round, and Morris organized his maps for the route they would be covering.

In the cockpit, Kit broke his news to his youthful assistant. 'I have a head like a blacksmith's forge, and my hands are playing an invisible piano. You'll have to take her over this leg.'

To his surprise, Joss responded with total confidence. 'Fair enough. You take it easy until we reach Athens.'

'You're quite happy?'

The youngster nodded. 'When we all carried you home last night, I knew you'd never attempt to fly today.' His boyish smile broke through. 'It was some party, wasn't it?'

'My head tells me it must have been, but I honestly don't recall many details. Thank God our passengers were nowhere near. Much faith they'd have in their captain for the rest of the flight!'

Joss turned away to occupy the pilot's seat, where he began studying the instruments intently. 'When the fabulous Kirklands, their wealthy influential passengers, and the prototype of a sensational new aircraft can all be ignored in favour of Kit Anson, I'd say no one in the world could fail to have less than total faith in him. Shall we do the checks now?'

Taken aback at the youngster's unusual assertiveness, Kit meekly took the right-hand seat and concentrated on the ritual of pre-flight instrument checks. When that was completed, he left the cockpit to stroll through the aircraft for a final word with each member of his crew. His head still had a sledgehammer working full time inside it, so the chief steward mixed him a concoction he claimed would muffle it, if not silence it altogether. Walking on then to the boarding bay, Kit looked across at the jetty where the launch was waiting to ferry the passengers out. It was still tied up, and there was no sign of any movement along the approaches to the harbour. He frowned. Departure was scheduled for ten o'clock. It was now a quarter to ten. They were late.

By ten thirty he was in a morning-after-the-night-before rage. Radioing the harbourmaster's office to send a boat for him, he returned to shore in it to telephone the hotel for information on the delay. Demanding to speak to Mr Jarvis, it was not long before Maitland's precise voice spoke into his ear.

'Hallo. Who is this?'

'We're half an hour behind schedule, Maitland. What the hell is going on up there?' Kit asked heatedly.

'There appears to be some difficulty in rounding everyone up,' came the unruffled reply. 'Miss Kirkland is doing her best to urge Countess Renskaya and Lady Frencham to dress, and Mrs Farrell appears to have set off at dawn on a sightseeing expedition and hasn't yet returned. Most of the men were here at nine thirty, but several have wandered off again to inspect the gardens. Mr Kirkland is endeavouring to retrieve them.'

Kit could hardly believe his ears. 'This isn't a bloody Sunday-school outing, it's an inter-continental proving flight designed to impress prospective investors! I'm playing my rôle to the hilt, and I expect all of you to do the same. Tell Leone she must damn well order those

345

women into their clothes, and give this message to your master. *Flamingo* will be taking off at eleven fifteen – an hour and a quarter late – and anyone not aboard by then will have to find alternative means of returning to England.'

He slammed the receiver down, and stormed back to the flying boat with his head pounding twice as fast. Joss's expression was carefully controlled as he was issued with instructions to get under way at the revised time, with or without passengers. Silence then reigned on the flight deck as the minutes ticked past. At eleven, movement on the jetty heralded the laden launch on its way out to them. An audible sigh of relief could be heard from all crew members save the captain, who instead snapped instructions for them to stand by for imminent departure.

The recalcitrant passengers were full of high spirits, which hinted at immense tact on the part of the Kirklands. It was not extended to the pilot, apparently, for Donald immediately mounted the steps to the flight deck and strode through to the cockpit, his face white with anger. Halting a few feet from Kit, he let fly.

'Just who the hell do you think you are?'

It was the wrong tone to use towards a man in the wrong mood. He answered with matching animosity. 'I'm the captain of this aircraft. As such, I insist that you leave the flight deck immediately. We shall be departing within minutes, and passengers are forbidden here during take-off.'

'Now look here. . .'

'Please don't make it necessary for one of my crew to enforce my ruling.'

'I'm the one who gives the orders,' Donald cried furiously.

'Not aboard this aircraft. A flight captain has total command over his crew, and the passengers. You should know that strict aviation ruling without being told.'

'You're no longer captain of this aircraft,' raged Donald. 'I terminate your employment here and now.'

'That suits me,' Kit snapped, 'but you'll find Mr Hamilton will also insist that you leave the cockpit immediately. He knows the rules as well as any pilot.'

Digger rose to his feet significantly, but Donald was not prepared to let them gang up on him and swung round to leave like a man ready to explode. Thankful that Joss would be at the controls, Kit sat heavily in the boy's vacant seat, his entire body thudding in time with his head now. Even so, he glanced over at his second in command.

'Sorry about that. It hasn't unsettled you, has it?'

The young man, wearing earphones which kept him in touch with the shore as well as his crew, shook his head. 'I'll make this take-off a really good one, as it's going to be my last in *Flamingo*. If you're fired, so are we all.'

Kit made no reply to that thought-provoking comment, and Joss broke the silence several moments later by asking, 'Will you make the departure announcement to the passengers, or shall I?'

'I think my fragile condition will just about allow me to do that,' Kit murmured, reaching for the speaking tube which would relay his words throughout the hull. 'Good morning, ladies and gentlemen. We are now ready for departure to Athens. Our route will take us around the toe of Italy and right along the Mediterranean. My first officer, Mr Hamilton, will be at the controls today. He is now indicating his readiness for take-off, so I'll leave you safely in his hands to enjoy the flight.'

The roar of aircraft engines was always as sweet as the song of a bird to Kit, and his anger gradually melted away with the warm thrill of rising up into the sky. There, he could be whoever he wished until his descent. Although Joss looked tense, he performed a copybook manoeuvre, handling the heavy craft with as much confidence as Kit could wish. After circling above the incredible beauty of the Neapolitan scene, he set the course given by Morris and relaxed his stiff shoulders.

'Boy, it's warm in here,' he murmured.

'We'll change into tropical kit at Athens,' Kit commented, getting to his feet. 'If any of you should want me, I'll be chatting to Mr Kirkland.'

He found Donald with Maitland and Leone, in the small forward cabin reserved for their use alone. Maitland looked ashen. He was plainly suffering from airsickness once more. Kit was tempted to pray for a violent storm somewhere along this leg, which would throw *Flamingo* all over the sky, but resisted the temptation because Joss would be forced to cope with the hazards it would entail. Leone looked coolly beautiful in iceblue, and the filigree neckline enhanced her flawless skin. How pride had smothered her youthful irresistible vivacity, he mused. She was now a typical product of her class, playing at being a businesswoman until she grew bored again. Sliding into the empty seat beside her, he took off his cap to hook it over one knee as he faced Donald.

'I imagine you're all now discussing the best place in Greece to find a replacement crew – one which is highly experienced with flying boats,' he said quietly.

'How dared you speak to me in that manner in front of those men?' choked his adversary, still white with anger.

'Those men are members of my crew which I command. It's essential to hold their respect, so how dared you speak to me that way in their presence?' Kit retaliated. 'We were preparing for take-off, which is a vulnerable process. Young Joss could have been dangerously unsettled by that scene. If you had something to say to me, you should have waited until now and asked me to leave the flight deck first.'

'*Waited* and *asked*!' thundered Donald. 'I own Kirkland's: I own this aircraft. You are simply one of my employees.'

348

'As the pilot of *Flamingo*, that may be true,' Kit agreed, trying not to lose his temper again. 'Right at this moment, however, I'm Kit Anson, who lived and worked with you for over three years and who knows a damned sight too much for your sense of wellbeing. Now we're here in private, man-to-man, I suggest that you drop your insufferable arrogance and discuss our differences sensibly. If you sack me at Athens, my crew will also leave.'

'If you behave with the manners of a mongrel you must expect to be kicked out,' Donald advised in cutting tones, although clearly shaken by this aggressive approach from Kit.

'That's how I was always regarded, wasn't it?' he returned, with a glance at Leone. 'A stray mongrel.'

She looked every inch her father's daughter as she said, 'One who bit the hand which fed him, as I recall.'

'How dared you telephone such a message to Maitland?' her brother then demanded.

'I'd have telephoned it direct to you, except that you've been in the habit of speaking to me through a third person. Now that we're back to normal communication, I'll give you a few facts. Although the sky is endless, we can't fly through it as we please. There are rules and regulations to observe. Pilots have to know who else is moving around, where they're heading, and when they're likely to be passing through certain areas. Where flying boats are concerned, there are additional important factors such as tides which govern the ability to land or take off.' Kit leaned forward to emphasize his next point. 'This flight has been planned down to the last detail, with every port of call told of our intentions and requirements. We've been given concessions, in many instances, by airlines willing to let us use their facilities or moorings on condition that we do not clash with the arrival or departure of their own aircraft. Kirkland Marine Aviation gave an assurance that *Flamingo* would maintain her schedule so that there would be no such problem. This morning, the very first of this long flight, we disregarded our own assurances to our host company in Naples. An Imperial Airways flying boat was due to arrive there just before noon, and we were almost ninety minutes late in departing, simply because you allowed twenty-four people to run wild this morning.'

Leaving a moment or two for all that to register with Donald, he then continued. 'Mechanical failure, impossible conditions, or threatened danger to life are all valid reasons for delay, but I refuse to alter my flight plan because several bone-idle women decline to get up on time. Even if St Peter were in command of this boat, he'd have telephoned the same message to you. No doubt, you'd have accepted it from him. It's my presence on this flight which you can't take, isn't it?'

'I believe I dispensed with it a short while ago.'

Kit took a deep breath. 'Haven't you heard anything I've just said? If I walk away at any time during this trip, my crew will follow, leaving you high and dry.'

'Why don't you? Why don't you walk away?' cried Leone, with astonishing passion.

He turned to her, marvelling at how deeply she appeared to hate him now. 'Because *Flamingo* was designed by Warren, who deserves all the help I can give him to make the world aware of his brilliance. Is it too much to ask you to do the same?' Getting to his feet, he settled the cap back on his aching head. 'I must insist that you get your passengers aboard on time, in future, or you might find not only the crew gone but the flying boat as well.'

Donald rose to face him with terms of his own. 'On shore, you do as *I* say. Is that quite clear?'

'Quite,' he snapped.

'Then, in future, you'll behave in a decent and responsible manner. I heard details of your disgusting public exhibition last night, and the fact that your reserve pilot is presently at the controls speaks volumes. If you touch alcohol just once more during this flight, a report will be filed in the right quarters. We have two men from the Air Ministry aboard, don't forget, and they are well informed on your past drinking habits. One word from me to them, and I doubt you'll ever be allowed to pilot an aircraft again, anywhere in the world.' With his mouth tugged down into a grim gesture of dismissal, he added curtly, 'Now get back to your duty.'

Kit's eyes narrowed speculatively as he studied the man. 'Yesterday upset you even more than I suspected, didn't it? Afraid of what I might say when I'm too drunk to care? Poor Donald. Two years behind bars might have been harsh, but I've served my sentence and been freed. Yours is likely to go on for as long as you have a conscience.'

As he walked away he heard Leone ask, 'What did he mean by that?'

'Who the hell knows?' came the ragged reply from her badly shaken brother. 'We never should have let him come on this bloody trip.'

Back in the cockpit there was silence. Kit sat beside Joss and gazed around at the noonday brilliance of the sky. 'What a superb element this is.'

'Pity we ever have to go down again,' murmured Morris from behind them.

'I don't know,' he returned nonchalantly. 'Landing on the Nile tomorrow should be worth descending for, wouldn't you say?'

Joss looked across at him, grinning his relief at the news. 'Gosh, I can't wait to see the pyramids.'

'Bugger the pyramids,' swore Digger, in typical release of tension. 'Lead me to the Dance of the Seven Veils.'

'What *I'm* really looking forward to is a nice box of dates,' Morris informed them straightfaced.

They all threw something at him, which was hardly the decent and responsible behaviour their employer had just demanded.

The flight of *Flamingo* continued without a hitch, the aircraft gathering laurels as the days passed like a gold and blue dream. The qualities which only a long flight could prove were well and truly displayed, and the gilded sun-washed ports set against the blue waters on which the flying boat settled so expertly time and time again, beguiled all aboard her. None was more spellbound than Warren, however. Naples had enchanted him. Athens had rendered him silent with awe. Cairo, with a truly spectacular landing on the Nile, had put a lump of unbidden emotion in his throat.

They had just departed from Mombasa, where they had remained for three nights. The crew had earned their essential rest period, and the guests had made the most of their airy rooms opening on to the beach. There had been dancing each night to different bands which played in the hotel's three ballrooms. In one, elderly British exiles enjoyed the twostep and veleta to a string orchestra. In the second, lonely colonials who administered the vast bushland areas and came to Mombasa on leave threw themselves into the energetic European dances presently popular. For lovers and those who found the clash of cultures too disturbing in that place of wild African beauty, there was the darkened club atmosphere where couples held each other close while they swayed to the hypnotic rhythms of the continent.

Warren had danced with Leone in each. Yet, even in the dim room with the sounds of basic sensuality filling their ears, she had never referred to that night in Naples, never mentioned Kit or her feelings for him, never questioned his own declaration of love on that bewitching terrace. His growing passion for her, her clear rejection of anything but friendship from him, and the deepening guilt of having remained silent when he could have spoken to clear his friend's name were the only aspects of that dream time which spoiled his elation. His nights were restless, but the days had been exciting enough to compensate. He tried to ease his conscience by telling himself that giving the truth to Leone about Kit would not win him for her, but simply increase the anguish by divulging the wrong her family had done to the man she loved against her will. Half the flight was over. Another week and Kit would presumably go out of their lives once more. Better to tick off the days and keep to himself information which would cause more pain than happiness.

He was losing some of his awkwardness in exalted company, and his nightly performance on the trumpet had created the pleasure and interest Leone had hoped for. The prospects looked extremely good. The Countess had telegraphed her banker from Cairo, and the transaction should be completed by the time they reached England. The men from Anglo-Asiatic had recommended the purchase of Kirkland's flying boats for their Asian route, cabling the news from Mombasa. This, from a company growing in stature, would result in a substantial order. The Air Ministry officials admitted to being highly impressed, but any deal involving a government department took four times longer to negotiate than any other and even a favourable opinion, at this stage, was more than they had hoped for. Warren was inclined to agree with Leone that the American pair could be along for a spot of spying, although they had appeared rather piqued when the rival Anglo-Asiatic directors made such definite promises.

Lady Carlyon-Bree declared she had never travelled in such comfort or felt so safe in an aircraft before, and would certainly recommend her friends to take an interest in *Flamingo*. The main cause for her euphoric state might have been the rather un-secret *affaire* she was conducting with Randolph James, the Royal Flying Corps eccentric who had once blown up an enemy fuel dump by flying low and dropping lighted hurricane lamps when his squadron's supply of bombs had run out. Warren had happened to see Monique inviting the man into her room at Cairo, and prayed she would have time during the night to persuade her admirer to invest in the aircraft which had made available what she was presently giving him.

All in all, the sun was in its heaven and shining right down on Kirkland Marine Aviation, so everyone was totally relaxed during this flight to Lake Victoria. Everyone save Mrs Harmesworth, who had expressed her concern over a journey which entailed crossing great expanses of land for the first time during the trip. Donald had smiled charmingly as he assured her there were enough lakes and rivers in case of emergency, although there was little fear of it in *Flamingo*. Thus placated, she had then settled back in the comfort of her pink seat and closed her eyes.

Warren thought Donald had calmed down a lot since Naples, despite the illness of Maitland Jarvis throughout the trip. Armed with smelling salts and a bottle of sedative liquid provided by an army doctor in Cairo, he had been put on a ship heading for home. Donald seemed quite confident without him. There had been no further demonstrations of Kit Anson fever by the usual welcoming crowds at their ports of call, and Leone, Donald and their unwelcome pilot were all being ultra-polite towards each other now. There was no doubt that the charged atmosphere which had governed the trip as far as Naples had fizzed itself out. Warren prayed things would stay as they were until the end of the flight.

They had left Mombasa early this morning. The sun was now at its hottest. The cabins were artificially cooled, but the great spread of windows around the flight deck made it virtually impossible for the crew to find shade. To cope with the problem, the pilots each took the controls for an hour at a time while the other rested in the cabin reserved for them. Warren found Kit there three hours into the flight, and sat beside him with a smile.

'Is this your idea of work? I've never had the luxury of another pilot to do the flying when I feel like a rest.'

354

Kit smiled back. 'I should think not, you lazy blighter. All you ever do is potter about in trainers giving lessons to those with more wealth than sense – like our Miss Kirkland.'

Immediately on the defensive, Warren said, 'She's very good. Went solo after only eight hours, and shows great keenness.'

'Until she tires of it, like everything else.'

'You're wrong,' he insisted. 'There's more to her than meets the eye, Kit.'

The other man grinned in knowing fashion. 'That's very obvious. With luck, your turn'll come to see it.'

Warren's colour rose angrily. 'That's a bloody rotten thing to say about her.'

'Good God,' exclaimed Kit, studying him closely, 'you're not still dazzled by the girl, are you? Men are reputed to come and go rather swiftly, where she's concerned.'

'That's cheap social gossip,' he snapped. 'You, of all people, should know better than to believe what's reported in print.'

'Hey, cool down,' advised Kit laughingly. 'It's far too humid to get all het up over our boss. Forget I mentioned her.'

Unable to leave it at that, Warren went on, 'Underneath that rather cool manner she adopts, Leone is a vastly different person. I admire her determined attempt to become a working partner in Kirkland's. Be honest, she had no opportunity to do much with her life while her father was alive to keep her in her place.'

'Christ, you're more dazzled than I guessed,' came the exclamation from a man who more often than not did the dazzling. 'That girl had wealth, beauty and the whole of Europe at her disposal. In addition, she had been given the kind of expensive education I'd have swopped my eye teeth for, along with a great many other men. Of course she damn well had opportunities to do something with her life; more so than you and me at the same

355

age. When *I* was twenty-two, I was working to take the air speed record after struggling to qualify as an engineer and pay for flying lessons. I know old Kirkland made some of it possible, but I'd fought tooth and claw to make a success of my dreary failure of a childhood before he came on the scene. At twenty-two, *you* were giving lessons to earn enough to allow you to design aircraft which your batty old landlady trod on without a notion of what she was destroying. Oh, come off it, Warren, no man can be so dazzled he can't see that she's no more than a beautiful lost soul seeking purpose for existing.'

Warren's lips tightened. 'I didn't realize you detested her so strongly.'

Kit shook his head. 'I feel nothing whatever for her. It's she who detests me.'

That observation silenced Warren as he studied the man alongside him. Hours on the beach in Mombasa had deepened his tan, now emphasized by the pale-green tropical uniform. Kit would be physically beckoning to any woman, he supposed, and his immunity to their admiration somehow increased his fascination, from their point of view. Was Leone merely physically attracted, or was she nursing a dangerously strong passion for this man who claimed he felt nothing for her?

Shaking his head, Kit said, 'You're too valuable a person to waste time on a girl like her, Warren. Concentrate on your work; have a love affair with aircraft. They'll bring you richer rewards and a greater sense of fulfilment. I know, old lad. Anyway, you're going to be far too busy to languish after the lady boss when you get back home. *Flamingo* is a sensation. You're even more brilliant than my father was . . . and infinitely more down to earth. I feel honoured to be part of your flight of glory.'

With guilt once more burning in his breast at the genuine warmth of his friend's congratulations, Warren asked unhappily, 'What'll you do when this flight is over?'

Putting his hands up behind his head, Kit sighed. 'Go back to Lisbon and fly for Tom Digby, I suppose. It's possible that this trip might redeem my reputation enough to enable me to get a job with some British passenger line, but I owe Tom a lot and these lads with me are honest and uncomplicated. Not one of them would claim another man's design as his own.' Into the significant silence, Kit added, 'You do realize that was what Donald did with *Aphrodite*?'

'I . . . I guessed he must have had some help,' Warren said warily.

'Help be damned! He stole my . . .'

They were interrupted by a call from Morris, who urged Kit to join them in the cockpit. He complied with immediate alertness. Warren followed more slowly, and was just in time to hear Joss report receipt of a 'mayday' call from Mombasa. The young pilot looked up at Kit in concern.

'We're being asked to go to the aid of three people from a light aircraft, which crashed in thick jungle near Lake Kiju. Two of them were injured in the crash. It occurred when the pilot was attempting to reach a nearby mission hospital with a passenger suffering from a deadly virus. He'll die if not treated within twelve hours, they say.'

'Why us?' asked Kit tersely, tapping Morris on the shoulder to give a swift aside to ask for a map reference.

Joss frowned. 'It's impossible for anyone to reach them overland, and the river's so tortuous and difficult it'd take a week to get a doctor up there by canoe. By then, they'd all be dead.'

'No seaplanes available?' Kit asked then.

'Two, but with insufficient range. We were known to be in the area, and they want our answer on whether or not we could make a landing on the lake.'

Turning away from Joss, Kit gave his attention to Morris pencilling a circle on his map. Warren joined his friend to study it, as Morris gave them the vital information on the size of the lake in question and the nature of the surrounding terrain. A small expanse of water encircled by thick jungle was a difficult proposition. Kit let out his breath slowly and gustily as he stared at the minute blue patch on the map for a long moment. Then he looked at Warren, his eyes full of questions.

'You're the man who knows this aircraft better than any of us. Could she do it? Could she land there and, more importantly, take off again on such a short stretch of water?' Another thought occurred to him and he turned back to Joss to inquire if Mombasa had given any information on the present depth of the lake.

'Water level high,' said the youngster. 'The rain has been heavy recently. It was a violent storm which caused the aircraft to crash, but the weather is now clear and calm.'

Looking back at Warren with urgency, Kit asked, 'Well, will she do it?'

A surge of tremendous excitement filled Warren as he replied, with total confidence, 'She's capable of doing it fully loaded, and she's only half that now. She's capable of doing it, if the pilot can induce her to.'

'Without risking the lives of the passengers in any way?'

'They're in the hands of the pilot,' he responded frankly. 'She'll do it, Kit, if you can make her.'

His friend walked over to Joss. 'Tell them we're altering course in order to take a look. If it's possible to attempt a rescue, we will. Set the course Morris gives you. I'll take over just as soon as I've told Mr Kirkland our intentions. He'll have to know about it.'

'I'll tell him,' Warren offered. 'He may take a while to digest the facts, and you have far more important things to do right now.'

'Thanks,' said Kit briefly. 'If you'd like to come back after speaking to him, I'd be glad of your company. You designed the bloody thing and you're entitled to be up here during her moment of glory.'

Warren left the flight deck possessed by supreme elation. *Flamingo* had been given the most dramatic and unexpected opportunity to demonstrate her strongest selling points. She *could* land on that tiny waterway and leave it again, and one of the finest pilots of marine aircraft would be at her controls. She would do it. She would save the lives of three people, and hit the headlines once more. She would remove any last hesitation in the minds of those aboard, and her success would be completely assured. His dream had not only come true, it had exceeded the wildest hope of any man who sought the realms of conquest.

13

Leone was enjoying a quiet pre-lunch pink gin with her brother, when Warren came up to them from the direction of the flight deck. He had changed a lot during this trip, she thought, watching his approach. There was a new touch of sophistication, of self-confidence which, when added to his shy charm, had made him a popular member of the party. There was also no doubt that his expertise on the dance-floor, together with the magical touch he had when playing with the various orchestras, showed another side of this clever, gifted designer. His enthusiasm when speaking of aircraft in such knowledgeable fashion, had won over even the most cautious of the male members of their group. Leone supposed this ability to be the reason for Donald's reticence on the more technical aspects of *Flamingo*; why he concentrated on the business side. Warren would be useless in making financial deals, so Donald plainly left him to do the ground work on 'nuts and bolts'. It was a good arrangement; one which was paying off handsomely.

As for Warren's sudden declaration of love, she blamed herself for precipitating it on a night when her own emotions had been in such turmoil. All the same, his kiss had been astonishingly passionate. Beneath that diffident genius in loud pullovers and yards of woolly scarf was a lion prowling in his lair. That long-ago red-haired girl had tempted him from it, but he had retreated again until several nights ago. How foolish the gods were to make her love a man she could never have, when another far more worthy one was there for the taking. Warren's brand of devotion was what she had been looking for ever since she could remember. Now it was being offered, she declined it. Maybe it was she who was foolish, and not the gods.

Smiling up at him as he reached their seats, she said, 'Join us for a drink. There's just time before the stewards start serving lunch.' Above the steady drone of the engines, she elaborated. 'There's a chilled quince consommé, a light mixed grill of . . .'

'You'll have to delay lunch,' he interrupted with a curious air of excitement, as he sat facing them both on the pink seat. 'We've received an SOS asking if we can go to the aid of three people stranded in the jungle. The only means of reaching them is if we can land on a small lake, which the crew reckon they can find from their present position. Kit's agreed to take a look and attempt a rescue, if it's possible. He's altered course. We should be over the lake in about fifty minutes, so I think the meal should be delayed until the emergency is over.'

Donald looked suddenly tense. 'He has no authority to do this without my permission.'

'Your permission is superfluous,' said Warren, leaning back confidently. 'He's captain of the aircraft, and the responsibility for such decisions is his alone. He was on his way to tell you when I stopped him. He has more vital things to do, at the moment, and an argument over who's boss on this trip would hardly help his concentration. Anyway, can't you see what a splendid piece of luck this is?'

'A piece of luck?' asked Leone, already worrying so much about Kit's concentration she accepted Warren's unusual frankness towards Donald with no more than slight surprise.

'We have twenty-four important and influential passengers aboard this flying boat,' Donald pointed out crisply. 'Add us and the crew to make the number more

361

than thirty. His first duty is to us, not to three total strangers lost in the jungle. Will you go back and tell him, or shall I?'

As the starboard wing dipped low to give a clear view of the terrain below, and the port wing rose into the dark-blue heavens to indicate a decided change of course, Leone asked, 'Who are these three people?'

Warren shrugged. 'No idea, except that two of them were injured when their light aircraft crashed during a storm. It was on its way to a mission hospital with one of the men, who has a fever which will kill him within twelve hours if treatment is not available. They sound to be in dire straits.'

'What kind of fever?' demanded Donald angrily.

Anticipating his concern, Leone said, 'He's right to ask, Warren. In this part of the world, there are tropical diseases which spread like wildfire. We can't expose our passengers to any kind of danger.'

'Kit knows that,' he reasoned impatiently. 'If only one of the three has it, it can't be highly contagious.' Leaning forward earnestly, he appealed to her rather than to Donald. 'If we don't even take a look to see if it's possible to pick them up, what kind of people are we? All three will die before any other rescue party could reach them. Do you believe any single person aboard would demand that we ignore this call for aid?'

She shook her head slowly. 'What if it isn't possible to land?'

'Kit says he'll then fly as low as he can, while we drop food and anything else we are carrying which might keep them alive a little longer.' He smiled. 'I imagine he'd rather pick them up than bombard them with a quince consommé and mixed grill.'

Her brother stirred restlessly beside her. 'So much for his high-handed lecture on sticking to a schedule and not flying around the sky willy-nilly.'

'Mombasa knows exactly where we are, Donald, and he's not doing this for fun,' Warren said, with a continuation of surprising authority towards a man he had always treated with restrained civility. 'I'm thrilled over these circumstances, but he's the poor devil who has to make a snap decision on the element of risk, then take it.'

'So there is an element of risk! I won't allow him to take it,' Donald declared, getting to his feet angrily.

Leone stood in unison with Warren, and heard herself say coolly, 'The pilot is the only person who can decide whether or not he can land his aircraft in a designated place, Donald. You have never flown, so you must accept that both Warren and I agree that the matter is out of our hands. What we all have to realize is that, whatever reservations we might have about this particular pilot, he is highly skilled and unlikely to endanger either his aircraft or his passengers.' Looking frankly at her brother, she added, 'If anything should go wrong on this trip – anything at all – he knows he'd be finished for good. He's no fool. If he attempts this rescue, it'll be because he's confident of carrying it off and restoring his smashed reputation.'

'If he attempts this rescue, it'll be in order to save three lives,' put in Warren with surprising heat. 'You two have him cast as the villain, whatever he does. Just for once, try to believe that people sometimes act for the benefit of others. You Kirklands really are the limit!'

'I'll thank you not to use that tone to us,' snapped Donald. 'You have no authority on this flight. The sole purpose of your presence here is to answer questions put by prospective investors. You're an employee of this company.'

Warren flushed darkly. 'I'm the designer of this aircraft. As such, I can see the tremendous good fortune offered by this drama. *Flamingo* is the one flying boat able to land on that short stretch of water, and Kit is a pilot able to make her. The slight element of risk involved will enhance the feat, so that news of it will make world headlines. Not only that, the prospective

investors aboard – whom you're so worried about pro-
tecting – will actually be participating in the event which
will perfectly demonstrate *Flamingo*'s unique ability. It
will ensure the survival of the company. Perhaps that
consideration will allow you to accept that it will also
ensure the survival of three desperate souls.' His colour
was still high as he turned away. 'I'm going back to give
Kit any assistance he might need. Perhaps you would
unbend enough to move amongst your Very Important
Persons to acquaint them with what we're about to do.'
At the door to the flight deck, he turned. 'You might
also be generous enough to congratulate your pilot after
he's pulled off something a lesser man might shy from
attempting.'

'Bloody cheek!' breathed Donald as Warren vanished,
but he appeared curiously shaken as he turned to Leone.
'This trip has caused him to get a bit above himself, if
you ask me.'

'He's always like that over anything concerned with
his precious *Flamingo*. Because you remain aloof over
your brain-child, you don't understand how het up he
gets in defence of his work,' Leone told him. 'Is he
right? Can *Flamingo* land on remarkably short expanses
of water?'

'He says she can.'

'Don't you know? You helped design the aircraft.'

Donald looked evasive. 'I never allow myself to be
dominated by a machine. They're there to be built, that's
all.'

She sighed. 'Some men do seem to become obsessed
by their aircraft. "A love-affair" is how they describe
their feelings. Poor Warren is normally just a rather shy,
sweet person, but he turns into a veritable Lucifer in
defence of his flying boat.'

'And in defence of the blighter flying it.'

'They've always been friendly,' she pointed out.

'He didn't thieve anything from Warren.'

Unhappy at that reminder, she said, 'Come on, let's

364

tell everyone what to expect, then pray he pulls it off. Otherwise, all the good work so far might be lost.'

They moved through the cabins breaking the news, and apologizing for the unavoidable delay in serving lunch. Leone's unhappiness deepened when everyone reacted to the prospect with great enthusiasm, which dismissed anything as mundane as lunch in favour of a heroic rescue. It made her wonder if Kirklands really were as black as Warren had painted them. Why had she sneered at what Kit was about to attempt, by hinting that it would be simply in the hope of salvaging his career? Why, when love for him was making this whole trip a purgatory to be endured only by adopting a pose?

Where the passengers had been lazily passive during that pre-lunch period, they now clustered in animated groups watching for the first glimpse of the lake ahead. Not one of them appeared afraid or worried; even the tiresome Mrs Harmesworth had red spots of excitement in her cheeks, as she sat beside Elaine Farrell declaring that she had never experienced a comparable drama on other flights. After joining Monique and her beau for a few moments Leone realized she was an unwelcome third and moved on to where one of the Americans was studying a map spread on his knees.

Slipping into the seat beside him, she asked, 'Are you tracking our course, Jerry?'

For once, he seemed less than delighted at her nearness. The map occupied his attention. 'I guess we're right about here,' he murmured, placing a thick finger half an inch from a blue dot. 'There's only one lake within a hundred miles, so that's got to be it. If Anson can land on that pin-dot, he'll get my hand in hearty congratulations.' His broad face tilted to look at hers. 'They say a pilot's only as good as his aircraft, but it cuts both ways, Leone. There has to be perfect understanding between them to make it really work. A love-affair of man and machine.'

There it was again; this suggestion of utter commitment. She sighed. 'When I'm in the cockpit, I feel no more than I do behind the wheel of my car. Why don't I have a love-affair with my machine?'

'You're a woman,' came the blunt answer. 'Stick to love-affairs with the men flying 'em. No one expects a creature as glamorous and swanky as you to lose her head over miracles of engineering.' His hand slid on to her knee. 'That head of yours is too damn pretty to lose, anyway.'

Getting swiftly to her feet, she moved away down the hull with a sudden longing to be with Warren so that she could watch the landing. There were no lingering doubts in her mind. Kit *would* attempt to pick up those people facing death as an alternative. Seeing that everyone was well occupied and entertained by the thrill of expectation, she sat alone by a window, staring at the dense green jungle passing beneath them now. Kit had descended at least ten thousand feet, and maintained a steady downward run towards that blue pin-dot on the map.

Then it was visible, lying like a tiny diamond in the rippling emerald vegetation. Although she had never been at the controls of any machine larger than a trainer, the basics of bringing an aircraft from the sky to a firmer element were the same, and that glittering smudge loomed demandingly. Her heartbeat quickened. She knew how vital one's judgement must be, how steady one's concentration during those last moments before landing, even when an entire airfield was spread below. With these limits imposed on any pilot, how much keener must all his senses be as he dropped lower and lower! The voices around her grew louder with excitement as the lake was spotted, and the passengers crowded the windows to search for any sign of life around those distant shores. Leone remained isolated in her seat, telling herself Kit was one of the finest marine pilots in the world, and would land safely.

As she stared down at the vegetation drawing ever

nearer, an inner voice flung a question at her like a spear out of the darkness. He *was* one of the finest marine pilots in the world, so why had he done what he had six years ago? That laughing, exuberant, passionately professional young man had confessed to her that he counted himself one of the most fortunate men alive. He had been 'adopted' by a family with wealth and power; he had lived with them in great luxury, with money to spend, a fast car, and all the trappings of high living. Women had chased him in droves, and the whole world had claimed him a hero of the skies when he achieved laurels no other man could match in the one love which gave him his reason for living. Why, *why* would he throw all that away for ten thousand pounds? He could not have needed the money so badly that he would rob himself of everything, including his personal freedom. Growing cold as she continued to stare into the jungle now slipping past no more than several hundred feet below, that inner voice challenged her to recall the young man she had found in tears amidst the ruins of the chapel. Could he have done all those things of which he had been accused? The evidence against him had been overwhelming, and twelve people had unanimously found him guilty. That being so, surely it was perfectly natural to believe that he would attempt this landing for no other reason than to regain personal glory. So why had Warren been so blighting in his opinion of that belief? Why had he deplored their casting of Kit as a villain, when the world had been shown that he was?

Suddenly, green gave way to gleaming tawny water as *Flamingo* crossed the lake, throwing a giant shadow over its surface. Dangerously soon, they were again above tall solid vegetation at the far end of the waterway. Leone bit her lip. How could any pilot make a decision of such vital importance on one short run? It appeared that Kit had no intention of doing so, because the flying boat began a wide turn which would bring them on a course to cross the lake from the opposite direction. It still seemed far too short, even on that second inspection, yet that repeat run produced some result. A cry from some of the passengers drew her attention to movement on the banks bordered by mangroves. Someone was waving what looked like a shirt or jacket. At least one of them had reached the spot, and was fit enough to signal his presence.

A lump formed in Leone's throat as the full import of that signal dawned on her. Small wonder Warren had behaved as he had. There was human life down there in that killer jungle; people like herself and those on the seats surrounding her. At a distance, the affair had been impersonal. That desperate waving, that slight movement in a vast expanse of isolation, had put the responsibility of life or death in her hands, just as surely as it was in the hands of all aboard this aircraft. Whatever else Kit had done, she now felt certain there was only one aim behind his determination to rescue these people. He had fought in a war in Spain, she had been told. Perhaps that experience of life and death had changed him so much he was no longer moved to tears by his own triumph; no longer ruled by the desire for aerial glory.

Flamingo was making another turn, climbing as she did so. Next minute, she was heading resolutely away from the lake. A chorus of voices filled the cabins.

'He's going away!'

'Surely we're not going to leave them to die!'

'Why wouldn't he land?'

'We should have tried – at least *tried*.'

Into these cries came the sound of a voice with the familiar Devonshire accent, echoing through the hull from the speakers. It sounded confident and relaxed.

'Ladies and gentlemen, this is Captain Anson. As you'll have seen, there appears to be at least one survivor who has managed to reach the lake from the scene of the crash. We must hope all three are there. I've made two runs across the area to familiarize myself with the stretch of water available, and I'm now preparing to run in for a landing. It's very fortunate that *Flamingo* has the virtue of being able to settle on to a remarkably short stretch of water, otherwise no flying boat could attempt a rescue here. All the same, I must advise you that the next fifteen minutes may be slightly uncomfortable, from your point of view. It is imperative that you all remain in the same seats throughout. This will avoid any risk of falling and injuring yourselves during the rather violent de-acceleration period. I hope to take off again with three patients, but no more than three. Thank you for your essential cooperation.'

The announcement struck everyone silent with the anticipation of coming drama. Leone found she was trembling. Despite the calmness of his voice, she knew what he must be feeling at this vital moment of decision. Landing anywhere was a vulnerable process; trying to set down on an unfamiliar spot which offered any number of hazards took great courage. When so much else was at stake, it took even more. When one's entire future career and reputation hung in the balance, it was an exceptional person who could succeed.

They were turning once more and, as the sun flashed first through the windows to her right, then through those to her left, that beam of brightness brought sudden inner illumination. If Kit carried off this rescue successfully, she would try to forgive and forget. She would make a new start; give the name of Kirkland a different slant. Maybe pride was as much a failing as a virtue. If Kit carried this off, she would do as Warren hoped and congratulate him with unconditional warmth.

Someone slipped into the seat beside her. 'I hope to God he knows what he's doing.'

'He wouldn't be doing it if he didn't, Donald,' she said quietly. 'It would have been so easy to tell Mombasa it couldn't be achieved in a flying boat.'

'He hasn't done it yet,' came the reminder. 'All the same, this is certain to focus attention on *Flamingo*.'

'Damn *Flamingo*,' she said with soft vehemence, concentrating on her view from the window and relating the movements of the aircraft with her own knowledge of landing procedures.

They were dropping quickly, looking set to pancake on to the roof of the jungle at any moment. She guessed Kit had to come in this low because the growth reached up to the lake in every direction, giving no open approach to that vital stretch of water. *Flamingo* began to shudder and weave as she slowed quite drastically. Leone gripped her hands together. This was the time when a stall could easily occur. It did not, of course, because Kit was at the controls and not a novice like herself. The engine noise grew deafening, and the china in the galley began rattling continuously as they dropped so low, she believed the broad belly of the aircraft must be brushing the treetops.

Next minute, there was nothing but cloudy brown water no more than fifty feet below. *Flamingo* dropped like a stone, steadied with a great roar of power, then dropped again to hit the surface with a thud which jarred Leone's teeth together and brought cries of excited alarm from the passengers. The hull was filled with an ear-splitting roar as reverse thrust was applied with maximum force. With outstretched arms, Leone stopped herself from tumbling headlong into the opposite seat as the aircraft began to shudder violently. As they continued to hurtle forward, the cabin grew alarmingly dark. Water rose high over the windows to obliterate all light and give the impression that they were sinking.

'Dear God, we're going down,' cried Donald, seizing her protectively. 'He's crashed!'

In a dark, deafening purgatory, she clung to her brother, unable to believe what was happening. Then, she sensed a lessening of the violent struggle against propulsion, a less agonizing note to the roar of the engines. Her lashes grew moist as she gripped Donald's arms. Emotion prevented her telling him that she knew

Kit had done it. Gradually, *Flamingo* eased into a glide as she settled more naturally on to the element she had encountered with such suddenness. The engines quietened further until they gave no more than a contented hum, and the surge of brown water subsided enough to let in light through the top half of the windows. Unheeding of the advice they had been given, everyone stood to peer through at the view. It was hardly reassuring.

Casting her gaze over the full scope of vision, Leone saw disturbing isolation. Thick jungle surrounded tawny water scattered with floating vegetation. The banks were hardly that; merely stretches of tangled mangrove roots which separated water from solid earth. The whole place bore an air of menace. The vegetation seemed to close in on them like the greedy growth of a carnivorous plant. Somewhere out there, three men had been facing a terrible fate until now. Swallowing convulsively as she fought back the tears, Leone suddenly realized why that young man had been crying in the ruins of a moonlit chapel. If she was presently overcome by the success of what had just happened, how must he now feel, as agent of it?

'He's done it,' said Donald in a curious tone, as he stared from the window beside her. 'He's damn well done it!'

'Of course he has,' she replied in wobbly tones. 'I knew he would.'

From every part of the hull came elated voices as the aircraft came to a stop, each passenger thrilled by that sense of achievement. Into the buzz of their conversation came Kit's voice, over the relay system.

'Sorry about the rough ride, ladies and gentlemen. I trust no one suffered bumps or bruises. As we are likely to be here for some time, while two members of the crew go ashore in the hope of picking up those awaiting us, you may now move about the craft as much as you wish. I must rule that you stand clear and in no way hinder Mr Hamilton and Mr Rathbone when they return

371

with people who are in immediate need of medical attention, however. As soon as they are aboard, I shall take off for Mombasa again. Meanwhile, if any one amongst you has any knowledge of medicine, I'd be grateful for any assistance you might be able to give. Thank you.'

Leone looked at Donald. 'If only we had a doctor on board.'

He looked back at her with a slight frown. 'He sounded pretty damn cool about it all.'

'Yes, he did. Perhaps his experiences in the war in Spain taught him to be that way.'

'Mmm, perhaps. Come on, we'd better go forward and see what's happening.'

Leone followed her brother along the central gangway, excusing herself from those who wanted to detain her, until she halted beside Donald at the wide cargo door. The Australian, together with the young co-pilot who tended to blush whenever she spoke to him, was climbing into the dinghy which already contained flasks of water, a first-aid box, and a folding stretcher. Kit might have sounded cool, but his shirt stuck wetly to his back and his face looked set and worried as he watched his men start to paddle away from the aircraft.

'Go easy,' he called after them. 'There can be some nasty creatures in equatorial waterways. Don't take any risks.'

'Hark who's dishing out advice,' responded the Australian caustically.

'We'll signal our findings from the bank,' the Hamilton youngster promised, his eyes glowing as he gave a quick backward glance. 'Gosh, I hope they're all still alive.'

Nothing more was said, as they watched the progress of the small boat across muddy water towards the area where waving had been seen from the air. Smothering heat moved in to set them all sweating. The monotonous repetitive noises of an African swamp were all around them, yet the utter stillness of the atmosphere held a sinister quality which increased the tension of waiting for the unknown. Leone felt the full significance of human drama, as she watched the two men in pale-green uniforms draw closer and closer to the mangrove roots edging the water. Next minute, mosquitoes came swarming in to settle on any area of exposed flesh. With the risk of malaria particularly high in this part of the world, Kit had no option but to close the hatch swiftly.

Without a word, he turned and made his way to the flight deck with urgent energy. Leone followed, with Donald in tow. It was even hotter up there, for the sun directly overhead beat down relentlessly through the hemisphere of windows. Warren was standing beside the navigator when they arrived there, but their attention was concentrated on the scene outside. They indicated to Kit something which had not been visible from water level. A kind of canopy was draped over the trees at a point some twenty yards from where the boat was heading. It indicated human presence.

Kit crossed the cockpit to take a loud-hailer from a clip on the bulkhead. Then he returned to Warren's side, where he slid open one of the windows, Speaking into the cone, he advised Joss Hamilton to change direction accordingly. His voice echoed bizarrely in that watered jungle clearing, and Leone jumped when his amplified words were followed by a cacophony of harsh warnings screeched by hidden creatures from all around them.

'They don't care for your dulcet tones,' murmured Morris Snaith, still gazing at his colleagues now guiding the flimsy craft further to their left.

'They'll care even less for the sound of gunshots, if Digger has to use that pistol,' Kit commented, in equally casual tones.

'He's seen plenty of crocs where he comes from. Says he isn't likely to pop off at any movement in the water, because they don't scare him.'

'Famous last words!'

This exchange demonstrated to Leone the camaraderie between these men, and emphasized the difference between them and those with whom she normally mixed. It was clear to her now why they regarded themselves as a team; and why they each had perfect trust in their leader. The trust of everyone aboard had been unequivocally given to the pilot during this rescue attempt, and whoever remained alive on that shore would also put their entire faith in the man who must return them all safely to Mombasa. Yet he had been convicted of theft, treachery and assault, and imprisoned for it. Studying that broad intent face as he watched with the loud-hailer at the ready, she wondered uneasily once more why he had surrendered the world for ten thousand pounds.

Movement on the bank caught everyone's attention. A khaki-clad figure materialized from the dense vegetation, gesticulating energetically. The boat veered towards it and the lithe first officer scrambled across the mangrove roots, while his companion fastened the craft to a low branch. Before following Joss ashore, the Australian waved a small flag from side to side three times. Excitement rippled through the cockpit.

'They're all alive,' breathed Kit. 'Thank God for that!'

Leone felt close to tears again, but the arrival of a brisk figure took care of her threatened weakness. Mrs Harmesworth, flushed by the heat building up in that stationary hull, pushed roughly past Leone to walk up to Kit.

'Captain Anson, I've come in response to your request for assistance,' she told him, in a voice brimming with authority.

He turned to her with only vague attention. 'Yes?'

'I was a VAD during the war, serving in the wards of a large military hospital at Gravesend. I'll do whatever I can to help those poor people you've rescued.'

Kit's strained expression softened, as he smiled warmly at a woman who had irritated and annoyed everyone during the course of the flight.

'I'm very grateful, Mrs Harmesworth. We've been signalled that all three are alive, but we won't have any idea what state they're in until the boat gets back. Perhaps you'd prepare impromptu beds for them. Take-off is liable to be very rough, so they'll need as much protection as you can devise. The medicines we carry are very basic and limited, but anything you can do will certainly aid their chances of survival.' He glanced at his navigator. 'Morris, show the lady what few comforts we have available, will you? Then you'd better get along to the galley to see what food can be provided.'

'I'll see to that,' volunteered Leone, her attempt to smother her emotion making her words sound somewhat haughty.

Kit's dark glance met hers briefly and impersonally. 'Thanks.' As she turned away, he added, 'Make it something simple. They won't want lobster and *crêpes suzette*.'

Spinning round, she released her tension with anger. 'Don't insult my intelligence! I may have no nursing experience, but I do know what constitutes an invalid diet.'

Visibly taken aback by her sudden vehemence, he merely nodded and said, 'Yes, of course.'

It was good to be doing something. Activity relieved tension and helped her to recover from that momentary confrontation with Kit before the eyes of too many others. His implication that she would have no idea what to give people in this emergency had touched her on the raw. He had shown such warmth towards that Harmesworth woman after her revelation of war experience as a nurse, his subsequent treatment of her own offer of help had seemed doubly dismissive.

It was particularly frustrating, in view of that, that there was very little on board by way of invalid food. With lunch menus already planned and supplied in Mombasa, and dinner due to be eaten in the hotel on Lake Victoria, there had been no need to load on many provisions. The best Leone could do was to tell the chef to stand by with his supply of eggs, milk and sponge cakes to augment the consommé already on the menu. She also advised him to chill jugs of barley water to serve to all the passengers once they were airborne again.

'After suffering this heat and the rigours of taking off, they'll need something cold and non-alcoholic,' she concluded. With a smile, she turned away. 'I know you'll do the very best you can under these emergency conditions.'

As she left the galley, she bumped full tilt into Warren.

'Sorry,' he exclaimed, holding her steady. 'They're coming alongside now. Let's get down to the cargo hatch.'

'Are they all right?' she asked, hurrying along behind him in an atmosphere now growing extremely unpleasant, as they roasted in the midday sun within that airless hull.

'Don't know,' came his brief answer, above the clatter of his shoes on the metal steps leading down to the cargo bay. 'One appeared to be sitting up as they came across. The other two must be in a bad way, because they were lying in the bottom.'

Kit, his navigator, and Donald were there ready to help them all aboard. As Leone and Warren reached the large hold where mosquitoes were again swarming through the open hatch, the dinghy appeared alongside.

Mrs Harmesworth materialized beside Leone, saying firmly, 'Step aside, Miss Kirkland, so that I can assist Captain Anson with the casualties.'

Leone remained where she was. 'I think he has enough help to get them all from the boat. Too many crowding the area will only be a hindrance.'

'I have had a great deal of nursing experience, you know,' came the indignant reminder.

'And Captain Anson has had equal experience in dealing with emergencies,' she responded quietly. 'I suggest we leave him to do so until he asks us to come forward. That dinghy is dangerously overloaded, and this lake conceals all manner of venomous elements. Let's leave them enough space to get everyone safely inside, shall we? This is one time when men really are best fitted to cope.'

Further words between them were halted by the realization that the figure being assisted from a seat in the stern, wearing khaki shirt and trousers, and a heavy masculine pith helmet, was a woman. Leone could see little of her face, because she was anxiously watching the transfer of the stretcher bearing the unconscious body of a bearded man. He was placed on the floor while the second man, conscious but clearly in great pain, was passed cautiously from the rocking boat to those inside the cargo bay. The terse single-word commands between the men highlighted their tension, and Leone was mildly surprised at Donald's participation, stripped to shirt sleeves and acting under the orders of any member of the crew. Prompted by her brother's activity, she went forward to the woman in soiled and crumpled khaki. She jumped nervously at Leone's touch on her arm.

'I'm sorry, I didn't mean to startle you,' Leone apologized. 'Perhaps you'd like to come along to one of the cabins and recover a little.'

Silver-green eyes stared blankly from a freckled face streaked with grime, as they took in the sight of Leone's peppermint-green sleeveless dress in fine Swiss lawn, her heavy gold bracelets, beautifully manicured pink-tipped fingers, and elegant hand-made Italian shoes.

'I must first see that my brother and Paul are comfortable,' the woman said tonelessly, in accented English.

'The crew will do everything possible for them, and this lady has had nursing experience,' Leone told her reassuringly, realizing how overwhelmed the poor creature must be by her dramatic experiences. 'Do come with me. I'll show you where you can have a wash, while I get you some tea or a cool drink.'

'I see first that the men are comfortable,' the woman

insisted, turning back to the injured pair lying side by side on blankets while their rescuers clambered aboard, then hauled in the dinghy.

Mrs Harmesworth went forward to kneel beside the men, taking up the wrist of each in turn. While Donald and Warren closed the heavy door, which then made the interior rather dim, Kit addressed the woman in quiet tones.

'There are limited medical supplies and a passenger with nursing experience at your disposal. We shall do all we can for you during the flight to Mombasa, where I'll arrange for an ambulance to be waiting. Are you hurt, in any way?'

'No.'

'How sick are the men?' he asked then. 'Can you give us details?'

'They are Paul Christianson and my brother Knut,' she said, scratching her left side fiercely. 'They have made a study of rare fever since two years in Africa. Now Paul has this fever. I am called to fetch them to the mission hospital. There is a bad storm. We make the crash. I am not hurt at all, but Paul now also has the bleeding inside, I think. Knut has the broken foot and much pain in the back. He will live. Paul maybe will die. I am not certain.'

Kit turned to Mrs Harmesworth. 'Did you catch all that? Will you need assistance?'

She glanced up at him. 'From the Almighty, preferably, but I'd be glad of help from one of the stewards to keep the fever patient cool. That's the best we can hope for, where he's concerned. Internal bleeding is extremely difficult to cope with under these conditions. I'll do what I can to immobilize the broken foot, once the patients have been settled on the beds I've made up. They should be moved there as soon as possible, please.'

Donald organized the transfer of the men, because he knew where the stretcher should be taken. He was joined by Warren to carry the man with the broken foot. The crew were busily stowing the dinghy, and Leone was left waiting to escort the somewhat independent woman to a quiet cabin. Kit was questioning her further.

'Were you piloting the aircraft when it crashed?'

'Yes.'

'If both men were injured, you must have got them to the lake single-handed.'

'Yes.'

'That's a remarkable achievement.'

'I wanted to live, that is all.'

He seemed disconcerted by her statement. 'We all want to live, Miss . . . ?'

'Sylva Lindstrom.'

There was a curious hesitation before Kit spoke again, in a voice containing faint excitement. 'You're surely not the Norwegian girl who did the Arctic flight in 1934! Didn't she also take the record for the polar run from Nicholson last year?'

'Yes, I did . . . and I am she.'

'You really are Sylva Lindstrom?' he exclaimed. 'I can scarcely believe it. Do you mean I've picked up a girl most pilots would give their eye teeth to meet? You are the famous woman aviator?'

'Yes.'

With his face alive with expression, Kit whistled through his teeth. 'Great Scott! Tell me I'm not dreaming! Whatever are you doing in Africa?'

'Flying . . . or crashing, to be most truthful.' She turned away from him, saying, 'Now I must drink some tea before we speak together more.' Reaching Leone, she glanced at Kit over her shoulder. 'Thank you for coming to save us. I think you must be a pretty damn special pilot yourself to make such a landing.'

His smile sizzled across that cavernous compartment. 'Wait until you've experienced the take-off before making final judgement on that. It's liable to be pretty rough.'

'So was the landing, my friend.' Facing Leone, she

said in more impersonal tones, 'I will like your tea and washing things now. I think I have many louses.'

Feeling overdressed, inadequate, and very definitely antipathetic to this woman's dominant personality, Leone led her to the tiny cabin reserved for the Kirklands. On their way, they passed the smoking saloon, where the injured men were being settled on makeshift mattresses by Mrs Harmesworth, Donald and Warren. Asking a steward to bring tea, Leone indicated the small toilet compartment.

'You'll find soap and towels, as well as various other things, Miss Lindstrom. Please use anything you need. Tea will be out here in about five minutes.'

The woman disappeared, and Leone sat awaiting her return with a curious sensation of wariness. Of all people they could have picked up in equatorial jungle, it had to be another record-breaking pilot, and a female one, at that. There was no doubt, her presence would increase the sensational aspect of the daring rescue. Donald and Warren would be pleased. Kit even more so. She supposed that she ought also to rejoice, but she had not seen Kit smile quite like that at anyone since he had lived with them at Sheenmouth Abbey.

Augmenting her thoughts, his voice reached her over the relay system. 'Thank you for your cooperation, ladies and gentlemen. The crew and I are now preparing for our return to Mombasa, but I must warn you that take-off will be less smooth than usual. As the surface of the lake is too calm, I shall have to create an artificial swell by making *Flamingo* imitate a wounded duck. There's no need to feel alarm at these manoeuvres. The aircraft will be fully under my control, but you will all be required to remain seated until we are airborne and flying level. I rely on you all to respect this vital request, for your own safety and that of us all. Please take your seats now. Thank you.'

The great engines burst into life one after the other. Despite the sweltering heat inside the cabin, Leone felt suddenly chilled again. Kit had sounded so confident, yet taking off was always a vital moment even when the conditions were perfect. Here, not only was there a minimum stretch of water, it was far too calm and there were too many trees surrounding it. Was he really as confident as his voice had suggested? *Flamingo* began to taxi slowly forward, turning as she did so in order to face the full length of the lake.

At that moment, Sylva Lindstrom came from the toilet and sat facing Leone. 'The captain says I must now sit. I will chase away the louses later,' she announced.

Leone regarded the Norwegian with a faint sense of shock. With her face washed clean, and the pith helmet removed, it was now possible to see that she was no more than twenty-five. There was determination as well as youth in her deeply tanned face with its sprinkling of freckles, and the warm brown hair coiled in braids around her head gave the girl an air of Nordic peasantry. Even in the crumpled khaki stained by foliage she had a compelling quality which Leone recognized as basic sensuality. Thank God she would be off-loaded at Mombasa!

Having completed the turn, *Flamingo* then moved forward in a very definite zig-zag pattern to create deep furrows through the murky calm stretching away on both sides. It was as well that Kit had warned his passengers, for the sensation was rather alarming and suggestive of total loss of control by the pilot. 'A wounded duck' had been an excellent description, and *Flamingo* dipped and floundered her way to the far end of the lake in this fashion. Another sharp turn pressed Leone against the window, giving her a view of water which was now as choppy as a lively sea. Then they were off and swiftly into maximum accleration, causing *Flamingo* to bump and bounce over her own artificial swell. The engine noise grew painful on the eardrums, and Leone felt her heartbeat take up the urgency of that desperate drive for enough power to lift them above the trees they were racing to meet. The hull began shaking alarmingly, and the interior was suddenly blacked out by great walls of brown water which leapt up to cover the windows and leave them imprisoned, blinded to what was happening outside.

A weird scraping noise began. It quickly developed into a thunderous boom which suggested breakers crashing on to a wild shore. Then, as Leone became convinced that instead of going up, they were diving to the gruesome tangled depths of Lake Kiju, she felt that unmistakable surge which told her the nose was lifting from the water. With dramatic suddenness, the cabin was flooded with brilliant light as water dropped away from the windows as if a plug had been pulled from a full bath. Temporarily blinded, and practically deafened by the labouring engines, she caught herself willing that great hull to rise faster than it was. Pressing back in her seat, the physical effort of her own impotent urging caused perspiration to run down her face and her pulsebeat to thud in her ears. It was then that her vision cleared enough to see green vegetation barely a few feet below her window. They were up and clear! No matter that the starboard float had a dressing of foliage, they were safely on their way. *Flamingo* had just proved her own greatness, and Leone felt like crying.

Sylva Lindstrom looked across at her, those light-green eyes no longer blank. They were blazing with primitive excitement.

'He *is* some pretty damn special pilot.'

'He should be. He's Kit Anson,' Leone told her, still very emotional.

'Kit Anson who took the speed record, then disgraced himself?' marvelled the girl. 'Was he not punished with prison? What can he be doing in Africa?'

'Flying . . . and *not* crashing,' was her tart response.

It fell on deaf ears. The Norwegian girl lost in a glorious world of her own imagination. 'What a truly splendid man he is! I will give *more* than my eye teeth for this. It is fate that we have been brought together like this,' she claimed fervently.

Leone turned to gaze out at the sea of jungle dropping away as *Flamingo* climbed more gently after her spectacular lift-off. Fate had a great many things to answer for, in her book, but this was more than she could take.

14

Flamingo returned to Mombasa already destined for the annals of aviation history. That a flying boat of her size, with such a collection of distinguished people aboard, should effect the dramatic rescue from so small a lake was a sensation in itself. When it then became known that the notorious Kit Anson had been at the controls, and that one of the lives he had saved was that of Sylva Lindstrom, the fearless, headstrong female pilot who was a law unto herself, sensational was too mild a word for such a journalistic scoop. On their arrival at Mombasa, the jetty had been packed with pressmen, photographers, British and Norwegian officials, excited sightseers, and society hostesses each determined to be the first to parade the colourful pair before her dinner guests. Ambulance crews had had to fight their way through with stretchers to take off the injured men.

Kit had felt very tired after the long flight, in the midst of which he had made the landing of his life and a take-off the like of which he never wished to experience again. Unwilling to face an unruly mob, he had sent Joss and Digger to supervise the transfer of the casualties, one of whom had deteriorated to the point of danger. Because of the uproar surrounding their arrival, the three Norwegians were taken off, and the passengers disembarked to return to their original rooms held for them by the hotel at which they had been staying, while Kit remained in the seclusion of the flight deck.

When he finally left the aircraft to take a taxi back to the beachside lodging he had occupied before, journalists followed him and the crew in a fleet of three cars. Knowing they would not go until he gave them what they wanted, Kit spoke to them all for roughly twenty minutes, posed for photographs, then told them he was in dire need of a bath and sleep. To his relief, they took up their paraphernalia and went in search of fresh victims. The bath was soothing, but rest was of the body and not the mind, as he lay reliving the drama of the day over and over again. *Flamingo* had risen effortlessly to the challenge, as Warren had vowed she would, but Kit Anson had been obliged to struggle.

Two years in prison, then two more as a virtual down-and-out had taken their toll of that skill which had been at its peak to take the air speed record. In Spain, he had flown obsolete war aircraft with wheels instead of floats. Only when Tom had set up Western Mediterranean Air Services had his own experience with marine aircraft resumed. A natural aptitude rarely vanished with disuse, so he had quickly got back into his stride. However, he was not the man he had once been. His ability had been considerably tested during the flight trials in *Flamingo* at Sheenmouth, although he had kept the fact to himself. Only during the trip from there as far as Mombasa had he really mastered her to his own satisfaction. Even so, what he had done today had been extremely risky, and he had known it. The aircraft was admirably equipped to perform such manoeuvres, but he had taken a big chance on his own ability to carry them off successfully.

The event was being publicly hailed as a heroic bid to save human lives, but only he knew why he had ignored common sense and professional caution to perform a feat which now had him marvelling at his own madness. Of course he had hoped to save three souls from slow tormenting death, but he had been forced to leave men to their terrible fate enough times in Spain to harden him against the stress of turning resolutely away when rescue proved impossible. Today, it was his professional reputation as much as the three Norwegians that he was determined to bring back from the dead. He had succeeded on all counts, but he lay offering a relay of thanks to the patron saint of all aviators for watching over him as he had challenged his own skill.

Sleep finally overtook him. He awoke an hour later and took another cool bath, before dressing for dinner. Seeking the telephone in the vestibule, he rang the number of the hospital. An official informed him that Paul Christianson was in a critical condition, but expected to survive. Knut Lindstrom was resting peacefully under sedation, and was in no danger from his injuries. Kit was disappointed by the news that Miss Lindstrom had gone to the apartment of a friend, from where she would telephone later that evening for news of her brother and his friend. The official did not know the address of the apartment.

Kit replaced the receiver slowly. It was an incredible coincidence to find himself responsible for saving the life of a woman whose flying exploits were known worldwide; an aviator with a reputation for Arctic flying whom he had found stranded in equatorial Africa. It almost seemed like fate, their meeting. During the return flight to Mombasa, he had handed over to Joss and gone in search of her. Leone had barred the entrance to the cabin, claiming that Sylva Lindstrom was sleeping after her ordeal and should not be disturbed by him. There had been no alternative but to return to the cockpit, for her cool attitude had vied with the heat of his sense of triumph.

He joined his friends at the dinner table, with disappointment still heavy on him. They would be off early in the morning, and the Lindstrom woman would remain no more than a vague impression of a brown face beneath an over-sized pith helmet, and a personal suggestion of authority which had aroused the desire in him to explore it further. She had disappeared into a place somewhere

386

within this city, denying him the opportunity. While his crew talked animatedly of the events of that day, he was quietly working out how he could discover the address of the apartment from which she was due to ring the hospital later this evening. The doctor must have it, in case of emergency. Unhappily, hospitals were the same the world over; extremely unwilling to give information beyond routine phrases which said very little. Even so, he determined to try coaxing from someone a telephone number at which she could be reached, if nothing else.

That slender hope was dashed when a message arrived from Leone, summoning himself and the crew to join the passengers in a celebration of the day's successful outcome. Kit was the only one who walked the short distance to the hotel filled with resentment at being obliged to comply. This evening would merely be an extension of duty, saying and doing all the right things required of a hired pilot. Sylva Lindstrom seemed even more beckoning as his chances of meeting up with her faded away.

Resentment flared into anger when he found the foyer filled with photographers, who immediately blinded them all with the flashes from their cameras while their colleagues scribbled notes. The Kirklands were certainly making great capital from the affair. He knew it was what anyone with sense would do. Nevertheless, he was tired, disappointed over the Lindstrom woman, and in no mood for artificiality from his employers for the benefit of the world's press. A hotel porter conducted them along a hushed corridor to a large airy lounge lit by masses of tall pink candles where white-coated waiters were serving drinks to men in evening dress and women in a rainbow dazzle of gowns with jewels worth a collective ransom. Their entry was greeted with enthusiastic applause, and the cameras flashed again from all sides. Drawn into the room, Kit had a drink pressed into his hand before being manhandled by pressmen posing groups for additional pictures. He was photographed with the men from the Air Ministry, with the group from Anglo-Asiatic, with Countess Renskaya and Lady Carlyon-Bree, with his crew, with Mrs Harmesworth – 'that brave nurse from the trenches of 1914' – and, eventually, with Warren and the Kirklands.

With his eyes aching from the flashes, he was then bombarded with questions from reporters eager to revive old glories and bitter scandals. His head began to spin as it moved from side to side to answer voices all speaking above each other. The effort of returning noncommittal words on dangerous subjects, and trying to revive memories of his wartime exploits in Spain, all made him extremely tense. By the time his questioners got around to today's dramatic rescue, he hardly knew what he was saying. Finally, Leone arrived beside him to dismiss them all with charming efficiency. Even then, they could not resist one final shot of the fabulous Kirkland girl alongside the aviator her family had good cause to hate.

As the newsmen reluctantly melted away, Kit looked for his friends. They were all being fêted and supplied with drinks by *Flamingo*'s elated passengers. It was attention well deserved, he thought, and they would have a night to remember when they all returned to Lisbon after this unsettling flight. Good luck to them. All he wanted now was to go to bed, where sleep would blot out thought. Movement beside him took his attention back to Leone, still standing close and looking up at him with a puzzling softness of expression.

'I'd like to add particular congratulations on your tremendous achievement today,' she said, with undeniable warmth despite the absence of a smile.

In a figure-hugging gown shimmering with amethyst beads, and with her pale hair waved back into a chignon sparkling with diamanté, she looked fragile and stunning enough to take any man's breath away. He was the exception. All he saw was Sir Hector Kirkland's daughter.

'Was that speech on behalf of the company you half own?' he asked deliberately.

She drew in her breath as her wide gaze searched his face closely. 'If those are the only terms on which you'll accept it, it will have to be.'

'Thanks,' he murmured, feeling that brevity was the easiest way to deal with this girl tonight.

She did not appear to share his view. Nodding at the full glass in his hand, she said quietly, 'Please don't take Donald's hasty words too seriously. You have every justification for celebrating this evening.'

The curious suggestion of a temporary ceasefire left him unmoved. He had experienced Kirkland bonhomie before and knew how swiftly it could turn to venom. Noting the amethysts surrounded by diamonds which flashed on her ears, he wondered which of her lovers had bestowed them on her during those years in which he, himself, had slept with vagrants and alcoholics in any place offering shelter.

'As it happens, I hardly touch the hard stuff now. That business at Naples ran out of control, that's all.' He held up the full glass. 'Three of these and I'm paralytic. Prison and poverty tend to cure the habit.'

Taking that on the chin, she said, 'They did nothing to impair your flying skill. You proved that so gloriously today.'

'Yes. Amazing, don't you agree?'

Faint colour crept into her cheeks at his sarcasm but, despite the chatter of the shifting crowd around them, and the light-hearted laughter of those who shared her social status, she remained determinedly facing him. It angered him more than if she had walked away without another word.

'Kit, I'm trying to be friendly,' she told him, with surprising diffidence. 'You're not making it easy.'

'No, I'm not,' he agreed. 'It's far too late for friendship with any member of your family. You don't understand the requirements of such a relationship.'

'We might, if you gave us a chance,' she countered swiftly.

'A chance? Ha! That's rich, coming from you.' He slammed the glass on to an adjacent table. 'I've no intention of being a fool twice over, Miss Kirkland. Keep your damned olive branch. I've nothing you'd find worth stealing now.'

As he turned, she swiftly barred his path, the colour in her cheeks now fairly blazing. '*You* were the thief, as I recall.'

'*As you recall?*' he repeated tight-lipped. 'You were no more than a desperately lonely child, ignored by your father and completely shut out from any knowledge of what was going on in the company. You can't possibly *recall* anything. You simply believed what you were told . . . and you've continued to believe it whilst prancing around Europe like a doe in season, living off the ill-gained riches of Kirkland Marine Aviation.'

The jewels in her ears almost dazzled him as she stepped back with a distressed shake of her head. 'No . . . no. What are you suggesting?'

'Ask your brother!' As she continued to gaze at him in evident shock, he added fiercely, 'If Donald hasn't the guts to confess, ask Warren. You'd never believe me.'

By the time he was halfway across the room, he realized Leone was not the only one in an impossible mood tonight. Reaction was setting in with a vengeance. This afternoon, he had risked more than thirty lives in order to prove something to himself. In doing so, he had revived the past too strongly, not only in his own mind but in headlines an inch high. His name was synonymous with heroism once more, and he was faced with that same elated confusion he had experienced after breaking the speed record. What did a hero do when the ultimate deed was done? Where did he go after reaching the pinnacle? That young boy who had slept with the Sheenmouth donkeys and worn darned bathing trunks, had risen to the heights six years ago. The subsequent fall had proved near fatal. Now, the ex-convict who had stood in line for a bowl of soup was back on the pinnacle. To glory in it was dangerous. Was a second fall inevitable?

He wandered the large room, speaking automatically, being clapped heartily on the back by men and shamelessly vamped by women, even those old enough to be his mother. He could have been in Sheenmouth Abbey after flying *Aphrodite*, it was all so reminiscent. Music began somewhere. Everyone moved towards the sound, sweeping him along with them. It was dim and noisy in the huge ballroom. People shifted in lively fashion before his aching eyes. Faces smiled at him, mouthing flattery. Women touched him with subtle, unexpressed invitation. One dragged him forward, melted against him, moved sinuously to a hypnotic rhythm. When it ended, someone gave him a glass of chilled liquid which nevertheless raced through him like fire when he defiantly drank it.

Before long, a mood of greater defiance ruled him. He had no wish to be with these people tonight. All he wanted was to relive those moments giving true freedom of identity, when *Flamingo* had responded to his desperate urging to rise up and over those trees. For several hung moments, he had believed that the great blunt white nose would plough into them with screaming, terrifying force but, as he had dragged on the column with all his strength and determination, it had lifted like the answer to a prayer. There was an ache in his arms and shoulders to remind him of that battle, and another in his throat which was growing too strong to contain. Relief could only be gained through surrender to emotion. Solitude was essential.

The lounge illuminated by pink candles was now almost empty. He headed across it towards the doors standing open to the terrace leading to the beach. The warm air hit him as he walked to the stone balustrade, to grip it and stare at the huge yellow moon hanging in that element in which he felt he truly belonged. Today, he had made the name of Anson respected again. Today he had pulled off one of the most dangerous pieces of flying he had ever attempted. It was as well that those roistering inside, by now convinced that they had personally played a major part in the rescue, were not aware of how close they had been to heaven over that African lake. His long sigh of mixed anguish and pleasure helped to relax the muscles of his stomach, which had been tightened to full extent by the pressures of the evening, as he continued to gaze at the moon, seeing way beyond that light into another world.

'So, I finally meet Kit Anson, the wicked boy of aviation.'

Those quiet words sent Kit spinning round to face a girl in a white silk Grecian robe which left one shoulder bare. Her brown hair, swept back severely into a tight band of pearls, then fell long and straight to her waist like the silken tail of a thoroughbred mare, and her brown freckled face was arrestingly sensual in its lack of true beauty. With a sense of incredulity, Kit realized that he was discovering Sylva Lindstrom in full female guise.

'I intended trying to find you tonight,' he confessed, still dumbfounded that she should be there before him on this terrace.

'And I.' She smiled. 'Success was first mine. They told me at your lodging that you would be here.'

'You actually went to my room in search of me?'

Moving to stand at the balustrade beside him, she also gazed at the moon. 'Oh yes. I knew how you would be feeling tonight. As I have been after something which turns the blood cold but sets the heart on fire.' Angling her face towards him, her eyes looking more silver than green, she added, 'We are two alike, aren't we?'

He knew it, but the question was rhetorical and

needed no agreement from him. 'Shall we walk along the beach?'

They moved off together across the flagged terrace to the steps leading to the sands, then turned on to a path parallel to the sea. This huge moon was tropical yellow, not the cold silver of that which had revealed his tears to a girl in a ruined chapel after the flight of *Aphrodite*. The warm air was filled with the rustle of breeze-tossed palms, and the sonorous thunder of glittering gilded breakers crashing on to the shore fifty yards from them. Such enchantment set the seal on his emotional state. Looking down at this girl who also communed with the heavens and found identity by daring the unknown in a solitary cockpit, he wanted to share more than tears with her.

'What are you doing in Africa?' he asked, in tones which betrayed his wonder at their meeting. 'It's a long way from the polar regions.'

She had discarded her shoes at the bottom of the steps, and now walked barefoot with languid grace beside him. 'I married a doctor, who swore I could be free to do as I wished. He came here to the hospital, and there was no freedom. I must do this, I must do that. I am his wife, after all,' she chanted derisively. 'He broke the promise; then I must break mine. We have the divorce, and now like each other very well.'

'You're living in his apartment?'

'Of course.'

Smothering a ridiculous stab of envy, he probed further. 'How did you come to be out near Lake Kiju?'

Smiling up at him, she said, 'I have been working, as you are. Sometimes it is necessary to take a pause and think what is best next to do. My brother Knut is making a study here with his friend. They are for two years already searching for the germs which make a rare tropical sickness. They are not doctor, you understand.'

'Biologists?' he suggested.

'I could not think the right word. See how you confuse

393

me, Kit Anson.' She smiled again. 'But it is a good feeling.'

Confusion was too mild a description for what she was creating in him, and it was a very good feeling indeed. 'So you've been flying supplies to them, and so on?'

'Yes, and bringing back to the hospital the tubes and bottles they have filled with the germs.' A soft sigh escaped her. 'I know that it is a work of great importance, but it is so dull and so *long*. Now Paul has the germs and maybe will die. Yet he will be satisfied in himself. I cannot understand this.'

'Not even if you equate it with your own endeavours?' he asked above the chorus of elements which sang along that beach as they strolled. 'Any one of those Arctic flights could have resulted in your death, yet you would have died fulfilled. Wouldn't you?' he challenged.

She halted to turn and study him with troubled eyes. 'I believe I shall never be truly fulfilled. I have an eternal hunger.'

'Haven't we all?' It was the comment of a man as well as an aviator.

She moved off again. 'The snow routes some men do not like,' she mused, her long fall of hair flying in the breeze. 'I find them mysterious, irresistible. To be alone in that pure, white world is like finding virginity once more. The peace, the sereneness, the untrod distances, give me an ecstasy I find from no lover.' Glancing across at him, she asked, 'Can you understand this?'

He nodded, thrilled that she had experienced aerial consummation and could speak of it so enthrallingly.

'You feel this same thing?'

'Not exactly. A man senses the ultimate conquest rather than rediscovered virginity . . . but it brings similar heights of ecstasy.'

'Ah, to a man virginity is no prize. He aches to lose it.'

'He's no man until he does.'

They walked on in silence, until she said, 'You have

been so splendid a man; too much for you now to waste by flying people like these on a pink journey.' Halting again, she tilted her vividly sensual face up to challenge him in more ways than one. 'You have been wicked, but that must be forgot. This is quite wrong for you. You must be free to dare the skies again. When this flight is over, what is to happen to you, Kit Anson?'

He had no hesitation in baring his soul to this creature, whose own breath of life came from daring the skies, also. 'Until this afternoon, I believed my days of glory were over. Landing on that lake was terrifying only because I doubted my ability to do it. Once down, I doubted I could get up and clear away. That take-off was the most hazardous thrilling experience I've ever known. I'm now longing to live fully again.' He frowned. 'From the moment I heard prison gates closing behind me, I've avoided considering the future. It seemed more vital to concentrate on getting through each day as it came. I now know the past six years haven't robbed me of my skill . . . or of my love for attempting what might prove impossible.'

Putting his hand beneath her elbow, he led her towards a cluster of palms at the far end of the beach near to where he and the crew lodged in an annexe. 'Sylva, you know as well as I do that during those grey years of my life, men and women have continued pioneering. Amelia Earheart crossed the North Atlantic, Jean Batten flew from Australia to Britain; men have flown over Everest, and broken record after record for long distance non-stop flights. All the great aviators have found new routes, new challenges, new feats of daring. You dreamed up a few of your own.' Reaching the trees, he stopped beneath the whispering fronds to confront her. 'What is there left to do?'

Leaning back against a tree trunk, she studied him avidly. 'A crossing of both Poles. The Arctic, then the Antarctic. No woman has done it. Together we could make a new exciting record.'

He stood with the breeze lifting his hair, the moon dazzling his eyes, and the thunder of the sea matching his heavy heartbeat, as he surrendered unconditionally to the first woman who had lured him with her courage as well as her body.

'We?'

'We, Kit Anson. You and me together,' she declared, with a surge of immense fervour. 'Can you not feel this pulse between us; this communion? I knew it from the very first moment.' Drawing close to him, she put her hands up to his shoulders and gazed urgently into his face, mouth slightly parted and her eyes glowing with Arctic fire. 'We shall make history together. Say that we shall!'

He was beyond words. In his arms, she was all he had sought and never entirely found. The madness and elation of this day went to his head as he kissed her with mounting fever. Those six years melted away into insignificance during their long mutual embrace.

When he finally lifted his head, it was to murmur, 'I seem to have encountered an unexpected hazard. All four engines are on fire, and I'm spinning out of control.'

In the golden moonlight, she gazed back uncompromisingly. 'Then you have two choices, darling. One is to jump to safety. The other is to keep spinning until you regain control . . . or until you hit the ground.'

Leone stood in an alcove with a champagne cocktail in her hand, watching the celebrations which looked set to continue until the small hours. Hour after hour, day after day, she had waited on these people; flattered, cajoled, sympathized in order to keep them sweet-tempered and spellbound. All her persuasive influence had been used on hoteliers and their underlings, to create the essential enchantment over men who held the future of Kirkland's in the palms of their hands, and over the women who held the men in the palms of theirs. She had danced with partners who turned her feet black and blue, or who had roaming hands, and forced herself to smile through it all. On a flight taking them from the cool May weather of Sheenmouth, through somnolent Mediterranean warmth to the sweltering equatorial temperatures of today, she had moved around the aircraft in elegant clothes, high heels and the perfect accessories, checking that the passengers were contented, in accord with each other, and especially with the Kirklands. At night, she had lain awake going over the plans for the next day, worrying about small areas of friction between those on whom everything depended, praying they would all rise for breakfast in time for the scheduled departure, and nursing her tender feet.

Yet, in a few devastatingly cutting sentences this evening, Kit had reduced her to nothing, made her invisible again. He had spoken derisively of that lonely child ignored by her father and shut out of family affairs. He had made her sophistication into a vice, and suggested that her disastrous love-affairs had been simply the adventures of a whore. His personal attack had been so violent and unexpected in the face of her overture to peace, she was still shaking with reaction. After the strain of all today had brought, she was fighting complete emotional breakdown by drinking cocktails one after the other. If only they would act on her as they did on him. She had downed four already, and was still on her feet.

With the pain he had inflicted biting deeply into her, she wondered wildly what he could have meant by charging her with living off ill-gained company riches. What had been behind his sneering comment about there being nothing she could steal from him/now? Why had he claimed so bitterly that Donald had too little courage to confess some mysterious truth? His whole conversation had suggested a reversal of rôles, making her the villain; it had hinted that he had been the victim of theft rather than the perpetrator. But he *had* stolen ten thousand pounds. The money had been found in his car. So had the plans of a seaplane. So had Stephanie Main. She closed her eyes momentarily, as the memory returned of the hero who had betrayed a young and vulnerable love by going off with another woman. That love was now mature, but clearly still as vulnerable.

The quickstep ended. Dancing couples broke from each other's arms and strolled from the dance-floor with animated conversation and laughter. Leone drank the champagne cocktail swiftly, then crossed to her brother who was visibly loath to release the blonde wife of a local colonial administrator ten years her senior. Jessica Reynolds had been enjoying a flirtation with Donald over the past three days, and appeared delighted at the unexpected bonus of this dramatic return to Mombasa. Watching them closely as she approached, Leone felt certain they would do more than dance in each other's arms tonight.

'Donald, I'd like a private word with you,' she said, reaching his side.

Her brother turned, his charming smile fading. 'What on earth warrants a private word right now?'

Ignoring the rapacious Reynolds woman, Leone replied, 'When we have it, you'll find out.'

'Can't it wait?'

'No, it can't. It really can't.'

Jessica clung to Donald's arm. 'You simply can't drag him away tonight, sweetie. He's the star of this celebration.'

'I can make it a public discussion, if you insist, but I feel sure you'd regret it,' she told her brother tautly.

The tone of her mood appeared to manifest itself to him then, but still he scowled. 'This is meant to be a party.' He released his partner with the promise to return in a few minutes, then walked beside Leone to the alcove she had just vacated. 'I hope this isn't simply some stupid nonsense about a soufflé or a pink blancmange,' he murmured.

She swung to face him, highly incensed. 'Would you

prefer to exchange words on adultery with a colonial wife?'

His good-looking features hardened. 'Pot calling the kettle black?'

'I've never dabbled in that. Neither should you. What would Yankee-Doodle Anita think?'

'Whatever she pleased,' he replied deliberately. 'Nothing has yet been announced.'

Leaning back against the silken wall-covering, Leone studied him with rising enlightenment. 'I see. Now *Flamingo* is such an unqualified, sensational success, the injection of American cash is no longer needed.'

Taking a cocktail from the tray of a passing waiter, her brother sipped it with restored composure. 'Can we get to the root of this mysterious business. What's it all about?'

'I'm hoping you'll enlighten me . . . although I've just been told you won't have the required guts to do so.'

His hand stilled with the glass halfway to his lips, and his blue eyes took on a curiously apprehensive expression. Even so, he sounded calm enough as he asked, 'Who imparted that piece of vindictiveness?'

'Our hired pilot.'

Her brother reacted strongly. 'You fool! Although I agreed with you that we had no option but to invite him here tonight, in the face of pressure from everyone, there was no necessity for you to socialize with the brute. I noticed he sloped off early. Couldn't stand the sight of wine flowing and being obliged to say no, no doubt.'

'He doesn't drink any more. He claims prison killed the habit.'

'Ha!' came the derisive response. 'What about Naples? He admitted that he was incapable of flying that day because of a hangover.'

What had happened at Naples was unimportant now. She had to pursue something deeper altogether. Taking a breath, she asked, 'Donald . . . has the company ever stolen anything from him?'

Her brother froze as he stared back in obvious shock. 'What's that bastard been saying? What has he insinuated?'

Taking the glass from his hand, Leone drank from it herself as her heart began thudding apprehensively. There was no doubt she had touched an exposed nerve, yet she suddenly dreaded to probe further. For several moments she remained silent, facing his hostility, both of them oblivious of the waltz music to which dancers were now dreamily moving.

'I was quite young when he was put on trial, and my awareness of his skill was probably limited. I now know the basics of flying, and today gave me indisputable proof of that rare ability which puts him at the top of his profession,' she began, leading up to what she must ask, at all costs. 'Donald, why would any man throw away what Kit had six years ago? Over that lake this afternoon, I suddenly found it made little sense to me.'

'Of course it made little sense,' he snapped. 'You've admitted that you were no more than a child . . . one who was hopelessly smitten with him.'

'I'm not now,' she lied, 'and I've discovered that men aren't the creatures they're often cracked up to be. During the past few years, I've met some very unscrupulous people and some with silver tongues. I can tell the genuine from the false, these days, and there's no doubt in my mind that Kit wasn't bluffing when he challenged me to demand from you an explanation of his charge of ill-gained company riches.'

Donald took back the glass, and drained the contents before saying, 'You prefer to believe an ex-convict rather than me?'

'You've said nothing on the subject yet,' she pointed out. 'All you've done is talk around it.'

Taking a deep steadying breath, he said, 'The company accounts are with Larchforth and Bodmin, as you know. When we get back, ask young Edmunds to bring them all down for you to study.' Glancing over his shoulder at the dancers, as if impatient to join them, he added, 'You'll find nothing in the least irregular – for that period or any other.' A thin smile twisted his mouth. 'The ten grand that bastard stole from our safe was missing for too short a time to warrant a double entry in the ledgers. Now, if you've finished this over-emotional cross-questioning, I'll return to our guests.' Walking off, he said, 'You *are* still carrying a torch for him, that's more than obvious.'

'He told me to ask Warren, if you refused to confess.'

Donald pulled up, then turned to her with eyes blazing. 'Warren is carrying a torch for *you*. The fool will say anything he thinks you want him to say.'

She moved forward, willing him to understand. 'I want him to say what you've just said; that Kit is a bastard through and through, that he still drinks to excess, and that everything he said to me this evening was vicious slandering insinuation. Will he say that?' When no answer was forthcoming, she went on, 'If he doesn't, I shall start being afraid for us . . . and for Kirkland Marine Aviation.'

Her brother did not understand, for he walked away without another word. She caught herself trembling over his dismissal of the subject. Evidence, plain facts told her a man had been justly punished six years ago, yet troublesome instinct hinted that the evidence might have been misleading, that the facts might not be as plain as everyone thought. Even allowing for the way she felt about Kit to colour her judgement, there had been such authority and passion behind what he had said to her, she could not dismiss it as vindictiveness without foundation.

The waltz came to a lingering close, and she spotted Warren escorting from the floor a chaste-looking girl in white georgette. He had danced three times in succession with her, and both looked happy to be together. Nevertheless, she would have to intrude. When she did, the girl became sulky. Warren appeared quite willing to

401

accept her suggestion of a chat on the terrace, however, and they went out through the french doors watched, from across the ballroom, by Donald.

'Phew, it's getting pretty hot in there,' Warren exclaimed. 'Not that it's much cooler out here with that breeze coming from the interior.' He smiled happily. 'It's a lovely party, isn't it?'

'Yes. You and Donald are the beaux of the ball, if one can say such a thing. You must be feeling over the moon.'

He leaned against the balustrade, his gaze on that huge yellow sphere suspended over a coppery sea. 'Over it, and far beyond. I keep pinching myself to make sure I'm not dreaming.'

His words echoed those of another young man, who had said the same to her in the bell tower of Sheenmouth Abbey. She moved up beside him. 'What *I* keep doing today is asking myself why Kit threw away all the glittering prizes a man could want, for the sake of ten thousand pounds. You're now in a situation similar to his of six years ago. Warren, wouldn't you hold on to what you've got, at any cost?'

His scrutiny dropped from the moon to the level of the sands. 'You're in a strange mood tonight.'

'Yes, aren't I?' After a pause, she asked, 'Do I get an answer to my question?'

Angling his head towards her, he nodded. 'Yes, I'd hold on to it no matter what it cost. Something like this comes along rarely more than once, and only a fool would give it up without a struggle.' Studying the sands again, he elaborated. 'I was born and brought up in the heart of London. The only father I ever knew was a Canadian flier who was married to my widowed mother for three years, most of which he spent away at war. He had no money, but left me the legacy of a dream. That dream became reality with the help of your father, Donald and Kirkland's. Today, reality turned into total triumph through the skill and courage of Kit Anson. I owe you all so much. Even so, none of you would be here now if I hadn't designed *Flamingo*, so it cuts both ways. We all need each other, so I think we should adopt your father's maxim of what's done is done. Raking up the past is pointless.'

Had she hoped for some revelation which would prove Kit's innocence? If so, it would surely have faced her with the guilt of wrongful imprisonment and destruction of a hero. Was that what she wanted, to discover that they had broken a man without true cause; that her family had hounded down their stray mongrel to brand him too dangerous to run loose? Unidentifiable fears, probing uncertainties prevented her from letting the matter rest, as Warren suggested.

'I no longer trust your advice,' she told him hollowly. 'At Naples you told me to bring my feelings into the open. I did so just now and it proved disastrous.'

He turned swiftly to take her hands in his. 'What happened?'

'I was . . . I was given a very frank opinion of the kind of person I am, along with a savage suggestion that I should ask Donald for an explanation of his charge that the company is involved in some kind of fraud.'

'Have you asked him?' Warren queried after a pause.

She nodded. 'He very nervously talked his way out of what was clearly a tight corner. Kit said he'd do that.'

'I see.'

'Kit also said I should ask you if Donald lacked the guts to speak.' She gripped his hands tightly. 'Whatever it is, I want to know. Tell me, Warren. Please tell me.'

His face was in shadow so she could not see his expression, but something about the stillness of his body and the long silence before he spoke suggested that he was as nervous as her brother had been. Her fears deepened. Was it true? Had Kirkland's engaged in illegal dealings?

'Leone, I'm a designer, that's all. I don't handle any part of the business side; Donald and Maitland together

403

with your banker and accountants would deal with sales and investments. I've no head for financial transactions, but they'd never discuss such things with me, anyway.'

'Then why was Kit so certain you'd know?' she demanded, frustrated yet again.

He sighed heavily. 'I doubt if he's certain about anything tonight. You know something about the exhilaration of achievement in the air, and its aftermath. Put yourself in his place. He pulled off something quite astonishingly skilful at that lake, and the press reception of his feat together with the noisy acclaim of everyone here has probably made him so tired his brain is confused by it all.' His thumbs caressed the backs of her hands while he allowed that point to sink in. Then he added gently, 'You chose the worst possible time to bring your feelings into the open. The poor devil may not have been able to cope with it in his weary state.'

She was so weary she could not cope with it, either. Suddenly, all she wanted was comfort, reassurance and a means of escape the cocktails had failed to provide. Looking up at him, she said, 'I wish this damned flight was over and we were back at Sheenmouth, don't you?'

'There'll be plenty to do,' he said, clearly relieved at her change of subject. 'Orders are sure to come flooding in, so there's every possibility that we'll have to build another hanger to cope with the work. We'll have to scour the country for skilled men; there won't be enough local lads for the job. Donald is talking about a sales trip countrywide. I can't see why you couldn't take that on. The brochures give all the technical details, and this flight has banished any doubts there might have been about performance. It simply entails taking prospective clients out to lunch and being very persuasive. As they'll all be male, you'd make a better job of charming them into submission than Donald. That's your strong point, isn't it?'

'It doesn't appear to be affecting you,' she cried, reaching the end of her tether. 'We're standing here

404

in the most absurdly romantic setting: tropical shore, whispering palms, whopping great moon, and a sky filled with stars like diamonds. You claim to be in love with me . . . yet all you can do is rattle on about that bloody flying boat!'

Her outburst silenced him, which made the situation worse. The need for an outlet, a release for her pent-up passions, drove her to step so close to him their bodies were touching as she looked up into his shadowed face.

'If I asked you to take me to bed, would you say you don't do that by invitation, either?'

Into a lengthening silence, he said roughly, 'It wouldn't help either of us. When you eventually opened your eyes, you'd realize it had been me all the time.'

The storm inside her turned into a tornado as she stepped back. 'Damn you, Warren,' she said through a tight throat, before turning to take the steps down to the beach. Kicking off her sandals, she walked swiftly away from the lights of the hotel to the shadier areas washed by moonlight. The wetness on her cheeks quickly dried in the warm breeze, but the thunder and lightning within continued despite the soothing rustle of fronds and the regular beat of waves on sand. She turned wild eyes to the rising crests of water glistening gold and black as they rolled in from that vast, fathomless ocean. If she walked into those breakers and continued to eternity, who would care? Donald would merely sigh with relief and put in hand the formalities of taking sole charge of the company. Warren might shed a tear between producing aircraft after aircraft. She had needed him tonight. Oh, how she had needed him, but he had let her down. If it was truly love he felt for her, then it was vastly different from her brand of it. He had had no understanding of the shattering pain of Kit's attack this evening. He had had no notion of the wounds for which she desperately wanted balm. Whenever she reached out, there was nobody to touch, nobody to take her hand and clasp it in comfort.

At the far end of the beach she turned back with dragging steps. The inner storm was blowing itself out, but the damage it had wreaked was considerable. Still confused, uncertain, desperate for the truth of so many things, she realized her steps were taking her past the annexe which lodged the crew. There was a single low light from a french window facing the beach. She was drawn towards it in the certainty that Kit was there. He had left the party some while ago and must have returned to his room. Moving towards that light, she told herself he would explain his accusations if she demanded that he should. Away from the crowds and flashing lights, he would be prepared to say more. Her steps quickened as she sensed that elusive answer almost within her grasp. Then she halted, as the fine voile curtains moved in the breeze to reveal two figures inside the room. Kit stood naked, facing a woman whose brown hair hung loose almost to her waist. As Leone watched with mounting desolation, the woman's white robe fell to the floor leaving her naked, also. For several absorbed moments, the pair gazed at each other in a world of their own, then they merged into an embrace so passionate, it verged on obsession.

With her clenched fist pressed against her mouth to smother the cry she dared not give, Leone backed away from that oblong of pale light. This had happened before; she had walked in on a pair of lovers, each splendid in their nakedness. That scene six years ago had haunted her unawakened senses. Tormented, sensual dreams had finally driven her to the bell tower to re-enact it with the man who was to have been her first and only lover. Finally, that scene was being played again. The hero was all she believed he would be; the heroine had been miscast.

Her bare feet encountered chilly wetness, and she looked down in alarm. The sea had surged up the beach to meet her, before retreating again to gather into another gigantic crest. She began to run towards the hotel, head thrown back, her throat working. The hem of her shimmering amethyst dress grew heavy with the creeping, unstoppable tide as it lapped spasmodically around her ankles. That woman had claimed fate had brought about their meeting today. *Of course* he was obsessed! Sylva Lindstrom embodied all he lived for; all he had ever valued. Sylva Lindstrom could never be invisible.

15

Flamingo made her triumphant way home, although an air of anticlimax was unavoidable and the temperatures kept everyone aboard in a lethargic mood. In an effort to prevent any element of tedium, and to dispel that feeling of the main event being over so that all that remained was to get home as soon as possible, Leone worked hard to provide diversions. There were bridge matches, evening sightseeing trips or visits to local casinos; even an impromptu concert given by the passengers themselves, who produced recitations and monologues, Victorian ballads, piano-pieces, and a humorous mime devised by the two RFC pilots well used to amusing themselves during their service days. Members of the crew were not invited to join them. Although passengers had occasionally suggested they should, both Kirklands ruled that the men were nearing the end of a long gruelling flight and needed to rest whenever they could.

There was much truth in that. Not only had it been a long gruelling flight, there had been the additional stress of the daring rescue to take toll of their stamina. All the same, it had been a long time since Kit had felt so relaxed and at peace with himself. During those final days of the flight of *Flamingo*, a remarkable change was seen in him by those men who were his friends and crew. Smiles, which used to be rare, appeared with great regularity. He was even caught smiling at his own thoughts, whilst gazing from the windows of the cockpit.

They knew the reason for this sunny aspect of their captain, and reflected ruefully on the power of women who could do in one night what had seemed impossible before.

Even his friends did not know that it was more than the wild sexual union with Sylva which had made him come alive again. She had given him a future; revived a man who had been living in shadows. A record-breaking polar flight! An aircraft with skis rather than floats. A small aircraft more like those he had flown in Spain. A route across snowy desolation, where a person could die within a few hours of exposure to the elements, and where any pilot forced down in such terrain had little hope of survival. Sylva was an expert in this field; he was experienced in many. They would make a formidable aerial team. He knew it, and so did she. The fact that he was possessed by desire for her also, made the future look dazzling.

Sylva would join him in Lisbon next month. They would plan the flight in every detail, then she would go on to Norway from where she had made her other polar flights. There, she hoped to find a backer to finance their proposed attempt at a record. She would also find living quarters near the airfield they would use for preliminary flights. Meanwhile, Kit's task would be to find a suitable aircraft they could adopt to their requirements. He hoped to recruit Tom Digby on that, because his friend and employer had many contacts in that line. The main problem would be finance. Sylva had confessed quite candidly to being in debt, because she could never be bothered to read letters from the bank, and Kit had no money whatever behind him. That being so, until the date of the vital flight, he would continue working for Western Mediterranean Air Services, and then for anyone who would employ him when they moved to Norway. Small wonder the pilot was one man aboard *Flamingo* not diverted from the longing to have this flight over and return home. In his isolated cottage in Lisbon they could start making their plans, and he could lose himself in the glory of her, day and night.

As he took off from the blossom-covered island of Madeira on the final leg back to Sheenmouth, the longing for Sylva was especially strong. He was on home ground, so to speak. It seemed particularly irksome to set a course for the south-west coast of England which would take him past Lisbon, where his thrilling reunion with her would take place. Telling himself that he was a man of twenty-eight, not a lovesick boy, he smiled at the view of Funchal harbour falling away below as he put *Flamingo* into a right-hand turn after her initial abbreviated take-off. He might be a man of twenty-eight but he was as eager as a lovesick boy. That one fiery night with Sylva had been like a proving flight. He now wanted to go into regular service. The simile made him smile again.

'Is there some joke I'm missing?' asked a youthful voice beside him, and he turned to see Joss with eyebrows raised at him.

Kit's smile deepened. 'Yes. Both floats have just dropped off, and you're going to be asked to do the landing at Sheenmouth.'

'Oh, very jokey,' came the light-hearted response. '*Nothing* could fall off this gorgeous machine. She's perfect, and so well-behaved it's like driving a Ford,' he sighed. 'You don't suppose you could persuade Tom to buy a couple for our fleet, do you?'

Easing *Flamingo* into her more sedate climb now they were clear of the volcanic hills, Kit shook his head. 'There'll be so many clamouring for them, he'd be well down on the waiting list.'

'This flight has been a stupendous success, hasn't it?'

'Not half!' Casting a sideways glance at the youngster, he asked, 'Sorry it's almost over?'

'Flying the Alexandria route won't seem anywhere near as exciting,' Joss confessed. 'I'll also miss flying with you.'

'Darn!' he exclaimed, in laughing tones. 'I damn near

410

killed you all at Lake Kiju. Anyway, young Hamilton, you're a first-class pilot in your own right. You could have handled this flight as captain.'

'I couldn't have handled the rescue at Kiju.'

Concentrating on the altimeter for a moment or two, Kit then said, 'Joss, if you're ever faced with a similar situation, don't do what I did. It's too damned dangerous.'

'Then why did you do it?'

He faced the boy. 'To prove something.'

Joss grinned. 'You proved it, all right. Things are going to seem pretty dull when we get back to routine.'

'I think we deserve a week off first, so I'll tell Tom he'll have to wait for his super crew.'

They sat quietly for a while as the aircraft climbed to cruising altitude, and then the engines settled into a contented growl. Joss soon broke the silence.

'You're far too good to carry on flying for Western Med. We all knew that before, but supposed there were reasons . . . well, we'd all heard what everyone else had heard,' he elaborated with slight awkwardness. 'After this, you could do anything you wanted. I'll accept that I'm a pretty good working pilot, but you have a quality lacking in me. Is your friendship with Tom so strong that you couldn't pack it in with us and do something more exciting?'

'Friendship should never be restrictive,' Kit responded. 'If it is, then it's not true friendship. Tom and I understand that. He'd never use blackmail on me. After all, he'd never have frogmarched me to Sheen-mouth for this event, if he hadn't guessed it would restore my reputation.' He settled more comfortably in his seat. 'All the same, there is a close bond between us which neither would ignore if the other really needed help.'

'Like saving the life of the other?'

Kit smiled, shaking his head. 'Dear me, don't turn me into a hero over that. In war, you save the lives of

411

total strangers if it's within your power. I saw Tom go down, so was able to pinpoint the spot for muleteers. Nothing valiant in that.'

'What was it like in Spain? I've often wanted to ask you, but never got around to it.'

'Now, I'm more approachable?' He chuckled. 'All right, I guess I've been a bit boorish, at times. What was it like in Spain? Confused; sometimes terrifying. I volunteered for the sole reason that I'd be flying again, and would have the chance to be with other men crazy about aviation – something I'd missed for four years. Somehow, I ended up fighting with genuine feeling for the cause.' Recollecting those incredible months, he went on, 'Battle flying is vastly different, you know. Firstly, you're the only chap in the aircraft and have to do the bloomin' lot – fly it, fire the guns, drop the bombs, and navigate, all at once. Secondly, you have to remember there's another set of chaps doing the same, who are out to knock you from the sky. Unfortunately, they did it all too often. Mostly German, with pretty effective machines, the enemy fliers were a well-trained regular air force.' He smiled ruefully. 'Beside them, we were a rabble. Half of us couldn't converse with the other half due to language problems, which led to orders being misunderstood, on occasion. We flew an assortment of aircraft in which most of us had had limited experience, and our supplies were so irregular we were sometimes grounded for vital days over lack of fuel. Our one big virtue was that we all had that certain characteristic which puts daring above safety. They were dangerous times, but highly exciting.'

'The war's still going on, so why did you pull out?'

Kit shrugged. 'I suppose Tom and I were growing a little disillusioned after Franco had taken over more than half the country. The Communist Russians who fought with us appeared to be doing so only in order to take over the country themselves, and their creed sounded to us as unattractive as Fascism. When Tom lost his eye, and dreamed up the notion of starting his own airline operating from Portugal, I took the first opportunity which came my way to follow him to Lisbon. Yes, Joss, the war is still going on, but Franco's undoubtedly won it. With the Germans and Italy openly pouring in their troops to aid him, and with no more than a handful of loyalists backed by adventurers set against him, he can't fail. If only we and the French, or even the Americans, had officially intervened on the side of the government troops, would Franco have thought twice?'

'Why didn't we . . . or the French?'

'Because, lad, we would have played into Adolph Hitler's hands. It would have given him the prelude to the war he's determined to have. Just one Hun killed officially by an Englishman would have been regarded as a continuation of something adjourned in 1918.'

Joss thought that over. 'If he's determined to have a war, won't it come anyway?'

'Unless something develops to change things, I suppose so.'

'Gosh, then I'd be caught up in it.'

'We'd all be caught up in it. That's why diplomacy will be exercised to the limit to avoid giving him his head.' Kit gently punched the young pilot's shoulder. 'Enjoy flying the Alexandria route, lad, and get your kicks from the female of the species. They can be as exciting and dangerous as any battle foe.'

The conversation was lulled for a while, until Kit noticed dark clouds on the horizon; a huge bank of them obscuring the sun.

'Hallo,' he murmured, 'I don't much like the look of that up ahead.'

Joss studied it through binoculars. 'It's a storm gathering, all right. On our present course, we're liable to hit it fair and square.'

'Mmmm. Which direction does it appear to be taking?'

'It's hard to tell,' the youngster replied, still with the

413

binoculars to his eyes. 'If anything, I'd say it's cyclonic. Could move anywhere, at any moment.'

'Damn!' Kit said with feeling. 'An entire trip flown in near-perfect weather, then we have to hit something like this just a few miles from home.'

'Home' to the one man would always mean Sheenmouth; the other automatically assumed the word to mean Lisbon. 'We ought to get there without much trouble,' said Joss. 'I know it'll mean a detour, but that's surely better than risking a great deal of bumping about on the edge of that monster.'

He nodded. 'I agree. Ask Morris to give us a new setting, will you? And tell him to make it snappy, because we're either going faster than the instruments show, or that swirling column of cloud is coming straight for us.'

Joss left his seat and slid expertly down the ladder to reach the navigator. Kit picked up the binoculars. There was no doubt it was a fearsome clash of elements of the kind every pilot avoided at all costs. It did appear to be approaching alarmingly fast and, if anything, veering east towards Portugal. A wide detour to the west would merely add an hour or two to their flying time to Sheenmouth. The delay would increase the fervour of the crowd certain to be awaiting the first sight of the flying boat, created and built in the tiny resort, he thought caustically, and the Kirklands would regard that as the cherry to place atop their beautifully iced cake. Joss returned to set the new course as Kit kept his troubled gaze on the gigantic tower of looming darkness. Already, the sun was dimmed by the shadow it was casting, and the first sensations of turbulence in the atmosphere caused *Flamingo* to tremble slightly. Almost immediately, the tremble became a shudder. Patches of flying cloud whisked past the windows, and the main section of the cloudbank was now like a huge satanic mountain directly in their path.

Apprehension crept through Kit's veins. Either they

had made a severe misjudgement, or the storm was now moving in an entirely different direction. They were heading right into the heart of it.

'Christ!' he swore. 'Five minutes ago that bastard looked set to hit Portugal. Now it's swung to the west. We should have run for Lisbon, instead.'

Joss looked across at him. 'We are.'

'Are what?'

'Running for home. Morris estimates we'll be there within two hours.'

The apprehension deepened into real fear as Kit realized what had gone wrong. Morris had unwittingly been asked to give them a course straight into danger. There was no time for explanations, recriminations, or even the plotting of a new course. Hurtling towards *Flamingo*'s nose was a seething explosive mass of electricity generated by the violence of the elements. All Kit could do was prepare to fight it whilst shouting for Digger to send a radio message giving their position and predicament. Even as he did so, lightning sizzled towards them to hit *Flamingo* with the sound of rending metal. Digger yelled that the radio was crackling so much he could hear no response from it, and had no idea whether or not his messages were being relayed. At the same moment, Joss pointed out that the compass needle was now jumping around in crazy manner, rendering it impossible to keep to the given course.

Kit wasted no words on replies. They were in dire straits and his entire concentration was needed to fly them through this hazard and into clear skies beyond. He had never experienced anything like this before, and could only rely on instinct. Hitting the full force of the cyclone was like flying headlong into the sea. The cockpit grew as dark as night. *Flamingo* rose and plunged as violently as if tossed by forty-foot waves, and rain thundered on her sides with the deafening force of an incoming tide. The cockpit lights failed to come on, so he sat in darkness gripping the column and trying to estimate his altitude. Sweat gathered on his body, created by fear and the physical battle with the heavy machine.

Light suddenly pierced the gloom. Joss had snatched the rescue-lamp from its bracket, and was struggling to cross the cockpit so that he could illuminate the instrument panel. Another violent plunge threw him off his feet, and the lamp spun from his hand to smash against the bulkhead. The darkness was next pierced by vivid bright flashes, which raced along the nose towards him. Kit ducked the lightning instinctively, slackening his hold on the stick just as the aircraft was tossed in the air. Next minute, they were in a steep dive and the nearside starboard engine had flames streaking from it. Hauling on the stick and yelling to Digger to send continuous distress signals in case someone heard them, he fought to pull out of the dive. The turbulence was so immense, it was impossible to complete any manoeuvre successfully. They yawed to port when the flaming engine failed completely, putting extra stress on his arms and shoulders as he braced himself with his feet to stay in the seat. He hardly gave a thought to what might be happening back in the cabins, although his aviator's sixth sense told him there would have to be an emergency landing. His crew knew the drill well enough, and would implement it when he gave the word.

Lightning was flashing continuously, fizzing across the white aircraft with deadly power. One bolt struck the propeller of the offside starboard engine, and the subsequent reduction in power dispelled his last hope of forging through the storm before having to put down on the sea. They were losing height spasmodically due to the buffeting which tossed them helplessly up and down, and Kit had his work cut out to avoid stalling or from entering a dive which he now had insufficient engine power to counter. To make matters really desperate, he had no idea of his height. Joss was back on his feet and peering closely at the altimeter in the half light, but he reported that it appeared to have gone mad and was stuck on maximum.

Kit could not help thinking of his words to Sylva, and her reply. *One chance is to jump to safety. The other is to carry on spinning until you regain control . . . or until you hit the ground.* There was no question of jumping, and little hope of regaining control in such violent conditions.

He yelled to his co-pilot, 'Tell all crew members to now prepare for an imminent emergency landing. We're going into the drink, Joss, and I've no idea when.'

With his whole body aching unbearably, he fought to retain command of his machine while gazing through the rain-washed windows for the first sight of the sea. He hoped to God they still were over the sea. They had a chance with water beneath them; very little with solid earth. It was the most terrifying of all the hours he had spent in the air. Landing was always a tricky process; landing blind was tantamount to suicide. He clung on with a prayer on his lips. His ears were full of the sound of labouring engines, the whipcrack of lightning, the pounding of rain; his eyes ached from the strain of peering through the darkness. His nerves were so tense, they sent a message of instant alert when the dark-grey obscurity began heaving in great watery ridges only a few feet below.

'*Flaps!*' he roared to Joss. 'Here it is.'

Although he fought valiantly, there had been too little warning of their proximity to the cold waters of the Atlantic. *Flamingo* hit the sea with bone-shaking impact, bounced high, then raced forward into a huge rising wall of water. Kit's last thoughts were of a sorrow so great, tears stood on his cheeks as the world drew away from him.

It seemed as if there would never be another sound in the world save the awesome roaring, as sea-water surged into the punctured hull. The screaming and shouting had stopped. The only indication of life around Leone

417

was a vague blur of paler life-jackets moving in the near blackness. The sea was icy. She had kicked off her tight skirt along with her shoes on discovering how they had hampered her movements. In the air, she had been petrified. Now the crash had occurred and she found herself alive and apparently unhurt, a curious calmness had overtaken her. Water held no fears for an exceptionally good swimmer, especially when wearing a life-jacket. The first priority seemed to be to escape from *Flamingo* before she sank to the ocean bed, taking them all down, too. The lack of human voices now became eerily unsettling, and she longed for just one person to speak to her.

Treading water, she called out, 'Is anyone there? Is anyone else there?'

'Here . . . Yes . . . Oh, thank God,' came voices from various directions.

'Let's all gather over by the bar,' she suggested. 'See where the fire outside is being reflected in the mirror above it? Make for that.'

Swimming strongly towards the spot which vividly recorded the flames on the wing in the looking glass, Leone reached the bar and found she could rest her feet. She waited for the others to join her. Before they could, however, the aircraft shifted dramatically to roll on to her side. Leone was thrown against the bulkhead with some force. The blow must have knocked her out. The next thing she knew, she was floating on her back and there was a bright light swaying in the air some distance away.

A man's voice cried out, 'Anyone left in there? Any more passengers still inside there?'

'I am,' she cried desperately. 'Leone Kirkland.'

'Are you able to swim, Miss Kirkland?'

'Yes.'

She made for the light, still feeling slightly muzzy. The man holding the lamp was Digger Rathbone, the Australian engineer.

'There are others with me,' she panted, clutching a ledge and looking up at his craggy face.

'No, you're the last,' he told her. 'We pulled out everyone we could find. They're all in the boat. Come on, it's safer out here. Give me your hand.'

He pulled her up to the edge of the open hatch, and she stood precariously on that small foothold. She shivered in her blouse and panties as the wind began to buffet her. The scene was sombre. In that doomsday light, the sea stretched away into the distance in a series of cold grey-green undulations overhung by cloud which reached almost to the peaks of the huge waves. Rain lashed down to bite into her bare flesh like ice-needles. Tied to the white carcase of *Flamingo* was a small lifeboat crammed with people, several being violently sick over the side. The boat was being dashed against the broken hull by the heaving waves, and would surely be smashed asunder unless it were cut loose.

'Get in, Miss Kirkland, we daren't hang around here much longer.'

On the point of doing as she was told, she asked the man, 'Where is my brother . . . and Mr Grant? I can't see them in the boat.'

'We're seeing to that,' came his brief reply. 'Please get aboard.'

'*Where are they*?' she insisted.

'I don't know,' he confessed bluntly. 'The crew will find them. You're endangering these people's lives with this delay.'

'Send the boat off,' she cried against the driving rain. 'I'm a very good swimmer. I'll stay and help you look for them.'

With a round oath, the engineer untied the rope. The tiny craft raced away from them on the crest of a wave, then vanished from sight into a trough as if it had been swallowed up by the sea.

'Where's the other boat?' she demanded of the grim-faced man.

'Lost . . . and the dinghy would overturn in this swell. All we can do is use it to cling to, once we're sure there's no one else left alive here.'

Only then did she dare ask, 'Is Kit?'

He gave a slow shake of his head. 'Can't reach the cockpit. The nose has practically sheared off.'

'I see.' How could she take it so calmly? 'Can you swim well, Mr Rathbone?'

'Champion of Millamoola Cove,' he shouted above the roar of waves breaking across *Flamingo*'s fractured back. 'The name's Digger to my friends. Keep with me, and we'll see what we can do.'

A storm-tossed Atlantic Ocean was not like the swimming pools of the wealthy or the limpid Mediterranean, and Leone found it difficult to stay with the Australian as he dropped from his perch on the hatch to swim beneath the flaming wing sticking from the water like a fiery finger pointing to heaven. The most fearsome prospect was that of being thrown against the hull, then being sucked beneath it by the force of the waves. It was a close battle to remain clear as she used all her strength to move forward. Her companion was heading for the upper cabin near the nose, where Donald and Warren might well have been at the moment of impact. As they neared it, however, she guessed the chance of anyone being alive in there must be slight. The fire had travelled down to the hull. That part above the water level was blackened and charred. Yet, even as she prepared to swim on, she caught sight of movement revealed by the rise and fall of water sucking around the half-submerged machine. A body was floating nearby, in imminent danger of being pulled beneath the wreck and lost for ever. Without hesitation, she struck out towards it, knowing the danger yet somehow feeling little fear. Each time the undulations allowed her a view of it, it seemed even nearer the wave-washed hull, but she reached the spot to discover that the bobbing figure kept afloat by the life-jacket was Warren.

'Thank God,' she breathed unemotionally, seizing hold of the straps across his shoulders and preparing to tow him, not knowing if he were alive or dead. He was certainly unconscious of his dire plight as she inched slowly away from the dread undertow. Putting all her strength into fighting the power of an angry ocean, she dragged Warren out to where she had last seen the Australian. She knew a moment of deep panic when the sea ran apparently empty in every direction. Then, rising on a crest, she spotted the man who appeared equally relieved to see her.

'I've found Warren,' she yelled against the tumult.

With energetic signals the engineer beckoned her to him, mouthing words snatched away by the wind. The circumstances gave her energy beyond her normal capacity to enable her to reach him. To her surprise, he was smiling, albeit somewhat grimly. Next moment, she discovered the reason for his smile. Three yards from him, her feet touched a solid surface which allowed her to stand when in troughs between the giant waves.

'Sandbank,' he yelled. 'We can't be far from land.'

The next wave swept them up again, but he signalled Leone to be ready for the next trough. When it came, he seized Warren's harness with one hand and then pushed her up to the roof of *Flamingo* several feet from where the nose, buried in the shallows above the sandbank, had been wrenched almost completely from the body of the craft. Finding a secure perch, she prepared to assist her companion up beside her with Warren who, she could now see, had a deep cut in the side of his head.

'Is he alive?' she cried.

'Just knocked cold on impact, I guess. He's bloody lucky you saw him when you did.'

'Will he be all right?'

'No idea, lady,' came the frank response. 'Do what you can for him while I take a look around.'

The prospect of his leaving her alone, perched high

above a sea licking at her feet for fresh victims, filled her with fear.

'No, don't leave me!'

His shocked eyes said more than any words. 'My mates are in the cockpit.'

She took a deep breath. 'Yes . . . of course.'

His hand covered hers momentarily, cold and wet, yet infinitely warming. 'I would never have believed you had it in you to do this. Stay where you are. It's safer than a boat, and they'll find you the minute the storm clears.' His drawn face creased into an encouraging smile. 'You are a damned wonderful girl.'

When he went, she finally understood what he had been telling her. His friends' bodies were in the cockpit, and he needed to get them out. Kit's body was in there. Tears joined the rain on her face as she sat clutching Warren, and gazing unseeingly at the angry world surrounding her. That tumult was nothing to the one racing through her senses. Kit was dead. It was too late for hope. She rode in despair on that white wreck stranded in a grey ocean, and the minutes passed while the elements in a final onslaught did their utmost to dislodge her. Her attention was taken by the sound of a moan, and she glanced down to find blue eyes clouded with pain and bewilderment gazing up at her. Bending to put her cheek against his, she sobbed in abandoned fashion, 'Oh, Warren . . . dear Warren, your lovely *Flamingo* is dead. I'm so sorry. So very sorry.'

The sensational side of the newspaper reports on the crash of *Flamingo*, with the tragic loss of life, had now diminished in favour of the German–Czech crisis over control of Sudetenland, which Hitler was determined to annexe. However, the financial columns continued to speculate on the future of Kirkland Marine Aviation, now solely owned by a twenty-two-year-old girl after the death of her brother, along with two Portuguese stewards, Countess Renskaya and Nicholas Harmesworth.

The sandbank had saved the lives of the flight crew, who would almost certainly have drowned if the nose of the aircraft had gone into deep water. The navigator and first officer had suffered less than the pilot, who had remained at the controls until impact. Kit Anson had broken both legs, and received head injuries from which he might not fully recover. Doctors said he would never be fit to fly again. He was now in a Lisbon hospital, too ill to know anything outside his own shocked half-world. Donald Kirkland's body had been flown home for burial at Sheenmouth. His stunned sister had requested a quiet private funeral, but morbid sightseers and pressmen determined to get the full story had made the event harrowing for the mourners.

There was to be an inquiry into the cause of the crash. Until the findings were known, the insurers would make no payments to Kirkland's, or to those who had been injured. The executors of Countess Renskaya's estate had frozen the transaction to invest in the company, and Anglo-Asiatic had gone no further with placing orders for a flying boat in which one of its directors had been killed. Faith in the prototype had been shaken; investment in its manufacture was now less likely. The cost of the luxury flight had been extortionate, adding to the company's financial problems. If the inquiry proved the disaster to be due to pilot error and/or adverse weather conditions, some of the more enlightened financiers might still put money in the aircraft or the company. However, if there was the slightest evidence of a major fault in *Flamingo*, the future for Kirkland's would look extremely black.

Throughout the first dazed weeks, Leone had been bombarded by letters from commercial vultures who saw the chance to buy the company for a ridiculous sum from a feather-brained girl certain to grab what she could in return for a white elephant. Although she was astute enough to ignore such offers, they nevertheless added to the burden of responsibility which had dropped so heavily and unexpectedly upon her shoulders. Donald had never been a deeply beloved brother, but he had always been there, first as the heir presumptive, then as an unwilling partner. Since her father's death, she had merely been playing at being a company director. Admittedly, five months was very little time in which to change from a party-girl to shrewd executive, and Donald together with Maitland had excluded her whenever possible. She knew that the decisions she made now, however, would concern her personal future as well as that of Kirkland Marine Aviation. During the proving flight so many doubts and questions had arisen; so many unavoidable truths had confronted her. She had been wrong so often. This time it was essential to head in the right direction.

On a stifling July morning, she sat in Sir Willard Jameson's suite of offices facing the family solicitor, in company with Spencer Bligh, senior partner of the accountants Larchforth and Bodmin. Despite the heat, the two ageing men wore the dark jackets and pinstriped trousers befitting their positions in the City. If they thought her pale floral crêpe-de-Chine dress unsuitable for a bereaved sister, they made no sign of it as they offered her tea.

'Miss Kirkland, your brother's death leaves you as Sir Hector's sole heir,' Sir Willard explained, in grave but kindly tones. 'Mr Donald Kirkland had made no will, although I had often pressed him to do so. The important problem of how to attract investment in his flying boat took precedence over what he considered to be a legal document best postponed until a later date. I understand there was the possibility of marriage to an American lady.'

'Yes,' said Leone dryly, remembering Donald's careless dismissal of that possibility in Mombasa, when the dire need for cash no longer seemed to threaten.

Sir Willard frowned. 'Of course, one could not have foreseen Mr Kirkland's demise within five months of his

424

father.' He sighed gustily. 'The terms of Sir Hector's will state that everything should pass to his daughter if his son should die intestate. I'm afraid that means you inherit both Sir Hector's and your brother's debts, in addition to their assets.'

She stared at him, waiting for him to continue. Money had always been available from as long ago as she could remember. Had her father accumulated debts? It seemed inconceivable. Yet, as Sir Willard and Spencer Bligh unfolded the state of her inherited finances, it appeared that both her father and brother had run up huge liabilities in the name of Kirkland Marine Aviation. Sir Hector had prudently invested large sums abroad, but they were in holdings for which interest would only be paid every five years. Donald had used last year's increment to partially finance the proving flight.

'We could, of course, realize on these investments, Miss Kirkland,' the accountant told her in sombre tones, 'but I would strongly advise against such a move. Your father was an intelligent participant in stock-exchange manoeuvres. Our broker never hesitated to advise him of movements in shares, knowing he had a sharp knowledge of business growth.' The rotund bespectacled man leaned forward across the desk to indicate a sheaf of papers. 'These are your security for the future, my dear lady.'

Leone did not understand. 'Sir Willard has just told me I've inherited debts. Presumably, they have to be settled by selling some of those shares.'

The two men exchanged a glance which spoke volumes concerning the simplistic attitude of this girl towards the complexities of business. Sir Willard prepared to enlighten the uninitiated.

'The "debts", as we shall call them for the sake of this conversation, were all incurred to finance Kirkland Marine Aviation. Sir Hector built up the company from nothing, and was very proud of the achievement. He had good cause for pride, but . . hem . . . shall we say he was inclined to put it before prudence. When Mr Kirkland's seaplane gained the speed record in 1932, your father's confidence in his company seemed vindicated. However, the trial and imprisonment of the pilot took its toll of orders for the aircraft.' The legal giant stroked his chin as if to forgive himself for what he was about to say. 'Regrettably, Sir Hector allowed emotion to override perspicacity. Against our advice, he began work on a new flying boat.'

Leone gave a faint smile. 'Father took advice from no one save Sir Hector Kirkland. I should have thought you were used to that trait.'

Sir Willard continued as if there had been no interruption. 'Your brother had little choice but to incur additional liabilities in a bid to sell *Flamingo* to investors and gain some return on the ill-conceived venture. Both Mr Bligh and myself advised him to rid himself of the company which was draining his wealth. We did not share his hopes for the proving flight, although we did not dream how tragically disastrous it would be, naturally.' He shook his head sadly. 'It's a great pity that our advice was not heeded, Miss Kirkland, for we now have an ailing company to dispose of. We cannot hope for any serious offer until the inquiry has been completed, which means temporary measures must be devised to help us over the second half of this year.' He took some sheets from a pile of documents, tapping them with a finger. 'I have drawn up a plan which will suit us very nicely, I believe. As production is in abeyance in anticipation of definite orders for *Flamingo*, it will be simple to close the workshops forthwith and terminate the employment of the workforce. The new owner may wish to take them on later, of course, but we cannot afford to pay wages to idle men. Mr Bligh has made a fair assessment of what he believes we can get for the company, according to the findings of the inquiry. If the pilot is blamed for the crash, we shall be in quite a strong position. On the other hand, if a major fault is found with the aircraft, we shall be unable to sell the production rights along with the buildings. In that case, it will be necessary to . . .'

'Sir Willard, may I interrupt to ask who you mean when you mention "we"?' put in Leone. 'You spoke just now of my being the sole heir. Surely I am the only person to make any kind of decision concerning the company.'

Raising thin eyebrows in obvious surprise, the solicitor informed her that he was not perfectly clear on the point she was making.

'You have both been courteous and sympathetic towards me this afternoon; you have offered me tea and condolences. You've looked and seen a young woman who must be reassured that she can leave her financial worries in your capable hands; a girl who must wish to rid herself of an aviation company now she no longer has a brother to help her run it. You're wrong. I've inherited my father's pride in the company he built from scratch. I want to hold on to Kirkland's, even if it means selling those foreign investments you prize so highly. Along with implicit faith in Warren Grant's skill and Kit Anson's ability as a pilot, I have every confidence that the inquiry will absolve from blame both the machine and the man who flew her. When that happens, orders will surely come in for our flying boat. I have every intention of meeting them.'

There was stunned silence from the two men, until Sir Willard spoke into it with a touch of impatience. 'Miss Kirkland, you must see that retaining your holdings in this aircraft company will certainly result in draining away the funds invested in solid projects abroad. Selling is really the only answer.'

'The only answer to what? Being assured of the means to live in indolent comfort until I marry advantageously?' She shook her head, repeating firmly, 'I want this company. I want to continue manufacturing flying boats, whatever it costs.'

The elderly man sighed, recognizing her determination but plainly not approving of it. 'Very well . . . very well, if that is the way you truly feel. But I must ask you this: there are many factors to take into consideration. Please allow us to outline them for you, then take a few weeks to dwell on them before making your final decision. It is not one you should make in haste, dear lady. It will affect your entire future.'

Leone gazed back at him frankly. 'As I waited on the wreckage of *Flamingo* for rescue or death by drowning, Sir Willard, it dawned on me that my life is destined to be linked with marine aircraft. The greatest turning points in it, so far, have been created by these machines and the people who are connected with them. I believe the decision has been made for me by forces out of my control.'

Arriving home late in the evening, Leone had a light supper in her rooms then sat on in the midsummer dusk considering all she had been told of the alternatives facing her. It was apparently out of the question for her to consider remaining sole owner of Kirkland's. Her ignorance on aircraft manufacture could be overcome by employing a knowledgeable general manager, who would run the industrial side of the business; the commercial side could be handled by her present team of secretaries headed by Maitland. However, there was the most important factor, which would prove an insurmountable obstacle. Deals were made in boardrooms, over the lunchtable, and in gentlemen's clubs; differences were ironed out on the golf course, whilst playing squash, or out on a yacht. Where Sir Hector or Donald Kirkland could tread, a twenty-two-year-old girl could not. In short, business tycoonery was available to the male sex alone. Finally, without mincing words, Sir Willard had warned her that confidence in a company owned solely by a young woman with no commercial experience would be nonexistent.

She lay in bed postponing sleep as long as possible. Her dreams were always haunted by recollections of the crash; she often relived those terrible hours spent clinging to Warren as they waited to be rescued. Tonight, she was glad of these problems to keep her awake. It was futile to be angry over Sir Willard's advice. She could not change the ways of the world overnight. Yet she wanted it so much; wanted this unexpected chance to counterbalance her unhappy past with a future of some worth. Donald was dead; Kit almost so. All that remained for her was the hope of *Flamingo*. She would not believe faulty design caused the crash, although poor Warren was driving himself almost crazy as he waited for the findings of those examining the wreck. He had been wonderfully supportive throughout this period, despite his own deep despair over the loss of all the initial interest in his brain-child. She had swiftly put an end to his thanks for saving his life, by saying she wanted a shoulder to lean on, not an ode of gratitude. He had not asked her about the possible fate of Kirkland's, and she had said nothing to him of her ideas. Whatever her desires, the future really depended on this vital inquiry. If technical fault was ruled out, surely the virtues displayed by the proving flight, with its dramatic lake rescue, would bring investors back. Meanwhile, she must manage to survive without withdrawing those foreign investments. They would be needed to finance expansion when orders for *Flamingo* rolled in. Only when that happened would she decide whether to take on partners, or whether to go public with the company she had now taken as much to heart as the man who had created it.

By morning, she had formed several ideas which would go some way towards easing the financial problems. After breakfast she decided, with pleasurable determination, to act on one plan without delay. Making her way to the large office which had been Sir Hector's sanctum, then Donald's, she rang the bell then stood beside her desk waiting. What she had to say to Maitland would be easier if she faced him eye to eye.

He arrived with the inevitable folder beneath his arm. There was little change in his expression as he said, 'These papers should have gone off on Monday, Miss Kirkland. I did warn you before you left for London. It will now be necessary to send one of the secretaries in to Axminster with them.' To facilitate her task, he set the papers out and unscrewed the top of the gold fountain pen to hold it out. 'Please! The final collection is at seven thirty.'

Without moving, she said, 'Did you know that I tried to persuade my brother the company couldn't afford you, when I joined it and discovered how well rewarded you were for what you did? Donald insisted that he couldn't possibly manage without you, yet he did so quite easily when you were so airsick he had to send you home from Cairo by sea.'

'A constitutional weakness I deplored but could do nothing to remedy,' he replied coolly, still offering the pen and indicating the papers. 'Please, Miss Kirkland.'

'Unlike my brother, I'm prepared to make economies which, in view of the unhappy legacy I'm facing, are essential. I wish I could say I regret having to dismiss you, Maitland, but the prospect of an end to your unctuous self popping up wherever I go in this huge building is extremely attractive. I shall pay you a month's salary and you may keep the car. I'd like you to be gone by tomorrow evening.'

He stood unruffled, not a single sandy hair turned, as he said, 'I don't think you would, Miss Kirkland. I know far too much.'

'I'll agree with that. In fact, you're almost too perfect for this world,' she told him calmly. 'I aim to find someone normally efficient to replace you, and intend to learn the business myself. In time I shall find out all there is to know.'

'Even the truth concerning your father and Geoffrey Anson?' he asked in the same cool, unemotional tones.

Leone grew still, her sixth sense telling her that the faintly sinister quality she had always suspected in this man was about to be revealed.

'Especially that,' she told him, hiding her apprehension.

'I thought you might.' Maitland threw down the pen and folded his arms confidently. 'Anson was a drunkard and wastrel, but he was undisputedly a brilliant designer. Sir Hector needed a new seaplane, but the man was going to the dogs after being thrown from his lodgings. In fact, he and his son were sleeping rough in the donkey stables. Your father offered them the old boathouse to live in, and gave Anson junior a job as a greaser in the workshops. In addition, he passed on a valuable tip on shrewd investment to Geoffrey. The old boy had to swear to keep on the wagon while he developed the new design in return for this largesse.' He gave a derisory laugh. 'He stayed sober for a while, mainly due to his son's threats, and Sir Hector's tip paid off rich dividends. The Ansons were in the money again, and riding high. However, the gambling streak in old Anson now saw a new form of sudden chancy wealth by playing the stock exchange. He began pestering Sir Hector for more tips, advance knowledge of company transactions, any opportunities for large profits on swift buying and selling. To keep him happy, and on the job, he was given a few quiet tips. They made him a very tidy sum, but he was then firmly in the grip of the fever to take bigger and bigger risks, for greater and greater profits. Finally, he did what every born gambler can't resist; bid everything on one certain winner.

'Sir Hector had told him of a new company being floated, which was starting quietly but was certain to hit the jackpot. Anson put his every penny in shares. Your father invested modestly. The company overstepped itself and crashed. A friend of Sir Hector gave him advance warning to sell, but he neglected to pass on this warning to Anson. The old boy lost everything. When he heard, he drank himself silly, then came here to the Abbey to confront the man he held responsible. Your father and I had gone down to the workshops early that day, so he forced Walter to take him down in the small launch, then staggered in to seek us out. Most of the men were outside taking their breakfast break, leaving just two in the shops to keep the machines running. Anson no sooner clapped eyes on Sir Hector than he went for him. There was no verbal abuse, just a silent murderous lunge at your father's throat. Sir Hector put up an arm to fend him off, and told the man to pull himself together. That's when Anson let fly with words, threatening retaliation unless he was given enough to help him recover from the disastrous investment. Of course, your father had no intention of paying him anything, and said so. Anson let fly a stream of vitriolic abuse such as I've never before heard, and vowed he'd sell his design to a rival. At that, Sir Hector's temper got the better of him. He hit out at the sot.'

Allowing a pause to highlight the significance of his words, Maitland then continued. 'Your father's second blow knocked Anson off balance and into the racing machinery, where he was instantly cut to pieces. Fortunately, I was the only person who saw what actually happened.' He smiled, something rare and almost bizarre from this man. 'Sir Hector always appreciated my silence. After his death, your brother heard the story and also appreciated it. I feel sure you will, too.'

Leone stood for long moments gazing into the past. At last, she understood why a man known never to do anything unless it would bring personal benefits, had taken in a stray mongrel. It seemed her father had had a conscience, albeit a rarely troubled one, and guilt had led him to offer a home to the destitute boy whose father he had accidentally killed. How could he have known that boy would become a man earning more respect from the world than any Kirkland? Was that why he had subsequently destroyed the son, as well? She turned away in anguish, her hand pressed to her mouth. In her own way, she had passively approved the order to place him under arrest. That made her as guilty as her father.

'Will you now sign these papers, Miss Kirkland?' prompted the smooth voice of the man who knew their guilt.

With her back to him, she struggled to say, 'I want you gone from here by tomorrow evening.'

After only a short silence, he said, 'Do you really want the truth published in every newspaper, and passed from lip to lip in social and business circles?'

Turning to face someone she had always resented for the place he had held in a household from which she had been excluded, she said, 'You've been dealing with the men of this family for the past twenty years. There's a new breed of Kirklands now, Maitland, and I'm the first of them. You may say what you like, you may gossip with whom you wish, you are at liberty to drag the name of Kirkland through the mud. It's been there before, and survived . . . but this will be the last time. Despicable creatures like you won't attempt to intimidate me, because they'll have no grounds for doing so. You'll never know how marvellous it is to feel free to rid myself of your presence in my home. When you've gone, I shall open all the windows and allow the breeze to blow away the ghosts. The monks have had their day here. The rest of them are going to be *mine*.'

16

After a glorious October when the banks of the Sheen
had been ablaze with autumn colours, and Sheenmouth
had enjoyed an extended season due to many people
taking a late seaside holiday while the weather was so
settled, November came in grey, damp and raw. The
days hardly changed from the first to the last of the
month. Mist hung over the river, forcing the ferry to be
cancelled on many occasions. In the resort itself, cafés,
ice-cream huts and souvenir shops along the promenade
had been shuttered for the winter. Only the Merry Monk
tearooms and restaurant remained open during the off-
season period, although the Imperial Hotel also served
dinner to non-residents who booked a table in advance.
The Roxy cinema alongside the Sheenmouth Palais de
Danse often had no more than three patrons for a
matinee now, and the dance-hall was closed for reno-
vations ready for the Christmas season.

In the quayside inns there was a great deal for the
regulars to mull over. With the tiny saloons to themselves again after the influx of holiday visitors, they could
settle happily each evening into their favourite corners
to discuss topics ancient and modern. With matters concerning Kirkland Marine Aviation temporarily quiet,
until the result of the inquiry into the crash of Sheenmouth's pride and joy was announced, the only bone to
pick in that area was the continuing sly references in
the *Sheenmouth Clarion* to 'certain questionable aspects

surrounding the Abbey'. These were apparently the fact of a girl whose reputation was known to be far from snowy white, living there alone with Kirkland's chief designer. Although everyone knew Warren Grant had turned the old boathouse into a smart home for himself, because Ethel Chubb 'did' for him and reported on every detail of what went on there, he *was* close enough to the Abbey to slip up there for a bit of fun with the Kirkland heiress whenever they both felt like it. Feathering his nest in two directions, was the verdict of those who set the world to rights over a pint of ale. The *Clarion* certainly seemed to have it in for young Grant, and for the family which had seen his potential and employed him. Jack Cummings had grown more bitter since his daughter had left one day to visit cousins in Bradford, and had not come back. Rumour had it that she had been badly let down by the designer when he went to work for Kirkland's, and Jack Cummings aired his malice weekly, in print. Anyone else who had had dealings with *Flamingo*'s creator spoke kindly of him, and agreed that what he chose to get up to with Leone Kirkland was his own affair.

On one thing, the residents were wholly agreed. The inquiry would never prove the crash to have been due to a fault in the flying boat; it was Sheenmouth's pride and joy, the finest marine aircraft ever designed. Opinions on possible pilot error varied. Some swore Kit Anson could never make an error of judgement at the controls of any aircraft; whatever else could be said of him, he was an exceptional pilot. Those who hated him, swiftly declared that he had clearly planned the whole thing as revenge on the family which had shown him up for the rogue he was, six years ago. The Ansons were rotten to the core, they pointed out, and he should be locked behind bars again. It had been robbery and violence before; now it was multiple murder. When Kit's defenders pointed out that he had suffered a terrible penalty from the crash, the only rejoinder was that the Almighty had wreaked just punishment.

In that November of 1938, however, the main topic of conversation was the threat of war. Czechoslovakia had just been sacrificed to placate Hitler in his demand for Sudetenland. Whilst no one in Britain wanted a war, with memories of the last still horribly fresh in the minds of many, the majority felt their own safety had been paid for by the betrayal of thousands of helpless souls. It could not have been wise for Neville Chamberlain to have given in to a madman who shrieked his fanatical speeches at his countrymen, and who was killing Jews out of racial hatred. Like any bully, who discovered he only had to threaten to be given what he wanted, this man would surely demand more and more.

The spectre of war hovered to cast a shadow over even such tiny, unsophisticated places as Sheenmouth. Twenty years of peace had not been long enough, for they had contained strikes, industrial collapse, hardship and the distressing plight of war wounded neglected and forgotten after the sacrifice they had made. Jack Cummings was really one of the luckier ones. He was doing well with the *Clarion*, because the townspeople read it to see who he would malign next, but huge hosts still filled asylums and workshops for the blind and limbless. Many more had been left to depend on hard-pressed relatives for a home and some kind of care. What Britain needed was continuing peace, a run of prosperity, and a shrewd, firm, far-seeing leader. What it got was an outbreak of virulent influenza, during that bleak month which had followed autumnal warmth.

Warren lay in bed feeling desperately ill. He had succumbed to the flu several days ago, and his weak chest ensured that he suffered the maximum degree from the virus. Today, however, he sensed that his condition had worsened even further. Mrs Chubb had packed up early yesterday, claiming that she felt 'like death warmed up', and had not put in an appearance today. Warren supposed she now felt like death without warmth, as he did. He had been too ill to eat for two days, despite the broth and egg custards Mrs Chubb had produced for him, so it did not matter that she was not there to do any cooking. There was little cleaning to be done, but her absence meant that there was no heat in that riverside boathouse. The stove had gone out early yesterday evening, and the place had been growing steadily colder and damper by the hour. Feeling too ill to stand, much less clean out the stove and relight it, he lay shaking from head to foot while sweat formed on his fevered brow. As it was growing dark, he supposed it must be around four in the afternoon. Another night ahead of him without light or warmth.

His weary brain tried to decide whether or not he really cared. He had been desperately tired for weeks now – months, even. Ever since Leone had dragged him from the sea in May. The disaster haunted him. People had died in his aircraft. Donald Kirkland had died. His sister was now left with a legacy of failure. What would the inquiry unearth? What had happened to the dream he had had? A roundabout of facts and images circled in his heated brain – drawings of aircraft components, pink flamingoes on jewelled leads, a lake surrounded by trees with gnarled arms outstretched to prevent them from leaving the water. The most recurring vision was that of a dead white bird on the edge of a seashore, and a small boy crouched over it with tears on his cheeks. He rolled over to blot out such images and felt himself falling, falling, falling.

He awoke to find himself in an enormous bed standing in a room of elegant luxury. A fire leapt in the hearth, the kind that should have a dog stretched before it. His eyes again focused clearly; his head no longer thudded in agony. Blissful comfort gave him an air of wellbeing, so he lay quietly enjoying the downy cradle beneath his aching body as he solved the mystery of his surroundings. Old stone walls and mullioned windows; seventeenth-century paintings, brocade curtains and bedcover, thick carpet dotted with Persian rugs, heavy gilt chandelier, and simple antique furniture. He could only be in Sheenmouth Abbey.

Leone came in some time later, pleased to find him awake. In a dress of scarlet wool with white angora bands around the neck and down the left side, she looked bright and lovely on a dreary day. Her scarlet mouth curved into a smile as she introduced the man with her as Dr Gibbs, who had apparently been attending him every day for almost a week.

'Give me a call when you've finished,' she told the medical man. Then, with another smile for Warren, she went out.

'Well, how are you feeling now?' asked Dr Gibbs, taking out his stethoscope.

'Better than before,' Warren confessed.

'I imagine so,' came the dry comment. 'You've had pleurisy, Mr Grant, and not for the first time, I should guess.'

Warren nodded on the pillow. 'In 1930. It left me with a weak chest.'

'You should have gone to the hospital, by rights, but Miss Kirkland insisted on your being brought here, with a nurse in attendance throughout the crisis.'

'What crisis?' he asked.

'Yours, young man. It was touch and go until yesterday. Your constitution is none too sturdy, as you've just admitted. I suppose you've been fretting over the business of the inquiry, and not looking after yourself properly.'

'I've been very worried, yes. The result ought to be announced soon. It's been more than six months.'

The fresh-faced man in heavy tweed nodded. 'Miss Kirkland went to the boathouse to tell you the news. Lucky for you she did. You were all alone there, in a critical state.'

His heart lurched. 'The news? She's heard the verdict?'

'She has indeed. Now, I'm prescribing a mixture which I want you to take . . .'

Warren heard nothing of what he should do with Dr Gibbs' mixture. Why had Leone said nothing just now? Was she keeping the blow from him until he was well enough to take it? Surely they had not discovered a design fault. There was none. He knew there was not. The crash had been due to the violence of the freak storm which had hit them. He could not believe in pilot error, either, not with that particular one at the controls. Kit had been flying his reputation and future hopes along with *Flamingo*. After that spectacular demonstration of skill at Lake Kiju, he would never have made a mistake so near to the end of a triumphant flight.

'As you appear to have listened to nothing I just said, Mr Grant,' said the doctor, bringing him from his thoughts, 'I have written down the dosage instructions. Don't overdo things for a day or two, but if you feel like sitting out for a while there'll be little harm in that. I'll call again on Thursday.' His smile was friendly and encouraging. 'No reason to get in a stew. You'll find Miss Kirkland's news very pleasant hearing.'

Leone came in several minutes after the man had gone from the room. Taking one look at him, she crossed to the bed to sit on the side of it and take up one of his hands.

'Stop looking so apprehensive. They placed full blame on the freak weather conditions. The crew have been cleared of any possible error or negligence, and *Flamingo* remains as marvellous as you've always claimed.' She smiled, and it was like the sun coming out. 'Preliminary inquiries are already coming in, which suggests that public faith in your beautiful boat remains unshaken. Warren, I'm such a new girl at all this, but I imagine it means we're back in business. If we want to be, that is.'

It was too much for him in his weakened state, and

after the long months of worry and despair. He turned his face away to hide the evidence of his emotion, and lay trying to accept that his dream had returned almost intact.

'I seem to make a habit of being on hand when men reveal that they're every bit as human as we are,' Leone said quietly. 'On the last occasion, I offered to kiss him better.'

'What happened?' he asked thickly.

'I fell in love with him.'

He rolled his head to look at her again. 'How is he?'

'I only know what the newspapers report of his condition. Now that he's emerged from the coma, doctors say they'll soon know if their fears are correct. Oh, Warren, what does a man born to fly do with his life when he's no longer able to use that great gift?'

He lay silent for a moment, then squeezed the hand holding his. 'Kit's a fighter.'

'This is probably something he can't fight.' She stood up, moving restlessly across the room to poke the fire. Then she sank into a small chair beside it, to gaze into the leaping flames as if a traveller in realms of distant thought. It was a while before she spoke next, and then it was with her face still turned to the fire.

'There's something I want to tell you. For several months I've been expecting to read of it in the pages of every newspaper in the world, but Maitland is either biding his time, or has given up all thought of what he threatened. All the same, I want you to know this. It's so important that you do.'

Puzzled by her enigmatic reference to Maitland, and still in the grips of incredible relief over the inquiry, Warren struggled to a sitting position. He felt initially giddy, but the sensation gradually subsided. Propped by the pillows, he discovered how weak he had become in so short a time, and lay waiting for the news she wished to impart, little realizing what form it would take.

Leone looked round at him then, and he was shocked

by the stress of her expression. 'When I told Maitland to go, he gave me the answer to why he was always so favoured by Father and Donald. He . . . he . . . Warren, Geoffrey Anson was pushed into the machinery by my father,' she confessed in anguished tones. 'They had a quarrel over investments Kit's father had been advised to make, but which had crashed. Poor Anson got drunk, then assaulted the man he held responsible for the loss of all he owned. Father apparently thrust him away and . . . and he lost his footing to slip down into the racing machinery. Maitland was a witness to it, and blackmailed first Father, then Donald. He expected to use the same pressure on me, but I . . . I truly didn't care if he made the news public. I was so numb inside, it didn't really seem important to uphold Kirkland integrity which was a myth.'

Warren felt giddy again. It was an appalling piece of information, and he protested. 'How do you know he was telling the truth? Your father can't deny it, nor can Donald.' He fought the sensation of floating up and down, as he went on, 'He's done nothing about it because it's a pack of lies. Of course it is. He can't prove any of it. Leone, he was simply trying to browbeat someone he saw as a distressed bewildered girl who had just sacked him.'

She shook her head, almost moaning. 'It's true, it's true. It all makes sense now. Why he was so privileged, why he was so generously paid. It also explains why Kit was taken in by a man with no benevolent tendencies whatever. It was Father's guilty conscience prodding him to do something for the son of a man he had virtually killed with his own hands.'

'No, don't think of it that way,' Warren urged with compassion. 'It was an accident, Leone, purely a terrible accident.'

'Then why didn't Father reveal the facts at the inquest?' she cried. 'I was there when Kit was brought to this Abbey, shocked and uncertain. I remember Father

441

saying that Teale would ensure that the circumstances of the death would be kept as quiet as possible for Kit's sake, because raking up details of Geoffrey Anson's past would be too upsetting for his son. There was no mention of pushing anyone, or of causing old Anson to lose his entire investment through neglect to inform him of the advisability to sell. No, Warren, Sir Hector Kirkland covered up his actions completely,' she continued, near to tears. 'There was enough heart in him to offer Kit a home and the chance to study, but the stray mongrel was so grateful and so filled with eagerness to ensure that his benefactor never regretted his generosity, he brought about his own downfall by outshining those who had polished off his corners and dressed him in the right clothes.' Fighting the emotion which threatened to overcome her completely, she confessed, 'I knew that Father compared Donald unfavourably with Kit, but I was too immature to see that if Donald couldn't be improved – which he couldn't – then the young man who was all the things his son would never be, had to be destroyed by the dissatisfied parent.' She broke down completely at that point, sobbing, 'If only I'd been older, or less in love with him. I might have stood by him and prevented Father from having him arrested that morning. As it was, I listened and said nothing – which condemned him as surely as if I'd put it into words. Oh God, no wonder he hated us all.'

Her distress tore him apart, particularly as it was over a man who was a friend, a rival and a source of personal guilt over the same kind of passive accusation Leone found so unbearable. What if she knew about that, too?

'Is that all Maitland told you?' he asked apprehensively, as she calmed a little.

'Isn't it enough?'

'More than enough. Why didn't you tell me all this before? I'd have sent Maitland packing pretty quick and with a flea in his ear,' he said. 'Why have you tortured

442

yourself all this time? I thought you trusted me enough to confide anything.'

Spreading her hands in a weary gesture, she said, 'I've stopped telephoning Lisbon. I'll keep out of his life from now on. He's free of the Kirklands and their abominable power.'

Loving her as he did, he longed to ease her pain. Putting out his hands, he said coaxingly, 'Come over here. We've had some good news. Try to concentrate on that instead.'

She came to sit on the edge of his bed again, speaking with great urgency. 'Warren, I've wasted the first twenty-two years of my life. I've done all the wrong things imaginable, because I could see no clear direction to take.' She seized his hand again, her eyes appealing to him for understanding. 'I can't undo what we all did to Kit, but I can ensure that no Kirkland ever does such things to anyone else. I want to make my future exciting, but very worthwhile, and the opportunity is staring me in the face. I want to hold on to Kirkland's. I want that more than anything. I've just sold my villa in Lugano, and the mews cottage in London. I intend to make my home here in a place I never dreamed I'd come to love, and the company workshops are just down the river. What could be more convenient?' she demanded, the words rushing from her in her fervour. 'Now the inquiry's over we'll be able to go into production with the flying boats, and I could sell some foreign investments for the cash to build a new hangar and workshop to cope with orders which are certain to come. There's just one gigantic snag.'

'Yes?' he murmured, struggling to follow all she was saying whilst still reeling from what she had confided about Geoffrey Anson's death.

'I can't run the company on my own. Since Maitland left, even the day-to-day volume of affairs has turned into a nightmare. I've an excellent female secretary, but it's daily more evident how very knowledgeable and efficient that snake was. In time, I know I'll grasp the office side of things, but it'll take a man to handle the industrial aspect of aircraft production.' Letting out her breath in a deep sigh, she went on, 'Having said all that, I repeat that I want to hold on to the company and make copies of *Flamingo*. I don't want to take on a large number of partners, nor do I want to go public until I see how things work out.'

'So what's the answer?' he asked, in a convalescent daze.

Gripping his hands tightly, the words came out in a rush. 'I want to do it with you. I'll work like blazes, I swear, but I need you, Warren. Don't let me down. Please, don't let me down. We'd make a perfect team, wouldn't we?'

What a moment to choose for such a declaration, he thought wildly. A man sitting in bed in winceyette pyjamas, still half stupid with the aftermath of fever, the relief of knowing he was not being held responsible for the deaths of five people, and the suggestion that the girl's father had killed a man and hushed up the fact, was hardly in a fit state to cope with this . . . or with her.

Taking advantage of his silence, she elaborated with growing enthusiasm. 'I've already worked out where we'd put the new buildings. That spare land to the south of our hangar is large enough – I've been down there and measured it – and Father held an option to purchase. I imagine that's passed to me now. We'd have to take on another foreman for the second workshop, and you'll now be head of the design office instead of Donald. I'll take on the clerical and social side of the business. Most important of all, though, is the addition of a managing director – someone fairly young, who knows the ropes and shares our enthusiasm for *Flamingo*.'

He was still overcome with too many emotions to say anything, and she searched his face anxiously before adding, 'Sir Willard insists no one would take me seriously without a man at my side . . . and you're the man I want. What's your answer?'

Feeling the effects of a vastly different kind of fever by now, he stammered, 'I'm not sure what . . . are you offering me a business partnership. . . or are you proposing to me?'

'Both, silly,' she said, smiling at last. 'Although I suppose you'll get on your high horse and claim you never get married by invitation, either.'

17

In the March of 1939 the Spanish Civil War ended leaving Franco as overall dictator, on friendly terms with Hitler and Mussolini who had given him such splendid aid throughout. With this outcome staring them in the face, the rest of Europe and Britain could no longer hope for a decline in aggression from a Germany so closely allied with Italy, who had just had proof of her military superiority. With Austria forcibly drawn beneath Hitler's warlike mantle, and Czechoslovakia handed to the Führer on a plate, it was clear to even the simplest mind that he would not stop there.

No secret had been made of the gigantic rearmament programme being carried out in Germany to create forces in the air, and on sea and land, which far outstripped those of any other nation. The obvious next victim was Poland – poor little Poland, who had suffered conquest by greedy neighbours so many times, her people hardly knew what national freedom was like. Everyone felt sorry for Poland, the British going so far as to sign a pact promising to protect her from Russian aggression. This was done in the mistaken confidence that the huge might of Communist Russia on one side, and the rest of Europe on the other, would make Hitler think twice about invading his Polish neighbours. So, throughout the early summer months of that doomed year, nothing more than uneasiness reigned as Hitler continued amassing his weapons, conscripting all able-bodied men into his three fighting forces, and persecuting Jews along with other groups of people who stood in the way of his plan for a super-race with himself controlling it.

Also during those early summer months of 1939, Kit was emerging the victor from his war against debility. For fourteen months he had struggled to recover from his serious injuries. The broken legs had mended, in time, but he had had to learn how to use them again. The head injuries he had sustained had severely impaired his powers of coordination, resulting in delay between signals from his brain and the movement of appropriate limbs. At first, doctors had believed coordination of any kind would prove impossible, but fortune had favoured him enough to spare him the worst by arranging that a Swiss doctor specializing in a somewhat revolutionary approach to such cases, should be living and working in Lisbon at just the right time.

Seeing this young pilot as the most providential guinea pig for his theories, Dr Kleist had taken over his case with enthusiasm and not a little eccentricity. Making no secret of the fact that to him Kit was simply an absorbing experiment without human emotions, the Swiss aroused a great deal of aggression in his patient. Anger being the perfect antidote to self-pity, swift strides towards recovery were made as Kit spent hours at such tasks as putting coloured blocks into the correct holes in a board, hammering at a small gong which swung like a pendulum, and operating weird mechanical gadgets with his feet. As if concentration and physical effort were not enough, Dr Kleist stood beside him with a large timepiece clicking relentlessly to register the time taken to complete the exercise.

There were long periods, however, when hopelessness did prevail, making Kit wonder why he was making such determined efforts, which often gave him a great deal of pain. Without his friends in Lisbon, he doubted he would have had the will to continue. Tom Digby was paying the sizeable fee demanded by Dr Kleist, and Kit could not let his friend down. Tom visited regularly, and so did Morris, Joss and Digger. Through them, he had heard the result of the inquiry a few weeks before Christmas. Partly because he had only recently emerged from his coma and his reactions had been very slow, nothing had been said by him about the misunderstanding over the location of 'home' when setting course. Later, he had reflected that there was no point in raising the issue when a decision had been reached. They would have hit the storm, anyway, if only on its fringes. He had been delighted to hear that orders were being placed for Flamingo-class flying boats. Warren deserved his success. The news of a marriage between the designer and his former employer left Kit unsure of his feelings on the subject. Leone could not possibly run the company on her own, and Warren certainly understood aircraft manufacture. However, his head was permanently in the clouds. Would he ever understand and take into account the financial aspects when creating bigger and better flying machines?

Towards the news of Donald's death, Kit had no doubt whatever of his feelings. The aggression induced by Dr Kleist allowed him to enjoy a certain grim satisfaction over the knowledge that the parasite of the family had met his end. Warren would now be free to rightly claim full credit for any future designs, and there was now one less Kirkland walking the earth. The only aspect of it Kit regretted was that one could not speak ill of the dead, and Donald would never receive his just punishment.

So Kit persevered and soon began to win through, although he did not know how he would ever repay his friend for the sum he was spending on medical treatment. Tom silenced him by saying the boot was on the other foot, because he was repaying Kit for saving his life in Spain. A more fruitful conversation between them had been on the subject of *Flamingo*, because Tom had contracted a salvage company to take her off the sandbank. The flying boat was presently in one of his own hangars being put together again.

'Kirkland's has enough on its hands trying to cope with the flow of orders for new ones, so doesn't want the wreck of their prototype,' Tom had told him with a grin. 'If I get a move on, Western Med could be the first company to put a Flamingo-class boat into service. What d'you think of that, old son?'

Kit was pleased for Tom, naturally, but now he was out of hospital the spectre his illness had kept at bay rose up to confront him. He would never fly the rebuilt *Flamingo*; he would never fly again. What was he going to do with his life? Unlike Tom, he had no huge nest-egg behind him. In fact, he was virtually broke. Only because his cottage was so far off the beaten track, and very primitive, had his landlord not considered moving Kit's belongings and re-letting it. The landowner also liked and admired his tenant and was reluctant to add to his tribulations, especially when he had no real need of the rent. Even so, as Kit tried to come to grips with the strangeness of being in a tiny two-roomed cottage once more, and also wondering what kind of job he could get which would allow him enough to give Mrs Valenques the usual sum to look after him and leave enough over to pay for the running of his essential car, he instead fell to thinking of what might have been. It was a fatal exercise for a man trying to accept what must be, but it proved impossible not to yearn for Sylva on a July day when the sun beat down on his bare head as he sat outside the cottage, gazing out over water so clear and turquoise he could see the dark shapes of fish moving in the shallows. In the past, he had been determined never to let any woman rule him. Yet she did, after only one night together.

A letter had arrived from Africa, to lie untouched in his locker for weeks. When he had finally emerged from the coma, Kit had hardly been aware of what was happening around him for many more weeks. Eventually, a nurse had told him of the letter, opened it, then held it up for him to read. At that stage in his recovery, Kit had not been able to write legibly. She had penned a reply for him. It had, of necessity, been restrained in tone saying merely that he was a great deal better, that he was very disappointed about the delay to their plans, and that he hoped she would write again soon. There had been two letters from Sylva in the following six months, each asking why it was taking so long for him to get back on his feet. She had filled the pages with urgent hopes that there would be good news from him in the next letter, then had gone on to list the number of flights being made by pioneers making and breaking records whilst they waited to embark on their polar adventure.

Realizing that she had no real notion of the seriousness of his condition, Kit had shrunk from telling her he would never fly again, much less attempt what they had planned in Africa. To aid his deception, he had cajoled the nurse into writing all the subsequent letters so that she would detect no change in the handwriting and question it. Unable to keep his replies restrained, he had written what he wanted to tell her, then handed it over to be copied. His nurse had never commented on the contents, but once asked if Kit was sure he knew what he was doing where Miss Lindstrom was concerned. A crisp affirmative had ended the topic, but Kit was nowhere near as confident as he had sounded.

Now, as he sat in isolation outside his coastal cottage on the twelfth day after leaving hospital, the naked truth hit him fairly and squarely. Sylva had captured his senses and his mind so totally, he could still see her clearly, recall the fascination of her forthright manner and the excitement burning in her as she had spoken about flying. Previously, he had known such profound affinity only with *Aphrodite* as they had risen into the sky together, to circle then streak through the air faster than any man had then travelled. With Sylva, he had

450

experienced a matching affinity with immense sexual attraction added. That combination had been overwhelming – so overwhelming he had been unable to sign its death warrant by telling her Kit Anson was doomed to stay on the ground for the rest of his days. He was of no use to her now; she would have to make her triumphant polar flight with someone else. It was time he plucked up the courage to write and admit it to her. The tranquillity of that day, the sight of the clear sparkling sea, put an ache in his breast as he thought of skimming that turquoise surface to make the spray fly before lifting into the heavens as vivid as the sea. The ache increased as his gaze lifted to the seagulls soaring and diving with such grace and agility, such perfect coordination of balance with strength. He would change places with any one of them right now, except that he was clumsy, slow and certain to plunge headlong into the sea again.

The sound of a car arriving along the lonely path brought him from introspection. One of the boys' company would get him out of this damned introspective mood, he told himself heavily. They had proved true friends. Even Morris, forever trying to solve the problem of his dominant Portuguese in-laws, had found time to meet up with him regularly over the entire fourteen months. Young Alia had several times arrived at his bedside with flowers, to tell him she was lighting candles for him. He had asked Morris to explain to his young sister-in-law that the slender relationship was over, and she must look for someone else to care for. The girl had come no more.

The sound of voices told him two of the lads must have come together today. With a faint sense of guilt, he abandoned the thought of writing to Sylva today and turned at the sound of their footsteps coming through the cottage to the small patio where he sat. It was like hitting that great wall of grey water for the second time, when he discovered who had arrived to see him. Slower to react than he used to be, Kit remained where he was while the impact of her reality kept him silent. In a beige straight-fitting dress and a wide-brimmed white-hunter's hat with a band of leopard fur around the crown, she looked so stunningly alive he grew weak with the excitement she created.

'My goodness, you look so terrible . . . and after so long,' she exclaimed in that breathy urgent voice he recalled so well.

Still he sat, unable to conjure up any words, as he studied her determined face, tanned and freckled, with its coral-tinted mouth and light-green eyes which saw the same things his saw. It was then he knew he could keep the truth from her no longer, because it was there before those perceptive eyes. If only he had been prepared for this!

Against the sound of a car departing, she gave a light laugh. 'The taxi man looked so strange at me when I said him this address. It is clear to me why. You are a peasant, Kit Anson, and did not write me the fact.' Crossing to him, she perched on a low wall and tugged off the shady hat. Her shining brown hair immediately cascaded to her waist, changing her image from that of cool, challenging achiever to *femme fatale*.

Instant, overwhelming excitement charged through Kit like an injection of richer fuel to a flagging engine, and his every sense grew sharper, more intense.

'I've been only half a man without you,' he breathed.

'You look only half a man still.' She reached out to touch his bare forearm. 'We crash, but we go on. Always we go on.'

He avoided her eyes, gazing instead at her hand as it lay against the dark hairs on his arm, grown pale after so long away from the sun.

'Why have you come here?'

'Why have you asked? You know the answer.'

Looking up then, he shook his head. 'No.'

'We go together, Kit. We are two alike.'

'No . . . not any more. I'll never fly again,' he forced himself to say.

'Phoo!' she cried, breaking contact in order to push away hair being blown across her face by the warm breeze. 'Kit Anson is born to fly.'

'Sylva, they've told me it's impossible,' he insisted in rising tones, which betrayed his tension at having to own it.

'*Impossible!*' Getting to her feet, she demanded, 'What is this thing called "impossible"? It is something to be made possible. It is the challenge we must all have.' Pushing back her hair again, she continued. 'Was it not impossible to fly faster than he who held the speed record? And did you not then show that it was possible? Was it not impossible to land on Lake Kiju? *And did you not make it possible?*' Her eyes blazed with the fire of her anger. 'I cannot believe that you sit there and deny such a challenge. I cannot believe it. Yes, you are only half a man . . . and I have wasted my time to come here to this peasant hut.'

Kit had not moved so fast for a long time. Pushing himself to his feet, he took the two strides to reach her and caught her against him to revive the magic of holding this compelling girl in his arms. With his face buried in her hair, he rode out the shock of her arrival. Then he began to kiss her with the hunger of fourteen months. She returned his fierce kisses, saying between them, 'Still spinning, darling?' and he replying between his, 'I'll always be spinning where you're concerned.'

Sylva achieved more than Dr Kleist could ever hope for. During the subsequent consummation of their mutual passion, Kit discovered that he could more than adequately satisfy a woman. When they finally lay lethargically in each other's arms, she began to persuade him that he could also control an aircraft.

'You can do it, because it is as natural to you as walking or enjoying a woman,' she reasoned, stroking his chest lightly with her fingertips. 'Loss of faith comes to every aviator, at some time, but always it returns. There is in us all a need to leave this earth behind and make communing with the gods, and so we go even if we are afraid. You *will* go, Kit. You will go with me across the great glittering white snows, as we have planned. I have made some maps and calculations, and already I have write to Steen for him to make application that we do this in the spring.'

Scrambling from his side, she took a small attaché-case from the pile of her luggage and brought it back to the bed. Kit watched her with continuing wonder and disbelief that a woman such as she actually existed, and had come from Africa when he most needed her. Running his gaze over her compact vital body he owned that passion with Sylva was an equal partnership. What she wanted from him she took, for as long and as often as she wished. He was welcome to do the same, and the result was heady; so heady he was unwilling for the sudden switch to cool, businesslike female aviator.

'See here,' she invited, taking from the case a sheaf of papers and selecting one as she sat cross-legged on the pillow beside him. 'I have plot two routes. We must decide which is best but, as I know the Arctic and you do not, you must trust me to say right.' Pointing to the map marked with red ink, she explained. 'This is easiest, but is long. The other crosses difficult areas – the weather can change disastrous very quick – but you must first see what machine you can buy before knowing the range we can have.'

'Sylva,' Kit intervened gently, 'you're racing ahead with plans we can't consider yet.' Sitting up beside her, he went on, 'I haven't done any flying for fourteen months, and I have no idea how much my skill will have been affected by the injuries. I do know that I'm slower to think, and to act, than I used to be. Before we can even consider this flight together, I'll have to put in a great number of hours in the air before coming to grips with my limitations. Darling, I've no notion what I'll be like in any aircraft now, much less how much use I'd be to you on a gruelling test such as you're planning.'

Studying him frankly, apparently unconcerned with how her nakedness might be affecting his ability to concentrate on serious matters, she demanded, 'You have been from hospital twelve days. Why is it you have not yet done some flying?'

He offered no defence. It would be pointless to say again that he had been led to believe it lay beyond his present capabilities. She had already ruthlessly flattened that theory. In truth, he was still too overwhelmed by the events of the past hour to think straight about anything.

'Kit Anson, do you wish to make this record with me?' she asked urgently.

'Yes, very much. You know I do,' he told her. 'But I'll need time.'

Throwing the papers back into the case and snapping it shut, she smiled. 'Then we shall waste none of it. Put on your clothes, then go out and fly.'

'I'd have to persuade Tom to let me try.'

'Go then!' she commanded, flapping her hands in a shoo-ing motion. 'Go and persuade.'

'It won't be at all easy,' he warned, still overwhelmed by her vitality.

'Phoo! You can persuade me easy. That means you can persuade anyone.' Grasping both his hands, she leaned forward to kiss him full on the mouth. 'We shall fly the snow route and have the whole world in wonder at what we have done. We are two alike, darling, and that is very rare. Go out and fly. I am so impatient for this.'

'I'd do anything for you, Kit – even cut off a leg – but nothing on earth would induce me to allow you behind the controls of one of my aircraft,' Tom said emphatically.

Prepared for such opposition, Kit reminded him that he was speaking to his company's leading pilot.

'My *former* leading pilot,' his friend countered ruthlessly. 'I refuse to be responsible for your aerial suicide. Besides, I can't afford to lose any of my machines.'

They were facing each other across the desk in Tom's office overlooking the slipways, each determined to win an argument only their close relationship made possible. Kit would not get even this far with any other aircraft owner, he was well aware.

'If I didn't have too many scruples to hit a one-eyed man, I'd land a punch to close the other one in retaliation for that insult to my skill,' Kit said.

'Ha! I'd have ducked long before it reached my face,' Tom informed him coolly. 'You're too damned slow, old lad.'

'You can't be sure of that until I give you proof of it.'

The big, rangy red-haired man shook his head. 'Herr Doktor Kleist gave me all the proof I need, thanks. If you couldn't hit that bloody great gong foursquare each time it swung past your eyes, you'd never take up one of my aircraft and bring it safely down again.'

Kit got to his feet restlessly. 'All right, I'll admit my performance with the gong was pretty pathetic, but I haven't been hitting them for a living since the age of eighteen, have I? I wasn't born with a fantastic gift for thumping gongs with a hammer, I didn't break the world gong-bashing record in 1932 and I didn't test a prototype medical toy all the way to Africa and back, did I? Wait until I go up and fail to return before you pass judgement on my ability.'

'No thanks, I like you too much to stand by and watch you kill yourself . . . especially in one of my own valuable machines.'

'To hell with your valuable machines,' Kit told him, growing angry. 'Before I take off, I'll sign an undertaking to pay for any damage caused during the flight.'

Tom tipped his chair back on two legs, as he studied Kit with a deepening frown. 'Dead men can't pay compensation, and even if you were still breathing long enough for me to have a hope of coming to collect it, you haven't a bean. Forget it, Kit.'

Kit was deeply shaken. He had expected opposition from his friend, but not total lack of faith. Yet, even as he faced Tom, he acknowledged that until Sylva had come this morning his own faith in himself had been nonexistent. She had restored it so swiftly, and the elation of feeling self-confident after fourteen months was so welcome, he was loath to surrender it again. With the fight going out of him, he leaned on the desk to appeal rather than demand.

'I *need* this chance to prove myself, Tom. No other man is likely to give it to me.'

The other man shook his head once more. 'Neither is this man. I'm sorry . . . more sorry than I can say.' As Kit straightened up filled with bitter disappointment, Tom added, 'I know how hard it is. How do you imagine I feel each time I hear engines roar into life, then stand at that window to watch some other man racing a sleek machine across the water to soar up into that most thrilling element of all?'

Kit walked to the window Tom indicated. From there, he could see the activity around the hangars, slipways and warehouses. Alongside number three jetty lay *Sunflower*, one of Western Med's yellow flying boats recently in from Alexandria. As Kit watched, a slim youngster in the light-green summer uniform of the company came from the hull carrying his overnight bag. His throat constricted as he followed Joss' progress along the jetty, recalling the boy's avowal that he would miss flying with one of the few pilots who could have carried off the Kiju rescue successfully.

Swallowing hard, Kit said over his shoulder, 'If I had lost an eye, I'd accept what you've been forced to accept. But I haven't lost an eye . . . or a limb. I haven't lost my nerve, either.'

'Neither have I, but it takes a hell of a lot more than nerve to be a good pilot,' came the quiet comment. 'Good

God, you saw the evidence of that in Spain. Remember Polanski . . . and young Cater-Smythe? Chock-full of courage and fiery dedication, but they went down on their first assault because they weren't quick enough in combat. You know damned well that half the art of successful flying is the ability to react instinctively and fast. You had that ability in full measure. Don't be stupid enough to imagine you still have it, simply because this Lindstrom woman has made it clear she doesn't want you unless you have.'

Kit swung round furiously. 'Leave her out of this.'

Letting his chair drop back on to all four legs again, Tom allowed a significant pause to elapse before saying, 'How can we? It's her arrival today which has prompted this very unwelcome conversation.'

Kit had no answer to that charge. It kept him silent for long enough to allow Tom to leave his chair and walk across to join him by the window. As they stood side by side looking out at the river where *Sunflower* rode peacefully after her flight through the Mediterranean, Tom said, 'I loved Margaret Ralston so much I virtually destroyed her husband's political career, I brought disgrace and dishonour to my entire family, and I gave up my country for her sake. After waiting six months for her to join me in Baghdad, as she had promised, I realized that she had no intention of coming. I later learned that she had returned to her husband, who had begun a new successful venture in the city, and that the scandal had blown over.' Glancing across at Kit, he added, 'I think I'm still in love with my memories of her, but I'm bloody glad I never went so far as to contemplate killing myself for the privilege of her affection.'

Digger and Morris were now leaving the flying boat to walk along the jetty, talking animatedly together. Kit thought of Naples and the party given by Benzini's family and friends for a man they still considered to be a hero. After that party, he had become a hero again to those men of his crew. Was he now going to accept defeat without putting up a fight?

Looking gravely at Tom, he said, 'If I lose her along with the only other thing which makes my life worthwhile, there are plenty of other ways to commit suicide.'

His friend gave an impatient gesture. 'You're a bigger fool than I imagined.'

'Tom, I served a two-year prison sentence which lost me my professional standing as well as personal respect, because I found out that a ruthless man had stolen my father's finest achievement to bestow on his spineless son. I served a further two years with a metaphorical begging bowl in my hand, until the war in Spain offered me the first rung in the ladder back to self-respect. You then offered the second rung by giving me a job I could have found with few other men. I'm now back again at the bottom of the ladder, and you're telling me you're going to pull it away altogether.'

'Too right, I am, and it's for your own good, believe me,' came Tom's unrelenting response. 'You can't take up one of *my* machines.'

Desperate, Kit asked, 'What about *Gina*? She's so old and shaky, you won't be risking much.'

'You're not old and shaky, Kit. You'd be risking everything.'

As Tom made to turn away, Kit caught his arm. 'Let me just taxi her out to sea and back. I'd see how I managed to handle the controls, but I'd not attempt to take her up.'

'*Ha!*' Tom exclaimed sarcastically. 'Pull the other one, lad. Once you got her well clear of the company buildings, you'd be off to Madeira without so much as a backward glance. I'm half blind, not half-witted, Kit. I won't do it, and that's final.'

As he watched Tom walk back towards his desk, Kit decided he had no alternative but to hit below the belt. 'That's what I said when you went on your knees to persuade me to give the company its finest break by captaining the flight of *Flamingo*. I won't do it, and that's final, I swore, but you all turned the thumbscrews until I gave in. If I had stuck to my guns and stayed here, I wouldn't have spent fourteen months in hospital suffering great pain . . . and I wouldn't now be on *my* knees asking for the chance to prove a point one way or the other.'

Tom halted with his back to Kit, and let out a long breath. 'As a school boxing champion didn't you ever learn the Queensberry Rules?'

'They only apply when it's a sporting contest. Once you start fighting for your life, they go out of the window,' Kit told him quietly. 'Well, Tom?'

The following four weeks proved to be some of the happiest Kit had ever known. Although he had used unfair tactics to coerce Tom into surrendering against his better judgement, and although he was driven by the need to prove himself to the woman he loved, he was too wise and experienced to ignore caution. With Tom in the right-hand seat, he did no more than taxi *Gina* from the jetty to open sea and back several times during the first two days. On the third, he declared himself ready to take her up. With Tom's remark that they were two crocks preparing to take another into the air ringing in his ears, Kit taxied *Gina* out to a lively sea on a day of endless visibility. Even with these ideal conditions, however, he was deeply dismayed by the clumsiness of the take-off.

'Christ, I'm little better than a student making his first attempt,' he swore, as he fought to lift the old aircraft from her bouncing run across the rippling surface.

Tom was silent until they were safely airborne and flying level. Then, he said dryly, 'If that was your idea of a take-off, I'm dreading the landing.'

He had good cause for his pessimism. Landing was always a very hazardous procedure in marine aircraft, and Kit found himself experiencing uncharacteristic panic as they dropped lower and lower to meet the shifting, dazzling waves. Telling himself that Tom was right, and he had suffered some brand of madness in believing he could still do what had once been a supreme skill, he pancaked *Gina* then almost lost control of her altogether as she ploughed onward with spray flying past the cockpit like a blizzard. By the time he brought her into the estuary and taxied to where Western Med had its base, he was sweating, shaken and ready to admit defeat. Back alongside the jetty by the warehouses, he cut the engines and looked across at Tom.

'All right, I know what you're about to say,' he told his friend heavily. 'And you're absolutely right.'

'Still got a high opinion of yourself, have you?'

'Eh?'

'I was about to say that I thought your flying days were over, but you've just proved me wrong. If I could do what you've just done, I'd be back in the pilot's seat like a shot,' Tom smiled. 'It was a bit rough, but at no time did I have the urge to take the controls. The first solo's always daunting. You'll do better tomorrow.'

'You're crazy!' exclaimed Kit, light-headed with reaction.

'Not half as crazy as you are. Go on, you silly sod, get on home and tell that girl of yours she's got a budding aviator for a lover.'

With every subsequent flight, Kit found his inborn skill slowly returning. With it came confidence, and a sense of growing elation. Impossible though he had believed it to be, his passion for Sylva had grown even more addictive. She had given him back his staff of life; she knew and understood all he confided to her about these flights of hope he was making. They talked on every aspect of aviation, each as eager and knowledgeable as the other. While Kit re-developed his flying skills, Sylva kept hers alive by accepting commissions to transport wealthy people on private business trips within the Iberian peninsula.

They also made love with matching skill and enthusiasm. More often than not, Kit would drive with reckless speed along the coastal track after longer and longer flights in *Gina*, aching to tell Sylva of his delight in success, only to find her lying naked on a mat in the sunshine, despite the presence of Mrs Valenques who cooked for them both. She could never understand his reluctance to strip and join her, because she saw no reason why they could not indulge their desire for each other beneath the eyes of someone she dismissed as a mere peasant.

'But it's so enjoyable in the open air with the sun on the skin,' she always protested, when he threw a towel over her then took her in to the bedroom, all thoughts of his recent flight forgotten.

'It's more enjoyable with no one looking on. You wouldn't want peasants in the cockpit during one of your Arctic flights, would you? This is the same.' Running his hands across her body still hot from the sun, he would always experience that feeling of spinning out of control. When they were alone, however, they would frequently scramble down the low cliffside to swim naked in the blue-green water, then return to the patio to sunbathe. Sylva would spread her hair out around her head to dry, and Kit would be intoxicated by her very lack of provocativeness. That she could lie totally nude beside his own naked body after an exhilarating swim, with utter unselfconscious relaxation, was a trait he found irresistibly exciting. Although she made no effort to lure him, her stillness beckoned more compellingly than any fluttered eyelashes.

Life was full of discovery and promise during those first weeks of August. If Sylva drove him to the heights sexually, she also did it practically, urging him to put in as many hours in the air as Tom would allow. Kit did his best to convince her that his progress was slower than she appeared to think, but she could not accept any suggestion of back-pedalling on the project so dear to her heart. However, the happiness Sylva brought allowed him to accept philosophically the knowledge that his injuries had indisputably placed limits on his natural skill. He was now a good competent pilot, if not a brilliant one. That was more than he had dared hope for, until she had arrived to make him a whole man once more.

During the third week of August, two things occurred which were to change Kit's life irrevocably. The free world was stunned by the signing of a non-aggression pact between Russia and Germany. That mighty threat which the European powers had counted on to keep Hitler contained on the eastern front, had agreed to take a neutral view of any activities by her warmongering neighbour. Real fears of wide-scale conflict now set Britain and Western Europe building defences, mobilizing territorials to augment their tiny fighting forces. No one any longer doubted that a second attempt by Germany to establish herself as the world's major power was inevitable. Free peoples stood holding their breath as they waited for the blow they knew would come.

In Lisbon, capital of a habitually neutral country, there was a sudden influx of additional staff at foreign embassies, plus an unusual number of influential civilian visitors taking an unscheduled holiday in Portugal. No one with intelligence was fooled for one moment, and this evidence of diplomats and spies taking up advantageous positions in this tiny country giving easy access to the Mediterranean, and to the Atlantic leading to the English Channel, served to convince onlookers that the world was already at war even if it had not been declared.

Kit was deeply concerned as he drove from the cottage to the Western Med offices three days after the news of the Russo–German pact. As an Englishman, his first duty would be to return home and join the fighting forces. Morris and Joss would face that same dilemma. Tom was medically unfit but, despite being treated shabbily by his countrymen in the past, there was no stauncher patriot. Kit was the same. Britain's press and many of her people had been merciless towards him, but that green island was still home to him. The thought of peaceful little Sheenmouth being filled with arrogant men in jackboots filled him with peculiar rage. However, against that underlying compulsion to defend all he had known since birth, was the tug of his love for Sylva. There had never been a woman like this; never a passion so all-consuming. He could not deny that she held him in thrall, or that he dared not contemplate life without her. Small wonder he was worried and distracted as he parked his car and made his way up the steps, through the operations room to the shaky lift, then up to Tom's office. Awaiting him there was the second development which was to affect him so dramatically in the years to come.

They discussed the situation with matching consternation for several minutes, then Tom changed the subject determinedly.

'Perfect flying weather today, old lad, so I've a favour to ask.'

Kit grunted. 'I know your "favours" of old, you rogue. You'll twist my arm and give me no choice. "Favour", be blowed. So what is it that no one else would be fool enough to do for you?'

'I'd like you to test fly *Flamingo* for me.'

After several seconds had elapsed, during which they regarded each other across the desk, Kit said, 'Would you mind repeating that?'

Lighting a cigarette, Tom drew on it and exhaled before saying, 'She's ready, I need her, and you know her better than anyone.'

'Give her to Joss. He knows her,' Kit suggested immediately.

'Can't. He's gone to Alex.'

'One of the others – Pele, Miguel . . . or even Constantin. They're all good pilots.'

464

'Sure they are. You happen to be the ideal man for the job.'

As Kit got to his feet, thrusting his hands into his pockets while he tried to take in what Tom had just offered him, his friend asked, 'Not afraid, are you? No silly notions about a jinx?'

Kit shook his head. 'Just knocked sideways. I never dreamed . . . I mean, you really have thought seriously about this?'

'The job of test pilot carries a salary. It should put a stop to your annoying habit of touching your friends for a fiver each time you need to fill up that car of yours.'

'You've paid out so much on Kleist's bills already. I can't accept any more from you.'

'Dope! Kleist gave me back my best pilot, so it was a good investment. Now you'll be doing an honest job of work instead of skylarking around in *Gina*, you're back on the payroll.'

'How will I ever repay you, Tom?' he asked, trying to mask his emotion.

The red-haired man stood with a grin. 'You can begin by using your first pay packet to buy dinner for your closest pals, and introduce them to this woman who has turned your head so badly you have no idea which course you're on. I've already waited far too long for the thrill of meeting the fabulous Sylva Lindstrom.'

'Just keep your eye and hands off her, that's all,' Kit warned, not without justification. 'That black patch somehow makes you devilish attractive to women.'

'Unsure of her, are you?'

Kit chose not to answer that, and instead turned to the prospect of testing the rebuilt *Flamingo*. She looked so different painted yellow as she rode at anchor just off the slipway, yet her sleek lines were unmistakable. Momentarily, he wished Warren could be there to see her, then he dismissed the thought. Neither he nor Leone Kirkland had contacted him since the crash. Presumably, they held him responsible despite the findings of the inquiry. When he climbed on to the flight deck from the empty hull, and walked through to the cockpit, that sense of unity with her he had had throughout the flight to Africa returned to fill him with fresh enthusiasm. She was a work of art, a marvel of engineering, and she was his again. Tom had no notion of the boost he was giving with this gesture . . . yet, perhaps he had. Kit would be for ever grateful to him, either way.

With Tom and an engineer aboard, he began his first test by taxiing out to open sea and checking the acceleration ratio. The engines, with two replacements sent out from England, sang sweet music to his ear as he increased then diminished power during the surface runs. Tom was already impressed, but he had not yet experienced the aircraft's greatest virtue. Kit could not wait to show his goddess off, and eventually announced his intention to take her aloft. With all else forgotten save the overriding thrill of that short, tremendously powerful take-off, he taxied to the starting point and put the machine into her spectacular manoeuvre. As *Flamingo* surged forward at his touch, he was back on Lake Kiju heading for those trees at the end of the short waterway. Spray flying, hull bumping and shuddering, and engines growling their power triumphantly, *Flamingo* raced for the wall of jungle then lifted from the water to climb up and over the top with mere feet to spare. He had done it!

A voice beside him returned him to the present. 'Christ, what's the bloody rush?'

He turned to Tom with a ridiculously proud smile. 'She's always like that. She's going places, this beauty.'

'Mmm, Miss Lindstrom has a rival, it appears.'

Fixing his gaze ahead once more, where the turquoise sea ran onward to the shores of England and Sheenmouth, Kit said, 'I was present at *Flamingo*'s conception, you know. I worked with Warren on the initial sketches, so I feel she comprises a small part of me. Unlike Donald Kirkland, I didn't claim equal credit with the man whose superb creation she really is. The only reason I'm sorry that man is dead is because he can now never be deprived of that claim. *Aphrodite* was different. My father was no longer alive to suffer the flames of suppressed anger at being the victim of Kirkland treachery. Warren was, and that flight to Africa must have given him as much pain as triumph. He's a bigger man than I am, because I could never have let that bastard steal half my thunder and get away with it.'

'He's married to the sister now. Perhaps she'll do something.'

Kit shook his head. 'He'll never tell her. He's far too nice a chap . . . and far too good for a girl like her.'

'You still hate the Kirklands, don't you?'

'Wouldn't you, in my place?'

'No,' Tom declared. 'I'd get on with my life and put them right out of my mind. If this war comes, as it surely will, you'll have far more formidable enemies to face.'

Turning *Flamingo* to the right over the top of his own cottage, Kit said, 'At least I'll know they're my enemies. It'll be a fair fight. That's something the Kirkland family has never understood.'

18

Kit had booked a table at one of Lisbon's leading hotels for an evening when Joss, Morris and Digger were free. It was to be a special occasion. Not only was Kit celebrating his return to the staff of Western Mediterranean Air Services, September first was Morris and Marie's wedding anniversary. With all the men threatening to drop heavy hints to the young Portuguese bride about Morris' marital rights which were being hampered by the presence in their home of her numerous relatives, and Tom claiming that he spoke fluent Norwegian so would monopolize Sylva for the entire evening, the occasion promised to be lively.

It began in very promising fashion. Kit felt absurdly proud leading Sylva into the hotel, where many interested glances followed their progress. She looked extremely striking in an African robe of bronze shot silk which left her arms and shoulders completely bare, and which emphasized the throat ornament fashioned to resemble the many rings women of certain tribes used to acquire elongated necks. Her hair had been arranged in a flat coil on the crown of her head, adding just the right touch to the ethnic effect, and her feet were enhanced by tangerine-coloured toenails displayed by flat sandals decorated with wooden beads. Kit would be the first to admit his mistress was not beautiful, but for sheer excitement and magnetism a man would have to look no further.

Morris, Joss and Digger had seen her only in filthy khaki at Lake Kiju, and later as no more than a face over a sheet when they had unwittingly walked into their captain's room in Mombasa to find out why he had left the celebration early. They now each looked as astonished as Tom, who had never before set eyes on this legendary female pioneer of the air. Sylva accepted their obvious reaction with her customary nonchalance, which Kit again felt added to her allure, but young, dark-eyed Marie was unable to hide her antagonism towards a woman who so immediately monopolized the attention of every male, including her husband. Kit noticed this, and whispered to Sylva that he suspected a little harmless jealousy might do Morris a good turn.

Giving him one of her typically forthright looks, she asked quietly, 'You wish me to flirt with him to make her love him more? Are you a masochist, darling? That is the right word? One who pleases to give pain to himself?'

'The pain is intended for young Marie. I would only be hurt if you were genuinely attracted to him.'

'With Kit Anson beside me? No, that would be impossible,' she said, with such feeling he wished the evening were now over.

After ordering aperitifs, Tom astonished Kit by speaking to Sylva in a language which was clearly Norwegian. She answered animatedly, then they both looked at Kit's expression and burst into laughter.

'Darling, if you could see yourself you would also be laughing,' she declared gaily. 'Tom has just asked me where is the best place for him to buy a comb, toothbrush and some hairdressing.'

Tom grinned. 'Nils taught me that when we were in Spain. It's the only Norwegian I could repeat to Miss Lindstrom, because the rest is rather rude.'

'Kit has learn some Norwegian,' Sylva announced to them all. 'I have teach him some hot love words, but they also are rude.'

All the men thought that extremely amusing, and Kit

felt it was time to change that subject. Turning to Joss, he said, 'I've been hearing rumours about a budding romance in Alex. Come on, out with it. Who's the lucky girl?'

The young pilot grinned self-consciously. 'A chap can't take a girl swimming more than once before his crew starts spreading it around that it's more than friendship.'

Tom fixed a stern look with his single eye on the embarrassed boy. 'I think I should be made aware of what goes on outside the area of my paternal control.'

'Paternal, my eye,' exclaimed Digger. 'Unless you've fathered a few on the sly, what would you know about guiding a feckless youth along the path of sobriety and chastity?'

'Don't you think this conversation is a bit . . . well, unsuitable? There are two ladies present,' put in Morris uneasily.

'I enjoy this,' Sylva told him. 'Men I like more than girls, but only until they want too much. My husband tried to make me do this, do that, as *he* wanted. Never did he understand that I must fly when I wished it.' Looking across at Tom, she went on, 'We divorce, you know. Then it is much better. We live together very happy, while I fly my brother and Paul for their horrible collection of germs. Ugh! Such a lifetime of work I do not understand, but I enjoy very much the flying while I wait to decide what next to do. Then we crash, and Kit comes down to the lake with such madness I think I shall watch *Flamingo* go apart, *pouf!*' She clapped her hands loudly, making Marie jump. 'But he is magnificent, of course.' Turning to look at Kit with such glowing warmth his toes began to curl, she added, 'I think I shall never forget that sight of you bringing so large a machine to so small a piece of water. I knew immediately that I did badly want the pilot who could risk all in such a landing.'

He gazed at her with a renewed sense of awe that she

had arrived here beside him after so long, to restore his faith in himself so miraculously and give him the love of a lifetime.

'What happened to your brother and the other bloke we picked up?' asked Digger, breaking the silent communion between them.

Sylva turned back to him. 'Paul died two days after you leave. I think it was the broken stomach, not the fever he had. My brother Knut is back home to work in the laboratory with the germs he has brought from Africa. He has made such study for many years. He is a clever man.' She looked around the group with a wide smile. 'That is what he has always tell me himself. But he is now made a professor by the university, so perhaps it was not a lie.'

'Any man prepared to study germs for two years in that jungle around Lake Kiju deserves some recognition,' declared Morris. 'It was steamy, vile and downright dangerous. I don't mind admitting I was glad to leave it . . . even if we took half the jungle with us on the floats,' he added, with a sly grin at Kit.

'You should try desert flying,' Tom told him. 'Steamy and vile it isn't, but it's equally dangerous if you're forced down. It can also get so hot, men have been known to pass out from heatstroke whilst sitting at the controls.' Making his way into the restaurant behind Kit, who had been told his table was now ready, he went on, 'I went down with engine trouble once, and by the time some Beduins came across me – friendly, I'm glad to say – I was suffering from sand blindness. Incredible thing was, I didn't recognize the fact. I thought it was still night time.'

Sylva sat in the chair held by the waiter, and nodded. 'The same you can have with snow. When I make the crossing to Alaska I wear the dark goggles, which makes me unable to properly see the figures on my panel. I make a bad mistake with altitude, and descend into a snow storm. When I take the goggles from my eyes, the white is so bright I am blinded. I think I nearly die.'

'Gosh, how terrifying,' breathed Joss, plainly over-awed by a compellingly feminine creature who was also a legendary aviator.

Sylva turned upon him a burning glance. 'It was the most thrilling time of my life. You are a pilot and can speak of "terrifying"? For a man to fly and think of fear, he has no soul, no communion, no passion for this wonderful thing. He could drive a bus and it will mean the same.'

Deeply mortified by her words, Joss concentrated on the menu while colour flared then receded from his fresh face. While Kit was sorry for the lad's discomfiture, he knew Sylva was right. To Joss, flying was simply an occupation he enjoyed. It was not his lifeblood; the pulsebeat without which he might well stop living.

'On the subject of narrow escapes,' said Digger into the silence, 'I reckon women are far more level-headed when facing danger than we care to believe. It's also often the most unlikely ones who reveal qualities you'd never suspect.' He looked across to Kit. 'You were still in a world of your own when accounts of *Flamingo*'s crash were in the world's newspapers, but I made certain they all knew of Leone Kirkland's courage.'

'Oh?' he murmured, frowning at mention of that name.

'To be honest, I thought she was one of your high-flown, hoity-toity dames, who flew into hysterics over no more than a dressmaker's error on her new frock.'

'Oh no, she's more intelligent than that,' Kit heard himself say in her defence.

'I'll say she is,' agreed Digger, ordering prawn pan-cakes from the hovering waiter. 'If you can still remem-ber the size of the sea that day, you'll know it needed great courage for anyone, especially a woman, to send off the lifeboat and volunteer to search for possible survivors when she knew there was no other boat available. That

472

girl did. What's more, she fought her way through mountainous seas knowing there was every danger of being sucked beneath the wreck and drowning.'

Thunderstruck by news he had not heard before because people tended to avoid the subject in his presence, Kit said, 'She was a superb swimmer as a girl, and totally fearless on a diving board, as I recall.'

'This was somewhat different, believe me. She saved Warren Grant from being pulled under, then sat on the wreck holding him clear of the waves until the launch came for us. She deserved a medal. I told the reporters, and repeated the opinion at the inquiry. She never got one, of course.'

'She got herself a husband, instead,' volunteered Morris, now happily holding Marie's willing hand. 'He'll be a valuable asset to her business. He's also a likeable sort of chap who might be a steadying influence. I always suspected he was dotty about her.'

Kit stopped the wine waiter from filling his own glass by putting his hand over it. 'Now he also owes her his life. Poor devil! No wonder he offered to marry her.'

'What nonsense!' declared Sylva, sipping her wine with gusto. 'I owe you my life from Lake Kiju, but never would I marry you for it.'

The comment came at Kit like an unexpected left hook, leaving him curiously shaken. Their passion was so mutually spontaneous and uninhibited, the lasting quality of it had never been questioned by him. So much had happened during the few weeks she had been with him, he had been more concerned with getting back into the air than dwelling on the nature of their love. The question of making her his wife had not had time to be considered, yet he now realized it had been firmly rooted in his behaviour from that night in Mombasa. Sylva was the great passion in his life, therefore it would last until death. To hear her publicly renounce something he had subconsciously taken for granted was a rude shock. He retaliated instinctively.

'I should think not. Why ruin a perfect arrangement with promises neither of us would keep?'

Marie spoke up quickly, as the Catholic girl celebrating the anniversary of her marriage. 'It could not be, anyway. In the eyes of the Church, you are still the bride of your husband.'

Sylva gurgled with laughter. 'Then he has made the bigamy, by taking another wife. In Africa, we have all been happy together.'

'I think I'll have the fricassee of lamb to follow,' said Digger heartily, looking at the menu. 'To go with it, I'll plunge into the entire selection of vegetables. I seem to have whipped up a hearty appetite. What about you, Joss me lad? Must build up those muscles to impress a certain someone during the next swimming session in Alex.'

Under cover of the general discussion of the next course, Kit struggled to throw off the shadow which had suddenly descended over his enjoyment of this evening. Despite the light-hearted banter of his friends, he found it difficult to banish the voices which whispered to him, *'Don't think of this lasting until death. She's yours until you've made the polar flight, at least. Don't look beyond that, or you're a fool.'*

As a result of these inner voices, he held her very close in his arms during the dancing which followed the meal. She was his now; he would enjoy all she offered.

'You do not dance well, darling,' she told him, gazing up at him dreamily, 'but I like it like this, slow and with bodies touching. That one called Digger goes like a prancing monkey, with feet first here then there. It is very energetic.'

With his lips against her temple, he murmured, 'Don't grow too exhausted. I have some rather nice plans for when we get home.'

'Mmm,' she sighed contentedly. 'You live like a peasant, Kit Anson, but I find it very stimulating. It makes

474

good practice for when we travel to Narvik and get to work on our modifications.'

As work was far from his mind with her body moving sensuously against him, he remained silent on the subject and thought instead of the coming night in his isolated cottage. It might be primitive, but he had the freedom to make love to her without restraint. Poor Morris had an entire family to fight for a chance to bed his Marie. Looking across at the married pair, he thought Morris should take the bull by the horns and book a room in this hotel to be sure of an anniversary to remember.

It was while they were relaxing between dances and Digger was bemoaning the fact that the girl he had just partnered had a most domineering mother, that they grew aware of some excitement amongst a group by the foyer. It was an excitement which spread like wildfire to reach everyone present within minutes.

Hitler has invaded Poland, Britain has given him forty-eight hours to withdraw, or she will declare war on Germany.

Kit felt his skin rise in goosebumps. Hitler would not withdraw. Although the threat had been there for a long time, the reality of it came as a shock. His country would be at war again a mere twenty-one years after the last horrific conflict. He could scarcely believe it. Looking around the public rooms now seething with people discussing the bombshell, he told himself that any Germans present would be his hated enemies by Sunday. Portugal was certain to remain neutral, although there was a bond of friendship with his own country stretching back many years. Just across the border, however, the Spanish had every cause to show passive support for the German leader who had helped to end their civil war. Fresh chill invaded him. Last time, half the world had been drawn into the mud and blood of bitter hatred behind the quest for power. Millions had died. Families had been torn apart and land devastated. What would happen this time?

Joss broke into Kit's thoughts with an extension of

that question. 'If it comes to wholesale fighting, I suppose we'll all have to go back and join up.'

'I'm Australian, lad,' said Digger immediately. 'What you choose to do in that tiny island of yours is nothing to do with me. Enough of our blokes got slaughtered last time getting your army out of trouble it couldn't handle. We've got more sense than to do it again.'

'Hold on a minute,' growled Morris, 'my father was killed on the Somme. He was as tough as they come, and could handle anything without the help of the Anzacs, believe me.'

'All right, all right, don't start a private war,' put in Tom placatingly. 'Don't start flocking to the colours yet, either. By Sunday, someone might have come to his senses and the trouble will blow over. In any case, Joss is the only one likely to go back and volunteer. I've only one eye, Digger's determined to cut himself free of the Commonwealth, Morris has a wife here. That only leaves Kit, and he's hardly fit enough for combat flying. We'll all carry on as usual.'

'No,' put in Sylva forcefully, drawing all their attention. 'I and Kit will be going to Norway immediately.'

'Eh?' he queried, still caught up in the drama of the evening.

'Darling, we must go now,' she told him urgently, turning a fiery gaze on him. 'If there is to be a war and fighting, it might be that we shall soon find no one to give us the money we need for this. We have to do it quick, before this Hitler can spoil it for us.'

'I don't understand,' he said, unable to follow her sudden change of topic with the speed he once knew. 'The flight can't go ahead now, Sylva. *There's going to be a war in Europe.*'

'But not in Norway, not in the Arctic,' she cried desperately. 'We go now. I have planned this so long, I will not give up for this.' Turning to face the others, she said, 'We shall go home at once. There is packing to do for our going to Norway.'

Tom, his face a picture of incomprehension, asked quietly, 'What's all this about Norway, Kit?'

He had no opportunity to reply, for Sylva was caught up in the height of her own enthusiasm.

'We have agreed in Africa that we shall fly the polar route to make a world record: Sylva Lindstrom and Kit Anson together,' she explained in swift breathless tones. 'He then crashes, and I wait more than one year for him. But when I come, he tells me he will no longer fly. This is nonsense, and I tell him he must make you give him a machine to practise in. You give him one, and he does fly well, as I have told him. Then, when he comes to tell me you have given him *Flamingo*, we know he is now ready to do what we have planned.'

Morris looked searchingly at Kit. 'I thought you'd just been put back on the payroll. Wasn't this dinner tonight intended to celebrate your miraculous return to Western Med?'

'Phoo,' cried Sylva heatedly. 'He is too good for such flying. I saw that right at the first with that pink machine. Any man can do this. Kit Anson is too great for such work. It is quite wrong for him. Surely you did not think he would return to it. We have all along planned this attempt on the snow routes, and he has been getting the practice with your machines so that he can make this world record with me as soon as he is ready. We leave tomorrow for Norway.'

His friends were all staring at him with something approaching shock, when Tom said, 'You might have had enough guts to explain why you stretched my friendship beyond acceptable limits, in order to get back into a cockpit. I might not have approved, but I would have retained my respect for you. Maybe the Kirkland family had a point seven years ago, after all.'

Kit drove fast along the lonely track, the headlights beaming out over a dark sea each time he turned sharply to follow the contours of the coast. He had marched

Sylva from the hotel, pausing only to pay the bill. They had exchanged no word, but there was a volcano of them surging up inside him as he raced towards the cottage. Sylva sat in the passenger seat apparently relaxed, which fact increased his desire to get home before he exploded. How could they have set out so contentedly, only to return with everything falling around his ears? They walked in to the place where they had been such joyous eager lovers, and he lit the two lamps with a hand that shook. Sylva walked straight through to the bedroom where, by the light from the main room, she stepped from her dress and began to unfasten the flat coil of hair.

When Kit moved across to the connecting doorway, she asked calmly, 'Why do you have a tantrum? This is the right word . . . tantrum?'

'Haven't you any notion of what you did tonight?' he demanded with great bitterness.

'We have had dinner with your friends, and everything was nice and very well until you seize me and walk away from them. I think you have behave very childish.'

'Aren't you aware that you betrayed my friendship with Tom – a close and valued friendship – and insulted three men who gave me incredible loyalty during the months I was in hospital? How dared you blurt out the plans we have not yet fully discussed or decided upon? How could you suggest that I'd simply taken advantage of their generosity in order to become fit enough to then walk off, leaving them to wonder what had hit them? How could you do it, Sylva?'

She turned to face him clad only in lace panties, as her hair fell loose to partially cover her breasts. That serene certainty of her own frankly sexual appeal had never been more apparent, as she picked up a hairbrush and began using it in long sweeping strokes down the shining strands.

'I spoke the truth. Do you deny that I did? You went to Tom so that you could prove that it was possible for you to still fly. This was for the purpose to go to Norway for our plan of a world record. You had no intention and no wish to stay here with flying that any ordinary pilot can do. Kit Anson is a champion. We both know that; we have decided that in Mombasa. We have both decided it again when you saw that you are still able to fly as a champion. Then we know we shall go to Norway. Are you saying that it is not true, that I am wrong?'

He gripped the door frame in his anger. 'Yes. At least, you were wrong to have come out with it the way you did.'

'A thing is there to be said,' she reasoned. 'What is a way, and what is not a way? I do not understand you.'

'Don't you?' he cried. 'Then I'll enlighten you. Firstly, we had by no means finalized our plans for the snow flights. They were still in the very early stages and nowhere near ready to be announced in public. Secondly, there was no likelihood of anything being done until next spring. We agreed in Mombasa, and again here, that I would have to continue working until almost the last moment in order to support us both. Bills have to be paid, and we have to eat, you know.'

She merely paused in her rhythmic brushing to raise her eyebrows at him. 'How can peasant living cost so much? In Mombasa, Andre has a wonderful apartment, with many comfortable things.'

'He also has a well-paid position as a qualified doctor,' he countered fiercely. 'Tom had offered to take me back on the staff of Western Med and I could have worked for him for at least six months before leaving for Norway. We could have accumulated funds, and I'd have given him some return for all he's done for me. Tom's been more than a friend for some years, and would have understood my decision to have a crack at the polar flights with you, wishing me luck in our attempts. I'd have introduced the subject gradually – probably soon after Christmas – and included all the boys in discussions of it so that they'd have felt part of the excitement. They would have wished me luck, too.'

He tried to ease the tenseness of his stomach muscles with a long sigh, but was too worked up to relax. 'Your premature announcement gave them quite the wrong impression. It suggested I had taken advantage of the main chance; that I was manipulative, grasping and lacking any sense of gratitude for the way they stood by me through thick and thin. You've made them all despise me tonight.'

Placing the brush back on the table, Sylva pushed her hair back to hang long behind her. With her disconcerting nonchalance over nudity, she then crossed to stand close while she studied him.

'Does it matter?'

'Of course it bloody well matters,' he fumed, turning from her in no mood to be sexually distracted.

'More than flying the poles with me?' came the question.

'You can't equate the two,' he told her, crossing to the roll-top desk where the maps and figures they had studied now spilled across it with many other papers. Atop the desk stood the photograph of himself in the cockpit of *Aphrodite*. The triumphant son in his father's stolen design! 'One is a question of friendship and loyalty; the other is a question of ambition.'

From the doorway, she asked, 'When has ambition taken friendship into account? Only to help make it possible; never to defeat it. To be great, to achieve, to explore and conquer, it is necessary to put everything else to one side. You cannot live above others, and still remain with them. If this is what you really want – these men and some miserable flying in a yellow boat with wings – you cannot be the Kit Anson I have thought you. We are not two alike. You are still half a man, and will always be so.'

He turned to face her, deeply shaken by what had happened with such suddenness this evening. 'Your ambition has certainly put aside any real recognition of what has happened since our first meeting in Mombasa.

I'm not the man you saw there, but it has nothing to do with friendships or lack of enough drive to seek the stars. I was extremely ill for a very long time – while you were enjoying a ménage à trois with Andre, apparently,' he added savagely. 'Only because you came to me as you did, and because I love you so crazily, did I go to Tom to ask something I really had no right to ask.'

Letting out his breath in another deep sigh, he found it still did not ease the tension in his body, which had become almost a physical pain. 'You'll probably never understand what an effort of will I had to summon up to take a machine into the sky again, or how appalled I have been to discover how clumsy and inept I am over things I used to do with such skill. When Tom asked me to test fly *Flamingo* I was so overcome with gratitude I almost made a fool of myself. That's an indication of how much I've changed since Mombasa, Sylva. Taking that superlative craft off the water and into the sky was as great an achievement for the Kit Anson of today as breaking the speed record was in 1932.'

Walking slowly towards him, her face was soft with love. 'Why have you not told me this before, my darling?'

He made a weary gesture with his hands. 'You expected so much of me. I suppose I shied from admitting that I was less than you thought. By next spring, I had hoped to be able to give you sterling support by putting in as many flying hours with Western Med as I could.' Unable to resist her any longer, he reached out to draw her close against him. Speaking into her hair, he said, 'This war has altered our plans irrevocably, but by the time it's over, I guess I shall have done so much flying we'll cross both poles in more than record time. That's a promise.'

He made many more promises during the passionate hours that followed but, when he awoke in the morning, she had gone. On the table was a note explaining that she now fully understood what the crash had done to him. It continued with the hope that he would understand that she now had to find another companion for her polar flights who would go with her to Norway without delay. The message ended with a vow of love for him which was saddened because they had no choice but to part.

PART THREE

19

Britain and France had been at war with Germany for eight months. With their forces lined up in those areas still haunted by the souls of the slaughtered millions who had made their sacrifice in the belief that their Great War would end such conflicts, there had been an initial stalemate. Optimists claimed that Hitler was having second thoughts now that he was actually facing the might of his country's former victorious enemies. Those with more insight waited to discover when and where he would strike next. When he did, it was swift, unexpected and entirely successful.

Early in the April of 1940, German troops swept in to occupy Sweden and Norway. Several weeks later, Holland and Belgium were also lost. By the middle of May, Hitler's triumphant army was greedily studying England through its binoculars from the French coast. The Allies had been outmanoeuvred in the most disastrous fashion. Europe had fallen, and the war had now arrived on the doorstep of those islands which had remained free for centuries. Although it seemed unlikely that such a mighty power could be halted by a small nation, the people of Britain prepared to defend their freedom down to the last man, woman and beast of burden.

When Kit arrived in London at the end of May, he was much struck by the change in the city. Most people were in uniform of one kind or another, and even the civilians carried gas masks in brown cardboard boxes slung on a cord from their shoulders. Sandbags were piled around the entrances to a great many buildings, barrage balloons formed a curious herd of grey elephants above the streets, and all signs giving information on destinations or place names had been painted over. After the colourful Mediterranean atmosphere he had left, Kit found this evidence of battle preparation disturbing. He had known war for over a year in Spain; he found it difficult to accept in his homeland.

After booking a room in the cheapest boarding house he came upon, he set out for a nearby recruiting office. The waiting room was crowded with men of all ages and types, most of whom clutched conscription papers and wore resigned expressions. After sitting for three hours awaiting his turn, Kit went out to buy a sandwich and cup of tea in a tiny café with marble-topped tables manned by a cheerful Cockney woman eager to chat. It was not long before she had coaxed from him the fact that he had arrived from Portugal to volunteer.

'Oh, you don't want to wait wiv all them 'oos bin called up, luv,' she told him. 'You'll be there all week, shouldn't wonder. No, you go straight up the stairs to the Raff bloke, and tell 'im 'oo you are. And say if *they* don't want you, you know some cocky little bugger wiv a black moostache 'oo'll welcome you wiv open arms.'

She broke into peals of unrestrained laughter at that, but Kit took part of her advice on returning to the stuffy room filled with smoke and the smell of stale sweat. Following the sign indicating the RAF department, he went up the stairs to approach a dour-faced corporal sitting at a table picking at his fingernails. The man showed immediate resistance because Kit had no call-up papers and had therefore not been 'processed' through the ground-floor sections. On hearing the explanation, he then declared that he had no instructions on the procedure for any other than normal cases, and returned to his fingernails. Annoyed by his attitude, Kit took the second half of the woman's advice, adding that the corporal he referred to would never have become a dictator if he had sat giving himself a manicure all day long. This goaded the airman into suggesting that Squadron Leader Harvey just along the corridor was the officer who dealt with odds and sods, so he had best go and knock. Kit did this, and entered an office to find himself facing a man he knew extremely well from his days of speed flying.

Max Harvey rose slowly to his feet, a smile dawning as he held out his hand. 'Good God, the last time I saw you, you were being carried shoulder high, and pursued by screaming girls bent on stripping you for souvenirs after taking the record in *Aphrodite*.'

'Hallo, Max,' greeted Kit warmly, shaking hands with him. 'It's good to see you again, but what the hell are you doing behind a desk?'

'Didn't you hear?' the short, fair-haired Cambridge graduate asked him, as he indicated a chair. 'Take a pew. I had a crack at taking the record from you twelve months later. The machine didn't stand up to the strain. I went down in the Solent and spent a year in hospital.'

'Tough luck,' sympathized Kit with total understanding. 'I'd forgotten. So much seems to have been happening since those early but thrilling days.'

'Hasn't it just!' Sitting again at his desk, Max said, 'I heard you were finished after that *Flamingo* business.'

'I damn near was.' He shook his head at the proffered cigarettes. 'No thanks, I gave that up long ago.'

A grin broke out. 'Bet you haven't given up the ladies, you young lecher.'

Kit let that pass. 'Max, it's a great stroke of luck meeting you here. I've been flying again in Portugal since last August – marine aircraft at first, but more recently some ancient wheeled transports for a freight company operating between Lisbon and Seville. I had a year's combat flying with the International Brigade back in 1937, and took the proving flight of the Kirkland's boat, as you know. Although I'm best with marine craft, I've put in a decent number of hours with other aircraft. I'm over here to offer my services to the Royal Air Force, if they'll have me.'

'I heard you were with Western Med.'

He sighed. 'We parted company last autumn, after a misunderstanding.'

'Ah . . . *cherchez la femme*, I take it. She's now in Britain?'

'No. Norway.'

Max whistled through his teeth. 'Quite a number got away just ahead of Adolph. We still manage to bring people out occasionally, especially those who would be of great value to us.'

'How?' Kit asked with quick interest, his pulse increasing.

'That's a national secret, old chap, but every country has its network of agents and undercover operations. Anyway, unless your girl is a scientist, a doctor, an inventor or a brilliant military tactician, she wouldn't qualify for a ticket to freedom.'

'It's her brother who's in the scientific line, although not in the sense you mean. He's a biologist. I picked them both up in *Flamingo* while overflying Africa.'

Max whistled through his teeth again. 'Your girlfriend is Sylva Lindstrom?'

'Was,' Kit corrected heavily. 'Now, what about my application to join you chaps in uniform?'

'Oh, that's simple enough. Your qualifications speak for themselves, so all you need to do is pass the medical and you're in. Look, why don't we have dinner together at my club? You tootle along to the doc meanwhile, and we'll meet up again at eight for a good old chinwag. What d'you say?'

Kit stood up, smiling. Not only would he enjoy an evening with this old acquaintance and rival, he would be glad of a decent dinner at Max's expense. 'Thanks, I'll look forward to it.'

'Good-oh. Where are you staying, by the way?'

'Haven't fixed anything yet,' Kit lied. 'My bags are at Victoria.'

'Better get yourself sorted out after the medical,' the other advised. 'Rooms in any decent place tend to get booked up by couples on unofficial honeymoons, these days.' He winked. 'A chap only has to look heroic and announce that he's off to some secret but dangerous destination on the morrow, and he can get pretty much whatever he wants.'

Kit spent the night alone in the lumpy bed of his room overlooking a fishmonger's warehouse. In a sultry early summer temperature, he had to decide whether to open the window and endure the stench, or shut it and stifle. He had enjoyed the convivial hours with Max Harvey, but they had spoken so long of old times he was plagued by all manner of memories during his sleepless hours. Max, a former RAF contender in the Schneider Trophy races, had openly broached the subject of the trial and imprisonment of his dinner guest and Kit, finding great rapport with this breezy man from those wonderful early days of seaplane racing, had told him the truth behind the affair.

'No one would have believed me then, nor would they now. My only evidence to support my claim was handed back to the Kirklands by the policemen who discovered the wreck of my car,' he had added. 'Old Kirkland and Donald are both dead, so the truth has died with them. My father was a bastard in many ways, but I should have liked to redeem his reputation with one last triumph.'

Thoughts of that old scandal, of past successes, of the flight of *Flamingo*, and of his estrangement from his friends in Lisbon kept his mind troubled while porters in the warehouse shouted to each other as they thumped boxes of fish one on top of each other. Inevitably, he thought of Sylva, with the usual agony of longing. On reading that note, he had gone after her and found her eating a breakfast of bread rolls and sardines in a *cantina*. She had refused to go back with him yet, two weeks later, she had been sunbathing nude on his patio when he had returned after yet another fruitless search for a job. They had been together for a month, and he had begun working for Mendes as a hack freight pilot, when she had written another note and vanished. This time Kit had discovered her in a hotel near the airport, where she claimed to be awaiting the arrival of an Italian air ace who had agreed to partner her on the polar flights. They had spent a passionate night together, and she had returned disconsolate to the cottage on Christmas Eve. Knowing he was a fool, yet unable to resist her magnetism, Kit had spent another period of uneasy happiness which had intensified his commitment to her. On the first day of February, he had awoken to find a farewell note explaining that she had to return to Norway before he took all her resolution from her. He had seen or heard nothing of her since that day, and did not even know if she were still alive. Life had been soul-destroying without her. His work with the freight company was dull and poorly paid; the cottage was haunted by echoes of Sylva and her forthright personality.

Kit had had no contact with Tom or any of his friends from Western Med. He felt that too wide a chasm had opened between them. Each month, he had sent the bulk of his earnings, accompanied by a slip of paper bearing his signature, to Tom's office. There had been no acknowledgement of his meagre repayment towards the sum spent on Dr Kleist's treatment, neither had the money been returned. Finally, the occupation of Norway had stirred him from his misery. Continuing to work for Mendes until he had earned his passage money, he had sold his possessions and returned to his homeland intending to fight for it, and for the liberation of Norway.

Max Harvey had set him another puzzle to keep him from sleep, however. In somewhat enigmatic manner, he had confided to Kit that he had spoken to one of his superiors about him during that afternoon. As a result, he had been charged to ask Kit to report to an address in Whitehall the following morning, where a Wing Commander Dryden would like to talk to him. Mystified, Kit had been unable to discover from Max the reason for the request, and he was still puzzled when he eventually strode through the summertime streets sobered by the trappings of defence to reach the sandbagged entrance of the address he had been given. The policeman on duty challenged his failure to carry the obligatory gas mask. On hearing Kit's explanation, he grew extremely suspicious.

'Where's your identity card, sir?' he demanded.

'I haven't one. As I just told you, I've come across from Portugal.'

'May I ask your business here?'

'Yes, you may ask,' Kit responded impatiently, unused to wartime suspicions, 'but I don't know the answer myself until I've seen Wing Commander Dryden.'

By now very belligerent, the policeman told him to wait where he was until further instructions on the matter could be gained, from officials inside the building.

'What name shall I give them, sir?'

'Kit Anson.'

The man went red in the face. 'Now come off it! He was once a famous airman. I know that very well because I used to live in Axminster years ago and saw him break the speed record in a yellow seaplane. Don't you start being silly with me, or I'll have you placed under arrest for suspicion of being an impostor.'

With a sigh, Kit reached into his pocket for his passport. Far from assisting his swift entry, it then sent the policeman into eulogies and reminiscences, followed by exclamations of disbelief that he had not recognized his local hero.

'Of course, Mr Anson, you look older and not altogether well, if you don't mind me saying,' the man continued, as Kit finally managed to move him inside the building and up to a messenger. This doughty employee soon prised him away from the garrulous admirer to lead the way up stairs and along corridors to his destination.

Colin Dryden proved to be a quiet intelligent man in his late forties. After thanking Kit for coming, he embarked immediately on the reason for asking to meet him.

'I have some rather negative news for you, I'm afraid,' he revealed, offering his cigarette case then snapping it shut when Kit refused. 'I've been advised by the medical board that they're obliged to turn down your application to fly for us.'

'I see,' said Kit, leaning back in the dark-red leather chair and trying to mask his deep disappointment. 'Since I was discharged from the hospital in Lisbon after the crash in *Flamingo*, I've been flying. For ten months. No one has complained of my performance.'

The man just nodded. 'Max Harvey told Sir Winfreth Calne that you fell out with Tom Digby and ceased working for his airline. Is that so?'

He was instantly annoyed. 'My conversation with Max was on a personal level. He had no right to . . .'

'I'm sorry, but in wartime certain ethics are necessarily disregarded,' put in the other man. 'Is the misunderstanding between you and your former employer too deep to be repaired, would you say?'

Kit was prevented from answering by the entry of a pretty girl in air force blue, who brought a tray containing two large mugs of coffee. The interruption gave him time to collect his thoughts, which had not yet recovered from the shock of his medical rejection. In consequence, when the girl left, he took the initiative before the other man could speak.

'Look, I'm not sure what this meeting is all about. I came over from Lisbon to offer my services to the RAF. Are you telling me the service is declining them?'

'Not at all. No, not at all,' was the calm reply, as the man sipped from the mug marked with his initials. 'We need as many men as we can get. There's no reason at all why you shouldn't be a navigator, a wireless operator, or a gunner. Your engineering degree would be of immense value as a member of our ground staff, and your experience as a former world-class pilot could be put to good working use in lectures to student fliers.' He paused before continuing, 'Your expression suggests you're less than wholehearted about any job I've just mentioned. However, you are an Englishman and your country is now at war.'

Still not as quick as he used to be, Kit finally returned to what he had been asked before the girl had interrupted them. 'What interest have you in the quarrel between Tom Digby and me?'

Colin Dryden smiled. 'Because the Royal Air Force would also not be wholehearted about employing a man of your unique ability, in a capacity others could easily handle.' Putting down his mug, he sprang a surprise. 'My department works hand in glove with the other two services on rather special assignments. Max Harvey spotted your potential usefulness right away, hence this meeting. We pounced on you, Mr Anson, because you're exactly the chap we need.

'For what?' he asked warily.

'To be our man on the spot in Lisbon.'

'*Your man on the spot?*'

Getting to his feet, Colin Dryden came round to sit on the corner of his desk as he explained. 'We have evidence that Mussolini is liable to bring Italy into the war against us very shortly. Hitler is certain to take advantage of that friendly access to the Mediterranean and, with the Balkans mostly in his hands, our strongholds there could be overrun or, at best, cut off, before we could move to save them. We already have men all along the Med firmly established and unsuspected of being what they really are. They can give us advance information when conditions are right, but a man flying between neutral Lisbon and neutral Alexandria, for a

493

civilian airline which is operating just as it has been for some years, could be of enormous help to us. He could see things from the air our men hiding in forests or mountain caves could not possibly observe. He could pass details with ease to an agent living freely in Lisbon – far more reliable than radio transmissions from secret shacks by men on the run from the enemy. He could transport vital commodities in a flying boat able to make rendezvous with small boats along coasts too isolated to patrol, and he could even pick up packages or the occasional person from places offering no other means of escape.'

He leaned forward to make his point. 'That man would be a hundred times more useful to us doing that, than he would be wearing a uniform and drawing on blackboards at a flying school. What is so very exciting about this is that our man would simply be doing a job he has performed for years, so suspicions would not be in the least aroused.'

Kit was stupefied. He could hardly credit the man was serious. 'You're suggesting that I should return to Portugal, patch up my differences with a man I like and respect in order to regain my job, then use his aircraft for spying purposes behind his back? You're mad!'

'No, Mr Anson, just very desperate. Hitler is right across the Channel. With Europe lost, and Russia and America declining to become involved, once Italy joins in against us there is a definite chance that this German madman might win the war.'

Kit got to his feet, unable to face the man confronting him so earnestly. Never had he deplored the damage to his quicksilver mind so deeply. It took a while to absorb and digest facts now. He walked the length of the room as he did so. It was something he had never ever contemplated when making the decision to come home and fight. He could not seem to contemplate it now. The whole idea was fantastic. It smacked of boys' adventure yarns.

Colin Dryden approached and touched his arm. 'I see this has come as something of a shock to you. You have time to think about it, naturally. Let me hasten to point out that you're under no compulsion to do anything you have no wish to do, and are free to change your mind and return to Portugal whenever you like.' He pursed his lips. 'However, I do pray you'll give this your most serious consideration. Shall we meet again at eleven tomorrow morning?'

Still in something of a daze, Kit walked to the door only to be halted by words which constituted another shock.

'You should take into account one other aspect of my proposal,' the RAF officer said. 'The only uniform you'd be wearing for this job would be that of your airline, so the Geneva Convention would not apply to you. If you should be caught by our enemies in the act of doing anything which breaks the laws of neutrality, you'd be shot, of course.'

The men in the operations room gave Kit a cautious greeting as he entered without knocking and crossed to the lift, as he had always done in the old days. His outer confidence was a pose. Facing Tom again after eleven uneasy months was certain to be uncomfortable; asking him for a job would be more awkward still. Back in a free Lisbon enjoying late July sunshine and the indolent pastimes which went with it, Kit found it hard to believe that he had agreed to something which seemed almost melodramatic in this peaceful city.

At first, he had declined Dryden's proposal on the grounds of his refusal to betray a friendship he had already used beyond acceptable limits – even if he could persuade Tom to give him a job, which he doubted. For a while, he had drifted around London tossing several alternatives around in his mind: should he join the RAF and operate a wireless or fire a gun? Or perhaps he should use his engineering knowledge to repair damaged

Spitfires. At one point he had even considered getting in touch with Warren with a vague idea of working with him in a design capacity. However, the possibility of reviving old hostilities in Sheenmouth had made him abandon the thought. Strangely, the thought of returning to the scene of his youth had added a pull of homesickness to his sensation of aimlessness.

Indecision had ceased when the war situation worsened dramatically. In a waterborne rescue aided by an incredible flotilla of fishing smacks, pleasure yachts and any small privately owned craft available to augment naval shipping, well over a quarter of a million troops had been brought from Dunkirk as France surrendered. Reading of that courageous action beneath enemy fire by all manner of civilian volunteers, who maybe only brought home two or three otherwise doomed soldiers in tiny pleasure boats, Kit realized the true seriousness of what he had been asked to do. The Wing Commander had been delighted by his change of mind, and several days of concentrated discussions and meetings had followed to familiarize the new recruit with the ways in which he would pass on any information gleaned during his Mediterranean flights, and how he would be contacted by various agents based in Portugal, if the need arose.

In the tense atmosphere of a Britain with her back to the wall it had all seemed vitally possible. Now, in the rattling lift taking Kit up to Tom's office, the notion of himself being some kind of aerial spy sounded utterly preposterous. It did nothing to aid the difficulties of the imminent meeting which *must* result in his being taken back as a company pilot flying the Alexandria run. Small wonder he felt apprehensive.

The door to Tom's office stood open, so he hesitated on the threshold watching the red-haired man seemingly absorbed in reading facts from a file on his desk. Tom soon sensed a presence in the doorway and glanced up.

He put the papers down, but offered no smile or word of greeting.

'Hallo, Tom.'

The response was a mere nod.

'May I come in?'

'The door's open.'

'I know . . . but may I come in?'

Tom gave him a long steely glance. 'Grown excessively polite, haven't you?'

'I always have been towards people I'm unsure of.'

Tom's mouth twisted. 'I should be saying that line, not you.'

Realizing that this was going to be as difficult as he had feared, Kit went in, saying quietly, 'I know how you must feel. I was once callously used by people I thought I knew. They weren't close friends, as we were, but I trusted them. There's an element of misunderstanding over this business between us, which has me painted blacker than I am.'

Tom reached for his cigarettes and took one from the packet to light. 'Taken you a hell of a long time to offer an explanation, hasn't it?'

'For a very good reason,' Kit said with feeling. 'Your immediate acceptance of my apparent treachery shook the foundations of our relationship. I'd been so confident of our mutual understanding, I was shattered by your unquestioning condemnation, especially in public.'

'Our mutual understanding, as you call it, had been seriously undermined by that woman. You were so besotted, the old standards of trust had been overruled by the desire to please her. I've seen it happen to other men – Christ, I'd been in the grips of it myself – and it makes the victim a stranger to his past self.' Leaning back to link his hands behind his head, Tom added, 'Passion for a woman has led gullible men to fight duels, steal, lie and cheat, betray their friends – even their country – and embark on wars. A king of England has

497

recently surrendered his crown for a passion he could not deny, if you recall.'

Kit looked at him in resignation. 'So you still believe that I used you in order to get back into the air, with the intention of going off the minute I felt ready?'

'Sylva Lindstrom lied about these sensational polar flights?'

'No . . . but . . .'

'You *didn't* plan it all with her in Mombasa?'

'Yes, we did . . . but . . .'

'But *Flamingo* crashed, and she'd been waiting a long time for something she'd set her heart on.'

'There was never any question of leaving you in the lurch,' Kit insisted. 'We had made tentative plans to start training in the spring of this year. Quite frankly, I had my doubts on my fitness for it. OK, I'll admit I was afraid of losing her by expressing my doubts, and I intended to face that when the moment of truth came. Until then, I had intended to work for Western Med, and certainly would have given you advance notice of what we were hoping to do.' He gripped the back of the chair to lean on it, as he said, 'I had no notion she would make such an announcement in front of you all. It . . . well, it certainly suggested that I was something of a rat. The worst blow, however, was that you all believed it.'

'As I said before, men become fools in the hands of manipulative women. Look at Morris. I've heard you deride his lack of assertiveness on numerous occasions. You've expressed utter incomprehension that any man could allow himself to be ruled by a parcel of in-laws. Yet Kit Anson, former playboy of the skies, dances to any tune played by a Scandinavian aerial goddess.'

Anger rose above his determination. 'That's quite enough on the subject. She went to Norway just before it was occupied. For all I know, she could be dead.'

'Not Sylva Lindstrom,' Tom averred, but in much gentler manner. 'She'll always fall on her feet. I'm sorry, however. You're plainly still under her influence, and must be going through hell without news of her.'

Kit nodded. 'To make matters worse, I gave up my job with Mendes to go to England. I had this ridiculous idea of fighting for my country, and for a king who wears the crown abandoned by his brother for love.' His laugh was somewhat brittle. 'Douglas Bader can pilot a fighter with two tin legs, but Kit Anson is apparently too slow and uncoordinated for combat flying. They turned me down.'

'Tough luck.'

Deciding that it was now time to sit and get down to the true reason behind his friendly overtures, Kit settled in the chair which was almost shaped to his contours by now.

'I need a job, Tom.'

'What as?' he asked coolly.

'A pilot, naturally.'

Tom unlinked his hands and lowered them to the desk. 'Are you serious? Am I to understand that this humble rigmarole you just dished up was simply to butter me up ready for this?'

Knowing that losing his temper would put paid to all hope of gaining this vital appointment, Kit said as levelly as he could, 'Flying the Med is going to get tricky now the Italians have come in against us. I'm still a damned competent marine pilot who doesn't lose his head in a crisis.'

'Except when the crisis is female. How would I ever be sure you wouldn't meet up with another woman flier in Alex, and go off to break world records with her, leaving me in the lurch?'

Ready to let fly at Tom, Kit gripped the arms of his chair to control the urge as he replied hotly, 'Because the world is at war, damn you. I refused to go to Norway with Sylva for that very reason, and lost her because of it. I might have been strongly under her influence, but not to the extent of the man who ruined a politician's career, disgraced his family, and abandoned his country for the sake of another man's wife. Don't put me in your shoes, Tom. They're too big for me.'

'Mmm, touché', said his friend, with surprising lack of reaction. 'Tell me, what's the tremendous attraction of my particular company? Your former crew now despises you, you're in my debt to the tune of some hundreds of pounds, and you've just admitted that flying the Med is liable to be tricky. There are any number of small airlines operating in areas well away from danger, like South America or Central Africa. They'd probably be only too glad to take on a washed-up former champion like you.'

Grimly holding on to the remnants of his control, Kit demanded, 'Will you take me on; yes or no?'

'No.'

'All I'll take from you will be enough to pay my rent and Mrs Valenques' wages, plus the cost of running the car to get me back and forth,' he offered urgently. 'The rest you can keep as part payment of my debt to you.'

'I'm not hard up for pilots.'

'I'm hard up for a job,' Kit admitted, 'and I want one with Western Med.'

Tom seemed finally struck by his determination, and looked him over shrewdly. 'All right. I'll give you a job as a storeman.'

'*What?*'

'You said you were hard up for a job.'

Kit got to his feet again, trying to work out the best way to proceed now. How far could he push Tom before he lost patience and told him to forget the whole thing? Walking to the window overlooking the slipways, he knew he wanted this opportunity as much as he had once wanted to fly the poles with Sylva. For once, he wanted to use his skills for something other than personal glory or achievement. His countrymen had gone in small boats to Dunkirk without hesitation. Surely he could do this for the same kind of patriotism.

He turned to face Tom across the width of the room. 'Because of personal pride, I suppose, I wanted you to offer to take me back before I told you this. Once you had agreed to let me fly the Alex run, I intended to let you in on something I felt you should know before I started the job. Keeping quiet about it would have constituted a betrayal of someone I still feel deep affection for despite the rift between us. It seems that rift remains, so I have no alternative but to confide in you and hope that what I'm about to reveal will succeed where my past friendship for you has failed.'

'Go on,' Tom invited calmly.

'Although the RAF had reservations about my usefulness, others in London felt that I was potentially valuable as a Western Med pilot flying between Lisbon and Alex. They put a proposal to me which initially took me aback. However, Dunkirk made me realize the full implications of their request, and I agreed to have a crack at it. Although I said nothing to them, my personal terms for taking it on were that I would only do it with your knowledge and agreement. I don't need just any job, Tom. It has to be as a pilot on the Alex run.'

'I've been giving that problem some thought,' put in Tom. 'It's pretty obvious that passengers are going to be a hell of a lot scarcer in the days ahead. There's nothing for it but to cut the service drastically.'

Dismayed by that news, Kit hurried on with his explanation. 'When I've told you what. . . .'

'Instead, I thought I'd switch to freight,' Tom continued blithely. 'The demand for food and other commodities is going to be huge, and shipping will be slow, overburdened, and in danger from mines, and so on. I'll make a fortune by ripping out seats and making my boats into freight carriers. Apart from that it'll make things much easier for you, old lad. Passengers have eyes and ears. They'd also have tongues to report your curious activities to unfriendly authorities here and in Alex. No, my friend, if you really are hellbent on this glamorous spying caper, you'll do it far easier if *Flamingo* is used for freight.'

As Kit stared at him, lost for words, Tom grinned. 'Colin Dryden's an old friend of mine. We went to the same school. One of his people contacted me yesterday, and I agreed to the scheme right away.'

'You . . . you *knew*?' Kit stammered. 'Then why the devil did . . .'

'I wanted to see how long it would be before you let me in on this vital secret. Colin guessed you'd tell me. He's a very good judge of character.'

As full realization dawned, Kit grew furious. 'You bastard! You knew why I was here, yet you made me practically crawl for a job.'

Tom grinned. 'I considered that your ego had been flattered quite enough by this proposition, and thought a little humble pie would do you some good in bringing you back to the level of we lesser mortals. Besides, you deserved to be told a truth or two, you lovesick dope.'

'You *bastard*,' cried Kit again, unsure whether to laugh or punch Tom on the chin. 'You deserve to have your other eye closed for this.'

Tom's grin became a hearty laugh as he rose to his feet and held out his hand. 'Now we're back on the old footing, thank God. Welcome back to Western Med, Kit . . . although I'm thinking of changing the company name to Spies Anonymous.'

It was late afternoon before Kit drove an old second-hand car filled with provisions back to the stone cottage. It had been arranged that he would fly *Flamingo* along the Mediterranean with Morris and Digger as his crew. Joss was now in the RAF and stationed somewhere in Scotland with a flying boat squadron but, far from despising Kit, as Tom had suggested, the other pair were in on the secret and raring to start back on the old footing. Exciting, dangerous days lay ahead. Young Joss was facing worse perils, but he would be a prisoner of war if caught by the enemy: they would all be shot as spies.

As he crossed the coastal track in the brilliance of a clear, hot summer day, Kit reflected suddenly that his life had followed an uneasy pattern of triumphant successes which always ended in failure. As a boy, he had been swiftly elevated to wealth and reflected fame when his father had been hailed as a genius for designing *Diadem*. From those heights it had been a slow degrading descent to a bed with the donkeys on Sheenmouth sands. Then had come the astonishing 'adoption' by Sir Hector, with all the amazing advantages which went with that curious status. The cornucopia of good fortune had filled to overflowing during the days following the gaining of the coveted speed record, until Warren had handed him the material which had resulted in his own destruction rather than those who should have suffered. Failure following in the footsteps of triumph, once more! Prison, vagrancy, the Spanish war, and Tom's friendship had all constituted the next gradual climb to success. The flight of *Flamingo* had taken him to the peak again. Hailed as a hero of this pioneering age for his spectacular rescue at Lake Kiju, he had then plunged to the depths almost immediately as a result of a freak storm. If he was destined to follow a tortuous path through life, where would this uncertain new direction take him? If he became highly accomplished as an aerial agent for the British government, would the inevitable reverse lead to his death?

Spotting the cottage on the horizon, he sighed heavily. It was good to be back, but longing for Sylva dimmed the peace of the scene around him. Tom might call him a lovesick dope, but she had brought to his life a quality he had never before known, and probably would never know again. It was that very quality which had somehow made her unattainable. The only time she was ever truly possessed was when she was alone in a cockpit flying across the snowfields, she had stated. If she was still

503

alive, and ever made those flights across both poles, there would be no one with her. Sylva Lindstrom was an independent spirit. No man would ever totally match up to her demands, whether as a soulmate or an aviator. He was not so blinded by love he could not see that. Knowing, however, in no way eased the loss of the most complete passion a man could encounter. It had arrived unannounced at a Mombasa hotel, and walked out on him from a simple Portuguese cottage, but he had not yet come out of that uncontrolled spin. It was possible he never would.

Pulling up on reaching the cottage, he began unloading the car. When everything was neatly stacked by the door, he pushed down the latch and opened it on to the familiar room still containing a few items of rented furniture. Sylva stood inside that room, her gaze fixed on the doorway. Wrapped in a towel with her hair hanging long, she was the embodiment of all his haunted dreams. He stood quite motionless for some moments, paralysed by the fear that the vision was born of his intense longings in this place where they had been so tumultuously united.

'I thought you were lost,' he managed, at last.

She shook her head slowly.

Moving forward, his arms closed tightly around her. 'Thank God. I'm nothing without you.'

'We *are* two the same, Kit Anson,' she murmured against him. 'I have found that, and must return.'

They stood holding each other close for as long as it took to recover from the joy of reunion, then she took his hands and led him through to the patio, where she had been enjoying the last of the sunshine. They sat, absorbed in each other, on the rug spread over the stone surface.

'I thought you were lost,' he said again, studying the face he had been unable to forget. 'How did you escape?'

A faint smile touched her coral-tinted mouth. 'I flew, of course.'

'*You flew?* Where did you get an aircraft? Wasn't it highly dangerous? Dear God, they could have brought you down at any time.'

Lightly placing her fingers over his mouth to silence him, she shook her head. 'Steen is a good friend of me and of my brother. He gives me this old machine to come with his small grandchild to safety. I leave just before dawn from this place where the Germans cannot be, and fly first to Scotland. I put the child with her grandmother, then go on to Ireland. It is there I have engine trouble. No one is happy to help me, at first, then I meet one of the men who was on *Flamingo* when you land to pick us up at Lake Kiju. He was very glad to see me and, when I tell him I must come here to you, he finds me what I need. Now I am safely here, darling, and everything will be good.'

'Very good,' he agreed unsteadily. 'I've been nearly crazy with anxiety.'

'Still spinning?' she asked softly.

His kiss answered that question for her, but she had many of her own which prevented his full expression of what it meant to him to have her back. By the time he had explained why he was not still working for Mendes, why he had gone to England but come back, and why he was taking up residence in the cottage she believed he had deserted, the sun was lowering dramatically in the orange sky.

'I have the machine in a hangar with Mendes,' she then told him. 'When I heard you were in England, I did not then know what to do about it. Now we can plan, darling, now you are back. The north pole will have to be left, for now, but we can still make a record in the Antarctic. You must inspect the aircraft to see what we can do to make it suitable; or we shall sell it to buy one which is. I have already worked out a safe route. We go from here to West Africa, then cross to Brazil. We follow down the coast of South America until . . .'

'No, Sylva,' he said swiftly, and with a firmness which

505

surprised him. 'I've signed on with Western Med today. Tom's planning to carry freight instead of passengers. I can't go anywhere with you while this war lasts.'

She looked totally puzzled. 'But you went to London to fight for the war, and they did not want you.'

'Tom needs me, Sylva, and I won't let him down again. The war's caused a pilot shortage, and I have to do what I can to help. You should feel the same, especially with the enemy already in Norway.'

She stood up angrily. 'I cannot change that. It has happen. I am Norwegian, and I bring my country pride by making this record of flying.'

Some of his elation began to die as he suspected the true cause of her desperate return to him. 'Your country-men in England are set on making many more flying records than Sylva Lindstrom will ever accomplish, by piloting Spitfires and Hurricanes for the RAF. Norway will have every reason to be proud of them, darling, because they'll be doing it in order to return their country to freedom.' Rising to stand before her, he added, 'Wait for peace; wait for me to do what I must. Then I'll go anywhere in the world with you, and break as many records as you wish.'

Her determined freckled face challenged him. 'I can go to the Antarctic without you.'

'I know,' he agreed quietly, 'but I can't make any sense of my life without you.'

She stood uncertainly for some moments, as if trying to see behind his eyes to what thoughts hovered there. When she turned without a word to walk indoors, he thought she was rejecting such a sentiment. However, she had simply decided that it was time they brought in the provisions stacked outside the door. As they com-pleted the task in silence, Kit accepted that Sylva was back with him again. But for how long? One day, he might return to the cottage and find she had gone again. Only then did he realize it was possible that she might be the one left alone in the cottage, if Colin Dryden's warning about being caught ever came true.

20

The woman looked almost crazy as she gazed across the table at Leone with dark shocked eyes. Even the most consummate actress could not summon up such depths of distress, surely, yet the woman had no means of proving either her identity or her story. It happened so often Leone should be hardened to such cases, yet she always felt akin to a hanging judge each time she was forced to recommend internment in a camp for aliens. This particular refugee from the horrors of war claimed she was thirty-eight, yet looked fifty. That was not unusual in peasant dwellers in harsh, underdeveloped districts, but this Polish woman spoke the French of the cultured classes and claimed to have travelled extensively in Europe during her youth. Her story was unbelievable in its tragedy, yet Leone sensed that it was true. An elopement with an impoverished army officer had ended in his death, leaving her with a baby. Gaining employment with a local tailor who had forced her to become his mistress, she had had two more children in quick succession before her elderly lover told her to go because he could no longer stand the crying of the infants. Then the Russians had come to the small town. She and her firstborn daughter had been taken to a barn and raped repeatedly until the unit had moved on. The little girl had died from her brutal treatment; the two smaller children had not been seen again. The woman had made her degrading way to Sweden and thence to Britain, where she hoped to join the Polish resistance fighters. She had been picked up by a Civil Defence officer because she had no identity papers, and brought to this interrogation centre which had given her a meal and a shower before the detailed questioning.

Filled with compassion, Leone began to explain in precise French that there was insufficient proof of her true nationality and loyalties to allow her freedom in this country. Watching the face which had witnessed things Leone prayed she, herself, would never have to see, she outlined the fact that although the descriptions of Europe were clearly those gained by personal experience, her memories of Poland seemed confused, uncertain or completely blank. With growing distress over the woman's expression as she listened, Leone said she perfectly understood that the experience suffered could have produced merciful loss of memory and the inability to recall precise details and dates. Even so, she concluded gently, the safety of the British people must be protected. Internment in an aliens' camp had to be recommended, until such time as the Polish authorities in London could guarantee her loyalty.

As Leone finished speaking, the woman uttered an almost inhuman cry and practically threw herself across the trestle table in a furious attack. Unprepared, Leone found her wrists caught in a wrench which almost unseated her. In a flash, two armed military policemen were there, hauling the woman upright to hold her arms pinioned.

'Sorry, ma'am,' apologized a red-faced corporal. 'She was sitting there so quiet, we wasn't expecting any trouble.'

Leone sat perfectly still as they dragged the hysterical woman away, but her apparent composure hid an inner anguish over what she had just done. Every week, it seemed harder to retain the unemotional approach necessary to the job. She wondered if it would be wiser for her to give it up. It took a clever tongue, a deal of intelligence, and a heart of stone. Hers was far too sympathetic.

Looking at the large clock on the wall of the hut, she was relieved to see the hands pointing to twelve thirty. The benches were all now empty. She could go home; her contribution was over for this week. She began collecting her things together, deciding to have a sandwich lunch and catch the earlier train to Axminster.

'Don't take it too much to heart,' said a voice from across the table, and she looked up to see the head of this particular group, Wing Commander Curtiss, regarding her with concern. 'She could well be telling a pack of lies, you know. Those engaged in espionage are very highly trained.'

'I know; too well trained to wander around England without papers of any kind. She was telling the truth . . . and I think I might just have condemned her to the kind of madness she's been fighting for many months.'

He reached out to take up her small case in gentlemanly fashion, and fell in beside her as she walked from the room. 'You haven't condemned her to anything, Mrs Grant, it's the rules of war which have done that. The enemy is doing far worse to people over there. Your sessions with us must have made you aware of that.'

She frowned up at him. 'A thief can never be excused simply because he points out that there are murderers in the same world.'

'You're really upset,' he said then. 'I'm sorry.'

'Something about her eyes bothered me,' Leone confessed. 'They had witnessed so much, and seemed to beg me to see it, too.'

The RAF officer held the door for her to go through to the corridor, and changed the subject in a way which surprised her. 'I'd like to invite you to lunch. I trust you have no plans to return to Devon immediately.'

'I had thought of catching the earlier train.'

'Oh dear, could you possibly revise that?'

Even more surprised, she glanced up at him curiously.

'This is very sudden, isn't it? Compensation for my being brutal to one of your refugees?'

He smiled. He was very attractive when he did so. 'I have an ulterior motive, as it happens. A friend of mine is very anxious to meet you, so when he knew you'd be in London today he expressed a hope that we could all lunch together and save him a journey to Sheenmouth. I'd be very pleased if you could manage it. The Regency isn't far from here, and I'd enjoy your company, anyway.'

'Who is your friend?' she asked, as they reached the street.

'I'd sooner leave him to tell you himself.'

Leone decided that she could meet this mysterious person. With daylight lasting well into the evening now, she could afford to take time to enjoy a civilized lunch with this charming man and his friend. They strolled the short distance to the restaurant, enjoying the July warmth of an uneasy London waiting for an attempted invasion from an enemy now no more than twenty-two short sea miles from the coast of England. During the walk, her companion asked if she thought they were on good enough terms to use first names.

'I'd be delighted if you'd call me Philip. Each time you say "Wing-Commander" in formal tones, it bruises my sensitive soul. After all, if you were another man, I'd be calling you James and sharing a scotch and soda after our weekly meeting, by now.'

She laughed as he held open the heavy door of the Regency for her to enter. 'As you're about to buy me lunch, I think I could manage Philip.'

The arthritic silver-haired waiter greeted her escort as an old friend and led the way to a corner alcove, departing again as soon as they were seated and had ordered dry martinis. Leone found herself being treated to a study of considerable warmth.

'I hope my friend is impossibly delayed, Leone.'

'Oh? I thought the meeting was rather important.'

'I'd like to take the opportunity to get to know you better.'

'Really . . . why?'

He was too sophisticated to be disconcerted by her cool tone. 'You're a fascinating woman. Owner of an aviation company and a spectacular home which was formerly a monastery, a qualified pilot, fluent in most European languages . . . and disconcertingly attractive. I trust your husband appreciates his good fortune.'

'He's a gifted designer and engineer. He also provides a staunch shoulder to lean on in any crisis,' she returned. 'It's I who have to appreciate good fortune, Philip.'

He grimaced. 'Oh my, a truly loyal wife! Bang go all my hopes.'

'I trust there really is a friend who's anxious to meet me,' she said teasingly.

'Sadly, yes.' He paid the waiter for the drinks, then leaned back comfortably to ask, 'How do you manage to cope with everything? Each Tuesday and Wednesday you work for us on the refugee committee, taking additional translations home to do in your precious spare time, yet you somehow control a large aviation company in Sheenmouth. You must be astonishingly efficient. Tell me about your life.'

Sipping her drink, she said, 'You've an exaggerated idea of what I do. When my brother was killed, I was advised to sell the company. However, I felt that *Flamingo* was too good an aircraft to hand over to someone else, so I held on to Kirkland's in order to manufacture her myself. Warren and I built an additional hangar and workshop, then went into production with a long list of orders.' She made a rueful face. 'It was no end of a struggle, at first. We had to borrow heavily to buy raw materials and find the wages for extra workers. The young enthusiastic managing director we engaged sank a lot of his own money into the project, hoping for rich dividends. Poor Jim! He was killed at Dunkirk,' she said sadly.

'I suppose you lost most of your workforce when the war began?'

She nodded. 'It was amazing how soon afterward we were visited by men from the ministry. The entire company was requisitioned for war production, whether we liked it or not.'

'So what happened to your flying boats?' Philip asked, with interest.

'The two presently under construction were assigned to your RAF squadron, with instructions to complete them as soon as possible. The men were replaced by local women directed into factory work. It was total chaos for several weeks,' she admitted with a smile. 'The poor girls had to be taught welding, riveting, and all aspects of aircraft production right from scratch. To everyone's surprise, including their own, they proved to be excellent pupils. Not only are they cheerful and friendly, they work until they're ready to drop. I don't know what we'd do without them. Now, Kirkland's is engaged in producing components for Spitfires in the all-out drive for fighters.'

'No more flying boats?'

She shook her head. 'Not until the war's over.'

'Sorry about that?'

'Mmm, yes. We're a marine aircraft company with slipways leading down to the Sheen, which is a perfect estuary for machines with floats. There's no romance in mere components . . . nor in fighters,' she added wistfully.

Philip grinned. 'A softy at heart, despite all that cool efficiency? Whatever the company produces, it still doesn't answer my question concerning how you cope with it all.'

'It's very simple,' she told him. 'When the factory was requisitioned they installed their own overseer who ensures that the targets we're set are met in time. He's a marvel, and runs the production side with ease. My husband deals with any problems over supplies of raw

513

materials or technical defects, and he also works on design modifications for Sir Harvey Pringle's team. All I do is the paperwork. Anyone with a grain of intelligence and lots of patience can fill in the endless forms and returns demanded by the ministry. I occasionally have to deal with an officious civil servant who believes the war can't be won without rows of neat figures on pages of neat forms, but I know how to cope with people like that.' She gazed into space for a moment or two, picturing a sandy-haired immaculate man with a smooth tongue. 'My father used to employ an assistant of that type. They can be deflated, if one is really determined.'

'I'm sure they can,' Philip murmured, with a hint of amusement. 'I trust I'll never require to be thus treated by you.'

Leone was still thinking of her father and Maitland as she said, 'It's a terrible admission, Philip, but the war proved something of a godsend to Kirkland's. Far from struggling, as we did that first year, the company is making substantial profits from government contracts as well as establishing firm links with major suppliers all over the country. The stress for Warren and me has been almost totally removed: no threats by larger rivals, no fear of losing orders through lack of funds, no constant struggle to attract investors. We are told what to make, and are given the women and materials to do it. What could be easier?'

'What, indeed?'

Unable to hold back a smile, she added, 'There's also no longer any suggestion of masculine distrust of an aircraft company owned by a woman. In emergency situations, it seems we are adjudged capable of doing anything men find it convenient to bestow upon us. God knows how many years it would have taken me to be accepted in the industry, otherwise.'

'What villains we are,' he commented dryly. 'So what happens when the war is won?'

'Kirkland's will make marine aircraft again,' she told

514

him firmly. 'My husband had a dream of a passenger liner with wings. Together with my brother, he made it come true with *Flamingo*. He still has his dreams, and I share them. We'll make them reality when the war's over.'

'With a fortune to back them, this time.'

'Yes.' She grew troubled again. 'How very lucky I am compared with that poor creature who attacked me. The war has destroyed her, yet here I am lunching in civilized fashion and speaking of profits from the production of killer aircraft.'

His hand touched hers momentarily as it lay on the table. 'Those killer aircraft, my dear Leone, will wreak the vengeance she's been denied . . . and far more effectively than a single woman, believe me.'

'Ah, Philip, how very good of you to achieve what I proposed,' said a voice beside them, to betray the approach of an elderly man in the dark clothes favoured by the dignified professions.

Philip Curtiss rose swiftly to shake the newcomer's hand, but Leone's attention was taken by the woman with him. In a chartreuse silk patterned dress and a wide burnt-straw hat trimmed with matching material, Stephanie Main smiled down with the knowing expression of someone who had put her own interpretation on the innocent touch of hands between the pair at the table. Leone experienced a severe shock on recognizing this woman who had figured so prominently in an event which still haunted her with the weight of unforgiven guilt. The man was introduced to Leone as Sir Melville Pyne. He greeted her with courteous warmth, then turned to present Stephanie as his wife.

'How are you, Leone?' asked the tawny-haired girl, who still possessed that old-style beauty which had so attracted Donald . . . and Kit.

'Fine,' she replied, trying to recover from feelings aroused by coming face to face with this girl so unexpect-

515

edly. 'I had no idea you'd married. I must have missed the announcement in *The Times*.'

'I didn't miss a single detail in the press about yours,' Stephanie replied smoothly. 'How is Warren? Such a sweet, shy, *ingenuous* young man, I always thought. But perhaps he's changed.'

'Not really. He's still sweet and rather shy, but immensely loyal – something one can't say of everyone.'

Philip was now deep in a discussion with the waiter, who was explaining the merits of the dishes on offer, so Sir Melville smiled across the table at her to say, 'Far be it from me to venture to contradict a charming young woman, Mrs Grant, but I do feel that while your comment might have been true in the past, it should not be applied today. The war has brought to the surface an admirable demonstration of national loyalty which will stand us in good stead for the coming ordeal.'

Leone merely returned his smile, then turned her attention to choosing between lamb casserole or steak with salad. That done, she reflected that Stephanie had done well for herself. Whatever Sir Melville did, he had brought her a title, enough funds to dress well and flash an impressive emerald ring to complement the gold bracelet and necklace she wore. If her strong rapport with Philip Curtiss was anything to go by, she apparently also found that which her ageing husband could not give her, in the arms of willing partners. In these days of strange meetings and swift dramatic partings, it was easy to embark on affairs of the moment. No doubt, she could herself stay overnight in an anonymous hotel with Philip if she gave him a sign of encouragement.

With their chosen meals before them and after some general conversation, Sir Melville then revealed the reason for his interest in meeting her. His thin face took on a gravity of expression as he fixed his gaze on her through the gold-rimmed spectacles.

'Mrs Grant, my wife says your home has an amazing

network of tunnels and small chambers beneath its foundations. Is that so?'

Taken by surprise, she replied, 'Well, yes. They were reputedly used by smugglers to store contraband goods taken from wrecks. Rumour has it that the monks assisted them in their illegal trade, but there's no proof to substantiate it. The local fishermen spin the yarn in the quayside inn, hoping gullible holiday visitors will buy them a pint of ale. I suspect they often succeed.'

The man nodded thoughtfully. 'Dear me! The existence of these tunnels is generally known?'

'Gracious, yes.' Still mystified by his interest in the subject, she added, 'Of course, to my knowledge no one has used them for years. The access from within the Abbey has been locked and barred ever since my father bought the place. In fact, there's a stove of Polish design standing over it now. There is another way in; from the grounds. Only Father, Donald and I knew of its existence, so I suppose it's my sole secret now.' Pausing for a moment, she asked lightly, 'You're not proposing to smuggle black-market goods up the Sheen estuary, are you, Sir Melville?'

Dabbing at his pale lips with his napkin, he surprised Leone further by saying, 'You could call it smuggling, of sorts, dear lady.'

Stephanie touched her husband's arm. 'Darling, you won't have to wear a black eye-patch and carry a cutlass, will you?'

Smiling fondly, he replied, 'I'm no swashbuckler, my dear. I shall do it all in very proper manner.'

Leone put down her knife and fork. 'I'm afraid I'm still all at sea.'

Philip entered the conversation at that point. 'Perhaps I should have told you that Sir Melville is an art historian of great international repute.'

Light began to dawn. 'Of course!' she declared. 'Melville Pyne, expert on the restoration of ceramics. You once gave a lecture in Lucerne to which all Heiterman's

517

pupils were marched in crocodile. You'd not been knighted then, of course, and I'm afraid my attention during most of your lecture was devoted to the very good-looking young man who operated the projector. We all thought he was absolutely *divine*.' She smiled an apology. 'Please forgive me for not recognizing you today.'

'Of course,' he responded gravely, but with a twinkle in his eyes. 'I remember that handsome young fellow. Who could possibly compete with him?'

'If you're hoping to find something of interest or value beneath Sheenmouth Abbey, I think you'll be disappointed,' she told him, finishing the last of her salad. 'My father was not a man to let a chance pass him by. He would certainly have removed any treasures before closing the tunnels up for good.'

Sir Melville sipped fastidiously at his dry wine. 'I'm hoping to put treasures in, Mrs Grant, not take any out. Let me explain, if I may. You do not need to be told that this country of ours is presently facing the prospect of occupation by the enemy. As we are an island nation, such occupation can only be effected by sea or air. Our reputation for defending ourselves down to our last breath is well known, so it's certain we shall be attacked with such ferocity as the Germans imagine will demoralize us into surrender. That will never happen, but we are liable to be left with very little standing around us when our enemies finally abandon hope and go elsewhere to conquer. It is, therefore, imperative that we act to save the vast number of paintings and artefacts which comprise our heritage. Our splendid historic buildings will have to take their chance, but I have been appointed head of a committee charged with finding suitable wartime quarters for works of art without which the whole world would be the poorer. Mrs Grant, if you would permit us to send someone to survey your subterranean storerooms and, if he feels they could be made suitable for our purposes, allow us to place objects of great value within them, they would be saved for posterity.'

'Gracious!' she exclaimed in alarm, 'I shouldn't care to be responsible for works of art worth a king's ransom.'

'You would not be asked to do that,' the historian assured her, with a shake of his head. 'We would provide guards who would work in shifts around the clock, and also make regular checks on the condition of anything we might be permitted to store there.'

'I see.'

'I do not expect an immediate answer, naturally, but the coastal towns have already suffered bombing raids and time is now a precious commodity.'

'I agree, Sir Melville, and I can give you an immediate answer,' she said decisively. 'Send your man down, by all means. If he feels the site is suitable, you're welcome to use any of it you wish.'

The thin face flushed with pleasure. 'Most kind of you. *Most* kind.'

Leone shrugged. 'One grows used to changing rôles. In my father's day, Sheenmouth Abbey was as over-whelmingly masculine as the monastery it had once been. I hated it. When he died, and I was in partnership with my brother, I began to introduce a feminine influence. After Donald was killed, the task of reorganizing the company occupied me to the exclusion of all else. The Abbey slumbered on around me until my marriage.' She gave a rueful smile. 'I was just embarking on the happy task of creating a home, when the war changed every-thing once more. The ground floor of one wing has already been turned into additional schoolrooms for the evacuees; the upper meadow has been loaned to a neigh-bouring farmer, who now has crops growing well on it. The bell in the tower of the east wing has become the responsibility of our one remaining manservant who, as air raid warden for the district, has orders to ring it in the event of fire, danger, or invasion by the enemy from the sea. The people of Sheenmouth use the Great Hall for meetings and occasional concerts in aid of funds for the war effort, and the Magnum Pomeroy Home Guard sometimes practises repelling the enemies supposedly swarming up from the Sheen across the lower meadow, with the intention of establishing their headquarters in my home.'

'Goodness me, what sterling work you are doing, dear lady,' exclaimed Sir Melville.

'I'd never recognize the place now,' mused Stephanie, in light-hearted manner. 'I'm surprised the navy hasn't yet established a submarine base in the Roman swimming pool.'

Philip decided to join the frivolous approach. 'I wonder the Home Guard hasn't thought of filling it with piranhas in case the Jerries take a dip when they arrive.'

Leone shook her head. 'Someone has already thought of a use for it. It's the area's static water tank. I have to ensure that it's kept full, and covered in winter so that it won't freeze over.'

Stephanie gave her a sleepy-eyed look, saying, 'Is there anything you *don't* do for the war effort, Leone?'

'I haven't got around to knitting khaki balaclavas . . . or providing other comforts for our troops, as some women do,' she replied evenly. 'I never seem to have the time, or the inclination.'

'Mmm, you've changed as much as the Abbey,' came the smooth response.

The waiter returned with the menu at that point, but Leone had had enough of the woman who had driven her to condemn Kit all those years ago. Collecting her bag and gloves, she smiled at Philip.

'The lunch was very nice, but I really do have a train to catch. Forgive me if I leave you now. No, please don't feel you have to come with me,' she added, as he rose. 'I'm quite able to get myself to Waterloo, and I'm sure you'd prefer to stay with your friends and finish your meal.'

'As a matter of fact, my wife and I should really be

on our way also,' Sir Melville said. 'I must report the gist of our conversation, and Stephanie is due to meet some ladies who hope to raise funds for a concert in one of our homes for convalescent officers. Shall we all leave together?'

While Philip settled the bill, and the older man headed for the cloakroom, the two women were left together beside the table. Stephanie drew on expensive white gloves as she glanced up at Leone speculatively.

'I never thought you'd end up making a marriage of convenience, but I suppose you never did find that great all-embracing true love you imagined was just around the corner.'

'At least I've stopped looking,' Leone replied sharply. 'It's clear you never will, despite your marriage of very great advantages as well as convenience. Stephanie, we've been at this table together for well over an hour, yet you've expressed no condolences or regret over Donald's death. You were about to marry him eight years ago, if you recall.'

Stephanie rose, taking up her soft kid handbag. 'I never live in the past. Your father and I agreed on that, at least. Donald was firmly put out of my thoughts from the day I went off with Kit.' Those renowned sherry-coloured eyes lit with expression. 'I fully intended to stay with him for as long as it amused me, you know. Compared with your brother, he spelled excitement, entertainment and a damned sight more passion than Donald could ever produce. How could I have guessed the fool was so drunk he couldn't control that fast car of his?'

Growing cold, Leone said, 'You charged him with forcible abduction. You claimed damages amounting to hundreds to compensate for your "permanent scars". I see none now, and if they're in places normally covered by clothing, I assume they're only seen by your numerous lovers who have not been repulsed by them. If you thought anything of him, why did you do that to a man already facing ruin?'

Stephanie's eyebrows rose. 'My dear girl, I owed Kit nothing. Didn't I once say to you that men like him were simply for women to enjoy? Once that stops, one discards them, taking what one can to compensate for the loss.' Looking closely at Leone, she asked, 'You surely still don't carry a torch for him? After what he did to your family? You're incredibly foolish, if you do. He's worthless. He and others like him live by their charm, getting what they can from all who fall for it. The secret is to take from them first.'

'Didn't you read about the crash of *Flamingo*?' Leone demanded. 'He was seriously injured and lay in a coma for months. He might well be dead by now.'

'Then it's a waste of time to yearn for him – especially when you have a devoted husband and all those essential wartime occupations to keep you amused down at Sheen-mouth.'

The two men arrived back at the table then, and Leone turned to Sir Melville, still shaking. 'I will be glad to do anything to help your committee, if you feel I can. Send your man down whenever you like . . . but please don't ask me to meet your wife again. I'm prepared to do a great deal for the war effort, but being civil to someone my family has cause to despise doesn't come under that heading.' Turning to Philip, she added, 'Thank you for lunch. Goodbye.'

She walked away, the subject of interested scrutiny by other diners. Philip Curtiss caught up with her as she reached the main entrance. He looked very upset.

'Please allow me to accompany you to the station. It's the least I can do. If I'd had any idea that Stephanie would make you so angry I'd never . . .'

Leone turned on him as she reached the pavement and signalled a rare taxi, which was passing just when she wanted one. 'It's not your fault, Philip, but please let me give you some advice. That woman is dangerous.

522

If there is anything going on between you two, finish it without delay. She's a ruthless, selfish and rather expensive whore, and will think nothing of ruining your career along the way. She did it to a close friend of mine, and I'll never forgive her.'

Leone arrived home an hour before dinner was usually served. Merrydew informed her that Warren had not yet come up the river from the workshops, so she went up to their room to take a shower then change into a georgette evening gown patterned in flame, yellow and beige. It was one of Warren's favourites. As she brushed her short hair back from her face, a glance from the window showed her Walter still waiting in his chair on the jetty for the boat to come. With all their craft save two commandeered by the navy, there was really little for the old boatman to do. However, he had been with the family so long Leone had no thought of dismissing him. He needed the occupation as much as the wage.

When there was no sign of Warren after another five minutes, she did what she had been longing to do since arriving home. It was a mistake to go to the bell tower, yet the longing for him was so strong she could not suppress it. The circular rooms were filled with echoing voices and the flitting ghosts of past youth. Meeting Stephanie had revived that laughing young airman on the brink of world acclaim, who had occupied this suite for three short years. He would always occupy it, so long as he occupied her heart. Where was he now? Was he even alive? She gazed heavy-hearted around the rooms where cupboards and drawers had long ago been emptied of the expensive clothes he had left behind on that dramatic night. It would have been easy enough to continue telephoning Lisbon without Kit being aware of the fact. Keeping out of his life did not mean shutting him totally from hers. What if he had died in that Portuguese hospital? Going across to grip the back of a chair, she told herself that news would have been published in the international press. In any event, she would have known if he had gone from the world; surely her heart would have known without reading the fact in print.

The chair she gripped stood before the writing desk. It was no longer overflowing with papers, charts and drawings; there was no photograph of *Diadem* on top. *Dad's finest design.* The tears began suddenly and uncontrollably. How he would have hated them all on the night he had discovered the terrible truth. He must have been half crazy when he stole the money and advance drawings for Donald's new seaplane; must have seen theft as his only means of vengeance on the Kirkland family. Taking Stephanie along had been additional punishment for Donald, that was now clear, but he could not have told the girl the reason for his departure or she would have used the knowledge to great advantage long ago.

Clutching the chair even tighter, she recalled the proving flight. How arrogant she had been; how hard she had tried to punish him for her love which refused to die. All the time he had known the vile guilt of her family, and had said nothing until she had tried to offer friendship. He had charged her to ask Donald . . . or Warren. Yet Warren had known nothing of it; he had been truly shocked when she had related Maitland's story. Closing her eyes in an effort to stem the tide of tears, she then cried inwardly for something she could never have. Only by facing Kit could she attempt to find peace, but she had vowed to stay out of his life, however shadowed it might now be. He had made it plain he wanted none of her, so she was paying the penalty of her family's guilt by suffering it in silence.

'I thought I might find you here,' said Warren from the door.

He had spoken in quiet tones, but she jumped nervously at his unsuspected presence. How long had he been watching her? She turned to study his expression. It was grave, but gave no indication that he had wit-

nessed her tears. She hoped her face gave no evidence
of them.

'Merrydew said you'd arrived home an hour ago,' he
went on, 'so I came up right away to look for you. You
know how glad I am to see you safely back after a visit
to London.'

Mustering her composure, she went to him with a
smile. 'I watched for the boat all the time I was dressing,
then slipped along here thinking there'd be time before
you came.'

'Time for what?' he asked, still quietly.

She linked her arm with his and began to descend the
steps to the door standing open to the corridor. 'I met
someone today who asked if we'd give permission for
works of art and other treasures to be stored in the old
smugglers' tunnels here. I told him he's welcome to
inspect them for suitability, and warned that they'd been
shut up for some years. He's sending a man down to
take a look. We might have to put him up overnight, so
I thought the bell tower would be just right. The other
rooms are far too large.'

'How did this person know about the tunnels?'
Warren asked too casually.

'Oh, he'd heard the tales,' she replied evasively. 'You
know how the locals yarn about this place.'

'So he'd stayed in Sheenmouth at some time or
another?'

'I suppose so,' she murmured, as they walked along
the corridor towards their own rooms.

'How did you meet him?'

'Through the head of the refugee interrogation group.
A wing commander who knows more languages than
anyone I've met before. He asked me to lunch to meet
Sir Melville Pyne.' As they entered their bedroom, she
smiled at him. 'Rather tardily, I recalled that the old
boy had once lectured on ceramics when I was at Heiterman's. I honestly don't recall a word he said on the
subject.'

He stopped and turned to face her. 'Black mark! Who is this wingco who bought lunch for you all?'

'Philip Curtiss. Very charming, but more interested in Sir Melville's youthful wife than me, I promise.'

Taking her in his usual lusty embrace, he said, 'The man's either a fool, or Sir Whatsit's wife is Cleopatra's double.' His kiss was long, lingering and particularly possessive. When he finally spoke, it was to murmur, 'I'd be lost without you, Leone.'

Whether his mood had been prompted by what she had said about Philip Curtiss or as a result of finding her in the bell tower she was unsure. Striving for lightness, she replied, 'Nonsense, you'd have your beloved flying machines.'

'Just as well when my gorgeous wife mingles weekly with dashing cultured linguists.'

'Some of them are so elderly they're past dashing anywhere.' She drew herself gently from his hold, saying warningly, 'Dinner will be ready soon. Hurry and change.'

He began unbuttoning his shirt. 'How was London?'

'The same as usual. Sandbags everywhere. People all in uniform of one sort or another. Strangely hushed with such limits on traffic.'

'No feelings of inadequacy because you're not in uniform?' he asked, taking off the last of his clothes and going towards the bathroom, picking up his robe as he went.

Knowing his frustration about being turned down for the fighting forces, she said sincerely, 'I don't let something like lack of proof of my war effort worry me, as you still do. I know many men and women are exposing themselves to danger – heavens, I have evidence enough of what some poor devils are suffering when I do my work with aliens – but feeling guilty because I'm not sharing that suffering helps neither me nor them. Warren, we're all doing what we're best equipped to do. It's all equally valuable to the general battle to beat the enemy. It doesn't bother me if some passing stranger imagines I'm useless because I'm not in a khaki or blue uniform. And it shouldn't bother you.'

With a sigh, she began picking up the clothes scattered on chairs and floor. He was hopelessly untidy. She might have understood it if he had been used to a valet, but carelessness was clearly the habit of a lifetime. With no personal servants now, it meant she had to tidy up after him each day.

'I thought you promised to fold your things neatly,' she remonstrated.

'Sorry,' came the unrepentant reply above the sound of running water. 'I was thinking about something else.'

Once more, she wondered how long he had been in the bell tower before speaking to her. Kit was never mentioned between them, but there were times when she was certain Warren felt his presence as much as she. This evening was one of those times. Her excuse for being in the rooms he had once occupied was weak. Warren was now being far too polite. And she? She was still shaken by the meeting with Stephanie which had revived shame, guilt and longings impossible to subdue immediately. Folding her husband's flannels and grey knitted cardigan, Leone held the woollen garment to her cheek momentarily. Her marriage was a good one. As business partners they worked together very successfully; as husband and wife they were happy and fulfilled. Shy and incurably unsophisticated Warren might be, absentminded and obstinate he could become on the subject of his work, he was nevertheless a surprisingly exciting lover. Refusing to share a bed with her until after the wedding, he had then taken her senses by storm. Someone finally loved her for herself, sincerely and deeply. It was what she had longed for during those confused isolated years and despaired of ever finding. She loved him for loving her, and cherished the loyalty she knew he would never forsake.

Warren returned wearing the open robe, towelling his

527

hair so that it sprang in even more unruly fashion. Leone put down the cardigan swiftly, but not before he had seen her caressing her cheek with it.

'Am I forgiven over the clothes?' he asked, subjecting her to an intently curious look.

'Not in the least . . . but that won't change you,' she told him lightly.

'I've no desire to change you. I adore you just the way you are.'

Striving to keep things light, she retorted, 'Only because I pick up after you. I dread to think of the state you lived in at the old boathouse.'

'A very lonely state.'

'Not too lonely,' she teased. 'What about Mona Cummings?'

He flushed, a trait she always found peculiarly endearing. 'It only happened once.'

'Then it must have been an exceptional experience to teach you all you know about such things in that one afternoon.'

Flashing her a vibrant glance, he murmured, 'I know a lot more you haven't sampled yet. After dinner, I'll prove it.'

'Yes, do,' she replied softly, thankful that he had stopped being polite.

'What about now?' he suggested. 'I'm not anxious for dinner, and I'm in the correct state of undress for what I have in mind.'

'I'm not . . . and Merrydew said Mrs Chalmers had planned something very good for tonight. Let's wait, Warren. I'd hate to have the dear old soul thumping on our door because whatever it is is getting cold. Besides,' she reminded him, 'you know I prefer to drift off to sleep afterwards. There's nothing less romantic than leaping up the minute passion ends, and carrying on as usual.'

'All right,' he conceded, dropping the wet towel to the floor then discarding the robe. Taking underwear from his drawer, he continued in conversational tones, 'I had a call from old Pringle this morning. The RAF has some kind of special mission planned, and they want my advice on several points.' In the act of pulling on the trousers of his dinner suit, he appealed to her. 'Must I wear these? It's such a warm night.'

'The temperature has nothing to do with it,' she said sternly. 'You wore them in Athens, Cairo and Mombasa, when it was hotter than this.'

'I had to impress people then. Now I'm at home.'

'Wear them,' she insisted. 'You're certain to be knighted one day, so you should practise behaving like a true gentleman.'

'Does that mean I should wear gloves when I make love to you?'

Going across to him, she picked up the black tie she always arranged. 'Don't be facetious! Go on about Pringle. Why have you been asked for advice on this mission?'

Tilting his chin upwards while she tied the bow, he spoke to the ceiling. 'One of their squadrons has acquired a Flamingo-class boat which they want to use for something rather hush-hush. I've been asked to go to Scotland to see what mods could be done on it.'

'How thrilling. When?'

'They'd like to start on Wednesday. I agreed to go up there.'

She smiled fondly. 'It wasn't a request, Warren, it was an order.'

'I still agreed to go,' he replied incorrigibly, squinting down at her. 'Haven't you finished yet?'

'Yes. How will you travel up?'

'I've cleared it with the RAF to fly myself.'

Without thinking, she said, 'Don't get caught up in a dogfight.'

'No chance of that. They'll route me well clear of any trouble.'

One look at his expression told her he was still upset

over his inability to follow his stepfather's wartime service. Aside from his weak chest which would have exempted him from the services, anyway, he was in a reserved occupation. Leone agreed that he was of more importance to his country in his present capacity, but had soon realized that was not really the point at issue. He simply felt that he was somehow letting down that long-ago Canadian, who had made such an impression on his small stepson. It was a problem only Warren could overcome, and she regretted having unthinkingly rubbed salt in the wound with her words.

'I'll miss you while you're away,' she said, smoothing the dinner jacket across his shoulders. 'How long will you be gone?'

'It depends on the complexity of the problem. They've given me no clues.' He caught her around the waist as she made to walk away, 'I'll miss you, too.'

'You won't have time. You'll be so engrossed in designing some clever modification, everyone and everything will be forgotten,' she claimed.

'Even when I'm working, I never entirely forget you. The same way you never entirely forget him,' he added significantly.

'I . . . what makes you . . .' she floundered, held firmly in his clasp.

His right hand touched her hair gently in a comforting caress. 'You've made a commendable effort to stay out of his life, as you vowed to do. I didn't think you'd be strong enough to keep it up. But, loving you as I do, I know you haven't managed to keep him out of your thoughts. Something happened while you were in London; something which upset you enough to send you straight to that damned bell tower. I gave you several chances to tell me, which you avoided. Now I want to know before I'll let you go down to dinner.'

She should have known he would see through her pretence. The secret of their successful life together was that they were always open and honest with each other.

She had hated lying to him – she was not very good at it – but had shrunk from hurting him. It was a relief to confess.

With a sigh, she said, 'Sir Melville Pyne's wife was Stephanie Main.'

He whistled, not expecting anything like that. 'Bit awkward for you both, wasn't it?'

'Not for her. She knew who she was meeting for lunch. I was totally unprepared.'

'Poor darling,' he said, kissing her temple. 'She was the one who knew about the smugglers' tunnels, of course.'

'Of course. Warren, she joked about them, about the war, and about what she considered our quaint country war efforts. When we were alone, she was extremely offensive about Donald . . . and even more so about Kit. Coming so soon after a particularly distressing encounter with a refugee woman whose life has consisted of loss and horror, I found her brand of self-centred immorality unacceptable. I suppose I was foolish to allow her words to get under my skin, but I'm afraid I was rather rude to Sir Melville and Philip Curtiss.'

'Attagirl!' he said warmly.

Her smile was rueful. 'When you're Sir Warren you won't approve of such conduct from your wife.'

His arms tightened around her even further. 'Anything you do is all right by me . . . anything except one thing.'

'Which is?'

'That when we've eaten this wretched special dinner Mrs Chalmers expects us to go down for, and you finally let me make love to you, you don't close your eyes and pretend I'm someone else. I'd rather forget the whole thing.'

Close to tears immediately, she put up a hand to touch his mouth reassuringly. 'I'd never do that . . . and you can't forget it. After boasting so patiently, I can't wait for what you've promised.'

531

They all stood in the hangar beside the huge hull of the Flamingo-class flying boat completed by Kirkland's twelve weeks ago. When she had left the workshops there had been simply a numerical identification. She had since been painted pale-blue with the name *Florida* on her side. Warren still thought her the most wonderful machine ever created. So, too, did the men with him.

'A truly spectacular aircraft,' commented a squadron leader named Fletcher. 'When I first saw her fly, I couldn't believe that initial climb. She leaves the water before you know it.'

Warren nodded, practically purring as a result of the eulogizing on his brain-child. 'You should have seen the take-off from Lake Kiju during her proving flight, after we'd rescued three people from the jungle. I knew she could do it, but the pilot had to have equal faith in her ability. Kit Anson did have, fortunately. He pulled off a superb stunt.'

'We all read of it,' put in Wing Commander Gregg, who was hosting Warren during his visit to the RAF station on the west coast of Scotland. 'It might come as a surprise for you to hear we have on strength young Hamilton, the co-pilot of that flight. He was sent up to us because he's had experience of these craft. You'll meet him later on.'

'Good lord, what a small world!' marvelled Warren.

'Not where marine aircraft are concerned. The pilots are a rare breed, and Hamilton is even more special because he's the man who's had more experience in your boats than anyone, so far.' Indicating a flight of steps at the far end of the hangar, Brian Gregg said, 'Let's go up to the office. I'll give you some idea of what we're after and you can mull it around.'

They climbed to a large area enclosed by windows, and sat around a sizeable square table on which lay numerous rolls of drawings. It was an atmosphere Warren liked and understood. In it, he was supreme. In the officers' mess, he had not been so happy, although the few members present during afternoon tea seemed friendly and not inclined to stand on ceremony. He sat now, eagerly awaiting the explanation for his presence on this station. Enthusiasm was well and truly roused.

'Although I can't give you actual details of something so secret I don't even know them myself yet,' the wing commander began, 'I can reveal that your aircraft is to be used for special missions in the months to come, due to her ability to land and take off on reasonably short stretches of water. There's no need for me to suggest the likely destination for these missions; you can guess that easily enough. What I have been told to do is see that *Florida* is adapted for her new rôle. Mr Grant, your flying boat has to be modified so that she can carry up to fifty men, with supplies, guns, etcetera. We require bays suitable for the transport of wheeled vehicles, inflatable boats or even small snow-caterpillars.' He gave a grim smile at Warren's expression. 'Yes, I know it's a tall order – probably too tall – but we'd like you to do some sums and drawings which will add up to the nearest answer to our requirements.'

Warren was staggered by the prospect. 'Yes, it is a tall order.'

'Here comes the punchline. The brass hats don't want to lose the advantage of that fast climb on take-off.'

'You don't want much, do you?' commented Warren heavily.

Brian Gregg sighed. 'The situation demands that we ask the impossible of our men, too. They're presently giving it to the full. Without men like you with the brains and skill to give them the best machines for the job, their efforts won't be enough. This office will be placed at your disposal night and day for as long as you need. Our mechanics and engineers will be on hand around the clock, should you want to consult them. If there's anything else you deem necessary, we'll do our utmost to get it for you.'

'There is one thing,' ventured Warren.

'Yes?'

'If you hear of anyone with a spare magic wand, race him up here on the double.'

It certainly seemed to be the only means by which he would produce what they required, and Warren retired early to his room in the officers' quarters that night to study his design plans and make initial weight calculations. He was still working when dawn produced so much sunlight his eyes ached. An uneasy sleep was broken at eight a.m. by a uniformed batwoman, who brought him tea. Embarrassed by her unconcerned chatter as she picked up his strewn clothes to fold on a chair, he remained well beneath the bedclothes until she made to depart with a reminder that breakfast began at eight and would be served until nine.

'We're only allowed to serve it in the officers' rooms if they're sick. I don't know if that applies to civilians, sir, so if I was you I'd get over to the mess before nine or you're likely to go hungry,' she advised, regarding his covered form with curiosity. 'Unless you're sick, of course. You don't look too good, I must say.'

'I'm fine,' he insisted, wishing she would go.

'Well, all right. If you're really sure.'

The girl left, and he sat up to drink the tea gratefully. Only when the same girl came back to make his bed and clean the room did he realize that he was still in his pyjamas and had missed breakfast. After a stammered apology from him, the batwoman went off promising to ask her friend in the mess kitchen to do a quick cuppa and a fried egg sandwich. Warren washed and dressed in record time, with his door locked against further unexpected entries. His thanks for the breakfast were diffident in the face of the girl's breezy friendliness, but when he collected his papers and went across to the hangar to work he soon forgot all else. People came and went during the day with mugs of coffee or tea. He declined lunch when a young pilot-officer who looked no more than a schoolboy came to remind him of the hour. However, Brian Gregg himself arrived in the upstairs office to drag him away, declaring that starving himself was no substitute for a magic wand.

'Take a break, man,' he urged. 'Come across to the mess. We'll have a drink, then eat a good dinner while you relax for an hour or two.'

'Dinner?' he queried, his mind still on what he was wrestling with. 'It can't be that late.'

The other man grinned, his round face looking more cherubic than ever. 'If it isn't, there are twenty-eight ravenous officers doomed to disappointment. Come on. You can leave all that just as it is. I'll lock the office, and there's a guard patrolling the hangars.'

The tidied room was soon dotted again with his discarded clothes as he took a quick bath, then changed into the dark suit Leone had insisted he should bring. Missing her suddenly and intensely, he combed his hair as his thoughts winged down to Sheenmouth. The modifications were likely to take some time, and he had been unhappy at leaving her. His reluctance at parting had been intensified by her response to his ardent farewell, which had suggested that her meeting with Stephanie Main was still bothering her.

He was destined to be reminded of Leone once more during that evening. Sitting with Brian when Warren entered the ante-room was Joss Hamilton. The youngster got to his feet with a smile and an outstretched hand.

'Hallo. It's marvellous to meet up again like this.'

'You look extremely smart,' said Warren, shaking his hand warmly. 'When did you come over from Portugal?'

'Right at the start. Well, I had to really, hadn't I? What'll you have to drink?'

Sitting next to Brian, Warren said apologetically, 'I'm afraid I've never really taken to the swanky drinks. I prefer a glass of ale.'

'Ale coming up,' responded Joss. With a grin in the direction of his CO he added, 'The swanky drinks are only indulged in by those who stay on the ground, or who can afford them. Most of the boys drink beer of one kind or another. We airborne chaps are perpetually hard up.'

'Shame,' put in Brian sarcastically.

Warren watched Joss thread his way between others in blue uniforms, who were either talking earnestly with expressive hand movements to suggest aircraft manoeuvres, or who were skylarking with each other. He envied them all. They were depending on his talent to produce what they needed for special operations, but they would be flying them. He could not banish the feeling that his stepfather would be more impressed by such courage than by miracles produced safely on a drawing board.

'He's a nice lad,' commented the man beside him.

'Also a very good pilot. He often took the controls during the flight of *Flamingo*, and flew her like an expert.'

'He'll be piloting *Florida* when you've done the mods.'

'Lucky devil!'

Brian gave him a shrewd glance. 'If he *is* lucky, it'll be due to your brains and hard work. We have hundreds like young Hamilton, very few like you. We're going to need you desperately as the war progresses.'

'You think it's going to be a long business?'

'Don't you?' Nodding towards Joss, who was returning with a steward carrying their drinks, he said, 'He'll very probably be lost, along with thousands more, but we'll train others as soon as they leave school. If men like you should be lost, we'd have a hell of a job finding replacements. Don't ever underrate the importance of your contribution, old chap.'

'I took it you'd like another of your swanky drinks, sir,' said Joss, as the steward set out the glasses before them.

'Impudent bugger!' growled Brian. 'Didn't they teach you manners in that ropey Portuguese airline?'

Joss laughed. 'It was a damned sight warmer and more

comfortable flying for Western Med than it is here.' Turning to Warren, he asked, 'Had you heard that *Flamingo* is back in the air?'

'No,' Warren exclaimed, thrilled by the news. 'We've had no contact with Tom Digby since he offered to take her off the sandbank and rebuild her.'

Joss wiped the froth from his mouth after drinking. 'Actually, she's been flying for around eleven months. Kit did the test flights last August.'

Warren felt his stomach tighten. '*Kit* flight tested her? But my wife was told by the doctors in Lisbon that he had such serious injuries, he would never fly again. In fact, they suggested he would be fortunate to walk, much less fly in the future.'

'Gosh, you're dreadfully out of touch. He was treated by a mad Swiss doctor with some kind of revolutionary theory to test. Kit was one of his guinea pigs. After leaving hospital, he met up with Sylva Lindstrom again. She apparently persuaded him he could fly if he only made the effort.' Joss grinned. 'They say love conquers all. After some hair-raising capers with an old flying boat, Tom gave him *Flamingo*. It was the best medicine he could have.' Taking another pull at his beer, he then added, 'I had a letter from the lads this week. She's been adapted for freight, and is regularly flying to Alex with Kit piloting, Morris and Digger forming his crew.' Wagging his head, he said, 'It takes some guts to pull back after being declared half dead, I reckon.'

'Yes . . . I'll say,' Warren agreed, somehow shaken by the news. Kit had recovered from that earlier affair, and bounced back to take *Flamingo* to Africa. Now, he had apparently bounced back again. The old sense of guilt washed over Warren anew. He had done little to help Kit the first time, and damn all this time. However, Kit seemed well able to fight his own battles, and maybe Leone was wise to steer clear of them. *But did that mean he also had to do so?* an inner voice demanded. There had really been nothing to stop him making discreet inquiries about his friend's progress, without Leone being aware of it. It was too late now, and the news had finally reached him in the most coincidental fashion. He slept badly that night, and returned to his work feeling jaded.

For three days and most of those nights, he concentrated on the problem he had been set. Mostly, he worked alone in the upstairs office, but he occasionally had sessions within the flying boat with mechanics, engineers, and the aircraft's crew captained by Joss. Only when he was dragged away for dinner by Brian did he relax for a while. Despite the man's words on his own valuable wartime rôle, Warren found that the lively, smoke-laden atmosphere of the mess filled with men in the uniform of the skies made him restless, uncertain even.

After one such evening, he escaped his companions early, vowing he had to get back to a half-finished problem. The July evening was balmy and filled with the fading sunshine of high summer, so the glory of the surrounding scenery beckoned too strongly. Instead of returning to the hangar, he began strolling around the perimeter of the station to reach the shoreline where squadron flying boats were moored. The sinking sun was turning the sea a rosy-peach shade, against which the distant hills stood high, gently rounded and dark green. There was an overlying hush broken only by the cry of curlews and the far-off rowdy songs of the airmen, as he walked with his hands in the pockets of the dark suit Leone insisted gave him the aura of a gentleman.

The evening was achingly peaceful. It was hard to believe that people were being killed, imprisoned or tortured just across the sea in Norway; hard to accept that half the world was now at war and would be for some years to come. The pretence that all was well proved too strong to resist. He walked on, lost in thrilling recollections of those years during which he had been allowed by Sir Hector to realize a dream, then fabricate the reality from his own drawings. Would he ever repeat that initial triumph? Would future ones ever recapture the excitement of launching his passenger liner with wings into the Sheen, then taking her out through the estuary to open sea and thence into the sky? If he was ever knighted, as Leone predicted, would he grow blasé and pompous, lose the fervour of a young man with a dream for sale? Would Sir Warren Grant lose all sight of a boy who had given flying lessons by day, to work on a balsawood model of a seaplane named *Seaspray* in his shabby digs by night? Those had been golden days, he now realized with a sense of surprise, for such thoughts belonged to the aged. He was only thirty-two. Yet he continued to reminisce with a curious ache in his breast for the simplicity which was overshadowed by fame.

Reaching the curve in the bay, he decided that it was time he went back to his work. It should banish introspection. Turning, he saw two girls in uniform walking towards him. On their way to meet secretly with boyfriends, he concluded. Who could blame them when the nearest town was forty miles away, with nothing more than a kirk surrounded by a hamlet between? Their animated conversation interspersed with giggles strengthened his supposition, and he prepared to nod in response if they happened to notice him and speak. They seemed too interested in the subject under discussion to be aware of another presence, he decided. Then, when he was little more than three steps from the pair, one glanced his way and slowed to a halt.

'Hallo, Warren,' she said quietly. 'I didn't recognize you from a distance.'

He looked at the girl intently. Round face, rather pretty, red hair tucked neatly around the soft, pleated cap. She would be eight years older, of course, and this one had little of that ingenuous rural appeal, but he knew only one girl with red hair.

'Good lord, are you really Mona Cummings? You look awfully different in uniform.'

'So do you in that swanky suit,' she replied, 'but I'd heard on the station grapevine that a boffin from Sheenmouth had arrived.'

'A *boffin*?' he echoed, at a loss as to how to handle this surprising meeting. 'Whatever's that?'

A smile touched her mouth coloured with brighter lipstick than her father would ever have allowed. 'Someone with more brains than most, who does clever things in laboratories or drawing offices.' The smile was replaced by a hint of sadness. 'You got where you wanted to be then, after all.'

'Mona,' said the other girl urgently, 'we've got to meet the boys in ten minutes. Come on!'

With her gaze on Warren, Mona said, 'I'll catch you up in a mo.'

Her companion wasted no time in argument, plainly keen to meet her sweetheart. She walked off smartly, leaving them alone on the rough shoreline path.

'Shouldn't you go with her?' he asked awkwardly. 'Some young man is waiting for you.'

'He'll survive.'

'Well, this is a surprise, Mona. I had no idea you had joined the WAAF.'

'Why should you? I left Sheenmouth a long time ago, and only went a couple of times to visit Dad. You were well involved with the Kirkland family by then, and never came near the *Clarion* office.'

He saw that tiny office so clearly, with Jack Cummings in his wheelchair behind the counter. 'I'm sorry about your father.'

She shrugged. 'They gave him two warnings before putting him in prison. They couldn't let him carry on printing all that stuff about pacifism, saying that the last war had been nothing more than a plot to reduce the world's population, and that Chamberlain had agreed with Hitler that it was time to reduce it further. Some people might have begun believing it; then what would have happened?'

'I don't think anyone would have believed such a ridiculous theory, but those who'd lost fathers, husbands or sons might have joined their sense of bitterness with his to spread a mood of despair just when it would be most dangerous. All the same,' he conceded, 'your father preached a sermon just a little too close to the truth. As a survivor of the last war, with the loss of a leg to remind him of all he's suffered, he must truly despair at this evidence of the rise of an enemy they all believed to have been vanquished. I had a great deal of sympathy with his views.'

'So had a lot of people, I suppose, which was why it had to be stopped.' She pursed her lips. 'In a way, I think he's happier locked up like that. Martyrdom is another way of using up his anger over everything.'

Warren was surprised by her reasoning. 'You've changed a lot.'

'So I should hope,' she returned energetically. 'I used to think Sheenmouth was the whole world, until I left and saw other places and discovered that people had wider ideas about things.' Changing the subject swiftly, to take him unawares again, she said, 'So you married Leone Kirkland, as I guessed you would.'

'I . . . yes, I did. Her brother was killed in an air crash.'

Her pale smile returned. 'I read the papers, Warren.'

He sighed. 'I suppose the Kirklands are prone to get their affairs in all the papers. Of course, if you were the same, I'd know what you've been doing since we last met.'

'Are you interested?' she challenged.

'Of course. We were very good friends, weren't we?'

'Rather more than friends on one occasion,' came her quiet reminder.

He felt himself grow hot with embarrassment. 'I'm

sorry about that, Mona. I've been ashamed of the way I treated you every time I thought about it.'

'And I've been ashamed of what I did out of revenge. Did it upset anyone?'

'Only Sir Hector. I managed to wriggle out of it all right.'

Studying him closely in the light of dying day, she asked, 'Did it make you hate me?'

'I don't think I'm the sort to hate people. If anything, that letter of yours made me sad to think I'd hurt you so deeply.'

'I was very fond of you, Warren.'

Gazing down at her in an isolation filled with the cry of homing sea-birds, he confessed, 'I was very fond of you, too, Mona. The timing was wrong, that's all.'

'And now it's too late.'

'Yes.'

'Are you happy with her?'

'Very.'

'Is she with you?'

'I think so.'

'You seem uncertain.'

He shook his head. 'I suppose I can't believe my luck.'

'Tell me what's happening in Sheenmouth these days,' she demanded. 'Is the Palais de Danse still open . . . and what about the Roxy? Oh gosh, do you remember the teas we used to have at the Merry Monk?'

He grinned. 'Not half! They still do them during the summer, but the whole place has changed. Mary Dell sold the café to a woman who's tried to make it posh. No more home-made scones and Victoria sponges. It's all vol-au-vents and teacakes and petits fours now. You'd never believe what she charges.'

Mona tut-tutted as she shook her head. 'I wouldn't like it now. What about the boats? Do they still hire them out by the hour?'

'A few, but it's not as busy as it used to be.'

'You used to leave your motorbike by the ticket-office

so's Dad wouldn't know we'd been on it. Amazing how no one ever told him, because enough people saw us go past.' She smiled. 'I suppose you've got a big car now.'

'Yes . . . but hardly enough petrol to run it on.' He was lost in recollection. 'The old bike was more fun, in a way. I could take it over fields and so on when I needed to take a shortcut. I was always late for the lessons at the flying club, so many's the time I'd bump across old Ponsonby's meadow and frighten the life out of the cows. He caught me once, if you recall, and blamed me for the drop in his milk yield.' They both laughed, and he went on, 'You always grumbled when I went cross-country, but you weren't so angry that you didn't scream with excitement when I went really fast. You loved speed.'

Chatting on about old times, he was hardly aware that they had begun walking back towards the station buildings, side by side, Mona's date forgotten.

21

By the middle of September the Germans had well and truly launched their campaign for the conquest of Britain. The first stage of their plan was to knock the RAF from the skies, so that landing would be unhindered by aerial defence. Day after day, aircraft were locked in battle over the east and south coasts of England. Day after day, the numbers of fighters and pilots from Britain, the Commonwealth, and even some who had escaped from occupied Europe to fight on, grew less. Like David and Goliath, however, the few in air force blue determinedly continued to rise up from an island basking in a glorious Indian summer, to send twice their own number spiralling down to the golden harvest being gathered in the fields, or to the gentle green downland where sheep grazed in peaceful ignorance of man's madness.

The residents of those counties nearest to France and Norway grew used to the wail of air-raid sirens, the concentrated roar of attacking squadrons approaching from over the sea, and the whine of plunging aircraft before they exploded on reaching towns, villages, farms, schools or churches. They also grew used to the aerial flocks of white billowing parachutes, when men managed to jump before being incinerated. RAF pilots were given a willing hand when they landed, with cups of tea, mugs of beer, or kisses from worshipping girls before transport arrived to collect them. The enemy survivors were

544

rounded up by an assortment of citizens armed with pitchforks, kitchen knives, antique swords and all manner of ancient firearms snatched from collectors' walls. These men – curiosities to most who had never set eyes on a German before and had imagined them all to be ugly and evil – were then marched purposefully to the nearest police station or ARP hut to be guarded until the army arrived to take over the problem.

The initial plan to knock the RAF from the sky, which had appeared to be little more than a routine business to the German leaders across the Channel, proved to be costly and humiliating. They changed the plan, deciding instead to knock their stubborn enemies from the *ground* by sending wave after wave of bombers to destroy airfields with the machines on them. For those few who might succeed in taking off, there would be no station left to provide runways, fuel, mechanics to do repairs, or food and beds for exhausted fliers. The systematic destruction of the coastal bases began with massive waves of bombers blackening the autumn skies, and filling the air with the deafening thunder of heavily laden machines.

Stationary aircraft were blown apart, along with hangars, workshops, fuel stores and vital communications rooms. Runways were rendered useless by peppering them with giant craters. Servicemen and women were killed or maimed as they struggled to continue operating; civilians were also killed or maimed by bombs dropped wildly off target. This plan was no more successful than the first. Still the RAF managed to get enough fighters into the sky to cause the enemy losses and humiliation. When the RAF fliers returned to find their bases had become little better than areas of burning rubble, they simply landed somewhere else. Emergency stations were set up on areas of suitable downland, on level valley meadows, and at any small flying club along the coast from Plymouth to Newcastle.

Magnum Pomeroy airfield, where Warren had given

lessons to eager pupils including Leone, and where the company Auster was kept, became an RAF station overnight in that September of 1940. It was to remain such throughout the war. Leone did not need to be told of the fact by Merrydew on a morning of soft mists and red-gold foliage. She had heard the Hurricanes fly over late the previous evening, and guessed that they had found a haven up on the club airfield. She had sent a message by hand of a ploughman from the neighbouring farm, offering accommodation and a meal to anyone needing them. A very polite man had telephoned to thank her, but saying that everything had been organized.

Warren was back in Scotland for a few days, having been called to advise on some difficulties encountered when making the modifications to *Florida*. When he was absent, Leone always ate breakfast in their room. Sitting by the open window with a tray containing orange juice, scrambled eggs and coffee, she gazed out over the lower meadow to the grey-veiled river. Out of the blue came the memory of Stephanie eulogizing on the autumn fascination of Sheenmouth Abbey. *It has an ethereal beauty reminiscent of bridal veils and the sound of a church organ floating on the still, crisp air.* She now saw that the description was apt, but bridal veils and the church organ had been at Axminster for her own marriage to Warren. The chapel, completely restored by her father, had been the obvious place for a Kirkland wedding. She had instead opted for an old riverside church in the nearby town. Reminded now of Stephanie's words, she finally owned that she had shied from pledging her life to Warren in that place where love for Kit had first bloomed.

Forgetting her scrambled eggs, she leaned on the old stone window sill with her chin on her hands. She had believed Kit to be disastrously disabled, if not dead. Warren had returned from Scotland with the news that he was miraculously flying *Flamingo* on a regular service to Alexandria, and had been joined by Sylva Lindstrom.

She had been unbearably restless since hearing that. What incredible courage he had to enable him to fight back after the crash; what natural skill he must possess to start flying a huge machine like *Flamingo* after being told he was virtually finished as a pilot. She pictured that square face, heard that unforgettable voice telling her that Kit Anson was seeking fame, fortune and the pathway to the stars. Maybe Sylva Lindstrom would provide all three for him. Joss had not suggested that the pair were married, but she appeared to be the only woman who could hold Kit.

Leone was not sure why Warren had told her all this, despite their pact of honesty between them, particularly on the subject of that one man. He must have known the news would bring her both joy and pain. Perhaps he hoped it would kill all hope of an eventual meeting to confess and gain possible forgiveness. It had. If Kit was now fulfilled professionally and sexually, he would put the past behind him. Leone must now make a determined effort to do the same.

Apart from that conversation with Joss, and an unexpected reunion with the Cummings girl he had seduced in the boathouse, Warren appeared to have worked very hard on the modifications to *Florida*. She could well believe it. Whenever he had a particularly tricky problem to solve he often went down to those old quarters of his to work, staying night and day until he had found the solution. Normally, he was never happier than when trying to unravel a knotty problem, yet he had seemed reluctant to return to Scotland yesterday. Daily dogfights over the coastal cliffs resulted in a great many aircraft crashing across the area, often killing civilians and destroying private property. He worried about leaving her at such a time, especially when he knew she would be travelling to London for her usual work with the refugees.

The chiming of the clock told her it was time to stop daydreaming. Dressing swiftly in a green cotton skirt and a black, white and green patterned blouse, she headed for the offices on the third floor. The post had already arrived. Her efficient silver-haired secretary, Virginia, had gone through it to set out on Leone's desk in order of importance or urgency. After a friendly greeting and brief comment on the arrival of the Hurricanes last night, the older woman pointed out that a letter had arrived from Sir Melville Pyne notifying them that transports would soon be arriving with 'the merchandise we discussed at our meeting'.

'Not a moment too soon,' commented Leone dryly. 'If things carry on as they have been, Britain really will be flattened and all our treasures destroyed. Who knows, maybe the Magnum Pomeroy Home Guard will be obliged to repel the Germans advancing up the Sheen.'

'They would, too,' laughed the secretary. 'I've never seen such a fierce band of tin-helmeted old gents.'

'They're very sweet underneath all that bluster,' said Leone with a smile. 'But they're great patriots.'

After an hour with paperwork, a sense of restlessness sent her seeking the warmth and beauty of the morning outside. Draping a pale cashmere jacket across her shoulders, she took the steps to the meadow and on down to the jetty. Walter was leaning on the rail lost in his own musings and smoking his favourite pipe. Growing aware of her approach, he straightened and smiled.

'Mornin', Miss Kirkland,' he greeted, having never managed to grasp the fact that marriage had taken away the status created by that name. Warren thought it amusing, so Leone had ceased trying to change the old man's habit of a lifetime. 'What a rare fine day it's turnin' out to be now that mist is gone.'

'Yes, indeed,' she agreed. 'The trees along the banks are at their most spectacular right now, aren't they? I always love it when the river is deep and silk-surfaced. Those wonderful autumn colours are perfectly reflected, with the blue of the sky running through the centre.

The smell of it all is so pleasant, too, so invigorating. On such a morning, it's great to be alive.'

'Aye, that it is,' he grunted. 'That's why we won't never let it all be taken from us by they there Germans.'

'Of course, we won't,' she assured him. 'They'll realize that soon, no doubt.'

'You goin' down to the works?' he asked then.

She nodded. 'I have a few things to check. I'll be back by lunchtime. Is *Miranda* ready?'

'Course she is,' he replied indignantly. 'As I told Mr Grant t'other day, I keeps one of the boats shipshape and filled up. In case of emergency, d'you see. It's my duty given to me by Mr Merrydew, for the defence of the river.'

'Very wise of you both, Walter,' she told him encouragingly. 'I shan't take her away for long.'

In no particular hurry to arrive, Leone sat with her hand on the tiller letting the vessel purr along the quiet stretches of the Sheen. She had lived beside it since birth, yet had only come to know it well in the past two years. She now loved it in every season, and particularly on days such as this. The reds, russets, golds and yellows of the foliage were echoed in the chrysanthemums rioting in gardens running to the water's edge. Although the sun was warm on her hands and face, there was that unmistakable hint of coming frosts in the air which smelled of fir cones, damp undergrowth and garden bonfires. The river was quiet, these days. The few summer visitors had returned home, and many residents had handed over their boats for more vital purposes. Leone had only been allowed to keep two of her own because Kirkland's could be reached by river in a quarter of the time it would take to go by road. The only sign of life was the ferry heading for Forton, which passed her heavily laden. With bus services cut to a minimum, many others found it easier to use the river, even though the ferries had been commandeered for Dunkirk, leaving just two to ply back and forth twice a day.

Waving to the passengers, Leone continued down-river. The bows cut through the smooth water to ripple the reflected images, and she felt a sudden sadness that she had missed childhood and youth-time pleasures which could have been hers on this beautiful stretch of water, if she had not been too lonely to come home for holidays. At that moment, however, the peace was shattered. From up on the hills of East Sheenmouth came the wail of the siren, quickly joined by another sited on the roof of the Roxy cinema in Sheenmouth itself. Almost immediately, the concerted roar of twelve Hurricanes from Magnum Pomeroy drowned the sirens, as they climbed fast and headed out to sea. As always during these distant daily battles, Leone's heart went out to the men in those machines, whoever they were. She could not imagine piloting an aircraft whilst trying to attack another, which was attacking her. Flying was an enjoyable but concentrated business, she had found. To regard it as a way of killing or being killed was quite horrific.

The Hurricanes vanished swiftly, but she was little more than half a mile from the company buildings when she saw them returning. Deciding that it must have been a false alarm, she then realized that the aircraft looked bigger and decidedly different. They were also approaching in unusual formation, equally spaced one behind the other. A curious sensation of alarm had hardly been born within her, when a whistling sound was quickly followed by a thunderous explosion. Before her eyes, part of Kirkland's original hangar flew into pieces within a cloud of dust and smoke. With the boat taking her steadily closer, Leone turned cold when a second explosion caused the roof of the main workshop to collapse. Too stunned to act, she drew nearer and nearer the danger as each aircraft released two bombs on or around the company buildings. Inside those han-gars and workshops were people she knew, doing vital work: men and women in her own employ were dying there as she watched.

Close enough now to feel the blast of air and the warmth of the flames springing up, Leone realized her own danger and automatically turned the tiller. There was a fire-fighting and rescue team stationed at the factory, and Sheenmouth defence forces would cope with the casualties. At the Abbey there was little more than a first-aid box and hoses beside the swimming pool. Children were taking lessons there at this moment. Suppose the German bombers should fly over it and mistake the building for another factory?

Revving the engine to full power, she set the boat at the river with fear clutching at her throat. It had all happened so quickly, so unexpectedly. Never had she felt so helpless, but what could anyone have done from a small boat in the middle of a river? With the tumult of continuing destruction bombarding her ears from the bank dropping further and further behind her, she raced the vessel back, seeing none of the charm and peace of her outward journey. The throb of the boat's powerful engine was drowned by the pulsing roar of enemy aircraft passing overhead still in line formation and heading purposefully towards Magnum Pomeroy. How could they have known so soon that it had become a fighter base? The Hurricanes had only arrived there last night. Feeling dangerously exposed out on the water, with the dark shapes casting shadows as they moved like sinister monstrous bats steadily forward, she wondered wildly what had happened to the fighters she had seen heading out to sea in defence of Sheenmouth. Surely they had not all been destroyed so swiftly and easily. Casting a quick petrified glance over her shoulder, she saw black smoke and flames rising from Kirkland's. The reflection in the river now was one of destruction.

As she rounded a bend which cut off all sight of something her shocked senses could still scarcely believe, the peaceful scene ahead suggested that it could have been a nightmare from which she had just awoken. The bombers had disappeared from view leaving only a distant rumbling to betray their presence. Then her ragged nerves jumped at the swift scream of diving aircraft. Her head shot back to see half a dozen fighters streaking down from a blue sky criss-crossed with white vapour trails, then flatten out almost overhead to go in pursuit of their quarry. The Hurricanes had returned. At least, half of them had.

The last stages of her dash for home were accomplished with instinctive seamanship, because her mind was racing with so many wild thoughts. Kirkland's was gone – destroyed in a matter of minutes after years of creation and growth. Her workers, people she knew and liked, had just died in the most savage manner. They had turned up this morning, probably also filled with the pleasure of such a glorious tranquil day, little knowing it was to be their last. Most were women. Leone's eyes filled with tears. Oh God, how terrible! If the Germans accomplished the unthinkable and invaded, would anyone or anything be left?

Against her muddled feverish thoughts, she heard the thud of further explosions up beyond Sheenmouth Abbey and the whine of battling aircraft, which rose up above the skyline in chase, then plunged out of sight again. The fight for Magnum Pomeroy seemed to be at its height, when the battle chorus was deafeningly augmented by the crack of guns atop Sheenmouth cliffs as they began firing at the machines out at sea. Within seconds, the pom-pom guns at old Forton fort opened up, the stuttering salvos completing the destruction of autumn peace which had hung so breathtakingly over this small Devonshire town.

Leone was in such a state of nerves, she took the boat too close to the jetty, removing a chunk of wood from one of the piers. Walter hardly noticed; he was more concerned with her safe return.

'Thank the lord, Miss Kirkland,' he cried in a voice roughened by fear. 'Whatever be goin' on?'

Scrambling to the jetty, she turned towards him a face which felt stiff. 'They hit Kirkland's, Walter. They hit it while I looked on. There's nothing but rubble and flames.'

The old man's jaw began to work as his watery eyes filled with tears. 'I dursen't believe that. It be too wicked.'

'Those poor women,' she murmured tonelessly. 'They were inside when it happened.'

'Oh, dear Lord, whatever is happenin' in this world of ours?'

Feeling giddy, Leone reached out to hold the rail. Walter saw and immediately took her arm. 'You look just about done in, m'dear,' he said kindly. 'I should get yourself up to the house and take a drop o' summat that'd put you right. 'Twould be that Mr Grant is away up north at a time like this. Get him on the tellyphone would be my advice. He'll soon come back and deal with this.'

'Thank you, Walter,' she told him, pulling herself together. 'I'll certainly take your advice about a tot of whisky, but I must deal with this myself. Mr Grant is engaged on something vitally important. He has to remain and finish it.'

The old boatman's lined and sunburned features were still concerned. 'You sure you be all right now, Miss?'

'I shall be when our boys have driven the bombers from the area. God knows what'll be left of Magnum Pomeroy by then.' She started along the jetty on legs still wobbly. 'Better get *Miranda* inside the boathouse, and stay there yourself, Walter. It would be foolish to move around in the open until the all-clear sounds.'

Leaving him with that instruction, she was walking over the lower meadow when a dark clamorous shape loomed towards her over the row of trees bordering the western boundary of her land. The bomber was being chased by a Hurricane which was only vaguely visible shrouded in the smoke pouring from its quarry. Even as she dropped flat instinctively, Leone saw the two bombs being shed as a dying act of destruction by the doomed German crew. No more than seconds passed before twin explosions rocked the ground beneath her, and a powerful wall of air rushed across the meadow to flatten the flower-dotted long grass and buffet her body with an invisible force. Her head came up to stare in rage and horror as the grounds beside the north wing flew into fragments of earth, rubble and wood, as that side of the Abbey appeared to disintegrate amidst a huge cloud of dust. The Hurricane, which had been caught in the blast from below, began to weave out of control as it disappeared beyond the hilly woodlands to the south. At the same time, a fresh explosion in that direction indicated that the bomber had crashed, sending up a pillar of fire into the clear autumn air.

Leone scrambled to her feet, caught in that curious calmness which transcends shock when further danger still threatens. The weather had been exceptionally dry. A fire in the woods could spread very fast to engulf several villages, besides cutting off access to Sheenmouth by road. She began to run over the meadow towards the steps leading to the terrace as, like the proverbial drowning man, her past flashed before her. Once, this ancient building had appeared to shut her out. She now loved every stone and window; every alcove and stairway. In the past, the bell in the tower had rung out a warning to the smugglers. Today, it must ring a warning to those in danger of burning in the fire raging over the nearby slopes.

Her flying feet changed their direction on reaching the terrace, for the first solemn notes of the great bell began floating in the clear morning with rhythmic insistence. Merrydew was already at his post. Swerving to her right, she skirted the front of the Abbey until reaching the corner of the north wing. There she halted. An appalling scene lay before her. The tennis courts and Roman swimming pool had become a crater stretching from where she stood, right across to where the stables had once been. The gallons of water from the pool were fast emptying from the crater through a narrow channel, to pour into the Abbey itself at a point where a large area of the ancient stone wall had been blasted away. There appeared to be no glass left in the windows, yet the fragile antique lanterns on each side of the garden door remained intact. Breathing fast from exertion, Leone surveyed it like a girl in a trance. Breaking into that state, however, came the sound of distant screams and cries from the west side of the monastery.

'Oh, dear God, the children,' she breathed, remembering why she had raced back up-river.

Turning, she ran along the terrace to the main entrance. It would take too long to skirt that crater. Better to go through the interior to reach the room where they would have been at their lessons. Thrusting open the heavy door, she found the sombre tolling of the bell atop the hollow tower shaking her head with its resonance as she practically fell inside the great hall. As she charged across it, she registered with abstract dismay that there was a scattering of stained glass on the old flagstones. Those windows were several centuries old, yet shattered in an instant. How sad. How terribly sad! The corridors seemed unnaturally dark. How could two bombs have put out the sun? How could such a short burst of running have made her throat so dry and her chest so painful?

On she went past the octagonal room, then into the transverse corridor. Here, it was darker still. She pulled up just in time. There was no heavy oaken door leading to the rooms used for lessons. In its place was a wall comprising stone, glass and huge splinters of wood. Above it, about twenty feet up, she could just glimpse some of the furniture in the bedroom where she had proposed to Warren. The ragged edge around this gap in the ceiling was cracked, and one huge section hung dangerously at an angle. Beyond the rubble she could hear more clearly now the cries of distracted women trying to calm children who were not only hysterical, but possibly injured.

Seeing the impossible as her only possibility, Leone began to climb that wall before her, knowing that the slightest displacement of the rubble could bring further collapse of the ceiling. Grasping and slithering in the semi-darkness, she inched up towards that gap with her gaze on the overhanging piece of masonry. Her hands and arms were scratched by the sharp edges of stone, and glass fragments which lay hidden in the dust. Her polished fingernails broke as she clambered over the shifting surface, and her knees were grazed each time she slipped back. Dust arose from her progress to add to that already hanging in the atmosphere, to set her coughing. However, she had ceased to be afraid. As it had been after the crash of *Flamingo*, once she had acknowledged that her life was in the hands of the Almighty, she grew calm and clear-headed. Foot by foot, she mounted that precarious hill feeling confident that the loose slab would not fall. Something needed to be done. She must do it.

Reaching the top only two feet from the ceiling, she peered over into the room beyond. Her confidence then faltered slightly. The windows had been blown inward by blast from the second bomb, which had landed to the rear of the wing. Many of the children had blood on their skin and clothes from cuts inflicted by flying glass. In a far corner alongside one of the teachers, who looked unnaturally still and pale, lay several of the pupils more seriously injured. The youngsters were suffering from shock, some screaming and squirming hysterically; others huddled in squatting positions in a dark world of their own. There was a strong smell of urine and vomit, the result of delirious fear in children. The three teachers who were still on their feet seemed as bloody as their charges, and were vainly trying to calm the situation.

Leone's heart sank. The room beyond this one, where classes had also been held, had caved in to form an impenetrable wall cutting off access in that direction. Outside the empty windows of the first room was another crater, making the sheer drop from there a frightening prospect. The teachers might make it, but children could never be taken by that route without ladders and ropes brought by rescuers from outside. In truth, they were all trapped. Whilst in little danger from further collapse, some vicious injuries had been sustained. The cuts needed swift treatment. Glass fragments would have to be picked from the flesh, bleeding staunched, and bromides administered.

Spreadeagled on that mound of debris, Leone thought of the best course of action. She could slide back down, then go for help to bring them all out through the windows and across the crater. That would be a lengthy task requiring all manner of equipment and a large body of men. Time was of the essence. The little ones would suffer drastically the longer they were trapped. Minds might be permanently affected if they were forced to remain in their glass-splattered prison; others could lose blood in dangerous quantities. She had no true information on the extent of injury. Delay might even prove fatal in some cases, if treatment was not given swiftly.

Deciding that the alternative course of action was best, she cast an apprehensive glance at the tilting block of stone just above her as a creaking sound came from its direction. It remained where it was, but she moved beneath it faster than caution dictated to swing her legs over the peak of debris and descend in a slither of stone and dust, until fetching up on the floor glistening with glass. When she scrambled to her feet and turned to face the room, she realized silence had descended.

'My word, it's you, Mrs Grant,' exclaimed one woman, in astonishment.

557

Giving a faint smile as she dusted herself down, Leone said, 'Sorry to come in that way. I can see your predicament. It'll take far too long to bring sufficient rescuers by the outside route, so there's really only one way out for you all.' Glancing around at the blood-smeared children, she asked quietly, 'How badly hurt are they?'

A second of the elderly teachers, holding back tears with a struggle, said, 'Some are quite badly cut. The glass just flew *everywhere*. One boy has severe injuries with one eye a mass of blood. I'm certain his sight has been damaged.'

The third spoke in the toneless manner of those in shock. 'Miss Cadbury is dead. The two unconscious children lying over there with her seem to be in a critical condition.'

Drastically sobered by this news, Leone told them, 'You've all been marvellous, in view of the state you're in yourselves. I have a proposal to put, but you must tell me whether or not it's feasible in view of the children's condition. There is a way out which we could use, if they could do it with our help. From this room runs a network of underground passages leading to a concealed door in the grounds.'

'The smugglers' tunnels!' cried one. 'So they really exist?'

'Yes, indeed. If we each carried a child who might be unable to walk, could you persuade the others to form a line and follow us through dark passages as far as the exit? It's quite a walk, I must warn you.'

The three women exchanged glances, then the tearful one nodded. 'They were terrified by the noise, the blood, and the fact that they couldn't leave. Quite a lot grew hysterical, but a few have strong enough personalities to keep their heads. If we tell them all we're taking them to safety through tunnels once used by smugglers, they'll not only be eager to get out, they'll also see what we propose as an exciting adventure.' Looking at her colleagues, she said, 'We'll put Terry Symes at the end of the line to keep any stragglers going. Lilian Thwaites can lead them right behind Mrs Grant. We can space ourselves out along the line, carrying any who can't walk.'

'How are they going to see the way in these tunnels?' queried the quietest of the three.

'There are candles and a supply of matches in this cupboard,' Leone said, going to it and opening the door. 'It's incredibly providential that I had cause only a few weeks ago to open up the tunnels from this room after years of disuse. The candles were placed here recently, and I little guessed how they would be first used. We'll give one to as many children as possible, so there'll be enough light to banish any fears of the darkness.' Looking from one to the other, she demanded, 'Well, can we do it?'

'What about Miss Cadbury and those two poor creatures with her?' asked the one in shock.

Leone sighed. 'They'll have to be left until we can return for them. They're in no further danger here, and trying to move the children without a stretcher might prove fatal.'

'I'll stay with them,' decided the woman, in a tone which brooked no argument. 'If the children should recover consciousness and find themselves alone with Miss Cadbury, they'd be terrified.'

'Fair enough,' Leone said, 'but one less adult means one less child can be carried. We must decide which are the worst three.'

Studying the small victims as she walked about the room crunching glass beneath her feet, Leone realized what a difficult task it was. Small cuts often bled profusely to give a false impression. Some had rubbed themselves in their terror, spreading blood over limbs actually untouched by glass; others crouched in their pain and would not allow an inspection of their wounds. She was appalled by this evidence of suffering by children who did not understand war, nor why it had entered their lives so suddenly. As it turned out, the children made the decision themselves. The teachers, who were all local women brought out of retirement when the evacuees had arrived in the area, knew their profession well. By persuading their pupils that an adventure was about to take place, they changed fear into a curious form of bravery with no more than a few sentences. Only four of their pupils failed to get to their feet and line up for a candle. That number posed a further problem, until one of the bigger boys, who looked as tough as they come, declared that he could carry skinny Mary Postins with ease.

While the teachers lit candles to distribute, Leone started the 'adventure' off by revealing the secret entrance hidden beneath the layer of glass fragments. Marvelling that but for Sir Melville Pyne there would still be a stove across this door, and certainly no candles for illumination, Leone began hauling on the chain which lifted the stone slab in the manner of a drawbridge. Soon, holding a child in her arms, each adult checked that the children were ready to step down into the bowels of the earth holding their candles.

Leading the way, Leone trod down the ten steps to reach the earthen passageway. She carried a girl in a red-stained dress whose arms were covered in dried blood and plainly very painful. The child seemed awestruck and made no response to Leone's soft questions. However, she continued to speak so that the infant would feel confidence during her ordeal. The teachers were doing the same, their voices echoing in the tunnels freshened by an ingenious seventeenth-century air-conditioning system of funnels to the outside world. The monks had been clever men, unlikely to allow smugglers or their stolen goods to be affected by a poisonous atmosphere.

It was a procession she would never forget, illuminated by flickering light from candles, and accompanied by the echo of young awestruck voices from those who had forgotten hysteria in the excitement of doing something they had only read about in storybooks. When she eventually reached the exit, Leone found the child in her arms was asleep. Touching her dust-filled hair with a light caress, she told herself the distant mother still had her child . . . for today, at least. Halting, she looked back at the ragged bobbing line of candles slowly advancing. All their mothers could breathe again today.

As the leading children shuffled to a halt, she told them all in a clear voice, 'I'm now going to open the secret door only I know about. All of you will now share my secret, but you must tell no one else. You'll be very surprised when you see where you are, but you'll understand why the smugglers used to hide their barrels of brandy and bales of silk here.'

The door did not open easily, despite the oil recently smeared over the hinges before the visit of Sir Melville's art expert. Soon, however, she was stepping out into the boathouse where Walter had moored *Miranda*. The old man was nowhere to be seen, despite her advice to keep out of sight. Walking out to the grass of the lower meadow, she discovered why. Flames and smoke were billowing from the woods where the German bomber had crashed, and they appeared to be spreading. Walter was staring at the sight as if hypnotized; Leone reacted in much the same manner. She had forgotten that sinister doomed aircraft; forgotten the destruction of Kirkland's. Like the children, she had been caught up in an imaginary adventure which had banished reality. It now returned with a rush as the young ones, still holding their lighted candles, clustered around her to witness the conflagration as if it were a continuation of their storybook experience.

Shouts drew Leone's attention to the Abbey. Men were starting towards them down the steps from the terrace, and she recognized members of the Home Guard detachment which exercised regularly in the grounds. Never had she been so thankful to see them. Figures of

561

fun though they might be to some local residents, they rose to this emergency in commendable fashion. In no time, the two teachers were being led away with their pupils towards the south wing. There, first-aid treatment would be administered whilst waiting for an ambulance. Calling after them an invitation to tell her cook to make sweet tea for them all, Leone then led the three men who remained with her back into the tunnels in their bid to bring out those who had been left behind.

Explaining the situation swiftly as she hurried along, Leone began to feel the effects of her own shock this morning. Her legs now had a will of their own, taking her along those ancient tunnels faster than the beating of her heart could match. Breathing hard in an effort to ease the growing pain in her chest, she felt herself turning unbearably cold. Her teeth began to chatter, making it impossible for her to speak clearly. This journey was surely twice as long as the first had been. She began to suspect that a wrong turning had been taken, and that she would wander in a subterranean labyrinth for ever more. At the point when suspicion was turning into certainty, light flooding into the narrow walkway fifty yards ahead dispelled her fear. That welcome light spurred her on, as she acknowledged a dread of the third journey beneath her home with men carrying a dead body in her wake.

Mounting the ten steps, she emerged into that scene of chaos once again. The stench was now almost more than she could take. Desperately close to vomiting herself, she crossed on rubbery legs to the corner containing the lifeless Miss Cadbury, two unconscious blood-covered children, and the teacher who had voted to stay with them. Despite her brave resolution, the waiting had proved too much for her. Her face was ashen, beaded with perspiration, and working convulsively as Leone and the men wearing tin helmets approached.

'You can come away now, Ethel,' advised one of them

who knew her well. 'Just you go along with Mrs Grant, m'dear. We'll see to what has to be done here.'

In deep shock, Ethel Green must have seen them as the enemy. Rising from her crouch beside the three bodies, she flew at the friend who had spoken so kindly, screaming abuse and attacking him with her fists. Seizing her arms, the man held her off as he again assured her of their intention to help those she had watched over so well. When she was quieter, he turned his red-cheeked face to Leone.

'Take her on ahead, ma'am. We'll deal with this, and find our way back with the aid of our torches. No need for you to stay.'

Leone was thankful for that directive, although the prospect of that long underground walk was hardly attractive. It would take determination to submit herself to it, she realized with an element of surprise. Knowing it had to be done, she reached for Ethel Green and encircled the woman with her arm.

'Come along, we'll go out and join the others,' she managed to say with creditable confidence. 'They're all having a cup of tea.'

Her elderly companion was past hearing words of reassurance. Taking one look at the yawning gap leading down into darkness, the teacher first drew back in abhorrence, then broke free to run to the door she normally used. It was no longer there, of course. Encountering instead the wall of rubble Leone had surmounted to first reach the room, the hysterical woman began to claw at it frantically, heedless of the glass and wood splinters tearing her palms. Leone ran across to pull her away, but she was too late. Disturbed by the violent assault, the gigantic pile of debris began slithering ominously.

Shouting at her to come away, Leone seized hold of the woman's brown knitted cardigan and pulled desperately. The garment was left in her hands as Miss Green wriggled free then flung herself at the barrier which was preventing her from escaping horror. Leone dropped the woolly on the ground, then launched herself at the figure trying to climb the shifting slope. They fought for dominance, Leone's victim strengthened by fear. Aware of masculine voices shouting warnings, Leone embarked on a fresh attempt to control the other woman. Grasping her leg, she pulled the terrified creature from her precarious perch as rubble started to rush down into the room. At the same time, came a sound heralding disaster. As she grappled with a biting, kicking opponent, she glanced up to see the huge displaced slab of ceiling slowly breaking away from its hanging position. With her heart pumping alarm through to her limbs, Leone made a last attempt to save them both by tugging at the resistant body beside her. The teacher then sensed true danger even through her imagined ones, and stopped resisting. Instead, she clung to her rescuer with vice-like arms, making it difficult for either of them to move away.

With a feeling of numb inevitability, Leone heard that avalanche roar down to engulf her just as a wrenching, tearing groan of masonry heralded the plunging slab from overhead. She was swept off her feet, the teacher torn from her grasp, as part of Sheenmouth Abbey descended to bury her alive in a black suffocating world.

Warren had been warned that the club airfield he knew so well had become an RAF fighter base, so he flew over Magnum Pomeroy soon after midday quite prepared to see Hurricanes dotting the green meadow surrounding the clubhouse with its two tiny hangars. All he saw were some large marquees, a couple of ambulances, and small groups of shirt-sleeved men sitting or lying on the grass. As he circled, he did spot two fighters, but they were no more than half machines now.

In radio contact with the flight controller on the ground, Warren complied with the instructions he was given and began his descent. Only then did he notice that the Buck and Hounds was no longer where it used to be. It must have received a direct hit yesterday, he realized, with a pang that increased the leaden sensation within him since the telephone call last night. Coming in over Magnum Pomeroy church, Warren saw several deep craters near the waterworks and paper-mill, where bombs had fallen harmlessly in fields from which the harvest had already been gathered. Only as he banked and glided effortlessly over the copse-clad Turkey Hill did the full extent of the raid become evident to his shocked eyes. Dobbs Farm looked more like a battlefield than a large, prosperous property with a manor house dating as far back as Sheenmouth Abbey. The manor was rubble now, and the fields were littered with wreckage of aircraft and what had once been ploughs, tractors and combine harvesters. From what he could deduce whilst concentrating on his landing, it seemed that two German bombers must have collided to send fragments in every direction. A Hurricane, partly burned out and with its nose buried in the earth, stood at a forty-five-degree angle in the eastern corner of one large meadow. When he was down to less than fifty feet, Warren realized with a chill that the movement he had detected was, in fact, children climbing all over doomed aircraft in which men must surely have perished. They were treating these grisly relics of battle as an exciting new playground.

Landing, he then taxied the Auster towards a man in grey flannels and a blue shirt, who beckoned him purposefully towards a corner of the small field. Rolling to a halt, he switched off the engine and pulled off his flying helmet before jumping to the ground. The lolling airmen regarded him with something uncomfortably like disparagement. Their attitude increased the leaden sensation in his breast.

'Hallo, Jim,' he said to the owner of the club.

'Hallo, Mr Grant. Good thing you didn't try to get in yesterday.'

'Yes, it looks pretty fearful from the air,' he responded, by now used to the curious reversal of rôles with a man he had formerly regarded as an employer. Marrying a Kirkland brought many strange advantages.

'They missed the club,' the other man pointed out, mopping his perspiring face with a handkerchief. 'I'm very sorry about your wife, Mr Grant, and about Kirkland's,' offered Jim, as Warren walked swiftly towards the clubhouse. 'The perishers came in behind their fighters. Fooled our lads, I'm afraid, and were so low our guns on the cliffs couldn't reach them. They won't let it happen again, believe me. The Hurries are out now. I don't know how they keep it up, straight I don't. No sooner are they down than they have to scramble again. No time to eat, rest or even sluice down in this baking weather. They're bloody marvels.'

They had reached the clubhouse. Warren stared at what used to be the small bar and lounge. It was choc-a-bloc with service gear.

'Officers' Mess,' explained Jim proudly. 'When they get in, they'll flop into those chairs and go out like a light until that telephone rings again.'

Vastly shaken by the evidence of what he had been told last night by Dr Gibbs over the telephone, Warren asked, 'Am I permitted to call the hospital from here?'

Jim smiled. 'No need for that, Mr Grant. Soon as I knew you were coming in, I asked Gerry Maggs to come up here ready to drive you to the cottage hospital to see your wife. He's over there in his taxi waiting for you.'

'Thanks.' The single word was vague, and uttered as he set off at a run towards the black car standing by the club entrance now guarded by an airman with a rifle. All through the flight he had held himself taut, while sensations of guilt, anger and fear had taken their toll of his nerves. The call from the hospital had come at a time when he was not on hand to take it, and he found it hard to resist self-blame. After working non-stop on the modifications to *Florida*, he had allowed himself to be persuaded to attend a station dance with some of the younger officers. Having been refused permission to fly home last night, he had seen the prospect of some social relaxation as the best way in which to smother his frustration at being obliged to wait until morning to leave. At the dance, he had met up with Mona again. They had spent most of the evening together, talking of old times and of Sheenmouth. Warren had enjoyed the dancing, and he had enjoyed her company. Now that she was no longer a threat to his future or his emotions, he found great pleasure in an uncomplicated relationship. Mona's current boyfriend had been flying last night, so she also seemed glad of a partner who did not threaten her love-life.

The duty officer had tracked him down to tell him he should ring the East Sheenmouth Cottage Hospital, where his wife was receiving treatment for injuries received in a bombing raid. A kind of madness had descended on Warren on hearing that a doctor had rung half an hour ago, whilst he had been dancing with Mona and laughing over their respective youthful follies. Guilt had swamped him. He was still bowed down by it. Guilt that he could have been socializing while Leone lay suffering; guilt that he was not in uniform fighting the enemy who had struck her down.

Gerry Maggs chatted for most of the journey to East Sheenmouth, but Warren heard hardly a word. The doctor had assured him Leone was in no danger, yet he had hinted that her injuries were more than slight. His brain was in a ferment. Coming in just now, he had seen the evidence of death and damage – the landlord of the Buck and Hounds and his wife had been killed. Imagination had him seeing Leone crushed beneath a ruin of an abbey, crying out in agony and calling his name in vain. He should have been there; he should be defending her and others like her with guns and bullets. What use was a man with a pencil when people were dying?

The doctor conducted him into the same private room in which Kit Anson had slowly recovered from his car accident, way back in 1932. Warren was appalled at Leone's appearance. Her face, arms and hands were black and blue with bruising, which was slashed with red cuts. She was in a drugged sleep and looked like a corpse. As he stood watching her with an impotent fury rising within him, the doctor spoke quietly.

'Your wife was buried beneath a considerable pile of debris, Mr Grant. As you can see, she has received extensive contusions and was cut by glass. However, the most serious injuries were internal. The weight of the rubble caused quite severe damage to the womb and pelvis. We operated as soon as she was brought in, but I'm afraid there was little chance of total repair. I don't know how important this news will be to you, but your wife took it with commendable calmness. She will be unable to bear children.'

'I see,' said Warren, still appalled by what had happened so suddenly to the girl he loved so dearly. They had never actually discussed the subject of children. They had married at a time when Leone needed help and advice with the company, so all thoughts and endeavours had been directed into dealing with the effects of the crash of *Flamingo*. War had arrived to channel their partnership into other concerns. On his own part, the idea of having children had never entered his mind. He had been so content with Leone and the work he enjoyed to the full, it had not occurred to him that anything else was necessary to his happiness. Certainly, Leone had never mentioned a wish for motherhood to him – at least, he could not recall that she had – and he could not honestly guess her feelings on being denied it.

He sat by her bedside for half an hour, but she did not awaken. The doctor suggested that he should go home for a meal, then return in an hour or so. Gerry Maggs had waited. There was little trade at this time of year, and the ageing man was happy to sit in his car outside the hospital so that he could take home to the

Abbey a man well liked by everyone in Sheenmouth and the surrounding district. Warren was grateful, and gave him a large tip despite the man's protests that he made no charge for the waiting.

Warren was shocked by the sight of his home, and the fury burned even hotter as he imagined what must have happened here yesterday morning. Walking through the beautiful old building, he noticed the shattered stained glass with detached regret. When he reached the place where Leone had been buried alive, he stared at the pile of rubble with horrified eyes. How could anyone have survived beneath that? The teacher Leone had tried to save was dead, killed by a massive heart attack during the night. Leone could also have been dead when he arrived home. He could have lost the most precious person in his life, whilst he had been dancing and laughing with Mona. All at once, he was aware of the tenuous aspect of relationships now. Leone had been spared this time, but while war was being waged not one person was safe, *anywhere*. It was a sobering thought, which made him vow to value to the utmost his fortune in winning her.

The flight from Scotland had been tiring, so he took a bath then dressed in flannels and a thick woollen jacket in preparation for the boat trip down to the workshops. Leone was sure to worry over the company of which she was so fiercely protective. He would take a look at the damage so that he could report his findings, and maybe set her mind at rest this evening.

Walter broke down in tears when they met on the jetty. 'Oh, Mr Grant, I never knowed anything so wicked,' he claimed thickly. 'Miss Kirkland's done no harm to anyone in her life, yet they devils vent their spite on her. Such a lovely young person – always has been. I remember her when she was nobbut a tiny little soul, you know. Lonely, she was,' he confided with a sniff and a dab with his handkerchief. 'Sir Hector was always terrible busy, and Mr Donald, God rest his soul, was a grown man before she was a young girl.' Wiping a large brown hand over his eyes, the distressed boatman sighed heavily. 'Used to come down here, she did, and we'd talk. I can still picture her sitting on that there post, swinging her legs as if she didn't know very well she could easy fall off into the water, and askin' me to tell her about they smugglers. I couldn't add up, sir, the number of times I spun that yarn to her. . . and the pretty little creature took it all in as gospel.' The tears began again. 'Now she be up there in that hospital. I won't never forgive our enemies like the rector says as we must all do; not when they do such things to a lady like Miss Kirkland. You should've seen her, Mr Grant, leadin' out all they youngsters with candles in their hands after tellin' them they was goin' to be like the smugglers. It's fair broke me up, sir, I swear.'

Warren gripped the old man's shoulder. 'She's going to be all right, Walter. In no time at all, she'll be down here on the jetty, no doubt to tell you how your old yarns helped her to bring the children through the tunnels. Now, how about coming down to the workshops in the boat with me? I want to take a look at the damage and try to work out what can be done.'

On his way down-river, Warren tried to concentrate on business. He must do all he could towards resuming full production as soon as possible. Brian Gregg had given him a very frank assessment of the situation during his latest trip to Scotland, emphasizing that the RAF could only hold out for a matter of weeks longer. Their rate of losses far outstripped that of supply. If Britain was to be saved, fighters were desperately essential. Although he was no expert on that side of the business, which was Leone's concern, Warren felt he must devise some temporary means of continuing their vital output of spares and components. If he could not get at the enemy in the air, he must do so through the means available to him.

Resolution faltered on approaching Kirkland's. The

old slipway which had launched *Aphrodite* and *Flamingo* had vanished beneath the river. The jetty beside it had been ripped in two, but enough of it stood to enable them to take the boat alongside. At first glance, the entire workshop appeared to have been reduced to a mound of blackened bricks and metal. Shaken by the extent of the damage, he jumped ashore and walked forward across the cracked hangar apron. A team of women, in brown bib-and-brace outfits over plain blouses, were picking any complete bricks from the rubble to pass down the line, to where two of their number were stacking them in neat piles. Catching sight of Warren, they called a cheery greeting without ceasing their back-breaking work. He then spotted Eddie Myers, their overseer, who was busily organizing a team of men with winches.

After expressing his regret at Leone's injuries, Eddie said, 'All this must be another shock for you, Mr Grant. Should have seen it yesterdee, right after it happened. I thought the whole place had gone up, straight I did. I've had a bit of a poke around today, and there's possibilities. That being so, I put some of the girls on picking out bricks we can use again.'

'Isn't it rather dangerous work for women?'

'Course it is,' Eddie replied tersely. 'By rights, they should all be at home making a nice tasty tea for their hubbies. But the hubbies is all off fighting, and these girls are driven on by their fury over the killing of their mates. Everything's dangerous for women these days, but the worst thing for them is to grieve and do nothing to ease it. They need to hit back, d'you see?'

Warren knew the feeling; knew it painfully well. He inspected the site thoroughly, clambering over loose rubble and skirting craters filled with water from firehoses, in order to get a true picture of the situation. Eddie then invited him over to the mobile canteen for a cup of tea, while they chatted to some workers taking the afternoon break from the shift working in the remaining workshop. These women echoed the anger hinted at by Eddie, saying that yesterday's raid had only made them more determined to keep the Germans from invading, even if they had to work twenty-four hours every day. Applauding their courage, Warren then walked back with the overseer to the great slide of smashed masonry. There, he began to voice his immediate thoughts.

'Just as soon as the men can clear the site, we'll start rebuilding. Some of the machinery looks good enough to salvage for the new workshop. Meanwhile, we'll carry on as near to full production as we can.'

Eddie pursed his lips. 'Blimey, that's a tall order, sir.'

'I know, but we can improvise in certain aspects,' Warren explained. 'At the Abbey, there are several enormous marquees Sir Hector used for social events. They've been packed away for some years, but they can now fulfil a more useful purpose. We'll move the packing section under canvas, and leave that area of the workshop available for further production.'

'Sounds fair enough, but where do we get the additional tools and benches?'

Warren frowned. 'I'll ring the Ministry about the tools. I reckon we could beg, borrow or steal some benches from local garages or workshops which had to close for the duration. I'll visit all likely places in the morning. Any sturdy bench will suffice. There must be a number no longer in use around this area.' He turned back towards the factory building still standing, the other man falling in beside him. 'There's also space being wasted at the end of number-one hangar.'

'That's where your seaplane's kept!'

'The times I've cursed Gerald Freemantle for dying before he could take delivery of her. I adapted a Seaspray model especially for him so that he could take whoever was his current mistress as a passenger, and built bigger fuel tanks in the floats for longer range. We never found another buyer. The craze for seaplane racing began to fade just as we went into full production on *Flamingo*, and poor old *Seaspray 22* was left on the shelf.' He sighed with regret for his old-time love. 'However, if we dismantle her wings, I see no reason why she couldn't be towed up to the old boathouse. It's empty now, and big enough to stow her. Of course,' he continued with inspiration, 'there's also a fully equipped workshop beneath my old quarters. If we shipped up some raw materials, three or four women could work there.'

They discussed Warren's plans for a while longer, then he prepared to return to the Abbey and put some proposals in hand. Eddie walked back to the jetty with him.

'We'll all do our best, Mr Grant, you can depend on that. Your wife set us a good example yesterdee. We all heard how she brought those evacuee kiddies out. You've a fine courageous lady, sir.'

'I know,' said Warren. 'I've had personal proof of that. She once saved my life.'

Together with Walter, he set off up the river again in the hushed afternoon. The sudden contrast between the noise and ugliness they had just left, and the red-gold peace of an autumn river scene, kept them both silent. The dying glory of it all held a hint of sadness, Warren felt. Winter lay ahead. Cold grey days; long dark nights. What would winter bring? No one dared believe the answer was an occupying enemy. That thought was strengthened by the roar of approaching Hurricanes, as they followed the river to its mouth and thence out to sea again. All the time such men kept going, there would be no occupying enemy, he decided. As they passed in deafening formation, sirens from each bank began their chilling wail to add to the clamour disturbing the peace of a moment before. Tilting his head back, Warren watched the fighters enviously, feeling again a sense of inadequacy.

When he arrived at the hospital early in the evening, with an armful of yellow and bronze chrysanthemums, he found Leone awake and waiting for him.

'Hallo,' he greeted gently, bending to kiss her. 'I hear you were a female Pied Piper yesterday. The whole town's very proud of you, but no one's as proud as I am.'

She studied his face searchingly. 'They told me Ethel Green died during the night. I didn't save her.'

'You tried,' he pointed out, sitting on the edge of the bed and taking one of her bruised hands in his. 'Her weak heart couldn't take the shock, that's all.'

'The two children are going to be all right.'

'And so are all those you brought out through the tunnels.' He forced a smile. 'How could we guess they'd ever be put to such use, especially by the only female Kirkland? Poor old Walter was in tears this afternoon when we went down to the workshops.'

'How bad is it, Warren? Tell me the truth.'

He avoided a direct answer. 'Eddie and I worked out several ways of continuing almost full production. I spoke to some of the girls. They're all raring to go again.'

She was one step ahead of him in knowledge. 'I asked the doctor how many had been killed. *Twelve*, Warren. Did you know?'

'Yes. Eddie told me.'

'I saw it happen; saw the place cave in knowing people were underneath. It's a sight I'll never forget.'

He had no words to follow that, so he simply kissed her hand very carefully, thanking God that she had not been one of the dead.

'Isn't it sad about the Abbey?' she commented next. 'Father would have been so upset.'

'Not in the way you are, darling. He regarded it as just another of his successful achievements. You've grown to love the place.'

She nodded. 'Surprising, isn't it? Can the stained glass be replaced, do you suppose?'

'Oh yes, after the war.'

'Naturally. Other things are far more important now.'

A nurse entered with a large vase filled with water for

Warren's flowers, and began to arrange them. Leone appeared to notice them for the first time, and thanked him.

'When must you go back?' she asked quietly. 'To Scotland.'

'I don't have to go back. I finished the mods yesterday.'

'How clever of you. I felt very bad about being the cause of taking you from your vital work.' A faint smile touched her bruised mouth. 'My brilliant husband.'

'I'd be more use in a cockpit,' he said bitterly.

'Not if you were dead in it. Who else could have done what they wanted to *Florida*?'

The nurse departed again with a warning that Leone should not tire herself. Warren reiterated the warning after the door closed behind the girl.

'You've been through quite an ordeal,' he pointed out. 'Take all the rest you can. I can handle the business, with Virginia's help. All our employees are very loyal and willing.'

She looked at him consideringly for a moment or so. Then she asked, 'Have they told you yet?'

'Told me what?' he responded, thinking of the business matters.

'About my injuries.'

'Oh. . . yes, darling, they have.'

Her eyes began to shimmer. 'I'll never be one of those enigmatic creatures known as "Mother". I vowed I wouldn't be like Marina Kirkland, or Daisy Anson. I won't know now whether or not I'd be any better than they at living up to that image of a protective, loving model of perfection.' She smiled with a great deal of effort. 'Perhaps it's just as well. I might easily have been as dismal a failure as they both were, and our poor lonely child would have had a wretched time of it.'

Moved by her tears and evident distress over something he had not counted too important, he then recalled

575

the strange near obsession she had revealed over mothers, including his own.

'I shouldn't worry too much about it,' he said raggedly, thinking to comfort her. 'They all appear to be much the same. Mine was too free with her favours. I had so many "uncles" I lost count.'

She stared at him, her tears checked by his outburst. Then, her discoloured hand went up to feather his cheek in a caress. 'Poor little boy,' she whispered huskily. 'Why didn't you tell me all this before? I'm so sorry. . . so very sorry. You must have been as lonely as I was. And Kit.'

'I've forgotten all that,' he told her fiercely. 'I loved you from the moment I met you. You're all I want, darling. You've made my life worth living, and filled it with happiness enough to compensate for all the years before we met.' Almost in tears himself, he said, 'Do you know that each time I look at you, I count myself one of the most fortunate men in the world?'

In astonishing distress, she put her fingers across his mouth. 'Don't, Warren! The last person who said that to me, lost everything he held dear very shortly afterwards.'

22

They would be landing at Lisbon within the hour. Kit
began to relax. Each trip was becoming a greater hazard,
and the strain was starting to tell on them all. Flying the
Mediterranean was now like running the gauntlet. With
hostile forces on both sides, to say nothing of German
squadrons based within bombing distance of the vital
British base of Malta, they were very often closely
shadowed by enemy fighters. Once, on flying too near
the island, *Flamingo* had actually been fired on by a
Messerschmidt whose pilot had signalled that they were
hazarding a raid in progress. Neutral aircraft now took
to the air over that former blue playground at their own
risk. Military pilots were within their rights to attack if
such machines strayed too near hostile territories, or in
any way threatened to impede vital operations against
the enemy. If they were seen to be engaged in any kind
of military or espionage activities, of course, they could
be shot down without prior warning. As the war hotted
up in North Africa and Southern Europe, it grew more
and more difficult to fly a course which avoided such
dangers.

Easing his stiff shoulders, Kit reflected on this life he
was leading. His initial reservations about the rather
melodramatic absurdity of what he had been asked to
do had seemed unnecessary once he had embarked on
the job. For the first few flights he had merely done
what he was supposed to be doing. Then, he had been

577

approached by a man named Georges Riccard, a commercial artist resident in Lisbon, who had asked Kit to look for a ketch which would have an identifying arrangement of fish boxes on deck. This vessel would flash a coded message, which Kit should record and hand to an agent in Alexandria. On his return flight, he should send an answer given by his contact.

Still feeling that there was an element of unreality about it all, Kit had hardly expected the vessel to be there. It had been, however, and the message had been signalled from the bridge of this dirty, broken-down craft by a man looking every bit the typical Greek fisherman. The contact in Alexandria had added to the suggestion of melodrama by turning out to be an olive-skinned importer in a tussore suit and fez, who had spoken with an effeminate Etonian drawl as they drank coffee together on the terrace of a seafront hotel. Kit had questioned the need for such subterfuge in the British stronghold of Alexandria, but the reply had shaken him.

'This place is swarming with German agents, and common informers who'd sell used bath water to a man dying of thirst and ask an extortionate price. Oh no, old fruit, Alex is a hotbed of shifty, vicious chaps establishing themselves nicely for when the Germans take over. Everyone, save a few romantically patriotic fools like yours truly, believes it's inevitable. Now the jolly old RAF has thrashed the wicked Luftwaffe and sent them looking for some place other than England's green and pleasant land to conquer, our lad Adolph is going to hit us elsewhere. Total control of the Med is what he's after now. Watch closely for military movements around Greece, old fruit. They might have pushed the Eyeties out, but they'll fall to a mightier foe. . . and soon. With the Afrika Korps presently racing through North Africa in this direction, the future for Alex does look somewhat dicey, don't you think? If Rommel ever reaches the outskirts of this fair city, half the population will suddenly show its true colours and assist his entry, take my word. That's why it's necessary for us to make casual contact like this. What's more natural than a meeting between an importer and the captain of a freight-laden aircraft? You surely didn't expect to trot openly into Intelligence Headquarters with a piece of paper in your sticky little hand, then expect to be allowed to do it a second time, did you? Believe me, old fruit, you've embarked on a dangerous business when you dabble in espionage.'

Before he had returned from that flight, Kit had been handed a message to transmit en route to Lisbon. His colourful contact, whose flippant pose plainly disguised a very courageous man, had thanked him for his valuable information passed on his arrival, told him to watch his step, then gave him the coded words on a slip of paper.

'Thanks for everything. Signal this to Grecian Ern as you trundle back through the Med, there's a dear.'

'Grecian Ern?' Kit had spluttered.

The man's dark eyes had filled with amusement. 'Rather nifty, don't you agree? I'm known as Turkish Delight.' Sobering, he had added, 'If we didn't have a bit of a lark over it, we'd all die of fright.'

On the return, the ketch had been there, still trawling, so Kit had lost height ready to flash the message. At that point, however, he had noticed a powerful gunboat streaking towards the harmless-looking ketch. Next minute, the vessel had flown into pieces beneath a savage attack. The incident had shocked Kit with its suddenness, even as he had levelled out and headed for base as if nothing had happened. It served to show him it was no game he was playing, and the apparent casualness of those involved plainly hid a deadly serious business to which he was now heavily committed.

Since that day, he had exchanged messages with other boats, or with invisible men installed in forests cloaking isolated headlands, in rocky strongholds of Sicily, or from luxury villas on the Balearic Islands. Often, he had brought packages from Alexandria. Some were small enough to slip into the hollow support of the pilot's seat, others had to be wrapped in waterproof cloth to drop overboard on docking, ready to be collected later. Sometimes, *Flamingo* had carried passengers back and forth. Able to seat eight in the upper cabin which the Kirklands had reserved for themselves during the proving flight, it was permissible for Western Med to take civilians on non-military journeys.

Kit and his crew were growing used to treading a fine line, but they had seen a great deal of activity all along their route which gave evidence of a German build-up. With Hungary, Rumania and Bulgaria now allied to the Nazi fighting forces, the chances of Yugoslavia and Greece remaining free were slim. If the eastern end of the Mediterranean should fall to the enemy, Alexandria would no longer be easy to reach, even for a neutral aircraft engaged in secret intelligence work.

So far, the tide of war was against the British, who were stretched to the limit in trying to hold on to the North African oil supplies, keep the Mediterranean open, and defend their homeland from the waves of German aircraft attacking all the strategic cities with incendiary bombs. Britain was ablaze night after night, but every stick of bombs, every inferno, only served to strengthen the fighting spirit of the people, not diminish it as Hitler hoped. Their only triumph, apart from the amazing evacuation at Dunkirk, had been the defeat of the proposed invasion plan last autumn. The RAF, although virtually down to their last few pilots and machines, had pulled off an incredible defence against a powerful German aerial force boosted by excessive confidence. In the courageous tradition of the thin red line, once again a few had refused to be defeated, and won the day.

Kit had been thrilled by the Battle of Britain. From his days in Spain, he knew the difficulties and dangers of combat flying. That men had engaged in it day after day, with hardly any rest between, inspired great admiration in him. It also strengthened his determination to do all he could for as long as possible, to back their supreme effort. His friends shared that determination, knowing full well the dangers they faced. Kit was particularly grateful to his Portuguese first officer, who had willingly joined the crew as co-pilot and loyal fellow collaborator. Aldo Diaz was something of a daredevil. Running any kind of risk was the food of life to him.

Fifteen minutes behind schedule, *Flamingo* taxied gently alongside the jetty, where the company warehousemen standing in small groups in the March sunshine were waiting to unload the cargo. Kit cut the engines. He and Aldo then continued the usual routine at the end of a long flight, watching the activity ashore with frequent keen glances.

'Good,' commented Aldo. 'Beno has arranged to be on duty today.'

Kit nodded, pleased to see Morris' brother-in-law ready to board the moment Digger opened the hatch. War had brought many terrible things, but also some curious benefits. Beno Terrazzi, a local excise official, had been promoted several months ago. Consequently, his name had been added to the duty roster of those who inspected the cargo of all incoming Western Med aircraft. The first time he had come aboard had also been the first time the flying boat had picked up British fliers from the sea. The men had been hidden, but a locked compartment had aroused the suspicions of the young Portuguese. Kit had had no alternative but to reveal the truth. Beno had been so delighted to discover his English brother-in-law was some kind of hero, he had promptly embraced him and declared that he would ask a friend with a fishing boat to collect the airmen after dark and hide them until they could be returned to England.

Since that day, he had arranged to be on duty every time *Flamingo* came in, and any servicemen who had been picked up from the sea were all smuggled away after dark by Beno's friend. Apart from his invaluable help, he had persuaded his family that Morris was a man well deserving of a bed with his Maria. Glad though he was to see this swarthy young man in uniform awaiting them on the jetty this evening, Kit noticed others there who were not so welcome.

'Heinz and Fritz are lurking by the hangars, as usual,' he murmured, watching the Germans who were supposedly businessmen but who made no secret of the fact that they were under instructions to watch the comings and goings of Western Med aircraft. There was no reason why the pair should not. British observers kept an eye on all Lufthansa's flights, in addition to any German activities in this neutral city. Places such as Lisbon were centres of intrigue during the present hostilities. The rules of neutrality demanded strict observance of it, yet all manner of plots and activities were successfully conducted by nationals of countries at war. Sometimes, the neutral authorities chose to turn a blind eye, particularly if the perpetrator of the offending act was a nation with trading and friendship links going back many years. However, if an official charge of violation of neutrality should be placed by any diplomatic body against another, the charge had to be investigated and any culprits interned. To this end, a close eye was kept by teams of agents for the slightest evidence of espionage, or for the passage of military personnel who should rightly be interned for the duration of hostilities. Since the fall of France, a large number of British evaders had been returned home after reaching Iberia, and German vigilance was tightening.

With Beno's help the crew of *Flamingo* had been lucky so far, but Kit feared that the Germans they had dubbed Heinz and Fritz might soon force an official search of their flying boat by Portuguese police. His fears were instantly realized. As he watched the smiling Beno advance along the jetty to greet Digger, he also saw the Germans stroll forward from the shadow thrown by the hangar and signal to someone around the corner of it.

582

'Christ, now we're in real trouble,' he murmured to his co-pilot, as two policemen came into view.

Their human cargo today numbered two. One was a bona fide passenger, the other a British tank commander whose crew had perished in battle. Miraculously, he had survived to make his tortured way to Tunis, where the Western Med agent had befriended him. Kit had taken the man aboard without hesitation, but he now represented danger for them all. A twelve-stone six-footer in army uniform could not possibly be hidden from enemies determined to search every nook and cranny. Unlike the packages they often carried, he could not be lowered beneath the hull to be collected at nightfall. Yet, even as the thought crossed his mind, Kit realized it was probably their only hope. The lieutenant would have to dangle beneath the jetty until darkness covered his rescue. There was no alternative.

Leaving Aldo in the cockpit, Kit went down to the lower deck very smartly, seeking out the man sitting more than happily with their female passenger. Marianne Aziz was the daughter of a Frenchwoman and an Egyptian, both dead, who had offered her services to the British in Alexandria. She was now on her way to France with her Egyptian passport, where she planned to become a guide for Allied evaders attempting to reach England. Having lived in indolent luxury all her life, the girl had fallen deeply in love with a Scottish sergeant on leave from the desert campaign. He had proposed marriage, then returned to be killed on his first day back with his unit. On hearing the news, Marianne had gone straight to the nearest bar to approach the first British officer she saw. Four months later, she was on her way to avenge her lover's death.

Kit was full of admiration for her pluck. Young, slender, blonde, well-bred, she reminded him of Leone Kirkland who, according to Digger, had once displayed unsuspected courage. This Franco-Egyptian girl, with her stylish appearance and wide, innocent eyes, looked the most unlikely heroine. It was probably her greatest asset for the future she planned and, hopefully, for this present emergency. Even the most suspicious of men would readily believe she was no more than a good-time girl out to spend a holiday in Lisbon at some lover's expense. George Calder presently looked set to pay for anything she might want.

'Sorry to break up the budding friendship,' Kit interrupted tersely, making them both look up. 'Two Germans are about to board with Portuguese police. They've been watching us for some time. Now, they're forcing a search. If they find you, Calder, you'll be interned. So will we all. I've no choice but to drop you over the side and trust to luck that they don't look too hard beneath the jetty. Come on, they're almost here. Digger will put you through the aft hatch while I delay them as long as possible. I hope you're a good swimmer, chum.'

The muscular young man flushed. 'Actually, I've a psychological fear of water. Never learned because of it.'

'Hell!' swore Kit heartily. 'You'll have to learn now, or we're sunk.'

The girl rose swiftly. 'Leave it to me. I'll show him what to do.'

Hearing heavy footsteps approaching along the jetty, Kit said, 'Show him pretty quick. They're here.'

With that urgent advice, he turned and walked back to the main hatch, where Beno was making a long job of expressing surprise over additional officialdom when he was already on the job. Kit joined him, effectively blocking entry. Speaking in Portuguese, he asked what was afoot. Trying to appear as mystified as an innocent man would be, he nevertheless worried about the chances of Calder quitting the aircraft without being spotted. Yet, how could that girl rid him of a phobia he had been ashamed to admit? Worried and anxious, Kit listened with every semblance of growing indignation as one of the policemen explained.

'These diplomatic gentlemen claim they have evidence

that you and your crew are working for the British, Captain Anson. A charge has been laid, and must be investigated,' added the dark-moustached rotund official. 'A search of your aircraft must be made before any persons or cargo can leave it. Regrettable, but I have my duties.'

'We all have our duties. . . and I suppose these two feel they have theirs,' Kit replied frostily, 'but is it necessary for them to walk all over my flying boat? The fact that you are prepared to investigate their absurd charge should be sufficient.'

Once more, the policeman was profusely apologetic. 'They will not be satisfied, Captain, until they have been personally assured that you carry nothing which breaches your neutral status. Please! If you would be so good as to conduct us over your aircraft, we can finish this unpleasant business and be gone.'

Knowing he could delay the stony-faced Germans no longer, Kit stepped back wondering what had happened to the officer who could not swim. Digger would have dropped overboard the package brought from Alexandria; Aldo was in the pilot's seat which contained a roll of film hidden in the aluminium supports. Kit would deliver that to Georges Riccard this evening in the usual way. There was little chance of either being discovered during the search, but Calder was a large man to conceal if he had to crouch above the water on the cross-struts beneath the jetty. One glance from the aft hatch would spot him.

Deciding to keep them from the stern as long as possible, Kit invited all four visitors up to the flight deck. The Germans had other ideas, however, and demanded a split into pairs. Insisting that it would speed the search, they determinedly walked in different directions, forcing the policemen to do the same. Kit left Aldo and Morris to cope with the upper deck, and joined the pair heading towards the tail where Digger was waiting. The Australian's expression gave nothing away, and his response to

Kit's optical inquiry was simply a knowing smile. It told Kit very little, and his heart sank when the German imperiously gestured that the hatch should be opened. Digger took so long over the operation, Kit was certain George Calder would be in plain view, clinging to the posts of the jetty.

As tense as a man could be, Kit swept the area with his glance as he waited for the shout of triumph from his enemy searcher. None came. The underside of the wooden pier was innocent of human presence. Turning swiftly to Digger, Kit's cocked eyebrow asked him for an explanation. The response was the suggestion of a wink, which implied that Calder had carried off a sensational disappearing trick. The German stared from the hatch for an uncomfortably long time, as if waiting for submerged men to be forced to the surface to take in air. Kit grew anxious again, in case those eagle eyes somehow realized that a large package was presently concealed where he looked for uniformed troops. It seemed an age before the Portuguese persuaded his companion that he had other duties to perform, and urged a continuation of the search.

Letting out his breath in relief, Kit led the two through the cargo bays to identify the contents of crates and barrels. Even so, the German poked and prodded at any goods in sacks or nets, as if suspecting that they contained half the British fighting forces. The policeman raised his eyes heavenward as he glanced Kit's way, then further urged completion of this fruitless task. By this time, the scrutiny of the upper deck had been carried out. The second German, looking more stony-faced than ever in his frustration, descended with his official companion. It was at this point, that Kit informed them of his female passenger; a rich Egyptian girl with a taste for even wealthier men friends. The policeman tut-tutted at the immorality of modern youth, and mention of a female appeared of little interest to the Germans, who were looking for armed stowaways. Still puzzled about how Calder could have been spirited from sight, Kit threw open lockers and compartments which were too small to conceal a child, much less a grown man. Then, there was only the passenger cabin left to see.

Pulling back the curtain, Kit prepared to introduce Marianne. His words stopped short as he gazed at the girl clad in no more than brief silk panties, who was enthusiastically kissing a man stripped to the waist and wearing Western Med uniform trousers. She turned in well-feigned alarm to reveal full dark-tipped breasts above a waist which invited hands to span it, as George Calder's did now.

'Oh!' she cried, a study of affronted modesty as she crossed her hands over her delightful assets, and opened her eyes wide as she looked reprovingly at the three male intruders in turn.

The devout Portuguese was visibly shocked; the German looked contemptuously amused. Quicker-witted these days than he had once been, Kit recovered from his astonishment to think fast. There was no sign of Calder's army uniform. It was probably in Marianne's luggage. The trousers he now wore must be Digger's spare pair, produced during the delay created at the main hatch. The girl had certainly shown Calder what to do, and he plainly had no inhibitions in this direction. The tank officer was actually smiling fatuously at them all. Even so, the ball was in Kit's court. He played it to best effect, reasonably certain that the Germans would not know how many men comprised a flying boat crew.

'My God, so this is your idea of attending to duty, is it?' he roared at the half-naked army man. 'When I instructed you to give our passenger every assistance, I didn't mean that you should continue a relationship begun in Alex. What you indulge in during off-duty periods is your affair, but on board this aircraft you'll do your job and nothing more. I'll report this to Tom Digby. He'll skin you alive, you randy bastard.' He turned his attention to the bewitching figure in silk underwear. 'As for you, words fail me, Miss Aziz. I've tried to overlook your provocative behaviour towards every member of my crew, as well as myself, during this flight, but I'd have refused to carry you as a passenger if I'd known you'd go this far. Please put your clothes on and go ashore immediately.' Turning away, he added sourly, 'You may well have ruined the career of a good man, whose overriding weakness you've just exploited. I hope you're suitably ashamed.'

It worked. Ushering everyone back to the main hatch, Kit barked at Morris as he came down from the flight deck. 'Why don't you keep an eye on what's happening on my aircraft? When I'm up there flying the damn thing, I expect my crew to do their jobs as thoroughly as I do.'

Before Morris' incomprehension became apparent, Kit asked the senior official if he was satisfied that all was in order. 'I apologize for that disgusting scene,' he added, giving the man no time to reply. 'As you saw, the girl has no morals whatever. I must accept the blame for allowing her on board *Flamingo* when I knew she had been entertaining one of my crew in Alexandria. I believed the man had more sense than to endanger his career like this.' Summoning up a regretful smile, he finished by saying, 'I'll not make the same mistake again, believe me.'

The Portuguese sighed heavily, plainly disturbed by the entire episode. 'Let us hope others have the wisdom to learn by their mistakes,' he observed, looking pointedly at the Germans he then proceeded to chivvy from the aircraft. 'My apologies for delaying you after a long tiring flight, Captain Anson. I have my duty to do, and it is sometimes unpleasant.'

Watching all four progress to the shore, it was apparent to Kit that a lecture on making unfounded accusations was being read. It fell on deaf ears, apparently, for Heinz and Fritz lingered near the hangars after the Portuguese officials moved off. Kit felt little sense of relief. The pair had failed today, but they would not give up until they had proved their suspicions. Not only was the net closing in the Mediterranean, it was doing so here in Lisbon. Meanwhile, George Calder remained a problem until he was safely with those who would smuggle him home to fight on. Turning back to the passenger cabin, he knocked lightly on the bulkhead beside the closed curtain.

'Are you two in a fit state for visitors?' he asked.

The curtain was swished back to reveal Marianne dressed in her smart white silk suit, with turquoise accessories. The tank officer was tucking his uniform shirt into his own trousers. Digger's discarded pair lay on the seat beside him.

Marianne gave Kit her sad attractive smile. 'It was the only idea I had in the short time available. The poor man would have drowned.'

Kit smiled back. 'Instead, he suffered a fate worse than death. You were absolutely splendid.' Looking over her head to Calder, he went on, 'I'm sure you're suitably grateful to this courageous young woman. Her quick thinking, at cost to her reputation, saved us all from internment for the rest of the war.'

The lieutenant flushed again. 'The thing about water dates back to a tragedy in my childhood, but I'd have gone in rather than incriminate any of you. As it was, I felt that was far less likely if we did what Miss Aziz suggested.'

Kit nodded, murmuring dryly, 'I should have thought you'd be on first name terms by now.'

Beno came up to them at that point, saying heatedly to Morris, 'I could do nothing, *nothing*. I will speak with my cousin, who is working at the prison. He will allow you all to escape, rest assured.'

'Hold on, we haven't been arrested yet,' said Kit, in lighter vein. 'However, Lieutenant Calder will have to be collected tonight when your friend picks up the package. Those watchdogs are going to hang around for some time, that's obvious, so we'll not get him away until late tonight.' Turning to the army officer, he added, 'Sorry about all this, but you'll be perfectly safe aboard until a man with a fishing boat comes to take up the package presently dangling beneath the hull. You'll then be conducted to a house owned by someone who'll get you safely back to England. We've already sent eleven home by that route. They all arrived safely.'

George Calder offered his hand. 'Thanks. I appreciate all you've done on my behalf.' Turning to Marianne, he took up one of her hands and kissed it in gallant fashion. 'I'm sorry we were only acting, Miss Aziz. He's a lucky man who has the chance to court you.'

'The man I would marry was *un*lucky, but I am glad to have been of help to you,' she replied, taking up her bag. '*Bonne chance*, Lieutenant.'

Kit escorted her to the main hatch, carrying her small suitcase. There, she turned to him with a smile.

'Thank you for bringing me on this first leg of my journey. I think that what you're all doing is tremendous. I do hope you manage to continue without those devils catching you out.' Going on her toes, she kissed him lingeringly on the mouth.

Taken by surprise, Kit said, 'Calder's the one you're supposed to be keen on, not me.'

Her smile now took on a haunted quality. 'A hundred years ago, when I was a pampered adolescent at a French finishing school, I along with many of my fellows was in love with a dashing young aviator called Kit Anson. That kiss might have been long deferred, but it came from all of us who've known better times. Goodbye, and good luck.'

Kit was silent as he walked with Aldo and Morris to Tom's office. The girl who reminded him strongly of Leone Kirkland had struck a chord in his memory. A schoolgirl in an over-sophisticated black dress, and a very young man overwhelmed by tears on the most triumphant night of his life. Had he ever been so simplistic; had Leone ever been so innocent? Had those really been better times, as Marianne had suggested? Perhaps, but they had been too good to last.

Introspection was cast aside on entering Tom's office. His friend had witnessed the search, but waved aside Kit's suggestion of danger to the owner of *Flamingo*.

'Rot! I've told you a dozen times that I shall deny any knowledge of your scurrilous activities. I'm not putting my head on a chopping block for any of you. What my crew members choose to do once you leave my jetty is no concern of mine. I shall yell that at any person who suggests that it is.'

Kit frowned as he dropped the flight log and cargo manifest on to the desk. 'I sincerely hope you succeed in making your claim stick. Morris could never use that line, however, and I reckon he should pull out now.'

'I'm not pulling out of anything,' Morris protested.

'It's getting too dangerous.'

'It always has been.'

'They're getting too close, pal,' Kit told him sharply. 'It's clear they didn't relish failure today, so they'll be out for our blood now.'

'So what?'

'You have a gorgeous cuddlesome wife with a family of sterling worth. They could get at you through them, if you carry on.'

'We all know the risks,' pointed out Morris, from his perch on the corner of a nearby desk.

'Don't be a fool,' Kit snapped.

'Say that to all those in occupied countries who are hiding or assisting prisoners of war on the run. Say it to the agents working beneath the noses of the enemy, like those who signal as we pass overhead. Say it to all those resistance groups who are fighting their private wars to help ours. Say it to Aldo here. Look, Kit, if it weren't for Marie, I'd have gone to England with Joss. Let me do what little I can here.'

Kit held up his hands. 'OK. I won't say another word. You and Tom have always been obstinate bastards.'

'Where's Digger?' asked Tom then.

Kit gave a sour smile. 'Struggling to inflict his individual brand of charm on a very beautiful, very worldly young woman we brought from Alex. I won't tell you why she's really here, but it's for something a damn sight more dangerous than our lecherous friend.'

'I won't ask, in that case.' Tom lit a cigarette, squinting at Kit through the smoke. 'Any other passengers?'

'One, this time.'

'Anything hanging beneath the boat?'

Kit nodded. 'They'll both be collected by the usual method tonight. Tom, I don't like the look of what's happening along the Med. The build-up of enemy shipping points to some kind of concerted attack before too long. In addition, the air is full of buzzing fighters which object to our presence. On the outward flight, we were followed for over half an hour. When I tried to make a dog-leg near Greece, the bastard fired several bursts close enough to my port wing to change my mind.'

His friend whistled through his teeth. 'If they win the eastern Med, the situation will be really black. We might have to start operating the long way round. Not only would that upset your private arrangements, I'd lose money on each trip. After the disaster last month, it hardly seems safer in the Atlantic either.'

The disaster Tom referred to was the loss of one of his flying boats on its regular run to Madeira and the Canary Islands, which had been forced to make an emergency landing and hit a mine. The Portuguese pilot and crew had been lost, along with twelve passengers and the total cargo. Tom had taken it hard. Pele Guardino had been a friend as well as an employee. It had seemed particularly tragic for these men to die in such a way.

Kit stretched to ease his muscles after the long flight, suggesting that they should continue the present route for a while longer. 'They really can't mistake a bloody great unarmed boat painted bright yellow and bearing Portuguese markings, for a belligerent aircraft.'

'They will if you keep trying to make dog-legs over battle zones, you crazy fool,' came the pointed reply. 'You're not in the International Brigade in Spain now, and don't forget it.'

'Damn sure I'm not. I can't fire back, and it's not a happy feeling, Tom.'

'Give me one by getting down to the real business you're supposed to be conducting on my behalf,' suggested Tom, tipping his chair back on two legs. 'How did Nile International respond to the idea of an increased order?'

For a while, they all discussed the cargo presently being unloaded from *Flamingo*. Tom had made a wise move in switching to freight runs between base and Alexandria. Money was easy to make at a time when shipping goods by sea entailed running through minefields. Since Kit had begun the service six months ago, business had boomed despite the hazards of flying the Mediterranean. Even so, without the spice of the secret side of his job, he would have found the weekly service monotonous. Ferrying boxes, crates and barrels back and forth was a dull business. Passengers at least enlivened a regular flight with their unpredictable behaviour. Merchandise provided no excitement, and Sylva was right in her assertion that this was no occupation for Kit Anson. All the same, although his spirit yearned for adventure and challenge along the pathway to the stars, he was intelligent enough to know that six months of regularly flying a set route had been necessary for a man trying to regain his old skills. Each successful return flight had strengthened his confidence; each take-off and landing had recouped a little of that old magic he had once been able to create when flying. After half a year at the controls of one of the most exciting flying boats ever created, he sensed that Kit Anson was again a name to be reckoned with. Perhaps he still had not the brilliance of the youngster who had nine years ago flown his father's finest design faster than any other man of the time, but he was surely wasted on a freight run.

This inner conviction of his regained ability plagued him with the urge to use it more fully, which did nothing to help combat the pressure constantly employed against him by the girl he loved. As he drew away from Western Med in the early evening of that March day, he was filled with restlessness. Reminding himself that he was lucky to be living in a country free of danger and sudden death, that he was damned lucky to be alive, and to have the woman of his life to return to, did not banish that restlessness. Only when he was almost at the apartment did he realize that Marianne Aziz had caused it. A girl of the same ilk as Leone Kirkland had lost the man she hoped to marry, and was now preparing to risk betrayal, torture and death in order to help his countrymen escape to freedom. He wished she had not travelled in *Flamingo* with them. Her example forced him to compare her with Sylva. In consequence, he parked his car beside the small one owned by his mistress, then climbed the steps to the first-floor apartment feeling reluctant guilt over his delight that she was at home. Loving Sylva Lindstrom was a little like rounding Cape Horn in a masted brigantine, he guessed. For days he was becalmed, then a storm would blow up without warning to buffet and test him to the limit. In the manner of the captain of such a brigantine, he loved the capricious lady and would not allow himself to believe that she would ever leave him to drown.

Only a fortnight had elapsed after their passionate reunion last August, before Sylva had announced her intention to start a private hire service to earn money towards the cost of their South Pole crossing. Hoping occupation would help her to settle to their present situation, yet anxious over her hiring her services to possibly unscrupulous men, Kit had tried to advise her. Telling him that she had been flying for almost as many years as he and certainly had as much experience, she had warned him of her dislike of being ruled by men.

'I have had a divorce because of it, and have walked away from others who thought to love is to possess. Do not make that mistake, also, Kit. I could not bear it.'

Heeding her words, he had said no more. Within a month, she had erected a small office near Mendes' freight company where her aircraft was housed, and had three flights under her belt. Within another month, she had acquired the loan of an apartment near the airfield. Declaring that advertising a twenty-four-hour service demanded her proximity to the aircraft and an address with a telephone, she had moved from Kit's isolated cottage. He had been unable to quarrel with her reasoning. Consequently, when she was in Lisbon at the same time as he was there, he stayed with her in the apartment. When she was away on a trip during his rest between flights, he slept in his own cottage.

After Christmas, she had acquired a smart four-seater which enabled her to fly longer distances carrying a different class of passenger. At that point, Kit had grown too concerned to respect her ruling on interfering. Being loaned a smart apartment by an ageing admirer of a pioneering airwoman was one thing, he had declared, but the loan of an aircraft in which she was then expected to transport his dubious business acquaintants to meetings in out-of-the-way rendezvous was far too risky. In an attempt to make her listen seriously, he had revealed some of his own experiences with aggressive German fighters, pointing out that sorties into unoccupied France and places like Casablanca invited the same brand of danger.

Sylva had disarmed him by begging him to give up his hazardous flights through the Mediterranean, about which she was always frantic with worry for his safety. She then went on to urge him to fly with her to Argentina, where they could plan their polar crossing. It always came back to that; she never gave up hope of persuading him. Whenever he protested at what she was doing, she produced her ultimatum. All she was doing would be for them both, she declared. Her flights earned money for the equipment they would need. Her elderly benefactor had hinted that he would finance their venture, on condition that he was given all rights to the story of their flight and the film they would be required to make of it. He would also expect to select which companies would supply their provisions and equipment. Each time, Kit was forced to refuse her plea without being able to give his true reason for continuing to fly freight when he longed to go with her. Each time, he feared she would go alone.

She stayed, however, caught in a relationship neither could surrender. Seeing less and less of each other, those times they were together were correspondingly more precious. Kit was away for four days of every week, and Sylva often stayed overnight at a destination, picking up fresh clients who would then often want to travel further on. He never knew if she would be at the apartment on his return from Alexandria, or for how long if she was. Often, he came back after an exhausting trip only to find her preparing to leave. On the occasions that she had left a note explaining where she had gone, there was no guarantee that she would not embark on a further flight which would keep her absent until after he had left once more.

As he now let himself in to her apartment, he wondered if he would soon be driving out to his own cottage after saying goodbye to her. Stepping through to the large cream-washed room this evening, his spirits leapt. It was immediately clear that Sylva had no flight planned; there was an aroma which suggested they would be eating dinner at home together. She was lying on her stomach on the floor, one leg swinging idly up and down, wearing a loose robe of bronze chiffon through which the contours of her body showed clearly. She had been reading a book, but now looked up at him with glowing eyes.

'We are here together tonight, darling,' she greeted joyfully. 'Come and kiss me, then take a bath before we eat dinner. I cannot decide if I am more hungry for the pilau or for you.'

He dropped his bag and knelt on the floor to draw her up against him, in arms which had been empty for too long. 'You really are here tonight – all night?' he demanded between kisses.

'Yes. . . whatever will be left of me when you have finished will be here,' she gurgled delightedly. 'I had forgot how greedy you can be.'

'I'm not greedy, just ravenous after all this time without you,' he told her, holding her away and running his gaze over the inadequate robe which was somehow more alluring than if she had been naked. 'Why are we bothering with dinner?'

'Because you have come here tired and full of concentration. You also smell of fuel and the heat. To make love now would not be good, darling,' she said, lying back against his arm to look up at him with her usual candour. 'I will come and help you to bathe, then you will feel good. After that, we eat a nice dinner and you will feel more good. We shall then be lovers.'

'I'm not certain I can wait that long.'

She smiled. 'And so not I. So we shall eat just one dish, then make love. After that, we can enjoy some fruit and cheese before we go to bed again.'

'That sounds much more realistic,' he murmured. 'Let's begin the programme right away.'

As they later headed for bed armed with the fruit bowl, Kit realized Sylva had been right. With the sharp edge taken off his hunger for her and for food, he now felt relaxed but not exhausted. He could take their second union slowly, with all the delights along the way. The stresses and demands of the flight, the tension induced by the forced search of the aircraft on arrival, and the unease he had felt in the company of Marianne Aziz, had faded to the background. Charmed and seduced by sensual pleasures, he wanted nothing more than those tonight.

Leaning back against piled pillows while Sylva peeled oranges with her short practical fingers, which then popped segments into his mouth with curious incitement, Kit told himself she was really two women in one. Tonight she was all female, enjoying every aspect of sexuality with that total lack of guile he found so heady. In some women, her approach might seem vulgar, but there was a directness about Sylva which made his approaches less a conquest than participation in a partnership. It produced an excitement which he had only previously found when hurtling through the sky in a perfect machine. He knew, however, that the telephone could ring and his love would instantly turn into a creature of purpose, clear-headed, efficient and fearless, dressed in a shirt and breeches topped with leather flying jacket. If that should happen, passion would be channelled into her other great love immediately. There would be no long, lingering regretful farewell. She would be afire with impatience for that aerial fulfilment Kit understood so well.

Pulling her against him to brush her sweet orange-drenched lips with his own, he prayed the telephone would not ring tonight. This was the Sylva he wanted and needed after a flight bringing acute depression over what he had seen of the worsening situation. This was the antidote to his excursions into war. Here in Lisbon, he needed the feminine seductress, not the daredevil woman aviator. Yet he then realized his own duplicity. If she was two women, he must also be two men. Otherwise, he would have gone off to Argentina with her, as he longed to do, instead of continuing to carry packages such as the one he had tonight deposited in the night safe of Georges Riccard's bank, to be collected by him tomorrow.

'Do you wish another orange, or perhaps a grape?' queried Sylva.

He smiled lazily. 'I can think of better occupation for my mouth.'

'You hope to feast on me?'

'You're the most luscious fruit in sight.'

'Then eat, darling, quickly. The telephone might call me soon.'

Satisfied and happy, drowsy but unwilling to sleep yet, they lay in each other's arms by the low light of a bedside lamp. Kit stroked her long brown hair as her face rested against his chest.

'You smell of oranges,' he murmured contentedly.

'You smell of a man who has just enjoyed passion. That I like,' she told him, with her usual frankness. 'I do not enjoy scented men.'

'Thank God. That rules out most Portuguese and Spanish philanderers.'

'You are jealous?' she asked, raising her chin to confront him.

Gazing at her determined freckled face made fascinating by such variety of expressions, he nodded. 'All the time.'

'I have no sympathy with such a thing, Kit Anson. There is no jealousy from me of your mistress in Alex.'

He grinned. 'Just as well. I have four, dotted all over the city. Aaah!' he cried, as she seized him in a vulnerable place and demanded the truth from him. 'The truth is that I miss you so much, no other woman could compensate,' he confessed, as she freed him.

'What do you do there?' Settling her face against his chest again, she probed further. 'If there is no woman who coaxes you there, how can you do this so boring job every week?'

It was the question she had asked so many times, and he was presently relaxed enough to give a partially truthful answer. 'It's something I feel I must do. I've said that before, and I'm not convinced that you understand. Not only is it some means of repaying my debt to Tom, it's one way of being useful to my country. It's becoming far from boring. You must have seen something of the presence of enemy aircraft during your own flights – which you continue despite my telling you how worried I am for your safety. All along the Med their numbers are growing. *Flamingo* is frequently shadowed, and we're sometimes warned off with an actual burst of fire across the nose.' At her swift look of protest, he silenced her with his fingers on her lips. 'I won't have a pot calling the kettle black,' he told her firmly.

'Explain that,' she demanded, tugging his hand away.

Cradling her face with tenderness, he said, 'It means that you were about to accuse me of taking risks, while you persist in taking them yourself.'

'I am a *pot*?' she queried, pressing her body closer to his.

'A beautiful shapely work of art,' he assured her, 'but don't try diverting me from the point at issue, madam. *Flamingo* flies a regular service at the same time on the same day of every week. She's a huge beauty painted bright yellow, with Portuguese markings. Yet she still worries a few fighter pilots. What do you suppose a tiny sky-blue four-seater bearing very obscure identification instils in aggressive men in speedy arsenals? Each time you go off on one of your highly lucrative private flights, you damn well risk being forced down and searched, if not actually being shot at. I mean it, Sylva,' he added earnestly. 'You have so much intelligence, I can't understand why you defy all my warnings and continue to endanger not only your own life but those of your passengers.'

With a swift furious movement, she was out of his arms and facing him, as she sat back on her heels in a pose which was defiant yet extremely provocative in her naked state. There was even sexual provocation in her anger, Kit found, as she threw words at him.

'You can't understand. *You can't understand.* Then I

will explain you, Kit Anson. Once more I will explain you why I do this. It is for *us*. It is for what we have to do, and soon. I have been very patient with you in this stupid wish to make Tom the thanks for what he did. Is it also your wish to be killed by these men with speedy arsenals? Is it?'

'Sylva. . . '

'No, you must also not be the black pot,' she warned wildly. 'You must shut the mouth and listen what I say. I have been patient for eight months. This is for two reasons. Before we can leave, we must have money to buy all we shall take for such a flight. Second: I have been fool enough to love you so much. It is always a great mistake. To succeed, only one love must be allowed and that is for flying. It is because you are so close tied with this, that I have mix the two. You have make the same mistake with me.'

'No,' he said swiftly. 'Without you, there'd be nothing.'

She pulled a doubting face. 'If I did not fly, if I did not talk to you of wind velocity, rate of climb or aerodynamics, if I did not listen and understand all you tell me of richer mixtures, engine revs and marine landings, you would still love me? If I was like that silly little wife of your friend Morris, or that spoilt useless girl whose family ruined you, you would still love me?'

Knowing the answer, he avoided it. 'You wouldn't be Sylva Lindstrom, you'd be someone different. You can't ask me that.'

'I can ask you *anything*,' she cried. 'We are two alike. That is why we have to do this record flight together. Any man can fly a yellow machine filled with baskets, wine and pretty tiles, just to please Tom. You are too good for this.' Picking his hands up, she stretched them out before him. 'These have once control a tiny seaplane to fly faster than anyone. These have fly a. . . a speedy arsenal,' she declared, finally recalling his expression. 'In war for Spain they have done this. They have make an unbelievable landing and take-off at Lake Kiju. I was there. I saw. Why do you let these hands take a. . . a *shop* into the air, when I plead you to make history with me? *Why*, Kit Anson?' she ended on a throbbing note.

He must be acutely vulnerable tonight, he realized, for her words reached right to his heart. 'I'd sell my soul to do it. I've told you that so many times.'

'Sell your soul, but not make Tom unhappy,' she declared bitterly. 'Perhaps he is also your lover.'

'*Sylva!*'

'Are you a pilot or a shopman?'

'There's a war on,' he cried, as he had on previous occasions.

'You have go to England, and they do not want you. You can now be free to do other things. So what do you do? Fly this shop.'

'Stop calling *Flamingo* a shop! You don't understand.'

'You stop saying I don't understand,' she countered furiously. 'You make no sense. There is a war; you have been turn down to help in it. You say you would sell your soul; you sell wine and baskets instead. Without me you would have nothing, tonight you say me this. We live here eight months and you spend most time away from me. I think you are full of lies, and I too think you are afraid of the South Pole. It is easier to fly this yellow shop for Tom.'

Recognizing that he had run into one of the storms he always dreaded, Kit found himself unable to ride it tonight. Her words were wounding too deeply. Sliding from the bed, he slipped on his robe and tied the sash with savage force, saying, 'Let's have this out once and for all, Sylva. And for God's sake put something on before we do.'

Padding through to the main room on his bare feet, he cursed the fact that they were not in his cottage. Sylva's absent sponsor seemed to be there in spirit, unmanning him the way she had. When she joined him, wrapped in a sheet Caesar-style, the sight affected him

602

as much as if she had remained naked. He perched on the arm of a large settee feeling highly aggressive. When she sat facing him, and reached for an apple which had fallen when he had taken the bowl into the bedroom, he snatched it away.

'You provoked this, so bloody well sit there and listen properly. We're no longer on an extended sexual picnic.'

Sylva leaned back. '*You* provoked this. You called me a pot.'

The anger melted from him swiftly as he let out his breath on a sigh of exasperation. Yet, as he studied her with the pain of his love, he realized she was still furious. It made him incautious.

'My flights in *Flamingo* are not what they appear to be. When I went to England, they turned down my offer to fly a warplane but asked me to help them in another way. I agreed. I've been operating for them over the past eight months. It's growing difficult as more and more of the Med falls to the enemy, but I can't give it up however badly I want to do something else.'

'You are being a *spy*?' she asked, in disbelief.

'Something of the sort.'

With a swirl of the sheet, she stood up and moved to stand before him, eyes blazing. 'You fool! Will the war be won because Kit Anson flies to Alex with a letter no one understands? Will Hitler be stopped by one man in a yellow flying boat? He has defeat the French; he has walk into all those countries like my own. He has killed thousands in his own land. You have just said he will have all the Med soon. What are you doing with this silly dangerous affair, when you should be flying to the South Pole that no one else can do?'

He said quietly, 'If everyone felt that one person's efforts were useless, no one would be fighting this maniac at all. You have no argument, Sylva.'

'Yes, I have the argument,' she insisted heatedly. 'Everyone is not Kit Anson. Everyone is not a man I love.'

603

Standing, he attempted to take her in his arms. She walked away, shaking her head. 'You tell me I must listen properly. So must then you!' Reaching the end of the large settee, she turned back to face him. 'I do not believe in this war. There was one before. There was always one. Men are killed like the goose is killed for a feast. They are all the same, wars. Kill and kill. Centuries ago it was still the same. Other things are different. They change and get better each time. My brother and Paul have study the germs in Africa for two years so that people will *not* be killed. It is like that with flying. Once, a man could not rise into the air. Now he can.' She flung out an appealing hand. 'Your *Flamingo* is a wonderful machine that can do more than the old flying boats. She can land on Lake Kiju and *save* lives. The aeroplane will be made to go longer distance; carry more passengers. The world will be shown to those who can now never see it. The aeroplane will discover parts of this earth no one has yet seen. It will go on to do this more and more. *This* is good.' Challenging him, she demanded, 'Kit Anson, is there not a better thing to do than you are doing?'

He considered his answer for a while. 'Yes, there are lots of far better things, but they're not vitally necessary to the freedom of the world. The other is.'

'Then let some other man do it,' she cried. 'Some other man who cannot fly as you can.' Coming forward, she launched her full appeal upon him. 'Darling, this war will end sometime. They all do. What use will it have been except to make women widows and children orphans? No one will be better for it. No one. If we fly the South Pole, we shall make good history. We shall make film of places no one has ever seen. We shall give to the world something good, which will lead to more good. We shall risk killing no one but ourselves.' Reaching for his hands, she held them tightly in her own. 'But there is no chance of that, because together we shall succeed. Think, darling! Sylva Lindstrom and Kit

Anson together all the time, making something good for the world.'

She was right. He knew she was basically right. Every instinct urged him to turn his back on Lisbon and head for Argentina. He had signed no contract with Tom, or with Colin Dryden in London. There was no reason why he could not pack his things and go off with Sylva tomorrow. Yet, with agreement almost on his lips, he suddenly thought of Marianne Aziz and knew he must carry on doing what he could. That young record-breaker known as Kit Anson must wait a little longer to recapture his glory.

Sylva allowed him to draw her into his arms now, and she sighed with relief when he began, 'Of course we'll make something good for the world, my darling. . . but not just yet.'

Stiffening in his embrace she looked up with those frank silver-green eyes. 'Are you saying me no?'

'I'm saying wait just a little longer.'

'I have wait too long already. Someone else will do this soon.'

Choosing his words carefully, he sensed that their entire relationship hung in the balance in that moment. 'If the Med falls to Hitler, there may be nothing more for me to do here. I have to see it through to a definite conclusion first.'

'And what if you are killed before it?' she asked icily, stepping away from him. 'You have no thought for me or my wishes.'

'My every thought is for you. I love you beyond reason, you must be aware of that,' he told her desperately. 'But I can't walk away from this commitment. I have to have self-esteem, or my passion for you would make me little more than a faithful dog at your heels. Can't you see that?'

She shook her head. 'I have passion for you, also, but it is for the aviator and not just the man. In bed, you are the same as any other lover. In the air, you are a king. For that, I came to you after the hospital. For that, I came back again and again although you ask me delay. I cannot wait longer. I have money for what we need, and a backer, so I go soon. With all my heart I want to do this with Kit Anson; for deep love and because he will be the perfect partner in the air. I *beg* you to come with me.'

'Sylva. . . '

'If not, I go with Salvadore Delgardo.'

Kit stared at her in shocked surprise. 'The Spaniard who crossed the Alps alone and made that spectacular landing on a glacier? You've met him?'

She gave a brief nod. 'Last week. He wrote me today that he will go with me to Argentina.'

'You've already discussed it with him?'

Her eyes filled with desperate tears. 'I want to go with you. I want *us* to make this record.'

'We'll go,' he told her raggedly, reaching for her again. 'We'll go together, I swear. Wait just another week. Please wait until I've made one more flight. By then, the situation may make what I'm doing well nigh impossible. Please, darling, *please* wait for one more flight. Promise me you'll wait.'

She nodded against his shoulder, gripping him tightly in a desperate embrace.

When he flew the next trip to Alexandria, the situation had worsened considerably, but Sylva had gone when he arrived back in Lisbon.

23

The eastern Mediterranean was slowly being brought
under German control. Yugoslavia had been occupied,
then Greece. British forces had been unable to retain
their foothold on the land of the mythical gods and
ancient temples, so troops were taken off in a massive
rescue operation at the end of that April of 1941. Flying
through the area, even under neutral colours, became
inadvisable if not downright suicidal. With Malta under
constant attack in the expectation of forcing her surrender, and the coast on both sides either controlled by or
allied to Germany, military aircraft commanded the
entire route down to Alexandria. Such was the ferocity of
the battle for control by the Germans and the desperate
defence by the British, neither side wanted unarmed
neutral aircraft getting in the way of their ceaseless aerial
dogfights.

Throughout May, however, Kit and his crew continued to fly *Flamingo* through, relying on recognition
of the large yellow machine by military pilots constantly
in the area, to ensure their safe passage. In fact, they
ran great risks each time. Not only were they several
times forced to make a temporary landing by determined
fighters, both British and German, who saw *Flamingo*
as a threat to their imminent encounter with opposing
aircraft, they also determinedly picked up any men seen
floundering in the water, no matter who they were.
While they in no way flouted their supposed neutral

607

status by performing a humanitarian act, German suspicion of this brightly painted aircraft's activities flourished in Lisbon. The two unsmiling observers were always on the jetty when *Flamingo* docked, so it became increasingly difficult to smuggle ashore any large package, or numbers of British servicemen picked up en route. On one trip they had gone down to pick up four exhausted men drifting on a raft. They had turned out to be German submariners. On reaching Lisbon, Kit had deliberately led the men out to the pair they had dubbed Heinz and Fritz, making no attempt to report their presence to the Portuguese authorities. The two continued to watch their arrivals, however, and Kit realized the gesture had gone no way towards encouraging tolerance from them, in return. The number of their own countrymen they managed to help increased with each flight, as the battle for the inland sea was slowly lost. On the outward journey, there was no problem in landing them in the British-controlled port. They still had to be transferred secretly in Lisbon, however. Once safely ashore, these survivors joined the ranks of many more who had somehow made their laborious, often hazardous, way to Portugal from prisoner of war camps, or who had been smuggled to safety by organizations operating in occupied France in order to fight again. By a well-planned undercover method, they were all spirited away to England without ruffling the neutrality of this gentle country on the edge of Europe.

By the final week of May, the step towards total control was taken by the Germans. Crete was invaded, the population terrorized by savage reprisals taken against those who tried to resist gradual occupation of the island. The defending British force was helpless. With Greece and her adjacent islands to the north already taken, and the area across the sea to the south held by German and Italian armies, there was little hope of reinforcements or of escape. They faced capture and internment for the rest of the war, which was certainly going in Hitler's favour wherever one looked.

When *Flamingo* took off on what Tom and her crew all agreed would probably be her last flight over that route, Kit experienced a curious sensation of having reached a crossroads, once more. Each time he set out on a determined course, it never led to a final destination. His life had been merely a series of progressions towards yet another change of direction. It was as if destiny had not yet decided what to do with him. Accordingly, as he took off from the water this morning in the initial spectacular climb, he offered destiny a free hand. Devastated by the loss of Sylva, he hardly cared what lay in the future. Without her, life would be colourless. As he banked to put *Flamingo* on course, he told himself savagely that he was still flying Tom's yellow shop because he was an utter fool. Right now, he could be in Argentina with the woman he loved, planning the most incredible flight of his life. He could no longer blame the Kirklands for depriving him of all he valued. He had been crazy enough to ruin his own life, this time. Did it really matter where he went from here?

Tom had already spoken of going around the long route through Bathhurst, Accra and Cairo, thence to Alexandria, if it did not fall. Kit thought it unlikely that he could be of use to Colin Dryden on that totally neutral route, unless Hitler overran the whole of Africa, too, so he truly would be doing nothing more than piloting a flying shop, as Sylva had so scathingly called it. Yet, even as the idea formed, his admiration for *Flamingo* protested. If he was too good a pilot for such work, then she was too good an aircraft. She had first hit the headlines as a sensational pink-lined luxury boat, then again as the heroine of a daring lake rescue. She might not be the goddess *Aphrodite* had once been, but she was regal enough to be a queen of the air. He hated the idea that she had already known her finest hour. . . or that he had known his. Yet it looked very much that way.

Morris would most likely be glad of an honourable way out of this dangerous business before some drama occurred. Digger had allowed himself to be part of it only because they were a united crew, and because he relished excitement. He still steadfastly maintained his stance that, as an Australian, the war in Europe was not his concern. For Aldo, it was even less his concern. His crew would possibly be very happy to fly the long route, with some fun along the way at the neutral refuelling stops. Kit knew in his heart that he would not. Yet he had thrown away the greatest chance an aviator could have, and the greatest love he would ever find. Small wonder he was a man in emotional and professional turmoil as they passed Gibraltar to enter the former playground of the rich and titled.

His introspection led him to dwell on the proving flight he had made over these same waters, just three years ago. Recollection of his triumphant arrival in Naples twisted the knife in his wound. For a brief while, a hero had been revived. Sylva had offered him a second revival, which he had refused. Maybe it was time to let that youthful record-breaker return to the past, where he belonged.

The engines droned on for several hours, and the sun climbed high until it was almost overhead. On the blue surface below there was a great deal of shipping. Kit sympathized with the captains of these vessels. Treacherous waters, beneath even more treacherous skies. They were nearing Malta now, and Kit was not really surprised when two aircraft bearing the black cross appeared seemingly from nowhere, to fall in as determined flank escorts.

'Here we go again,' he murmured to Aldo. 'What I'd give for a machine-gun or two right now.'

The co-pilot grinned. 'To give them brrrr, like you did in Spain?'

'This isn't the Spanish war,' Morris pointed out. 'It's a damn bigger one.'

'And you're not flying a single-seat monoplane, mate,' Digger reminded him. 'If you want to indulge in heroics, wait until I get off. I like my skin just as it is, not peppered with holes.'

Kit was in no mood for such banter – he had not been since Sylva left – and now resented being forced off course by two sleek fighters armed to the hilt. Obstinately sticking to the compass bearing, he continued a course which would take him close to Malta.

'This *bandido* signals very strongly,' observed Aldo, watching from the starboard windows. 'We shall have to do as he wishes.'

Kit ignored the comment. However, he could not ignore the sudden break away of the Messerschmitt, which then flashed back towards them firing a burst across *Flamingo*'s nose.

'For Pete's sake, do as he wants,' cried Morris. 'He'll turn the guns on us next time.'

'He'll cause an international incident, if he does,' Kit said through a tight mouth.

'That won't bring us all back to life,' Digger remarked acidly. 'Don't be a fool. You can't win an argument with these two.'

The Australian was right. The feeling of impotence which had lived with him since the day he had discovered Sylva gone now increased to tighten his stomach muscles and produce a dull pain. He was no more than a flying shopkeeper. These grim-faced strangers in leather helmets and goggles could command him at will, and he had no way of hitting back. He pushed the control column over and veered to starboard. This was not the first time they had been ordered to clear air space over the direct route eastward, but today Kit found compliance unacceptable. The fighters stayed with them for fifteen minutes, to ensure that they kept well clear of the British island garrison.

After refuelling at Tunis, as usual, during which time the crew enjoyed a light meal and chatted to their agent about the threat to continuance of their weekly flight, they took off for the second leg to Alexandria. Aldo took the controls for the first few hours of the long haul, while Kit dozed uneasily in the cabin, troubled by tormenting dreams. When Digger made tea for them all, Kit took over from Aldo feeling very little refreshed by the break and more belligerent than ever. Accordingly, it was not long before he reached a decision and asked Morris for a course which would take them back on a central Mediterranean course instead of one hugging the coast.

'Are you totally mad?' demanded Digger immediately.

'No, I'm the captain of this aircraft,' he snapped back. 'You're simply a member of my crew. As such, shut up and leave me to fly to Alex whichever way I see fit.'

Morris began to speak. 'Digger's got a point. . . '

'The same applies to you,' Kit interrupted grimly. 'Give me the bearing I requested.'

Uneasy silence hung between them after Morris had complied. Kit continually swept the clear blue around him with a keen glance, half expecting tiny dots to appear on the horizon as the minutes passed. He also studied the clear blue below as they entered the widest part of this enclosed sea, before it narrowed again between Crete and Cyrenaica. There was the usual selection of small native craft, but he also identified the more sinister fast-moving gunboats which patrolled in the hope of preventing supplies from reaching the last British stronghold at the end of this vital access to the East. Without the Mediterranean, tedious passage around the tip of Africa must be made, adding weeks to the journey. There was a valid reason behind what his friends saw as his foolhardiness. If this was to be their last flight over a route Western Med had used for some years, he would use it to gain one last piece of information. Having sacrificed the woman he loved and an aviator's dream in order to fulfil this dual commission, he would ensure that this flight would comprise more than a mere delivery of goods. He determined to take a look at Crete as he passed.

At some distance from the island it became apparent that something was afoot. The sea was alive with an unusual number of small craft, and there appeared to be a complicated aerial battle under way. Heading straight for this activity, Kit took it in with a growing sense of excitement. A large military operation was evidently in progress. It suggested a concerted attempt to reinforce the island and save the trapped British troops by driving the Germans back to the mainland of Greece.

'Take a look at this,' he invited, over his shoulder. 'What do you make of it?'

Morris and Digger came up behind him to study the scene through the cockpit windows. One of them whistled through his teeth as all three watched the activity below, which left criss-crossing creamy furrows as boats passed back and forth, and the activity ahead, which left the heavens criss-crossed by pale contrails as battling aircraft sought to gain dominance. Amidst the fighters, small clouds kept materializing to signify gunfire from batteries on the island. As *Flamingo* steadily approached, the sound of distant thuds emphasized these artillery attacks.

'Christ, there's a whole war going on out there,' exclaimed Digger. 'We're heading right into it. You really are crazy, mate.'

'Not that crazy,' Kit assured him, keeping his gaze ahead. 'This boat isn't fast enough to join in, and we'll only confuse our own lads if we get too close. I'd like to find out exactly what's going on, just the same. They might like the latest report when we dock at Alex.'

'I don't like the look of it,' said Morris.

'I bet our troops trapped on that island like it, though,' Kit countered. 'Whatever's happening, it must be designed to help them. Get Aldo up here. I'll need him.'

For once, the belligerent aircraft were so intent on their own battle, *Flamingo* approached apparently

613

unnoticed. Kit was so intent on watching them, he missed something Aldo did not when he came from the cabin to take his seat full of excitement. Tapping Kit's shoulder, he pointed out to the left.

'Great Scott, flying boats!' said Kit, in surprise. 'They're ours, too. What the hell are they doing mixed up in this business, I wonder.'

With his sense of inner excitement increasing, he studied the pair of Sunderlands with RAF markings, which were presently flying in opposite directions on a straight course between Crete and Alexandria, as if operating a shuttle service. They must be ferrying arms and supplies, he decided.

'I don't like the look of this,' said Morris again, 'and I suggest the best way of discovering the ins and outs of it is to ask when we reach Alex. . . all in one piece,' he added emphatically.

'I agree,' said Digger slowly. 'This is too big for us. I'd like to know why we weren't warned by our people in Alex that there was something planned.'

'It might have blown up suddenly,' reasoned Kit. 'All attention would have been concentrated on the emergency. People like us would have been overlooked. However, I'm inclined to agree that we have no choice but to push on to Alex,' he continued, envy colouring his tone as he watched the progress of the military flying boats. They might, like himself, be ferrying supplies, but no one would call them flying shops. They had gun turrets fore and aft, and definite military markings.

It was with reluctance that he embarked on a starboard turn, which would put them on course for Alexandria. Thirty seconds later, his pulse raced as he saw the puff of an artillery shell appear by the wing of the southward-bound flying boat, quickly followed by the glow of flames. Fire soon engulfed the starboard engine of the stricken aircraft.

'She's been hit,' he exclaimed sharply. 'There's no way she'll reach Alex now.'

Without further words, he pulled out of the turn and began to head towards the aircraft from which smoke was now pouring. The sun had passed its zenith and was on its way down. The blinding glare in his eyes caused him to lose sight of his quarry momentarily. Knowing where she must be heading, he remained on a course he guessed would take him to her. The thunder of heavy guns was now even clearer above the sound of *Flamingo*'s engines. A backward glance through the port windows showed the wheeling, diving fighters marginally nearer now they had reversed direction and were closing on the vicinity of the battle. The coast of Crete lay stark, sheer and unwelcoming against the clear depths of unending blue sea stretching away to freedom. From that island came the hostile assault of anti-aircraft guns, and the boom of heavier ones as they fired at the ships drawing closer. It all reminded Kit of those things he had once experienced; wartime flying was a sensation never truly forgotten by any participant.

'Here she is,' said Aldo urgently, as the flight curve took them out of the sun's full glare to give a clear view of the other craft. 'She is going down very fast.'

'Too fast,' Kit said thoughtfully. 'It can't be just the fire. She must have been hit elsewhere. The pilot knows it's useless attempting to go on, so he's making an emergency landing while he can.'

'You're going down after him, aren't you.'

It was a statement rather than a question from the young Portuguese. Kit offered no answer, therefore. All he did was advise Morris and Digger to get below ready to open the hatch when *Flamingo* halted beside the doomed flying boat.

'We'll take the crew aboard as soon as they abandon ship,' he added. 'If the fire really takes hold, there could be an explosion. I don't want to be there if there is, so make the business snappy.'

While his friends clattered down to the lower deck, Kit concentrated on the aircraft he was pursuing. With the intention of landing as close to its setting-down position as he could, and thus cut down on valuable time, he had to study his fellow pilot's rate of descent and gauge his own accordingly. The other machine did not behave exactly as *Flamingo* did, of course, but Kit soon realized it could not behave normally. As it wove from side to side, dropping in a series of alarming manoeuvres which suggested descending a flight of steps, it occurred to Kit that the pilot himself must have been hit. It would certainly explain why he was making no attempt to run for home.

That suspicion became certainty when the aircraft suddenly dropped like a stone, bounced on the choppy surface, then slewed to one side as the port wingtip dipped deep into the water. Concentrating on bringing *Flamingo* down in her abbreviated descent to a lively sea, Kit listened to Aldo's account of what was happening and was dismayed when he said the other's wing had snapped beneath water pressure. With a great shuddering smack, *Flamingo* touched down to send a surge of water up almost as far as the cockpit windows as she raced towards the crashed aircraft which was certain to go under before long. Kit fought the resistance of the sea, until they were taxiing at a speed which allowed him to take her in a wide turn. He then headed back to where the other machine was already awash. What he then saw filled him with alarm. From the hatches which still remained above water, men in khaki were leaping into the sea in a continuous procession. He had been wrong to imagine supplies in that flying boat; she was packed with soldiers.

'Christ, she's a troop carrier,' yelled Digger from below. 'We'll never manage them all with this cargo on board.'

'Ditch the cargo,' instructed Kit, as he took *Flamingo* on a line which would allow them to approach as near as he dared. 'Start pushing overboard now anything you can handle.'

A blast of air rushed up to meet him as they dropped speed to no more than a gentle glide, enabling his crewmen to open the cargo hatch. His heart was thudding with a sense of urgency as they stopped, with just the starboard engines now running. The scene was extremely distressing. Heads were bobbing in the water all round the doomed aircraft, yet men still spilled from the hull. Then, as he was on the point of going below to help pull them aboard, he saw the other flying boat keel over and vanish as suddenly as if some unseen Neptune had reached up to pull her into his kingdom. Next minute, there was nothing but a swirling eddy to mark where she had been – that, and half a hundred men desperately splashing their way towards *Flamingo*. Kit grew icy. The crew and any number of soldiers must have been inside that hull as it sank. Curious terror froze him to the spot as he relived those moments before crashing into a grey nightmare off Lisbon. For those poor devils, there had been no sandbank to save them.

His hesitation was only momentary. Leaving Aldo at the controls, he took the steps to the lower deck, snatched two life-belts from the bulkhead, then hauled open the forward hatch to heave them with all his might towards the men struggling to stay afloat despite the impediment of heavy uniform and boots. Racing through the hull to where Morris and Digger were frantically jettisoning anything they could manhandle, Kit did the same with the life-belts in the aft section. Next, he inflated the dinghy to push away on the rise and fall of the waves.

Slowly, punishingly, the collection of pale faces drew nearer, changing direction as *Flamingo* drifted slightly in the lively sea. One life-belt had been swept wide of the survivors, but the other three were now supporting groups of men looking near the end of their tether. Some had captured the dinghy, climbed aboard, and used the paddles to cross to their comrades who welcomed the support offered by the ropes each side. Kit now stood in the open forward hatchway, ready to throw ropes as soon as any swam near enough to seize the ends. The stiff breeze ruffled his hair, and flapped the legs of his shorts as he braced himself against the motion of his craft. He watched the rise and fall of the waves with anxiety. As *Flamingo* swung round further, he could see the far-off coast of poor war-torn Crete. Above it, aircraft were still battling and wheeling, while the thunder of guns from the island batteries added a sinister background to the afternoon.

The survivors began arriving in small batches as the waves swept them suddenly close. Kit threw lifelines to those who looked most desperate, then secured the ends to enable them to haul themselves to safety, or to hold on until he did so. Those who had managed to swim right up to the yellow hull trod water with difficulty, as they waited for Kit to haul them the several feet to the lip of the hatch. There was no exchange between any of them. Urgency allowed no time for words.

Kit's arms and back began to ache. Nearing the end of this long flight, he was physically weary, and some of the larger men were a dead weight to lift from his position five feet above them in a rolling aircraft. Several of those who had already scrambled aboard now appeared beside him to help others up through an entrance normally served by a jetty or a launch. When the dinghy came alongside to deliver seven grateful survivors, Kit was briefly reminded of a similar moment when a girl in khaki had stepped aboard this same aircraft and into his heart. That mental vision was banished when the last man in the boat, a sergeant with thinning sandy hair, declared his intention of going back to pick up more and paddled away again.

It was whilst stretching up to ease his back that Kit became aware of a sound he knew well; a dread sound swiftly followed by another. Next minute, a diving fighter flashed past, raking *Flamingo*'s hull with bullets and setting the sea dancing with tiny splashes. A spasm of fury gripped him as he realized what was happening; his mind raced with the implications of an attack. *Flamingo* was the perfect sitting target. She had no guns, no means of warding off further attacks. Neither had the men in the sea. Yet *Flamingo* was the only hope of survival for those already aboard; the only means of returning to Alexandria.

At that point in his anguished thoughts, he heard the German fighter approaching once more. He and the others crowding inside the hull ducked instinctively at the ominous rattle of bullets on metal. Heartrending shouts and cries were now coming from those in the sea. Some looked to be drifting motionless where they had been swimming frantically before.

Kit's blood ran cold as he faced the unthinkable. As at Lake Kiju, he was now forced into a decision on which a certain number of lives had to be weighed against others. In Spain he had been forced to leave men to die, but today it represented possibly the hardest thing he had ever been made to do. He tried not to look at those terrified faces in the water as he resolutely tugged the hatch back into position. There was an immediate outcry from those around him; an aggressive vocal rage.

'You can't leave those poor buggers out there,' cried a shivering soldier, with a touch of hysteria in his voice. 'They'll die.'

'You *bastard*,' swore another ferociously.

'Sergeant Hamilton's gone back out there. You can't abandon them!'

The chorus rose as Kit punched the button which flashed a warning light as the cargo hatch closed automatically. Thrusting his way through the crowding belligerent troops, he avoided considering the thoughts of those about to be left to their fate as he charged up the steps to the flight deck, shouting to Aldo to start up the inboard engines for take-off. Even as he settled in his seat, another burst of fire hit *Flamingo* on the port wing, mercifully missing the two engines, so far as he could tell. Increasing throttle, he prepared to leave, feeling like a mass murderer. Reason told him even more lives would be lost if he allowed this aircraft to be put out of action, yet it was hard to accept that truth. Better by far, to save half than none at all, yet even that possibility hung in the balance while the attacks continued. If only he had the means of firing back!

Never had he been so glad of *Flamingo*'s initial superb take-off. Even so, his concentration on what was always an unpredictable operation, even in idyllic conditions, struggled against the images of those he had deliberately abandoned, which superimposed themselves on the instrument panel. Sweating profusely and fighting a sensation of nausea, he was then shocked into taking instinctive action which quickly banished the images of dying men. Their German attacker, plainly unprepared for such a rapid climb from a flying boat, had levelled out and now raced past overhead so close that only Kit's swift manoeuvre prevented a mid-air collision. Although *Flamingo* responded, she did so sluggishly. For a few alarming moments Kit believed she would stall and plunge back into the sea. She held, however, but a sharp tap on his shoulder and Aldo's pointing finger drew his attention to a series of rips across the starboard wing, which had caused damage to the forward strut holding the float below it. Landing would constitute a problem. With that unwelcome prospect came a cause for even greater concern, as a second dark diving shape flashed past too close for comfort.

'Christ!' he swore, trying to coax the machine into a climb again. 'They're all turning on us.'

'No, they're not,' roared Digger with excitement. 'That bloke's an Aussie. He's chasing the sausage-eater off!'

'It's one of ours?' queried Kit hopefully.

'No, mate, it's one of *mine*,' came the proud correction. 'There's a roo painted on the side.'

Taking *Flamingo* in a wide turn to gain even more

height, Kit scanned the sky around him. Sure enough, the German aircraft which had been attacking was now very definitely the victim of a Spitfire intent on sending it down to join the men on which it had been firing. It was not long before the pilot had his revenge, and a hollow cheer rose from the soldiers on the lower deck. That cheer crystallized for Kit what had been little more than an anguished wish from the moment he had closed the hatch against their comrades.

His gaze dropped to the sea, where tiny dots were now closing on a lozenge-shaped dinghy. It would never support that number, he knew. Raising his eyes again, he studied the sky in their vicinity. It was now clear, save for the one Spitfire circling above those dots in the sea. He had known wartime aviation, and recognized the message spelled out to him by that solitary fighter with a kangaroo painted on its side. Without hesitation, he acted on it. Heading back to the spot where the other flying boat had gone down, he began losing height in preparation for another landing. Taking *Flamingo* lower and lower, he shouted instructions to the friends comprising his crew.

'Open both hatches as soon as it's feasible. Each of you take some of the more vigorous men as helpers, then pull them aboard just as fast as you can. Leave the bodies. I want to be off again before our pal above is obliged to end his protection. He can only stay there so long.'

Morris and Digger departed, leaving Kit to glide down anxiously watching the starboard float, until the great yellow craft skimmed the water before settling on to the waves once more. He remained at the controls this time, wondering how he would ever get *Flamingo* up with such a load aboard. The really heavy cargo could only be shifted with winches, so those boxes and barrels already ditched would only have made minimal difference to the weight. As he sat sweating and tense, he recalled the take-off at Lake Kiju which had made his own hair stand on end. Warren had sworn then that his brain-child could make it, and Kit had put his faith in her. He would have to do so again. At Kiju he had had only a short stretch of brown water on which to perform a miracle. Today, he had an entire blue sea. *Flamingo* was about to be a passenger liner with wings again, and this was clearly going to be her finest hour. With a prayer, and a great deal of luck, added an inner voice.

It seemed interminable sitting in the cabin with little idea of what was happening below. Finally, Aldo appeared, his long sensual face alive with dramatic excitement.

'They are all aboard. We have made them spread out to help the balance, but there is one hell of a lot of them, Kit.'

'I know,' he said briefly. 'Short of pushing some back into the drink, we've got to get to Alex somehow.'

'They are not reinforcements, as we thought,' the Portuguese added loudly, as Kit ran all four engines ready for departure. 'Crete is being evacuated. Two British squadrons are going back and forth, to fly off as many as possible before they fall into German hands. These men are pretty damn grateful.'

It was something of a blow to realize that the last tenuous foothold along the eastern end of the Mediterranean was now lost. How long could Alexandria hold out now? With that thought in his mind, he prepared for the most doubtful take-off of his life, knowing how many lives he would be risking in the process. The engines were now giving sufficient power to begin his run. As *Flamingo* began to move forward sluggishly, he wished the surface was a little calmer. Giving power in the usual ratio, he was dismayed by the minimal effect it had on the forward surge. It was as if he were driving this superb machine through glue, from which he would never prise her into the air.

Slowly picking up speed, they nevertheless remained on the surface to bump and shudder alarmingly while

Aldo kept an anxious eye on the float to his right. Spray obscured it almost completely, but they would soon know if the strut snapped. The chances of lifting off would then be lessened even further. On and on they ploughed, with *Flamingo* noisily announcing her anguish, until the normal time for lift-off had been reached and passed. With his throat tightening, Kit fought to make the machine rise but, for once, she resisted his will. Aching, fearful, yet with iron determination that she could and would do it, he did all he could to coax her to lift into the air. Still she bumped across the waves with engines roaring a complaint, until he began to believe they would taxi all the way to Alexandria.

'Come on! *Come on*, you beautiful creature,' he murmured desperately. 'We can do it, you know we can. You're the queen of boats, and I'm Kit Anson. Of course we can do it!'

Of course they could! Well past the usual short run, *Flamingo* finally heaved herself a few feet into the air. Afraid she might instantly drop back, Kit hauled on the controls to create that unmistakable upward surge. With *Flamingo* unable to rise in her usual spectacular fashion, the climb was laborious and cumbersome. It was enough, however. Kit knew they were past the danger point; she would not let him down now. Whispering love words to her, wooing her with honeyed flattery on her grace and magnificence, he levelled out at no more than feet above the undulating waves. All at once, he felt like the young man who had long ago flown another yellow mistress in triumphant manner across Lyme Bay. The world and his wife might not be watching today, but the sense of elation was as great. In the manner of the water-bird after which she was named, *Flamingo* cast a rippling shadow on the blue beneath as she turned and headed for Alexandria.

Aldo flashed Kit a brilliant smile as his hand gripped his shoulder in congratulation.

'Bloody marvellous!' exclaimed Digger from the rear. 'I never thought you'd do it.'

'Oh ye of little faith,' responded Kit happily. 'No wonder you have such trouble with girls. You've no idea how to coax the best from them. It takes an expert like me.'

'Save the rejoicing until we're safely down,' advised Morris. 'Those boys might have another ducking when we land.'

'Many injured?' Kit inquired.

'Eight – two seriously.'

'OK. When we get within range, radio Alex to have ambulances standing by.'

'There's an officer with them, who wants to come up and recite a vote of thanks.'

Kit shook his head. 'Tell him he can recite it down there. *Flamingo* will hear it, wherever he is.'

The sun had almost dropped below the horizon when they eventually came in sight of their destination. It was a welcome sight in more ways than one. The overloading had slowed them considerably, and fuel was getting low. Not only that, the strut of the float looked to be weakening. How it would stand up to the landing was a source of worry to every member of the crew, not least the two pilots. A curious change had been wrought in one of them, however. Kit sat at the controls a man more in charge of his own future than he had been since that evening when he had discovered that drawings of his father's *Solitaire* had been used to build a seaplane named *Aphrodite*. He now saw that he did not need to fly to the South Pole to prove himself. Most directions he had taken at the crossroads of his life had ended in sadness or disaster. This time, he would take a step at a time, not looking for the end of the road but waiting to discover what he might encounter along the route. These men he had dragged from the sea could only live that way. Today could have been their last; tomorrow might well be. It had been a salutary encounter, so far as he was concerned.

Morris had radioed for ambulances and been promised them. He had also warned the port authorities that they were coming in dangerously overladen, with structural damage. Emergency services would be standing by, and small boats alerted for possible hazards on landing, they had been assured. Approaching the twinkling lights of the docks, Kit dared not fly his normal course in case of collision with cranes and towers. Passing close to the outer harbour still very low over the water, he headed for the company mooring. Sure enough, there were the ambulances, and a rescue launch beside a fire-fighting vessel. The coming minutes would prove whether or not their services would be needed.

Overshooting the mooring deliberately, he flew on until there was enough distance to make a wide sweep before regaining a direct course. Dusk was always tricky. It put shadows on the water, which disguised the exact position of the surface. Many a man had flattened out too soon, or ploughed into the water believing it to be some feet lower than it was. Straining his eyes to see the dark deceptive expanse as it flashed past below, Kit brought *Flamingo* in with the skill of a would-be lover coaxing his sweetheart into a secluded trysting place. The flying boat practically kissed the water, before surrendering herself to greater immersion.

However, with the water creaming peacefully around her bows, she suddenly went mad and began careering in a sharp turn leading to the stone wall of a nearby dock. Aldo shouted that the float had been whipped backward by the force of the water, but Kit had been holding himself ready for the emergency. Keeping the machine level with great strength, his arms took the strain as they raced headlong towards the wall. With the flaps down and the drogues out, there was little else he could do to decelerate except pray. He had forgotten the excessive load on board, and it was this which slowed their forward surge within twenty feet of the solid wall. Taking in a sharp breath to relax his taut stomach muscles, he told Aldo to quickly organize half a dozen men to sit on the port wing before they tipped over. While they scrambled through the overhead hatch to do his bidding, he remained where he was. *Flamingo* had given him her all today; he could hardly bear to leave her.

Morris spoke into the sudden quietness. 'What a time to choose, to demonstrate to us all that you're still one of the best marine pilots around. We've known that all along.'

Feet clattered on the steps as Digger arrived from below. 'It's bloody awful down there. Half of them have been as sick as dogs.'

Kit sighed heavily. 'That's nothing. They could now all be dead.'

His friend gave the usual craggy grin. 'Nah! I knew you'd get us here in one piece. After that pal of mine in a Spit made it possible, you just had to.'

'I thought you said this war is no concern of Australians,' Morris reminded him.

'*Was*, mate, *was*. After what I saw back there, I'm in it, believe me.'

Kit managed a faint smile, as he said wearily, 'You damn fool, you've been in it ever since our first flight along here. Why the hell do you think we've been doing it – for fun?'

They remained in Alexandria for three weeks. The crisis precipitated by the fall of Crete delayed the opportunity for repairs to a neutral aircraft, despite the courageous rescue of thirty-eight men from the sea. During the period of waiting, Kit spent a great deal of time with pilots of the RAF flying boats stationed in Alexandria, who had effected the evacuation of Crete under heavy fire. From them he learned of the many valuable services these marine aircraft performed in squadrons: air-sea rescue, convoy escort, submarine pursuit, and special missions for the various Intelligence departments. Many of these duties involved solo machines, which tended to breed a type of flier who was a law unto himself.

After talking to these men, Kit spent long solitary periods trying to come to terms with his resolution to command his own future. He had been unable to pull out of the spin he had been in since meeting Sylva, and had crashed to earth when she left. World newspapers had recorded her arrival in Argentina with Salvadore Delgardo, outlining their proposed attempt at an Antarctic record. Kit supposed she was now the man's mistress – she enjoyed sexual indulgence too much not to be – and had put their own magnificent relationship from her mind. In the search for fame and glory, there was no place for heartbreak.

His own heart was not exactly broken, just empty. Those waiting days in Alexandria caused him to analyse his obsessive passion for a woman who had entered his life at one of its most dramatic and highly charged moments. If he had not been responsible for saving her life at Lake Kiju, during an incident which had restored his reputation in the eyes of the world as well as his own, would her impact have been as great? If she had not come to him when he had been under the spell of a time remembered, the echo of a former triumph, would he have surrendered his soul so swiftly? If Sylva Lindstrom had not been part woman, part aviator could she possibly have enchanted him beyond reason? Finally, he forced himself to ask the ultimate question. If he had gone with her to create a new record by flying across both Poles, would she not then have walked away from him having exhausted his professional usefulness? The answers to those probing suppositions told him he could choose to remain crippled for life by the emotional crash he had sustained, or he could fight back as he had after the physical crash on a sandbank.

Hour after hour he mulled over which direction to

take from this present crossroads. To recover from his bodily injuries, he had worked exhaustingly at Dr Kleist's bizarre and curious tests so that he had had little time to think. Inner wounds could possibly be healed that same way, but a long safe route to Alexandria flying freight would not be taxing enough to stifle yearning he must not allow. Tossing restlessly at night, haunted by memories of Sylva, Kit gradually reached a decision. To consolidate it, he persuaded one of the RAF flying boat pilots to take him as his first officer when sickness had depleted his crew. Returning from a successful search for a U-boat skulking near the coast of Turkey, he knew he had found the cure he was seeking.

The repairs were eventually completed, and *Flamingo* was scheduled to leave at dawn on a late June morning. Before going to bed the previous evening, Kit had been asked to take four passengers to Lisbon. He had agreed, wondering who Messrs Duncan, Benedict, Simpkins and Waters could be. Fifteen minutes before take-off the men arrived by staff car, to be ferried out to the mooring where *Flamingo* rode the rippling surface. In civilian clothes, with briefcases, they looked like businessmen. Kit recognized their unmistakable features instantly, and guessed there must be a high-powered conference arranged in Lisbon with other leaders concerned in the Mediterranean situation. Respecting their incogniti, Kit welcomed each aboard and saw them settled before explaining the route they were now forced to fly.

'A long, uneventful journey will probably be a welcome change for you, gentlemen,' he concluded. 'After our outward adventures, it will even be welcomed by myself and my crew, I assure you.'

The first leg to Tunis was enlivened by no more than a passing squadron of British bombers, whose pilots first eyed them suspiciously then gave friendly waves. Aldo took them safely in to the company mooring, where the refuelling boat was already taking up her position. Leaving Digger to supervise the process, crew and passengers went ashore for a light meal before continuing. Kit headed straight for their agent's office, leaving the others to order a drink before lunch. Raymond Leck, a Eurasian, was engrossed in some papers when Kit walked in, hot and thirsty, with his shirt sticking to his back.

Dropping a small package on to the agent's desk, he said, 'There you are, Ray, me lad. The latest copies of *Picturegoer* straight from the delicate hands of the NAAFI girl in Alex, as usual. Have this lot on me, as a farewell gift. I shall not pass this way again.'

The man seemed unconcerned with the film magazines he loved to study from cover to cover. He frowned at Kit. 'You already know?'

'Know what?'

'About the trouble with Western Med.'

Kit leaned on the desk, suddenly alert. 'We're talking at cross-purposes. What's up, Ray?'

The agent got to his feet, holding out a sheet of paper. 'This came in from Tom Digby two hours ago. Read it.'

Kit scanned the terse communication with a growing sense of being once more in the hands of destiny. A diplomatic storm had arisen over *Flamingo*'s rescue of thirty-eight armed soldiers during a military engagement. The Germans in Lisbon had seized their chance to accuse Western Mediterranean Air Services of anti-neutral activities, using the indisputable incident off Crete as proof of their claim. The British were countering the charge with one of their own; that of unprovoked attack by a German aircraft on an unarmed neutral flying boat engaging in a humanitarian act. The next salvo had just been fired by the Germans, who insisted that an investigation must be made by the Portuguese into the airline run by an Englishman, who owned the aircraft crewed by his countrymen. All Western Med machines were temporarily grounded, and *Flamingo* was almost certain to be impounded on her arrival. The local authorities would have no choice but to place her crew under open arrest until the charge could be investigated. The message ended with Tom's recommendation not to return to Lisbon.

'Sounds bad, doesn't it?' commented Ray.

Kit pursed his lips as he re-read the message. Then he looked across at the other man. 'Without us, they have no leg to stand on, Ray. All other crew members are Portuguese, apart from two Irishmen and a South American. As far as I know, they have never engaged in questionable activities. We have. So long as we stay away, Tom will be in the clear.'

'What will you do?'

Kit gazed from the open window at the yellow craft being refuelled. 'Go on to Gib. I've four passengers for Lisbon, so they'll have to pick up another flight there.'

'Then what?'

'That's up to my crew,' he replied thoughtfully. 'I'd better tell them about this now.'

Digger, Morris and Aldo took the news philosophically, more concerned about the trouble facing Tom than the fact that the Germans had come into the open with a charge against them. They had known all along the risks they were taking. None of them seemed able to offer a solution to their predicament, beyond flying the passengers to Gibraltar, where they would be flown on by the RAF. Only after giving them all every chance to speak their minds did Kit voice something which had been formulating since reading Tom's message.

'You're all aware that the Med is now virtually closed to us, so we couldn't have continued the work we've been doing for British Intelligence. I gave the matter a lot of thought during those idle weeks in Alex, and decided that I wasn't keen to continue flying freight if the other side of our job ended. Picking up those chaps from Crete showed me what I really wanted to do. I intended to go back to England and offer to fly a boat with guns and military warpaint. This message from Tom adds a complication. What do I do with *Flamingo*

630

and her crew?' He glanced at each of their faces in turn. 'Any suggestions?'

They all looked back at him; three wary men in a small hot room on the coast of an alien country, with nowhere to go. Then Digger spoke.

'I don't think we'll come up with a better suggestion than yours.'

'I haven't offered one yet,' said Kit.

'Well, it's bloody obvious what you're asking, mate.'

'Is it?'

'Yeah. If you take *Flamingo* to England, do we want to go with you. That *is* what you want to know, isn't it?'

'I suppose so. . . but she's Tom's boat.'

'What else can we do with her?' asked Aldo.

'Take her as far as Gib, then leave her to be fetched by another crew when this business blows over,' suggested Morris.

Kit shook his head. 'Gibraltar's an even more vital military base than before. They'd never give permission for us to leave a static boat cluttering up the moorings.' Wiping his damp brow with the back of his hand, he focused on Morris. 'This puts you in a bigger spot than any of us. As I see it, the Jerries can't prove anything other than the rescue off Crete. The Portuguese authorities are certainly not going to investigate too deeply, and you can always claim non-participation in the Crete business. You couldn't have prevented a pilot from doing what he wished with his aircraft, so no one can dispute your word on the subject. Tom will back you to the hilt, you know that. If I should take *Flamingo* to England, it will provide further evidence of my sole culpability, and support your plea of innocence. You can leave us at Gib with Aldo, then fly on to Lisbon with our passengers.'

'I'm not sure as hell going back now,' vowed Aldo, in his hot-headed fashion. 'If you take her to England, I go too.'

'Don't be foolish,' Kit told him. 'This isn't your war.'

'You rather I go to jail? Morris may not prevent you from what you do with your aircraft, but I am second pilot. No excuse for me. Besides,' he went on, flashing Kit a persuasive smile, 'I have made this my war by flying with you. What is there for me if I go home? All Tom's aircraft are grounded. No, I come with you.'

'What about you, Digger?' Kit asked.

'I told you at Alex that I'm in it now. When I saw those poor buggers being shot up in the sea, I knew whose side I was on.'

Letting out his breath on a long sigh of decision, Kit then went back to Raymond Leck to ask him to signal Gibraltar with the news that four extremely important passengers for Lisbon would be delivered there instead. Giving his agent a code word provided by a passenger calling himself Bill Simpkins, Kit was not surprised at the swift response giving permission for them to land.

All the crew were unusually silent as they left the familiar mooring they had used for so long on this route. Kit felt almost bemused. No sooner had he reached a decision in Alexandria, than curious events dictated a course which would maintain his partnership with this aircraft. Maybe *Flamingo* was the true love of his life, not any woman.

Keeping well clear of Malta so there would be no risk to his high-powered passengers, Kit then took over from Aldo for the landing in Gibraltar's busy harbour. Gliding down towards the historic island rising from an expanse of sea touched by the westering sun, he felt a sudden unexpected surge of pride. An exile for five years, he was now proclaiming himself a true Englishman and returning home. *Home*! Visions of Sheenmouth rose immediately to fill him with unbidden yearning for that small resort; for its donkeys and Punch and Judy shows on the sands, its cosy cafés along the promenade, its rowing boats on the river, its end-of-pier minstrel show, and its tiny cinema where the seats squeaked with every movement. It had probably all changed now. One thing would remain, however. Sheenmouth Abbey, that great yellow stone building set in green surroundings along the river bank. It had been the best home he had ever known, until he had unrolled some drawings and changed his life irrevocably. Home would now be wherever the RAF sent him. The Abbey belonged to a girl who had never been happy there, and a man whose eyes saw little but dreams.

Landing, he taxied *Flamingo* in the wake of a small launch to guide them to a mooring. No sooner had Digger secured them to it, than a fast boat raced out to draw up alongside. The single passenger, a staff officer in immaculate uniform, climbed aboard to welcome and collect the VIPs before whisking them away to military headquarters. From the cockpit, Kit heard the army man dealing smoothly and competently with the four distinguished men from Alexandria, and something about the voice struck a chord in his memory. Telling himself it had to be imagination, he went down to the cabin for a formal farewell with those he felt privileged to have met. Three feet from the group he pulled up. His memory had not played tricks with him. The elegant, crisply uniformed, unctuous staff officer was Maitland Jarvis.

'Good God, it really is old "Maiters",' he exclaimed, using Donald's undergraduate term of address with great sarcasm. 'Don't tell me Warren actually kicked you out, leaving you no way of avoiding conscription.'

Maitland turned as green about the gills as he had been when flying in *Flamingo*. For once, he seemed lost for words as he gazed in matching disbelief at an old adversary.

Kit continued grimly. 'Not that you've ever lifted a rifle to your immaculate shoulder, I'm sure. Knowing your powers of ingratiation, and your filing cabinet of a mind, you doubtless leapt straight into a safe posting as the indispensable know-all of some senior officer in administration. Well, well, war brings strange meetings.'

'Played it pretty safe yourself, behind a neutral flag,' countered Maitland, rather late by his former standards.

'At least it's honest. Better than donning a brave uniform only to lick boots. You were always rather good at that, as I recall. If you're not a colonel, at least, by the time we've won the war, it won't be for the want of a ready tongue, I bet.'

Having collected himself by then, Maitland reminded Kit of his superb ability to make invisible anyone who had become a nuisance. Turning all his attention to the passengers, who had been fascinated by the exchange, he fascinated them further by addressing each with the correct pseudonym and promising them their individual personal requisites during their overnight stay in Gibraltar. Taking the fact that their visit had been announced only six hours ago, such intimate knowledge of their fads and fancies was a feat truly worthy of the man Kit had always disliked, despite being forced to admire his outstanding efficiency.

After shaking hands with all the crew, the four were guided attentively into the boat. Captain Jarvis gave no word of farewell, nor did he look back as the boat raced for the shore. Kit shook his head with rueful acceptance. The man was probably an invaluable aide-de-camp to an officer of the Hector Kirkland mould, and would come through the war as spick, span and unruffled as ever. All the same, Kit was surprised. Maitland would never have left Sheenmouth Abbey on a patriotic urge, yet who had had the temerity to fire him after so many years of claustrophobic employment? Even more puzzling was the prospect of how a useless society girl, and a designer with his head in the clouds, could run Kirkland's without him.

Due to the lateness of the hour, and the priority of service personnel, *Flamingo* could not be refuelled until the morning. Her crew, therefore, found overnight lodgings as near to the harbour as they could. There, they wrote letters to Tom, and to those who would pack up and send to England their essential possessions as soon as an address could be given. Kit found his missive to Tom difficult to word. He owed the man so much in the name of friendship, and this type of parting seemed inappropriate for such a bond. Knowing there was a strong possibility that they would never meet again, he struggled to express his feelings without going over the edge into maudlin sentimentality. He was listing those few things he would like Tom to ship over to him, when Morris appeared in the doorway of his room.

'Am I interrupting?' he asked quietly.

Kit shook his head. 'I've practically finished this letter to Tom. I haven't asked him to do his best to help you, because it's not necessary with a man like him. Similarly, I've no need to ask you to do what you can, to help him out of this damned business with the Germans.'

Morris sat on a chair near the bed covered with a Spanish blanket. 'You'll have to find another postman to deliver your letters. I'm going to England with you all.'

The news came as no real surprise, yet Kit felt bound to argue. 'You've a wife back there. The rest of us are unattached.'

'I knew you'd say that,' Morris told him. 'We've been together for some time, and had some hairy experiences. That makes a person very aware of how his companions feel and think. You knew damn well I wouldn't go back to Lisbon alone, didn't you?'

'What about Marie?' Kit asked, wondering how he would feel at the moment if Sylva were waiting for him in Portugal.

'She'll have her family with her. It was never like an English marriage, you know. I simply became an addition to the group after the wedding. She'll miss me, of course, but not as much as I'll miss her. All the same, I'm English. Thousands of my countrymen have had to leave their wives and children to go off and fight, so why not me? I'll have the advantage of knowing Marie is safe in a neutral country. The poor devils like those we picked from the sea are worried to death about bombs dropping on their loved ones while they're away. I feel the least I can do is give them a hand by trying to stop it happening.'

Kit smiled. 'You're right. I knew you'd come with us.'

'I had to, really,' said Morris casually. 'I couldn't let some other poor bastard navigate for a pilot who thinks he can land his machine anywhere, at any time. No man has the right to inflict such a fate on another.'

'Cheeky sod!' commented Kit lightly, getting to his feet. 'Come on, I think this calls for a drink.'

Morris joined him by the door. 'Only for those who can take it like a man.'

'One whisky and soda, I promise. And, since the drinks are on me, that's all any of you bastards will get.'

'It's all we'll need to drink to *Flamingo*'s new, exciting rôle.'

'This time, she'll be flying under her true colours,' said Kit, 'and she'll be able to fight back, at last.'

24

They finally left Gibraltar at four the following afternoon, delayed further by the arrival of a convoy crippled by U-boats. Kit decided on a direct route over Spain to reach the Atlantic. Still showing neutral colours, there would be no risk in crossing a country where he had once fought more for the chance to fly again than for a doubtful ideal. Only when reaching the coast of France were they likely to encounter German aircraft, who might take exception to their presence. Kit had no expectation of the entire Luftwaffe being acquainted with the charges against a yellow flying boat named *Flamingo*, but they might be jumpy enough to force them to land at some French port for an inspection of cargo and papers. That would prove fatal. The chances of escaping such a trap would be very slight.

Their plan was to fly to Plymouth. The RAF men at Alexandria had told him there was a flying boat base there, so it seemed to be the logical destination for them. They were all quiet as the aircraft banked away from their usual course to Lisbon and headed for the rugged interior of Spain. A memorable phase was ending in a sudden and dramatic manner. Making this decision had been one thing; acting it out brought home its finality. The only regret Kit had was being unable to bid Tom a decent farewell. Apart from that, he was leaving behind the ghost of an affair which had dazzled and tormented him. Lisbon held too many memories; better by far to break free this way. Sylva belonged to Mombasa and Lisbon. Where he was now heading, there would be no reminders of her elusive magnetism.

They left neutral territory to fly out over the Atlantic. Although they all felt happier over water, where emergency landings were far easier, the knowledge that they were once more entering the battle-skies off France made them tense as they scanned the coast, watching for hostile fighters approaching. None came. Instead, they were fired upon by the jittery captain of an armed merchantman uncertain of their identity. He was also uncertain of his cannon, for the shots were all wide of them.

Kit took the controls from Aldo just before they reached the Brittany coast, the closest they would pass to German-occupied territory. With evening well advanced, by then, Kit prayed their identification markings would be seen by anyone investigating their passage. He could not help recalling Maitland's accusation of hiding behind a neutral flag. How different it would be when they had guns to counter aggressive fighters' attacks. However, as *Flamingo*'s engines continued to sing their throaty quartet, there was no challenge to their progress through a clear milky evening sky, where the moon was already shining a silver welcome to those who had missed the sun.

Morris came forward with the news that the English coast should soon be visible ahead. Kit found himself ridiculously emotional as he strained his eyes for the first sight of it. His homeland had hardly treated him kindly, yet it suddenly seemed very precious. At that moment, something came at them without warning. With his heart jumping, Kit realized that an aircraft had approached to catch him totally unawares. Hot on that shock came another. A second fighter flashed across the top of the cockpit.

'Christ, we're under attack,' he choked. 'How many of the buggers are there?'

Aldo was practically upside down in his attempt to

638

look upward through the windows. 'Cannot be told,' he panted. 'Gone too damn fast.'

'Calm down, calm down,' yelled Digger, from his position at a porthole. 'I see them. They're Hurricanes. Must be a welcoming committee.'

'I'd have preferred a small crowd waving flags,' Kit said dryly. 'After that business off Crete, I've developed an aversion to diving fighters.'

Even as he spoke, he noticed one of the Hurricanes flying alongside the port wing. At the same time, Aldo remarked that the other was on their starboard flank. A swift glance told Kit they really did have an escort of British fighters. He wondered fleetingly if someone had mistakenly believed the four VIPs were still aboard. Why else would they have been met like this? He soon discovered his mistake in believing they were escorting machines. Both pilots were making signals with their hands which suggested they wanted him to land. He shook his head, pointing in the direction of Plymouth. Then, in case they did not understand, he asked Morris to signal the information with the Aldis lamp.

This clear message made no difference. The accompanying pilots made even more vigorous gestures with their hands, demanding a swift descent to the sea. Annoyed, Kit told Morris to flash the details of their destination once again. The response to that was startling. First veering away, the two fighters closed together to fly towards *Flamingo*, their guns chattering in unison.

'Stupid bastards,' fumed Kit. 'What the hell are they playing at? Signal our neutral status, Morris. Keep on until their thick heads register the fact.'

They could as well have signalled *Merry Christmas* for all the good it did. After several more very close bursts of fire which suggested that it would not be long before the warnings developed into outright attack, Kit had to bow to their demand that he should land. Fuming and cursing, vowing he would have them skinned alive for disregarding neutrality so aggressively, he embarked on a long shallow descent which would place *Flamingo* as close to the coast as possible. After evading German aircraft over the French coast, it was maddening to be the victim of the RAF when they were almost home. Dropping lower and lower in the developing dusk, Kit was suddenly struck by the absence of twinkling lights ashore. It seemed sinister and uncanny, until he realized there was a total blackout in force all over Britain. All at once, the war seemed more of a reality than ever.

The two Hurricanes circled overhead to enforce their directive. So intent was he on their manoeuvring and on making his own landing, it was not until *Flamingo* touched the surface, then ploughed forward with decreasing speed, that Kit grew aware of red cliffs faintly visible ahead and experienced that sense of unavoidable destiny once more. Almost immediately, a small speedy vessel began cutting through the calm sea, heading for their position some one and a half miles offshore. The RNVR launch was armed and, when it came alongside, signalled quite clearly that Kit should follow where it led. As Kit was wondering when Morris and Digger would realize the truth, Aldo asked the pertinent question.

'Where in the name of God are we? It is England, isn't it?'

'That's right,' Kit told him, as he taxied in the wake of the gunboat. 'It's a small seaside resort called Sheenmouth.'

'If it is England, why have we been forced down in such manner?' Aldo asked, mystified.

'I don't know,' Kit answered slowly. 'Whatever the reason, *Flamingo* has come home.'

They had finished dinner and were taking a stroll through the gardens of the Abbey, hand in hand. Leone breathed in the late evening air almost greedily.

'I adore times like this, don't you?' she murmured, gazing at the silver shimmer of the river against its dark background of trees. 'Everything's so hushed and filled with a curious promise of enchantment.'

Warren squeezed her hand. 'For a woman of twenty-six who controls a thriving aircraft company, runs a huge home and estate and, in what little spare time she has, does mountains of translating for another of Philip Curtiss' numerous influential friends, you've grown very fanciful lately.'

'Have I?' she queried dreamily. 'Maybe it's an unconscious attempt to relieve the seriousness of life. There's not a lot to lighten the heart these days, is there? Moments like this become extra special.' Halting, she extended the sweep of her gaze to take in the copse through which a path had been cut to the old boathouse. Warren spent a great deal of his time there, on secret Air Ministry work. 'Perhaps it's also because we see so little of each other now. Since you joined Lord Howden's committee, you're either at some out of the way RAF station, in London for meetings, or beavering away at your drawing board in the boathouse.' She smiled fondly at him. 'Clever old thing. You've become what is generally known as a boffin.'

Warren shook his head, laughing. 'Boring Old Fool Full of Idiotic Notions, is how Mona translated it.'

Leone also laughed. 'She's a bright girl.'

'Not so bright since her fiancé was posted missing, I'll bet.'

Her laughter faded. 'Poor girl, it must be terrible not to know. *Killed in action* is at least definite. One can grieve and try to get on with one's life. *Missing* creates the hope of a return some day, and that hope can last for years, only to be dashed eventually.' She sighed, turning away to gaze at the distant scenes. 'Let's not talk about the war, darling. Not right at this moment. It's far too serene and beautiful out here. Look at that superb sky with the last fading glow of the sun to the west, and the pale silvering of the moon hanging over East Sheenmouth. Evenings on the Riviera can be heavenly; dying day in the Alps is immensely stirring. Sunset in Mombasa was all fire and sensuality, but there's really nothing to compare with an English midsummer night.'

'There you go again,' he murmured, sliding an arm around her. 'But, for a girl who claims to love times like this, you sound rather sad.'

'Happiness always contains an element of yearning. Probably because it seems too good to last. Before long, this sky will be filled with German bombers on their way to destroy our lovely cities. This midsummer perfection will be marred by the horror of a thousand burning buildings.' Turning to him swiftly, she apologized. 'After asking you not to speak of the war, I've just ruined the evening by doing so myself.'

'It's impossible to live a life apart from it. This conflict has bound communities and nations together into vast industrious colonies – like those of the ants – where we're all inter-dependent.' He sighed. 'The work I do now is vitally important, I'm aware of that, but at the back of my mind is the knowledge that all I'm doing is devising clever ways to kill. If I stopped to think about it much, I'd join Jack Cummings in jail for pacifist beliefs.'

She stopped to confront him. 'What happened to your burning desire to put on a uniform and fly a Spitfire? You'd be personally involved in the killing then; much worse, surely.'

'Yes,' he confessed, 'but I'd be personally involved in the danger, not creating the means to provide it for others whilst I'm safely cocooned by sandbags. Leone, day after day, I sit at a drawing board making sketches and calculations which will result in some poor uniformed devils flying into eternity. I often wonder about their thoughts concerning the bastard who dreamed up the means of sending them on a doomed mission.'

She took his hands in a fierce grip. 'We all feel that way sometimes. When I go down to the workshops and see women in drab overalls making components for fighters, I have similar thoughts. One more aircraft in which a young boy straight from school will possibly die in agony, after attempting to kill a German boy straight from school. I have stood there on many occasions thinking to myself that if we refused to make any more, and *they* refused, too, the war would end. I know it's nonsense, however, because they wouldn't stop. That's why we have to go on. Darling, if you had only read what I have in the letters from refugees that I translate for Philip, you'd know how vital your work is.'

He gave a sad smile. 'We're a bright pair, aren't we? On a romantic evening like this, all we discuss is doom and gloom.'

Slipping her arm through his, she started back towards the Abbey. 'I can't wait for the war to end so that we can get started on the new flying boat. How are the preliminary ideas coming along?'

'Very slowly. I've had so little free time lately.' He made an apologetic face. 'I know you've set your heart on being the first to go into production with a new model when peace comes, but designing is pure guesswork, at the moment. Who knows what materials will be available by the time this is over, or what advances in aeronautics will have been made? The revolutionary boat I design today might well be obsolete by tomorrow. In any case, development of land aircraft is racing ahead. Future passenger liners with wings are more likely to have wheels than floats.'

'Oh, no.' She shook her head fiercely. 'Kirkland's will always produce marine aircraft. Who wants to cross the world and land in a field each time? How can that compare with the thrill of skimming the blue water with spray flying high past the portholes, then coming to rest on a tropical waterway, where a launch races out to take passengers to the elegance and comfort of a hotel overlooking the most spectacular marine sunset imaginable?'

'Spoken like a true Kirkland,' he commented fondly,

as they crossed the great hall dimmed by boards over the broken stained glass.

'I'm a Grant now,' she pointed out. 'Have you been so busy you've forgotten?'

'No one thinks of you that way. I was addressed as Mr Kirkland again this week, this time by a boy official still wet behind the ears.'

'You'll be Sir Warren before long,' she told him. 'Philip agrees.'

'Philip agrees with too many of your ideas.'

'Jealous?' she teased, as they wandered along the upper gallery.

'Not of him,' he answered enigmatically.

When they were inside the suite of airy rooms, he drew her into his customary close embrace to kiss her hungrily. 'Let's take the phone off the hook. Who knows when we'll spend a night together like this next?'

Responding to his overture, and still in a mood of restless yearning, she nodded. 'Let's make it one to remember.'

'Expecting fireworks? I won't disappoint you. I've waited too long.'

She drew away to unfasten her long dress of blue and white voile. Even the war did not deter her from dressing for dinner; the one concession to normal living left open to her. In no more than her panties, she crossed to her dressing table, unfastening the pearl and sapphire necklace as she watched Warren shed his clothes on to the floor, as usual. As she reached for the velvet jewel case, the telephone rang. Tempted to ignore it, as her husband did by moving through to the bathroom, she knew it could be a most vital call and reluctantly picked up the receiver. A man's voice apologized for disturbing her at a late hour, then told her he was speaking from Kirkland's, where the night-shift foreman had allowed him to use the telephone in his office.

'This is Sub-Lieutenant Grimes, ma'am. I captain a patrol vessel stationed at East Sheenmouth.'

Her excellent memory conjured up a picture of a plump, pasty-faced man nearing forty, who had bored her with interminable chatter about his hobby of pigeon fancying.

'Yes, Mr Grimes. We met at the Mayor's Easter Fête in aid of the Red Cross. What can I do for you?'

'Well, ma'am, there's been a rather awkward incident. I. . . well, I was given no choice in the matter, or I'd have. . . ' he explained in blustering fashion. 'It's those damned. . . darned Polish pilots up at Magnum Pomeroy. Their skill at flying is one thing, but I think they're all slightly crazy. Most of them are ignorant of English, save how to order a pint, or how to. . . '

'Mr Grimes, could you please get to the point?' she interrupted crisply. 'I can't believe you have rung me at this hour to complain about the Poles. Any complaints about their behaviour should be passed on to Wing Commander Keen. He's used to receiving them.'

'I've already rung him, Mrs Grant. He seemed to think the whole thing was rather amusing.'

'He's that type of man. *What* is rather amusing?'

'Two of his mad pilots forced down a neutral unarmed flying boat half an hour ago, despite clear identification markings and signals flashed from the incoming crew. The Poles' excuse is that they didn't understand the signals, and the flying boat was behaving suspiciously. They thought it was an enemy spy-machine. I ask you!' he added in tones of disgust. 'We went out to intercept the aircraft, and brought it in to your slipways so that we could board and search.'

'I see.' She was inclined to be as amused as the commanding officer of the unconventional Polish squadron at Magnum Pomeroy. 'Are you detaining the flying boat overnight?'

'I thought you should be informed of the fact.'

'It's very courteous of you, Mr Grimes.'

'There's one more thing I thought you should know, ma'm. It's one of yours.'

'One of mine?' she echoed, finding the jigsaw of information suddenly forming an unbelievable picture which quickened her heartbeat. Only one aircraft built by her company presently bore neutral colours, yet surely it could not be here.

'Yes, it's a Kirkland's machine, all right,' the voice on the line continued. 'She's been flying for a Portuguese company, but was apparently shot up in the Med and couldn't return to Lisbon.'

Sinking to sit on the stool, because her legs would no longer support her, she asked faintly, 'What's the pilot's name?'

'There are two,' he replied, apparently believing she knew nothing about flying. 'One's a Portuguese called Diaz, the other's a Captain Anson. He's English like his navigator. There's an Australian aboard who claims to know you, Mrs Grant.'

'Digger Rathbone,' she murmured, drastically robbed of breath by shock.

'That's right.' His surprise was evident. 'You really are old friends?'

'With the entire crew.' Excitement, apprehension and a ridiculous girlish thrill ran through her simultaneously as she heard herself ask, 'Have they been taken anywhere for the night yet?'

'I'm just about to send them up in a Jeep to Wing Commander Keen. Funny though he thinks it is, he's offered to give them a meal and a bed.'

'Send them here instead,' she told him swiftly. 'I've plenty of room. Both my husband and I would very much like to meet them again.'

'They are expected at the camp,' he pointed out uneasily.

'Ring the Wing Commander and tell him of the change of plan.' Adopting the firm tone she used when trying to get her own way at meetings, she continued. 'That machine is the prototype my husband and brother designed, and those men crewed her on her proving flight. The captain is the famous Kit Anson, in case you haven't cottoned on to the kind of flier who has just been treated as an enemy spy.'

'Oh,' came the exclamation from a man who clearly had never heard of air speed records, or the giants who broke them.

'The crew survived the crash on a sandbank outside Lisbon, and we've not met up since. If they are forced to spend a night at Sheenmouth, it has to be here at the Abbey. My husband will insist.'

The approach worked, as it unfailingly did, but she replaced the receiver with her mind in a whirl. When Warren came from the bathroom in naked state, she stared unseeingly at him as he approached.

'What's up?' he asked in curiosity. 'You look as though you've seen a ghost.'

She slowly shook her head. 'Not yet, but any minute now. Warren. . . *Flamingo* is down at our slipways. Her crew. . . I've. . . I've invited them here for the night. They're on their way in a Jeep.'

He seemed unable to take in the fact, so she relayed in disjointed sentences what she had just been told. When she finally ran out of words, he stood looking at her closely.

'He'll refuse to sleep here.'

'Who?'

'Don't be silly, Leone. I can tell from the state you're in that Kit's with them.'

She swallowed, watching his expression. 'Yes, he is.'

'He won't stay here.'

'I shan't attempt to persuade him.'

'I see. You just want to take a look at him, to see if he's shattered now the Lindstrom woman has walked out on him. Is that it?'

'Warren, don't,' she pleaded. 'Kit can't harm you, or destroy what we have. Let's just meet up for old times' sake. You two were good friends.'

'You invited him here for my sake?' he charged sarcastically.

'Now that fate has been responsible for bringing him here in such unexpected fashion, you surely wouldn't let him go up to Magnum Pomeroy without making contact. After all, he was the man. . . '

Turning away from her to walk to the wardrobe, he cut her off short. 'It isn't Kit I don't trust, it's fate. This has all been arranged far too neatly for my peace of mind.'

'I could say the same about your reunion with Mona in Scotland.'

'That's different. I'm not still in love with her.'

Upset, uncertain, she rose to go across to him. 'I'm sorry. I should have consulted you before inviting them all here.'

'Why? It's your home,' he countered, pulling on his underpants.

'It's our home.'

He shook his head. 'This place has the Kirkland stamp on it. It always will have.'

Taking hold of his arms, she said insistently, 'Ring the guardroom at the camp. Tell them to look out for an RN Jeep, stop it and tell the occupants the plan has been changed. . . that we have been called away suddenly.'

Warren gently drew her hands from their hold on him, his expression growing even more desolate. 'Now you're really worrying me. Get dressed, darling. They'll be here soon.'

With shaking hands, she slipped back into the dress she had just discarded, then did what she could to her face and the thick shining upswept roll of hair she had luckily not started to unpin. Turning back to face the room, she discovered that Warren had not put on the dinner jacket. It was still on the floor with the dark trousers he always railed against wearing. Instead, he had on an old pair of flannels and one of his favourite woollies over an open-necked shirt. She was inordinately angry. He might have tried to please her, under the circumstances. What circumstances? asked her fluttering brain. She was a happily married woman, and Kit Anson had every reason to despise her. Why, then, were both she and Warren suddenly afraid?

There was no clear answer to that, yet it caused her to shy from the coming meeting. Telling Warren that she must organize rooms, then arrange for a light meal to be served to men hungry after a long flight, she suggested that he should greet them and dispense drinks before they freshened up ready to eat. It was cowardly, she knew, and Warren's silent nod of agreement told her he read her mind all too well. Perhaps he also knew, without being told, that she would put Kit in the bell tower suite for the night. If he agreed to stay the night.

While she did all this, her mind worked feverishly. Warren might feel that fate had arranged this too neatly for his peace of mind, but she saw it as a heaven-sent opportunity to ease her own. When Maitland had told her the terrible facts of Geoffrey Anson's death, she had vowed to keep out of Kit's life from then on. Fate had brought them briefly together, and she must now make her peace with him. Somehow, she must get him alone long enough to . . . to what? To apologize because her own father had practically pushed his to his death in pounding machinery? To confess Kirkland guilt for all he had suffered as a boy? Small wonder her nerve failed her when they were about to come face to face.

When that moment could be delayed no longer, Leone found their guests in the small sitting room decorated in blue and lemon, with antique furniture, while Warren played host in his usual unaffected manner. Everyone rose at her entry, and her gaze flew straight to the dark, muscular man in crisp green uniform. He looked tired, strained, and a good deal older than when she had last seen him at Madeira, just before a take-off which had ended in a disastrous crash. The years melted away as she met his dark, distrustful gaze and knew nothing had changed for her.

'Hallo, Kit,' she greeted, in carefully controlled manner. 'What an incredible twist of fate that Peter Keen's mad Polish boys should have forced you to land right here.'

'Yes, incredible.' He nodded at the room he had once known so well. 'The monks appear to have been well and truly driven away.'

'Not before time,' she responded quietly. 'They had had things all their way for far too long.'

'So you always claimed,' he returned, taking in the delicate attraction of her evening gown bought in Rome and therefore at least three years out of date.

Leone immediately felt overdressed in the company of a husband who resembled a jobbing gardener, and four men in working uniforms. She had felt that way once before, when a woman in stained masculine khaki had stepped from a dinghy to a pink-lined flying boat to gaze in disparagement at her own immaculate appearance. At recollection of Sylva Lindstrom, Leone immediately searched for signs of heartbreak in the square face which had haunted her thoughts for so many years, but Kit had turned his attention back to Warren, leaving her none the wiser about the broken love-affair. If Warren was still apprehensive, he did not show it, and it was clear that the friendship between the two men, started on the night Kit had broken the speed record, had survived the years between. They talked eagerly about the great love of their lives as Leone renewed her acquaintance with Morris Snaith and Digger Rathbone, who introduced their new second pilot. The young Portuguese very obviously appreciated her presence, and his amusing Iberian effusiveness served to ease her tension.

By the time they all sat at the table, the host and hostess drinking a glass of wine while their guests ate a welcome meal, a warmly relaxed atmosphere generally prevailed. Leone was unsure whether Warren was putting on an act as convincing as her own, or whether he saw Kit's uninterest in her as totally reassuring. He certainly chatted without restraint throughout the meal. Leone noted that Kit declined the offer of wine, although his crew indulged enjoyably. The small point reminded her of the party to celebrate the rescue at Lake Kiju, when he had asserted that prison had cured him of the drinking habit. He had also that night challenged her to ask Donald for information he probably would not have the courage to give. Her brother had, indeed, dismissed her demand, and the answer would have died with him if Maitland had not tried to blackmail her with the shocking truth. As she watched Kit across the table, Leone suffered the weight of it with increased force. How he must have hated the Kirkland family all these years!

'You really do intend to offer *Flamingo*, complete with crew, to the RAF?' Warren was asking, returning to the reason why they had been flying off the coast of southern England this evening, and betraying to Leone his deep envy of their plans.

'I'm still not clear why you were advised not to return to Lisbon,' Leone said. 'Surely the Germans couldn't have had you all arrested just for picking up men who would have drowned. It was not as if you'd taken part in the battle.'

'We'd done a few other things over the past year,' Morris told her quietly, 'so they were hoping to use this incident as an excuse to mount a full investigation. Without us, Tom can't be charged with anything.'

'A few other things?' she asked with curiosity.

'When we landed at Gib, I had a surprise meeting with a dapper staff officer,' put in Kit, changing the subject adroitly. 'Captain Jarvis M – as oily and perfect as ever.'

'*Maitland*. . . in the army?' Warren looked even more dismayed over the news of their former assistant also donning uniform, when he had not.

'I found it hard to swallow myself,' Kit told him.

'However, the smooth, suave and very slightly inhuman "Maiters" has landed a perfect job; almost a continuation of what he did here, plus the heroic trappings of the warrior.'

'Donald used to call him "Maiters" way back during his Cambridge days,' said Leone thoughtfully. 'Fancy you remembering that.'

Kit turned to her. 'I remember an awful lot about this place.' Then, before she could rise to that, he turned back to Warren. 'What drove you to fire him after all those years of sickeningly efficient service?'

'Leone decided that, like the monks, he had had his day. She fired him, not me.'

Kit's glance rested on her again. 'Good lord, a formidable task for anyone, much less a woman. Congratulations. . . but how have you coped without him?'

'Very well. He was a brilliant organizer, but he wasn't God,' she said, plagued by thoughts of that painful dismissal and what it had revealed. 'I have a female secretary who is very capable. The rest I do myself. Of course, we're dictated to by the various government departments now, so company business isn't half as complex as before, but women are coping with formidable tasks all the time. War makes heavy demands on everyone, even those not in uniform.'

Flashing her a warm smile, Warren continued the theme. 'You've been out of the country too long, Kit, that's plain. Women do the most admirable things now. Leone, for instance, runs Kirkland's with great efficiency, and deals effortlessly with a workforce twice the size we had when you were here. In addition, she translates for a committee controlling registered aliens and refugees. As she speaks French, German, Italian and Spanish well, she's invaluable to such people. You've no idea the number of hours she spends going through letters and documents, after a full day's work. Then there are her numerous local commitments with various war charities, and with the evacuee children. You wouldn't have heard about the rescue she carried out. . . '

'I think that's enough about my work,' put in Leone, growing uncomfortable.

Warren was determined to continue, however. 'Remember those tunnels beneath the Abbey said to have been used by smugglers, Kit? Last September, Kirkland's and the airfield at Magnum Pomeroy were bombed and a doomed Jerry decided to drop his last two on us. The evacuees were trapped in those two adjoining rooms in the west wing, which Sir Hector always used for business discussions. My wonderful brave wife brought all the children out to safety through those tunnels, then went back with some Home Guard men for those unable to walk. She was buried under masonry whilst trying to save one of the teachers, and was badly injured. Sheenmouth reckoned she deserved a medal, and so do I.'

Digger nodded at her as he finished his large meal. 'That makes two of us. You should have got one for saving Mr Grant from being sucked under the wreck of *Flamingo*. I said so at the inquest.'

By now feeling embarrassed and very shaky over the way Kit was looking at her, Leone stood up. 'That's quite enough flattery, gentlemen. I suggest we return to the blue sitting room for coffee, and talk of pleasanter things.'

As they all walked back to the small salon, she asked Morris about the flying boat. 'I hear she's painted yellow now. Poor dear won't be happy with camouflage after the dainty colours she's used to.'

The navigator smiled as he shook his head. 'No, she won't. I don't suppose she'll think much of the cold grey Atlantic after so long over the Med, either, but we'll all be there to console her and keep her happy.'

'You really think you'll be allowed to stay with your machine?'

'There'll be trouble, if we can't. We belong together.'

'You feel a strong affinity with *Flamingo*?'

He looked surprised. 'Of course. She's our boat.'

'I've never understood this love-affair between man and machine,' she confessed with a sigh. 'To me, flying is much the same as driving a car, and I change them frequently. . . or I did when cars were easy to come by.' She smiled. 'I only drive one now because I'm a company director with a priority rating. It would be the horse, or shanks' pony otherwise.'

Once settled with their coffee, they began speaking of the proving flight. Apologizing to Aldo for reminiscing on an event he had not shared with them, they then laughed over some of the antics of their passengers, and over Monique Carlyon-Bree's *affaire* which had led to her third marriage. Soon – too soon for Leone – Warren commented on the fact that it was almost two a.m. and that his guests looked ready to turn in. They seemed to welcome the prospect, and said goodnight before splitting up to go to their rooms. Leone regretted her impulse to give Kit his old suite, as she and Warren walked with him the full length of the gallery to reach the bell tower. Too many painful memories were attached to that set of circular rooms – for herself, and probably also for him.

Warren appeared untouched by such thoughts, as he confessed to Kit, 'The proving flight was devised to bring in cash and orders enough to save Kirkland's from a very shaky future, as you know. That prospect was touch and go after the crash, of course. It's really the war which has done the trick. The company is more prosperous today than it was even in Sir Hector's time. We're making a fortune from government contracts. There's more money from making components than there was from producing whole aircraft. Ironic, isn't it?'

They all halted outside Kit's door, and he asked, 'What about those passenger liners with wings, Warren; the dreams? You had so many, as I recall.'

'Oh. . . I haven't forgotten them,' Warren murmured. 'They simply seem to have vanished beneath the drive to make machines that will kill. That's all I do these days; devise more and more ingenious ways to commit murder from the air, and receive enormous sums of money for doing so.' He sighed. 'Sometimes, I'd give anything for the old days at Ma Bardolph's making balsa-wood miniatures of my designs.' Summoning a wistful smile, he added, 'We still have a *Seaspray* we made to order for a customer who died before he could collect it. She's a two-seater, with a shortened wingspan and racing lines echoed in body and floats. I was proud of her. Proud as could be.'

'I'd like to see her before I leave,' Kit said.

Warren shook his head. 'She's dismantled and stored in the old boathouse for the duration. We needed the space when the workshop was bombed. I go and look at her sometimes, when I grow sick of warplanes. One of these days, I'll get her out and fly her; pretend the war doesn't exist.' With a sigh, he began turning away. 'We mustn't keep you awake talking about old times, when you must be almost asleep on your feet. Goodnight, Kit. I'm rather glad those crazy Polish boys forced you down so that we'd have this meeting.'

'So am I,' came his surprising reply. 'This place has changed. . . for the better. Goodnight.'

As he turned to open the familiar door, Leone caught herself quoting him from those old times, before she knew it. '*Goodnight. Sleep tight. Hope the bugs don't bite.*'

Kit turned back, an incomprehensible expression on his face. 'Fancy you recalling that old rhyme,' he said in that voice she would recognize anywhere, any time.

'Like you, there are lots of things I remember,' she returned, through a throat thickening with pain and regret.

In their own suite of rooms, Warren said little except to declare that he was tired and had a tricky development to tackle on the morrow. Leone had a good idea of his thoughts and feelings as they lay in the bed, gazing at the moon through the window from which she had drawn back the dark curtains. He made no attempt to embark on the lovemaking which had been interrupted by the startling telephone call, merely murmured a good-night before turning away. Leone was glad. He would not then see the tears gathering on her cheeks.

They had breakfast in the octagonal room. Rested and fed, their guests were eager to go down-river to their aircraft and begin their new life as a fighting team. The minutes ran away, and they were soon on the terrace ready to depart. Warren walked down the lower meadow to the jetty in order to rouse up Walter, leaving the men to bid Leone a warm, grateful farewell. Feeling desperate, and knowing she must not let Kit go without cleansing her own soul of reflected guilt, she seized the hand he offered in parting and fairly dragged him along the terrace.

'Do come and see what they did to the west wing,' she urged. 'You can't leave without taking a look, and Walter will be ages bringing out the boat. He's grown so ancient, everything he does takes twice as long as before. I can't bring myself to pension him off. He's been with us so many years, he's almost part of the fittings and fixtures.'

Words rushed from her as she led him away from his crew, and round the corner to where the swimming pool and tennis courts had been during his days at Sheen-mouth Abbey. Now there was a great stretch of open earth filling in the bomb crater, and vegetables grew in abundance. Kit went with her willingly enough, still caught by his hand, and made no attempt to interrupt her nervous monologue to cover her tension. They turned a second corner to see the damaged area, shored up with stout props for the duration of the war. Kit studied it for several moments in silence. When he turned to her Leone was surprised by the warmth of his glance.

'You were buried under *that*?'

She nodded.

'And you really did lead a host of children to safety through those old underground passages?'

She nodded again.

The warmth of his expression deepened as he went on, 'I never believed in their existence, despite those old yarns.'

'They're there, and in extremely good condition due to an antique air-conditioning system. At present, they're serving another purpose. In preparation for it, I had arranged to uncover the interior entrance, thank God. It lay beneath that old stove in what used to be the sacristy. Do you remember it?'

It was his turn to nod.

'Only because the tunnels had been inspected several days before, and because I'd put a supply of candles ready were we able to use that escape route. That's what I call a real twist of fate, don't you?'

Still regarding her with speculative interest, he said, 'As Warren told me last night, I've been out of the country too long. Things aren't the way I remember them, Leone. It was time I returned to correct certain ideas.' He turned back to the broken ancient stone, saying with regret, 'The bastards must have known what they were destroying. In daylight, it's clearly visible from the air.'

'Yes, it is,' she agreed.

Releasing his hand, at last, he looked back at her again. 'You have your pilot's licence now?'

'Warren insisted.'

He pursed his lips thoughtfully, then said, 'You appear to have made him very happy. I never thought you would. . . but you've changed.'

'Have I? In what way?' she asked, seizing this moment

greedily because it would have to last for the rest of her life.

'I can't say exactly. You've grown quieter, perhaps. . . more human. It was there beneath that Kirkland pride when you were a girl. Later, I thought it lost beyond recall. Warren seems to have brought it to the surface with a vengeance. Marriage suits you. So, apparently, does hard work.' He began walking back towards the terrace. 'You've become a woman of purpose, instead of an aimless social butterfly basking in the name your father so revered.'

'Kit,' she blurted out, catching his hand to halt him once more. 'Please wait a moment.' As he turned to her and disengaged his hand, she almost faltered in her resolution to say what she must. As the light morning breeze ruffled their hair and caressed their bare arms with the promise of heat to come, she forced herself to recall how it had once been between them. How it had been before life had overtaken her. 'I never dreamed I'd ever have the chance to speak to you again. Fate decided that I should, and I can't let you go until I've. . . ' The wariness of his expression robbed her of fluency. Distrust was back in his dark eyes.

'We have a flight to Plymouth ahead,' he reminded her dispassionately.

'*Please*,' she begged, 'please listen. After the crash, I telephoned the hospital in Lisbon three times a week for news of you. The reason I stopped was because. . . because I finally learned what you once advised me to ask Donald to explain. He never did, Kit, and the truth would have died with him if Maitland hadn't tried to blackmail me into keeping him by revealing it.' Gazing entreatingly at him, she confessed, 'The guilt for what he told me has haunted me ever since. Please believe that I knew nothing of the terrible affair until that moment. With all my heart, I apologize for what my father did to yours. It's impossible for you to forgive it, I know, but can there be peace between us, at least?'

Kit frowned, plainly very disconcerted by her confession and uncertain how to deal with it. Eventually, he gave a sigh and a shrug, as he resumed walking back to the terrace.

'There's no need for you to make apologies. You were only a child when it happened, and were in no way involved apart from blindly believing what Sir Hector and Donald chose to tell you of the affair. I suppose I'm glad it's out in the open with one Kirkland, but too much water has passed beneath the bridge and my rage has subsided. When I first saw those drawings Warren found in the old boathouse, and realized that *Aphrodite* was really my father's *Solitaire*, I suppose I went slightly crazy. I threatened to expose their theft of Dad's design, publish the facts in every newspaper in the country, and expose Donald as the fraud he was. Your father had me over a barrel, of course, and told me to get out within the hour. He laughed in my face when I offered to sell him the design for ten thousand, and when he threatened to make me drunk and dump me in the Sheen unless I went quietly, I foolishly took the sum I considered to be my due. I played right into his hands, and fate decided to assist him by staging a car crash.'

He paused momentarily at the corner of the west wing, frowning in recollection. 'My father was dead, and unable to bask in the glory of acclaim for his most brilliant piece of work, so I suppose my rage was mainly for the fact that no one would ever know the full record gained on that tremendous day – a man winning laurels in his own father's seaplane. It would have restored the respectability of the Anson family, and would somehow have bridged the gap which had widened between us during the last years of his life.' Returning from his recollections, he gave a hint of a smile. 'My rage is now directed elsewhere. When I saw helpless men being machine-gunned in the sea, I knew what was really important. War tends to put a great many things into perspective, doesn't it? All the same, I'm glad you finally know the truth. Yes, there can be peace between us, Leone, if that's what you want.' He began drawing away. 'Goodbye. Take care of Warren. . . and of yourself, of course. You're doing a great job here.'

As he walked briskly off to join his crew, Leone felt as if the west wing had collapsed on her once more.

25

Setting eyes on *Flamingo* again gave Warren a greater
thrill than he had imagined. It was like seeing his firstborn after three years. As the powerful launch
approached the jetty, the great yellow flying boat seemed
a vision from the past to her creator who now dealt only
with warplanes.

'Gosh, she's fantastic!' he breathed, adoring her lines
with eager eyes.

Kit beside him laughed. 'Of course she's fantastic.
Surely you hadn't forgotten.'

With his gaze still on the aircraft, Warren shook his
head. 'Not exactly. I've been modifying one up in Scotland – the third off our production line – but she's
camouflaged and armed. Can't think of her as mine as I
do this one.' Recollection of *Florida* caused him to turn
to the men with him. 'Good lord, I should have told you
last night. I met up with young Joss Hamilton. He was
given command of the boat because he knew the model
better than any pilot in his squadron. He rings us sometimes. The last we heard from him, he had just returned
from a special flight. There are no prizes for guessing
where he'd been. People are being brought out regularly.
The Germans are using Norway's resources to great
advantage, and her unfortunate scientific or engineering
experts are being forced to work for them.' As *Calpurnian* came alongside the jetty, he added heavily, 'I think
we have little idea what it's like to be in an occupied

country. Life must be hell. Thank God we managed to resist it.'

They all climbed ashore as he tied the vessel fast, and the discussion intensified as they strolled towards the slipway.

'We might have held on to Britain,' Kit said, 'but the situation is extremely grave. We've virtually lost the Med – we've seen it gradually fall over the past six months – and Europe's under enemy control. Despite Russia's peace pact, there's surely no doubt Hitler hasn't any intention of honouring it. With the nation totally unprepared for aggression, and with the madness of conquest ruling him, he'll find the temptation to have Russia irresistible. How can we stop him? Bringing a few people out of Norway in daring aerial missions is hardly more than a drop in the ocean.'

'Why don't the Yanks come in? That'd help,' put in Digger.

Kit grunted. 'Not so long ago, you were claiming this war was no concern of Australians. Maybe they feel the way you did.'

With a sigh, Warren confessed that Leone had asked him last night if the war would be lost. 'I reassured her, naturally, but I do have doubts. Like you, I watch the world being swallowed up and wonder how anyone can bring a halt to it.'

'Adolph'll get indigestion, that's how,' said Morris, in his quiet fashion. 'When you stop to think about it, you realize there just aren't enough German soldiers to go around. Each time some place is conquered, it has to be filled with enough troops to guard the people. Soon, Hitler's entire army will be used in that manner, leaving none to make fresh conquests.'

Warren nodded gloomily. 'You're probably right, but a great many will die before he reaches that stage.'

Aldo came into the discussion then, his youthful breezy personality an antidote to depression. 'What many long faces you all are! Surely we all know that when *Flamingo* and her magnificent crew has donned the battle colours of the RAF there will be no more problems. Is that not what we have come for?'

It brought a laugh all round, and Digger added that when the news reached the German High Command they would realize the game was up and sue for peace. On approaching *Flamingo* they were met by a member of the crew of the launch which had escorted them in last evening. He had been standing guard over the flying boat, and greeted Kit with a smile.

'Hallo, sir. Lieutenant Grimes has a message for you from the base at Plymouth. Would you step over to the office for a moment?'

Warren went aboard with Aldo, Morris and Digger, while Kit crossed to the utility office on the far side of Kirkland's. Warren found *Flamingo*'s interior quite altered, with passenger cabins reduced to one in favour of cargo bays. She was hardly the prototype he remembered, with pink seats and decor, bar, smoking saloon and roomy galleys in which to prepare gourmet dishes. She was no longer a passenger liner with wings, yet he told himself thirty-eight men had been taken from the sea to safety in her only last month. Surely, more deserving passengers could not be found. The thought fanned the flames of his envy once more. These men with him had saved lives under fire without hesitation, even though they wore a non-combatant uniform. They were now off to volunteer for further danger, while he continued to work in underground workshops and offices, well protected from any hazard, on drawings and complicated theories. Perhaps it was as well he could have no sons to ask what he had done during the world war. The intricacies of aircraft design would not suggest glory to any small boy, who would read of the courage and daring actions of other men, and compare. Kit Anson's sons would have every reason to be proud at the end of it all. He chose not to consider that there was an even chance

Kit would not live long enough to father children, once he donned that blue uniform instead of the green.

For half an hour or so Warren wandered the aircraft, noting with interest how she had been adapted from the original luxury passenger boat. Soon, *Flamingo* would be fitted with gun-turrets and bomb-bays. How her rôle had changed over the years! Kit returned to tell his crew that Plymouth had given them permission to proceed and land there before noon. After that time, operational activity would prohibit their approach and escort to a mooring.

Knowing they were now anxious to be on their way, Warren bade them farewell and the best of luck in their new, exciting life. Then he climbed ashore for a final word with the man who had been ultimately responsible for gaining him all he valued in life. Once there, facing Kit, he found words surprisingly difficult.

'Well. . . you're off to your new future,' he said awkwardly.

Kit gave a rueful smile. 'Another new future. My life seems to change course with alarming frequency. However, variety is the spice, so they say.' He held out his hand. 'I'm glad we met up again after so long.'

Warren shook hands. 'So am I. We telephoned for months after the crash for news of you. Then Joss kept us up to date with your movements. All the same, it's jolly nice to have had the chance to talk about old times. Little did any of us realize what lay ahead.'

'Your marriage is clearly a great success, and I'm glad for you both.' Kit grinned. 'It just shows what a lot of nonsense I spoke when I advised you to steer clear of a Kirkland girl. Take care, Warren. See you at the end of the war, perhaps.' With a wave of his hand, Kit turned back to his aircraft.

Unable to dismiss the curious impact of this unexpected meeting, Warren remained a lone figure to watch *Flamingo* get under way and taxi down to the mouth of the river. He was still there watching when the great yellow aircraft rose above the clifftop on a course for Plymouth. Only when his flying boat, his early dreams made reality, had become no more than a dot in the morning sky did he walk slowly back to the expensive launch tied up at the jetty. He was so lost in thought, he did not see Eddie Myers signal to him from the workshops. The roar of *Calpurnian*'s engines drowned the overseer's shout for attention.

Acting mechanically, Warren turned the powerful boat and gave her full throttle. The speed of his passage tossed his unruly hair and filled out his woollen cardigan around his body. He *had* been glad to meet up with Kit again, but he was equally glad of his departure. The natural rapport between them had in no way diminished and, although it had been clear that Leone was still deeply affected by this particular man, there had been no evidence that her feelings were returned. Admittedly, the animosity which had been between them during the proving flight had mellowed in the interim, but Warren had watched his friend closely throughout the visit and seen nothing to suggest grounds for unease. Yet he *was* uneasy, because Kit was back in England and would be no further away than Plymouth. It made no sense except that, as he had admitted to Leone, fate had arranged things far too neatly for his peace of mind.

Knowing he had a tricky project to face, one which had been tagged by Lord Howden's committee as vitally urgent, and being reluctant to intrude upon or witness Leone's present mood, he took the launch directly to the old boathouse with the intention of starting work immediately. There was no better way to forget vague fears than to concentrate on a seemingly insoluble design modification. Tying up the boat, he walked past the dismantled *Seaspray* and into the ground-floor workshop where some women had worked during the days following the bombing of Kirkland's. It was now his sanctum, the one place where he could grapple with the increasingly demanding requirements of a desperate air force.

Already thinking of the problem awaiting him, he mounted the steps to the trap-door entrance to his drawing office which also contained basic food supplies and a bed for extended visits. With head and shoulders through the opening, he forgot about work. Leone was standing in that familiar room, which had once housed the Ansons in their most desperate days, and she looked ashen.

'I guessed you'd come directly here,' she said in haunted tones. 'I've been waiting for the sound of the launch.'

He climbed the rest of the way into the room, unaccountably wary. 'What's the matter?'

'I need to talk to you, and I can't wait until you finish being unbelievably brilliant and emerge again into the real world the rest of us inhabit.'

'That's rather unfair, isn't it?' he asked, through a throat grown tight. 'I've never locked the door and refused you entry when I'm working. If you've not come down here, I assume it's because there's never been an urgent enough reason for you to disturb me.' He moved towards her. 'Now there is, I take it.'

She passed a hand over her brow distractedly. 'I'm sorry, Warren. I can't think straight.' Looking around the room, she asked, 'Have you any alcohol here?'

'Only a few bottles of ale. You know I don't go in for the swanky drinks.' Taking her upper arms in a gentle clasp, he asked, 'What's this all about, darling? You need a sympathetic ear, not a drink. Come on, out with it!'

She drew away, clearly too deeply disturbed for his chummy approach. 'I've had a terrible shock. I can't believe it, yet I sense that it's true.' Moving around the room in her distress, she went on, 'If it's true. . . if it's true, I don't know how I'll live with myself. Or with you.'

A chill of premonition told him fate had been even more devious than he thought, when sending two Polish pilots out hunting last evening.

'You said you came to talk to me. Perhaps you'd better do so,' he suggested, 'and I'll do what I can to help.' She looked so ill, he wondered whether to persuade her to lie down. Then he realized that she was so overwrought, only movement would prevent some kind of uncontrollable reaction. 'Please tell me what's upset you so deeply,' he urged. 'I've never known you to act this way before.'

She confronted him white-faced, as words tumbled from her stiff lips in erratic style. 'Did Donald design *Aphrodite*, or did he steal *Solitaire* from Geoffrey Anson?'

It knocked him right off balance, blurted out without warning and with no time to prepare himself. How could she have found out after all these years? Kit must have told her. . . but why?

'I joined Kirkland's long after that seaplane was designed and developed,' he caught himself saying.

'The drawings you found here and handed to Kit – were they for a seaplane designed by his father?'

So she knew about the drawings! It was useless to deny their existence. 'What has Kit said to you?' he demanded harshly.

'He said. . . Oh, Warren, he completely misunderstood what I was telling him,' she cried in anguish. 'I knew, as soon as I heard he was in Sheenmouth, that I had to confess to now being aware of how his father had fallen into the machinery and been killed. That's why I wanted them all here for the night.' Putting both clenched fists to her temples as if trying to relieve her distress, she said, 'I took him aside as he was leaving this morning, and apologized from the heart for what my father had done to his. He. . . he thought I was referring to something quite different, and explained that his rage over the theft of his father's design had diminished with time. He went on to say that after Father kicked him

out, because he offered to sell him the rights to the
design for ten thousand, he foolishly took the money he
felt was some compensation for being unable to tell the
world a man had flown his own father's seaplane and
broken a world record. He ended. . . he ended, Warren,
by telling me he was glad it was out in the open with
one Kirkland, at last.' Coming towards him, she held
out both fists in appeal. 'Dear God, it isn't true, is it?'

It rose up to confront him finally; that sense of guilt
he had always suffered over an affair which had broken
a man at the height of his brilliance and put him behind
bars for two years. His brain raced. He loved this woman
challenging him for the truth; loved her deeply. She
would believe what he told her now, because she trusted
him implicitly. For her sake, as well as his own, for the
sake of the marriage they had created so successfully, it
would be better to lie. Surely it would be better to lie.

'I found some drawings here when I was clearing the
place out,' he offered carefully. 'I handed them to Kit.'

'Without looking at them? Of course you would have,'
she charged.

'I glanced. . . yes.'

'Were they drawings of a seaplane?'

'It was years ago, Leone.'

Her anguished face grew even paler. 'Warren, this is
one of the most terrible moments of my life. Don't fail
me when I most need you. Tell me the truth, as you
always have.'

Feeling between the devil and the deep blue sea, he
knew it was also one of the most terrible moments of his
life. Something told him he would lose her, whatever he
said.

'The drawings were for a seaplane Geoffrey Anson had
named *Solitaire*. I wasn't familiar with the finer details
of *Aphrodite*'s design. She had been developed and built
before I ever joined the company. . . but I did see
remarkable similarities between Anson's drawings and
Donald's aircraft.' He sighed. 'I'd just been taken on by

your father and knew I had to tread very carefully if I wanted to keep my job. As it was really not my concern, I handed the rolls of plans over to Kit and left any action to him. For all I knew, old Anson had made some kind of deal with Sir Hector, allowing Donald to take credit for the design. He was always desperately short of money, from all accounts, so it wasn't inconceivable.'

Leone stood quite still, as if trying to make conclusions from what he had said. She seemed calmer, and he was on the point of reaching for her when she resumed her inquisition.

'The drawings found in Kit's car after the crash; were they the ones you handed to him?'

'I don't know. I suppose. . . well, they could have been,' he agreed slowly.

The wild look returned. 'Those policemen brought them back to the house; handed them over to Father. The only proof of Kit's claim was handed back to those who could turn the tables on him and charge *him* with theft. Is that what they did? Is it?'

'I wasn't there in the Abbey that evening. I have no idea what was said or done,' he reminded her. 'All I know for a fact is that your brother didn't design *Aphrodite*.'

'Why certain?' she demanded swiftly. 'You said just now that there were *similarities* between the drawings and Donald's aircraft. Now you're changing your tune.'

'No, I'm not,' he contradicted, trying to reason with her. 'I'm certain Donald didn't design that seaplane, because he was no more than a competent working engineer. He had no creative talent.'

She seemed uncomprehending. 'But. . . *Flamingo*. . . '

'Was all my own work, Leone, with a little initial help from Kit.'

In a shocked daze she moved to the bed and sank on to it, gazing at some inexplicable truth she did not want

669

to accept. After a long while, she glanced across to where he stood too fearful to go to her.

'Why did you let him steal your glory?' she asked brokenly.

'What choice did I have?' he cried in self-defence. 'I'd seen what they did to men who challenged them. If they could break Kit when he was the conquering hero of the day, what would they have done to a nobody struggling for recognition? In order to survive, I had to accept half the bone and keep quiet. That's what I did.'

'And you also kept quiet when a man was tried and sent to prison for something he hadn't done.'

The words were out, and his guilt became too heavy to bear. 'Nothing I said would have helped him,' he said miserably. 'He didn't even attempt to defend himself, knowing he could never win against Kirkland power and influence. All I would have achieved would have been my own destruction. Kit wouldn't have wanted that.'

'Did you ask him?'

'Leone, I no longer had the drawings. I had no more proof than he of what they had *possibly* done with his father's design. What purpose would have been served by my speaking up?' he cried.

'You could have told *me* the truth,' she whispered hoarsely.

He swallowed. 'You were a schoolgirl, and I'd been warned off.'

'But *I* condoned his arrest that morning; *I* allowed him to be sent to prison.'

'Don't be melodramatic! Your father had him arrested; the jury put him behind bars. You were considered too young even to give evidence on the affair.'

'Why didn't you tell me later, when he arrived here to take the proving flight?' she demanded wildly. 'I was no longer a schoolgirl. Why didn't you tell me then? Dear God, I treated him like. . . I lashed him with Kirkland arrogance and did all I could to humiliate him. I allowed Donald *and* Maitland to do the same. Why. . .

670

why didn't you tell me then, Warren?' she repeated in mounting distress.

'Kirkland's was facing a crisis,' he countered desperately. 'The proving flight had to succeed in order to save the company. The relationship between you and Donald was explosive enough without throwing in a handful of unstable gelignite. It was vitally important for the directors of the company to be in accord during the flight, and for the pilot to concentrate on his job. Leone, company survival was at stake. You had claimed your half of the responsibility for running it, and talked a great deal about women being able to cope with such things quite as well as men. I believed in you; I supported you, if you recall. The success of *Flamingo* was all that mattered.'

Unable to dispute his words, she still attacked. 'It was assured after the rescue at Lake Kiju. On that moon-washed balcony in Mombasa, when I asked you why a man would give up all his glittering prizes for ten thousand pounds, *why didn't you tell me then?*'

When he said nothing, she added, 'You were my friend. I trusted you.'

'I wasn't your friend, Leone, I was in love with you. There are different rules for each relationship.'

She came back fast. 'All right, but when I asked you to marry me, confessed what Maitland had revealed about the way Geoffrey Anson had died, why didn't you tell me then? Donald was dead, I was vowing to keep out of Kit's life, and we were about to become lovers.'

He stood silent, knowing the answer to that would not appease her. How could he be afraid of losing her to a man who did not want her? Yet he had been. He still was afraid.

She flung her final challenge. 'Would you ever have told me just how vicious and cruel the Kirklands could be?'

His continuing silence gave her her answer.

'I'll never be able to forgive you, Warren.'

He shook his head, saying quietly, 'It's yourself you'll

never be able to forgive. Loving him as you've done all these years, you nevertheless instantly believed him guilty.'

Contrary to their expectations, the RAF did not greet them with open arms. A yellow flying boat bearing Portuguese markings, complete with a suntanned civil airline crew, was viewed by the station commander more as an embarrassment than a welcome gift. Having offered his unexpected visitors common hospitality, he then found they were expecting to join his family. Harassed, overworked, suffering from systematic German bombing, the poor man wished they had chosen some other place to land. After an awkward interview with the captain of the aircraft, he had advised him to relax for a few days while he dealt with their request. Then he concentrated on his own squadron problems in the hope that they would decide to return to Portugal.

They did relax, despite the heavy air raids which came as a shock after peaceful Lisbon, but Kit had the sense to realize that nothing would be done unless he forced the issue. He telephoned Colin Dryden, who had already been told by Tom that the Mediterranean episode was over. Within two hours of that call, *Flamingo* and her crew had been added to the strength of the squadron, earmarked for special duties. Over the next few months, *Flamingo* was modified yet again. Machine-guns, bomb-bays, additional radio equipment and camouflage paint turned her into a warplane, yet she was different from the Sunderlands and Catalinas of the squadron. Her guns were recessed and removable; her identification markings could be changed from military to civil, at will. Her crew had two uniforms – RAF blue-grey with badges of rank, as well as the smart navy-blue with gold insignia of a civil airline. Kit was given the title of Flight Lieutenant and the rest of his crew appropriate ranks, but they were chameleons changing appearance to suit the job on hand. The fact that they received their orders from Colin

Dryden's department, not from the squadron commander, and enjoyed an unusual dual status made slight difficulties, in the early days. The members of the squadron tended to regard them as élitists, outsiders even, and were inclined to shun them. However, their friendly manner and complete lack of consequence broke through the social barriers, and they were soon affectionately dubbed 'The Sardines' because they had come from Portugal.

Kit found his new life exciting and stimulating. He never knew if he would be flying high-ranking men to secret meetings on neutral soil, or making risky flights over occupied territory to pick up Colin Dryden's agents. When the squadron was hard pushed, they sometimes joined the boring but vital patrols of the Atlantic to protect convoys from lurking U-boats. Other times, they bombed German destroyers in company with the flying boats from their base, in a concerted attack. All the same, whether *Flamingo* carried Winston Churchill and his ministers to a meeting in Nova Scotia, or landed without lights in a strange bay defended by enemy guns to offload men with blackened faces armed with silent weapons, or even flew for hour after unfruitful hour on a square route searching for a reported submarine, Kit felt he could no longer be charged with piloting a flying shop.

He thought of Sylva often, but the pain of such thoughts began to diminish as time passed. Every man was potentially liable to succumb, as he had, to a certain type of woman; most were lucky never to encounter one. But for Lake Kiju and his determination to prove himself by pulling off an incredible rescue, he never would have met one. There was an occasional paragraph in the newspaper detailing Miss Lindstrom's progress in Argentina. Her plans appeared to be going well. Kit was certain she and Salvadore Delgardo would gain the glory they sought. He would be glad for her. For himself, breaking records no longer seemed important. Perhaps it was merely a convenient attitude to suit his inability to do so, yet he presently felt more professionally fulfilled than he had ever been. Emotional fulfilment eluded him, however. As summer darkened into winter, he found himself once more engaged in the careless pastime of making love to a succession of eager experienced girls, who all seemed much the same save for the colour of their hair.

Christmas 1941 brought events which both shocked and cheered. The Japanese entered the war by sweeping through British Far Eastern territories. Hong Kong fell, swiftly followed by the occupation of Malaya. It seemed the beginning of the end, until America took up arms after the destruction of their Hawaiian naval base by Japanese ships and aircraft. Hope rose again. New Year celebrations were exaggerated, if tinged with the kind of desperation which encourages a desire to live as if tomorrow may never come. On leave, but with nowhere to go, Kit allowed himself to drink more than usual in company with a lively crowd in the local pub, and woke each morning with a different girl beside him. They exchanged the customary light promises to write and meet up on their next leave, but they knew the whole world could have changed by then.

On a bleak February lunchtime when Kit was in the mess reading of the fall of Singapore, with the capture of an appalling number of trapped servicemen and civilians, a steward called him to the telephone. As it was the outside line, not the internal one on which he was notified of service matters, he took his time crossing to the instrument while asking the man the identity of his caller.

'The lady merely said she was an old friend, sir,' he replied, his expression speaking volumes about aircrew officers who attracted girls like magnets.

In view of the grave news concerning Singapore, Kit was in no mood for a flirtation with some distant girl he had most likely forgotten, so he picked up the receiver to say in businesslike tones, 'Anson here.'

For a moment or so he believed the caller had hung up. Then a quiet voice said, 'Hallo, Kit. I wasn't sure I'd be able to ring you casually like this.'

'Leone?' he questioned experimentally, taken by surprise.

'I'm in Plymouth for a business meeting.'

'Oh.' Still surprised that she should ring him, he asked, 'How's everything at Sheenmouth? Nothing wrong, is there?'

There was further hesitation before she said, 'I was certain I'd be told you were unavailable. In fact, I didn't even know if you were still at the base. It's seven months since you arrived in England. People get posted elsewhere.'

'Not me. I had a tough enough job persuading this squadron to take us on. Now they're stuck with us.'

'Does that mean you have nothing much to do?'

Leaning his shoulders against the wall, he gave a casual wave to a passing pilot just in from patrol. 'They keep us busy enough.'

'But not today?'

'My day off. I haven't had one for three weeks.'

'Poor you.' Background voices filled her next pause, then she said, 'I'm ringing from a call box outside the building where the meeting is being held. It's likely to continue for most of the afternoon, so I've booked a room for the night. Rail connections to Sheenmouth are tricky after four, and it's miserable waiting on blacked-out stations in this bitter weather.'

'Good idea,' he agreed, in the absence of further comment from her.

'Kit. . . would you have dinner with me?'

He put a hand over his right ear to deaden a loud shout of laughter bursting from the ante-room as someone opened the door. The officers were a noisy bunch, very distracting when a man was at the end of an unexpected telephone call. On the point of making an excuse, he hesitated. Today's news was gloomy enough to

675

prompt a heavy drinking session in the mess tonight, followed by some of the wilder methods of letting off steam. Dinner with an attractive woman, even this particular one, seemed a better prospect.

'Only if I pay,' he said down the line. 'You did the honours the last time we met.'

'Can you manage seven? It's awfully early, I know, but the hotel allows its restaurant staff to get home before the raids start.'

'Which hotel?' he asked then.

She named the most exclusive, in the centre of the city, and he told himself he had been naïve to ask. Where else would a Kirkland stay for the night?

'OK. I'll come to the lounge just before seven,' he promised. 'Pity old Warren isn't with you. We could have had a real get-together about old times.'

'That's what I have in mind,' she said, almost inaudibly. 'Until seven, then.'

Parking his rakish car at the rear of the hotel, and tipping the aged attendant handsomely to keep a watchful eye for anyone trying to syphon the petrol from his tank, Kit then pushed through the thick curtain over the entrance to step into welcome warmth and brightness. He immediately spotted two officers from his own squadron, in company with an obvious mother and daughter. They waylaid him, one of his fellows introducing his parent, and his sister who was engaged to the other pilot. When Kit eventually excused himself and entered the lounge, he found Leone walking towards him. She looked pale, but very striking in a dark-green cocktail dress with unmistakable Continental chic, enhanced by a diamond clip no one would doubt was genuine. Her shining hair was swept into a thick roll like a halo around her head, and equally fashionable scarlet lipstick emphasized the whiteness of her skin. A Kirkland to the core, he told himself wryly. How different from the girls he had been dating recently.

'I saw you come in,' she greeted, unsmiling.

676

'Eagle eyes! I'm dressed like almost every other man here.' Indicating the bar, he asked, 'Would you like a drink before dinner?'

'I'd prefer to go straight through.'

He was not sorry. They would have wine with the meal, so his pre-dinner drink would have to be non-alcoholic and uninteresting. The head waiter led them to the most secluded table in the room, with a comment betraying the fact that Leone had requested it. Kit was intrigued. They had no cause to seek privacy. He refrained from remarking on it, however, and instead chatted lightly about the blue-plush decor which had seen better days, whilst studying a menu about which the same could be said.

'Their *Sole Meunière avec Pommes Afriques* is actually haddock and chips,' he told her with a smile. 'One of our chaps brought his prospective bride and mother-in-law here to impress them. The wedding has since been called off.'

His joke fell flat, and he suddenly sensed that there was more behind this meeting than her chance visit to Plymouth which had necessitated an overnight stay. Frowning slightly, he decided to tackle the mystery right away.

'There *is* something wrong, isn't there? Not with Warren, I hope.'

She put aside the menu. 'You think a lot of him, don't you?'

'He's a brilliant chap, and a very genuine one. Not in trouble, is he?'

She shook her head.

'So what's this all about, Leone? I have the feeling that you didn't invite me here because you happened to find yourself in the same city with nothing better to do.' Curious insight made him add, 'Your meeting didn't overrun, did it?'

She avoided a direct answer. 'I really am in Plymouth on business. I didn't even know if you were still here,

677

after all this time. I rang the station on impulse. When they went off to fetch you, I panicked and almost hung up. Then I told myself I'd leave things in the hands of fate.' She sighed. 'So here we are.'

He sat back in his chair thoughtfully, also abandoning the menu. 'Yes, here we are. Do you now propose to take over from fate?'

Fiddling nervously with the cutlery for a moment or two, she then said, 'This was a terrible idea. I'm not in the least hungry, and what I have to say can't. . . I mean, it's not the kind of thing one discusses over dinner.'

Puzzled by unease in a girl who had always displayed such assurance, Kit decided he must take command of the situation. He got to his feet and went to put a hand beneath her elbow.

'Let's go and have that drink. We can eat later. . . if the staff haven't all gone home by then.'

He led her back to the bar, which was now so crowded and noisy it seemed quite unsuitable for Leone's mysterious revelation, he thought. However, she appeared glad of the rowdiness and made for two stools just being vacated by a naval officer and his uniformed girlfriend. Perched on these high seats and staring at their own reflections in the long mirror ahead, they were now as exposed as they had been secluded before. Ordering a dry Martini for Leone, and a whisky and soda for himself, Kit waited for her to begin. It was her mystery, after all.

Leaving her drink untouched, she regarded him with eyes deeply troubled. 'Do you recall our conversation just before you left that morning?'

He knew which morning she meant, and nodded.

'The conversation concerning Donald's theft of your father's design; *Aphrodite* which was really *Solitaire*?'

'That's right,' he agreed, growing more curious by the minute. 'Maitland had told you about it when you sacked him.'

'Those drawings Warren found in the old boathouse.

Were they the ones discovered in your car after the crash?'

He started on his whisky, wondering why she looked so tense and strained over something he would rather not discuss. It would have been wiser to join the mess rough-house tonight.

'Were they, Kit?' she persisted.

He sighed. 'The supposed "secret designs" I stole from Kirkland's? Yes, they were Dad's drawings. The police handed them to your father with the ten thousand I'd helped myself to. I imagine he destroyed the evidence pronto. Ironic, wasn't it?'

'*Did* you assault Donald that night?'

The diamonds on her collar caught the light to dazzle him as he shifted position. 'Where's all this leading?' he demanded aggressively.

'Please answer,' she begged. 'It's *so* important.'

The events of that night might have been pushed to the back of his mind, but they were still clear in every detail. 'I grabbed him by the lapels and threatened to choke him. Wouldn't you have done, in similar circumstances?'

'What happened then?'

He drank more whisky as the scene grew clearer in his memory. Echoes of rage began to make themselves heard above the noise in the bar. He drowned them with his own angry voice.

'You might have some devious Kirkland reason for dragging this all up, but I've no wish to resurrect the past. Sir Hector and Donald are dead, and I served my sentence for daring to challenge them. It's over, Leone.'

'It isn't,' she cried, with astonishing passion. 'For me, it won't be over until I know the truth.'

Still aggressive, he said, 'You told me Maitland had tried to twist your arm by giving it to you.'

She shook her head, making the diamonds in her ears flash fire. Then Kit realized the fire was also within her.

As she gazed at him with burning scrutiny, it was as if she was searching for someone who no longer existed.

'We were unwittingly speaking of two different things on that morning last July. I knew nothing of the theft of *Solitaire* until you mentioned it.'

He drained his glass, attempting to make sense of what was turning into a bizarre meeting with an old adversary whose motives were unclear. Nodding absently when the barman asked if he wanted the same again, Kit racked his brains to recall the details of that conversation beside the shattered west wing of Sheenmouth Abbey.

'You apologized for what your father had done to mine. I told you it was unnecessary, because you'd been little more than a child when it had all happened.'

'I was referring to something else, Kit.'

It was said so quietly, he was obliged to lean closer to catch her words. Something of her intensity then transferred itself to him, and he knew the past was not in the least dead. Indeed, it was about to rise up and confront him once more.

'You're right, this isn't the kind of thing one discusses over dinner,' he said tautly. 'Did you ask me here to explain what you were really apologizing for that morning?'

Her hand, with its heavy gold wedding ring and band of opals bestowed by Warren, twisted the stem of her glass for a moment or two while she continued to search his features for his other self – that youthful, heedless record-breaker who had held the world on a string.

'You said there could be peace between us, Kit. I want that more than anything in the world, but when you hear what I must tell you, you may find it impossible – *ever*. No, don't say anything until I've told you what Maitland revealed to me; what he had used to blackmail both Father and Donald into maintaining him in very comfortable manner.'

So he sat silently, while a beautiful young woman in

silk and diamonds, sitting erectly on a high stool in a cocktail bar, told him that her father had been the cause of his own losing every penny of an investment; that he had subsequently countered his victim's drunken fury with a physical blow which had sent him staggering from a platform above racing machinery to his death within it.

'When Maitland gave me those appalling facts, I thought I finally understood why a white-faced orphan had been taken into my home and given Kirkland largesse,' she continued in brittle tones. 'I persuaded myself that Father had possessed something of a conscience. When you unwittingly spoke of the theft of your father's design that morning, I was filled with the horror of knowing my assumption was wrong. Far from being guilt-ridden over Geoffrey Anson's gruesome death, Father had seen it as the perfect opportunity to endow Donald with the brilliance he lacked. You were absorbed into the masculine machinery of the Abbey purely for the purpose of keeping you under Kirkland control. Instead. . . instead, you foolish innocent, you heaped further glory on my family by flying their damned stolen aircraft faster than any man of the day,' she added brokenly. 'After such treachery, how can there ever be peace between us?'

Kit was shattered. She now revived a rage he had tried to subdue during two years in prison, twelve months of war in Spain, a strenuous proving flight, and during an emotional battle with a woman who had consistently urged him to become again the man who had been destroyed by the Kirkland family so that he could help her gain further laurels. That rage had died only when he had seen drowning men shot to pieces before his eyes, but it now rose again to consume him. He recalled standing in the library at Sheenmouth Abbey, while the legendary Sir Hector Kirkland told his well-bred, handsome son that this orphaned greaser from the company workshops was to be suitably dressed and polished up for inclusion in their hallowed household. *The orphaned greaser had been awed and overwhelmed with gratitude! He had vowed to ensure that his benefactor never regretted his generosity.*

Swallowing the second whisky in a gulp, he slammed the glass back on the counter as he got to his feet. 'You're damned right, there can never be peace between us. You might have changed your name to Grant, but you're still a Kirkland and always will be, so far as I'm concerned.' Throwing some notes in the direction of his glass, he turned abruptly and headed for the door knowing an uncontrollable desire for violence. Before he reached the night outside, however, it was there all around him. The familiar shuddering thuds beneath his feet, the concentrated thunder of several hundred engines overhead, and the tardy wail of sirens told him the German raiders had arrived earlier this evening. He was pushed aside as some people dashed for the safety of an air-raid shelter. The hotel lights dipped, then rose again; the crystal chandeliers clinked musically as they swayed and trembled from the growing tremors. There was laughter and conversation still from those who believed in prearranged destiny, as they caroused around the brightly mirrored bar. In that brief moment of hesitation, Kit saw reflected the haunted face of a girl who had taken on the sins of her father and was now breaking beneath the weight of them. Their glances held by means of that mirror, while the night grew as violent and dangerous as the emotions ruling him.

Next minute, an ear-splitting roar was instantly followed by a blast of dust-laden air as the long mirror fragmented to collapse with a section of the wall behind it. The scene was plunged into darkness, relieved only by the fires burning in the hearths of the bar and dining room. Women began screaming; male voices rose urgently. Beyond the collapsed wall, searchlights were probing the sky as another thud shook the ground menacingly to bring a further fall of masonry. Kit began moving forward, calling Leone's name in a voice grown husky. Choking on the flying dust, and pushing through a mill of people all endeavouring to find each other, he groped his way in the near-darkness across a room where sections of plaster and droplets from the chandeliers fell without warning, into the layer of debris underfoot.

'Leone! Leone!' he called desperately, finding it hard to gauge where she had been sitting as he pushed past other men in uniform, who were leading shaken partners to the comparative safety of the dining room. As his eyes adjusted to the reduced light, he saw people digging frantically in the rubble, where he guessed the barman was buried. The barmaid was clutching her arm with a blood-stained hand as an army officer helped her to cross the shifting surface of glass and bricks. The initial panic was subsiding as war-hardened people pursued the familiar routine learned from other nights like this, and Kit had to force his way through the flow heading for the adjacent blue-plush salon, his heart hammering as he searched in vain for a girl in green within that moving tide.

The continuing thuds as Plymouth was systematically flattened and set on fire were now augmented by the deafening thunder of guns forming the coastal defences, and the clangour of ambulances, fire-engines and police cars as they raced through the stricken streets. These sounds of destruction increased Kit's urgency as he searched the area with eyes watering from the irritation of dust. Then he saw her, a blonde girl backed against a distant wall, staring at something beyond reality and shaking violently. In a flash, he remembered that she had been buried alive beneath a wall of her home in an earlier experience of this kind. Crossing swiftly, he took hold of her arms outstretched against the wall and spoke gently through his rasped throat.

'Leone, everything's all right now. Come with me. I'll take you out of this.'

Her eyes abandoned their visions of terror and saw

only him. Where she had been rigid before, she now grew so limp she would have fallen if he had not supported her. Clinging to him, she clutched the dusty uniform jacket convulsively with both hands.

'You're safe! Thank God. Oh, thank God.'

Holding her close against his side and covering her restless fingers with his left hand, he began leading her through to the dining room. There, staff were bringing branches of candles and oil-lamps, and two women wearing Red Cross armbands were dealing with the casualties. Thankful that Leone appeared to be suffering from no more than shock, Kit took his trembling companion to the table where one of the waiters was dispensing tea from a copper urn. Securing some for Leone, Kit then had to hold the cup to her lips because she was shaking too much to do so herself. Between her grateful sips, he drank from the cup to moisten his throat grown unbearably dry. As he watched the girl caught in the grip of paroxysms, he reached a decision. Bombs were still falling, but more distantly now. The enemy aircraft would be turning for home soon.

'What's the number of your room?' he asked, drawing her from the press of people around those offering comforts of one sort or another. 'I think you'd be better off up there where it's quiet.'

'Key's in. . . the. . . in the. . . purse,' she stammered, still clutching his jacket.

Opening the black moiré bag on her arm, he took out a key with the number 19 on it. Glad that her room was not at the top of a building whose lifts would now be out of action, he asked the direction of the stairs and coaxed her towards the broad flight illuminated by lanterns. Progress was slow, and she stumbled several times, but Kit eventually opened the door of what proved to be a suite of rooms. A maid had already been on the job. Two lighted candles stood on a low polished table. Several more, in heavy candlesticks beside a box of matches, awaited the guest. Still supporting Leone

684

with his encircling arm, he lit all the wicks from one of the flames to provide as much brightness as possible. Only then did he set her down in one of the armchairs covered in gold brocade, prising her fingers from their hold on him with the assurance that he was simply going to fetch something to wrap around her. In the adjoining room, he stripped a blanket from the bed and returned to tuck it around the shivering girl. That done, he took up the brass poker and attacked the smoking slabs of coal until flames bloomed to throw extra warmth and light. When he turned back to Leone, she was clutching the blanket tightly as she watched him with wide, luminous eyes. The spasms were growing less violent, but she still looked distraught.

'Are you warm enough?' he asked.

'Warmer than before. You must think me very feeble,' she added, as he squatted before her to remove her shoes and tuck the blanket around her feet.

Intent on his task, he said, 'I've seen strong men in shock. This kind of reaction is involuntary and nothing to do with feebleness.'

'You're covered in dust,' she murmured. 'Your hair is full of white plaster, and your face is filthy.'

He glanced up. 'You're not exactly bandbox fresh yourself, madam.' He was prevented from elaborating, because he realized that she was looking down at him with an expression no strong man in shock had ever displayed. Getting slowly to his feet, he turned from her to walk to the window where he stared through the gap in the dark curtains at the ruby glow of fires burning all over the city. He had done what he could for her, and should leave.

'I ought to get back,' he said over his shoulder. 'The station might have been hit.'

'Not while the raid's still on,' she countered swiftly. 'You can't go yet. It's too dangerous.'

'I've faced worse,' he told her. Only eight p.m. and the rest of the lonely night to get through. It must be a daunting prospect for her. 'We're supposed to report back after a raid,' he continued, still watching the conflagration which put a satanic glow in a sky where stars twinkled coldly, despite murder and mayhem on this planet.

'Wait for the all-clear,' she begged. 'Come over to the hearth, Kit. There's a lovely fire now, and you look remarkably shaken, too.'

'I'm no hero,' he declared abruptly, turning back into the room. 'Of course I'm shaken. Like everyone else. This is the kind of evening I can well do without.'

'I'm sorry,' she said in distress. 'I'm so sorry.'

'Oh, for God's sake don't start apologizing on behalf of the Germans, as well,' he snapped, surprising himself by re-opening the hostility from which he had been walking away half an hour ago. 'Give up trying to shoulder the blame for everyone's bloody sins. No one expects you to do that, least of all me.' In the face of her continued distress, he began to pace the room. 'I don't know why you decided to make a full confession of your father's iniquitous crimes against the Anson family, especially all these years later. Both he and my father are dead. Geoffrey Anson can't be brought back to life; *Solitaire* can never be claimed as such. What proof I had of the theft must have been destroyed, and no one would believe my word against that of a Kirkland to this day.'

'Warren studied the drawings. He knew the design had been stolen.'

That halted him. '*Warren* knew. . . right from the start?' It was an unacceptable concept. 'If he knew, why didn't he say anything?'

Her pale face in the candleglow grew even sadder. 'He says no one would have believed him, either.'

Deeply affected by the revelation, Kit gazed at her in protest. 'Why didn't he say something to *me*? At the time of the trial, while I was in prison. . . even during the proving flight. He could have told *me* he knew. We were good friends.'

'He could have told me,' she added softly. 'We were also good friends.'

Fighting a painful sense of disillusionment, Kit nevertheless forced himself to shrug. 'What does any of it matter now? The three main characters are dead, and the reptilian Maitland has shed that skin for another. Warren is putting his brilliance to good account, and will go on doing so for the glory of aviation. As for me, if destiny decides that I'll survive the war, she'll doubtless have some damn good prospect in mind.'

'What about me, Kit?' came the urgent question. 'You've left me out of the cast of villains.'

'You weren't a villain,' he retorted, 'just a precocious, rather arrogant adolescent, who so badly wanted to be a Kirkland she echoed the censure of those out-of-reach males who dominated the scene.'

'No, you're wrong,' she cried. 'You have no idea how wrong.'

Getting to her feet still clutching the blanket around her shoulders, Leone came right up to him. There was no longer any mystery about why she had wanted this meeting, he realized with a shock. It was suddenly clearly written in her face which gazed up at him in the soft flickering light.

'Father had just told me of your supposed ingratitude and treachery; said you had left Sheenmouth never to return. Loving you madly, as I did, I couldn't believe him. I told myself there was a misunderstanding, an elusive but satisfactory explanation for your behaviour. I protested, claimed that you would come back to show Father and Donald how wrong they were. Then two policemen walked in carrying some rolled drawings, and a bag containing the exact sum I'd just been told you had demanded in order to settle your debts.' The mistiness in her eyes formed into tears on her lashes as she put her guilt into words. 'I stayed true to you even then, Kit. . . but when they revealed that Stephanie had also been found unconscious in the car with you, I accepted your treachery instantly. Young, vulnerable love is stormy and intolerant. I wanted to make you suffer as I then suffered. Being a Kirkland, my pride overruled my heart and I allowed Father to destroy you.'

With the long strident call of the siren outside announcing that danger was over, and nothing but the soft splutter and crackle of the fire within that candlelit room, Kit looked back at the girl and realized that the danger was here now, confronting them. Marvelling that he had not been aware of it before, he tried to pinpoint the exact moment during this eternal evening when his subconscious mind had registered what was happening between them. Completely off balance, he remained silent as she completed the irreversible truth.

'My father and brother are dead, but I'm still paying for what I did. I knew I loved you when you returned to fly *Flamingo*. I love you now. I'll always love you.'

She was so close he could feel her breath on his lips. He looked and saw Leone Kirkland, who had been part of his life even when he had put her from it. He saw a child in crumpled shorts bursting into a circular room which was to be his new home, declaring that she was determined to befriend him. He saw a girl masquerading as a woman in a moonlit ruin, begging with tears on her cheeks to be kissed. He saw a beautiful, worldly-wise social butterfly yearning for fulfilment in a pink-lined aircraft of which she was half owner and therefore his employer. He saw an intelligent, courageous woman asking for peace between them, yet making it more and more impossible with every word she uttered. He saw another man's wife.

'I should go back to the station,' he murmured, fighting awareness with reason.

He must have betrayed himself in some way. Recognition was there in her eyes, and in the way she said without dismay, 'Yes, I know you should.'

They remained as they were, standing close enough to feel the vibrancy of this new relationship. It was as if the span of those aggressive years now demanded a lingering surrender, however. His kiss was little more than a searching, experimental contact, at first. Then, as the blanket dropped from her shoulders, and his arms closed around her, their last hope of peace was driven away by a passion more violent than any between the Ansons and the Kirklands, and as potentially destructive.

26

It was snowing hard. Warren gazed out at the white
expanse of the lower meadow to where the Sheen lay
like a great grey snake beneath a leaden sky. He saw no
beauty in the silent, breathless snowscape, where trees
stood like frozen sentinels beneath the caressing drift of
large swirling flakes. Despite the cheery log fire heating
the room, there was a coldness in every part of him.
Vital work awaited. He could settle to none of it. When
Leone had told him of the refugee reassessment conference at Plymouth, he had known instinctively that she
would try to contact Kit. Hoping desperately that *Flamingo* and her crew were no longer at the base, he had
feared they were when Leone's secretary had informed
him that his wife had telephoned her intention of staying
overnight due to the late running of the meeting. When
she walked in today, he would know immediately
whether or not the seven-month hiatus in their marriage
was over.

After that morning of revelation they had continued
their lives as before, except that they were merely business partners and no longer lovers. Leone had never
rejected his overtures, because he had been afraid to
make any. They still shared a room and a large double
bed, but no longer touched in intimate fashion. Love
for her was slowly destroying him; anguish over her
mantle of guilt was slowly destroying her. Kit's name
had not been mentioned since that July day, but it had

been there between them whenever they spent time together. Warren had worked for longer and longer periods at the old boathouse, and had not hurried back from various trips to aerodromes around the country.

Finding himself again in Scotland, he had enjoyed Mona's company to the extent of contemplating a revival of sexual partnership. He began making overtures, until Joss Hamilton had demanded an introduction to the red-haired girl. The foolish, heedless creatures had surrendered to what was these days known as lust at first sight, and had married on a special licence a week later. The news had made Warren's own situation seem even more painful. The prevailing sense of urgency between lovers who might not live to see the morrow, did not touch his relationship with Leone. She knew he was certain to be there. 'Boring Old Fools Full of Idiotic Notions' like himself were coddled and sandbagged so that danger could not touch them. Of course there was no sense of urgency in their marriage. Good old dependable, doglike *Mister* Grant would always be there when she called. If he were Squadron Leader Grant, how different things might be.

A shifting log fell to bring him from his reverie. He sighed. Leone had made no secret of her enduring love for Kit, and he had married her knowing of it. They had been happy, nevertheless. It had been a good partnership in many ways, and she had been generous in passion. His only hope of recapturing any part of that joyous interlude lay in the hands of the man Leone had almost certainly contacted yesterday. Although it would tear his wife apart, Warren prayed Kit would have killed any last hope of forgiveness she had. Only that, or his death in action, would put an end to Leone's tangled passion for a man who had never wanted her in return.

Snow deadened the sound of the taxi arriving from the station. The slamming of a car door drew him to the window again, but she was already hidden by the porch over the main entrance as she let herself in. He heard her stamping the snow from her shoes; the sound echoed in the vaulted hall. It was an effort to remain where he was, but he would not run out like a dog anxious for a pat of reassurance. She was unlikely to be impressed by such behaviour after her meeting with a uniformed hero. He heard her ask Merrydew to bring tea to the small sitting room, and braced himself for her entry. When she walked in unprepared to find him there, he knew with an appalling sense of shock that he had lost her. A woman who has been in the arms of her lover all night betrays the fact with a subtle radiance apparent in every aspect of her manner and movements. Leone did so now. It was like a stunning physical blow. He could not believe Kit would wreak such terrible vengeance for his own silence ten years ago. Guilt for guilt, an adulterer was a greater sinner than a man who said nothing at a time when no one would have heeded him. Leone pulled up instantly, her radiance being replaced by wariness. But it had been there. Warren had witnessed it, and knew he could not accept its implications.

'Why aren't you working?' she asked.

It was a gentle enough question, yet in his ears it sounded like a belligerent accusation – as if he had no right to be in her home, destroying her private joy with his presence.

'I'm not always chained to a drawing board,' he snapped. 'I also need to enjoy those things other people do when they're not working.'

She made no attempt to sit. Coming to warm her hands by the fire, it seemed to him that she was calculating what to say next. Then he noticed her mouth, and the faint, darkening marks on the side of her neck. She bruised easily in passion. He should know. Fury boiled up inside him, as it did only in defence of things he held dear.

'You're just another of his many easy conquests. I hope you realize that.'

Her head came round as her colour rose. 'Warren,

692

please don't attack me before I've had a chance to speak and explain.'

'There's nothing to explain. The proof is all too evident. Where are the other bruises to match the one on your neck? Would you care to strip off and show me, or shall I look for myself? Ah, I'd forgotten. Your husband isn't allowed privileges like that any more. They're reserved for heroes in uniform.' He thrust his hands into his pockets, where they would be safe. 'That's always been the attraction, hasn't it? Women are fools over daredevil, lecherous men of action. The oftener they risk their lives, the more besotted women become. When they don a uniform to do it, their fascination doubles. All they need to do is beckon, and even a Kirkland is lured.'

Her eyes pleaded with him. 'You're only wounding yourself with such words.'

'I don't expect to wound you,' he retaliated bitterly. 'You're wrapped in your own protective layer of sexual fulfilment. There are no raw, exposed emotions to weaken a woman who has just unconditionally surrendered to a man she's been longing to satisfy for years. Was it worth waiting for? Does he live up to his reputation?' Clenching his fists tightly in his pockets, he cried, 'Are heroes any different from we ordinary men when they're naked?'

'Stop it, Warren,' she shouted. 'I'll not be spoken to like that.'

'No, of course, I'd forgotten I was addressing a Kirkland,' he went on harshly. 'He can say anything he wishes to you, of course, because he once lived here as part of the family. The Ansons might have been nobodies who slept with the Sheenmouth donkeys, but he was a bright boy. He knew how to ingratiate himself. He never complained about dressing for dinner and keeping up appearances. He never went around in woollen cardigans to make you ashamed of him. The orphaned greaser turned into an assured pseudo-Kirkland with willingness

693

and ease. Oh yes, he was a bright boy then, and still is. I'm the idiot. I dared to fall in love with a girl above my station. Your father warned me of the fact, and I should have heeded him. Kit Anson's the sophisticated randy hero; I'm just a brainy stick-in-the-mud son of a whore. Small wonder you went to bed with him the moment he beckoned.' He swallowed painfully. 'You did, didn't you?'

Even then he hoped she would deny it, but she did not. Feeling like striking her, he lashed her with his tongue instead. 'Haven't you any pride?'

'Yes, my dear,' she said wretchedly. 'An excess of it has been my greatest failing. It was responsible for breaking a man at the height of his splendour, and for humiliating him unforgivably.'

'You're asking me to believe that he nevertheless has forgiven, not only you but your entire family? The man would have to be a saint, and even someone as enchanted as you can't cannonize him.'

'No. . . but I can vindicate him, Warren. There was no deliberate treachery on his part. There was a raid. The bar of the hotel was damaged. He helped me to my room because I was rather shocked. The. . . the rest simply happened.'

'*I'll bet it bloody well did!*' To his horror, he realized he was on the verge of tears. Turning away and crossing to the window, he fought them desperately as he wondered how to handle this bombshell. Before he was in a fit state to speak, she arrived behind him to appeal for his understanding.

'Please listen for a moment. I'm not going to attempt to excuse myself, but I must defend him. He was falsely accused ten years ago and sent to prison. I can't allow further injustice without speaking up. Kit may be all you say when it comes to women, but he agreed to have dinner with me because it happened to be his day off and because he believed my story of a prolonged meeting. It would have been a perfectly innocent evening, if I hadn't been determined to tackle the past. I told him how Father had pushed Geoffrey Anson, so that he fell into a machine. Kit then told me there could never be peace between us, and began walking out. He was almost at the door when a bomb landed in the street outside, bringing down the wall of the bar. He returned to search for me in the resulting devastation, found I was in shock, and did what he could to relieve it. He was about to return to his base when I told him I loved him, that I always had and always would. He tried to go, even then. It. . . well, it proved impossible.'

The tears were now on his cheeks and he was powerless to stop them. Leone put a tentative hand on his right arm, then another on his left. As his shoulders began to shake with his anguish, she laid her cheek against his back and held him close in her regret. They stayed that way until he felt weary with the pain of trying to hate her. Turning to take her in his arms, he knew he could not – whatever she did. Incredibly, he felt sorry for her.

'So what happens now?' he asked thickly.

Drawing away, she shook her head unhappily. 'I suppose fate will decide the final outcome. War tends to snatch people from life without warning, and without discrimination. I've loved you in my fashion, Warren, and I still love you that same way, but I can't give up this vulnerable happiness. I just can't. You've always known my true feelings for Kit. He now shares that passion.'

Warren thought of Mona and Joss Hamilton. Overwhelming desire had to be instantly satisfied. Tomorrow may never come. It was possibly this same madness ruling Leone now. He knew damn well what was ruling Kit Anson.

'You intend to meet him again?'

She nodded. 'Whenever it's possible.'

'I see. I'll move my things down to the boathouse.'

'No, Warren,' she cried in instant distress, 'there's no need for that.'

'There's every need,' he retaliated from the depth of his hurt. 'Sheenmouth Abbey has only just tolerated me, even with you as my wife. I'd find it totally hostile now you're another man's mistress.'

Leone was engaged in translating a long document into French for Philip Curtiss, when her secretary buzzed through to say Flight Lieutenant Anson was on the line. Joy raced through her as she snatched up the receiver, casting caution to the winds in her eagerness. It was May, and they had met only once since that unforgettable night in Plymouth. Kit had been flying when she was free; she had been at important meetings when he was. They had exchanged telephone calls, but private conversations from his base were strictly limited and ruthlessly cut off by the operator if they overran the allotted time. When Kit used a public call box, he invariably ran out of coins, or was accosted by a queue of angry people waiting to get in, long before they had said all they wished to each other. Careless of whether or not she was being overheard, Leone made no secret of her feelings with her first words.

'Kit, *darling!* What a wonderful surprise. The past four days seemed an eternity. Did they to you? Where are you speaking from? How long do we have?'

'Leone, I have Wing Commander Dryden here in my office,' his voice warned, dousing her excitement rather drastically. 'Sorry to ring you during office hours. I hope I'm not interrupting anything too vital.'

'A very boring French translation,' she told him, her own voice growing flat with disappointment. 'What can I do for you?'

His reply was made in businesslike manner, and concerned something quite unexpected. 'When I arrived in Sheenmouth last year, Warren mentioned a *Seaspray* which had been designed to seat two, but which had never been delivered due to the customer's demise.'

'Yes,' she murmured, gazing from the window at the buds of May putting bridal touches to all the trees, and finding it painful that he was listening to her voice yet she could say nothing of her yearning for him.

'Does he still have it?'

'Down in the old boathouse. It has been dismantled and stored there.'

'Then I suppose I ought to talk to him about it. Is he at home?'

Good God, she could not possibly buzz through to the boathouse to tell her husband that her lover wanted a conversation with him! Kit should know better than to put her on such a spot. He must be mad.

'Is this. . . ' She cleared her throat. 'Is this an official matter?'

'Of course it damn well. . . yes, naturally,' he amended, plainly finding this as difficult as she. 'It's also rather vital, otherwise I'd have sent a written inquiry.'

With her brain in a whirl, she merely said, 'Perhaps I can help. I know a little about this seaplane – who ordered it, the individual refinements, and so on. If your inquiries are more detailed, then you will have to speak to the designer himself. He's very engrossed in a problem concerning instability at speed, so I'd prefer not to disturb him unless it's absolutely essential.'

'Yes, I quite understand,' came the warm response.

Kit then went on to ask if she thought the seaplane could be swiftly assembled and flown, if she knew its individual range and fuel capacity and what, if any, were its performance statistics. Having recovered a little from the strain of the situation, Leone asked her secretary to bring in the relevant file. From it she was able to provide answers to his questions in her normal professional manner.

'How swiftly she could be assembled and ready to fly is one answer I can't supply,' she continued. 'There's nothing in the data about that, naturally, so I'd have to ask Warren. He's always vowing to put her together and take her up on a joy-ride, so presumably it's a possibility. Is the time element very important?'

'Absolutely vital. Will you hold on a moment while I convey all you've told me to Wing Commander Dryden?'

She heard him speaking to his companion, and tried to picture the man she deeply loved working hard not to betray his personal feelings during this contact. Away on thoughts of her own, she was abruptly recalled from them by Kit's next words.

'Leone, we believe *Seaspray* could be the answer to a prayer, but we shall have to discuss the matter more fully. We'll fly down to Sheenmouth in *Flamingo*. Should be with you by about three this afternoon. Perhaps you'd warn Warren, and we'd appreciate a boat waiting to bring us up to the Abbey. Adieu until then.'

He rang off leaving her staring at the receiver still in her hand, unable to believe she had heard aright. In a few hours, he would be here. He would behave as if they were merely old friends, and he would discuss aeronautics in a civilized manner with the man whose wife he had recently bedded. Warren would talk about his beloved *Seaspray* in a similar manner, as if he were not a betrayed husband. She would be with them, and they would expect her to handle the impossible situation the way they undoubtedly would. When it came to flying machines, all else was unimportant!

Slamming the receiver on to its cradle, she rose to her feet as a storm broke within her breast. Damn Kit! Damn Warren! Damn this Wing Commander! They had no right to do this to her. How dare Kit ring up and announce that he was arriving this afternoon to discuss some mysterious project with Warren? How dare he, after holding her naked body and driving deep within her in his passion? This damned incomprehensible relationship between men and the aircraft they flew, still took precedence over her union with the one she had loved for so long. Having thumped her fist on the wall beside the window to relieve her anger, she then took up the fat telephone directories and shied them one by one into a padded chair.

Leaning her temple against the window frame, she gazed out to where the restored chapel stood surrounded by blossom trees. Suppose Warren had never found those drawings and handed them over to Kit. Stephanie would have married Donald in that chapel. Now, as his widow, she would be sole owner of Sheenmouth Abbey and of Kirkland's. Kit would never have been imprisoned and disgraced but, instead, would have gained greater aerial laurels, chased even more women, and now would almost certainly hold very high rank in the RAF. Or he would be dead. Warren would still be as brilliant on the design front, without a Kirkland as his wife. What of herself, however? Gazing from that window with apprehension for the coming afternoon, she realized it was still a masculine world she lived in. Leone Grant might be a sharp businesswoman, efficient translator, good organizer and supporter of local fund-raising bodies, and a competent pilot, but she would still be emotionally torn while her husband and her lover discussed the principal love of their lives as if she did not exist.

As she had guessed, after the initial barely suppressed hostility, Kit and Warren put aside personal matters in favour of the main issue. Colin Dryden was a pleasant nondescript man, who nevertheless plainly held a position of uncommon responsibility. If he sensed the somewhat charged atmosphere, he gave no evidence of doing so. As they all gathered in the blue and yellow room where Leone dispensed tea, there was no attempt to exclude her from the discussion, her position in the aircraft manufacturing industry being enough to guarantee her reliability. It was a difficult situation for her, however, so she was more than happy when talk developed into deep technical theorizing by the men. At first, she sat back to study Kit hungrily. Then she realized such scrutiny was making difficulties for him, and abandoned it to concentrate on following their discussion. Before long, she grew fearful. They were not talking about aeronautics, but Kit's life.

'When Colin first approached me, I told him it couldn't be done,' Kit said to Warren. 'We think there might be a chance with your machine.'

'Here's the problem in a nutshell,' Colin Dryden continued, leaning forward in his chair as if to emphasize his urgency. 'You've done mods on *Florida* so that she can operate to and from Norway on special flights, and must know a fair bit about the type of passenger we bring out. This one is rather more tricky. We have just ten days in which to do the job, and only one hope of reaching him. It's a pig of a prospect, but if we can even make an attempt at it we must. That's why we have to commandeer your seaplane, if she's fit to fly.'

Warren nodded, concentrating on the wing commander. 'She'll fly. Over the last couple of months I've been working on her in my free time. She's oiled, checked, and in tip-top shape. I simply have to assemble her.'

'OK. We've established that she's available. Let's get down to the finer details, so that you'll know why we've come to you as our last hope. Our passenger is one of these men of science who believe their knowledge should be shared by the world. At least, he held that belief until a few weeks ago. When the Jerries first occupied Norway, he happily continued working in his laboratory, delighted with the facilities they afforded him.' Dryden's mouth twisted cynically. 'Four weeks ago, everything suddenly changed. Our man was told he would be sent to Germany to work with scientists there on further development of his successful breakthrough on bacteria. It then dawned on him that his findings were to be used in the field of germ warfare; that abominably filthy form

700

of mass murder. That's something even his scientific liberalism can't stomach.'

'So he wants to come over to us?' asked Warren.

Leone was surprised by his calm acceptance of facts which were deeply disturbing to her. Who was Colin Dryden? How did Kit come to be so closely associated with the man, and how did Warren know so much about bringing people out of Norway? Even without the answers to those questions, instinct told her this all spelled danger for Kit. In any attempt to bring this man out of Norway, he was plainly the chosen pilot. Fear now knotted inside her to create real physical pain.

'Yes, he wants to come over to us,' Dryden confirmed. 'The alternative is to be tortured and killed for refusing to cooperate. The death they would devise for a specialist in killer germs would be particularly horrific, I imagine. He is due to be shipped to Germany on the twenty-fourth of this month, which is ten days from now. The laboratory is closely guarded – he lives on the premises – so his absence would be swiftly noticed and a search mounted. He has just one chance of being picked up by us. Thirty miles south of the laboratory there's a narrow fjord. The leader of the local partisans says they can get him from his quarters at the end of his working day, and down the steep sides of the fjord under cover of darkness. It's up to us to do the rest, but it's a very tall order, I fear.'

'Isn't it always,' commented Warren, surprising Leone further with his aplomb. 'What's the main problem about the landing area, lack of depth or length?'

'Both,' Kit told him heavily.

'I might have guessed.'

'There's an additional drawback,' put in the wing commander. 'Halfway along the fjord there's a bottle-neck. This rules out a flying boat with huge wingspan. A small seaplane could be taken through, with a genius at the controls, but the craft has to be a two-seater to take the passenger.' Casting a glance at Kit, he added,

'I have the genius to fly the damned thing, but no machine with the right combination of properties. Your dismantled racing model is our last hope, Mr Grant.'

'What about a submarine?' asked Leone. The men all turned in startled manner, having forgotten her. Fighting the sensation of once more being invisible in her own home, she posed a second question. 'Why must it be a marine aircraft, not a boat?'

Kit explained, trying to sound impersonal. 'A sub would never navigate the bottleneck. There are underwater rocks. I'm not even sure I'd care to chance flying through it. Depending on Warren's advice, I think up and over it, with a deep swooping landing on the far side sounds less of a risk.'

Anything sounded an unbelievable risk, to Leone. She longed to say as much, but had to remain silent.

'Before we go further with maps, flight timings, moon phases, and so on,' the senior man said to Warren, 'I must ask the vital question. Assuming that *Seaspray* is mechanically capable of carrying out this mission, can she be made ready to do so within ten days? Remember, Kit will need to test fly her so that he perfectly understands what he can demand of her, and also what she'll refuse to do. He'll be laying his life on the line for this biologist, so we must do all we can to ensure his success. Not only will Lindstrom be snatched from the Germans, he'll be invaluable to us in developing a defence against the horror he himself has created.'

Leone was now totally anguished. 'Did you say the man's name was Lindstrom?' she asked tensely.

Colin Dryden nodded. 'Knut Lindstrom. It'll be a strange coincidence if Kit pulls this off. Saved his life once before, out in Africa. Picked the man up from a ridiculously small lake, together with his partner and sister. She's Sylva Lindstrom, the Amazonian flier presently tackling the South Pole.' Then he collected his thoughts. 'How foolish of me! You and your husband

702

were present during that rescue, of course. You'd be acquainted with the Lindstroms.'

'Not really. I played very little part in the affair,' she murmured, gazing at Kit, 'and my knowledge of Miss Lindstrom is minimal.'

Kit gazed back at her, but the angle of the light from the windows made his expression unreadable. Warren then suggested that they should all take a look at *Seaspray*, and the men rose to their feet as if eager to be gone. Leone did not accompany them to her husband's retreat, neither did she return to her French translation. At ten p.m. she was so tense she buzzed the boathouse. Warren took a long while to answer, then sounded abstracted in answer to her question on what was happening.

'We're assembling the seaplane. It'll probably take us all night, so don't wait up for him.'

With her nerves raw, she reacted heatedly to his implication. 'Don't insult me, Warren!'

There was a slight pause before he said, 'Sorry.'

'Do they think *Seaspray* will suit their purpose?'

'He's planning to test fly her tomorrow. Then he'll know.'

Leone noted the avoidance of Kit's name, and recalled how Donald used to do the same thing. A sign of guilt? 'I see. Will you let me know the outcome?'

'Ask him. You're looking for a good excuse, aren't you?'

Tired, afraid of the unknown, and depressed over this unhappy situation in her life, she appealed to him. 'Please don't be hostile. The world is hostile enough already.'

'I have to go,' he said briefly. 'Time is vital.'

She spent a restless night haunted by nightmares, and waking spells containing fears worse than nightmares. In the morning, she had to fight the urge to go immediately to the retreat Warren had made his home again. They would not want her there. It was a day of gusting wind which blew the blossoms from the trees in a shower of pink and white, and of sudden squally showers. Too restless to work, she drove to the cliffs above East Sheenmouth. The wildness of the pewter sea below suited her mood. Was Kit to be snatched from her in this bizarre manner now she had finally found true fulfilment of her love for him? He had vowed the affair with Sylva Lindstrom was over, yet he was contemplating the ultimate sacrifice in order to save her brother from his own ethical blindness. Why? Why Kit, not some other clever pilot? So many doubts and questions were bombarding her at a time when Sheenmouth Abbey appeared to have reverted to its old style. Had the ghostly monks made a bid to return, showing her she was still unimportant in the masculine world around her?

She remained on the isolated cliffs until an armed soldier, accompanied by an officer with greying hair, approached the car from the direction of the artillery battery a quarter of a mile away. The senior man seemed relieved to find a female occupant, but still maintained an official tone as he asked her what she was doing there.

Giving an apologetic smile, Leone said, 'I didn't mean to cause you alarm, and I am aware of the notice forbidding loitering on the cliffs. Please forgive me. I have something on my mind, and this seemed the perfect spot in which to try to get to grips with it. I'll move on now.'

'Yes, Miss. I'm sorry, but we can't be too careful, you see,' the officer explained. 'Even a lady like yourself could be up here making sketches of the defences and beaches, or signalling to the enemy. Seems a shame not to be able to enjoy a view like this one, but you must blame the Jerries for that. We just do our duty.'

As she started the engine and gently backed ready to turn, she overheard the corporal saying to his officer, who was clearly new to the district, 'That's Mrs Kirkland. She practically owns Sheenmouth.'

The other man's reply was whipped away by the wind, but as Leone raised a hand in farewell, she reflected on Warren's assertion that she was still a Kirkland in everyone's eyes, so Sheenmouth Abbey would always be hers alone. Heavier-hearted than ever, she conceded that he was probably right. Had he also been right in his decision to remain silent all these years? All she had achieved by determinedly reviving something even Kit himself had buried in the past, was a situation making none of them entirely happy. Warren was deeply hurt, estranged from a relationship which had brought understanding and contentment. He was her husband, yet he lived in a small boathouse whilst continuing to be part owner of Kirkland Marine Aviation. Kit had been brought to realize a true love which brought him no more than uneasy pleasure, in a life which promised only each hour as it came. He could make no lasting commitment to her; she could not to him. Her father had always ruled that the past should be forgotten whilst getting on with the future. Easier said than done, when the future was entirely out of her hands.

The rain cleared to bring sunshine later in the afternoon. Walking in the grounds, Leone heard what she thought was one of the boats out on the river. It proved to be *Seaspray* taxiing slowly and experimentally. Both cockpits were occupied. She realized that Warren was in the rear seat to explain the aircraft to Kit, who was piloting. They would be lost in the complexities of what they were doing, forgetting all else. The seaplane taxied back and forth for a while, then the engine suddenly roared into full revs as Kit took her in a bouncing run over the choppy surface and up into the air above the Abbey. The significance of that first flight hit Leone then. Kit really was going to attempt to bring out Sylva Lindstrom's brother within the coming ten days.

Three of them passed agonizingly for the girl who watched, then waited for some word from the men preparing to launch a mission which could end her happiness so recently found. *Seaspray* was towed down to the workshops, where she was sprayed grey and given RAF roundels for identification. Kit made further test flights over Lyme Bay, demanding slight modifications which were immediately carried out by Warren and a duo of mechanics. Knowing how vital such tests and adjustments were, Leone merely made telephone inquiries of the overseer and did not attempt to go in person to her workshops. When there was still no call from Kit, she rang the airfield at Magnum Pomeroy where he and Colin Dryden had been given temporary accommodation. The officers' mess orderly told her that Flight Lieutenant Anson was asleep and had given orders not to be disturbed. She left a message. Later the same evening, she rang again. Mr Anson had left a short time before and was unlikely to be back before breakfast. She left another message.

When five of the precious days had passed without any word from him, or from Warren, Leone embarked on something she very rarely did. Ringing Wing Commander Keen at Magnum Pomeroy, she reminded him of the many times he and his officers had been entertained at Sheenmouth Abbey, then asked for a favour in return. Two hours later, the telephone rang and Kit's angry voice asked if she had gone completely mad.

'No, darling,' she replied, with a touch of bitterness. 'I simply thought it was time to remind everyone of my existence. *Seaspray* was certainly designed by Warren, but she was built by Kirkland's and therefore sixty-five per cent owned by *me*. When I phoned Warren, he rather boorishly told me to consult you about what's happening. You ignore all my messages. Colin Dryden calmly mentions "commandeering" the aircraft, if she's suitable. While I dutifully pour tea, you three talk glibly about something so melodramatic it sounds like a story from *Boys' Own Paper*, then off you all go to carry out your vitally important secret plot and behave as though I don't exist. Don't you think it's time one or other of you had the courtesy to consult me about *Seaspray*, what work is being done in *my* workshops, and whether or not she's about to be "commandeered" by Colin Bloody Dryden for your stupid death or glory antics in order to save *her* brother? After all, I. . . '

Kit interrupted her monologue made in tones which were rising dangerously. 'All right, Leone, calm down. This phone's in a damned public place. Keen gave me a half-crown look when passing on your message. I really don't want the entire station also knowing how you feel.'

'Do *you* know?' she challenged emotionally.

'Now I do.' His voice softened slightly. 'I'm sorry. It's a hellish situation for us all.'

'I must see you.'

'Where, for God's sake? Not there on the man's own territory. . . and you can't come here.'

'What about the Buck and Hounds?'

'And have the whole of Sheenmouth scandalized? We're both too well known.'

'So you intend to go off with your aerial mistress leaving things like this? Goodbye, and thanks a lot for Plymouth! I always have come a poor second to flying machines where you're concerned.'

'Who's being melodramatic now?'

'You may never return from where you're going.'

The urgency in her voice must have touched him then. After a short silence, he said quietly, 'Drive along the Forton Road. I'll be beside the old watermill in about thirty minutes.'

He was there when she arrived. He looked tired and worried, so she was immediately repentant and apologized for putting him in an embarrassing situation.

'I was desperate, darling, and women do unexpected things when they're in that state.'

Kit managed a pale smile as he settled in the seat beside her. 'I think old Keen is smitten with you. He passed on your message in the tones COs use to tear a strip off a chap. He's a stickler for good manners, and backed up your complaint of our high-handed use of

Kirkland's facilities without having the decency to consult the owner.'

'You didn't return my calls. I had to make you contact me, and that was all I could think of.'

'You're right, though. We've all been so absorbed in this thing, we've forgotten who's the real boss here.'

'That isn't my problem, and you know it,' she said softly.

After studying her expression briefly, he suggested that she should drive on to the downs beyond Forton. 'Your kind of problem can only be solved in a place less public than this.'

As the sun went below the rim of the green ridge overlooking the old market town of Forton, they kissed with a hunger which could not be satisfied as they both wanted.

'This is an intolerable situation,' he murmured against her temple, as he held her close. 'One minute, we're discussing technicalities with the ease and rapport of old friends, the next, we're like stags in the rutting season. If we weren't on his home ground, it wouldn't be quite so bad for me. God knows how he feels.'

'What about how I feel?' she asked, drawing away to study him in the gathering dusk. 'Have either of you considered that?'

'I daren't,' he confessed. 'Look, we've already agreed to count no further than today where our love is concerned. I can't offer you anything more than an occasional night in some out of the way inn, or furtive groping in the back of a car like this. Oh, Christ,' he swore furiously, gazing from the window away from her, 'this is humiliating! Leone Kirkland being kissed and cuddled like a cheap floosie picked up by a serviceman who's half cut!'

'Darling, don't,' she begged. 'Let's get out and walk. The kissing and cuddling is over for the moment. I want to talk to you.'

They left the car to stroll hand in hand along the

smooth turf of the downs, now illuminated by the rising moon. Leone remained silent until she thought he had recovered from his outburst. Then she asked a whole string of questions.

'Who exactly is Colin Dryden?'

'He's the head of a department specializing in affairs like this.'

'How do you come to know him well enough to drop rank and use his first name?'

He tightened his clasp on her hand. 'I've been working for him since just after the outbreak of war. The Jerries had true cause to be suspicious of our flights through the Med.'

She glanced up at him quickly. 'Are you saying you've been acting as some kind of agent?'

'More or less.'

'And now?' she asked fearfully.

'Now I'm with the RAF.'

'But you still work for him and this mysterious department?'

'Yes.'

'Why didn't you tell me this before?'

He stopped and faced her. 'It's supposed to be a secret. You only know now because we needed *Seaspray*.'

She waited a moment before asking, 'Are you going to do it; this flight through a fjord, which requires a genius at the controls?'

'Yes.'

'When?'

'I can't tell you that.'

'Oh, for heaven's sake!' she cried. 'I know the rest. Don't start being so ridiculously secretive now.'

Taking her by the shoulders, he gave her a gentle shake. 'Listen! I can't tell you, because I don't know myself. It must be before the twenty-fourth, but the weather has to be considered. As you can see tonight, the moon is in its brightest phase. I'll need as much light as possible, so a cloudy overcast evening is one to avoid. It'll be a last-minute decision.'

Moving into his encircling arms, she murmured against his jacket, 'I hate the whole idea.'

'So do I, but I hate the idea of germ warfare even more.'

Pressing closer, she asked, 'Does she know what her brother's been working on?'

'How could she? She's in Argentina.'

'When she was with you.'

He shook his head. She felt the movement as she pressed against his body. 'Sylva disowned the war; claimed it didn't much matter who won it because there'd be another, and then another. She said it was more important to devote one's energies to pioneering and discovery, which brought good things to the world and risked no lives but one's own. She has a point.'

'Was she aware of what you were doing in the Med?'

'Only right at the end.' He gave a short mirthless laugh. 'She had no time for a man who believed Hitler could be defeated by dropping messages and taking pictures from what she called "a flying shop".'

Leone drew back to look at him in the pale glow of night. 'She must have hurt you very deeply.'

'Yes, I'm afraid she did.'

'Poor Kit,' she whispered. 'Were you so much in love?'

'I thought I was, but I was wrong. With Sylva, I lost my head. With you, I'm in danger of losing everything.'

They kissed passionately, then he circled her with his arm to lead her back towards the car. 'We're going up to Scotland tomorrow – both of us – in *Seaspray*. Colin's arranging for a ship to take us to a point well within the seaplane's range. I'll fly in, pick up Lindstrom, then get back and land as close to the destroyer as possible. I feel sorry for poor old Warren. He'll have to kick his heels aboard the ship, wondering what's happening. I'll know.'

'Kit, what will. . . ' she began swiftly, but he cut her off with a gentle kiss on her mouth.

'You forced this meeting in order to prise the facts from me. Now face them, like a true Kirkland.'

'I'm not a Kirkland, I'm a Grant,' she reminded him hollowly.

'Don't I know it,' he responded. 'If you weren't, I'd have had you in a bed in the Buck and Hounds long ago.'

She heard *Seaspray* depart the following morning; saw the grey seaplane circle twice over the Abbey as if in salute, before heading north for Scotland. In the dual cockpit were the two men in her life. By the twenty-fourth of this month she would know whether or not the number had been reduced to one. For the first time since hostilities began, she knew the fear and prayers of millions of women whose loved ones might have said their last words and bestowed their last kisses.

27

They slipped away from the Scottish coast without ceremony. Warren remained on deck after everyone else had gone below. Lashed securely to the stern was *Seaspray*; he wanted to stay with her. He also needed solitude to indulge his thoughts. A week ago, he had been thrilled by the knowledge that his very first design had produced a machine which, alone, answered the demands necessary to pull off a flight of such importance. For several days he had told himself that everything people had said about his invaluable wartime rôle was true. Without *Seaspray* Knut Lindstrom could not be rescued. There were thousands of pilots, but only one aircraft suited to the vital task. Putting her together had been exciting and totally absorbing. He had even forgotten sexual hostilities for hours at a time, whilst working against the clock with the man who was to fly her. Later, when the full enormity of what was involved became all too clear, the entire project took on a sombre aspect. It smacked of lunacy. Surely there was some other way to bring the man out.

Turning to lean back on his elbows against the side, he studied the sleek racing lines of the special aircraft he had modified for sporting purposes. When he had rather shyly shown the famous Kit Anson his first drawings all those years ago, in Mrs Bardolph's attic room, how little either of them had guessed how strangely their lives would be linked; parting yet inevitably coming

712

together again in dramatic circumstances. None had been more dramatic than these.

Only now did he fully appreciate those qualities he had envied in Kit, and had consequently derided to Leone. Being a hero involved more than receiving public adulation and female worship. It demanded iron confidence when success seems impossible, the nerve to face danger in isolation, and the ability to hide one's doubts from those who believe one superhuman. If *Seaspray* had never been built, if the customer had lived to claim her, if he, himself, had not mentioned her existence to Kit last year, they would not now be steaming towards a point on a nautical chart whence this dainty aircraft would depart on a flight fraught with hazards. A sensation of deepest foreboding had settled within him, from the moment this destroyer had left port. He could not guess how Kit must be feeling.

Moving across to his aircraft with the intention of checking her over just once more, he got no further than a quick inspection of the floats, which acted as fuel tanks for the super-charged engine, when a voice made him turn almost guiltily. Kit stood beside him.

'Irresistible, isn't it? I did the same with *Aphrodite*. Although you know she's bloody perfect, you can't stop fussing over her.'

'I'm not sure she likes being tossed around like this,' Warren muttered awkwardly.

'It's a bit undignified for such a delicate creature, I agree. Like any highly strung lady, she hates being tied down.' He began checking a few points, also, bracing himself against the decided movement of the decks as they rode the Atlantic swell.

Warren watched him covertly. A sturdy man in uniform trousers and a thick roll-necked pullover, he seemed perfectly calm as all his attention focused on the machine he would soon fly. What were his thoughts and feelings beneath that outer confidence, Warren wondered. For a while they worked silently together,

713

checking details which needed no checking. Then Kit spoke over the sound of the wind and water surrounding them.

'If life had panned out differently, we'd have made a good team, wouldn't we?'

Warren ceased inspecting the ailerons. It was suddenly clear that Kit was deliberately attempting to make peace between them. Wary, at first, he then realized it was once again as it had been on that first evening at Sheenmouth Abbey, when instant rapport had sprung between them. Regrets flooded through him.

'I should have burned those drawings instead of handing them over. A small decision which had overwhelming repercussions.'

Kit stopped what he was doing, and perched on the beaching wheels. 'Over the years I've found that fate makes the decisions,' he said quietly. 'We believe that we're in charge of our own lives, but that's not so. You were meant to arrive on a motorcycle at the right moment to pick up a girl stranded by the roadside. From then on, the plan unfolded as fate intended it to. It'll continue to unfold, carrying us along with it.' Glancing down at the oily rag in his hands, he added, 'I've often wondered about the course of events, if you had simply thrown Dad's drawings out with the other rubbish from the boathouse.'

'So have I,' Warren admitted.

Kit glanced up at him again. 'We'd have realized soon enough that Donald was no designer, and grown suspicious over *Aphrodite*. Although we'd probably never have guessed the truth, I'm sure I'd have confronted old Kirkland with his son's incompetence – roped you in on it, too – and I'd have been out on my ear, just the same. He needed you; pilots are two a penny. So you see, it was bound to happen. Your decision over the plans for *Solitaire* had very little effect on the ultimate outcome. For years, I burned with a sense of injustice. One day, I realized it scarcely mattered whose name was associated

714

with that seaplane; it was the machine itself which was important. In the centuries to come, my father's design will simply be a single rung in a massive aviation ladder leading to bigger, faster machines.' He gave a rueful smile. 'Sylva once told me she regarded the war as unimportant because it was a recurring destructive force, while aerial pioneering produced enlightenment and discovery to benefit mankind. She's right, you know. Her brother won't give a damn about the name Warren Grant. All he'll care about is that a flying machine is able to penetrate an inaccessible fjord, in order to save his life tonight. He won't give a damn about the name of the pilot, either. He's right, too. It's what we do, not what we're called that's important.'

'Except when the name happens to be Kirkland,' Warren said, unable to help himself. 'Leone's burdened with the obsession to right all the family wrongs.'

Kit's dark eyes studied him for a moment across that windswept deck. 'You think that's all it is?'

Warren had imagined this moment many times over, and knew exactly what he would say to the man who had stolen his wife. Now he sensed that Kit was somehow saying farewell to him, and the chill of foreboding crept through his veins to keep him silent.

'She's seeking the echo of a youth that never was,' Kit said. 'You love her; you must be able to see that.'

'You love her and can?' Warren challenged.

Kit nodded. 'Probably because I'm seeking the same thing. I'm sorry, Warren, deeply sorry.' Getting to his feet, he added, 'Don't be too cruel to her. She's going to need you one day.' Turning away before Warren could respond to that, he said in more normal tones, 'I'm going to get my head down for a while. Look after *Seaspray* for me; I'm going to need *her* tonight.'

Warren remained on deck, gazing unseeingly over the grey sea. *It's what we do, not what we're called that's important.* Right now, he'd have given anything not to have designed and built this particular aircraft. Knut

Lindstrom meant nothing to him, but the man preparing to rescue him was the only true friend he had ever really known. If life had panned out differently, they *would* have made a most marvellous team.

There was a cold sky, scattered with brilliant stars. The moon rode high, silvering the seaplane so that she looked a wondrous mythical machine ready to ascend to that luminous planet where she truly belonged. Kit knew that indescribable mixture of fear and excitement as he pulled on his leather helmet and walked to the stern, shivering in the sudden coldness after the warmth below decks. There was an entire team clustering around the dainty aircraft. In their midst, he could just see Warren wearing an expression of anxiety similar to the one he had shown before *Flamingo*'s initial departure from Sheenmouth, on the proving flight. Not for this man fears of narrow clefts or the deceptive bottleneck; engine failure, or any manner of mechanical fault constituted his dread of the hours to come.

Men clapped Kit on the back, wished him good luck, and promised a gargantuan binge on his return. The ship's captain shook his hand, reminding him of the arrangements for his rendezvous with the destroyer after collecting his passenger. Then he was helped up the ladder to the forward cockpit, with the aid of a hooded lamp. He settled in the cramped seat, finding yet another reminder of that time when he had been victorious in a machine designed by his brilliant, unstable father. Cheering crowds had turned out to witness his success or failure on that occasion. Tonight, there would be no more than a legendary troll or two. Just as well, perhaps, for he was nowhere near as confident as he had been then.

Seaspray was a superb machine, but it was a long time since he had flown anything as small and speedy as she had turned out to be. Used to the majestic size and power of *Flamingo*, he had not yet gained that sense of

716

mastery when making precise and risky manoeuvres. There had been insufficient time. The fjord bottleneck was worrying him. A reconnaisance aircraft had taken photographs, which he had studied along with the maps until he could visualize details in his mind, but he would be flying through the narrow cleft at night, when hazards tended to loom at a pilot from out of the darkness. During the past few days, he had flown *Seaspray* along the Devon coast to a famous landmark providing a physical formation similar to the bottleneck. More than a dozen times he had attepted to pass between the high, craggy cliffs and the tall chimney of rock standing just offshore. Only on the last run had he found the courage to head for the dangerously narrow gap. It had been so hair-raising, he was now deeply concerned about the prospect of performing such a stunt by moonlight, through a gap he had never seen before. Ruling out a practice run at night in case he had smashed up the aircraft to make the mission impossible, he now found that one aspect of what he was about to do produced more fear than excitement.

On the inward journey, he could fly up and over the bottleneck. Coming out, with the additional weight of a passenger, he had no alternative but to go through it. *Seaspray* would never lift in time on that short stretch of water, despite her super-charged engine. It really was a brute of an assignment, in all respects. Colin Dryden had given clear, unemotional instructions. The prime objective was to get Lindstrom out of German hands, preferably alive. If anything went wrong before the pick-up, the biologist would be killed by the partisans trying to smuggle him out. If anything went wrong once he was in the seaplane, Kit had orders to shoot his passenger rather than allow him to be recaptured by the enemy. When he had light-heartedly suggested to Colin that trying to fly through the bottleneck would probably result in killing them both, the brief response had been, 'Make certain he's dead before you expire.'

717

'Are you ready, sir?' inquired a voice in his ear.

Brought from his thoughts, Kit turned to see a lad of no more than eighteen on the ladder alongside the cockpit. He nodded. 'Yes, quite ready.'

The young sailor jumped to the deck, and the naval team began rolling *Seaspray* forward on her beaching wheels until she reached the brink of the specially designed ramp. There was a great deal of shouting and grunting as she was carefully eased from her supports until the floats touched the first of the rollers. Winches took the strain as the machine would have raced forward, and Kit tensed as he stared down at the dark water swirling around the stationary ship. Foot by foot, he was lowered towards the black fathomless surface until the sea began to wash over the tips of the floats. Men in thigh boots came down the sides of the ramp to disconnect the ropes; disconnect all contact with that ship providing the only human link in a vast nocturnal ocean. Soon, he felt the familiar rocking which indicated that he was entirely waterborne. Drifting slowly from the warmth and comradeship on that destroyer, Kit experienced a momentary sense of desolation. There was no cheery crew to accompany him on this flight; no friends to share whatever danger lay ahead. It was a long time since he had flown alone.

His hand went to the ignition switch. *Seaspray*'s single engine roared, and the racing propeller set the water dancing with its power. The aircraft bumped a little over a greater swell than she had encountered at Sheenmouth. Kit had to fight to hold her steady as she hurtled into the air before he was ready. It was a stern reminder that this lady of the skies was capricious enough to recognize that he was not entirely her master yet. Once in the air, he found the balance of power growing more even as she responded to his demands obediently. He was not fooled for a moment. The lady was happy to purr gently through the moonlit serenity, but once he entered that narrow passage through high craggy cliffs, she would not be so amenable.

Putting himself on a course for the fjord, he glanced over the side at the dull silver sea. The destroyer was no more than a distant dark shape. Strangely, the sense of loneliness now that he was completely alone took on a different aspect. There was excitement in isolation. He recalled Sylva saying that it was like rediscovering virginity. For him, at this moment, it was rediscovering Kit Anson. That youthful, eager seeker of aerial laurels was once again attempting to prove that he could do the impossible. There might be no friends with him to provide company, but he had only his own life to consider when taking risks tonight. Knut Lindstrom's was in other hands, he felt. Fate would almost certainly make the decision on that man's future. With everyone poised to kill him the moment anything went wrong, Kit was happy to leave the responsibility with that mysterious force which had ruled his own fortunes so ruthlessly.

Fanciful thoughts were swiftly banished, when he realized the dark smudge ahead must be the heights of Norway's hinterland. A swift glance at his luminous watch told him he had been dreaming far longer than he imagined. The rendezvous was timed for thirty minutes from now, and he was right on course. This serene interlude was over.

In brilliant moonlight, he neared the coast then crossed it. His mind conjured up the physical features recorded on the map and aerial photographs. They should be easy to identify on a night as clear as this. He slid back the hood to lean over the side for a clearer view. The shimmer of water had gone, to be replaced by the darkness of mountains. He searched for a gleaming ribbon which would identify the fjord, and eventually spotted it further to his left than expected. Either the compass was out, or he had been given an incorrect bearing. He changed course, losing height as he did so. To avoid being spotted by the intermittent artillery posts known to be in the area, he must fly low through the chasm until reaching the bottleneck.

Dropping between the steep barren walls, visibility was instantly restricted as light from the moon was blocked by the heights. Kit realized it would not be as easy as he had hoped. How would he identify solid physical features from his memory of maps? In this gloom, it was impossible to see anything clearly. The rocky sides of this narrow corridor were hardly discernible from his cockpit. *Seaspray*'s engine magnified from a purr to a roar as sound was thrown back by solid rock. He might just as well be flying past the mountain batteries fully illuminated; the gunners would almost certainly hear him. So much for secrecy.

With the hood pushed back the cold wind buffeted him, yet he was sweating profusely as he flew on through that shadowed place where a wing could scrape a jutting crag, or a float could touch an unseen ledge to send him spiralling down to the rock-strewn water. Even so, excitement was pumping through him as *Seaspray* raced on, while his eyes strained to spot and recognize what should be clear landmarks. It proved a vain attempt. The moon rode the sky too far north to provide clarity. Only if it had been directly overhead would there have been a silver wash to create a living scene out of semidarkness.

A blank wall of rock was suddenly there ahead, rearing up as high as he could see. His heart raced; his reflexes tensed, but his mind told him he had come upon the dreaded bottleneck. There was no time to 'jump' it, as he had planned. *Seaspray* would never climb fast enough. He must take her straight on through it. There was no alternative. Now was the testing time, for she must put herself in his hands unreservedly. The slightest display of temperament on her part would result in them both smashing on to the rocks below. He told her this in stern tones, as they raced headlong at the wall, his eyes searching for the fissure which would offer them passage through it. When he saw the cutting, all sense of excitement deepened into pure dread. Only a madman would attempt to fly through there; a madman who knew his machine intimately and who held his own life to ransom. A madman, or Kit Anson who had no alternative.

With the roar of the engine filling his ears, and feeling very much like a pale moth seeking escape from a cathedral through a tiny crack in the wall, Kit gripped the control column and tensed himself for the sound of tearing metal. Used to the huge wingspan of *Flamingo*, he expected to make contact with the jutting rock no more than feet away on each side. Yet the seaplane few on, her backswept wings designed for speed missing the hazards as Kit's nerve held. Hair's-breadth manoeuvring was essential to negotiate the bottleneck's slight irregularities, and the little aircraft responded to his touch with total obedience. His throat grew dry; his head spun, yet he experienced that elation of existence only ever found with a mistress of the sky. By the time he grew aware of space, greater vision and a diminishing echo of sound, ten years had faded away to make him the champion he had once been. The bottleneck lay behind him. He had done the impossible. Leaning forward, he kissed the instrument panel.

'You little beauty, we made it. Together we made it!' he told her.

Triumph was brief. He was only five miles from the rendezvous, and other men's lives were now in the balance. What he had just done could not be attempted again. With additional weight to make precise manoeuvres that much slower, it was out of the question. Colin Dryden's orders were to kill Lindstrom if threatened by the enemy, not to murder the man unnecessarily. Somehow, he must go up and over the hazard. He had precisely fifteen minutes in which to think of a way to achieve the climb needed to do it. Right now, his brain could think of no solution whatever.

Due to the difficulties of night landings, when the

surface was so deceptive, the partisans had been instructed to float flares on the water when they heard the seaplane approach. Kit looked for these pinpricks of flame in the blackness below. There was no sign of light or life. Another swift look at his watch told him he should have passed over the rendezvous three minutes ago. Either they were late, or the rescue attempt had failed. His own orders were clear, and based on *Seaspray*'s capacity. He must delay no longer than ten minutes over the pick-up point, or there would be insufficient fuel to get him back to the destroyer. Frowning, he prepared to turn and overfly the spot once more. It would be daunting to be forced to return without knowing the fate of Sylva's brother.

There was insufficient air space for a turn within the chasm, so he climbed towards the stars and the bright moonlight flooding the crest of the heights. After the gloom of the fjord, he found a magical lunar atmosphere above the snow-tipped range which suggested Norwegian myths and legends. Gazing over the side as he made a wide turn, he jumped violently as the peace was shattered by concerted rifle-fire. Reacting instinctively, he dived for the protection of the fjord, the familiar ring of bullets on metal telling him *Seaspray* had been hit by his unseen attackers. Cold air rushed past his head as he plunged into the comparative gloom again, his brain teeming with possibilities. Had the partisans been trapped as they reached the fjord? Was Lindstrom now dead? Must he return alone to the ship, to report failure? As he pulled out of the crazy dive, faint blobs of light appeared a few miles ahead. They spelled a clear message to a man used to clandestine meetings. Lindstrom's absence must have been noticed sooner than expected, and the German pursuers were on the lip of the ravine. How long would it take them to climb down to the spot now clearly marked by flares? How long would it be before they reached a point from where they could fire down on *Seaspray*, as she rode the water

illuminated by landing lights? He had no idea of the
damage already inflicted by the rifles; so long as his
machine continued to respond normally he must assume
there to be no serious problem. He would soon know if
there was.

Seaspray was now on a steady downward glide towards
the flares, which put dancing lights on the black water.
Even with illumination, landing was no simple job when
rocks were known to be plentiful just beneath the surface. He had been assured that the Norwegians had
selected a stretch where hazards were few, but they were
not bringing the craft in. He dropped warily from one
element on to another, the streamlined floats cutting
through the water easily, until the machine slowed to a
halt without encountering obstacles. The dank coldness
at the bottom of this cleft struck at his bones; the echoing
pulse of the engine was unnerving to those intent on
stealth. Struggling up to perch on the fuselage, Kit then
saw a small rubber dinghy containing three shadowy
figures appear from the darkness. An overcoated man he
could not recognize was bundled up the ladder to the
rear cockpit, where he settled so clumsily he set the
aircraft rocking. Lindstrom was now aboard, expecting
to be flown to safety, and still Kit had no idea how
to avoid the bottleneck. Perhaps he should explain the
problem and give the Norwegian the choice of how to
die, or should he simply take off and fly the man, in
ignorance, to eternity? While he hesitated, one of the
partisans called softly to him.

'We have no time to thank you for your courage.
Please go quickly. Our enemies are not far behind us.
If they have ropes, like us, they will be down here at
any moment. Good luck.'

Faced with an insoluble aeronautical problem, Kit's
engineering knowledge then allowed him to see a possible solution. Leaning over the side, he asked urgently,
'You have ropes with you?'

'For climbing.'

'Are there any trees down here?'

'Many trees,' answered the man, whose pale face looked alert but strained.

'Good. I can take off all right, but I need to climb very fast. With the aid of your ropes, I think I can do it.'

As briefly and precisely as he could, he explained his theory. They were intelligent men, who understood his instructions and nodded their reassurance as they paddled away swiftly into the darkness whence they had come. Kit spoke no word to Lindstrom, who crouched as an unhappy figure in the tiny cockpit behind him. All his concentration must be on this one hope of avoiding a crash against the great thrusting walls each side of the bottleneck. As he waited for these strangers who presently held two lives in their hands, he told himself it would surely work. If it did not, his bones would lie here with Sylva's brother in the land of her birth.

It seemed an age before the sound of faint splashing heralded the return of the boat. Acting on Kit's low-voiced instructions, the partisans began tying the ends of two ropes around *Seaspray*'s elegant tailplane. As they were engaged in this, however, several of the drifting flares came close alongside to illuminate the scene quite clearly. Almost immediately, a volley of shots rang out revealing that their pursuers were closer than they had guessed. One of the Norwegians jumped into the icy water to swim across and douse the nearest flares, but those on the far side still highlighted their activity too well. More shots were fired, the bullets splashing in the water around them. One must have hit the dinghy. It collapsed and began to sink. Fortunately, the ropes were now fast around the tail. Knowing he must go now or not at all, Kit increased revs. The engine, which had been ticking over contentedly, began to speak with the voice of its super strength. Hoping desperately that the remaining Norwegians on the bank had done exactly as he had directed and knew what they must still do, he

724

firmly ignored the floundering of those being fired upon in the water and concentrated on the luminous dials in front of him. This would only succeed if he gauged the precise moment to give the signal, and those men on the bank who he had not even seen tonight, acted on it immediately.

With his gaze glued to the dial indicating engine power, he reached for the distress pistol kept in the pocket beside his seat. *Seaspray* was now uttering such a tremendous roar for so dainty a machine, he was unable to hear rifle fire above it so had no idea of what might be happening ashore. The crucial moment was near. He could feel his machine fighting the restraints put upon her, could feel the cockpit growing hot from the repressed power he was deliberately creating. Dear God, could she possibly stand such treatment? What if her tail fractured, or the engine caught fire? The hand on the dial crept nearer and nearer the red danger zone and still he waited, heart in mouth, until *Seaspray* began to groan with structural stress. He dared delay no longer. Up went his hand holding the pistol, to fire a distress flare.

It burst high above him, filling the darkness with blinding white light which revealed to him, for the first time, the sombre awesomeness of this Scandinavian waterway. There was no time to dwell on what he saw. *Seaspray* shot forward at a speed which robbed him of breath, as the ropes attached to trees on the bank were severed by the partisans' knives. The makeshift catapult worked. So suddenly released, *Seaspray* hurtled through the air with such force, she was off the water and climbing almost before Kit could recover from the shock of impetus. The flare blinded him, as it should also blind everyone in the vicinity, so all he could do was keep her in the steepest climb and pray. The ability to see would be of little help to him, really. If the climb was insufficient, he would sooner not be aware of when he was about to smash into the rocky wall ahead.

Up and up they went, he almost lying flat on his back due to the angle of climb. Then the aircraft began to labour, the initial launching speed slowly being lost. He would soon have to face the inevitability of levelling out or stalling. His eyes were now growing accustomed to darkness once more, and scrutiny of the dials before him produced a mild shock. They could not have reached such height so swiftly! The engine gave a warning cough, and he risked a glance over the side. His head then slowly swivelled in every direction, and in each of them stars appeared to be twinkling. He gently levelled out until he was flying steady on a course for the destroyer, but his outward calm covered an inner rioting excitement. He had done it; he had bloody well done it!

He began to laugh as he imagined Lindstrom's reaction to being catapulted from a fjord. Even his pioneering sister would never have done such a thing. He laughed even louder as he pictured the expressions on the faces of the Germans when the night had unexpectedly blazed with light, and a little grey moth had shot up from the water and clear over the mountains before their dazzled eyes, taking off the man they badly wanted.

By the time he crossed the coast to face the welcome expanse of silvery sea, laughter had quietened into an encompassing sense of joy in having found that echo of youth he had told Warren he was seeking. It did not matter that his name would not be recorded in the log of aerial achievements – men in aircraft were doing all manner of amazing feats today which the world would probably never know about. The important thing was to have done it. If his father was looking down at this moment, he would feel the balance had been restored for the Anson family.

As *Seaspray* purred onward, he began to grow aware of a dull burning pain high up between his shoulders. A vague recollection of feeling a thump at the back of his neck, during the nerve-racking moments whilst timing the precise second to sever the ropes, suggested that he had been hit by a bullet fired when he could hear nothing but *Seaspray*'s engine roar. Elation dimmed slightly. There was a long flight ahead, followed by a tricky landing on the sea near the destroyer. However, he did not appear to be losing blood, so the wound must be slight. Pain was an old companion, and this was nothing in comparison with some he had suffered. He had put his entire life in the hands of fate tonight: she had handed it back polished and shining brightly. If this was the price of success, it was wonderfully low. He murmured his thanks to her, there and then. His thanks to Warren for creating this aerial mistress would have to wait until he was back aboard the destroyer.

It was growing cold in this hour before dawn. As he no longer needed to watch for possible pursuit aircraft – they would have appeared by now – he decided to close the hood until nearing the ship. His arm felt a leaden weight as he tried to raise it. The demands of this hazardous flight had certainly taken toll of his strength, but surely not to such an extent. After another attempt to lift the arm, he was forced to close the hood with his left. The awkward movement caused the seaplane to wobble, and Kit then realized that he could no longer grip with his right hand. It fell from the control column as the machine tilted, and lay on his knee as an uncontrollable weight. He began to worry. Injuries received in the crash of *Flamingo* had impaired his power of coordination; the ability to match actions to thoughts. Action itself now seemed impaired. The burning pain between the shoulders had ceased to bother him, but a tentative rocking movement in the tiny seat brought little sensation in his back. Numbness appeared to have afflicted parts of his body.

He then tried to move his right leg. When that proved impossible, worry deepened. Lifting his useless right arm with the other, to place it back on the control column, he tried to explore with his left hand that area where the remembered thump had occurred. With the hood now over, there was insufficient room for the exercise. He was forced to abandon hope of discovering the cause for his strange condition. Still convinced that he had been hit at a time when all his concentration had been on the getaway, he recalled men in Spain saying they had felt no pain at all even when suffering severe wounds to the spine. The word 'paralysis' swam through his weary brain. Had fate demanded a higher price for his success tonight, after all?

Knowing nothing could be done until the ship's surgeon could take a look at him, he tried to concentrate on the probable difficulties of landing beside the vessel, so that *Seaspray* could be hauled aboard via the ramp. Warren's seaplane had no radio transmitter fitted, of course, so he had no verbal contact with the destroyer. All he could do was fly around the vessel several times, until it became apparent to those watching that he had a problem. He must hope that they would stand by to act as best they could when he finally reached the sea. At that point, he told himself to stop anticipating trouble. He had solved one insoluble difficulty tonight; he would get around this one when the time came. After pulling off the dangerous rescue and returning to the ship, the question of how best to land was not going to stand in the way of his total success.

Time passed serenely enough as he wondered what Lindstrom would work on for the Allies, now he had been snatched from those who intended to use his knowledge for the production of biological weapons. How had the man allowed himself to be led away from the beneficial studies he had made in Africa, to enter such deadly production? The same way he, himself, had been persuaded to use his flying skill for warlike purposes, and Warren had been forced to abandon his dreams and design killer aircraft, instead. They were all victims of war, like everyone else, he realized. Would it ever end, and who would win? He mused on that theory until he saw the dark ship on the dull silver sea ahead, waiting

728

patiently for him. Dawn was breaking off to the east, and he was looking forward to a rest. To hell with the gargantuan binge promised by the ship's officers! He wanted a bed with clean sheets, a deep pillow, and a locked cabin.

In order to have them, he had to get from up here to down there, he reminded himself. A quiet word with *Seaspray* on the subject ended with his promising ever-lasting devotion if she gave him her fullest cooperation. She replied with a cough and a splutter. It was not the answer he expected, but a glance at the fuel gauge showed that the fuel tanks were almost empty. One of the floats must also have been hit, leaving petrol to dribble out all through the return flight. Thank God the hole had not been bigger, or there would not be enough to support his landing. It was going to be difficult enough as it was.

He made a swift decision to enter a gentle descent now, even if he touched down some distance from the ship. He could always taxi the last stretch leading to the ramp. It would be safer than making a wobbly landing right beside the huge armour-plated vessel.

In that cramped cockpit fashioned, for speed, to fit round a man's body, the leaden right arm impeded movement to such an extent, Kit moved it to one side as he held the aircraft in the dive with his knees. It was at that point that he realized he could no longer swivel his head. Perspiration swamped him as he accepted that he was paralysed down one side of his body. Low in the cockpit, it meant he could not look over the side to locate the position of the ship. His vision was restricted to the area directly and distantly ahead. The dive was not steep enough to allow him sight of the water yet, but he continued to go down while he came to grips with the situation facing him. There was no longer any question of making decisions. All he could do was con-tinue this shallow descent until he was low enough to glimpse the sea beyond her nose, then do his utmost to pull her out at the right time to bring her to rest on the surface. The navy would have to take over from there.

He forgot his passenger, forgot the bed with a deep pillow, as he endured the endless waiting for a sight of the sea to which he was heading. Perspiration ran into his eyes, and he had continually to blink it away. His vision soon blurred again as he sweated out this 'blind' landing, unable to clearly see the figure on the altimeter. He felt no fear, however. Kit Anson was reputedly one of the finest pilots of marine aircraft in the world. If anyone could make this landing, he could.

All at once, there was the sea right below and shifting in deceptive fashion. He dragged heavily on the column to pull *Seaspray* up, but she did not take kindly to such violent commands after all she had done tonight. Lurching upwards in a gigantic loop, she then smacked down on the water with a thud which jerked Kit's useless arm across his body to jam his left hand between the column and his knees, rendering him totally helpless. It was in that state that he saw the shimmery image of hooded lights, a ramp running down to the sea, and a great dark ship towering right ahead.

Seaspray raced towards all this, impetuously returning home, and he could do nothing to curb her high spirits. She hit the ramp with a force which set her screaming as metal rasped on metal. Slewing round, her port wing became trapped between rollers to hold her fast, although her propeller continued to race. A surge of water lifted her free, minus the wing, and she ploughed crazily in a circle to finally smash against the grey wall of the warship not far from the ramp. Men rushed to the side of the ship. Klaxons sounded; ropes were lowered. Several dangled inches from him, but Kit could only watch them and hope someone would swiftly realize his plight. Lindstrom was rescued from the rear cockpit nearest to the ramp, then attention was drawn to Kit's inactivity. They shouted instructions to him, but their words were whipped away on the breeze. Two seamen started down the ropes, but they swung dangerously with the motion of the ship to thump against the side as they slowly descended.

As he watched their precarious approach, a figure rose up from a risky position on the wing, wet through and white-faced.

'What's wrong?' cried Warren above the general noise. 'Are you hurt?'

'Can't. . . move,' he managed.

'Oh God! I'll give you a hand.'

'You'll need help,' Kit told him.

A slight hesitation. 'I'll get some others.'

As Warren vanished from sight, Kit had his first indication of the true situation facing him. The glow of fire was suddenly alongside. Although he could not see the flames, he recognized that hazard dreaded by every man who had ever been in an aircraft. The leak in the float must have spilled the remaining fuel on the water, which had then ignited to drift and surround the wreck. He knew then that fate had planned the most fearful price imaginable for the recapture of his youth tonight. Even Kit Anson could not take this on the chin. He began to scream for someone to help him. Warren was there immediately, having abandoned his quest for assistance in the face of this direst of dangers. Clambering up to straddle the fuselage behind the cockpit, he bent to grip the collar of Kit's flying jacket.

'Come on,' he yelled, tugging hard but in vain. 'You've got to get out quickly. *Come on! Come on!*'

Kit tried to tell him to shift the useless right arm and so release the hand which he could possibly use to push himself up, but there was too much noise as hoses were played on the flaming sea and the crew shouted warnings to their fellows dangling on the ropes. A boat was being lowered twenty-five feet ahead, but it was now unbearably hot in the cockpit as flames began to lick around the grey fuselage. The night flared into a lurid hellish glow, as Kit willed his friend to find the superhuman strength needed to pluck him from this death-seat. When he accepted that there was no hope of it, he sobbed a command for Warren to jump clear while he could. The man refused to go, continuing to drag at Kit's coat like a madman, even when *Seaspray* began to tilt and sink beneath that layer of flames on water.

Leone had ensured that she was near a telephone during the last two days and three nights. She had lived a nightmare of fear and anxiety throughout that time. It had proved useless to tell herself that Kit had made countless flights into danger, which she had known nothing of. She did know about this one, and it made her realize there would be no peace of mind or heart from now on. Love created pain in times of war. The worst aspect was having no idea of what was happening; which night had been chosen for the rescue attempt. Had he made it and failed to return, or had he still to go? Kit had promised to ring her from Scotland when it was all over, but only at her insistence and because she feared Warren would not. Her nerves were stretched to breaking point on this third morning, when the telephone rang for the fourth time since breakfast. As she snatched it up in the hope of hearing Kit's voice, the caller identified himself as Colin Dryden.

'I'm using military priority to make this call, Mrs Grant,' he told her quietly. 'I regret to tell you that there was an accident early this morning, in which your husband received serious burns. He is in a ward of the naval hospital here, being given the best care available. The doctor assured me that he is in no danger but we thought you might care to come up and see him.'

Bewildered, and strangely fearful at this unexpected development, Leone could not take in what she was being told. 'My *husband*. . . in an accident? What kind of accident?'

'I'd prefer to explain when you get here, ma'am.'

'Yes. . . of course. I'll come right away,' she murmured, her mind in total confusion. 'He. . . he wasn't flying, was he?'

'No.'

Thoughts began to fall into place then, making her even more fearful. Why was this man, and not Kit, telling her news of this nature? Growing icy, she asked, 'Was Flight Lieutenant Anson involved in this accident?'

'I'm afraid so. Your husband very courageously fought to save Kit's life. Doctors are continuing the fight at this moment.'

Leone flew herself to Scotland in the company Auster, but she found the Kirkland name held no sway with the Almighty. Kit died an hour before she reached him.

Epilogue

There had not been crowds like this at Sheenmouth for a very long time. Even when the war had ended, three years ago, those who had thronged the streets and let off steam at the ferry parties on the Sheen had merely been local residents or servicemen stationed in the area. After the initial excitement of the German surrender, followed by that of the Japanese several months later, life in Britain continued to be grey, Spartan and fraught with even greater privation than before. The only difference was that loved ones were no longer being sacrificed in the fight for peace. Getting Britain back on her feet seemed to be secondary to getting the defeated standing securely again. The victors could be excused for sometimes wondering who had really come off best in the six-year struggle. Poverty, food-rationing and unemployment were the legacies of victory for a vast number of people in the islands which had resisted occupation so fiercely. In the little Devonshire seaside resort, however, rations were greatly augmented by the bounty produced by fertile country soil. Unemployment was non-existent. So, therefore, was poverty.

On this August afternoon in 1948 the town was decked with bunting and the sands were as crowded as the promenade. It was a day of sweltering heat. The sea was full of children screaming with delight and splashing each other. Mums and dads frolicked in provocative fashion, whilst keeping an eye on their energetic offspring. Grandmas and grandads paddled contentedly at the water's edge, the men with their trouser legs rolled to the knee and the women with their floral print dresses tucked defiantly into silk stockinet bloomers. If there were also those in wheelchairs, or with a trouser leg or jacket sleeve empty, the sense of fun was in no way lessened. Visitors had swarmed to Sheenmouth to see the Air Show and, for once, the weather was perfect for it. The one great advantage of an aerial performance was that it could be seen clearly by everyone below, and if there was an opportunity for some traditional seaside fun into the bargain, so much the better.

Ice cream was not as good as it had been before the war, of course, but it was refreshing on a day of high temperatures. The vendors did a roaring trade. The cafés were also doing well with ham and salad lunches, and cream teas were planned to coincide with the conclusion of the show. The Sheenmouth donkeys were back, for the first time since 1939. Old Mr Moxy had passed on, but his niece and her mentally handicapped husband had revived this standing attraction of the resort. Boats could again be hired for half an hour's rowing on the river, and picnickers on the cliffs at East Sheenmouth vied with courting couples for the best vantage points. Yet, it was not quite the same as it used to be. Nothing was quite the same as it used to be. Nostalgia was all right, but one had to move with the times. Take the town's main industry, for instance.

Kirkland Marine Aviation had become Grant Kirkland Aviation Limited. The original works by the river continued to produce marine aircraft, but the new mammoth factory up on the site of the original Magnum Pomeroy Aero Club which had been a fighter base during the war, concentrated on the development of civil airliners. Warren Grant had gained a knighthood for his work on amphibious aircraft, which had been used extensively in the Far Eastern campaign. He and his wife had also made a fortune from government contracts throughout the war. This had been used to build the new aircraft works. Local men had had no difficulty finding jobs after being demobbed, and even old Jack Cummings had failed to stir up union trouble after being released from prison at the end of hostilities. He was in a mental home now, ranting and raving to his heart's content. Grant Kirkland had brought prosperity to the area, although there were people who grumbled about the noise of aeroplanes performing endless manoeuvres.

No one grumbled about the man who did these aerial stunts. Roger Lisle, the company's test pilot, was a quiet man of thirty-six with a quiet wife, and four well-behaved children. The family had settled into the sleepy village of Magnum Pomeroy as if they had been there for years. Old-timers still talked of the days of Kit Anson, Sir Hector's first test pilot, who had had a quality of élan this man Lisle lacked. Time had honed the sharp edges of criticism, and it was generally believed now that there had been more behind young Anson's supposed treachery than anyone guessed. After all, a man who had started as a hero and died as one, could surely not have betrayed his benefactors in such a way. Stories were legion concerning the war exploits of Geoffrey Anson's son. Some had him as a spy under direct orders from Churchill, flying special misions behind enemy lines. Others suggested that his trial and imprisonment had been arranged by the Secret Service, so that when he had supposedly been in jail he had actually been in Spain reporting Intelligence information on the war which had preceded the world conflict. What was indisputably true was that he had piloted Sheenmouth's famous *Flamingo* flying boat, to pick up survivors from Crete whilst being machine-gunned, for which he had been awarded his first decoration. He had then flown her to England for use with the RAF on special assignments. What no one knew for certain were the details of his last flight, which had earned him a posthumous DFC to add to his impressive row of medals. So, whatever the truth about that affair with the Kirkland family, no one could deny he had been the stuff of which true heroes are made, and had shone as brightly as the stars he had never given up trying to reach. The days of such men were over; now it was the turn of builders and reformers. All the same, the world would be a little less exciting without them.

Today was as exciting as anyone in the crowd could wish, and when the aerial show began there was hardly a throat which did not grow hoarse with cheering as all faces were turned to the clear sky. Those who recalled the proving flight of *Flamingo*, with all the pink ballyhoo and ostentation, thought the Grants had pulled in their horns somewhat this time. It was, nevertheless, an impressive way to launch a new flying boat, and the glamorous days were over. First came *Aphrodite*, rescued from the scrapyard and restored by Sir Warren personally. She looked slow by today's standards, but she had had her days of glory and many who watched her felt great affection for this yellow goddess who, like themselves, was past her prime. Following her were two noisy giants, side by side, still in their camouflage with RAF markings. *Flamingo* and *Florida* raised shrieks of pride for these two battered old ladies who had withstood so much to survive.

Leaving enough time for these comparatively slow machines to cover the course, there next came a formation of Hurricanes which had been based at Magnum Pomeroy, and another of Spitfires for which components had been made at Kirkland's by a force of women throughout the war. Several heavy bombers from the existing RAF station beyond Forton thundered past above the sands, tailed by a long line of *Clarions*, the swift, compact passenger planes being turned out in the new factory at Magnum Pomeroy. Roger Lisle was listed next on the programme, and the ocean of upturned faces watched him perform fantastic stunts from which it seemed he could never emerge alive. His display raised

737

cheers and applause, yet young lads had no desire to seek his autograph and the girls never pinned his picture beside the bed to kiss it goodnight with an ache in the heart. He was not that kind of man.

Then, at last, came the star of the show; Sheenmouth's latest pride and joy. A new flying boat developed by Warren Grant from an original design by Geoffrey Anson, and named *Solitaire*. Taxiing from the mouth of the river came the majestic craft painted blue and silver, looking like a great passenger liner with wings. She was exciting, breathtaking, a symbol of lush adventure which had been put aside since 1939. Here was that mysterious quality which was missing in the wheeled *Clarion*. Here was the epitome of romance, once more. The cheering of the crowds was drowned when the rest of *Solitaire*'s six engines started up, and she began to move forward raising glittering white spray as she cut through the azure water with the regal grace of a queen of the air. When she rose effortlessly from the sea and headed towards the sun, the cheering people slowly grew hushed. By the time *Solitaire* had made a wide sweeping turn to fly back level with the top of Sheenmouth's red cliffs, those watching had been totally silenced by an emotion they could not name. It was one which affected them seldom, but when it did even the men found moisture in their eyes.

The cocktail party at Sheenmouth Abbey for VIP guests and personal friends of Sir Warren and Lady Grant soon indicated the total success of the day. *Solitaire* had been triumphant in advance of her debut, for orders had been placed at the semi-construction stage. More were certain as a result of today's show, and a decision would then have to be made on whether or not one of the workshops at Magnum Pomeroy would have to switch to making components for the flying boat rather than for the standard *Clarion*. First, however, the directors were taking a holiday, something they had not found time to do before.

Leone reminded Philip Curtiss of this when he invited her to a luncheon of the Royal Aeronautical Society. 'We shall be in Africa. All the arrangements are made and can't be changed,' she said firmly. 'Sorry, Philip.'

The group captain laughed. 'You've always been a woman who makes irreversible decisions, Leone.'

'Not where my husband is concerned,' she responded dryly. 'The minute I start trying to pin him down, he escapes to the old boathouse and becomes engrossed in something else.'

'Good thing, too, or he would never have discovered the old plans of Geoffrey Anson's and created *Solitaire*.'

'Yes, of course,' she agreed, so used to the white lie now it no longer threw her.

'I bumped into Sir Melville yesterday,' Philip continued, taking a vol-au-vent from a nearby tray. 'Did you know he'd suffered a stroke?'

'Yes, I visited the house soon after Stephanie left him for her American diplomat. I wanted to thank him and the other members of his committee for commissioning a stained-glass expert to restore the Abbey windows, in gratitude for storing their treasures here during the height of the bombing. I thought it very generous.'

Colin Dryden approached at that point, and Leone soon excused herself to leave the men discussing American development of military aircraft. Nearby was Mona Hamilton, who had been widowed in 1944 and now ran the *Sheenmouth Clarion* whilst rearing her two children. The little newspaper had increased its circulation, but tended to retain some of the bitterness from the days of her father's editorship. It was not surprising. Mona had lost a fiancé, and her husband Joss. Many women felt bitter, these days. The red-haired girl conducted no campaign against the residents of the Abbey, however, and she promised a glowing report on today's show.

'I saw your Ben wandering around with a dreamy look on his face this afternoon,' Mona said with a smile. 'I

739

recognize that expression all too well. He'll be flying the minute he's old enough, Leone.'

'I suppose it's inevitable,' she agreed. 'He's surrounded by all the temptations, isn't he? I wish he longed to be a musician or a painter, instead.'

'Belinda doesn't. She tags along after him like an adoring shadow.' Her eyebrows arched dramatically. 'If she's as wanton as this at the age of five, I dread to think of her future.'

'The time to worry is when she tags adoringly after someone at the age of sixteen. By then, she'll have lost Ben to flying machines.' Leone observed pensively, 'Isn't it curious that my life has been dominated by aircraft from birth, and I now devote almost every day to the production of them, yet I've never experienced this love-affair men seem to have with them.'

'You're a woman, that's why,' declared Mona. 'We've got our feet firmly on the ground, thank God. Where would the world be if we all surrendered to the search for an elusive dream? Warren's very brainy and certainly deserves the recognition he's been given, but where would he be without you?' she demanded. 'Let them have their love-affairs with machines. Women have a love-affair with life, and that's far more important.'

Mona's words stayed in Leone's mind as she wandered the Abbey entertaining her guests. Her father had sought power and personal consequence; Donald had searched for the strength to emulate him. Kit had pursued the pathway to the stars, and had found it never to return. As for Warren, he was on a ceaseless quest for perfection. All she had wanted was to become visible and defy loneliness. That, she had achieved, but did she yet have a love-affair with life?

Leaving the last few official guests with Warren, Leone mounted the branched staircase lost in thought. What more could she have? Grant Kirkland Aviation Limited was expanding, prosperous and in the forefront of British aircraft development. Sheenmouth Abbey was truly a delightful home created by her own feminine touch, and she led a full, interesting life professionally and socially.

Reaching the bell tower, she entered to climb the steps. His presence was there immediately, as it always was when she looked around this circular room with the writing desk and chairs covered in ruby velvet. No one had occupied it since that night when *Flamingo* had been forced to land at Sheenmouth by headstrong Polish fighter pilots. So close did she suddenly feel to that young man who had led her along such a stormy path, tears she had not shed for a long while rushed to her eyes and would not be checked. The pain of her love for him, which had been gained and lost so dramatically, overwhelmed her again as he occupied her heart and mind to the exclusion of all else. She saw so clearly a young girl rummaging through shabby suitcases to discover facts about a boy who was to become a curious kind of brother. How little that lonely vulnerable girl had suspected that the mysterious Kit Anson was about to change her entire life.

Moving up to the bedroom, she recalled the anguish of adolescent passion denied while that same girl, older but still lonely and vulnerable, had sought ravishment on his empty bed. Standing at the sconced window, Leone gazed with blurred vision at the lower meadow with the Sheen beyond. He had been suffering his own torment that night, in the knowledge that he and his father had been betrayed in the most appallingly callous manner by men who had exploited his trust. They had stolen *Solitaire* and called her *Aphrodite. Dad's finest design*. Today, another fine design had been shown to the world, with Geoffrey Anson's name accredited to her. Out on the lower meadow, Leone could see that laughing young aviator surrounded by eager adoring girls heading for the jetty ready to go down-river for his attempt at breaking the world air speed record in his own father's seaplane. Finally, the Kirkland debt had been paid. It had taken seventeen years, but *Solitaire* had flown over Sheenmouth in triumph this afternoon.

Returning to the sitting room, she remained swamped by memories until Warren came in to fold his arms around her and draw her back against his chest, as she continued to gaze from the window at the renovated chapel.

'I guessed you'd be here,' he murmured against her hair. 'It's really been *his* day, hasn't it?'

She nodded, still unable to speak. Then he turned her to face him, searching her face and saying gently, 'Don't you think it's time we used these rooms; time we let him go?'

Her hand went up to feather his face scarred by burns suffered on that last night with Kit. 'Not many men would have made a gesture as generous as you did this afternoon.'

He caught her hand in his. 'I allowed Donald to steal half the credit for *Flamingo*, and he had no talent whatever. Geoffrey Anson was a great designer who deserved recognition for his skill.'

'But you really did it for Kit, didn't you?'

'No,' he confessed quietly. 'No, Leone, I did it for you. . . in the hope that there'd be peace between the Kirklands and the Ansons, at last.' His steadfast gaze was full of hope. 'Is there?'

Her answer was the farewell she had never been able to make before. 'Yes, darling. I found it here just before you came in.'

He let out his breath in a long sigh of relief, then took her arm to lead her from that place of memories. They walked in understanding silence along the upper corridor, past the rooms occupied by Ben, whom they had adopted as an orphaned evacuee four years ago. He was now fourteen, strong and happy, with his gaze already on the skies. Leone's mouth softened into a faint smile. Ben was another stray mongrel who had been taken in and polished up to meet Kirkland standards. This one was here to stay, however. Stay until he fell in love with a goddess of the air, she reminded herself hollowly. Then she recognized that missing element which would make her life complete.

'Warren,' she began quietly, 'isn't it time we thought of adopting another child – a girl?'

He grinned as they reached the door of their rooms. 'I wondered how long it would be before you felt outnumbered by men, and wanted to even the balance in this place.'

'That's no answer,' she declared, confronting him.

Drawing her into his embrace, he kissed her with that steadfast love she had found so supportive. 'We'll discuss the details when we're in Mombasa next month, darling,' he promised. 'Now, please can I take off this penguin suit and get into something more comfortable, before we join our son and his friends for their schoolboy bun-fight downstairs?'

For those who have enjoyed this book, may we recommend the following coming shortly from **Rowan**.

THE QUIET EARTH
Margaret Sunley

For decades the Oak family have carved a living out of the tough and beautiful Yorkshire Dales, but now Jonadab Oak is facing rebellion from his children who want lives of their own. Margaret Sunley's tender and truthful pastoral saga celebrates mid-Victorian family life—its strengths, its tussles, its losses and gains—in a novel which rivals *The Shell Seekers*.

ELITE
Helen Liddell

Ruthless, politically ambitious, beautiful and clever, Deputy Prime Minister Ann Clarke is the modern Joan of Arc of the Scottish Labour Party. But has her dizzing rise to power been too swift? Helen Liddell's stunningly powerful drama of political and sexual intrigue keeps the reader guessing until the very last page.

A BOWL OF CHERRIES
Anna King

Frail and often in pain from a chronic disease, Marie
Cowley grows up in London's East End surrounded by a
large and lively family who feel that Marie is a novice when
it comes to holding down a job — or choosing a husband.
But Marie is determined to live a normal life, and she sets
about it with typical courage and determination...

THE SINS OF EDEN
Iris Gower

Handsome, charismatic and iron-willed, Eden Lamb has
an incalculable effect on the lives of three very different
women in Swansea during the Second World War that is
to introduce them to both passion and heartbreak. Once
again, bestselling author Iris Gower has spun a tender and
truthful story out of the background she knows and loves
so well.